COMPETENCE IN PERFORMANCE
THE CREATIVITY OF TRADITION
IN MEXICANO VERBAL ART

COMPETENCE IN PERFORMANCE

THE ▫ CREATIVITY ▫ OF ▫ TRADITION ▫ IN ▫ MEXICANO ▫ VERBAL ▫ ART

CHARLES L. BRIGGS

UNIVERSITY OF PENNSYLVANIA PRESS

PHILADELPHIA

UNIVERSITY OF PENNSYLVANIA PRESS
CONDUCT AND COMMUNICATION SERIES

■■■

Erving Goffman and Dell Hymes, *Founding Editors*
Dell Hymes, Gillian Sankoff, and Henry Glassie, *General Editors*

A complete listing of the books in this series
appears at the back of this volume

■■■

Library of Congress Cataloging-in-Publication Data
Briggs, Charles L., 1953–
   Competence in performance : the creativity of tradition in
Mexicano verbal art / Charles L. Briggs.
      p.   cm.—(University of Pennsylvania Press conduct and communication series)
   Bibliography: p.
   Includes index.
   ISBN 0-8122-8088-1.   ISBN 0-8122-1260-6 (pbk.)
   1. Mexican Americans—Folklore—Performance.   2. Folk literature—
New Mexico—Cordova—History and criticism.   3. Folklore—New
Mexico—Cordova.   4. Cordova (N.M.)—Social life and customs.
I. Title. II. Series.
GR111.M49B75   1988
398'.08968720789—dc19   88-14427
                                                              CIP

Designed by Adrianne Onderdonk Dudden

for Dean John Donald Robb
composer, scholar, and grandfather

and for my wife, Barbara Fries,
and my children,
Feliciana, Jessie, and Gabriel
beloved fellow travelers

CONTENTS

List of Plates   ix
List of Illustrations   xi
List of Examples   xiii
Preface   xv

1   Introduction   1

2   Mexicano Northern New Mexico   25
        APPENDIX: Methods of Transcription   55

3   Historical Discourse   59

4   Proverbs   101

5   Scriptural Allusions   137

6   Jests, Anecdotes, and Humorous Tales   171

7   Legends and Treasure Tales   233

8   Hymns and Prayers   289

9   Conclusion   341

Notes   377
Bibliography   387
Index   415

PLATES

1. Quemado Valley, 1979   27
2. Córdova Plaza, 1974   28
3. San Antonio de Padua del Pueblo Quemado Chapel   29
4. Uplands above Córdova   32
5. Córdova Plaza, ca. 1900   33
6. Sheep pens in the Quemado Valley   35
7. *Rancho* homes, 1974   40
8. Interior of San Antonio de Padua Chapel   41
9. Miguel Sandoval, Inez Córdova, and Victor Córdova   48
10. San Antonio Day procession, 1976   51
11. Threshing wheat with goats, ca. 1935   76
12. Young Córdovans carrying water, 1939   78
13. Transportation in bygone days   79
14. George López and Silvianita Trujillo de López, 1986   88
15. Lópezes' home in the Quemado Valley, 1974   89
16. Dry farm area of Las Joyas, 1979   95
17. Melaquías Romero, 1984   138
18. Romero home, 1984   139
19. Costancia Apodaca de Trujillo, 1986   144
20. Trujillo home, 1986   145
21. *Fuerte* owned by José Dolores López   150
22. Federico Córdova and Lina Ortiz de Córdova, with one of their grandchildren   174
23. Córdova home, 1986   175
24. Death cart   325

ILLUSTRATIONS

MAP

1 Northern New Mexico 26

FIGURES

1 Marked and unmarked senses of *antes* 73
2 Comparison of four types of historical discourse 90
3 Topical progression in pedagogical discourse 93
4 Relationship among genres of the talk of the elders of bygone days 223
5 Structure of the Rosary service 310
6 Alabado used in Rosario 315

TABLES

1 Summary of proverb performance features 129
2 Summary of scriptural allusion performance features 151
3 Summary of chiste performance features 224

EXAMPLES

■■■

(3.1) Benjamín, Ignacio, CLB; 29 March 1986   66

(3.2) George López, Silvianita Trujillo de López, CLB; 22 July 1983   84

(4.1) Silvianita Trujillo de López, George López, CLB; 3 October 1972   106

(4.2) Silvianita Trujillo de López, George López, CLB; 9 October 1972   112

(4.3) Federico Córdova, CLB; 21 July 1974   116

(4.4) Federico Córdova, CLB; 21 July 1974   122

(5.1) Melaquías Romero, CLB; 28 July 1981   140

(5.2) Aurelio Trujillo, Costancia Apodaca de Trujillo, CLB;
       8 October 1972   146, 160

(5.3) George López, CLB; 22 July 1983   152

(6.1) Federico Córdova, Lina Ortiz de Córdova, Samuelito Córdova, CLB;
       3 October 1972   176

(6.2) Fabiola López de Domínguez, Benjamín Domínguez, Leonarda Lovato
       de López, José Paz López, CLB; 24 July 1983   182

(6.3) Lilia Pacheco de Vigil, Lázaro Vigil, Julián Josué Vigil, CLB;
       18 August 1983   188

(6.4) Lilia Pacheco de Vigil, Julián Josué Vigil, CLB; 18 August 1983   194

(6.5) Federico Córdova, Lina Ortiz de Córdova, Samuelito Córdova, family, CLB;
       2 October 1972   204, 226

(6.6) Federico Córdova, CLB; July 1974   212

(7.1) Melaquías Romero, CLB; 24 August 1983   234

(7.2) Bernardo, Juan, CLB; 26 March 1979   254

(7.3) Carlos Córdova, Julián Josué Vigil; 17 April 1984   278

(7.4) Francisca, Estevan, CLB; 9 October 1982   278

(8.1) Segment of Rosary Service of Holy Wednesday   306

(9.1) Aurelio Trujillo, Costancia Trujillo, CLB; 8 October 1972 (continued)   364

PREFACE

My focus in this work is on the verbal art of Spanish speakers in New Mexico. Historical discourse, proverbs, scriptural allusions, jests, anecdotes, legends, hymns, and prayers are analyzed in arguing that performers create complex poetic forms in conveying provocative interpretations of themselves and their society. My goal is to draw on a host of particulars in addressing a basic problem. Folkloric performances are not simply repetitions of time-worn traditions; they rather provide common ground between a shared textual tradition and a host of unique human encounters, thus preserving the vitality and dynamism of the past as they endeavor to make sense of the present. This raises the general question that is addressed in the following chapters: What do performers need to know in order to be able to bring these two spheres together creatively in performance? Addressing the issue in this way places the folkloristic enterprise of exploring the form and meaning of oral genres within the context of ongoing attempts by linguists and others to explore the nature of the communicative competence that enables us to use language in creating and sustaining human communities.

We now stand at a particularly opportune juncture to be able to take up this question, because two recent theoretical advances have suggested means to celebrate rather than obscure the creative and complex interplay of voices that constitutes verbal art. Under the aegis of ethnopoetics, scholars, performers, and poets have worked together in forging new means of appreciating the aesthetic form and cultural significance of myths, folktales, and other genres. New methods of transcription have been developed in attempting to preserve the prosodic and grammatical structure of the spoken word as it is transformed into written texts. Attention has also been directed to the variable ways in which verbal art forms are performed within communities. Influenced by Bateson, Goffman, and the ethnomethodologists, the performance perspective emphasizes the interaction among performers, audiences, creative uses of language, and the social situations that connect them.

This study attempts to extend ethnopoetics and performance theory in two ways. First, I will look at a range of genres that are performed by the members of a particular speech community and at the relationships among these genres. Such a focus places this work closely in line with three studies: Glassie's *Passing the Time in Bal-lymenone,* Gossen's *Chamulas in the World of the Sun,* and Sherzer's *Kuna Ways of Speaking.* I will argue that comparison of systems of genres is essential if we are to gain a more in-depth understanding of the nature of competence that underlies perfor-mance. Second, the Spanish-language folklore of the Southwest is particularly rich in conversational genres, such as historical dialogues, proverbs, scriptural allusions, jests, and anecdotes. I hope to show that research on the contextual or situated di-mensions of conversational folklore must complement studies of myths and folktales if we are to achieve an adequate understanding of the way that linguistic form and cultural significance, textual tradition and social interaction become one in perfor-mance. Exploring this facet of performance is similarly necessary if we are to appreci-ate the way that the study of verbal art can contribute to our understanding of the nature of communication.

I do not mean to suggest, however, that my concern with these issues springs from theoretical sources alone. I have spent a great deal of time over the last fourteen years in Córdova, a small community in northern New Mexico, and have recorded perfor-mances in a number of other communities in the region. I will refer to the performers and their neighbors as *Mexicanos;* my rationale is simply that this is the term they most frequently use in reference to their own ethnic group. This area was part of Mexico until 1846, at which time it was invaded by the United States; since then a culturally and linguistically distinct population, which is usually called Anglo-American, has joined Native Americans and Mexicanos in the region. Mexicanos have tried to create a dialogue with the newcomers in order to express their vision of themselves and the land that surrounds them. Mexicanos have been particularly con-cerned with the need to help Anglo-Americans see what a profound impact their presence has had on life in communities such as Córdova.

Performances of historical discourse, proverbs, scriptural allusions, jokes, and leg-ends play an important role in creating this dialogue, as means both of portraying Anglo-Americans and of engaging them in conversation—when they will listen. Verbal art also provides a central forum for discussions between Mexicanos in which the past is used in critically reflecting on the present and future. Appreciating the complexity and flexibility of this process has prompted me to draw heavily on perfor-mance theory and ethnopoetics in developing a dynamic, context-sensitive approach that is sensitive to stylistic detail; it has also motivated me to question certain limita-tions of this body of theory and method in order to adequately interpret the perfor-mances that are transcribed on the following pages. This effort has also drawn me beyond the confines of my background in linguistics, anthropology, and folklore in exploring issues raised by literary critics, sociologists, philosophers, psychologists, and others.

The goal of adequately interpreting the contextual dimensions of these performances brings me into the picture, since I was a participant in nearly all of them. I have not mustered a notion of "scientific objectivity" to the task of writing myself out of the analysis, hiding the effects on my presence on what was said and done. My own responses, even the many yes's and uh huh's, are faithfully recorded in the transcripts. This book is not, however, about me; my own actions and reactions are relevant only insofar as they affect the course and the meaning of the performance. This procedure is not always comfortable, since a great many examples over a fourteen-year period give rise to a fair number of faux pas. But failing to treat my own involvement with the critical attention that I accord to that of other participants would obscure the reflexive manner in which performances comment on the situations in which they emerge.

I alluded earlier to the fact that the research on which this book is based was carried out over a fourteen-year period. This means that adequately expressing my appreciation for the help that I have received along the way is not an easy task. My greatest debt is to the people of Córdova, New Mexico. The insistence and clarity with which they taught me what it means to be Mexicano has been the strongest force behind my research. They allowed me to become a member of their community and tolerated (often with great interest and humor) the way in which I filled my rather peculiar niche. I thank them for showing me how effective language and folklore can be in resisting hegemony. Especial credit is due three couples: Lina Ortiz de Córdova and Federico Córdova, Silvianita Trujillo de López and George López, and Costancia Apodaca de Trujillo and Aurelio Trujillo. They taught me so much while I was still so young that it is hard to imagine who I would be if I had never met them. I am pleased that they asked me to use their names in this book, since this enables me to help extend their reputations as performers. It is sad indeed that Federico Córdova and Aurelio Trujillo died before I could show them what I did with their words.

Outside Córdova, Fabiola López de Domínguez and Benjamin Domínguez of Chamisal gave me a pointed lesson as to how one can use the past in confronting injustice in the present. Lilia Pacheco de Vigil and Lázaro Vigil, their son Julián Josué, and Julián's wife Irene Gurule de Vigil were more than warm friends and kind hosts. Lilia Vigil taught me how humor can be used in subverting gender-role stereotypes. Julián worked with me a year, lending his fine ear and impressive knowledge of New Mexico Spanish and Mexicano folklore to the task of transcribing a number of performances; he made several of the transcriptions and translations that are used in this book. Since I have revised them in keeping with an ethnopoetic format (explained below), final responsibility for any imperfections must remain my own. I am also grateful to the many performers throughout northern New Mexico whose words are not included in these pages (due to limitations of space). Others do appear here, but not by name; in such cases one or more of the performers died or became seriously ill before I was able to ask whether or not they wished to have their names appear in print.

Several institutions generously supported the research financially. The International Folk Art Foundation funded the 1972–1973 fieldwork. The National Science Foundation supported my doctoral research in 1978–1979 as well as a summer in the field and time for analyzing the data in 1983–1984. Additional funds for doctoral research were provided by the National Institute of Mental Health. Vassar College has provided a number of small grants in assisting both the research and the publication itself. I am particularly grateful to H. Patrick Sullivan, Dean of the College, to Colleen Cohen, Walter Fairservis, Judith Goldstein, Lucy Lewis Johnson, and Lilo Stern in the Department of Anthropology, and Michael Murray in the Department of Philosophy. Harvard University provided me with an Andrew W. Mellon Faculty Fellowship in the Humanities in 1983–1984. My time there was rendered more stimulating and enjoyable by virtue of the chance to work in the Committee on Degrees in Folklore and Mythology with Hugh Flick, Albert Bates Lord, and Gregory Nagy.

Quite a number of individuals have criticized my initial formulations. Roger Abrahams, Richard Bauman, Iain Boal, Thomas Buckley, Paul Friedrich, Barbara Fries, Kenneth Goldstein, Bill Hanks, Dell Hymes, Virginia Hymes, Joel Kuipers, Enrique Lamadrid, John McDowell, Michael Murray, Michael Silverstein, Thomas Steele, Julián Josué Vigil, and Marta Weigle provided valuable comments on specific chapters. The ideas were also presented in papers given at the Universidad de Oriente (Cumaná, Venezuela), the University of California at Santa Cruz, the International Summer Institute for Structural and Semiotic Studies (at Indiana University), the Center for Psychosocial Research (Chicago), the University of Arizona, the University of Pennsylvania, Harvard University, the University of New Mexico, and the Mellon Faculty Seminar on Literary Criticism at Vassar College; I thank my interlocutors at all of these institutions for their critical attention. Nancy Smith Hefner, Joan O'Donnell, and Catherine Hiebert Kerst provided stimulating responses to early versions of the chapters as they unfolded in lectures at Harvard University.

A number of individuals have played special roles in bringing this work to completion. Enrique Lamadrid and Greg Accialoli uncovered last minute bibliographic materials and sent them to me in South America. Enrique Lamadrid also provided a close reading of the Spanish transcriptions. James Armstrong, Jr. kindly checked the musical transcription that appears as Figure 6. Marta Weigle has used her folkloristic expertise and bibliographic wizardry countless times over the years in challenging me to broaden the folkloristic base of my research. Michael Silverstein taught me a good deal of what I know about language; the challenge with which he presented me—to grasp the pragmatic dimensions of performances—was crucial. Dan Ben-Amos, Dell Hymes, and Jeff Opland read through every line of the manuscript. Preparing the final version gave me the feeling that I was engaged in an ongoing, high-geared dialogue with these three individuals. Their comments enabled me to work on a number of weak spots in the argument as well as to broaden its theoretical breadth. Dan Ben-Amos and Dell Hymes also provided crucial encouragement and offered suggestions that pushed me to consider crucial implications of performance theory and ethnopoetics for my research. At the University of Pennsylvania Press, Alison Anderson, Carl Gross, and Patricia Smith gave generously of their time and expertise in seeing this manuscript into print.

Finally, this book is dedicated to my grandfather, Dean John Donald Robb. He has provided a model of artistic creativity, as a composer and conductor, as well as of scholarly dedication, as a student of Southwestern folk music. I owe much of my interest in the study of verbal art and the confidence that I could bring such work to fruition to him as well as to my parents, Nancy Robb Briggs and Bill Briggs. The dedication also points to the role of my wife, Barbara E. Fries, and our children, Feliciana, Jessie, and Gabriel, in making all of this worth the effort.

Nabaribuhu
Caño Mariusa
Territorio Federal del Delta Amacuro
Venezuela

1

INTRODUCTION

Imagine that a number of individuals are sitting in a kitchen, crossing a field, or driving to town. Their talk is unfocused, touching on recent events or tasks to be accomplished. When one of the participants, an older person, begins to speak, the tone shifts. Her voice rises suddenly, then falls. Her eyes become fixed on a younger person, her grandson, who has just spoken, and he responds in kind. Her words break the hold of the here and now, drawing the group through the window of the community's past. The words are no longer hers alone, for they have taken the shape of a quotation. The expression embodies a familiar form and content. All watch and listen closely as the pace and the pitch of her speech rise to a peak, then suddenly descend. She continues, more slowly now, with a relaxed and even tone; the family members laugh or smile, and their gazes become unfocused. As she finishes speaking, most murmur words of assent. The grandson is the last to respond, nodding and replying, *sí, es cierto* 'yes, it's true'.

The talk returns to the present, but it is no longer the same. This is the power that lies in the grandmother's words. She has not *described* the past—she has *quoted* the words of the people who lived it. She ceased speaking in her own right at this point and became instead a sounding board for a chorus of innumerable voices. The elderly woman has advanced her own position on an issue at hand by revealing the moral questions it raises. As a result, the present can stand alone no more, bearing a false self-sufficiency and limiting the imagination to seeing what is present to the senses. The ghosts of *los viejitos de antes* 'the elders of bygone days' linger, interpreting what they see in terms of the values that they themselves represent. The landscape now evokes the historical events to which it once played host more strongly than it does the houses, cars, and fences visible today. These voices use their historical force to confront the present with a value-laden interpretation of itself.

This family portrait of a moment in a Hispanic community in northern New Mexico may seem quite divorced from the experience of the reader. An analogy may bring it closer. Whether alarmed by the ever-increasing threat of a nuclear holocaust or plagued by a personal crisis, we sometimes feel oppressed by our own present. As literati, we often find solace in fiction. Neither Woolf nor Shakespeare nor Cervantes lived in our time or faced our specific problems. Yet one of the marks of a masterful writer is the ability to use language in such a way as to take a dated situation, one that may hold no intrinsic interest for us, and reveal the basic human dilemmas that lie within. Retreat into a fictional world does not give us clear answers to our problems any more than Woolf, Shakespeare, or Cervantes presented unequivocal solutions to their characters' tribulations. Still, when the book is closed and we are confronted anew with the same old problems, our preoccupations may bear the traces of another world. Literature presents us with the opportunity to broaden our understanding of the recurrent existential questions and social dilemmas that face the members of Western society. We thus bring a broader frame of reference to the interpretation of our own particular situation.

The problems facing the bearers of a folkloric tradition are really not so far removed from the process of creating a great work of literary art. One part is imaginative. The artist uses the spoken word to transport her or his audience to another world. Skillful use of stylized language prompts the hearer to look beyond appearances to grasp the meaning with which the creator has imbued this world. Such artists also have the ability to "read" the "real" world in which their audiences live and thus to find the sorts of imaginary scenes and existential problems that will fit the experiences of their interlocutors. The interpretive task that confronts the artist is thus twofold—interpreting both an imaginary sphere and the perceiver's own world. But oral performance has a third component as well. The gifted artist uses stylistic devices in such a way that the form and content of the performance reflect the artist's view of the way these two worlds, imaginary and real, are connected.

To seek an understanding of the nature of this gift, I have focused on a small group of artists who live in a small rural community in northern New Mexico. I refer to these people, in keeping with their own usage, as *Mexicanos*.[1] Their primary language is Spanish, and their predominant medium for verbal artistry is the spoken word. A great deal of respect is accorded to those members of the community who are skillful in using language aesthetically and persuasively, particularly to those who can perform in such genres as proverbs, scriptural allusions, jokes, legends, hymns, and prayers. By and large, only the oldest members of the community are believed to have the *don* 'gift' needed to perform in these genres, and few are endowed with the 'gift' to use different genres. My goal is to reach an understanding of these gifts or, in other words, to explore the *competence* that underlies the ability to perform verbal art.

This chapter presents a theoretical framework for the study of competence in performances of verbal art. My goal is to establish the importance of this approach to performance and to draw together the various scholarly traditions that have informed my perspective. I must admit, however, that my initial realization of the importance of competence was catalyzed not by this body of theory but by the failure of my efforts in understanding Mexicano verbal art performances.

I conducted a preliminary study of Spanish-language folklore of New Mexico in 1974,[2] when investigating the production of images of Catholic holy personages, particularly in the community of Córdova (see Briggs 1980). Because of my related interest in verbal art, I had collected scattered examples in various genres. My initial efforts were informed by study of the wealth of folkloristic texts from New Mexico and southern Colorado. The work of Campa (1946, 1963), Aurelio M. Espinosa (1910–1916, 1953), José Manuel Espinosa (1937), Lucero-White Lea (1936, 1953), Rael (1937, n.d., 1951/1957), Robb (1954), and others had yielded a large collection of proverbs, jokes, folktales, ballads, hymns, riddles, folk dramas, legends, and other genres. Having read this literature, I thought I knew what this body of folklore was and how to find it.

In my initial study, I sought to apply a contextual or ethnography-of-speaking-folklore approach in illuminating the way proverbs are used in social life.[3] For two years I had been working closely with Costancia and Aurelio Trujillo, who were skilled in using various types of verbal art. I asked them to provide me with examples of situations in which proverbs might be used and how they would be performed. Mr. Trujillo replied most apologetically that he could not recall a single one, even though he had heard them all his life. Mrs. Trujillo concurred.

Later in the conversation when Mr. Trujillo used a familiar proverb, *hay gente pa' todo* 'there are all kinds of people' or 'it takes all kinds', I asked him if this expression was not a proverb. He refused to accept the idea that this counted as a proverb, adding that *no más palabras es* 'these are just words.' He then suggested that I speak with the two elders who enjoy the greatest reputation in the community as proverb performers.

Frustrated and confused, I turned to one of the proverb specialists, Federico Córdova, who was already a good friend. Exploring the 'just words' phenomenon, I provided him with a text found in the literature (cf. Cobos 1973b; Aranda 1975): *por dinero, baila el perro* 'for money, <even> the dog dances'. He noted, however, that 'they rather used proverbs that conveyed the sense, significance, or meaning' (*traiban el sentido*) of a given situation. Thus, according to both Trujillo and Córdova, the mere utterance of a proverb text does not illuminate the participants' understandings of a particular conversation. Mr. Córdova focused on the ability of elderly performers to use proverbs in convincing their interlocutors of the validity of their own point of view.

The concept of *sentido* extends simultaneously in two directions. The best speakers in this community can command a vast range of the textual tradition of their society. This ability is measured in terms of both the number of genres in which they can perform and the variety of examples that they can draw from each type. In addition to a range of knowledge, it is equally important to be able to select just the right genre to fit a given situation and then choose an item that speaks to the problem at hand most directly. The form of the text is then shaped in such a way that it fits the most minute details of the interactional context of its performance. *Sentido* thus points to the manner in which performances integrate elements of the Mexicano *conscience collective* and the unique, fortuitous circumstances of a particular moment in time.

What had I learned in these two encounters? Mr. Trujillo and Mr. Córdova rejected my a priori, text-centered view of folklore—my assumption that I could start with a set of proverb texts and then see how they might be used in social interaction. They emphasized the difficulty of producing a proverb text apart from a social context that provided a raison d'être. Isolating a text from the discourse that surrounds it simply produces 'just words.' Mr. Córdova went on to argue that the nature of performance lies not in repeating texts but in developing the competence to embed textual elements in an ongoing interaction.

This book is an attempt to understand *trayendo el sentido*. My focus will remain fixed on performances of Mexicano folklore. I will present the reader with transcriptions and translations of tape-recorded or videotaped performances. In each case, I will take an interaction that may seem either opaque or seducingly straightforward and try to reveal the richness of structure and meaning that lends rhetorical force to such performances. Once a number of such instances have been explicated, I will outline the basic features of the genre. The scope of the study will extend beyond proverbs to include other genres, particularly historical discourse, scriptural allusions, jokes, legends, hymns, and prayers. Together these form *la plática de los viejitos de antes* 'the talk of the elders of bygone times'. One major thrust of this book is thus descriptive. I hope to isolate the features that characterize each body of performances as a genre as well as the commonalities that they share as varieties of this 'talk.' In other words, I am interested both in the fact that trayendo el sentido plays a key role in all of these genres and in the substantial differences in the way this process works in each case.

A second thrust of the analysis is theoretical. The analytic core of the work lies in the new field of ethnopoetics. Ethnopoetics focuses on the way in which formal or stylistic elements go hand in hand with meaning in verbal art traditions. Researchers have explored new techniques of transcription and analysis in attempting to interpret performances on their own terms. Work in ethnopoetics has focused primarily on the study of the myths and tales of native North and South Americans. The present work expands the scope of ethnopoetics by comparing the form and meaning of narrative genres with the form and meaning of shorter, more conversational genres, such as proverbs and scriptural allusions, and by dealing with Romance language materials.

This broadening of the empirical focus has prompted the inclusion of a wide range of theoretical frameworks. I draw on the areas of sociolinguistics, pragmatics, discourse and conversation analysis, performance theory, and phenomenology. My goals in presenting this mode of analysis are twofold. First, I hope to construct a framework that will enable us to grasp the fundamental processes that underlie performances in a given set of genres without falling into reductionist traps. My thesis is that the way performances interpret textual traditions contrasts sharply with the way in which they are rooted in social interactions.

Second, a broader theoretical goal emerges from my concern with the way these two processes come together in performance. The two-sidedness of performance parallels a bifurcation in communicative processes in general. Linguists have long been concerned with the way that the act of speaking presupposes command of complex arrays of elements and rules that are shared by all speakers of the language. Anthropologists have similarly pointed to basic social and cultural premises that underlie speech and action in a given society. None of these theories indicate what we will say at a particular time. This entails a sensitivity to the minute details of unique encounters as they unfold from moment to moment.

Linguists, anthropologists, sociologists, and others have generally stressed either the shared, recurrent patterns *or* the pragmatics of particular interactions. We are accordingly far from understanding how speakers relate the two each time they speak. My contention is that the study of verbal art performances affords particularly interesting data on this problem in that the formal or stylistic elements of performances provide something akin to a blueprint from which one can see how each process operates in the production and comprehension of discourse. My larger goal is thus to draw on a study of the abilities that underlie performances in providing insight into the nature of communicative competence in general.

BUILDING AN ETHNOPOETICS OF CONVERSATIONAL FOLKLORE

Some ideas enter the intellectual landscape with great force, providing a common orientation for formerly disparate studies and motivating researchers to rethink old questions. Students of verbal art have often felt a sense of academic ennui; the study of such forms may intrigue the odd person, but it has not been perceived by "the mainstream" as illuminating the fundamental social, cultural, and linguistic processes that guide thought and action. In the 1970s, however, a group of folklorists, linguists, anthropologists, and others developed a shared interest in the concepts of *performance* and *ethnopoetics*. Because these approaches called for novel techniques of collection and analysis, the study of verbal art was imbued with a new sense of methodological rigor. Like many structuralist and poststructuralist movements, the glamour was derived in part from the appropriation of a new linguistic "model," sociolinguistics. However, the process was multidirectional, because linguists, anthropologists, literary critics, and others were gaining a new sense of the insights that the study of verbal art could offer in pursuing their own concerns.

I believe that these developments provide us with a new understanding of the nature of verbal art. The work of Parry (1930, 1932, 1971) and Lord (1960) on epic fostered a crucial shift in the way performance is conceived. They suggested that verbal art forms are *composed* in the course of their performance by the application of recurrent formulas in specifiable formal and thematic environments. Lord (1960:99–102) argued that performances are also shaped by audience participation. These insights helped overcome the prevalent reification of performances as objectified texts in favor of explorations of the processes that underlie oral composition.

Lord was careful to note, however, that one cannot generalize from a model of epic production to the study of other verbal art genres. Similarly, this change in perspective drew on a number of other theoretical sources as well. It is thus important to examine the contribution of performance theory, ethnopoetics, and other fields in developing an approach that will enable us to appreciate the nature of the performance process as it is realized in each individual genre as well as to identify basic similarities and differences.

COMMUNICATIVE COMPETENCE

The concept of communicative competence is drawn from the work of Hymes. He uses it in contrasting his own approach with Chomsky's emphasis on *linguistic competence*. Chomsky argues that "we must abstract for separate and independent study a cognitive system, a system of knowledge and belief that develops in early childhood and that interacts with many other factors to determine the kinds of behavior that we observe . . ." (1968:4). Hymes redefines the concept as sociolinguistic or communicative competence, noting that in addition to a grammar, "a child acquires also a system of its use, regarding persons, places, purposes, other modes of communication, etc.—all the components of communicative events, together with attitudes and beliefs regarding them" (1974:75).

This reorientation is crucial for the present study. Chomsky isolates the study of competence, which he sees in purely abstract and cognitive terms, from interaction and even from communication itself (cf. Chomsky 1975:53–64). I hope to show that the structure and meaning of Mexicano verbal art can never be grasped apart from an understanding of the way in which mental representations unfold in performance. The present study questions the possibility of gaining insight into the nature of competence when performances are stripped of their spatiotemporal and social relevance and analyzed in purely general and abstract terms.

The concept of communicative competence provides a central focus for the task of describing and analyzing a particular speech community. This perspective helps researchers avoid reifying language varieties as static, self-contained objects, and directs their attention to the processes that underlie both type and token dimensions of particular bodies of discourse. Interestingly, the performers themselves are concerned with precisely this problem. The way they conceptualize the performance process challenges the researcher to go beyond a mapping of texts to contexts or an analysis of stylistic features that does not grapple with questions of meaning. The concept of sentido points to the creativity that is needed to bring fundamentally different types of communicative processes together in a unique manner on each occasion.

Both competence and sentido thus point to a basic proposition that underlies this research: performers are not passive, unreflecting creatures who simply respond to the dictates of tradition or the physical and social environment. They interpret both traditions and social settings, actively transforming both in the course of their performances. Use of the term *communicative competence* challenges the analyst to penetrate beyond the viewpoint of the outside observer to explore the nature of each individual's participation in particular interactions and the factors that shape such involvement.

PERFORMANCE THEORY AND ETHNOPOETICS

Hymes has extended the concept of communicative competence in relating it to genre and performance (1971, 1981/1975). He argues that competence assumes many different forms both within and between speech communities. Performing in two different genres may involve quite different abilities. In the Mexicano case, competence in a given genre is seen as involving a specific type of *don* 'gift', and individuals develop reputations for excelling in particular genres. My own analysis reaches the same conclusion: the processes that underlie different genres are quite different, particularly as one contrasts shorter, more conversational genres (such as proverbs) with those genres in which narrativity is more pronounced (such as legends).

Such differences only come into focus, however, once the distinction between genres and analytical types is drawn. According to Ben-Amos (1976/1969), analytic types are concepts constructed by scholars as an aid in classifying and comparing different folkloric repertoires. Genres, on the other hand, are specific to individual speech communities, constituting "a cultural affirmation of the communication rules that govern the expression of complex messages within the cultural context" (1976/1969:225). Identification of genres thus entails analysis of events in situ for sets of relations between "formal features, thematic domains, and potential social usages." This task forms the descriptive core of this book.

Hymes's expansion of the notion of competence is equally crucial. He argues that knowledge of a given body of information comes in many forms. Drawing in part on the work of Labov, Hymes contrasts the ability to interpret, report, or repeat a given speech act with the ability to perform it; performance is distinguished "as cultural behavior for which a person assumes responsibility to an audience" (1981/1975:84). Hymes is not alone in emphasizing the importance of performance; the work of

Abrahams (1968a, 1971, 1983b, 1985), E. Basso (1985), Bauman (1977/1975, 1986), Ben-Amos (1971, 1977), Dundes (1964, 1980), Glassie (1982), Goldstein (1964), Gossen (1974a, 1985), Kirshenblatt-Gimblett (1974), Lomax (1968), Sherzer (1983), and others has been influential in this regard. The performance framework changes the way one addresses the issue of competence. Rather than attempt to isolate what it takes to produce a particular type of text, performance theorists seek features that identify when speakers are signaling their assumption of responsibility for invoking shared patterns of form and meaning. Three types of characteristics have been identified as primary components of performance.

The first of these relates to the concept of *responsibility* as articulated by Bauman (1977/1975:11) and Hymes (1981/1975:84). All members of social groups do not have equal access to particular traditions. Such factors as age, gender, occupation, ethnicity, and political or religious status often define the range of possible performers for a given genre. Among the Kuna of Panamá, for example, only the chief can deliver the *namakke* 'chant', whereas the act of translating the chant into the "ordinary" Kuna is reserved for the chief's spokesman (Sherzer 1983). In many cases, however, not all individuals of the appropriate age, gender, or status will be accorded the right to perform; as in the Mexicano case, individuals must earn this right by displaying their verbal virtuosity. Aurelio Trujillo's refusal to provide examples of proverbs did not emerge from ignorance. He was quite capable of repeating proverb texts as well as interpreting and reporting performances; he did not, however, consider himself to be a competent performer of proverbs. As later chapters will attest, he was one of the most accomplished performers of prayers, hymns, and scriptural allusions in the community.

Whether a particular utterance qualifies as a performance does not depend, however, on the social characteristics or even the virtuosity of the speaker alone. A person who is an accomplished performer may invoke tradition without actually performing it. The difference lies less in the nature of the content that is conveyed than in the way the speaker articulates it vis-à-vis the ongoing social interaction. Austin's (1962) concept of *performativity* points to the way that the meaning of an utterance emerges from more than the referential content of the words; language is not a passive instrument for describing a world that is independently constituted. Through its performative force, language can effect action, whether it is the baptism of a baby or the delivery of a command. In performance, an individual assumes responsibility for invoking the tradition itself, not just pointing to its existence.

The nature of this invocation differs between genres and communities, but several characteristics are common. According to Bauman (1977/1975:11) performance involves "an assumption of accountability to an audience for the way in which communication is carried out." Performers thus direct attention to the act of speaking itself as well as to the content of the speech, and their communicative competence will be evaluated in accordance with genre-specific criteria. Hymes (1981/1975:83–84) and Bauman (1977/1975:24) argue that the assumption of responsibility for performance can differ in intensity; only some performances or parts of performances will achieve full authenticity and authoritativeness.

How, then, does the audience know whether a performance is in progress? Here performance theorists draw the concept of the frame, articulated by Bateson (Bateson et al. 1972/1955; 1972/1956) and elaborated by Goffman (1974), that certain features are metacommunicative in nature. Their function is thus to define, interpret, comment on, or in some way shape the ongoing communicative event. This role is evinced by opening and closing formulae in verbal art. "Do you know the one about X?" alerts the listener that a joke is to follow, whereas "Once upon a time" and "And they lived happily ever after" signal the opening and closing of a fairy tale. The point is that verbal art traditions include frames that stand as conventional signals for indicating the existence of performance and for specifying what type of performance is under way.

The second major characteristic of performance is the existence of particular formal or stylistic patterns. I noted previously that performance involves a heightened awareness of the manner in which sound, gesture, and perhaps other media are used in conveying a body of content. This foregrounding of form, which Jakobson (1960:356) refers to as the poetic function, is combined with a stylistic elaboration of speech. Bauman (1977/1975:16–22) lists a number of common forms of elaboration. Some genres are marked by special codes; among the Warao of eastern Venezuela, male medico-religious practitioners use a special lexicon in addressing spirits, just as women draw on special grammatical forms in funerary laments (Briggs 1987b; also see Barral 1964; Lavandero 1972, 1983; Suárez 1968:157–82; Wilbert 1972). Performances are also commonly marked by a heightened use of figurative language that forces listeners to penetrate beyond the "ordinary" definitions of words in discerning the speaker's meaning.

A third common characteristic, parallelism, consists of the repetition of elements drawn from any level of linguistic structure (cf. Jakobson 1960). Alliteration and rhyme form common examples, but lines or larger stretches of speech may be organized in relations of equivalence as well (cf. Espinosa 1985:154–60; Urban 1986b). Performances also frequently feature special features of prosody (pitch, loudness, stress, vowel length, phrasing, rate, etc.); styles of oral delivery; and uses of gesture, body motion, and other paralinguistic and nonverbal features. Performances are often framed through the use of special formulae, such as the opening and closing formulae cited previously. Performers may make a direct appeal to tradition; Mexicanos thus note that their words are taken from *la plática de los viejitos de antes* 'the talk of the elders of bygone days'. Ironically, some traditions use a disclaimer of performance as a mode of framing performances; for example, a Warao chief, who is a master story-teller, began a lengthy and complex mythic performance by noting, *naminanaharone, sanuka ine warate* 'even though I don't know [any myths], I'll tell a short one.'[4]

A related field, ethnopoetics, has focused specifically on stylistic features. The work of Hymes (1981, 1985b) and Tedlock (1972b, 1983) has played a central role in shaping the field, and studies by E. Basso (1985), Bauman (1986), Bright (1979), Gossen (1974a, 1985), K. Kroeber (1981), McLendon (1982), Sherzer (1982, 1983), and others have been influential as well. As Hymes and Tedlock have noted, the absence in Native American mythology of the formal features of Western poetry has often led to the conclusion that it lacked any formal structure or poetic properties at all. Ethnopoetic research has demonstrated, however, that verbal art is characterized by recurrent patterns at all levels of structure from micro to macro. Tedlock has focused on characteristics of oral performance, particularly pause, pitch, loudness, vowel length, and voice quality. For Tedlock, such "paralinguistic" features hold the key to understanding narrative traditions.

Hymes contrastively draws attention to grammatical details that reveal the poetic structure of the text. The Northwest Coast materials that form the starting point of his research often employ sentence-initial particles that point to the existence of poetic lines, verses, stanzas, scénes, and acts; this discovery led him to uncover a broad range of underlying patterns. One of the aspects of Hymes's work that forms a particularly important basis for the present study is his emphasis on exploring the way that formal structures signal meaning; he refers to this relationship as the "systematic covariation of form and meaning." "The poetic purpose is to come as close as possible to the intended shape of the text in order to grasp as much as possible of the meanings embodied in this shape" (1981:7, 10). A good example of such form–meaning covariation is provided by recurrent patterns in narratives of the unfolding of action in cycles that move from exposition to complication and climax and then finally to denouement (cf. Hymes 1981/1975:200–59).

Ethnopoetics has pointed to the existence of identifiable patterns in narratives from the level of lines to that of the overall structure of performances. It reveals the way stylistic features provide a map, as it were, of the discourse structure of performances. One of the major contributions of the work of Hymes (1981) and Tedlock (1972a, 1972b, 1983) is to show that received methods of transcription reduce narrative to simple prose, thus obscuring the formal structure of texts. Their work spells out the theoretical assumptions that are generally implicit in the transcription process. Each scholar has proposed techniques that are theoretically grounded in an appreciation of the nature of oral narratives and that seek to indicate the formal structure of texts by the way that type is aligned on the page. (See Fine 1984 for a review of different theories of transcription.)

A third focus of performance theory lies in the concept of emergence. Here we are concerned with the way that the structure and content of performances are shaped by the specifics of the social interaction in which they occur. Lord (1960) emphasized the importance of the audience's involvement in the performance. In the performance of Serbo-Croatian epics, one of the central determinants of dramatic style and of the length of the song is audience reaction. The singer must use "his dramatic ability and his narrative skill in keeping the audience as attentive as possible" (1960:16). If the singer is not successful in sustaining audience interest, he will be forced to shorten his song. The importance of Lord's work in this regard is the insight that the social setting of performance is far more than an external set of conditions into which a predetermined text is inserted.

Abrahams (1968a, 1971, 1978, 1983b), K. Basso (1979), Bauman (1977/1975, 1986), Glassie (1982), Labov (1972a, 1972c), Sacks (1974), Sherzer (1983), Urban (1986a), Woodbury (1985), and others have moved beyond these initial insights to deepen and broaden our understanding of the way that the setting of performances, including audience participation, constitutes a set of communicative resources that play an important role in the process of oral composition. These writers have drawn on the understanding of contextualization that has emerged from Bateson's work on metacommunication, Hymes's ethnography of communication (1964, 1972), and Goffman's dramaturgical model (1959, 1974, 1981).

Ethnomethodologists, such as Cicourel (1974a, 1982, 1985), Garfinkel (1967, 1972), Jefferson (1972, 1974), Moerman (1972, 1974, 1988), Sacks (1967, 1973, 1974, 1978; Sacks, Schegloff, and Jefferson 1974), and Schegloff (1968, 1972, 1982; Schegloff and Sacks 1973), have been among the most insistent in emphasizing the need to examine the way that social interaction shapes discourse. They argue that many of the "rules" or "norms" that are often treated as preexisting determinants of speech and action are themselves created or renegotiated in the course of human interactions Cicourel (1974b, 1982) and Sacks (1967, 1973, 1974) have noted that sets of common-sense assumptions that we use in making sense of what others say and do frequently vary between different types of speech events. The present work pursues these concerns in attempting an in-depth study of the factors that underlie variations in interactional patterns and background assumptions within a given set of types of speech events—the genres that constitute the talk of the elders of bygone days.

Context-sensitive approaches have been developed within the field of folklore. The work of such scholars as Abrahams (1976/1969, 1971, 1983b), Bauman (1977/1975, 1986), Ben-Amos (1971, 1977), Dundes (1964; Arewa and Dundes 1964), Georges (1969), and Goldstein (1964, 1968) has been referred to as the "contextual" school. Ben-Amos (1971) defines folklore as a "communicative process" in which the interaction between performer and audience is crucial. A recent work by Bauman (1986), subtitled "Contextual studies of oral narrative," is concerned both with the way that context shapes performance and with the way that performance can transform context. Abrahams (1968a), Hymes (1981/1975), Seitel (1972, 1977), and others have followed Burke (1941, 1945, 1969/1950) in analyzing verbal art as involving strategic uses of rhetorical resources in advancing the performer's point of view, whereas Abrahams (1985, 1986a, 1986b) has recently drawn on James (1907) and Dewey (1925) in developing "a pragmatic approach to folklore."

REMAINING PROBLEMS

I have summarized some of the advances that have been made in the last two decades in the study of performance. Drawing on the work of Bakhtin, Bateson, Bascom, Burke, Jakobson, Lord, Mukařovský, Parry, Sapir, and others, students of performance theory and ethnopoetics achieved an integration of these many insights that has moved the study of verbal art away from concern with texts as decontextualized and static. The result is a new framework that understands performance as the dynamic interplay of individual competence in traditional forms, stylistic resources, and a unique interactional environment. This approach has helped overcome the prevailing tendency to reduce verbal art to a single axis, such as the problem of narrative content, stylistic detail, or social or psychological function. The goal is rather to grasp the role of each component in the performance process.

This body of scholarship thus brings us close to providing a framework for studying the process of trayendo el sentido. This is particularly true in that both the Mexicano concept of el sentido and the scholar's notion of performance highlight the individual's relationship to tradition, the role of stylistic features, and the interaction between performer and audience. Unfortunately, the fit is far from perfect. Both the concept of el sentido and the performances that are judged to convey it successfully present problems that extend beyond the limits of the received theory. It is accordingly necessary to identify these limitations and to modify and expand the framework in such a way as to permit a more adequate appreciation of Mexicano verbal art.

PROBLEMS IN THE DEFINITION OF CONTEXT

One problem pertains to the manner in which the *context* of performances is defined. Students of ethnopoetics and performance theory have argued persuasively that context plays a crucial role in performance. Unfortunately, definitions of "the context" are seldom provided, and those that are offered are far from precise. Malinowski's (1923, 1935) work has been quite influential in increasing awareness of the importance of context as well as in informing explicit and implicit definitions. He distinguishes the "context of cultural reality, . . . the material equipment, the activities, interests, moral and aesthetic values with which the words are correlated" (1935:22) and the "context of situation" or "social context," the "purpose, aim and direction of the accompanying activities" (1935:214). His use of the term context is exceedingly inclusive, embracing all aspects of cultural life and the social and physical environ-

ment that surround a given speech event: "I think that it is very profitable in linguistics to widen the concept of context so that it embraces not only spoken words
but facial expression, gesture, bodily activities, and the whole group of people present during an exchange of utterances and the part of the environment on which
these people are engaged" (1935:22).

Some definitions presented by performance-oriented scholars follow Malinowski
closely in stressing both "cultural" and "situational" context. Ben-Amos, one of the
most forceful proponents of context-based analysis in folklore, argues that "the study
of folklore in its cultural and situational context does not only broaden the empirical
field of research, but also provides the basis for explanation and exploration of the
diversity of verbal creativity in society" (1977:47). Others limit context primarily to
Malinowski's "context of situation." Dundes (1964:23) states that "The context of
an item of folklore is the specific social situation in which that particular item is
actually employed." Note that such definitions seldom provide any limitations as
to what is to be included in descriptions and analyses of the context. According to
Toelken (1979:50), for example, "no text can be fully understood without consider-
able reference to the dynamics of context, the total live situation, in which it came
forth."

This body of work has greatly increased the sophistication of theoretical and descriptive studies of performance. I believe, however, that it has failed to grapple with
two central problems, those of inclusiveness and false objectivity. Ben-Amos (1977)
has noted that the growing awareness of the importance of context has yielded relatively little in the way of adequate descriptive studies. One reason for this empirical
deficiency is a basic theoretical shortcoming—definitions of context are overly vague
and inclusive. Even when context is limited to Malinowski's "context of situation,"
the aspirant "ethnographer of speaking folklore" is presented with little idea as to
where to stop—that is, how to know when an adequate range of situational factors
has been included. The task of describing the context thus takes on the form of an
infinite regress. Because breath groups can enter into poetic structure, shall we monitor the physiological changes that accompany the respiration of performer and audience? If the talk is exchanged across a table, are the table's shape, size, color, texture,
construction, and possibly even its molecular structure to be reported?

These are obviously absurd suggestions. But the fact remains that exhortations to
include "the total life situation" of objects and persons present at the time of the
performance provide scholars with no idea as to what elements warrant inclusion.
Once the definition is expanded to include the culture as a whole, then the task of
describing a performance must await the emergence of a total ethnography of the
society. Because such a total study is itself an impossibility, practitioners will be
forced to admit failure. This leaves them with the choice of remaining true to the
task and despairing of ever providing an adequate description of even a single performance, or of making do with a cursory, general description of "the context."

CONTEXT VERSUS TEXT

I would like to suggest that the inclusiveness problem is founded on a deeper fallacy. The problem of false objectivity constitutes a misconstrual of the very nature of context. Most definitions of context are positivistic, equating it with an "objective" description of what exists in the situation of a performance. This definition has two implications. First, the researcher, who is generally not a member of the performer's community, reserves the right to decide what counts as "the context" on the basis of what she or he observes to be "actually there." Thus the analyst is left without a means of assessing whether a given contextual element actually enters into the participation of the performer and the audience in the performance. Second, this definition of context is external to language. Researchers are urged to supplement tape recordings with observationally based descriptions of everything that surrounded the flow of words.

The result is the creation of a dangerous chasm between text and context. Practitioners have been concerned with the way that text and context interact in the emergence process. However, the problem is that defining the context apart from the text and vice versa creates a hiatus that is hard to overcome in later analysis. Such a view also circumvents any real understanding of performativity, as Austin (1962) defines it. In other words, many researchers see the context as a set of conditions that exist *prior to the emergence of the performance.* This renders it much more difficult to recognize the way in which contextual frames shift from moment to moment.

A number of performance-oriented researchers are aware of the problem; as Glassie (1982:33) has aptly noted:

Loose colloquial usage can trick us into employing "context" to mean no more than situation. Then the power of the idea evaporates, and studying context we enlarge and complicate the object we describe but come little closer to understanding than we did when we folklorists recorded texts in isolation. Context is not in the eye of the beholder, but in the mind of the creator.

A number of scholars have drawn on the work of Bateson (1972), Goffman (1974, 1981), Schutz (1967), and others in constructing a more phenomenological concept of context. Bateson's (Bateson and Ruesch 1951; Bateson et al. 1972/1956) research on metacommunication and Goffman's (1974) notion of interactional frames draw attention to the ways in which participants in a communicative event provide each other with cues that signal how words and actions are to be interpreted. These insights have prompted some practitioners, such as Young (1983, 1987), to replace an external, objectifying notion of context by a phenomenologically based concern with the way that context links situation and discourse.

What is needed is a way of studying context that does not create a text/context dichotomy and that enables researchers to identify which elements are actively involved in the contextualization of discourse. Cook-Gumperz and Gumperz (1976; see also Gumperz 1982) provide an approach to the problem that incorporates the insights of Bateson, Goffman, and others and present them in a form that is amenable to empirical analysis. They argue that communicative contexts are not dictated by the social and physical environment, but are created by the participants in the course of the interaction. Communication is punctuated with "contextualization cues" that signal which features of the physical, social, and linguistic setting are being utilized at the time in creating interpretive frameworks for deciphering the meaning of what is being said.

Because such frameworks are products of negotiation, speakers and hearers are constantly monitoring each other's behavior for auditory and visual clues as to how the other person(s) is contextualizing the discourse. The concept of contextualization links the study of poetic features and the participants' own interpretive processes in a new way. The study of contextualization reveals the status of interpretation as an emergent, interpersonal activity that relies on such features not solely for patterning form and content, but also for structuring the process of negotiating a shared frame of reference.

GENRE, STYLE, AND CONTEXTUALIZATION

Note that the movement from "context" to "contextualization" has the potential for bringing this facet of our study in line with other tenets of research in ethnopoetics and performance theory. Viewed as contextualization, assessment of the role of the ongoing social processes that provide the setting for a performance involves looking closely at the forms of discourse themselves to see how the situational resources at hand enter into the performance. The point is not simply to correlate formal features with elements of the surroundings. Performance features do not merely reflect situational factors; rather, they interpret the social interaction, thus opening up the possibility of transforming its very nature.

Note also that the contribution of ethnopoetics lies in its emphasis on sensitivity to poetic or stylistic features. The work of Abrahams (1983b), Bauman (1977/1975, 1986), Ben-Amos (1976/1969), Gossen (1974a, 1985), Hymes (1981, 1985), McLendon (1982), Sherzer (1982, 1983), Tedlock (1972b, 1983), Urban (1986a), and others has provided us with insights into the formal features that enable bearers of traditions and scholars alike to identify a given stretch of discourse as verbal art in a given genre. Such practitioners as E. Basso (1985), Bright (1979, 1986), Hymes (1981, 1985a), McLendon (1982), Sherzer (1982, 1983) Silverstein (1981b, 1985), Tedlock (1972b, 1983), Urban (1985, 1986b), and Woodbury (1985) have indicated ways that stylistic features provide a metacommunicative framework for grasping the discourse structure of performances. Both these and other writers (e.g., K. Basso 1976, 1979, 1984) have used such insights to examine the way that stylistic features provide interpretations of social and cultural patterns.

Unfortunately, close readings of formal features seldom focus on those elements that interpret the social interaction itself. This failure relates to the problems of inclusiveness and false objectivity that I criticized previously. Most analyses of performances include only general and superficial descriptions of the social interactional setting. Such information often comes in the form of a brief introduction that precedes the transcription and analysis. The stylistic analysis may inform our view of the way formal features elucidate textual structure and cultural import, but they are rarely analyzed systematically as keys to the contextualization process. The text comes to stand apart, once again, from its context. There are some notable exceptions (cf. Brukman, 1975; Cicourel 1982; Hanks 1984; Hymes 1981/1975:129–34, 138–41, 1985; Tedlock 1983:285–301; Urban 1986a, 1986b; Woodbury 1985) in which the apparent gap between style and social interaction is bridged. There is still a pressing need, however, for analyses that draw on poetic features in teaching us as much about the participants' understanding of the ongoing social interaction as they do about discourse structure and social and cultural meanings.

The point is not simply to provide more lengthy descriptions of "the context." Malinowski's own work should alert us to the dangers of providing ever more detailed descriptions of "the context," seen from the observer's perspective, without relating the setting to the discourse. The problem lies in developing an adequate means of integrating the two. One major hindrance in this regard is methodological. Despite advances in transcription techniques, most transcriptions and translations still delete back-channel cues spoken by the audience, such as "uh huh," "yes," and "really?" As conversation analysts and ethnomethodologists have shown, these sorts of interjections provide invaluable means of understanding the contextualization process (cf. Duncan 1972, 1973; Duncan and Niederehe 1974; Jefferson 1974; Sacks 1967; Sacks et al. 1974; Schegloff 1982). For example, in his work on Yucatec Mayan narrative, Burns forcefully established the "dialogue nature" of Yucatec narratives (1980, 1983:19–24). Nonetheless, his own volume of ethnopoetically inspired translations of these narratives fails to include these crucial responses, thus turning dialogue into monologue.

This paucity of attention to the relationship between style and contextualization is also related to the generic focus of ethnopoetics. Most practitioners have focused on myths and tales.[5] The emphasis has accordingly been on genres that foreground narrativity and often reserve the role of performer to one individual. Although narrative texts are certainly contextualized, extended narratives are contextualized to a lesser degree and in a different manner than highly conversational forms such as proverbs. By concentrating on myths and tales, scholars have been able to defer the challenge to examine systematically the relationship between style and contextualization to a greater degree than would have been possible if proverbs and riddles had formed the initial focus of ethnopoetic research.

ON THE FUZZY FRINGE OF PERFORMANCE

The study of conversational genres draws our attention to the difficulties that emerge from the manner in which practitioners segment performances from other types of discourse. As Hymes (1981/1975:84) and Bauman (1977/1975:8) have argued, the term *performance* would be devoid of explanatory value if it were used to cover the entirety of spoken discourse. To be considered an example of performance (particularly of "authoritative or authentic performance"; see Hymes 1981/1975), a speech event must differ in significant ways from other types of discourse. Likewise, it must be possible to segment the stretch of speech that is to be labeled as performance from the nonperformative speech that precedes and follows it.

One of my concerns in this book is with the difficulties imposed by received definitions of performance for certain types of speech events. Such Mexicano forms as pedagogical discourse and collective recollections, for example, clearly fall within the aegis of 'the talk of the elders of bygone days', and they evince a number of features that are not shared by conversations that lie outside the bygone days frame. By their very nature, however, they are structurally quite similar to ordinary conversation (see Chapter 3). Most important, it would be impossible to make sense of these two types of speech events without examining the connections between utterances that are framed as performances and those that are not, and this is true for proverbs and scriptural allusions as well.

In other cases, parts of performances may contrast sharply in form and content from other communicative modes. Nonetheless, clear lines that demarcate the end of other speech event types and the beginning of such performances or the end of these performances and the transition to other types of discourse are very difficult to identify. This problem is particularly true of proverbs and scriptural allusions (Chapters 4 and 5). The point is that most of the meaning of the performance would be lost if equal weight was not accorded to the manner in which performative and nonperformative modes intermingle as well as the ways that they are distinct.

These phenomena I term *fuzzy boundary problems*. I emphasize them because they challenge performance theory and intersect with many of the issues that I raised previously. I have noted that received analyses of stylistic features are concerned with the way that formal elements frame performances, reveal their discourse structure, and indicate the performer's view of cultural and social patterns. This approach tends to limit perception of the way stylistic features also point to relations of coherence or relatedness between performance and other types of discourse.[6]

The methodological problem is also crucial here. Transcriptions generally begin at the point at which the performance is deemed to have begun and ended, thus leaving out the discourse that precedes and follows it. In the case of proverbs, riddles, and the like, quotations of the proverb or riddle text are often accompanied by the author's summaries of "the context." When performances of myths and tales are provided in situ, transcriptions similarly delete the "ordinary conversation" that precedes and follows them and that may also come between stanzas. This technique strips performances of the data needed to explore fuzzy boundary problems. Notions of performance that focus only on the way it is distinguished from other speech modes ultimately reintroduce the same sorts of system (*langue*) and usage (*parole*), text and context dichotomies that they were designed to circumvent.

COMPETENCE, INTERPRETATION, AND METACOMMUNICATIVE COMPLEXITY

My goal in raising these questions is not to deprecate ethnopoetics and performance theory. As I have noted, these two related bodies of literature provide the theoretical and methodological backdrop for this work. My comments are rather motivated by the need to look at and to understand a wide range of Mexicano performances. My goal has been to show how the theoretical framework can be revised and expanded so that it can deal with performance at the same level of sophistication that is evident in the notion of trayendo el sentido and in those performances themselves. My concern is that performance theory and ethnopoetics sometimes place a barrier between researchers and performers. Whereas scholars stress the *discontinuities* between performances and other modes of interaction, performers emphasize the *continuities*. I believe, however, that the adoption of two major theoretical tenets can bring the two conceptions of performance into a fruitful rapprochement.

PERFORMANCE AS AN ACTIVE, INTERPRETIVE PROCESS

The basic postulate that underlies my work is a conception of performance as an active and interpretive process. The view that "natives" produce meaning that must in turn be interpreted by scholars is, in my estimation, an ethnocentric and class-based conceit. Performers do not simply "reflect" the natural and cultural world around them, unconsciously replicating structures of which they have no understanding. The materials of performance, including traditions, texts, and settings are not presented to the performer in predigested form. The performer draws on these resources as needed, selecting those elements that prove relevant to the purpose at hand. These are then interpreted by the performer and thereby provided with a meaning that is responsive both to shared beliefs and values and to the individual's own perspective. The performer's concern is both with the vast array of meanings that each component holds and with the production of a whole in which each part is consonant with the others. Being a performance, style is foregrounded; the performer is thus also concerned with making this conceptual fit a formal or stylistic fit. The formal structure will yield as much information regarding the interpretation that is embedded in the performance as will the referential content of the words themselves.

This interpretive process reaches into the role of the audience as well. As Cicourel (1982), Gumperz (1982), and others have shown, background information and communicative resources are not always shared by speaker and hearer. The achievement of understanding between performer and audience is not automatic. The Mexicano materials suggest that one of the most important determinants of the form and content of performances is the performer's estimation of what the audience will be able to understand. Performers are particularly concerned with the responses that they receive from the audience in the course of the performance, even if these may be as banal as nods of the head or monosyllabic equivalents. The analysis must consider that members of the audience have their own interpretive task; the shape of the performance will reflect the way the audience conveys its own interpretation and the way the performer interprets this response (cf. Goodwin 1981).

The work of interpretation, as Tedlock (1979) has argued, is not that of imposing an interpretation on blocks of heretofore uninterpreted discourse. My first principle is that *performers embed interpretations of the meaning of their utterances in the form of the discourse itself.* The interpretive process does not even begin with the performer. As phenomenologically inclined philosophers and literary critics have noted, the performer's interpretation is itself informed by a long line of preceding interpretations. The audience draws both on this tradition and on the performance itself in its interpretation. My role in presenting these performances in a scholarly treatise is to continue this work of interpretation. Given the nature of my audience and differences in the character of this speech event, the way I articulate my understanding of the performance will be dissimilar. The underlying goal is, however, the same—to discover the interpretation that the performer has embedded in the discourse and to make sense of it.

THE DIVERSITY OF INTERPRETIVE PROCESSES

My second tenet relates to the nature of this interpretive task. Mexicano performances draw on a number of basic communicative resources. A central role is accorded to 'the talk of the elders of bygone days', the verbal traditions that convey the people's view of their past. Performers have a heightened awareness of the form of their discourse, the way that the various linguistic units fit together into a coherent whole. They also command an extensive repertoire of stylistic devices for elaborating the discourse structure. A vast body of knowledge concerning the contemporary residents of the performer's community, including their genealogies, personal reputations, and communicative competence is similarly of importance. Speakers incorporate knowledge of modern American society and world affairs into performances. Audiences and performers alike draw on close readings of a unique set of circumstances, the ongoing social interaction.

Performance thus entails coordination of a number of distinct types of communicative resources. This is not a mechanical process, but an active, interpretive one that extends principally in two directions simultaneously. Individuals gain the right to perform by mastering one or more genres of the talk of the elders of bygone days. This involves learning how to interpret the beliefs and practices of the elders of bygone days as well as the formal devices that are used in conveying them, a domain that I term the *textual sphere*. Performance features that index this sphere are termed *textual features*.

My definition of the textual sphere and textual features applies some classic measures of textuality (cf. de Beaugrande and Dressler 1981) to the culture-specific importance of the elders of bygone days. To be seen as indexing the textual sphere, a feature must exhibit three basic properties. First, the feature must be intertextual—that is, in the present case, the utterance in question must be framed as a token of the talk of the elders of bygone days. Its meaning will thus hinge on its relationship to speech acts that presumably took place in bygone days; it will also bear important similarities to past performances of the talk of the elders of bygone days.

Second, the coherence of textual features derives from the way in which the relationship between features is seen as being analogous to the relationship between elements of the world of the elders of bygone days. For example, utterances that are linked sequentially in a legend are connected by virtue of an iconic relationship that they are believed to bear vis-à-vis series of events that took place in bygone days.

The third criterion draws on the notion of cohesion, the way that words, gestures, and prosodic features as sign vehicles (rather than objects of representation) are connected. In the present case, textuality implies a recognition that a set of words, gestures, and prosodic features go together by virtue of the fact that they jointly form a particular token of the talk of the elders of bygone days. A high level of textuality will enable performers and audience members to identify a given group of utterances as constituting a particular text (e.g., the joke about Antonio Córdova's Indian servant, the Tale of the Lost Mine of Juan Mondragón [cf. Briggs and Vigil 1989], or a hymn entitled *Al pie de este santo altar* 'At the Foot of this Holy Altar').

Performers will not be able to convey el sentido, however, unless they are astute students of unique, ongoing social encounters. Interpreting the social interaction in which a performance takes place and conveying that interpretation in the form of the performance brings the *contextual sphere* into being. To be considered a *contextual feature*, an utterance must be uninterpretable without reference to some facet(s) of *ahora* 'nowadays', the world that currently embraces the participants. Contextual features are indexically tied to nowadays in three ways. First, some contextual features index one or more elements of the social, linguistic, and physical setting of the performance. Second, such features may be linked to some specific interaction that preceded the performance; contextual features commonly point to a previous conversation between the participants. Third, contextual features may index nowadays as a whole—that is, the general social, cultural, or political-economic conditions that characterize the present. A perceived loss of religious faith in the world today is, for instance, a recurrent theme in performances.

Having made this distinction, I can now present a number of hypotheses about Mexicano performances. I believe not only that all performances contain both contextual and textual features, but that they provide indispensable means of making sense of performances; this is true for participants and researchers alike. Another claim is that textual and contextual features play highly contrasting roles in performance. Performances are accordingly not unitary, homogeneous entities; their structure rather revolves around a dialectical relationship between textual and contextual realms. One of the most important ways that genres are distinguished is with regard to the relative importance of textual and contextual realms in performances. I will argue that these two realms are rooted in quite different sorts of communicative processes. Finally, the complexity of performances lies in the fact that these two distinct interpretive processes are linked by a third one, an interpretation of the way that textual and contextual spheres intersect at one particular time.

My quibble with performance theory and ethnopoetics is that this body of literature is one-sided. Most practitioners have concentrated on the workings of the textual sphere, and many have provided brilliant insights into its richness, complexity, and diversity. The contextual sphere is, however, little known. Even those researchers whose interest lies mainly in the contextual sphere have largely failed to base their efforts on close analysis of how the form of discourse reveals the way that the participants have phenomenologically constructed the context of their interaction. Regardless of whether one favors the textual or contextual realm, the problem is still the same. Performance consists of the simultaneous exploration of both of these realms and the building of an architectonic that maps their rapprochement. We thus cannot claim to have adequately understood the performance process until we have grasped the nature of both textual and contextual components and the way they interrelate. This problem has not been entirely neglected by researchers; studies by Abrahams (1976/1969), Bauman (1986), Hanks (1984), Hymes (1985), Sherzer (1983), Silverstein (1985), Urban (1986a, 1986b), and Young (1987) have explored various ways in which performance unites contextual and textual elements. But we are far from understanding the basic processes that are used in generating text-context architectonics and the way that these processes are differentially realized as we move from genre to genre.

El sentido is precisely that architectonic, which takes me back to the issue of competence. My consultants were quick to point out that recitations that reach in only one direction fall short of inclusion in 'the talk of the elders of bygone days'. Unless

our analyses can make sense of textual and contextual realms and the way they intersect, our efforts will similarly fall short of an adequate understanding of the complexity of the interpretive processes that are learned in the course of becoming a
competent performer.

The complexity increases when we take genre into account. The role of the contextual sphere diminishes and that of the textual sphere increases as one moves from
performances of historical discourse to proverbs to scriptural allusions to jokes to legends to hymns and prayers. The problem is qualitative and not simply quantitative—
the place of these two spheres in performance shifts radically as one moves from the
more contextually to the more textually focused genres. This pattern suggests that
only an appreciation of the threefold nature of the interpretive process that constitutes performance will enable the analyst to grasp the similarities and differences in
the nature of the competence that is associated with different genres.

PLAN OF THE BOOK

The remaining chapters except two examine the nature of performance in a particular genre. The first of these exceptions is Chapter 2, a discussion of the field site,
Córdova, and of Mexicano culture in northern New Mexico. The focus here is on
the way that history, political economy, religion, and sociolinguistic patterns inform
performance. I also describe my fieldwork in Córdova and other Mexicano communities, discussing the issues that arise when the collector is a member of the audience.

Chapter 3 examines what I have termed historical discourse. Such discourse consists of no set texts, and its formal structure is flexible. This "looseness" enables performers to shape their discourse to fit the level of knowledge and interest of their
interlocutors. *Antes* 'bygone days' is contrasted with *ahora* 'nowadays' with respect to
key features of how people relate to God, the land, and each other. A dialectical
movement between these two roles is fueled by the inclusion of central images of life
in bygone days. The rhetorical structure centers on the synthesis of these oppositions
in the form of basic moral principles that serve as fundamental guideposts for conducting oneself in any age.

Chapter 4 focuses on proverbs. *Dichos* 'proverbs' are embedded in a wide range of
different types of conversations. They are used by elders in attempting to legitimize
their position on a given issue. Proverb performances draw on the talk of the elders of
bygone days in citing moral precedents that apply to a current situation. Performers
frequently spell out the relevance of an element of bygone days for the problem at
hand. This powerful juxtaposition of past and present is made in the space of a short
stretch of discourse. Proverbs are quite unforgiving in interpretive terms; missing one
syllable may well prevent an audience member from comprehending the performance
as a whole. If successful, proverb performances constitute the final word on a given

subject, and the addressee(s) has little choice but to admit the cogency of the speaker's point of view. They accordingly provide potent demonstrations of rhetorical virtuosity.

Scriptural allusions, which are discussed in Chapter 5, use a quotation as precedent for argument and action. The authority in this case is not the words of the elders of bygone days themselves, but the words of God or Christ. The scriptural quotations may be taken from catechisms or other written texts, but they are more commonly drawn from texts that have been transmitted orally. Scriptural allusions are often used in the course of pedagogical discourse. Here they focus the ongoing past/present dialectic by providing a poignant axis of comparison—a moral principle embodied in a divine quotation. A performance in this genre embodies a particular kind of hermeneutic. Ostensibly reiterating a previously stated contrast, a scriptural allusion in effect points out the sacred meaning that underlies the problem at hand. Performances of scriptural allusions are not necessarily as evanescent as those of proverbs. The quotation may be quite lengthy, invoking, for example, a conversation between Christ, the devil, and death; attention is often refocused in the course of scriptural allusions from the situation at hand to the explication of abstract theological questions.

In the case of *chistes* 'jokes', narrativity grows in strength. As is described in Chapter 6, some jokes are used in the same vein as proverbs and scriptural allusions, illustrating (although seldom proving) the ongoing topic of conversation. Many jokes are performances of lengthy if humorous tales, and their telling is not motivated by the need to legitimize one's position. Jokes are also exchanged in joke-telling sessions. Unlike the preceding three genres, there are no restrictions on who can tell jokes—children can swap jokes with their grandparents. The structure of performances differs considerably from setting to setting. Grasping the nature of Mexicano joking entails explaining what is funny and why, as well as accounting for the multiplicity of ways that jokes link bygone days with the present.

Legends, which are treated in Chapter 7, teach about the past, bringing tradition into the present. Their pedagogical strategy does not, however, involve the incorporation of historical events, figures, and values into characterizations of the performance setting. Raconteurs are rather concerned with using the tale to transport their audience into the once real, now imaginary world of bygone days. I will concentrate on two types of legends. Historical narratives take their raw materials from a particular event or series of events and lodge them in a dramatic structure. Once the setting has been described, a narrative complication, such as an Indian attack, places the dramatis personae in a precarious situation. Descriptions of crucial details join forces with enactments of the characters' words and vocal qualities in heightening the dramatic tension, bringing the audience closer to the events. The denouement traces the forces that lay behind the outcome as well as the way in which the legend encapsulates basic features of life in bygone days. Another set of legends focuses on buried treasure and lost mines. Interestingly, these tales are performed both by believers and by those who deny their veracity. Although the content is the same in either case, the performance features of the telling differ in accordance with the rhetorical intent of the raconteur. Both groups thus use treasure tales in articulating their respective stances on basic social and philosophical questions.

Chapter 8 traces this movement toward the textual pole to its most complete realization. In performances of hymns and prayers, concessions to the present are minimized as worshipers seek to move from an earthly to a spiritual plane of existence. With the aid of written texts, the words are fixed, increasing their resistance to current events. Context does play a limited role through recruitment for the roles of prayer leaders, hymn leaders, image bearers, and the like. Once the roles have been filled and the sacred drama has begun, however, the context is more a creation of the scriptural texts than of the exigencies of the moment. If an individual plays the part adequately, even this level of involvement in the here and now will be superseded in the individual's consciousness in the course of achieving a symbolic unification with Christ.

Chapter 9 moves away once again from a genre-specific focus. Here we return to the issues raised in Chapter 1. The conclusions regarding the role of textual and contextual spheres that emerged from Chapters 3–8 are compared in attempting to comprehend the differences and similarities in the nature of the competence that is entailed in performing in the various genres. The chapter concludes with a discussion of broader comparative and theoretical questions in exploring the implications of research into Mexicano performance for the study of communication.

2

■ ■

MEXICANO NORTHERN NEW MEXICO

As New Mexico State Route 76 climbs onto the mesa above the Santa Cruz Valley, the Sangre de Cristo Mountains fill the horizon (see Map 1). After two miles of winding curves, a deep valley dotted with small farms is visible below. A right turn at the fork in the highway affords entrée into a steep escarpment that plunges onto the floor of the Quemado Valley. Small isolated *ranchos* 'farms/ranches' dot the fields (Plate 1). Continuing east on the dirt road, one passes a tiny post office and two general stores, one defunct and the other nearly so. Another fork divides roads that encircle a town plaza of enjambed adobe houses that are fitted with bright metal roofs (Plate 2). Turn left at the defunct Quemado Bar, and you will find yourself facing the wall of the cemetery of the San Antonio de Padua del Pueblo Quemado Chapel (Plate 3). If school is not in session, children will be walking or riding bicycles or motorcycles on the rough earthen lanes between the houses. A group of young men with longish hair and polished old cars will probably be studying you closely.

Some visitors apprehend this scene with curiosity, enjoying its "quaint" or "exotic" appeal. Others become uncomfortable, feeling that they have inadvertently intruded into someone else's world without knowing what to do or say. In any case, few newcomers have the sense that this community is like any other small American town. The paradox thus emerges. Córdova lies in northern *New* Mexico. Its residents go to school, work for wages, pay taxes, vote, and watch television just like everyone else. Most are dependent upon a modern, capitalist economy for both the basics and luxury items. The lights of the Los Alamos National Laboratory, where the first atomic bomb was constructed, are visible to the west, and most Córdovan workers are employed there.[1] Although they live in the midst of modern America, Córdovans and other rural Mexicanos are not just like any other Americans, either in the eyes of other Americans or in their own eyes.

In my fourteen years of seemingly constant migrations between Córdova and what residents call "the outside," I have found four facets of life in Mexicano northern

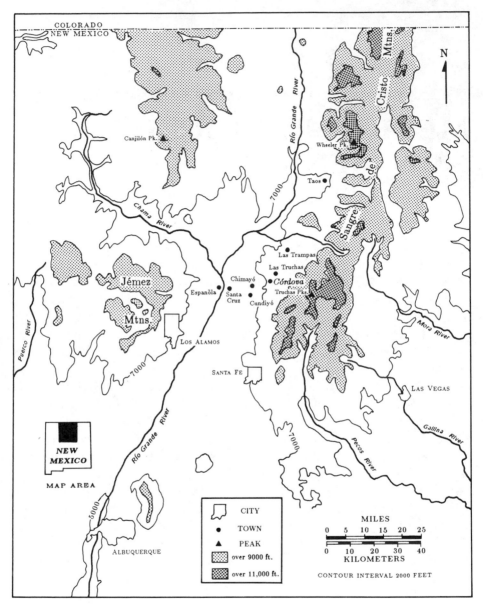

Northern New Mexico. From Charles L. Briggs (1986), Learning how to ask (Cambridge: Cambridge University Press). Used by permission.

Plate 1. The Quemado Valley which surrounds Córdova, 1979. Photograph by Charles L. Briggs

Plate 2. The Córdova plaza, 1974, a view from the south. Photograph by Charles L. Briggs

Plate 3. The San Antonio de Padua del Pueblo Quemado Chapel, located in the center of the Córdova plaza, ca. 1935. Photograph by T. Harmon Parkhurst, courtesy of the Museum of New Mexico, neg. no. 9037.

New Mexico to provide the best sense of the differences and the similarities between Córdova and "mainstream" America. These consist of history and the role that historical consciousness plays in their lives, the effects of the expansion of capitalism on economic and social relations, the way that Mexicano Catholics worship Christ and venerate the Virgin and the saints, and the manner in which Mexicanos use and appreciate language. These four areas provide crucial information for understanding the oral genres that form the focus of this study.

HISTORY

Comprehending performances of *la plática de los viejitos de antes* entails knowing at least the general outlines of the history of Córdova. Even when Córdovan elders talk about the present, *antes* provides a framework for analyzing why events have taken a particular course. The first step in learning about Córdova's history is to examine the basic principle that has shaped it—corporatism. I am not referring here simply to some vague sense of esprit de corps. The point is that Mexicanos do not envision society, à la Hobbes, as an artificial aggregation of individuals who join together in order better to obtain their individual ends. Mexicano corporatism provides persons with a sense of themselves first and foremost as members of a historically produced community. Articulating one's identity entails not so much stating one's individual experiences, goals, or place within the educational, occupational, and social levels of American society as it does locating oneself vis-à-vis this social community and the events that shaped it. Córdovans do not see history as a succession of "one damn thing after another," nor does the past hold only antiquarian interest for the living. Mexicanos are fascinated by their history and by the moral values it embodies for them, and it is a major topic of conversation, particularly for elderly persons.

For Córdovans, each historical period is characterized by the degree to which and the manner in which this corporatistic principle was expressed. Its expression, in turn, is reflected in the way the residents related to each other and to their natural environment. A distinctive set of relations of production is evident, for example, during the initial years of the settlement. The settlement was founded between 1725 and 1743, and it was known until 1900 as Pueblo Quemado.[2] Although the original grant papers have not come to light, the nature of social relations in the community during this period emerges in a decree issued by the governor in 1749. The residents had left the community in the face of increasingly hostile relations between Spanish citizens and "nomadic" tribes in the previous year. The settlers requested permission "to go and plant our fields, such that only the men and the older boys would ascend all together and collectively (*todos juntos y en común*), some to do the planting and those who are not involved in cultivation to watch from the peaks." In granting the petition, Governor Codallo y Rabal admonished them to proceed "well united and armed" (*bien unidos y armados*) (Spanish Archives of New Mexico, No. 718).

This pattern emerges clearly in Córdovan accounts of the period. The settlers' concerns were twofold. First, they required a subsistence base, but the small irrigated fields in the Quemado Valley never produced enough to feed the residents. Córdovans also had access to common lands that were used for hunting and fishing, grazing goats and sheep, cutting fuelwood and timber, and the like. Córdovans enjoyed control over the uplands that stretched between the community and the Truchas Peaks to the east that rise 13,102 feet (Plate 4). This common area, which served for grazing livestock, cutting timber, and hunting and fishing, was thus deemed *libre* 'free', meaning that it was open to exploitation by all. The irrigated fields in the Quemado Valley, on the other hand, were privately owned during the growing season.

The most important feature associated with this era is the high degree of cooperation. The work of the community was a communal enterprise. Individuals assumed various roles—as farmers, hunters, and guards—in accordance with the needs of the settlement as a whole. Each family received an equal portion of what the community produced. Unlike the present, there was no monetary remuneration for services: 'they didn't pay them anything, they just helped. Nowadays there is no one who would help out anyone else. "If you want me to work, pay me," they tell you.' Although the settlers are seen as having been extremely poor, their lot was made easier by an abundance of natural resources and a strong communitarianism.

The settlers' second concern was defense. The settlement consisted not of isolated *ranchos* 'farm/ranches' but of houses grouped in a single plaza with one thick adobe wall abutting the other (Plate 5). Entrance to the plaza was possible only through two openings, and these were sealed with high gates. Windows were high and small, and doors to the individual houses opened into the plaza enclosure. Invaders would fall upon Córdova from the mesa above the plaza. Lookouts were posted at each of the two *torreones* 'circular guard towers', and their cry of alarm would bring Córdovans from the fields and, if they could make it, from the nearby hills. A number of the settlers were particularly good fighters, and legends are still recounted about the most valiant (see Chapter 7). The *Indios* were, however, both determined and *muy tiradores con la flecha* 'good marksmen with bows and arrows', and they killed many men and either killed or made off with numerous women and children.

This situation contrasted sharply with that of the succeeding period. The transition between the two is signaled by the ascendancy in the 1830s of Pedro Córdova, a resident who came to own nearly all of the land and livestock in the community. Córdova had land holdings in Santa Cruz, Chimayó, Las Joyas, el Llano de los Quemadeños, Las Truchas, and Las Trampas. He was able to gain such an economic hold over Córdova and surrounding communities due to the dire poverty of the inhabitants and because he was *inteligente,* meaning that he had an innate, God-given talent for amassing material possessions. Having no resources of their own, the remainder of the Córdovans are believed to have worked for Córdova. The men tended his crops and flocks, the women worked in his large household under the supervision of his wife, Ramona Mondragón. Pedro Córdova assigned *mayordomos* 'foremen' to

Plate 4. *Uplands above Córdova, with piñon-juniper vegetation in the foreground and the Truchas peaks in the background, 1986. Photograph by Charles L. Briggs*

Plate 5. The Córdova plaza, about 1900, prior to the advent of metal roofs. Photograph courtesy of the Museum of New Mexico, neg. no. 58847.

oversee the workers, and his household contained a number of Indios captured or ransomed from "nomadic" tribes as well. The laborers received a portion of the crops and meat, and special allocations were made when a wedding, baptism, or the like was being celebrated (see Brown with Briggs and Weigle 1978:99–105).

The 'reign' of the late Pedro Córdova was a time of great abundance, it is said. He sold grain to area farmers, and his cattle and sheep were driven as far away as Taos for sale or barter. Trading caravans headed south in ox-driven carts to Juárez, Chihuahua, Lagos, Zacatecas, and other destinations, and they would return with gold, silver, and luxury items.[3] Because nearly all of his needs were met by his flocks and fields or through trade, Córdova merely placed the gold and silver that he acquired into *ollas* 'jars' and hid it. He was a good *rico* 'rich person', however, and he also used his wealth in sponsoring such community events as the casting of a bell and the celebrations that followed the completion of such projects (cf. Brown et al. 1978:101–105). Although the contradictions inherent in such a pronounced social inequality are recognized (see Chapter 7), Pedro Córdova is believed to have exhibited the sort of *caridad* 'charity' and generosity that are believed to have rendered this period so fertile. At the time of his death in 1858, Córdova's estate was valued at $9,243.88 (Rio Arriba County Clerk's Office, 1852–62:295–307), many times greater than the holdings of wealthy residents of neighboring communities.[4]

Pedro Córdova died after eating fruit that he had accidentally contaminated with poison. In passing, he took his treasure with him, so to speak, because he never told anyone of its whereabouts. Córdovans still occasionally look for it; only one person, however, is believed to have ever found any of it, and that was a small cache. (These legends will be discussed in Chapter 7.) As a result, Córdova's widow and children were left with his land and cattle alone; their fortune was hardly comparable with that of Pedro Córdova. This situation came to characterize the whole of the period that stretches from Córdova's death until 1915.

A few individuals, including several of Córdova's sons and their descendants, were somewhat better off than the remainder of the Córdovans. There were, however, no ricos—'all of the people were poor.' The ones who did amass any surplus did so in terms of wealth on the hoof, as it were, because the well-to-do of this period were the keepers of large flocks of sheep (Plate 6). Most ran their sheep *al partido* 'on shares', renting them from Frank Bond of Española in return for a given number of pounds of wool per sheep per year. This industry was fostered by the growing availability of breeds of livestock that were more suited to commercial ranching, and by the connection of New Mexico by rail to larger markets to the east and west in 1878–1880. These events were part of a growing commercialization of production in the area.

Like the preceding period, this era was a good one. Cooperation prevailed, and help was always available with planting, harvesting, and the like. A large group of people would harvest one person's fields, then the neighbor's fields, and so on. The

Plate 6. *Sheep pens in the Quemado Valley, with barns of* fuerte *construction. Photograph by Charles L. Briggs*

people exemplified the concept of caridad in their daily lives, helping out those who were in need. An orphan or imbecile would be cared for, not just by relatives but by the community as a whole. The people were strong, because they ate the good food of the land—*atole* 'blue cornmeal gruel', beans, wheat, and vegetables—and their herds and the wild game of the uplands provided them with meat. The sheep brought a double harvest, first the wool and then the lambs. There was little cash in sight, but nearly all of the Córdovans' requirements were met through agriculture and pastoralism, the production of handicrafts, and barter. This prosperity emanated, as it had before, from a combination of hard work and faith in God; the latter was particularly expressed in ritual observances, collective labor, and the extension of caridad.

LAND LOSS AND SOCIOECONOMIC TRANSFORMATION

The demise of the Córdovan sheep ranchers can be attributed to two factors. First, as I noted previously, the pastoral component of the villagers' livelihood depended on the availability of the surrounding uplands for grazing. Having taken the area in 1846 during the Mexican-American War, the United States formally committed itself to respecting the property of former Mexican citizens in article VIII of the Treaty of Guadalupe Hidalgo of 1848; nevertheless, the territorial surveyor general, the Court of Private Land Claims, and the U.S. Congress later rejected most of the Mexicanos' claims to land grants in New Mexico and southern Colorado (cf. Briggs and Van Ness 1987; Van Ness and Van Ness 1980; Wesphall 1983). Even in those cases in which the grants were confirmed, lengthy legal proceedings and the lack of protection from unscrupulous attorneys/land speculators resulted in the loss of large portions of these grants to the attorneys and others (cf. De Buys 1985; Ebright 1980).

Córdova fared poorly in the land struggle. The community was founded earlier than most of the surrounding settlements, and its legal recognition by the appropriate authorities is confirmed by a host of documents. Unfortunately, when the heirs petitioned the Court of Private Land Claims for confirmation of the grant in 1893, they could not produce papers relating to the settlers' original petition and the governor's and *alcalde*'s approval. Although grants with even scantier documentation had been confirmed, the case was not pursued by the Córdovans' attorneys, the notorious Thomas Benton Catron and his partner Charles Coons. The petitioners were thus forced to accept a rejection of their claim in 1893 (Court of Private Land Claims, Case No. 212). The Quemado Valley which contains the house and garden plots and the nearby fields, had already been included in the survey of the adjoining Nuestra Señora del Rosario, San Fernando y Santiago Grant in October 1895 (Case No. 28 and Surveyor General, File 227). Córdovans gained title to these lands as heirs to the latter grant, and no efforts were made to deny them rights to valley lands or home sites.

Such was not the case, unfortunately, with respect to the uplands. Córdovans, along with the residents of neighboring communities, had always depended on the area between the village (at 6,900 feet of elevation) and the Truchas Peaks (13,102 feet) for firewood, timber, and hunting and fishing grounds. The produce of the small farm plots in the valley had never entirely fed the population, and the goats and sheep had always been a vital part of subsistence. The uplands also provided the only lands available to Córdovans for grazing the flocks of sheep during the summer. This area became part of the Pecos River Forest Reserve on 11 January 1892. Although some grazing restrictions were imposed, enforcement was nil, and Córdovans were not even aware of changes in administrative jurisdiction and regulatory policy. Once the uplands were included in the newly created Santa Fe National Forest in 1915, however, a series of changes in grazing regulations severely restricted the local Mexicanos' access to these lands.[5] This eventually deprived Córdovans of nearly all of the subsistence that they had derived from livestock. According to the elders,

A Everything has ended. Oh, there used to be lots of goats, sheep, and. . . .
B There used to be lots of everything.
C The uplands used to be open, but that is no longer true. Now there is the fence and there is the government.

This undermining of the subsistence base forced Córdovans to depend on outside employment. This phenomenon was not wholly new; Córdovans had worked outside the community since the Spanish colonial era. After 1915, however, Córdovans had to sell their labor to an unprecedented degree and to work for employers of a different cultural background. This situation, along with the transition from a predominantly barter to a predominantly cash economy, the imposition of land taxes, and the replacement of locally-produced with mass-produced goods, created a growing need for cash income.

Córdovans resorted to various types of migratory wage labor to cope with this situation. Opportunities for outside work were provided by the building of railroads and the expansion of mining and other nonagricultural enterprises in the area; the harvesting of sugar beets, onions, potatoes, and other crops during the Colorado harvest; and the sheep camps of Colorado, Utah, Wyoming, Montana, and New Mexico (Harper, Córdova, and Oberg 1943:77; Siegel 1959:38; Soil Conservation Service 1937:2). It has been estimated that before the Depression, seven to ten thousand workers from the villages of the middle Rio Grande Valley (the land drained by the Rio Grande River between Elephant Butte and the New Mexico–Colorado line) left each year to engage in these types of migratory labor (Harper et al. 1943:76–77). This pattern created a large dichotomy between the experience of those born around the turn of the century and that of previous generations.

Although Córdovans and other Mexicanos had become highly dependent upon such employment, this source of income was sharply curtailed with the onset of the

Great Depression. After the Depression gained momentum, earnings from outside work were reduced by as much as eighty percent (Harper et al. 1943:77). Widespread starvation was prevented by the implementation of many federal work and aid projects, but this was merely a stopgap measure.[6] The Depression was a bitter pill to swallow for many rural Mexicanos, especially because the constriction of outside employment made the residents even more painfully aware of the expropriation of land resources.

World War II and the succeeding years witnessed an influx of population into New Mexico. Much of this growth was associated with the federal installations in Albuquerque and Los Alamos. The Los Alamos National Laboratory and the service industries that grew in its shadow provided opportunities for daily wage labor, a new source of cash income for residents of the area. The participation of Córdovans in the national economy was further enhanced by improved accessibility to the community. Before 1946, the road to Córdova was little more than a trail, and daily travel to Santa Fe or Los Alamos was impossible. In that year, however, the road that traverses the plain above Córdova was graded and maintained with gravel, and in 1953 it was paved.[7]

Depriving rural Mexicanos of their subsistence base placed them in a position of political-economic dependence upon 'the outside world'—that is, modern industrial society. This in turn induced great changes in the way people related to each other. As Van Ness has shown, the social, cultural, and historical character of rural Mexicano communities is inseparable from the complex system that tied the people to ecologically distinct types of land through a host of different means of ownership and exploitation. The central feature of this system was the character of the community as a corporate unit, as expressed through community ownership of key resources, patterns of collective labor, and a cycle of feast days, dances, and other events (Van Ness 1979a, 1979b, 1987a, 1987b; Kutsche and Van Ness 1982; also see Ebright 1987; Swadesh 1974). Corporatism, stressing the identity of individuals vis-à-vis their membership in the group, was a central feature of Mexicano society well into this century. Corporatism similarly pervaded interpersonal relations; a person who refused to give or lend a possession to someone in need was sanctioned.

The land has been important in other ways as well. Ortiz's (1969) ethnography of nearby San Juan Pueblo clearly demonstrates the way that land can provide crucial reference points in the cultural system of the people who occupy it. K. Basso (1984) and Kuipers (1984) have recently pointed to the rich associations that emerge between events and the places in which they take place; landmarks thus evoke names and stories that are closely connected with cultural values and patterns of interaction. These observations are no less applicable to rural Mexicano communities. A trip through Córdova and the surrounding countryside brings to mind myriad names that point to geographic features or historical events. Crossing the Alto Huachín above Córdova often prompts an elder to talk about the Tano Indians who inhabited this area before its settlement by *los Españoles* 'the Spaniards' and about the Tano leader for whom it was named. The site is also likely to spark a historical discussion of the way that Córdovans used to plant wheat and other crops there in bygone days.

Loss of the uplands thus dealt a severe blow to the community in sociocultural as well as political-economic terms. The uplands surrounding the community provided central communal resources; Córdovans thus lost their control over a major source of subsistence resources as well as of collective identity. Talking about the land continues unabated, as will be seen in the succeeding chapters. But the role that these places play in the lives of Córdovans was transformed as soon as fences and forest rangers stood between the people and the land. Living off the land became practically impossible, and, as the elders still tell you, this has led to many changes in the way people relate to one another. As Córdovans were increasingly forced to spend months away from the community as migrant laborers or to leave each day for Los Alamos, they found it harder and harder to exchange labor and its fruits and to be on hand for community-sponsored events. Working for wages in an Anglo-dominated world also fostered the adoption of individualist and materialist values whose expression has been reflected in recent decades by the construction of more "modern" homes on isolated valley or hillside plots away from the plaza (Plate 7). The geographically close-knit character of the community and the ubiquity of face-to-face interaction on a daily basis with other residents have thus been eroded by changing economic, social, and residential patterns.

As a result, Córdovans have found it increasingly difficult to express basic Mexicano values in production and social relations. Nevertheless, two other domains in which these values are realized—the way Córdovans exercise their religious beliefs and the way they use language—have remained central.

MEXICANO CATHOLICISM AND FRANCISCAN VALUES

The St. Anthony of Padua of the Pueblo Quemado Chapel stands in the center of the plaza, and it has formed the heart of community worship for more than a century. Passing through the walled cemetery and the two sets of doors, the visitor is immediately struck by the brightly painted altarscreen that stands on the back wall of the sanctuary (Plate 8). It was made by a Córdova resident, José Rafael Aragón, one of the most prolific and skilled image makers of the nineteenth century. Flanked by images of the saints, the central panel contains two hands, each bearing the stigmata, placed before a cross. This sanctuary provides a small sign of the great influence that the Franciscan Order of Friars Minor had on the development of New Mexican Catholicism. Although the Franciscans were expelled in 1834, their religious and moral legacy is still very much alive in communities such as Córdova.

Plate 7. Rancho *homes, 1974. Photograph by Charles L. Briggs*

Plate 8. Interior of the San Antonio de Padua Chapel, showing altarscreens and freestanding images, 1977. Photograph by Charles L. Briggs

The Franciscans were integrally involved in efforts to conquer, convert, and colonize northern New Spain from the start. Once Cabeza de Vaca convinced the viceroy that the northern fringes were storehouses of treasure, it was a Franciscan, Fray Marcos de Niza, who traveled to present-day Zuni in 1539. Francisco Vásquez de Coronado left four Franciscan missionaries in New Mexico after he explored the area in 1540–1542; all were killed during the next few years. Franciscans accompanied Juan de Oñate and his band of soldiers and settlers in 1597–1598, and there were twenty-four Franciscans in the region by 1622. The Pueblo Revolution of 1680 brought missionary efforts to a halt until de Vargas reestablished Spanish hegemony in 1692–1694. As the missions were rebuilt following the Reconquest, the Spanish program was turning from the zeal of the sixteenth and seventeenth centuries to a concentrated effort to build self-supporting, permanent settlements. After several conflicts in the late seventeenth century, relations with the Pueblo Indians who lived close to the Hispanic settlements grew less hostile, although Spaniards and Pueblos alike were frequently at war with the Apaches, Navajos, Utes, and Comanches.

The missionaries were concerned with converting the inhabitants to Christianity and suppressing native religions. But the work of the mission was much broader. An apt summary emerges from one of the stipulations of Oñate's contract: "You shall charge the Spaniards to teach the Indians how they may assist and become useful in the . . . preservation of the Spanish organization" (Hammond and Rey 1940: I, 67). Beyond teaching Catholic doctrine and worship, this entailed instruction in music, reading and writing, crafts and trades, home economics, agriculture, and other pursuits.[8] The missionaries' educational resources were limited. Catholic images were fashioned first by the missionaries and other Spaniards and later by native New Mexicans, such as José Rafael Aragón.[9] Córdova (1979:122) argues that the absence of textbooks and the low level of literacy were offset by the use of folklore as a major pedagogical device.

Because the Franciscans' efforts were primarily devoted to converting the native inhabitants, the nature and extent of their work with the settlers who came up from central Mexico and their descendants is less clear. Smaller communities such as Córdova were visited by priests relatively infrequently, often as little as once a year. Córdova was included in the Santa Cruz Parish until 1959; parish records indicate that Córdovans traveled to the Santa Cruz church or other churches to obtain the sacraments. Thus, although contact with clerics may not have been frequent, it was hardly absent. On the other hand, the day-to-day religious needs of the community devolved largely upon the community itself.

Sacristans cared for the chapel and its furnishings, including the religious images. One of the most important lay religious officials was (and is) the *rezador* 'prayer leader'. Rezadores cooperated with the older women of the community in leading the Rosary services on Sunday. The rezadores also assumed primary responsibility for the different *velorios* 'wakes'. A *velorio de santo* 'wake for a saint' was an all-night vigil in honor of a saint, generally beginning of the eve of the feast day. On the feast day of St. Isidore, the patron of the farmer, the saint's image was carried through the fields to the upland dryfarms of Las Joyas. *Alabanzas* 'hymns of praise' alternated with prayers during the night, interrupted only for a communal meal at midnight. The next morning a procession crossed each field, asking St. Isidore's blessing (cf. Brown et al. 1978:185–87). *Velorios para los difuntos* 'wakes for the dead' occurred before an individual was buried, as the community watched over the body, sang hymns, shared food, and told jokes (cf. de Córdova 1972:48–50; Jaramillo 1941/1972:75–76; Rael 1951:16–18).

Mexicano communities have also hosted a wide range of Catholic lay societies, including cults to Our Lady of the Rosary, the Holy Family, Our Lady of Mt. Carmel, the Holy Altar, St. Joseph Patriarch, the Sacred Heart of Jesus, and St. Francis of Assisi. Some sodalities are organizationally informal, revolving around the care and veneration of a local image or shrine. Others involve annually elected officers and a host of activities, including charity and mutual aid. A cult devoted to the passion of Christ, generally referred to as *La Cofradía de Nuestro Padre Jesus Nazareno* 'The Confraternity of Our Father Jesus the Nazarene', has been the largest and most institutionally complex of these lay organizations since at least the beginning of the nineteenth century.

The Confraternity or Brotherhood is generally referred to in the literature as the *Penitentes*, a term that points to acts of corporal penance that brothers perform in the course of Holy Week devotions. I eschew this term because most brothers see it as being pejorative; they use *cofrados* or *hermanos* 'brothers' instead. Penitente also reinforces the sensationalist stereotype of the Brotherhood as revolving solely around acts of corporal penance. Although this practice constitutes only one aspect of Brotherhood devotions, this is the one that has proved most striking to outsiders. Because of this unwanted and unflattering attention, the Brotherhood has adopted rules of secrecy that are aimed at protecting the privacy of penitential devotions. The arena that the brothers are most interested in explicating—the theological tenets that form the basis of their practices—has been almost totally neglected in the literature. Yoder (1974) suggests that this lack of systematic study of the "folk beliefs" associated with "official" religions is a general phenomenon, although the work of Tambiah (1976) and other scholars promises to fill this hiatus. Because interpreting three of the genres treated in this work requires an understanding of this theology, I am mainly concerned with these beliefs.

A major focus in the scholarly literature on the Brotherhood concerns the issue of its origins. Five major theories have been presented; these point to Native American religions (e.g., Lee 1910; Lummis 1893); religious dramas, particularly passion and morality plays (e.g., McCrossan 1948); fanatical medieval flagellants (e.g., Deane 1884); Spanish confraternities that existed during Colonial times (e.g., Chávez 1954; Woodward 1935); and a lay society, the Third Order of St. Francis (e.g., Boyd

1974:440–51; Darley 1893; Espinosa 1911; Weigle 1976:37–51). The last two hypotheses find the greatest documentary support. The question of the date of the ascendancy of the organization is also moot. Firm documentary evidence of its existence is available from at least 1833,[10] but it may have been present many years earlier. The Brotherhood enjoyed a rapid increase in membership after this date, and this may be related to the replacement of the Franciscan missionaries with diocesan or "secular" priests in the first half of the nineteenth century (cf. Bloom 1914:359–60).

One thing that is abundantly clear is that the Brotherhood encountered resistance from Church authorities quite early on. Bishop Zubiria denounced the group in 1833. His stance was even more adamant in a pastoral letter of 19 October of that year, when he referred to the organization as a Brotherhood of "carnage" (cf. Weigle 1976:24–25). He objected to their reunion for penitential exercises, because their activities were not supervised by the clergy and their penances exceeded accepted canons of moderation. Following the American conquest of 1846, a Frenchman, Jean Baptiste Lamy, was appointed as bishop of the new Vicariate Apostolic of New Mexico. Because he found the group to espouse no heretical ideas, he concentrated on regulating rather than suppressing the Brotherhood.

His successor, Jean Baptista Salpointe, adopted a more hostile stance. He wrote that the Brothers' Holy Week processions "were never countenanced by the Church; on the contrary, since there have been bishops in New Mexico, they have denounced the practice and made of it the subject of some very strong circulars" (1898:163). Members who refused to submit to Church authority on the matter were to be refused the Sacraments, and Mass would not be celebrated in chapels that housed such individuals (cf. Weigle 1976:58–62). Enforcement of these guidelines was up to the local clergy, and implementation appears to have been both sparse and largely ineffective. The split between the Brotherhood and the Church ended only with formal Church recognition in 1947; some chapters refused to submit to Church regulation, and they remained independent (Weigle 1976:110).

The principal activities of *moradas* 'local chapters' are described in Chapter 8. In brief, the cult is devoted primarily to commemorating the passion of Christ and the suffering of the Virgin Mary. This involves meeting during Lent to pray the *Via Crucis* or Stations of the Cross and the Holy Rosary. Beginning on Wednesday night of Holy Week, the Brothers cloister themselves in their *morada* 'lodgehouse'. They are almost constantly moving during the next three days, visiting other moradas, conducting rituals, and making processions to the Córdova chapel and elsewhere. It is a time of intense ritual devotion and of great solidarity with one's Brothers, leaving worldly concerns aside in favor of seeking a symbolic unification with Christ. Many activities occur behind closed doors, owing to intense group solidarity and the need to keep out intruders who lack respect for the Brothers' privacy. Others involve the community as a whole; here, Brothers and other parishioners play complementary roles. The Brothers also grant nonmembers' requests to accompany them as they fulfill vows or perform other devotional acts. Membership in the Brotherhood is open only to men. Applicants must be in good standing with the Church; single men must obtain the consent of their parents, whereas the approval of one's wife is necessary for married petitioners. Approximately ten per cent of male Córdovans over the age of sixteen belong to the local chapter, and its strength does not appear to be waning.

The Catholic Church itself has lost many of its members in this century in the wake of the entrance of Protestant missionaries following American conquest. The Presbyterians converted a number of Córdovans in the opening decades of this century, and a church (without a resident minister) was established in 1924.[11] The Presbyterians and Methodists could offer substantial educational advantages to Mexicanos at, respectively, Menaul School in Albuquerque and McCurdy School near Española. Recent decades have witnessed the conversion of several Córdovan families to evangelical sects, and they worship in small churches in the neighboring communities of Truchas, Río Chiquito, and Chimayó (see Map 1).

Conversions have lessened the extent to which religion provides a centripetal force within the community. Protestant and Evangelical churches disdain the veneration of religious images as well as Brotherhood rituals. Some converts accordingly divorce themselves entirely from such activities as the feast day of the community's patron, St. Anthony of Padua (13 June) and Holy Week ceremonies, while others take a more ecumenical attitude. These divergences have had important effects upon the performance and interpretation of Córdovan folklore. Performances involve connecting a set of moral precepts with the situation at hand, and many of these moral precepts are rooted in Catholicism.

The role of religion in this oral tradition is accordingly both critical and twofold. Drawing out the moral and religious roots of a particular problem, whether implicitly or explicitly, is a crucial feature of performances in a number of genres, but not in all. Most elders clearly state their allegiance to the world of the elders of bygone days, and they assert the validity of the entirety of this talk. Others, including some Catholics, will perform in some genres but judiciously avoid evoking others. Some elders seek to distance themselves from the talk of the elders of bygone days as a whole; these individuals may refer to folkloric texts as a means of declaring them to be falsehoods. Awareness of this complex nexus is requisite to overcoming the false stereotype of folklore as a passive echo of tradition. I will be particularly concerned with the way that religious and social differences affect such performances in Chapters 6 and 7.

LANGUAGE USE IN MEXICANO NORTHERN NEW MEXICO

Another important means by which rural Mexicanos have been able to retain a grasp on the elements that provide them with collective identity is their language and the way it is used. All native Córdovans are fluent in Spanish, which is still the predominant language. Many residents over fifty years of age know little or no English. The intimacy of the connection between language and Mexicano identity is enhanced by the distinctiveness of the dialect. The features of New Mexican Spanish were recognized through the pioneering work of Aurelio M. Espinosa, Sr. (1909–1914, 1917, 1930, 1946, 1985) and Juan B. Rael (1937, 1939) as well as research by later scholars, particularly Ornstein (1951) and Bowen (1952, 1976). New Mexican Spanish contrasts with the standard on a number of phonological, lexical, and suprasegmental grounds.

Phonological features include the production of voiceless velar fricatives [x] in place of [s] and [f] in some words (e.g., *ji* [xi] for *sí*, *jui* for *fui*), dipthongization of stressed words (*pais* for *país* and *maiz* for *maíz*), the addition of a paragogic [-i] at the end of infinitives and oxytones ending in [l], [n], [r], and [s] when in isolation or at the end of a breath group (*¿quiéni?* for *¿quién?* and *a veri* for *a ver*), and the loss of medial [y] (spelled *ll*) in such forms as *e(ll)a*. Lexically, some forms have been retained from sixteenth- and seventeenth-century Spanish (*asina* for *así; croque* for *creo que*). English loan words, such as *troca* 'truck' and *yonque* 'junk', are common. A number of scholars, however, have noted that some nonstandard features, such as the loss of intervocalic *-d* at the end of past participles of *-ar* verbs (e.g., *tirao* instead of *tirado*), are common in other parts of Latin America and Spain (cf. Peñalosa 1980:108–11).

Dialectal differences are closely related to social and cultural experience. The use of Castilian or Standard Mexican Spanish in northern New Mexico immediately alerts native speakers of New Mexican Spanish that the person in question is from a different social, cultural, and educational background and, more than likely, a higher social class. A person does not acquire the dialect in Spanish classes, but by living with Mexicanos. A stranger who speaks New Mexican Spanish is thus assumed to have a substantial body of experience in common with those who share the dialect. In some cases, this process operates on an even more intimate level. Córdovans systematically substitute [š] (like English *should*) in words containing [č] (like English *chop*); *chango* thus becomes *shango* and *muchacho* becomes *mushasho*. The residents of surrounding villages can accordingly tell that a person is from Córdova simply by detecting this feature. I have accordingly attempted to record dialectal forms that appear in performances.[12]

The association between language and social identity does not lie simply in structural aspects of the dialect. One of the first things that strikes a newcomer to the community is the emphasis that is placed on communicative competence. Verbal skill plays a major role in determining the degree of respect that a person is accorded by the community. Speech itself forms a frequent subject of discourse. A political meeting, for example, will form the subject of debate for days or weeks afterwards. Discussions will center both on the force of each speaker's claims and on the élan with which they were presented. Mexicanos are no less concerned with the substance of a person's remarks and their bearing on future events than anyone else. But the language acquisition process affords a great deal of sensitivity to stylistic cues, particularly those that alert the hearer that a message carries implicit meanings.

Children are expected to observe the discourse of their elders and, as soon as they are able, to repeat their words. Such modeling is encouraged through the use of repetition elicitation formulae. The caregiver provides a child with an utterance that is seen as appropriate for obtaining the child's needs; this is framed with a formula—*dile* "X." As children reach adulthood, the ability to produce their own utterances becomes essential. In such settings as community meetings or political discussions, individuals gain respect for the ability to use diplomatically indirect allusions to sensitive or divisive issues in such a way as to unite the community around their vision of what should be done (cf. Briggs 1986:77–83).

Upon reaching about seventy years of age, speakers gain the right to draw upon a powerful source of legitimacy in advancing their point of view. Performances of the talk of the elders of bygone days involve the ability to select just the right genre and the specific item needed to fit the situation at hand and to show just how it applies. Putting past and present together in a convincing manner also entails mastery of a complex set of formal devices. As I argued in a study of the acquisition of communicative competence in this speech community, this process is markedly metacommunicative in character, because it involves embedding a host of messages about the meaning of one's utterances in the utterances themselves (Briggs 1986:62–88). In this study I focus directly on one facet of communicative competence—the ability to perform la plática de los viejitos de antes.

METHODOLOGICAL CONSIDERATIONS

Before embarking on this task I will outline the fieldwork on which my analysis is based. Providing this information forms an important part of my descriptive and analytic task for a number of reasons. I have been involved in Córdova for a long time and have engaged in a wide range of activities. Because of my involvement, I do not pretend to stand apart from the performances that are presented and analyzed on the following pages—I was a participant in nearly all of them. In a number of cases, the performer's point revolved around my actions or ethnic (Anglo-American) background. Familiarity with this material is crucial in understanding these performances and evaluating my analyses.

FIELDWORK

My fieldwork in Córdova began in September and October of 1972. My primary interest at the time was the local wood-carving industry. Córdova is the home of the López family, internationally known carvers of Catholic images and secular figures (cf. Briggs 1980). I worked most closely with Silvianita and George López, with

Plate 9. Miguel Sandoval, Inez Córdova, and Victor Córdova (clockwise) in conversation. Photograph by Charles L. Briggs

whom I had made arrangements the previous summer. I spent a great deal of time during these two months in their home. In view of the tremendous age gap (Mrs. López was seventy-one, Mr. López seventy-two, and I nineteen), Mexicano socio-linguistic norms placed the responsibility for structuring our interactions in their hands, not mine. As a result, my initial attempts at formal interviewing proved un-successful (cf. Briggs 1986:44–45, 57–59, 64–65). I accordingly began to carve with the Lópezes. I frequently left my cassette tape recorder running when conversa-tion was taking place, and a number of the performances described below were re-corded in this manner. I also tape-recorded conversations with other carvers and with elders who were not artists. I continued the fieldwork during the summer of 1973, although I resided in Santa Fe. Research on wood carving was completed while I resided in the community from July through November of 1974 and during the sum-mers of 1976 and 1977.

I had lived in rented houses on all of these occasions before 1976, when a number of Córdovans suggested that I had been around so long that I ought to establish a more permanent residence there. Consequently, when a small, unassuming house just above the plaza came up for sale, it was suggested that I buy it, which I did. My commitment to the community became apparent in another way in 1978 when I returned with my wife and two-month-old daughter for eighteen months of doctoral fieldwork. Close friends, Angie and Rubel Martínez, served as godparents in the bap-tism of my daughter. It was at this point that I came to be recognized as a member of the community, albeit a rather odd member.

My focus during this period was on la plática de los viejitos de antes. During these eighteen months I worked with nearly every elder in the community, trying to docu-ment the full range of ways that Córdovans talk about bygone days. Few of these interactions constituted interviews. The elders knew that I was interested in antes, but they were in control of the way that they taught me about it (see Chapter 3). The conversations lasted anywhere from one to five hours. I frequently went alone, but I was occasionally accompanied by a friend from Córdova. Some elders were alone at the time of the recording, but other elders or younger relatives were generally present.

I continued to study the talk of the elders of bygone days while living in the com-munity during the summers of 1981, 1982, and 1983. During the entire fieldwork period (1972–1986), I also made short trips of several days to two weeks to Córdova, particularly during such culturally important times as Holy Week. Between 1981 and the present, my focus has been threefold. I have tape-recorded discourse in as wide a variety of situations as possible, many of which did not include any performances of la plática de los viejitos de antes, in order to obtain systematic data on sociolinguistic patterns and on the acquisition of communicative competence (cf. Briggs 1986). These included casual conversations that took place in work contexts (fixing cars, building houses, stacking firewood, canning fruit, etc.), in the small local grocery stores, during recreational outings into the mountains, and elsewhere.

My second goal was to record performances in all the genres that are part of this talk; this involved placing myself in situations in which such performances would be likely to occur. I did obtain exegesis from a few individuals on the various performances, but this was strictly secondary to recording unsolicited performances. Finally, a grant from the National Science Foundation enabled me to purchase audiovisual equipment and to spend the summer of 1983 in Córdova. It was accordingly possible to supplement the audio recordings that I had made in 1972–1982 with approximately twenty-five hours of audiovisual recordings. My objective was to gauge the role of gesture, gaze, facial expression, and body movement in performance.

My research on la plática de los viejitos de antes involved observation and recording in a host of situations in addition to conversations in the elders' houses. As will be described in Chapter 3, elders shift into historical discourse in a host of settings. As Brown (Brown et al. 1978:201–202) has noted, groups of *ancianos* 'elders' gather during the day for conversation. Although their discourse covers a wide range of topics, talk about bygone days is central. A number of elders, usually men, converge in the local post office each weekday morning for about twenty minutes while the mail is sorted. Their references to antes often take the form of competitive exchanges of proverbs and historical vignettes. I similarly observed and at times recorded exchanges between elders that took place over lunch in the senior citizens' center in Truchas. I also loaned my equipment to a number of families in Córdova and nearby communities so that they could record discussions of bygone days with their parents. While I have compared the performances contained in these recordings to my own in analyzing the materials I collected, I am not able to quote them in print.

Bygone days similarly come alive during trips into town or to bring fuelwood from the mountains, during the annual cleaning of the irrigation ditches, and in the course of casual meetings in the community. It was seldom possible to have a tape recorder on hand during such encounters, because of the unexpectedness of their occurrence and my own reservations about intruding too much into people's personal lives. When tape-recording was not possible, I took careful notes on what had been said as soon after the discussion as possible.

Ritual performances provided a special case. I encountered no difficulties in obtaining permission to record such events as the annual feast day for the community patron saint, St. Anthony of Padua (see Plate 10). Josie Luján, secretary of the Holy Family Parish (that serves Córdova), kindly gave me access to her recordings of a procession that accompanied the Archbishop of the Archdiocese of Santa Fe, Roberto Sánchez, through the community and the Mass that followed.

The data on Holy Week rituals are drawn from my participation in these rituals as they were observed in Córdova in 1972, 1973, 1974, 1979, 1984, and 1986 as well as from conversations with Brothers of all ages. It was possible to obtain permission to tape-record in certain contexts; all transcriptions are taken from such recordings. My request to videotape one of the more public ceremonies was, however, denied. I have

Plate 10. Matachines dancers and musicians and the Mayordomos bearing the image of San Antonio de Padua in a San Antonio Day procession, 1976. Photograph by Charles L. Briggs

also had access to the *cuadernos* 'notebooks' of *alabados* and *alabanzas* 'hymns' that were made by George López (obtained by J. D. Robb) and Aurelio Trujillo. These data have been checked against the recordings of alabados and alabanzas by George López that were made in 1950 and 1966 by J. D. Robb and in 1952 by Reginald and William R. Fisher (J. D. Robb Collection, 244–46, 249, 259–60, 1017–34, and 2147–70).[13]

All of the tape recordings were analyzed in locating performances and classifying them according to genre, and the performances were transcribed (see the section on Methods of Transcription). The performances in each genre were then compared with my notes on performances that had not been recorded, with recordings made by individual families, by recordings of Mexicano performances that I made in Santa Fe, Guadalupita, Peñasco, Chamisal, Española, and Medanales (all of which are located in northern New Mexico). Julián Josué Vigil also kindly provided me with a copy of recordings by Mexicano collectors that were made in Las Vegas, New Mexico, and surrounding communities and are housed in the Carnegie Public Library in Las Vegas. Access to these recordings enabled me to compare the materials I had collected with performances in which neither I nor any other Anglo-American was present. All of these materials were used in analyzing performance features for each of the genres and in generalizations regarding the nature of the competence that underlies Mexicano performances of verbal art.

Two points are useful to keep in mind when one is reading the performances included in this book. First, I was only nineteen years of age and a college sophomore during my first period of fieldwork (i.e., in 1972). My age and lack of professional status placed me in the role of a youth who needed to learn a great deal about practical skills (fixing cars, building houses, hunting, slaughtering game and livestock, harvesting and preserving food, etc.), how to relate to others, and basic truths about life. Three couples in particular took on the task of teaching me—Silvianita and George López, Costancia and Aurelio Trujillo, and Lina and Federico Córdova. Many performances included in this book were recorded in conversations with them.

By the time I conducted my doctoral fieldwork, I was six years older, married and a father, spoke the dialect fluently, owned a house in Córdova, knew nearly everyone in the community, and had listened to a large number of performances of the talk of the elders of bygone days. Peer relationships with men and women of approximately twenty-five to fifty years of age now joined with pedagogical interactions with elders as primary modes of participation in the community. I was called upon to take an active role in community affairs; I was accordingly elected to the board of directors of the community water association (which oversees the operation of the community's well) in 1978. After several years of such involvement and much additional work on la plática de los viejitos de antes, elders became aware of my knowledge of the subject; this prompted some individuals to believe that I was in fact twenty to thirty years older than I was at the time, a perception that surprised and somewhat disconcerted me.

REFLEXIVITY AND THE ROLE OF THE COLLECTOR

The second issue that arises from the fieldwork pertains to the fact that I, an Anglo-American researcher, play a significant role in most of the performances transcribed and analyzed in these pages. Sorting out the implications of such involvement is an extremely complex process, and an acute polarization is evident in the literature with respect to the empirical and theoretical implications of the collector's participation in the performance process.

On the one hand, many researchers attempt to circumvent the problem entirely. Even though they present us with transcripts and with notes on "the context," their own role is entirely overlooked. We often have no idea whether the researcher directly elicited the item, played the role of audience in a performance, or was simply one person present at a "naturally occurring" event. The deletion of back-channel cues from transcripts makes it even harder to answer this question. Analyses frequently fail to examine the ways in which the form and content of the performance may reflect the collector's presence. As I noted in Chapter 1, this approach is usually combined with overemphasis on the role of textual over contextual features; as I have argued at length elsewhere, the approach emerges from an objectivist ideology that hinges on the assumption that the object of scrutiny is "out there" and operates independently of the research encounter itself. This conveniently excuses collectors from the task of assessing their own role in such interactions and the factors that shape their actions and interpretations (Briggs 1986; also see Karp and Kendall 1982).

Folklorists in particular have criticized this naive approach. Goldstein's (1964: 80–87) distinction between *natural contexts* and *artificial contexts* has been influential. The natural context is defined as "the social context in which folklore actually functions in a society" (1964:80). The artificial context is "the context in which the folklore is performed to order at the instigation of the collector." Goldstein stresses the need to obtain at least some of one's data in the "natural context": "Unless a collector is sure that there is no appreciable difference between informants' performances in artificial contexts and in natural contexts, then a report of observations made only in artificial situations may be almost worthless" (1964:86).

Some practitioners take this position to an extreme. It has been asserted that only data collected in "natural contexts" that are unaffected by the participation of the collector provide valid data on performance. Goldstein notes that the collector's "very presence changes to some degree every situation in which he participates" (Goldstein 1964:73; see also Segal 1976). The desire to obtain untainted data and awareness of the observer effect lead some researchers to make their recordings with hidden microphones while they themselves are not physically present. Dégh (Dégh and Vázsonyi 1976/1969:103) describes the way she collected some of her data on Hungarian legends as follows:

The text below does not involve the collector. She did not participate in the general talk on that winter evening, December 30, 1962, when she recorded the continuous conversation between people who were swapping legends. . . . The tape recorder was outside of the room, and the microphone was camouflaged with a shawl; only the hostess knew of its presence.

It is certainly important to obtain as wide a variety of data as possible; observing or recording some performances in which the collector has as little effect on the performance as possible is similarly a tremendous asset. Dégh's work on belief in legend amply demonstrates the benefits of sensitivity to observer effects, particularly in the case of genres in which the presence of an outsider will substantially change the character of the materials.

If this practice is taken to extremes, however, two problems arise. First, I personally am bothered by the ethics of purposefully misleading one's consultants. I prefer to subscribe to the statements of ethical principles adopted by the American Folklore Society and the American Anthropological Association, which assert that field-workers are obliged to be explicit about the nature of their goals and procedures.[14] I believe that hidden microphones violate the right of consultants to choose if and how they will participate in a research project. I have similar reservations about Goldstein's "induced natural context" method (1964:87–90). Here the collector collaborates with a member of the speech community who acts as an "accomplice" in creating a social encounter that is likely to produce a natural context for performances. However, the role of the "accomplice" is specified as "calling together a group of his cronies or friends . . . without informing the participants that the purpose of the session is to allow a collector to observe them in action" (1964:88). Although I laud Dégh's and Goldstein's concern with the role of the collector's presence in shaping performance, I think it quite unfortunate if researchers came to believe they can obtain adequate data only by intentionally misleading their consultants.

Likewise, acceptance of the view that only performances in which the collector is absent or peripheral provide acceptable data may lead researchers away from the consideration of crucial theoretical issues. Fieldworkers are participants in the research process even if they are absent from the setting of the performance. The researcher still decides what to collect and how to record, transcribe, analyze, and publish it. The researcher thus continues to play a central role in the interpretive process. Similarly, even if the collector's presence plays little or no role in the contextualization of discourse, the discourse is still contextualized. My fear is that such procedures may lull researchers into a false sense of objectivity, thus fostering the illusion that they are collecting social facts that can be perceived "objectively." Bauman has eloquently pointed out the conservative theoretical base of this position.

Folklorists demonstrate a persistent impulse to strive for the so-called natural context of a folklore form, an impulse generally resting on a conception of the way things were in an ideal time before progress or the intrusive presence of a folklorist corrupted the folk. . . . The concept rapidly becomes unproductive if it fosters the notion that any departure from our traditionalist conception of natural context is therefore unnatural, and outside the purview of folklore (1983:366).

This perspective is methodologically conservative as well, because it neatly excuses investigators from the need to examine the way performances emerge from particular interactions and from their own role in the research process.[15]

I endorse Goldstein's contention that the study of verbal art entails the collection of as wide a variety of data as possible. As Dégh and Vázsonyi and Goldstein assert, the collector's presence necessarily affects the performance. I share their skepticism of the naive belief that one can analyze data on performances in which the collector plays the role of audience without seriously considering the effect that this has on the performance. Our disagreement pertains to the proper means of overcoming this problem.

I do not believe that the answer to this problem lies in extracting the researcher insofar as is possible from the setting of the performance, although studying some performances in which the role of the collector is minimal is important. Rather, I believe that including reflexivity in studying the way performances are contextualized is essential. Researchers must be able to show what effect their participation has in shaping the performance, just as they need to analyze the role of every other major participant. In fact, given the availability of information on performances in which the collector is peripheral, data that show how performers change both form and content in keeping with their perception of the researcher can afford significant insight into the performance process (cf. Bauman 1983:366; Darnell 1974; Hymes 1981/1975).

This perspective explains two facets of my methodology. First, the analysis of each genre is informed by data on a wide range of performances, including instances in which I constituted the audience or was a member of a group audience as well as examples in which I was either absent (as in the recordings made by family members) or in which I was only a peripheral member of the audience. Second, I have tried to be as explicit as possible in showing how my participation affected each performance. The comparison with performances in which I was absent or marginal leads me to conclude that the performances in which I participated fit into the range of variation that is observed for each genre. In any case, it seems unlikely that people would invent a new set of verbal art forms to use on a researcher and then use them consistently for fourteen years. It is equally true, however, that the fact that I am a gringo who began living in the community at nineteen years of age affected nearly every performance in which I participated in some way. Detailing the nature of those effects is thus a necessary component of the interpretive task.

APPENDIX: METHODS OF TRANSCRIPTION

Although the transcription of oral performances was long seen as a purely mechanical process, we now realize that transcribing involves a powerful act of interpretation and that choices regarding transcription format and style reflect basic assumptions about the nature of verbal art. E. Fine (1984), Gold (1972), Hymes (1981), McLendon (1982), Rothenberg (1969), Scheub (1971), Tedlock (1972b, 1983), and others have experimented with techniques for capturing as much of the poetic and rhetorical texture of the original as is possible. The question is not simply one of producing an aesthetically pleasing text or of capturing the "flavor" of the performance. Research has shown that the stylistic characteristics of a performance bear a great deal of information about its meaning in the eyes of the participants. This includes such dimensions as prosody or "intonation" (including volume, pitch, and duration), demarcation of poetic units (lines, verses, etc.), repetition of key elements, and the dialogic involvement of the audience. One of the most neglected components of performances is the role of visual communication, particularly gestures, body posture, gaze, and facial expression, in conveying the meaning of what is said (cf. Scheub 1972).

Overall, my goal in the transcriptions and translations has been to lose as little of the information that is contained in the audio- or videotape as possible. My intent is not to indicate as many formal characteristics as is possible on paper but to provide the reader with a means of perceiving those formal elements that constitute the rhetorical structure of the performance.

The following conventions are used in both the Spanish and English texts.

⟨　⟩	Material enclosed within brackets has been placed within the text to clarify meaning
((　))	Double parentheses enclose words or passages that are unclear; here the transcription and translation are uncertain
[[　]]	Double brackets are used in narratives to mark the introduction of a back-channel cue (e.g., *sí* 'yes') by the fieldworker (used only in explanatory asides that appear in narratives)
italics	Italics are used to show that the italicized words were spoken in English
CAPITALS	Text is set in capitals to show that it was delivered with greater volume (loudness);
/	A slash at the end of one utterance and another at the beginning of the next speaker's turn indicates an overlap, that is, a point at which two people are talking at the same time

In transcriptions of historical discourse, proverbs, and nearly all scriptural allusions, the text begins flush with the left margin. Stylistically defined lines are represented by typographical lines except where the spoken line is too long; continuations are slightly indented. Back-channel cues are indented.

Important differences emerge when a narrative structure is apparent. Narratives are marked by distinct uses of prosodic characteristics, rhetorical particles, and other features. Groups of prosodically marked lines are unified by an overall prosodic contour; these have been aligned vertically. The transition to a new group of lines is generally signaled by a decrease in both pitch and volume; such transitions are marked by an indentation to the right. Once the narrator shifts to a new theme, pitch and volume return to a higher level; the change is indicated by a return to the left margin. (This is the general pattern; the exact prosodic markers of groups of lines and of narrative progression differ somewhat between speakers and genres.) In other words, narrative form in the performances is made apparent by the horizontal placement of the text on the page.

The constraint posed by the width of the printed page requires an adjustment of the transcription for portions of the examples in Chapter 7. Where the indentation pattern if followed blindly would force the text too far to the right, the affected blocks are moved to the left and set off with a double vertical bar.

The flow of the narration is interrupted from time to time as the speaker explains some element of the story, for example, to relate a character's genealogy or to describe the location of an event. Such interventions are marked by a "flattening" of the pitch and loudness changes that characterize the narration itself. Such speech is not marked poetically (in Jakobson's 1960 sense of the term); I have accordingly distinguished it from the stylistically marked discourse by further indentation and setting it off with a single vertical bar.

Prosody takes on a different set of characteristics when it becomes fixed by a melodic structure; this is the case in performances of hymns and prayers. A rather different set of conventions is necessary for transcribing and translating these forms, as is described in Chapter 8.

In the performances that were videotaped, a column has been added to note important gestures and facial expressions. Highly abbreviated descriptions of these visual forms are placed alongside the utterances they accompanied.

3

HISTORICAL DISCOURSE

In Córdova, elderly persons are not seen simply as retirees who are no longer in touch with "the real world." Córdovan elders rather bear principal responsibility for ensuring the vitality of Mexicano culture and the survival of its bearers through la plática de los viejitos de antes. This task is fulfilled through performances by elders in the company both of their peers and of their juniors. This 'talk' is seen as embodying the collective identity of the community and of Mexicano society in general. If the elders fail to transmit it to succeeding generations, the people will be engulfed by 'the outside world'. This fear is not viewed as a romantic clinging to the ways of the past just for the sake of what is old and familiar. Modern industrial society fosters values of individualism and secularism that are seen as destructive of the fabric of social relations. The problem is Hobbesian, but the Mexicanos' solution is not. The talk of the elders of bygone days strengthens the values of cooperation and respect for human dignity that prevent the emergence of a "warre of all against all." The elders consider it to be their duty to warn the young against the dangers posed by egoism.

The talk of the elders of bygone days emerges in performances of proverbs, scriptural allusions, jokes, legends, hymns, and prayers. Another form consists in discussions of bygone days that are relatively free-form, involving no preset text. These discussions consist, in general, of the statement of some fact about the past, its comparison with a feature of life nowadays, and then the assertion of an underlying principle that relates the two. They are of particular interest to this study in that this historical discourse, as I refer to it, exhibits the least textuality of any form that is included under the aegis of la plática de los viejitos de antes.

Historical discourse emerges in four basic types of interactions: competitive displays of oral historical knowledge and rhetorical skill between small groups of elders; allusions to bygone days in conversations between persons between thirty and sixty years of age; noncompetitive discussions between elders; and pedagogically oriented exchanges between elders and their juniors. The elders' competitions and the discussions of the middle-aged occur infrequently, while the last two types of events are quite common.[1]

BATTLING WITH WORDS: ORAL HISTORICAL COMPETITIONS BETWEEN ELDERS

Brown (Brown et al. 1978:201) provides a fascinating portrait of the exclusiveness of oral historical duels between elders in his description of a clique of Córdovan men that flourished in the 1930s.

A group of four *pensionistas* ⟨recipients of World War I veterans' benefits⟩ gather every afternoon at the home of their senior member. They have been dubbed *Los Senadores* ("the Senators") by a wit of the village. They gather in the shade in the summer and in winter seek the *resolana* or sunny side of their host's humble home.

"Election" to such informal groups is not based on age alone; participants must hold a substantial command of Córdovan oral history and great facility in its articulation. The goal of these discussions is not primarily cognitive or referential, in Jakobson's (1960:353) terms (i.e., to provide the hearer with new information). The emphasis is on enhancing one's status as a repository of the talk of the elders of bygone days— and thus as a distinguished elder—at the expense of one's interlocutors. Brown's description similarly captures the fiercely competitive character of these debates and the importance of the participants' social statuses and overall relationship in determining the alacrity with which they pursue their own rhetorical goals (Brown et al. 1978:202):

The old men live again the days of their youth, and many glimpses may be gained of a bygone day by implication contained in some chance remark or by direct relation of events long ago. It is amusing to hear the rebuke administered by the oldest of this quartet to the *Pícaro* ⟨'Rogue'⟩ who happens to be his godson and therefore must take the rebuke with good grace. "*Pendejo, ¿qué sabes tú?*" ('Fool, what do you know?') It was thus or thus." The godson is apparently as old as his *padrino* ⟨'godfather'⟩ and blind besides. Perhaps this is fortunate, because his *padrino's* little blue eyes kindle to pinpoints of wrath as he rebukes this presumptuous one who dares question his statements concerning the duel between the *difuntos* ("deceased") Juan Antonio and Manuelito who fought on the Cuestecita, of the superiority of mules over horses, or that the Negro ⟨'Black'⟩, Pata de Palo ⟨'Peg Leg'⟩, was a much better schoolteacher than Simón.

The only examples of full-scale oral historical competitions that I witnessed in Córdova occurred during lulls in religious/festive events. In one instance, the Archbishop of the Archdiocese of Santa Fe (which includes all Catholic parishes in New Mexico) made a special visit to Córdova on 15 July 1979. Archbishop Roberto Sánchez is a favorite among Mexicanos, being a New Mexican who was named archbishop partly in response to popular choice. The significance of the visit was heightened by the fact that he chose Córdova as a site for making a demonstration of solidarity with rural Mexicano communities in northern New Mexico.

The oral historical competition occurred before the archbishop's arrival. The people of Córdova had walked in procession from the chapel to a wide point in the road that leads to the main highway. Because the archbishop did not arrive for forty-five minutes, a number of persons broke ranks, so to speak, and began conversing with friends. An eighty-year-old *rezador* 'prayer leader' and a man of about sixty-five, who is one of the wealthiest and most politically powerful members of the community, started up a conversation about twenty-five feet from the head of the procession. With another ten or so men between twenty and forty years of age, I moved within earshot but remained ten to fifteen feet from the interlocutors. The older one began the series of exchanges. He stood upright, leaned his head back, exhibited a somewhat challenging smile, and said to his conversant, *Pues, ¿sabes tú que esta capilla tiene más que 200 años? Porque la capilla tenía 50 años cuando vino el primero padre pa' acá* 'Well, do you know that this chapel (the San Antonio de Padua del Pueblo Quemado Chapel in Córdova) is over two hundred years old? Because the chapel was fifty years old when the first priest came up here'. This constituted an overt challenge to an oral historical competition, and it was appropriately initiated by the older of the two.

The other contestant responded with a similar datum, *Pues, ¿sabes TÚ que esta capilla es más vieja que la iglesia ahi en Las Trampas?* 'Well, did YOU know that this chapel is older than the church in Las Trampas?' The initial speaker then came back with an assertion that Córdova is older than its neighbor, Las Truchas. By this point, two other elderly men had taken positions within the primary interactional sphere, creating a rough square of about five feet on each side. These new contestants also offered oral historical information, although they responded only about half as often as the original entrants. Each turn was initiated by *pues, ¿sabes TÚ que* 'well, did YOU know that'. Interestingly, there were no overlaps whatsoever. Each turn at talk was succeeded by a pause of at least two seconds, and a prospective speaker would gain the floor by leaning slightly back, standing more upright, and smiling before beginning his utterance.

This interaction was clearly an important event. Those of us who had moved to within earshot (although staying far from the circle of the participants) listened both intently and silently. Both those persons who had remained in the processional line and other small groups of conversants looked at the competitors frequently, and a few were listening to the repartee. The duel ended abruptly about twenty minutes after it began when the archbishop's car approached; participants and observers alike returned to their respective positions in line. Although there was little chance for comment on "winners" or "losers" at the time, evaluations of such discussions by participants and spectators generally follow. On this occasion I visited the oldest participant the following day, and he took this opportunity to dispute the validity of his principal opponent's statements and to assert the veracity of his own.

Although all of the competitions I witnessed took place during lulls in ritual events, groups of elders also engage in such debates when no one else is around. This secretive character is clearly absent in the competitions that accompany festivals. It seems plausible that such events are more likely to occur and to occur publicly during those times at which the community's interest in displays of rhetorical skill, whether in reciting prayers, singing hymns, making public speeches, or other communicative events, is heightened. Note also the esoteric rather than pedagogical character of these competitions. This mode of speaking provides no opportunity to explain the meaning of what is said or the social and historical information that it presupposes. The intent of the discourse rather lies in the opposite direction—using very brief historical references as a means of indexing the extent of the speaker's own knowledge of la plática de los viejitos de antes. Only the most highly skilled can participate, and only those who already know a great deal about this talk can appreciate the significance of what is said.

TOWARD PERFORMANCE: HISTORICAL EXPLORATIONS IN THE MIDDLE YEARS

This absence of pedagogical focus is also characteristic of a second type of historical discourse—discussions of past persons, events, and conditions by women and men between thirty and about fifty years of age. These commonly occur in casual situations, such as taking a rest in the shade during a deer hunt in the mountains or relaxing with close friends over a beer. These historical explorations, as I call them, evince a number of characteristics.

First, they involve friends or relatives of approximately the same age. All participants are roughly equal in their knowledge of and ability to articulate oral historical material. Historical explorations do not take place when elders are present; it would be presumptuous for a middle-aged person to assume control of a presentation of information about bygone days in the presence of a viejito. Persons who are substantially younger than the peer group that is engaged in an historical exploration may well be present; even if they were involved in the preceding conversation, however, they will be excluded from active participation in the dialogue once this type of discourse begins.

Second, historical information is presented not as the talk of the elders of bygone days itself, but as a series of personal recollections. Each utterance is prefaced with a formula for indicating the evidential basis of the account. *Me acuerdo que* 'I remember that' and *me acuerdo cuando* 'I remember when' are the most common frames, and one of these is frequently followed in the second or third sentence of a turn at talk by *yo no tenía más que como X años cuando* 'I was only X years old when'. It should be noted that the elders also sometimes use the *me acuerdo que/cuando* frame in speaking of bygone days. Nevertheless, the elders also invoke the words of their predecessors more directly through the use of such frames as *decían los viejitos de antes que* 'the elders of bygone days used to say that', whereas middle-aged persons do not.

Third, the speakers' words are directed toward the entire group of active participants rather than toward one or more persons who are selected as respondents. Here historical explorations contrast with both historical competitions and pedagogical discourse, because the last two types generally require the role of one or two individuals as respondents. The more generalized interactional focus of historical explorations is apparent in gaze and other visual signals; these are directed at the group of participants as a whole. This type of interaction is characterized by a relative paucity of back-channel cues (cf. Duncan 1973) such as *sí* 'yes' or *¿sí?* 'really?'. Fourth, historical explorations never constitute the predominant focus of entire conversations; they form just one of the numerous topics that are broached in such interactions.

Taken as a whole, these characteristics suggest that historical explorations constitute reports of such events rather than performances of historical knowledge. The distinction is neatly captured in Hymes's (1981/1975:84) definition of performance: "cultural behavior for which a person assumes responsibility to an audience." Historical competitions are clearly performative; speakers stand as the recognized bearers of historical information, they use stylized speech forms that are specific to such occasions, and they place the full weight of their authority behind their words in presenting them to their fellow participants and to bystanders. In the case of exchanges of historical information between middle-aged persons, none of these conditions are met. Here the material is presented as facts about the elders of bygone days but not as the words of the deceased elders themselves. Historical explorations may bear the claim "this is what I saw," but they do not purport to be authoritative. Younger persons do not assert that their information is unimpeachable. If a question arises, such persons will say 'I don't remember very well, I was very young' or even 'I don't really know. You should go talk to so-and-so' (naming an elder). This is why I have used the term *explorations* in labeling this type of historical discourse. I found it impossible to record such discussions; the presence of a tape recorder would induce a shift of topic and a suggestion as to whom I should record instead of the speaker.

To cite one example, a historical exploration emerged during a conversation with Rubel and Filiberto Martínez that took place in 1982. These brothers are both close friends, and Rubel is my *compadre* (he is my daughter's godfather). We conversed and drank beer in my house for two hours, in the course of which Rubel and Filiberto spent about twenty minutes exchanging recollections of agricultural practices in Córdova when they were children. Their turns at talk constituted minimonologues on some aspect of farming, each framed with *me acuerdo que* 'I remember that' or *me acuerdo cuando* 'I remember when'. Most of these statements placed the speaker alongside their father, Octavio Martínez, or another member of his generation. The speaker then described how the two of them used to plow, plant, irrigate, or the like.

Some remarks recounted some feature of agricultural technology or custom without assuming narrative form, such as a description of how Córdovans used to thresh wheat by running goats over piles of grain.

Even though I had listened to a good many historical discussions by that point, I obviously had no personal experience to offer. I was virtually silent during the discussion, and Filiberto and Rubel made very little eye contact with me. No attempt was made to include me in the conversation or to explain what was being said. Rather, as the historical exploration drew to a close, they looked at me and noted, 'it's too bad you weren't here back then.'

In sum, historical explorations arise occasionally in conversations between Córdovans during the middle years of the life span. Residents in this age range have personal experiences to draw on, and most are interested in this material and enjoy discussing it. Nevertheless, explorations make up only a small percentage of historical discourse and draw on a very restricted range of speech forms.

COLLECTIVE RECOLLECTIONS

Historical explorations are not, at first glance, so very far away from noncompetitive exchanges of historical information between elders. The encounters also involve individuals of approximately the same age and level of historical expertise, and they are thus similarly distinguished from pedagogical encounters. Beyond this initial similarity, however, there are a number of important differences. The elders *do* assume responsibility for their accounts of bygone days, and their words are marked by distinct stylistic features. The noncompetitive historical dialogues between elders are, like the competitive events, clearly performances. One of the most important differences between the way that middle-aged and elderly Córdovans discuss the past lies in the nature of turn-taking. Whereas historical explorations take the form of a succession of minimonologues, noncompetitive discussions of bygone days between elders are highly dialogic. Because the participants cooperate closely in developing their vision of the past, I refer to these events as collective recollections.

Unlike historical competitions, collective recollections generally emerge in everyday situations. Two or more elders may enter into a collective recollection while driving to town, sitting by the woodpile, or relaxing in their living room. Such events are unlikely to emerge, however, when people's attention is largely devoted to a focused activity (e.g., when a ceremony is taking place or a task is to be performed). Similarly, collective recollections arise in the course of conversations between elders. Younger persons may be present; if they are taking an active part in the conversation, however, historical discourse is likely to take the form of pedagogical discourse. As is the case with historical explorations, collective recollections create marked differences with respect to the roles that are assumed in the discourse between a core set of interactants and a peripheral group (if present).

An example of a collective recollection is provided by a recording (example (3.1)) that I made of a conversation that took place in 1986 between two elders, whom I will call Benjamín and Ignacio.[2] Benjamín, who is from the nearby town of Truchas, spends part of the year with his daughter in Córdova; he is 81 years of age. Ignacio, a native Córdovan, lives close to Benjamín's daughter; Ignacio is 67 years old. The two were seated outside Ignacio's house, enjoying the sunshine on a chilly spring day. The two had been talking with Benjamín's son-in-law and several other individuals. These persons left for about a half an hour in search of a six-pack of beer, leaving Benjamín, Ignacio, and myself alone. The two of them sat close to each other, and they began to converse. I was sitting several feet to one side, and they did not make eye contact with me, nor did they address any remarks to me. My compact cassette recorder, which had been running during the previous conversation, was out of their range of vision; later conversations revealed that they did not realize that it was still recording. The dialogue focused on World War II and its impact on their lives and those of their relatives and friends. (Benjamín was drafted into the service, whereas Ignacio was refused enlistment on medical grounds.) After an 11-second pause, the two moved to the discussion of bygone days shown in example (3.1). After the material presented, Ignacio and Benjamín continued their discussion of *punche* 'home-grown tobacco' for 4 minutes. Their collective recollection, which went on for 7 minutes more, included discussion of dances, architecture, donkeys, and sheep in bygone days. It was interrupted by Benjamín's son-in-law and several other friends.

THE STRUCTURE OF COLLECTIVE RECOLLECTIONS

This dialogue appears at first glance to be mundane and amorphous, thus fitting into our category of "ordinary" conversation. The structure of the discourse is not dominated by a narrative, and it does not evince the sort of structure that is apparent in the mythic texts that have formed the focus of ethnopoetic analysis. In the absence of any obvious framing devices, performance features, or evidence that Benjamín and Ignacio have assumed any particular type of responsibility for their words, I doubt seriously that many analysts would deem the exchange an instance of performance. I believe, however, that this example possesses central features of both "ordinary" conversation and performance and thus questions assumptions regarding the way in which these two categories have been differentially defined.

Providing a Frame. The transition from the discussion of World War II experiences to the collective recollection is marked by use of the term *antes*. Antes provides, to

(3.1) Benjamín (81), Ignacio (67), CLB (32); 29 March 1986, Córdova, New Mexico

I   Antes,
cómo había CABRAS,
BORREGAS aquí,
¡uuh!
Pero CABRAS sí tenían más MUCHAS,   5
¿no, BENJAMÍN?
B   Allá en TRUCHAS TAMBIÉN,
casi TODOS tenían CABRAS.
I   Sí, no, no, no POQUITAS, . . .
de CIENES. . . .   10
Trillaban con ellas,
oh,
entonces sí era BONITO.
B   Sí, ¿no?
I   Vuelti-vuelta atrás de la—   15
en la pila de TRIGO. . . .
Y luego arriba la azotea ahi,
cuando cosechaba uno mucho FRIJOL,
B   ((ahi sí))/
I   /ahi está uno MASHUCÁNDOLO,   20
¿no?
B   sí
I   AIGRIÁNDOLO
arriba la AZOTEA,
le sacaba uno un frijol LIMPIO   25
con una bandeja las VIEJITAS,
bzzzzzzzzzzzzzzzzzz,
y el TRIGO.
B   Ansina cuando yo era un muchacho,
trillaban ALVERJÓN.   30
        Oh, ¿sí?
I   Y pa' eso de TRILLAR,
yo sí era BRUTO.
B   Sí.
I   Oh, por voltear la, la PAJA,   35
pa' que no se revolviera con el TRIGO,
B   oh, sí,
I   oh, estaba bruto YO.
Yo no sé POR QUE;
APRENDÍ.   40
Aquí venían todos los VIEJOS,
a que fuera yo,
y yo estaba JOVEN.
B   Yo también me fui a ((trillarla)).
I   Sí, pues,   45
estabas oreando, oreando, oreando,
hasta que vaya la ((   ))
y se quedó la medulita.
B   Y el/
I   /y luego se tira el grano abajo,   50

English translation

___

In bygone days,
there sure used to be a lot of GOATS,
SHEEP here,
  uuh!
But they used to have many MORE GOATS,
  right, BENJAMIN?
Up in TRUCHAS TOO,
nearly EVERYBODY used to have GOATS.
Yes, not, not, not just A FEW, . . .
HUNDREDS. . . .
They used to thresh with them,
oh,
in those days it used to be GREAT.
  Yes, right?
Around and around behind the—
in the pile of WHEAT. . . .
And then on the roof up there,
when a person used to harvest a lot of BEANS,
  ((ah yes))/
/up there you'd BEAT THEM,
  right?
  yes
WINNOW THEM,
on top of the ROOF,
with an enamel pan THE OLD WOMEN
used to get the beans CLEAN,
bzzzzzzzzzzzzzz,

laughs   and the WHEAT.
That's how, when I was a boy,
they used to thresh PEAS.
  Oh, really?
And I was REALLY GOOD
at THRESHING.
  Yes.
Oh, in turning the, the STRAW,
so that it wouldn't get mixed up with the WHEAT,
  oh, yes,
I was really GOOD.
I don't know WHY;
I ⟨JUST⟩ LEARNED.
The old folks would all come OVER HERE,
so that I would go ⟨and work for them⟩,
and I was just a KID.
I used to ((thresh)) too.
  Yes, well,
you used to winnow, winnow, winnow
until you got rid of the ((chaff?))
and only the kernel was left.
And the/
/and then the grain drops down,

```
        y la paja se saca después,
        la paj—
        la aigrea.
B       Nosotros como chiquitos como
        quedar con las CABRAS                                        55
        en la cañada;
        mi papá también tenía cabras en la otra BANDA/
I             /SÍ, SÍ, SÍ,
        y, y, y con una PAJUELA,
                ¿no?                                                 60
        ¡PWAASS!
B       Todos corrían tras de ELLAS.
I       Ah, pero
        ah pa' CUIDARLAS,
        SANAMABI,                                                    65
        como ANDABAN. . . .
        Andaba uno con TEGUAS,
                ¿no?
B             Sí.
        Se paseaban,                                                 70
        paseaban uno en ELLAS,
                ¿no?
I.      ¡Cabró-!
        Y luego/
B       /agua/                                                       75
I       /y, y agrarraba el AGUA/
B       /el agua, yah/
I       que agarraba el agua en el MONTE, . . .
        venían las teguas ((bien mojadas)),
                ¿no?                                                 80
        Y luego en la MAÑANA,
        cuando se las iba a poner estaban BIEN DURAS.
        ¡Eeeeeh! . . .
        ¡Qué venía a pasar cuando estaba joven!
        Entonces sí trabajaba,                                       85
        AHORA ¡QUÉ!/
B       Ahora ya los jovenes no quieren trabajar.
I       /Ahora no trabaja la PLEBE.
        Ahi viene LEOPOLDO,
        con la plebe rezongando ahi en la ACEQUIA,                   90
B             sí
I       que no—,
        que no sacan la acequia.
B       Ahora no sabe trabajar la plebe.
I             No, no. . . .                                          95
        Oh, ¡qué también trabajaran como trabajábamos NOSOTROS.
B             Oh, no.
I       Me, me levanté a las TRES de la mañana,
        me despacharon pa' Rito la Gallina
        con cinco BURROS,                                            100
B             ¡uuuh!
I       VACIOS,
        ya pa' venía con CARGA,
        en la TARDE.
```

and the straw is taken out later,
the stra–,
it gets blown away.
When we were small
we used to stay with the GOATS
in the canyon;
my father also had goats on the other SIDE/
              /YES, YES, YES,
and, and, and with a TORCH,
              right?
PWAASS!

both laugh   Everybody used to run AFTER THEM.
Oh, but
TAKING CARE OF THEM,
SON-OF-A-BITCH,
the way they USED TO GO. . . .
We used to go around in MOCCASINS,
              right?
              Yes.

I laughs   We used to go around,
we used to go around in THEM,
              right?

I laughs   Hell!
And then/
/the rain ⟨or water⟩/
/and, and they used to get SOAKED/
/the rain, yeah/
they used to get soaked up in the MOUNTAINS, . . .
the moccasins would come back ((really wet)),
              right?
And then in the MORNING,
when we used to put them on they would be REALLY HARD.
Eeeeeh! . . .
The things that used to go on when ⟨I⟩ was a kid!
Then a person used to work,
NOWADAYS WHAT!/
Nowadays the kids don't want to work.
/Nowadays the kids don't WORK.
There comes LEOPOLDO,
with the kids grumbling over there in the DITCH,
both laugh   yes
they don't—,
they don't clean the ditch.
Nowadays the kids don't know how to work.
              No, no. . . .
Oh, if they just worked like WE USED TO WORK,
              Oh, no.
I, I got up at THREE in the morning,
they sent me to Rito la Gallina,
with five BURROS.
              uuuh!
EMPTY,
so I could come back LOADED,
in the AFTERNOON.

    Y luego me tenía que ir otro día en la mañana   105
    MUY de MAÑANA tenía que ir.
    Allá tenián PEONES,
    trabajando en la PAPA/
B   Jalaba uno leña en BURRO,
        ¿no?   110
I   Sí,
    yo tenía DOS.
    Oh, yo lo tenía lleno de pura leña.
    Con mis CHAMACOS,
    ellos me seguían en el BURRO,   115
    ya después,
    que estaban GRANDES.
B   Sí.
I   Ahi vienen en el BURRO. . . .

I   Muy BONITO era ANTES.   120
    Y luego se íbamos a cuidar CABRAS,
    y nos poníamos a pescar ahi en el RÍO.
B   Uh huh.
I   Y no,
    no se—,   125
    no sentíamos la cabras
    cuando salían de la SOMBRA,
        ves,
B   sí
I   en la TARDE.   130
    Y se bajaban pa' La Cañada de la ((   )),
    Las JOYAS
    a los FRIJOLES,
        mano,
B   ¡oh!   135
I   ¡eeeee!
    un DAÑO,
    híjola.
    Y luego nos castigaban aquí los VIEJOS.
B   Oh, ((sí nos castigaban)).   140
I   MUCHOS,
    muy ATROCES eramos.
    Y luego no había CIGARRITOS,
        ¿no?
B   uh uh   145
I   PUNCHI de la SIERRA.
B   Sí.

And then I used to have to go back the next morning,
I used to have to go VERY EARLY in the MORNING.
Up there they used to have WORKERS,
working in the POTATOES/
We used to haul wood with BURROS,
      right?
I laughs   Yes,
I used to have TWO.
Oh, I used to load them up with lots of firewood.
With my SONS,
they used to follow me on the BURRO,
later on,
when they were GROWN UP.
      Yes.
Here they come on the BURRO. . . .

[I have omitted 90 seconds in which they discuss how many goats and cattle there used to be in bygone days]

It used to be GREAT in BYGONE DAYS.
And then we used to go herd GOATS,
and we would go fishing up there on the RIVER.
      Uh, huh.
And we,
we didn–,
we didn't notice the goats
when they left the SHADE,
      you see,
      yes
in the AFTERNOON.
And they used to go down through ((   )) Canyon,
⟨to⟩ Las JOYAS
to the BEAN FIELDS,
      brother,
      oh!
eeeee!
a DISASTER,
damn.
And then we used to get whipped back here by the OLD FOLKS.
Oh, ((they sure did whip us)).
We used to be REALLY,
really ATROCIOUS.
And then there didn't used to be any CIGARETTES,
      right?
      uh uh
⟨we used to have⟩ MOUNTAIN-GROWN TOBACCO.
      Yes.

use Goffman's (1974) expression, a crucial framing device. Antes is used in a marked sense in the talk of the elders of bygone days. Here it generally appears as the first word of an utterance that shifts the topic to bygone days. The word is spoken with unusual force, beginning at a higher pitch and then falling rapidly, and a distinct pause then comes before the utterance continues. Antes signals a number of communicative functions. Once the expression appears in this fashion, it tells the participants that a change in the structure and content of the conversation is taking place. Topically, referents that relate to Córdova and surrounding communities before 1915 will predominate. Engaging in an extended discussion of a new fast-food restaurant in Española would accordingly necessitate a conversational reframing. The term antes also frames the ensuing discussion of bygone days as a performance, reflecting the elders' assumption of responsibility for speaking on behalf of their predecessors, the presence of special stylistic devices, and the emergence of the talk within the ongoing social interaction.

Introduction of the antes frame changes the nature of the points of reference that will guide the flow of conversation. One way in which we structure speech is through the use of chronology. By placing our referents in temporal order, we establish coherence relations. Córdovan elders generally follow this course when describing events that occurred after 1915 or away from Córdova and nearby communities. A personal narrative that relates a journey to Colorado in search of mining employment, for example, will generally begin and end with, in Labov and Waletzky's (1967:32) terms, orientation and evaluation sections. These provide respectively an account of the factors that motivated the trip and an assessment of the relative importance of the various narrative units. The body of the narrative will consist of a blow-by-blow account of the major events of the journey in the order in which they occurred. Narrators often note the year in which events in the story took place, and dates may be used to show the temporal relationship between the events.

Chronology is, however, irrelevant when it comes to the talk of the elders of bygone days. A question concerning how long ago (or in what year) an event occurred will be met with either *uuh, hace MUCHO* 'ooh, it was a LONG time ago' or with a response that signals the inappropriateness of the question such as *¡quién sabe!* 'who knows!' Events are frequently placed with respect to a tripartite division of bygone days (see Figure 1). The term antes is used in a minimally marked sense to refer to bygone days as a whole; it also refers, in a more marked sense to the latest period of Córdova's history, the epoch that extended from the time in which the present elders' grandparents were children until the time of the latters' death. Here it contrasts with *mucho más antes,* the first era of the community's history (c. 1730–1830), and *más antes,* the middle period (c. 1830–1880).

Verbal Inflection and Bygone Days. One of the most striking things about the talk of the elders of bygone days is a systematic grammatical alternation that is apparent as one moves from characterizations of bygone days to nowadays. Events that occur

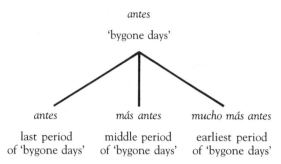

Figure 1. Marked and Unmarked Senses of Antes

nowadays are inflected in what is generally referred to as the present indicative tense. As soon as the antes frame appears, a consistent change can been seen in verbal inflections. In the transcribed passage and in collective recollections in general, verbs that are used in reference to acts that took place in bygone days are marked for past tense and for what is generally termed imperfective or imperfect aspect.[3] As Hockett (1958:237) notes, aspect has to do with the "temporal distribution or contour" of an action, event, or state of affairs, not with its "location in time." (See also Comrie 1976.) Aspect often marks verbs with respect to whether the action is completed (perfective vs. imperfective) and the extension of the action in time (durative vs. nondurative).[4]

Molho (1975) argues that the fundamental aspectual distinction in Spanish is between the *campo de inmanencia* and the *campo de transcendencia*, which we may gloss as the 'sphere of immanence' versus the 'sphere of transcendence'. These provide quite different perspectives on action. Immanence *suscita la imagen de un acontecimiento vivo, devanando la sucesividad de sus instantes* 'evokes the image of a living event, spinning out the succession of its moments'. Transcendence looks back on *un acontecimiento muerto . . . que el pensamiento vivo, que lo ultrapasa, ha dejado tras sí* 'a dead event . . . that the live thought, which transends it, has left behind'. (The translations are my own.)

Note that the imperfective endings that are affixed to verbs that characterize bygone days are highly marked for the sphere of immanence. As Molho (1975:268) notes, the imperfective can do what the perfective cannot—*view actions as they are occurring*. This takes the participants in a speech event out of their immediate spatio-temporal location and places them in the middle of the action in question. The imperfective carries this interpretive penetration of the event even further. The perfective *suscita la imagen del acto en su estricto desarrollo* 'evokes an image of the act in its precise unfolding', focusing on its termination (1975:269). The imperfective, on the other hand, is concerned with *una actitud, que no es un acto sino el* modo *de un acto* 'an attitude, which is not an act but the *mood* of an act' (1975:269; emphasis in original).

The antes frame and the use of imperfect inflections point to a crucial feature of historical recollections. These devices preclude the possibility of viewing the world of los viejitos de antes from a distance, looking back to the past from the perspective of the present. Participants are placed squarely in the middle of the action, and their attention is focused on the factors that give rise to such events. The grammatical machinery takes this movement one step further, invoking a special form of the imperfective aspect. Most of the verbs that are marked for past tense and imperfective aspect refer to iterations or repetitions of actions (such as threshing or hauling wood) rather than to actions that take place only once. Such actions do not appear as a series of isolated events, however, but as actions that constitute, in Molho's (1975:271) terms, *un programa de habitual actividad.*

Use of the habitual aspect lends added force to characterizations of life in bygone days. Collective recollections revolve around the selection of elements of bygone days that are particularly evocative of this era (see below). To inflect the verbal elements of such expressions as *trillaban* or *andaba uno con TEGUAS* in the habitual aspect is to reinforce subtly the notion that such actions (as `threshing or wearing moccasins) occurred so regularly that they are characteristic of bygone days. We are thus left with the image of depth and continuity as embodied in actions and values that saturated the past and are projected toward the present.

The past habitual leaves open the question whether this progression extends into the present. This provides an effective backdrop for articulation of the other half of the elders' basic message—that it is tremendously important for current generations to preserve these actions and values. This side of the equation is grammatically marked, of course, by shifting to the present indicative when describing the present situation. The tense/aspect alternation thus sharpens the past/present contrast that emerges from the content of the discourse. The effect of this alternation is not simply referential; use of the habitual aspect highlights the movement that is apparent in collective recollections between antes and ahora. Like the term antes itself, the past plus habitual inflections provide the participants with entrance into the world of bygone days, while both ahora and present-tense endings draw them back into nowadays.

Mutiplex Signs: Points of Reference for Bygone Days. One of the most important types of building blocks for the construction of collective recollections is a set of expressions that refer to elements of bygone days. In the case of example (3.1), these include references to goats and sheep, threshing, moccasins, hard work, bringing fuelwood, and home-grown tobacco. These topics and the terms used to describe them recur frequently in collective recollections. Beyond their referential value, these expressions possess an unusual degree of pragmatic force; this fact emerges in their ability to bring to mind a great deal of information about bygone days and their role in structuring this type of discourse.

After introducing the antes frame, Ignacio mentions goats and sheep. Alluding to these types of livestock is a nearly ubiquitous feature of collective recollections; goats and sheep often provide a starting point for such discussions. As I noted in Chapter 2, Córdovans have never been able to subsist entirely on the produce of their small fields in the Quemado Valley. Nearly every family had a herd of goats, which supplied them with meat, milk, and cheese, and a lesser number of sheep, which were used for wool and meat. As we discover further on in example (3.1), Córdovan boys spent a good deal of time in their preteen and teenage years herding goats and sheep in the uplands during the spring and summer. When elderly men think back to their youth, goats and sheep stand as a leitmotif. The goats and sheep were generally returned to the village each night; both the animals and their rough wooden pens thus provided a dominant visual element in Córdova and other communities (refer back to Plate 6).

Such emphasis on the importance of goats and sheep in bygone days points in a different, more political direction as well. In Chapter 2, I described the process through which Córdovans lost control of the uplands that surround their community. Once this land became part of the Santa Fe National Forest in 1915, the goats and sheep were the first casualty. Forest Service officials asserted that goats were more destructive of the range than cattle. Note, however, that goats were of subsistence rather than commercial value, and it was rural Mexicanos, by and large, who owned the goats. Cattle, on the other hand, were part of the Anglo-dominated capitalist expansion that was occurring in the region. Goats were thus excluded from the Forest Service lands that surrounded Córdova. The number of sheep that could be placed by Córdovans on the forest was at times restricted, while at other times they were completely excluded.

Because Córdovans lacked other summer grazing areas, they were forced to dispose of nearly all of their goats and sheep. This accordingly cut their subsistence resources in half. Loss of the goats and sheep also had a disastrous impact on agriculture. The valley fields had served as a communal pasture during the winter, thus fertilizing the land. Without the animals, the fields became much less productive. Within a short period of time, it became impossible for most Córdovans to support themselves through these pursuits. The men thus left in great numbers to work outside the community, first as migratory laborers and later as workers in Los Alamos and elsewhere.

It is small wonder, then, that allusions to goats and sheep form a recurrent feature of collective recollections. They evoke a great deal of information about life in bygone days in addition to standing as abbreviations for the chain of events that deprived Córdovans of the self-sufficiency that they had enjoyed for nearly two hundred years.

Ignacio's and Benjamín's description of the way that Córdovans used to thresh wheat and beans extends this portrait of self-sufficiency in bygone days. Goats played

Plate 11. Threshing wheat with goats, ca. 1935. Photograph by T. Harmon Parkhurst, courtesy of the Museum of New Mexico, neg. no. 9059.

another role in the Mexicano subsistence economy. A threshing floor was prepared of hardened earth. As shown in Plate 11, the wheat was piled on the threshing floor. The goats were then driven in a circle on top of the wheat, thus separating the grain from the straw. Ignacio then notes that beans were often winnowed on the roofs of the houses. He uses gestures and a sound symbol, bzzzzzzzzzz, in demonstrating the manner in which the crushed plants were dropped in an enamel pan (*bandeja*), thus allowing the wind to blow away the chaff.

The word *azotea* 'roof' appears in nearly all collective recollections. It is a powerfully evocative synecdoche for the physical and social character of Córdova in bygone days. Most houses in Córdova now feature shiny metal roofs (see Plate 2). Before the 1920s and 1930s, they consisted of timbers, layers of sticks, and several inches of mud. The roofs were all level, and most were of the same height (see Plate 5). When the plaza served as a fortress, it formed a rectangle; the line of abutting houses was broken only by the two plaza gates. The elders are thus fond of saying that 'a person used to walk all the way around the plaza without getting down from the roofs'; one could even cross above the two gates, because planks were placed across these gaps. The old roof style thus evokes the visual appearance of the plaza in bygone days, the physical and social closeness of the residents, and the fact that the roofs were used as work spaces for such tasks as winnowing beans.

The reference to *teguas* 'moccasins' is also quite common in collective recollections. They point, on the one hand, to the poverty of the people in bygone days. Teguas were produced in the community because Córdovans were too poor to afford shoes. The elders generally describe moccasins in derogatory terms, noting that they absorbed moisture from the rain or snow and then stiffened as they dried. Moccasins evoke, on the other hand, the way that the elders of bygone days compensated for their poverty through hard work and resourcefulness.

A third feature that emerges in this dialogue is the back-breaking work that characterized life in bygone days. Starting at about six years of age, children became an integral part of the labor force of the household. Water for domestic purposes had to be hauled from the Río Quemado in the valley below or from one of the ditches. Most of the large number of trips to the river or ditch that were needed each day fell to the children (Plate 12). Children also helped with planting, watering, weeding, and harvesting the crops; tending the livestock; and doing household chores. Transportation of fuelwood, crops, and other vital resources was either by burro or by wagon (Plate 13). It thus often proved necessary, as Ignacio notes, to start at three o'clock in the morning in order to travel both ways and to load the animals.

Benjamín's reference to hauling firewood similarly brings to mind the fact that wood had to be cut for use in heating and cooking. Cutting fuelwood with an axe and hauling it on burros or in wagons was an arduous and time-consuming activity that had to be undertaken regularly. Children who are growing up today take the presence of power saws, trucks and cars, tap water, refrigerators, and grocery stores for granted.

Plate 12. Young Córdovans carrying water from river to home, 1939. Photograph by B. Brixner, courtesy of the Museum of New Mexico, neg. no. 9060.

Plate 13. Transportation in bygone days. A young goatherd is visible in the background. Courtesy of the Museum of New Mexico, neg. no. 9053.

Ignacio and Benjamín thus agree that the young no longer labor in the same way that their grandparents did.

The power of these expressions for structuring collective recollections and conveying the speaker's meaning emerges from their multifunctionality. They possess three major types of significance. First, each operates as a referential sign, pointing out some object or state of affairs. They are equivalent at this level to other designations for the same entity. They contrast with referentially equivalent signs with respect to an encyclopedic function, that of evoking the entire referential frame in which they are included. Drawing on Peirce's (1932) second trichotomy of signs, these two functions are respectively symbolic and indexical. The encyclopedic function of such expressions derives from the way they encapsulate basic features of bygone days. The discussion of goats, for example, raises issues of how crops were threshed and winnowed, what crops were raised, the assignment of young boys to the task of herding goats, the use of moccasins, the degree to which children worked antes, and so forth. The apparent breadth of these topics is not surprising, nor is the fact that reference to goats frequently provides the opening gambit in examples of historical discourse. Making reference to the ubiquity of goats antes provides a synecdoche that indexes much information on agriculture, animal husbandry, age-related social roles, and the like. These expressions are thus ideally suited to realizing the task of drawing the participants into the referential universe of bygone days.

A third discourse function is indexical. These expressions constitute, in Jakobson's (1957:131) terms, messages that refer to the code. The code in this case is conversational structure—the demarcation of turns, topics, openings, closings, and so forth and their combination in higher-level units. Such signs are interpretive frames; their appearance indicates a shift of topic to the encyclopedic domain that they index. Statements that are made after that point will be interpreted in terms of their bearing upon this domain. Antes, used in reference to bygone days, is the most powerful in this regard. Inclusion of antes will indicate that a shift to the talk of the elders of bygone days has occurred, regardless of the nature of the previous dialogue, and will inform the manner in which the other participants and any spectators will interpret the elders' remarks.

These expressions thus operate communicatively in three different ways, effecting referential, encyclopedic, and discourse-level functions. I accordingly refer to them as triplex signs. They provide us with a tool for exploring the way that collective recollections are structured in the absence of a fixed narrative structure. The sum total of triplex signs is not exceedingly large, and key expressions occur in nearly all tokens of the genre. The most important triplex signs are the antes frame along with references to *cabras* 'goats' and *borregas* 'sheep', *sembrar* 'planting', *cosechar* 'harvesting', *trillar* 'threshing', and *teguas* 'moccasins', although others are used less commonly.[5] In collective recollections, grasping the function of these expressions as synecdoches is contingent on familiarity with this type of discourse. The structure and content of a given example will depend on the interests and competence of all parties, the specific interests that each brings to the conversation, and the way these come together as the discourse progresses. Participants do not know in advance which topics will be included in a given interaction, or in what order they will appear. By knowing the central triplex signs and by grasping their communicative functions, however, participants can establish the topical status of a series of referents and can place them with respect to a large body of information about bygone days.

The Dialogic Nature of Collective Recollections. What, then, is the structure of collective recollections? First and foremost, they are dialogues—communicative exchanges between two or more elders who collaborate in generating an account of bygone days. Although one participant may produce more of the discourse during one part of the dialogue (as is the case in the transcribed section), the social organization of the interaction does not accord any one elder greater control over turn taking or topical selection. The discourse is rather punctuated with markers of conversational involvement. After making a point about bygone days, the speaker will hesitate, look at his interlocutor, and ask *¿no?* 'no?' or 'really?' The other then will respond by nodding his head, smiling, laughing, perhaps saying *sí* 'yes', *¿sí?* 'really?', or a similar expression. Alternatively, the respondent may continue to develop the previous topic or shift to a new topic. Collective recollections thus strike the listener as something of a verbal ballet, proceeding through close coordination of conversational involvement.

Topical selection also plays an important role in structuring collective recollections. Initiated through use of the antes frame, an initial central topic is broached through the introduction of a triplex term (e.g., *cabras*). Another triplex term then explores the same topic by considering another facet of that part of bygone days (e.g., the use of goats in threshing). Alternately, one of the elders may relate some personal experience that pertains to the topic. Note that such reminiscences never become personal narratives, isolating a particular event and developing a specific series of events. Such a shift would be marked by the emergence of repeated uses of past tense and perfective aspect (e.g., "I went"), a grammatical mechanism for placing actions in a discrete temporal series (cf. Hopper 1982). Allusions to the speaker's experience rather advance the work of characterizing the nature of action in bygone days.

Ahora 'nowadays' is not entirely absent from collective recollections. It enters, in some instances, as an interruption. This particular recollection was interrupted twice, once to discuss the possibility of a trip to the local horse race the next day and once in talking about odd jobs that Ignacio is sometimes able to secure. In the latter case, Ignacio turned to me and included me in the conversation. When he shifted back to antes, I was once again effectively removed from participation in the discourse. In other instances, references to *ahora* are an integral part of the collective recollection. In (3.1:87–97), Ignacio assesses the limited acquaintance of today's youth with the sort of labor that was required of Benjamín and himself as children. He has thus moved from an interpretation of a feature of bygone days (hard work) to an interpretation of nowadays vis-à-vis this same feature.

Ignacio's remark about Leopoldo and his young co-workers (89–93) comments on an event that is taking place while he is speaking. Leopoldo was serving as the foreman in directing work during the annual spring cleaning of one of Córdova's irrigation ditches. Every landowner is required to send at least one worker. Many claim that it is now hard to find youths willing to do the work. Reports are also heard that once a party has been assembled, some of the young workers are not willing to do their share. Ignacio knew that Leopoldo and his band of workers were approaching the section of the ditch that is opposite his (Ignacio's) house at that moment, thus Ignacio's timely comment, *ahi viene Leopoldo* 'here comes Leopoldo'. This suggests the nature of collective recollections as dialogue not only between two or more elders, but also between antes and ahora.

PEDAGOGICAL DISCOURSE

Collective recollections can be comprehensive in their discussion of antes. Such information is designed for the appreciation of initiates. Little flesh is placed on the bones of the triplex signs. Because all of the participants are thoroughly familiar with the talk of the elders of bygone days, there is no need to proceed from general to more specific topics or to explicate the meaning of what is said. This is, of course, equally true of historical competitions and explorations. If only these three forms existed, the elders would find it much more difficult to realize one of the central tasks that confronts them in waning years—transmitting the talk of the elders of bygone days to their descendants.

The problem is complicated by a real dilemma that confronts the elders in their pedagogical attempts. The difficulty lies in the fact that the young lack a common basis of experience with the elders of bygone days. By the time that Córdovans under the age of forty were born, the viejitos de antes were dead, the uplands had been lost, and agriculture was no longer the major means of subsistence. In order to comprehend this talk, the young must cross an experiental chasm that separates them from the world of bygone days. The present viejitos could simply *describe* what transpired in the past, but this would fail to show the young why it is important to learn about bygone days. They would also fail to grasp the sentido of what was being said. If the younger generations miss the deeper significance of the talk, the elders will be unable to realize their basic goal—helping people to see the meaning of the past for the present. One of the elders' central concerns (as revealed by their meta-communicative comments) is thus to help the young cross this experiental hiatus, drawing them into the world of los viejitos de antes. How can this be accomplished?

The answer lies in a fourth type of historical discourse, one that I will refer to as pedagogical discourse. It is similar to collective recollections in a number of ways, including use of the antes frame, many of the same triplex signs, and its status as dialogue. In pedagogical discourse the juxtaposition of antes and ahora becomes even more pronounced, reaching the level of a centripetal force. There are, however, a number of important differences between the two types of historical discourse; most of these emerge from the fact that pedagogical discourse relates elders and younger persons, not peers.

Example (3.2) contains pedagogical discourse drawn from a conversation with George López that I videotaped in 1983. Silvianita Trujillo de López and George López are pictured in Plate 14. Mrs. López was cooking lunch in the kitchen while Mr. López was sitting in the living room, and she offered an occasional remark. Asked what life was like when the elders of bygone days were alive, Mr. López compared the ways Córdovans provided for their subsistence in bygone days and more recently. He emphasized the way the viejitos de antes had been able to provide for their needs with their flocks of goats and sheep and by planting as many small pockets of arable land as they could find. (See example (3.2).)

Two of the basic features of collective recollections, the antes frame and triplex signs, are also apparent in pedagogical discourse. Although their use is in many ways parallel in these two types of speech events, important differences appear in the way that these features relate to the ongoing social interaction. Pedagogical discourse is also characterized by two important characteristics that are not shared by collective recollections, namely, a special structuring of topical progression and a focus on the rhetorical competence of the participants. The distribution of a number of features between all four varieties of historical discourse is schematized in Figure 2.

THE ANTES FRAME

The term antes appears five times in example (3.2). As is the case with collective recollections, the antes frame shifts the discourse to a discussion of bygone days, imposing topical constraints and selecting for the use of certain stylistic features. In the case of pedagogical discourse, the antes frame also changes the nature of the access that the different participants will have to the conversational floor. Once the term antes is introduced, elders enjoy a great deal more control over topical selection and turn taking. Junior participants may use some feature of the topic under discussion in

(3.2) George López (83), Silvianita Trujillo de López (82), CLB (30); 22 July 1983, Córdova, New Mexico

CB Sí.
    ¿Y cómo era la gente antes?
GL Pos,
    a–, la gente antes,
    pos, todos usaban unos zapatos,   5
    usaban zapatos teguas.
CB   Hm.
GL   Sí.
CB   Sí.
GL Su papá de, dif–, del Evaristo, el difunto Fernández,   10
    los Chupaderos, Chupaderos/
CB   Sí
GL que están allá arriba,
    era, era de él,
    ahi sem–, ahi sembraba de todito.   15
    Se daba papas y todo.
CB   Um hum.
GL   Sí.
    Como pa' Las TRUCHAS,
    ves.   20
    En Las Truchas cosechaba MUCHA GENTE.
    Ya 'ora no quieren sembrar,
    ya 'ora no,
    ya 'ora no,
    ves.   25
    Ya 'ora mejor trabajan por otro.
CB   Sí, ¿es verda'?
GL   Sí.
    Sembraban de por sí.
CB   Sí.   30
GL   Sí.
    'Ora no.
    Nh-hn.
CB   Hm.
GL Yo me acuerdo cuando,   35
    cuando iba del difunto Juan Córdova,
    tenía un patrón en Chama Arriba.
    Ahi venía yo a venir
    junto con él
    a los hijaderos ahi en Chama Arriba,   40
CB   ¿sí?
GL a hijar BORREGOS.
CB   Hm
GL Oh, era muy diferente antes a lo de 'ora.
    Era más pobrecita la gente.   45
CB   Sí.
GL 'Ora no.
    Ahora está todo al ESTILO.
      ¿Eh?
CB   Sí.   50

English translation

	Yes.
	And what were people like in bygone days?
points toward feet,	Well,
then brings hands up	ah, in bygone days, people,
in expansive gesture	well, they all used to wear mocc–,
	they used to wear moccasins.
	Hm.
	Yes.
	Yes.
	The father of, the la–, of Evaristo, the late Fernández,
points repeatedly	the Chupaderos, Chupaderos/
nods	Yes
	that are up there,
	that ⟨place⟩ was his,
	he used to pla–, he used to plant everything there.
	⟨It⟩ yielded potatoes and everything.
nods	Um hum.
	Yes.
indicates entire	Like up in Las TRUCHAS,
Truchas area with	you see.
sweeping gesture	In Las Truchas, A LOT OF PEOPLE FARMED.
	Nowadays no one wants to plant,
shakes finger	not nowadays,
vigorously	not nowadays,
	you see.
points	Nowadays they'd rather work for someone else.
nods; laughs	Yes, is that so?
nods	Yes.
	They used to plant for themselves.
	Yes.
nods	Yes.
	Not nowadays.
	Nh-hn.
	Hm.
	I remember when,
	when Juan Córdova used to go,
points	he used to have a boss in Chama Arriba.
	I used to come along
	together with him
points	to the lambing up there in Chama Arriba,
	really?
	to help with the LAMBING.
	Hm.
shakes head	Oh, it used to be quite different from the way things are nowadays.
nods	The people were much poorer.
	Yes.
	Not nowadays.
laughs; shakes head	Nowadays everything is in STYLE.
	Eh?
	Yes.

CB   ¿Vivía más a gusto la gente antes?
GL   Pos sí.
    Pos, de todo COSECHABAN,
    de todo SEMBRABAN.
    Pos, ahi,   55
    ahi en el Cerro de los Córdovas,
    ahi sembraban,
    ahi sembraban también.
    Las Joyas en Medio también sembraban.
    En el punto de Rito La Gallina sembraban.   60
    Sembraban ahi en Rito La Gallina.
    Sembraban pa' allá pa' Los Pozos.
CB   Sí.
GL   Todo eso de ahi sembraban,
    ahi se–, era ranchos,   65
    siembras,
    pero
    ya ahora no quieren sembrar.
CB   ¿Por qué?
GL   Porque ya el mundo está diferente.   70
ST   Ahora no se da.
GL   Ya ahora no quieren sembrar,
        no, no.
    Mejor trabajan por otro.
        ¿Eh?   75
CB   Sí, es verdad.
GL   Pos sí.
    Antes no.

---

conjunction with a question frame in attempting to elicit more information on a particular subtopic. By and large, however, pedagogical discourse places the elder in the position of principal speaker, while younger persons are responsible for supplying the back-channel cues (e.g., *sí* 'yes', *¿sí?* 'really?', etc.) that signal comprehension. In the case of pedagogical discourse, the antes frame creates an asymmetry between the participants that is not present in historical competitions, historical explorations, or collective recollections.

TRIPLEX SIGNS

The use of triplex signs in pedagogical discourse and collective recollections is quite similar. These features play important roles in structuring both types of speech events, encapsulating a great deal of information about bygone days, providing conceptual landmarks, and structuring the discourse. Such basic triplex signs as goats and sheep, planting and harvesting, and moccasins occur in both examples (3.1) and

smiles	Did the people live better in bygone days?
	Well yes.
	Well, they HARVESTED EVERYTHING,
	they PLANTED EVERYTHING.
points	Well, there
begins counting	there on Córdova's Hill
different locations on	they used to plant there,
fingers	they used to plant there too.
	They used to plant in Middle Las Joyas too.
points	They used to plant near La Gallina Creek.
points	They used to plant there by La Gallina Creek.
points	They used to plant over there in Los Posos.
	Yes.
	They used to plant all those places,
	they plan–, there were farms,
	fields,
	but
	nowadays they don't want to plant.
	Why?
emphatic gesture	Because the world is different now.
	⟨The fields⟩ don't produce these days.
shakes his head	These days they don't want to plant,
	no, no.
both smile	They'd rather work for someone else.
	Eh?
	Yes, it's true.
	Well yes.
	Not in bygone days.

(3.2). (These examples were not selected for such correspondences but were selected nearly at random from recordings of the talk of the elders of bygone days.)

Two subtle differences are apparent in the role that triplex signs play in pedagogical discourse and collective recollections. References to goats and sheep and to agriculture play a central role in both examples. Mr. López places these references conceptually in two principal ways. On the one hand, he adumbrates the places where these activities were carried out. I have visited all of these locations, either in Mr. López's company or in trips taken with members of his family. In the course of such visits, Mr. López would generally discuss the historical significance of the site and point out any artifacts (buildings or their foundations, plows, corrals, etc.) that bear witness to their past uses. He accordingly knows that I will be able to evoke a mental image of the locations and that I ought to be able to imagine people planting, harvesting, and herding goats and sheep there. Mr. López's use of triplex signs in thus custom tailored, so so speak, to fit the extent of my knowledge.

This mode of contextualization is, of course, not necessary in collective recollec-

Plate 14. George López and Silvianita Trujillo de López, 1986. Photograph by Charles L. Briggs

Plate 15. The Lópezes' home in the Quemado Valley, 1974. Photograph by Charles L. Briggs

Type of historical discourse	Participants	Performance	Antes frame	Triplex signs	Antes/ ahora dialectics	Topical progression ordered	Focus on rhetorical competence of participants
Historical competitions	elders only	+	–	–	–	–	+
Historical explorations	middle-aged only	–	–	–	–	–	–
Collective recollections	elders only	+	+	+	+	–	–
Pedagogical discourse	elders and younger persons	+	+	+	+	+	+

Figure 2: Comparison of Four Types of Historical Discourse

tions. Here the elders bring a host of memories of bygone days and a substantial corpus of talk that they themselves heard from the elders of bygone days to bear on generating and interpreting historical discourse. As such, a brief allusion to the fact that 'up there they used to have WORKERS, working in the POTATOES' (3.1: 107–08) is adequate for persons who can remember how and where potatoes were grown, but younger persons are unlikely to make much sense of it.

The second means of placing these triplex signs is through reference to what has taken the place of this aspect of bygone days at present. Although I never lived in Córdova while it was primarily an agricultural and pastoral community, I understand what it means to give up farming and herding and get a job in the city. I am also well acquainted with the positive moral significance that is attributed to 'working for oneself' as opposed to 'working for someone else.' Arbitrary decisions by foremen or bosses can demean the worker, placing the employee in a situation that compromises her or his *dignidad de la persona* 'personal dignity'. The image of the mass exodus that now occurs each morning as wage laborers leave in carpools for Los Alamos in turn brings into sharper focus a picture of hard-working farmers who labor within their community and its environs. Clearly, collective recollections also develop antes/ahora contrasts. In pedagogical discourse, however, this movement from past to present occurs more frequently, and it plays a greater role in explicating the meaning of the past.

Triplex signs provide "students" with a tool for grasping the way that pedagogical discourse is structured in the absence of a fixed narrative structure or content. The sum total of triplex signs is not large, and key expressions occur in all examples of the genre. Familiarity with these signs provides younger participants with a vital tool for grasping what an elder is telling them about the past and how she or he is doing so. Once the students are acquainted with this set of expressions, they can draw on a set of familiar guideposts for grasping the meaning and coherence of facts that they have not previously encountered. Learning to recognize triplex signs and discern their conversational significance is thus a vital component of the competence that is requisite for comprehending pedagogical discourse.

Herein lies the difference in the way that triplex signs function in the two types of speech events. In collective recollections they access a large body of information that is known in detail by all participants, whereas in pedagogical discourse they are like directions that a seasoned traveler gives to those who are setting out on their first journey. As with all directions, the more they are suited to recipients' present knowledge of the terrain, the greater the likelihood that they will prove to be useful in helping those who are just starting out find the paths that their precedessors have blazed.

THE DIALECTICS OF PAST AND PRESENT

My discussion of pedagogical discourse thus far has been microscopic, explicating individual features of this variety of talk about the elders of bygone days and characterizing their communicative functions. Pedagogical discourse is, however, not patterned at this level alone. A careful structuring of topical progression that provides another important means of organizing the discourse occurs at the level of treatment of individual topics, the movement from one to another, and the way this process changes as the student learns more about bygone days.

Grasping the structure of this dialogue requires enlarging our frame of reference beyond the segment that is transcribed in example (3.2). In the beginning of the discussion, Mr. López cited the importance of agriculture antes, using the *sembrar/cosechar* triplex sign. This allusion included reference to one detail regarding cultivation antes—the fact that they used homemade wooden hoes, sometimes inserting pieces of metal. He then turned immediately to a discussion of the large herds of sheep and goats that Córdovans owned in bygone days. This point was illustrated by a statement that his father, José Dolores López, had herded sheep. This material on livestock leads him to note that goats were also used in threshing wheat and other crops and then to remark on the great differences that separate life in bygone days from nowadays.

The beginning of this example of pedagogical discourse thus evinces four major features of this genre. First, the term antes frames the conversation as bearing on the talk of the elders of bygone days. Second, such conversations begin with allusions to the basic features of life antes, articulated through the use of triplex signs. Nearly all dialogues begin with references to the importance of both agriculture and pastoralism antes; initial references to goats are particularly common. This is complemented, sometimes in the opening lines, by a statement of the antes/ahora contrast. This hiatus becomes a major force for structuring the discourse. Once a central feature of life in bygone days has been articulated, the elder will turn to a characterization of nowadays. This juxtaposition is generally used in demonstrating the fact that this important element of antes is of diminished importance or missing altogether ahora. The elder will often proceed to interpret the adverse effects of the failure to preserve this element of the past.

Pedagogical discourse is thus guided by the following pattern. Conversations begin with the statement of a major premise regarding bygone days, which is complemented by one or more specific examples of persons or practices from antes that illustrate its importance. The speaker then turns to nowadays, pointing out the absence of this trait ahora. This may be exceedingly brief, as in examples (3.1) and (3.2), stating a basic contrast, such as 'working for oneself' versus 'working for someone else.' It can also lead to a lengthy interpretation of nowadays, articulating the effects of such factors as land loss, government relief programs, or wage labor on the people. Because younger persons are also familiar with such subjects, they are free to take a more active role in such discussions. Such contributions consist of the provision of additional examples from ahora that support the elder's position. (Only very rarely have I seen a younger person use such an opportunity to deny that this facet of bygone times is absent nowadays or to argue that its loss is of no moment.) The conversation will then focus on another feature of life antes; the new topic frequently pertains to some facet of the preceding one.

In short, topical progression in pedagogical discourse evinces a dialectical structure. It moves back and forth from antes to ahora, pointing out cultural features that are present and absent in the two periods. In and of itself, such a movement between two poles would not realize the elders' goal of conveying the sentido of this material. Pedagogical discourse combines this oppositional dynamic with a periodic synthesis, which consists of the derivation of a basic moral value that underlies the opposition. The elders' point is not simply that this value was present antes and is absent ahora but that such values are of equal importance to survival nowadays. Note that elderly pedagogues are not simply interested in convincing the young that their generation is going astray; they are exhorting them to internalize these values and to reflect them in their behavior. These value-laden syntheses thus bear three types of communicative functions—descriptive, interpretive, and exhortative.

This focus on the student is also evident at the level of the conversation as a whole. Once a basic antes/ahora contrast has been stated, the discourse moves quickly from topic to topic, and breadth outweighs depth. This stage is apparent in the section transcribed in example (3.2). As the discourse progresses, however, it moves further and further in the direction of greater specificity, often in the form of a progression to more detailed, concrete topics. Figure 3 summarizes the topical pro-

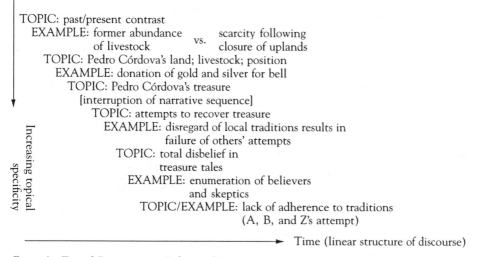

Figure 3. Topical Progression in Pedagogical Discourse

gression in a conversation that I had with two Córdovan elders in 1979. (A segment of this dialogue appears in Chapter 7.) It begins with the statement that Córdovans used to be better off than they are at present, before the loss of grazing lands in the uplands above Córdova, as measured in terms of land and livestock. This contention is then supported by material on Pedro Córdova, detailing his land and livestock holdings. An allusion to the gold and silver that he donated at the time the community's bell was cast prompts a discussion of how much gold and silver he had and where he buried it. Increasingly detailed accounts of efforts to recover the treasure culminate in an account of a treasure hunt in which the two speakers participated.

Example (3.2) evinces a movement toward a different sort of specificity. Mr. López's descriptions do not themselves become increasingly detailed in this conversation. His focus is more on interpreting one facet of the meaning of past/present contrasts. The upland fields that Mr. López mentions were entirely dependent on rainfall, and they are located at 8,000 to 9,000 feet of elevation. (See Plate 16) Planting an area like Las Joyas or Los Chupaderos in this semiarid and variable climate involved risk. The assumption here is that los viejitos de antes did so not simply out of economic necessity, although this was quite real, but also as an act of faith in God's omnipotence and generosity. The images of St. Anthony, the local patron, and St. Isidore, the patron saint of farmers, were carried through all the fields as a means of invoking the saints and God's protection (cf. Briggs 1983; Brown 1941).

This notion bears important implications for the present, given the current reluctance to till the land—'nowadays they don't want to plant, no, no.' This loss of faith in turn indexes an apocalyptic theme. Most elders believe that the growth of commercialization, technological advances, and secularism in modern society represents a turning away from religious and corporatistic values. The desire to gain material goods by 'working for someone else' thus aligns Córdovan wage workers with this tendency. The elders draw on scripture in asserting that the spread of individualistic and secular values will eventually lead God to destroy the world (i.e., in the second coming of Christ). As the conversation progresses, Mr. López focuses less attention on enumerating basic antes/ahora contrasts and more on explicating the coming millennium and its scriptural basis (see Chapter 5, example (5.3)). Mr. López's discourse thus centers increasingly on the moral theme that he is advancing throughout this conversation.

The extent to which a dialogue will move from the general to the specific is dependent upon the elder's assessment of the competence of his or her interlocutors in the talk of the elders of bygone days. When the younger participants are comprehending the "lesson," the discourse can continue to move in this direction. If it becomes apparent that one of the participants has failed to grasp the last point, the elder will go back a step, returning to a more basic point. If the junior asks a naive or general question, the conversation will probably return to square one, that is, to basic contrasts between past and present. This means that beginning students seldom

Plate 16. Dry farm area of Las Joyas in the uplands above Córdova, 1979. Photograph by Charles L. Briggs

progress beyond the level of generalities. This certainly proved to be the case in my early attempts to learn about the elders of bygone days (cf. Briggs 1986:56–59). As they gain in experience and sophistication, students can move more and more quickly to ever greater conversational depths. Pedagogical discourse is thus not only structured by the elders' representation of bygone days; the course of a given example also reflects the most immediate present—the course of a particular social interaction.

Pedagogical discourse is thus quintessentially interpretive, and it revolves around a dialectical process of examining the meaning of past and present. These features are not lacking in collective recollections. Elders jointly produce an interpretation of the facets of life in bygone days that rendered it distinct from contemporary society; they similarly use the past as a framework for examining nowadays. This interpretive and dialectical thrust is less apparent in collective recollections. The focus there is less on analyzing the cultural and religious values that shaped conduct in bygone days than on reaffirming a shared sense of personal involvement, articulating a sense of the impact that their early life experience has had upon their own identities. The basic goal of pedagogical discourse, on the other hand, is to teach the young how to undertake this dialectical and interpretive process themselves. The latter type of speech event thus evinces a different sense of dialogicality, the one illuminated by Bakhtin (1981); here the exchange between interlocutors (real or imagined) represents dialectical engagement of conflicting ideologies, such as those emanating from antes and ahora.

Both pedagogical discourse and collective recollections are far more than simple idealizations of the past. The elders are quick to point out that life was hard, the people were generally poor, and that they 'used to work like mules' in bygone days. One of the recurrent themes in both forms is that today's youth often act selfishly and foolishly because they are less committed to basic values. Nevertheless, Benjamín and Ignacio point an accusatory finger at themselves in noting how their irresponsible actions as youthful goatherds cost their community a portion of its subsistence resources on at least one occasion. Merely romanticizing the past and condemning the present would not serve the critical and dialectical ends of these two forms, particularly those of pedagogical discourse.

DIALOGIC CONTEXTUALIZATION

Thus, the form and content of pedagogical discourse are structured, in part, by the need to render it intelligible to younger participants. This situation raises the question of how the elders can know whether their interlocutors are comprehending a given point. The answer is that the younger persons are constantly signaling their reactions to what is being said, sometimes in response to queries by the elder. In la plática de los viejitos de antes elders regularly request confirmation that their interlocutors are following the conversation. Some requests are verbal. In example

(3.2:49, 75) Mr. López solicits a response with *¿eh?* Elders commonly use *¿ves?* 'see?', *¿sabes cómo (te digo)?* 'do you know (what I mean)?', *¿sí?* 'yes?' or 'really?', and other forms for this purpose.

Numerically speaking, the most common queries are visual. The crucial factor here is gaze. Elders generally look in the direction of one of the juniors at the beginning of an utterance; most then look away as their statement progresses. The important thing is that the elder will gaze directly at one younger person when reaching the end of a triplex sign. The elder then pauses, continuing to look at the junior, until a response is obtained. As I noted in the section on triplex signs, these expressions are laden with pragmatic meaning. If the younger person does not realize that a triplex sign has been uttered and thus fails to signal comprehension, he or she is unlikely to be familiar with the information on bygone days that the sign indexes. The elders thus wait before proceeding with a new topic until they are sure that the younger person understand the message.

Students do not provide such responses only when asked, whether verbally or nonverbally. Transcripts reveal that juniors punctuate their elders' remarks with such expressions as *hm hum, sí* 'yes', *¿sí?* 'yes?' or 'really?'. A rising inflection can be used to signal a lack of understanding, inducing the pedagogue to explicate the point. Younger persons also use gaze, shakes and nods of the head, movements of the eyebrows and forehead, and changes in posture as conversational signals. This combination of visual and auditory signals provides the elder with a constant stream of signs as to the nature of the juniors' participation in the discourse.

If two or more juniors are present, one of them will assume responsibility for providing the elder(s) with these signals at a given time. Selection of the respondent is basically in the hands of the elder who is speaking, the choice being signaled by gaze. As the elder looks at one interlocutor, that person will provide the verbal and visual back-channel signals. It is, however, not entirely up to the elder. Occasionally a younger person will petition for the role of respondent by nodding and providing the um hm, sí, and similar responses. The back-channel signals are generally uttered a bit more forcefully than usual at such points, a tactic that usually induces the elder to look directly at this person who then assumes the role of primary respondent. This sequence of events often precedes a junior's attempt to ask a question or offer a statement.

THE POWER OF THE PAST

Appaduri (1981) recently noted that the rules or conventions that societies use "to regulate the inherent debatability of the past" still stand as largely uncharted territory. Fortunately, a number of studies have appeared that provide us with a sense of the similarities and differences in the ways that people articulate their history and the role that talking and singing plays in daily life. Cohen (1977), Denning (1980), Rosaldo (1980), and Sahlins (1982, 1985) draw on a diverse range of historical, ethnographic, and folkloric sources in reconstructing cultural histories. Glassie's (1982) study of Ballymenone and Gossen's (1974a, 1985) work with the Chamula of Mexico place style, content, and performance in cultural context. The appearance of a new edition of Vansina's (1985) classic study reminds us of the importance of historical tradition in Africa, while Levine (1977) and Price (1983) demonstrate the way that historical consciousness has enabled Afro-Americans to survive oppression.

Studies by Finnegan (1967) and Price (1983) discuss a number of features of African and Afro-American historical discourse that bear a high degree of similarity to their Mexicano counterpart.[6] First, the past or some part of it frequently provides a locus for the validation of cultural action. The Saramaka of Surinam, descendants of escaped slaves, are centrally concerned with traditions concerning those ancestors who helped them win their freedom. As Price (1983:6) notes, "First-Time (*fési-tén*)—the era of the Old-Time People—differs most sharply from the recent past in its overwhelming inherent power." The Limba of Sierra Leone similarly believe that "it was from the old people [i.e., the dead], it is constantly being stressed, that they first learnt their traditional culture which they now keep 'in their heads' to 'bring out' on a particular occasion."

Second, Wittgenstein once noted that "Ethics and Aesthetics are One and the Same," and it seems likely that Saramakas, Limbas, and Mexicanos would agree with him. In each case the past is not viewed simply as a set of events or processes that exist independently of the means by which humans remember them; rather, historical information is closely identified with the speech forms through which it is conveyed. For the Limba, *maboro ma* 'old times' or 'ancient ways' are believed to have given rise to the stories, songs, historical narratives, riddles, proverbs, analogies, and figures of speech that artistically reflect the past in analogic form. The Saramakas embed First-Time in genealogical nuggets, personal epithets, commemorative place names, personal names, lists of land holdings, proverbs, drum slogans, songs, and prayers. The identification of history and discourse is so close here that calling out the names of the Old-Time People evokes their presence, sometimes with fatal results. The forms that preserve historical information are closely guarded, and one never fully reveals all that is known. This same connection between rhetoric, aesthetics, and historical reality is apparent in the way that Mexicanos connect antes with the genres that comprise la platica de los viejitos de antes.

Third, for all three groups the past provides a crucial source of collective identity. First-Time, maboro ma, and bygone days are used in validating claims to lands and other resources as well as in providing legitimation for belief and action. As Glassie (1982:155) argues, the unifying force of history is also apparent in the way that social groups are generated through performance. In the three cases, performances are collective—participants collaborate in accordance with special social roles and interactional patterns. Although one performer sometimes predominates, others are at least responsible for providing back-channel cues, if not for singing choruses (Limba) or echoing phrases as well. The embodiment of history through artistic expression is seen in these (and in many other societies) as a basic prerequisite for cultural and often physical survival.

The placement of such emphasis on the force of tradition might provide fuel for scholars who would identify folklore with the conservative, passive repetition of what has come before. This vision is far from what Mexicanos, Saramakas, and Limba have in mind. As Price (1983:5) notes, "Saramakas are acutely conscious of living in history, of reaping each day the fruits of their ancestors' deed, and of themselves possessing the potential, through their own acts, to change the shape of tomorrow's world." The Limba are similarly aware of the fact "that there is continual recreation or improvisation and yet that this takes place within the framework of traditional style and theme" (Finnegan 1967:102). This "dual nature" is tied both to differences of individual style and to use of stories to " 'give someone sense' (*thi funun*), showing him in a parable either that he has acted wrongly himself or that he, and others, should try to act in a certain way in the future" (1967:30). Like Mexicanos, Saramakas and Limba view the past as a dynamic force that can respond in flexible ways to the task of making sense of the present.

These three examples point to the existence of an interesting dialectic. Folklorists, anthropologists, and others have often identified a strong focus on "the ancestors" and their legacy with cultural conservatism—a desire to keep things "just the way they are." Even if the members of a particular society may worship the past (literally or figuratively), this does not mean that they are enslaved by it. The past rather stands as a communicative resource, providing a setting and an expressive pattern for discussions that transform both past and present. The data suggest that all three societies see this process as intrinsically interpretive; both performers and audience members must deduce the basic principles that generated action in the past and then apply these to the present and future. The participants thus provide us with an excellent lead that we can follow in our attempts to develop adequate theoretical models for the study of folklore. They do not treat the past as a set of objects that must be shielded from change; developing performance competence seems rather to engender an emphasis on the basic processes that underlie the production and interpretation of patterned, artistic expression and on the social interactions in which they emerge.

4

■■

PROVERBS

Historical discourse provides us with a sense of the world of the elders of bygone days and of the ways the past can inform our understanding of the present. The means by which it invokes bygone days is somewhat indirect, however, in that the performers continue to speak on behalf of their predecessors. This points to a major difference between historical discourse and the other forms of la plática de los viejitos de antes. These other genres bring the voices of the elders of bygone days into the performance by quoting this talk. Historical discourse thus retains some distance from bygone days. It provides us with a window on the past, but the door remains closed. Proverb performances, on the other hand, open the door and invite the elders of bygone days into the room. Not all elders can use proverbs. For those who possess this *don* 'gift', however, proverbs constitute exceedingly powerful devices for connecting past and present.

This difference between proverbs and historical discourse is matched by a striking methodological dissimilarity. Study of the latter form of the talk of the elders of bygone days had to grapple with the task of demonstrating the existence of a discernible pattern of folkloric speech that bore no correspondence to the analytic types that have been elucidated by folklorists. The proverb, on the other hand, is one of the best established analytic types, and a vast literature exists on its form, content, and social functions. The problem here thus becomes one of avoiding the trap of imposing the characteristics of the analytic type on the culture-specific data.

All of us have encountered proverbs in conversation, and proverbs have figured in the literatures of the ancient Sumerians and Egyptians, the *Talmud* and *Bible*, the Renaissance Commonplace Books, and those of recent decades. Such intimacy may lead us to believe that we know what proverbs are and how to identify them. This sense of familiarity has not translated into scholarly success in defining the proverb. The kernel of the contradiction emerges in the classic work, Archer Taylor's *The Proverb* (1931:3):

The definition of a proverb is too difficult to repay the undertaking; and should we fortunately combine in a single definition all the essential elements and give them each the proper emphasis, we should not even then have a touchstone. An incommunicable quality tells us that this sentence is proverbial and that one is not.

This position, which Taylor later reiterated,[1] uses an admission of defeat in justifying a remarkably powerful claim, namely, that researchers can use a priori and intuitive criteria in the identification and analysis of proverbs.

A great deal of work on proverbs has emerged during the intervening decades. Many writers have attempted definitions; Mieder's *International Proverb Scholarship: An Annotated Bibliography* (1982) lists 245 books and articles that deal with definitions of the proverb. Researchers have examined proverbs from literary, poetic, semiotic, logical, semantic, sociolinguistic, rhetorical, psychological, historical, and functional points of view, and we have accordingly gained a much more sophisticated understanding of the nature of the proverb and how it relates to other genres. The last two decades have witnessed the appearance of a number of dissertations and books that focus on an in-depth ethnographic study of the way proverbs are used in a single society (cf. Murphy 1976; Okezie 1977; Penfield 1983; Seitel 1972; Yankah 1985).

Nearly all of the attempts that have been made to define the proverb or characterize the nature of a given body of proverbs have, nevertheless, encountered one or more of the following problems. First, researchers generally focus on either textual *or* contextual dimensions. Studies by Arora (1968, 1972, 1977), Barley (1972, 1974), Dundes (1975a), Giovannini (1978), Goodwin and Wenzel (1979), Kussi (1969, 1972), Milner (1969, 1971), Murphy (1976), Permyakov (1979), and Zholkovskij (1978), for example, focus on linguistic structure, semantic content, and logical relations, whereas Abrahams (1968a, 1968b), Arewa (1970), Arewa and Dundes (1964), Barakat (1980), Burke (1941:293–304), Evans-Pritchard (1962), Firth (1926), Gossen (1973, 1974a:111–15), Jason (1971), Kirshenblatt-Gimblett (1973), Messenger (1959), Paredes (1982), Penfield (1983), Seitel (1969, 1977), Yanga (1977), and Yankah (1986) concentrate on the social and communicative functions of proverb use. A number of works, however, have attempted to relate textual and contextual elements (cf. Abrahams 1972; Abrahams and Babcock-Abrahams 1975; Finnegan 1970; Krikmann 1974a, 1974b; Mukařovský 1971; Seitel 1972; Yankah 1985).[2]

A second problem is the conflation of analytic types and culture-specific genres as the focus of definitions (cf. Ben-Amos 1976/1969), which has led many scholars to believe that proverb-like genres in a given society must conform to the basic features that have been proposed for a cross-cultural comparative model. A third problem is most telling in terms of the present argument. All but a few of the definitions that have been offered are tautological. Taking a given body of proverbs, researchers analyze them for common features and present the summary as a definition of the proverb. The problem is that the same a priori and intuitive grounds guide identification of the initial corpus of proverbs and the analysis itself.

Note that this sense of "an incommunicable quality" also informs the differentiation of proverbs from the discourse that surrounds the proverb "text." This assumption has failed to receive badly needed critical attention. Close ethnographic studies of societies in which proverb performances remain an accepted type of speech event suggest that a number of linguistic features regularly accompany the text itself in performance (see particularly Seitel 1972:142–43, 153, 175, 201, 219, 225; Penfield 1983:22). From the time of such Renaissance collections as Erasmus's *Adagia*, however, the textual core of proverb performances was singled out for preservation and analysis. Given the referential biases of literacy-oriented cultures, this element was regarded as the most deserving of preservation and comparison. But, as many proverb studies have shown, the text itself seldom provides a clear statement of the rhetorical intent of the performer (cf. Abrahams 1967; Kirshenblatt-Gimblett 1973; Krikmann 1974a, 1974b; Mukařovský 1971:285–87; Penfield 1983:7).

Studies of the social context of proverb performances have demonstrated the importance of contextual information in discerning the meaning of proverbs. Unfortunately, such analyses have been based primarily on consultants' attempts to match texts with judgements as to their correlative hypothetical situations (see especially Arewa and Dundes 1964). Even the best studies, such as Seitel's research on the Haya (1972, 1977), are based on the assumption that the relationship between a given proverb performance and its conversational context "is readily available for study in proverbs in that one may intelligibly ask a proverb informant what (kind of) situation a particular proverb refers to" (1972:5–6). Similarly, one of the basic assumptions that underlies Penfield's study of Igbo proverbs is that "the external function of quoting behavior [including proverbs] in Igbo society can be inferred from folk conceptions offered by Igbo speakers through guided recall and hypothetical cases" (1983:23).

The problem here is that the rhetorical force of proverb performances emerges from a subtle and complex use of the pragmatic functions of language. As Silverstein (1979, 1981a) has argued, pragmatic or indexical features generally lie beyond the conscious "limits of awareness" of native speakers. The less context-sensitive elements are more readily susceptible to the sort of conscious recall and reinterpretation that transpires in interviews (cf. Briggs 1986), such as those used in collecting lists of proverbs or commentary on proverb usage. This is not to say that proverb users lack any awareness of the dynamics of performances. Indeed, as I argued in Chapter 1, Mexicano "oral literary criticism" (cf. Dundes 1966) both evaluates particular performances and explores the basis of such rhetorical effectiveness. Nevertheless, many of the stylistic cues that relate a given proverb to the subtle details of interaction cannot be elicited in interviews, which suggests that an adequate analysis of the structure and meaning of proverb performances will only emerge once interview and other types of data are supplemented by the use of transcripts of actual occurrences as a primary source of data. (See Seitel 1972 and Yankah 1985, 1986 for examples of studies that present transcriptions of performances.)

My purpose in presenting these remarks on proverb scholarship is not to denigrate a long, multidisciplinary tradition of painstaking research that has informed a broad range of issues. My criticism emerges from the fear that this body of literature is still plagued by a number of theoretical and methodological assumptions regarding how one locates proverb performances, analyzes their form and meaning, and traces their relation to the surrounding discourse. In particular, these assumptions prompt researchers to identify "the proverb" with the text alone; even if "the context" in which the text appears is described, crucial information that is located in the discourse that surrounds the text is relegated to secondary importance or overlooked entirely. I hope to show that the proverb genre in Mexicano society cannot be adequately identified or analyzed apart from discourse features that precede and follow the proverb text in performance. I will argue that recognition of such features, when present, can greatly enhance our understanding of the manner in which textual and contextual elements are related in proverb performances.

PRINCIPAL SETTINGS OF PROVERB PERFORMANCES

Mexicano proverb performances occur primarily in two types of settings. First, proverbs appear in conversations between elderly speakers. Two or more of the primary participants, male and/or female, interject proverbs into ongoing discourse, and a number of performances may transpire in quick succession. The proverb texts are generally given without elaboration, and little or no explanation of their meaning is offered. These performances presuppose the large body of linguistic, cultural, and often biographical information needed to interpret the proverbs. This type of setting parallels what I referred to in Chapter 3 as historical competitions; exchanges of proverbs between elders do not always occur within historical discourse, however; they are also capable of standing on their own.

A second and more common situation involves one or more elderly speakers and younger interlocutors. The overriding purpose is pedagogical, elders intending to influence juniors in thought or deed. These settings include both pedagogical discourse and conversations that do not focus on bygone days. Proverbs generally appear either singly or at widely separated intervals, the proverb text is generally elaborated, and the relevance of the proverb to the topic of discourse is usually made explicit. In other words, the younger (and thus, presumably, the more ignorant) the hearers, the greater the need to emphasize information needed to interpret the meaning of the proverb performance. Such proverb uses may come either within examples of pedagogical discourse or in elder-junior interactions in which other forms of the talk of the elders of bygone days are absent. Although I witnessed exchanges of proverbs between elders, all the performances recorded were of the pedagogical type.

TWO MEXICANO PROVERB PERFORMANCES

I will focus on two proverb performances that took place in the home of Silvianita Trujillo de López and George López. The first was during my initial field stay in Córdova in 1972. My research focused on the local woodcarving industry (cf. Briggs 1980), and we were carving while the recording was made. The setting was a conversation in which Mrs. López described a group of local youths who had reacted with hostility to the arrival of a number of Anglo-American *jipes* 'hippies'. The *jipes*, the only young Anglo-Americans who had resided in the community before me, exhibited great insensitivity toward local residents, rendering them easy targets for thefts by somewhat unruly local youths. Fearing I would be classified as a *jipe*, the Lópezes counseled me on comportment and advised me to avoid these particular young Córdovans. Mrs. López characterized the youths' means of placing the unsuspecting in their grasp in the opening lines of example (4.1).

The second performance transpired six days after example (4.1). Mrs. López had served me a piece of commercial jerky, noting that it was venison. She was subsequently informed by her great-nephew, Elvis, that it was beef. Mrs. López obviously felt that she had lost face through her *mentira* 'lie'; example (4.2) was her second attempt that day to extricate herself from this situation.

I will leave the task of interpreting these two performances until later, turning first to an analysis of the features that these examples share with other proverb performances.

FEATURES OF PROVERB PERFORMANCES

FEATURE 1: TYING PHRASE

The first performance begins with a "tying" element, a device that usually initiates a performance and links one or more of the preceding utterances in the conversation with what is to follow (cf. Moerman 1972; M. Rosaldo 1973; Sacks 1967). 'That's why I tell you, that's why he says'. (4.1:105–06) effects three ties to utterances of the conversation. First, the analogy I present in (4.1:96–104) is cited as an example of the point that Mrs. López has been making throughout: these 'kids' are dangerous. Second, Mrs. López has asserted that the statement she is about to make in (4.1: 107–16) will explicate my analogy. Finally, Mrs. López has suggested that her remarks in (4.1:107–16) will further clarify the issues she raised in (4.1:1–69).

Some tying elements also constitute performance frames, for example *había otra cosa que decían los viejitos* 'there used to be something else that the elders used to say'. This frames the succeeding utterance(s) as an instance of la plática de los viejitos de antes. A minority of performances, illustrated here by example (4.3), invoke the label that is most frequently used for the genre, *dicho*,[3] in the tying phrase. Both *tenían tambien otro dicho* 'they had another saying as well' and the opening lines of this example linked two consecutive proverbs within the same conversation.

Such phrases as *tenían tambien otro dicho* '⟨the elders of bygone days⟩ used to have another proverb as well' connect the succeeding performance with the immediately preceding discourse; they serve other anaphoric functions as well, such as indicating which elements of the preceding discourse (e.g., genre or source of quotation) remain in force. Some tying phrases, such as (4.1:105–06), signal the status of the succeeding discourse as an explication of that which preceded it. If the audience accepts the use of this feature as valid, the applicability of the proverb to the ongoing conversational topic is acknowledged.

FEATURE 2: IDENTITY OF OWNER

Another feature that appears toward the beginning of proverb performances is the citation of a person(s) with whom the proverb is associated. This identification emanates from the belief that proverbs are, in a sense, "owned" by individuals. Some speakers control a greater range of proverbs than others; they are more *dichosos* 'have more proverbs' (in this sense of the term) than other performers. Nevertheless, proverb specialists are said to be primarily associated with a particular proverb—*cada uno tenía su dicho* 'each one had her/his own proverb'. When such a proverb is performed by someone else, its "owner" will be cited; Mr. Córdova thus notes that 'I used to have a COMPADRE, now he's DEAD, but his proverb was. . . .' The unnamed deceased elder of Truchas (see Map 1) was similarly associated with the horse beans proverb. If a specific social relationship exists or once existed between the speaker and the "owner" of the proverb, this relationship is stated as well. Ties of kinship and "fictive kinship" (cf. example (4.3)) figure most prominently in this regard.

(4.1) Silvianita Trujillo de López (71), George López (72), CLB (19); 3 October 1972, Córdova, New Mexico

---

ST   "No me GUSTA ⟨LA CERVEZA⟩."
CB   Yah.
ST   ¿ENTENDITES?
CB   Sí, sí claro.
       "No me GUSTA."   5
ST Tú te puedes,
    tú te puedes decirles
    que "en mi vida NO,
    a mí no me gusta
    una CERVEZA,   10
    un WHISKEY,

Feature 2 is always overtly marked in performances. The form of such marking is contingent, however, on the degree of competence of the audience. Relationship terms are often used in lieu of the proverb "owner's" name ('my father', 'an uncle of mine', etc.); given Córdovans' familiarity with each other's genealogies, the referent is seldom obscure. A newcomer to the community would not be expected to be aware of the kinship and fictive kinship network in Córdova and surrounding communities. Feature 2 was thus elaborated in the performances that were staged for my benefit, and first and last names, place of residence, and occasionally a short description of the person were often included. In some cases, a given proverb is not associated with any individual, living or deceased, who is known to the speaker; such proverbs are accordingly associated with la plática de los viejitos de antes in general.

FEATURE 3: QUOTATION-FRAMING VERB

The proverb text is invariably introduced by one element of a small set of verbs or verb phrases. In most cases, this consists of the quotation-framing verbs *decir* 'to say' or *platicar* 'to speak' or 'to converse'. *Decir* is used in framing the proverb texts in examples (4.1), (4.2), and (4.3). In (4.3), the *decía* frame is coupled with a less frequently used device, *tenía su dicho* 'he used to have his proverb' and *su dicho era* 'his proverb was'. These expressions alert the audience to the status of the proverb as a quotation and to the attribution of the quotation to the "owner" of the proverb.

Inflection of the verb for tense and aspect is also a crucial element of the performance. Quotation-framing verbs are nearly always marked for past tense and habitual aspect. This usage subtly reinforces the notion that these proverbs were spoken with great frequency in bygone days. This intersection between tense and aspect leaves one with the sense that the proverb was used so often in the past that both it and the values it embodies characterized bygone days. Unlike "past perfective," past + habitual leaves open the question whether the proverb (or the talk of the elders of bygone days as a whole) has retained its moral force in the present.

English translation

"I don't LIKE ⟨BEER⟩."
    Yah.
    GET IT?
    Yes, yes of course.
"I don't LIKE IT."
You can,
you can tell them
that "In my life, NO,
I have never liked
BEER,
WHISKEY,

un VINO, no,
no me GUSTA," diles.
"Nunca lo he TOMADO."
Y no lo HACES que te tomes,   15
no lo TOMES en algo.
Porque pueden venir, . . .

GL la VUELTA.
ST   Sí.
CB   Yah, uh huh.   20
ST Y asina es como se cuide UNO,
          ¿ves?
    Un EXTRANJERO tiene que CUIDARSE.
CB   Yo sé, porque/
ST   /Y luego porque   25
    quiero a tu MAMÁ,
    quiero a tu GRANDMA
    como mi VIDA.
CB   Yah.
ST   Sí. . . .   30
    DECÍAN los viejitos de ANTES,
    de ANTES decía su papá de ÉSE ⟨=GL⟩,
          ves,
    era viejito,
    ahi está retratado,   35
          ves.
    Y decía, "MIREN, . . .
    si van allá por un RATO,
    dígales que usted no lo TOMA,
    usted no lo BEBE.   40
    Y no los deje que lo miren.
    Pero si ustedes tienen
    un trago en su HELERA,
    les dan PRUEBA,
    'a ver si lo tiene aquí.   45
    A ti te GUSTA'."
CB   Um hum.
ST   ¿Ves?
    Y asina es,
    porque SON CANANJILES.   50
    "Dame un vaso de AGUA,
    de la HELERA."
    Quieren VER,
          ves.
    Quieren ver a lo que hay en la helera. . . .   55
CB   Yah.
ST   Sí,
    no más la ABRES, . . .
    y ES TODO.
    "¡VEN la cerveza!   60
    Y no DICES que no te GUSTA.
    Mira, ALLÁ TIENES—
    a ti te GUSTA."
CB   Yah.

WINE, no,
I don't LIKE IT," tell them.
"I have never DRUNK IT."
And DON'T go ahead and drink,
don't DRINK anything.
Because they can come, . . .
AROUND.
      Yes.
      Yah, un huh.
And that's how A PERSON is CAREFUL,
      you see?
A STRANGER has to be CAREFUL.
I know, because/
/Because
I care about your MOTHER,
I care about your GRANDMOTHER
as I do for my own LIFE.
      Yah.
      Yes. ; . ;
The elders of BYGONE DAYS USED TO SAY,
in BYGONE DAYS this fellow's ⟨=GL⟩ father USED TO SAY,
      you see,
he was elderly,
there is his picture,
      you see.
And he used to say, "LOOK, . . .
if they go over there ⟨to your house⟩ for AWHILE,
tell them that you don't DRINK,
you don't DRINK.
And don't let them see it.
But if you have
a drink in your REFRIGERATOR,
they'll TEST YOU,
'let's see if he has it here.
You LIKE IT'."
      Um hum.
      You see?
And that's how it is,
because THEY'RE SCOUNDRELS.
"Give me a glass of WATER,
from the REFRIGERATOR."
They want TO LOOK,
      you see.
They want to see what there is in the refrigerator. . . .
      Yah.
      Yes,
you just OPEN IT . . .
and IT'S ALL OVER.
"SEE the beer!
Don't TELL us that you don't LIKE IT.
Look, YOU HAVE SOME THERE—
you LIKE IT."
      Yah.

ST	¿Ves?	65
CB	Vamos a la cantina."	
ST	Sí,	

"vamos ALLÁ."
Y asina NO.

CB	Mi amigo,	70

mi amigo muy BUENO,
el BENITO,
me dió un consejo muy BUENO.
A mí me dijo,
"si quieres hablar   75
con uno de ellos,
vete tú a donde está UNO,"

ST ALLÁ
CB "y no BORRACHO.
UNO,   80
sin cerveza.
Y puedes hablar con UNO.
Pero con más que UNO,
o si esté BORRACHO,
nada, nada."   85

ST	Sí. Sí, ¿VES?	
CB	Sí.	
ST	Es la MESMA.	
CB	Yah.	
GL	Es la MESMA, sí.	90
ST	Es la MESMA.	

CB El sí sabe.
ST Y yo también SÉ.
CB   Yah.
ST Han pasado aquí COSAS.   95
CB Yo sé también,
porque ⟨pa' allá⟩
ST   ¿sí?
CB pa' allá en ⟨X⟩, en ⟨X⟩,
en ⟨X⟩,   100
ST   ¿sí?
CB había MUCHA plebe como ésta.
ST   ¿Sí?
CB Mucha/
ST /POR ESO TE DIGO,   105
por eso dice EL,
que "DONDEQUIERA SE CUECEN HABAS."
Como decían ANTES,
en TRUCHAS se cosechaban MUCHAS HABAS. . . .

You see?
"Let's go to the bar."
Yes,
"let's go THERE."
And that's BAD.

[Mr. López then related an incident in which two jipes who purchased one of the small ranches just above the central plaza treated several of the *plebe* to a beer. Their household possessions, including the remaining beer, were soon found missing. Moved by the urgency of Mrs. López's statements, I interjected two similar examples into the conversation in an attempt to convince her that the advice had been taken to heart.]

My friend,
my GOOD FRIEND,
BENITO
gave me some very GOOD ADVICE.
He told me,
"if you want to talk
with one of them,
go to where ONE of THEM IS,"
THERE
"and ⟨who is⟩ not DRUNK.
ONE,
without beer.
And you can talk to ONE.
But with more than ONE,
or if he's DRUNK,
nothing doing."
                    Yes. Yes, you see?
                    Yes.
                    It's the SAME.
                    Yah.
                    It's the SAME, yes.
                    It's the SAME.
He knows.
And I also KNOW.
laughs   Yah.
Things have happened HERE.
I know too,
because ⟨over in⟩
                    yes?
over there in ⟨X⟩, in ⟨X⟩,
in ⟨X⟩
                    yes?
there used to be A LOT of kids like these.
                    Really?
Lots/
/THAT'S WHY I TELL YOU,
that's why HE SAYS,
that "HORSE BEANS ARE COOKED EVERYWHERE."
Like they used to say in BYGONE DAYS,
in TRUCHAS they used to harvest A LOT OF
    HORSE BEANS. . . .

```
        Y decía un VIEJITO de ANTES,                          110
        de TRUCHAS.
        "Sí.
        NO, NO MAS AQUÍ SE CUECEN HABAS,
        donde las COSECHAMOS;
        en DONDEQUIERA,                                        115
        en TODO EL MUNDO."
                Y es VERDAD,
                es CIERTO.
CB              Yah, yo pienso.
ST              Es CIERTO, . . .                               120
                es CIERTO. . . .
GL  Muchos de estos vienen haciendo,
        esos PENDEJOS,
        a VER. . . .
CB              Yah.                                           125
ST              Sí.
        Y luego hacen MAL,
                ves,
        hacen MAL.
        Porque BIEN no hacen.                                 130
                Nuh uh.
CB              Yah.
ST              Muy TRABAJOSO.
```

(4.2) Silvianita Trujillo de López (71), George López (72), CLB (19); 9 October 1972, Córdova, New Mexico

```
ST  Dicía ⟨sic⟩ una vecina MÍA,
        ahi en, eh, la PLACITA.
CB              Hm hum.
ST  Dicía,
        "cuando dicía uno una mentira,"                         5
        y luego,
        "pronto salía la VERDAD.
        BUENO," dicía,
CB              um hum,
ST  "SABEN USTEDES                                             10
        que DIOS . . .
        USA las personas,
        pa' que digan la VERDAD?" . . .
        Dios usó la persona del ELVIS,
        pa' que saliera la verdad,                             15
        Y CARNE VENADO.
CB              Asina es/
ST              /¿VE? ¿VE?
        Sí DICE,
        porque ella es PENTECOSTAL.                            20
        No es católica,
```

And an ELDER of BYGONE DAYS USED TO SAY,
from TRUCHAS.
"Yes.
NO, THEY DON'T JUST COOK HORSE BEANS HERE,
where we HARVEST THEM;
but EVERYWHERE,
ALL OVER THE WORLD.

laughs   And it's TRUE, . . .
                    it's CERTAINLY TRUE. . . .
                    Yah, I think so.
                    It's TRUE,
                    it's TRUE.
Many of them come around to do that,
those FOOLS,
to LOOK. . . .

laughs   Yah.
                    Yes.
And then they behave BADLY,
        you see,
they behave BADLY.
But they DON'T behave well.
        Nuh uh.
        Yah.
        It's very DIFFICULT.

English translation

A neighbor of mine used to SAY,
she used to live up there on the PLAZA.
        Hm hum.
She used to say,
"when a person tells a lie,"
and then,
"the TRUTH would soon COME OUT.
WELL," she used to say,
        um hum,
"DO YOU KNOW
that GOD . . .
USES people,
so that they will tell the TRUTH?" . . .
God used ELVIS,

laughs   so that the truth would come out,
both ST and CB laugh AND VENISON.
                        That's so/
                        /YOU SEE? YOU SEE?
She DOES SAY ⟨THIS⟩,
because she is PENTECOSTAL.
She's not Catholic,

es PENTECOSTAL,
en la RELIGIÓN.
Y dice,
"OH, DIOS USA TODAS LAS PERSONAS.   25
CB   Um hum.
ST "Y cuando uno tiene buen CORAZÓN,"
dice
"Dios usa la PERSONA
pa' que traten la VERDAD."   30
    Y es VERDAD,
    es cierto.
    ¿Ve?
Yo he pensado/
GL /Porque ama la VERDAD y no la MENTIRA.   35
ST   Sí,
      ¿ve?
Yo te dije MENTIRA, porque,
pos, en pensablemente,
yo pensé que porque la carne era NEGRA,   40
pensé que era VENADO,
    ¿ve?
Yo te estaba platicando una MENTIRA,
    ¿ve?
Bueno, pues, se PASÓ,   45
    ¿ve?
No sé si lo creerías o NO.
Bueno,
pero yo sí lo DIJE.
CB Pero no es como/   50
ST /Y luego entró el ELVIS,
yo le ((hablé))
"Anda, ven a CENAR.
Anda, ven a cenar.
Y luego yo misma saqué la plática del VENADO,   55
    ¿ve?
de la CARNE.
CB   Oh.
ST Y me dijo,
"NO, ES DE RES."   60
    ¿Ve?
Pues ahi salió la VERDAD,
    ¿ve?
CB   Yah.
ST Pa' que no se notificara la MENTIRA.   65
CB   Um hum.
ST   ¿Ve?
CB   Uh hum.
ST Dios usó la persona. . . .
Y muy JOVENCITO,   70
    mira.
CB   Um hum.
ST   ¿Ve?
All' se DESATÓ la MENTIRA.

she's PENTECOSTAL,
by RELIGION.
And she says,
"OH, GOD USES EVERYBODY.
     Um hum
"And when a person has a good HEART,"
she says
"God uses that PERSON
to foster the TRUTH."
     And it's TRUE,
     it's certainly true.
     You see?
I have thought/
Because he loves the TRUTH, not LIES.
     Yes,
     you see?
I told you a LIE, because,
well, in my mind,
I thought that since the meat was BLACK,
I thought it was VENISON,
     you see?
I was telling you a LIE,
     you see?
Well, it HAPPENED,
     you see.
I don't know if you'll believe this or NOT.
Okay,
laughs   but I did SAY IT.
But it's not like/
/And then ELVIS CAME IN,
And I ((said)) to him,
"Come on, come EAT.
Come on, come eat."
And then I myself brought up the subject of the DEER,
     you see?
of the MEAT.
     Oh.
And he told me,
"NO, IT'S BEEF."
     You see?
Well, that's where the TRUTH CAME OUT,
     you see?
     Yah.
So the LIE wouldn't be spread AROUND.
     Um hum.
     You see?
     Un hum.
laughs   God used the person. . . .
And ⟨Elvis is⟩ so YOUNG,
     You see.
     Um hum.
     You see?
That's where the LIE came UNRAVELED.

```
              ¿Ve?                                              75
              ¿Ve?
       Y dice ELLA,
       dicia ELLA.
       "Sí usa DIOS las PERSONAS."
              Y es VERDAD,                                      80
              es CIERTO.
CB            Tiene que ser.
ST            Sí. . . .
       De manera que TÚ TE VAS A ACORDARE
       algún día si te,                                        85
       que andas por AHI,
       tú vas a decir,
       "dijo la Mrs. LÓPEZ
       que 'DIOS USABA LAS PERSONAS . . .
       pa' la VERDAD.'"                                        90
              Y es VERDAD.
CB            Um hum.
ST            Sí las usa,
              ¿NO?
CB            Yah,                                             95
              yo creo que sí.
```

(4.3) Federico Córdova (ca. 75), CLB (21); 21 July 1974, Córdova, New Mexico

---

```
FC  Lo mismo que
       estaba un hombre aquí
       que tenía su DICHO.
       Yo tenía un COMPADRE, . . . [4]
       ya es MUERTO,                                            5
       pero su dicho era,
       ¿qué es ese dicho, hombre? . . .
       "Así es el MUNDO, compadre,"
       decía,
       "así es el MUNDO, compadre,"                            10
       me decía,
CB            sí
FC  "unos LLORAN por sus HIJOS, . . .
       y otros LLORAN por sus MADRES,
       me decía. . . .                                         15
CB            Hum.
FC            ¿Ves?
              Esta es una cosa muy CIERTA.
CB            Sí.
FC  Y era compadre MÍO,                                        20
       pero ese era su DICHO.
```

CB *laughs*   You see?
ST *laughs*   You see?
And she SAYS,
she used to SAY,
"GOD does use PEOPLE."
    And it's TRUE,
    it's CERTAINLY TRUE.
    It is surely so.
    Yes. . . .
So then YOU'LL REMEMBER
someday if you,
that you are going THERE,
you will say,
"Mrs. López SAID THAT
'God uses PEOPLE . . .
for the TRUTH.'"
    And it's TRUE.
    Um hum.
    He does use them,
    DOESN'T HE?
    Yah,
    I think so.

English translation

It's just like
there used to be a man here,
who used to have his PROVERB.
I used to have a COMPADRE, . . .[4]
now he's DEAD,
but his proverb was,
what is that proverb, man? . . .
"That's the way the WORLD is, compadre,"
he used to say,
"that's the way the WORLD is, compadre,"
he used to say to me,
    yes
"some CRY for their CHILDREN, . . .
and others CRY for their MOTHERS,"
he used to say to me. . . .
    Hum.
    You see? . . .
    This is CERTAINLY TRUE.
    Yes.
And he was a compadre of MINE,
but that was his PROVERB.

Note that Silvianita Trujillo de López uses both present (*dice*) and past + habitual forms (*dicía*) in example (4.2). This provides the exception that proves the rule (to use an English proverbial phrase). In my corpus, only in example (4.2) is a proverb attributed to a living elder. Note that Mrs. López used *dicía* in the initial framing of the proverb, while she adopted *dice* later, when discussing the woman's religion (4.2:19, 24). This alternation suggests that Mrs. López is characterizing her as a bearer of the talk of the elders of bygone days in (1–13). The woman returns to her role as a member of the community, however, in discussing her religion (19–23), and the *dice* marking is used. In beginning the final, exhortative part of the performance, Mrs. López returns to the *dicía* form (*Y dice ella, dicía ella*). The association of proverbs with the elders of bygone days is thus so strong that Mrs. López partially assimilates the woman to the status of a deceased elder.

Features 2 and 3 form crucial elements of proverb performances. They signal persons who are familiar with the talk of the elders of bygone days of an impending change in the form of the discourse and the speaker's relation to what is being said. Stylistically, the succeeding utterance will not be unmarked, "ordinary" speech. Special canons of interpretation will apply, depending on which genre of this talk emerges. If the dicho label is used, the generic status of the speech is clear in advance. If not, this question will soon be answered as the performance unfolds.

With regard to the role of the performer, the evidential basis of unmarked speech is provided in general by the personal experience of the speaker. With the exception of the quotation from George López's father (4.1:31–63), the Lópezes assume personal responsibility for the information they have given me. Mrs. López similarly draws on her own experience in explicating the series of events that led to her 'lie'. Once the *decía* frame appears, however, the speaker shifts the locus of authority for what is said to the elders of bygone days generally as embodied in one member of that group. This category does not merely consist of deceased individuals; these persons lived to maturity in their communities, and they were recognized during their waning years as respected repositories of "traditional" Mexicano wisdom. This role was assumed at the time of their deaths by the present viejitos, including the Lópezes. The ability of the oldest living individuals to serve in this capacity depends on their capacity to convey the words of the viejitos de antes.

The communicative effect of the use of these two features is to transfer the basis of the legitimacy of the succeeding utterance from the personal authority of the speaker to the collective authority of the elders of bygone days. This group, along with God and Christ, is seen as the major source of legitimacy. In performing a proverb, an elder thus invites a member of this group into the midst of the conversation; the proverb "owner" obliges by attesting to the validity of the performer's point of view. There is an interesting paradox here in that the speaker's own role in the presentation must temporarily be diminished in order to underline the importance of what is being said. Conveying the talk of the elders of bygone days becomes one's major obligation after the age of about seventy, and an elder's social status depends partly on her or his skill in invoking this talk. In mediating between past and present, the current elders strengthen their position, both in that particular conversation and in the community as a whole.

FEATURE 4: PROVERB TEXT

The quotation-framing feature is generally followed by what is generally referred to as the text of the proverb, the element that is usually isolated for collection and analysis. As I will suggest, the form of proverb texts is constrained in a number of ways. Nevertheless, texts are not always presented identically. In example (4.1), for instance, the text is first given in a simple form and then repeated in an elaborated form. Likewise, the same proverb text is presented in another form (*en dondequiera se cuesen* ⟨sic⟩ *habas* 'horse beans are cooked everywhere') by Aranda (1975:26) and in two different forms (*en cada casa se cuecen habas* 'horse beans are cooked in every home' and *en todas partes se cuecen habas* 'horse beans are cooked all over') by Cobos (1976:53, 55).

The text itself also contributes to the ability of the audience to identify utterances as constituting tokens of the proverb genre. Although both the form and the lexical and semantic content of proverb texts are of importance in this regard, they operate as constraints rather than as fixed requirements. With regard to content, nearly any element of Mexicano life can be singled out for proverbial comment, although recent cultural innovations and off-color allusions do not constitute acceptable topics for proverbs. An expression that includes reference to the new fast-food restaurant in the nearby trade center of Española would thus be unlikely to be accepted as a new *dicho*. Similarly, the inclusion of lexical items that are considered obscene or that are included in juvenile argots would render an utterance non-proverbial. English loan words often appear in Mexicano jokes, but they are not used in proverb texts.

Some proverb texts are marked phonologically, morphologically, lexically, and/or syntactically. Phonologically, alliteration is rare, but assonance and the repetition of word-final syllables or phoneme clusters are common. For example, /as/ appears in word-final position in the last three words of *Dios usa todas las personas*. Similarly, the final two clauses of *así es el MUNDO, compadre, unos LLORAN por sus HIJOS y otros LLORAN por sus MADRES* yield the structure:

$$(a + /os/) + b + c + d + (e + /os/)$$
$$(f + /os/) + b + c + d + \quad g$$

The semantic contrast between *hijos* and *madres* is heightened by the absence of the expected /os/ ending in the last line as well as by the syntactic and prosodic parallelism. Syntactic and morphological parallelism is matched by lexical parallelism in such proverb texts as

> En la casa que reza,   todos rezan.
> En la casa que reniega, todos reniegan.

These formal mechanisms assist in conveying the meaning or sense of proverbs by delineating semantic equations and contrasts, thus echoing Jakobson's (1960:358) remark that "the poetic function projects the principle of equivalence from the axis of selection into the axis of combination."

Interestingly, the majority of texts that were used by the proverb specialists contained such formal markers, whereas the opposite was true for those uttered by nonspecialists. It should be emphasized, however, that my consultants readily accepted proverbs whose texts lacked formal markers as tokens of the genre (and vice versa), provided that they were properly contextualized. The only obligatory formal constraints relate to the length of the text. Expressions that do not form complete clauses do not appear in my corpus, and texts that exceed about forty syllables are absent as well.

FEATURE 5: SPECIAL ASSOCIATION

The proverb text is often followed (although it is sometimes preceded) by a statement of the provenance or specific association of the proverb, if one is known to the speaker. In example (4.1), the horse beans proverb was associated with the neighboring community of Truchas. Even contiguous communities can be separated in this mountainous area by several hundred or even thousand feet of altitude and have substantial differences in the amount of annual rainfall. Limited agricultural specialization and an accompanying system of intercommunity barter were formerly of some importance. Truchas is thus known as a particularly well-suited location for cultivating horse beans. In example (4.2), the expression *Dios usa todas las personas* 'God uses everybody' is typical among members of the Assembly of God Church. Their Catholic neighbors use the expression in proverb performances as well but note that the "owner" of the proverb uses this saying "because she is Pentecostal" (4.2:20). The situation that gave rise to a proverb is occasionally recalled (Brown et al. 1978:226–30) and may be indexed in the performance.

Feature 5, that of special associations, also enhances the legitimacy accorded the proverb performance. The connection of a proverb with a particular group increases the authority wielded by that proverb when the group is known to be especially knowledgeable in that regard. In example (4.1), for instance, because Truchas is known as a center of horse bean cultivation, a Truchas elder would thus be especially well equipped to use a horse bean metaphor for social relations. Similarly, because

Pentecostals are reputed to maintain that God is intimately involved in the details of everyday life, they could speak with authority about the involvement of humans in the fulfillment of his intentions.

Feature 5 does not appear in every performance. When such an association is recognized, however, the presence or absence of overt marking depends on whether the speaker believes that the audience is aware of the association of the proverb with a given group. If this information can be assumed, the association will remain implicit.

FEATURE 6: GENERAL MEANING OR HYPOTHETICAL SITUATION

The general meaning[5] of a proverb is frequently foregrounded in the course of performances that are staged for the benefit of young persons. This process often consists of an explication of the logical implications of the proverb. Federico Córdova thus explicated the proverb *en la CASA que se REZA, TODOS REZAN. En la CASA que RENIEGA, TODOS RENIEGAN* ('in the HOUSE that PRAYS, EVERYONE PRAYS. In the HOUSE that CURSES, EVERYONE CURSES') in the manner shown in example (4.4). This example also illustrates a second mode of explicating the general meaning of a proverb, the construction of one or more hypothetical situations to which the proverb applies. As is apparent in example (4.4), the two modes of interpretation often overlap in performances.

As the literature has shown for proverb traditions generally (cf. Abrahams 1967; Kirshenblatt-Gimblett 1973; Krikmann 1974a, 1974b; Mukařovský 1971:285–87; Penfield 1983:7), the same proverb text can be accorded various general or hypothetical meanings. Aranda states that the text concerning horse beans suggests that "if you try hard enough, you can accomplish almost anything" (1975:26), whereas Cobos asserts that the proverb's import is that "everyone has his faults and we should look first at our own" (1973b:53).

Feature 6 points to the way in which the proverb conveys a general principle. Features 2, 3, and 4 connect the performance to the talk of the elders of bygone days. By explicating the general meaning of the proverb, the speaker links the performance to the moral values that are embodied in this talk. This feature thus furthers two of the elders' goals. First, it adds moral force to their position in the conversation. The hearer may be able to prove that the utterance is not a proverb of the elders of bygone days, that the proverb does not apply to the situation, or that the proverb does not express this moral value. This task is not easy, and only participants who are also competent performers can attempt it. In the absence of such a counterclaim, failure to accept the performer's interpretation of the situation and to act accordingly will constitute a violation of a basic value. Second, feature 6 advances what the elders see as their main motivation for conveying the talk of the elders of bygone days, including proverbs, to younger persons—the inculcation of these principles.

(4.4) Federico Córdova (ca. 75), CLB (21); 21 July 1974, Córdova, New Mexico

---

FC	Fíjate, que en tu CASA . . .	
	había, ju–,	
	en la casa se va muy BIEN,	
	allí más REZABAN.	
	Pero otra CASA 'onde había . . .	5
	este, allá te–,	
	aquí hablando esta TONTERA,	
	el otro una PICARDÍA,	
	o no RESPETAR.	
	Todo eso quiere decir que 'onde pe–,	10
	'onde se REZA,	
	en la CASA que se REZA,	
	se rezan,	
	son las casas que son HONESTA,	
	la GENTE,	15
	¿sabes cómo?	
CB	Sí.	
FC	Hay RESPETO,	
	pa' que ENTIENDAS.	
	Aquí hay RESPETO en la casa.	20
CB	Sí.	
FC	Y 'onde se RENIEGA,	
	pos, NO HAY RESPETO.	
CB	Sí.	
FC	Porque siempre HABIDO	25
	clases de GENTE,	
	¿sabes cómo?	

FEATURE 7: RELEVANCE TO CONTEXT

Most Córdovan proverb performances also contain an explicit statement of the manner in which the general meaning of the proverb applies to the present situation. Previous utterances within the same conversation figure prominently among the elements of the context that are singled out for comment. This feature expresses the "point" of the performance, and it provides significant insight into the relevant alternation rules (to use the term proposed by Ervin-Tripp 1972:218–20). In the case of proverbs, such rules pertain to why an elderly speaker decides to use a proverb in arguing a point rather than an unmarked expression or a token of another genre; and, if the proverb genre is selected, why a given proverb is chosen.

Having established the legitimacy of the general principle in features 2, 3, 5, and 6, the speaker now asserts that the situation being addressed in the conversation is included in the class of situations that it governs. Feature 7 also serves to elucidate

English translation

Look, in your HOUSE . . .
there used to be, ju—
in the house ⟨where⟩ everything is FINE,
they USED TO PRAY MORE.
But ⟨in⟩ the other HOUSE where there used to be . . .
this one, there te—,
one speaking FOOLISHLY,
the other one a CRUDE REMARK,
or lacking RESPECT.
All this means that where pe—
where they PRAY,
in the HOUSE that PRAYS,
they pray,
these are the houses that are DECENT,
the PEOPLE,
       do you know what I mean?
       Yes.
There's RESPECT,
in other WORDS.
Here there is RESPECT in the home.
       Yes.
And where they CURSE,
well, THERE ISN'T ANY RESPECT.
       Yes.
Because there have always BEEN
⟨different⟩ kinds of PEOPLE,
       do you know what I mean?

---

the *manner* in which the general principle applies to the present situation; an explicit statement of how it should be translated into future action is sometimes given. This is the crucial point at which the performer creates a rapprochement between past and present. As I noted previously, performers are not evaluated solely on the basis of the number of examples they can perform or the aesthetics of their performances. The point of using the talk of the elders of bygone days is to convey the *sentido* 'meaning, sense, or significance' of a given situation. A skillful speaker weaves enduring, shared elements with unique encounters in such a way that the tightness of the weft is unimpeachable. At this point in the performance, just before its formal ending, the tightness of the twining must become apparent.

Features 6 and 7 are rarely marked overtly when both the performer and the audience are either proverb specialists or all elderly nonspecialists. On the other hand, specialists almost always mark these features when their performances are directed toward nonspecialists of any age. The former believe themselves (and are in turn believed) to possess greater knowledge of the proverbs, the type of situations to which they are normally applied, and the mode of applying a proverb to a specific situation than is controlled by nonspecialists. Variation is apparent in such situations, however, with respect to the degree of elaboration of these segments. Performances that are directed toward nonspecialist peers are characterized by minimal elaboration of these features. Maximal elaboration obtains when the performance is intended to avert a member of the audience from a potentially dangerous course of action and when children (or ethnographers) are among the intended hearers.

FEATURE 8: VALIDATION OF THE PERFORMANCE

Proverb performances conclude with statements by various persons as to the truth of the proverb. This feature minimally consists of an assertion of the validity of the proverb by the performer. The most commonly used phrase is *es verdad, es cierto* 'it's true, it's certainly true'; *tiene que ser conforme* 'it must surely be this way' is also common. As is apparent in example (4.2), the speaker may validate the performance several times, especially if the proverb text is repeated. This will be followed by a validation by another elder, should one be present. Some elders, such as Mr. López, often validate their peers' performances by restating the point (or some part of it) in their own terms (cf. 4.1:122–24; 4.2:35).

Finally, if the performance takes place in a pedagogical context, a response is elicited from the audience. The performer will generally utter a one- or two-word interrogative, with *¿oíste?* 'did you hear?', *¿entendiste?* 'did you understand?', *¿sabes cómo?* 'do you know what I mean?', *¿ves?* 'see?', and *¿qué no?* 'right?' being the most common. When the performance addresses the behavior of a younger listener, that member of the audience is expected to respond, either visually (nods of the head) or verbally (e.g., *es verdad* 'it's true', *es cierto* 'it's true', *pues, sí* 'well, sure'). Although I could discern when a response was appropriate, I did not use the appropriate forms at this point in the study. I thus responded to Mrs. López's *¿sí las usa, no?* 'He does use them, right?' (4.2:93–94) with *Yah, yo creo que sí* 'yah, I think so'.

Each proverb performance that I recorded contained a validation of the proverb by the speaker. This feature appears central to performances in the genre on both formal and functional grounds. Formally, the utterance of one or more validating phrases marks the termination of a performance (and the control of the performer), thereby permitting new topics to be introduced and providing other speakers the chance to predominate. Feature 8 constitutes the final step in the process of binding the general moral principle to the present situation. If features 1 and 7 (the tying phrase and the statement of relevance to context) are valid, the applicability of the general proverbial principle to the situation at hand is certain. Given the use of the talk of the elders of bygone days as precedent and the importance of rhetorically powerful speech, acceptance of the validity of the first seven features leaves the audience with little choice but to accept the performer's point of view. This is precisely what is signaled in feature 8. The most appropriate gloss for such validations might thus be *probatum est*.

INTERPRETING PROVERB PERFORMANCES

The mere enumeration of these features would not provide an adequate analysis of Mexicano proverb performances if one's goal were to show how these features provide keys to the interpretation of specific performances and to the role of proverb usage in the speech community. Successful proverb performances are akin to logical proofs of the performer's position in the conversation. Features 2, 3, 5, and 6 accomplish the first half of such "proofs." The logic runs as follows: i) the previous "owner" of the proverb was a respected elder; ii) the proverb text is a quote from the deceased elder, thus constituting a segment of the talk of the elders of bygone days; iii) the speaker has the right to perform the proverb; and iv) the general principle that is presented by the speaker is accepted as being implicit in the proverb. If the audience accepts the validity of each of these points, then the binding force of the general principle is deductively certain.

The second half of the proof is established by features 1, 7, and 8. Feature 1 asserts that the performance is relevant to the preceding discussion. Feature 7 establishes the bearing of the proverb text and the general meaning on the situation at hand. However, the performer does not simply describe some element of the ongoing interaction, but interprets it. Once the performer establishes a firm link between an irrefutable precedent and a particular point of view, the proof is complete. If another elder validates the performance, it becomes even more difficult for a younger person to oppose the performer's contention. Proverbs that are used pedagogically nearly always constitute the final word on the subject—they are followed by silence or by the introduction of a new topic.

Consider, for example, the first performance. Mrs. López was concerned that I successfully gain entrée into the community. Her consternation did not emerge from her knowledge of the history of jipe involvement in Córdova alone. She had learned "through the grapevine" that I had recently accepted an invitation to join in one of the 'kids'' late-night sojourns. I had also told the Lópezes that I would be out of town the following weekend. Mrs. López thus surmised that I might have marked myself as the target for a robbery, and that my residence might be broken into during the weekend. Indeed, her remarks are quite unusual in their directness. She wanted me to grasp the precariousness of my situation and stay away from the 'kids'.

Another difficulty arose in the course of the discussion. Mrs. López had been so direct and so persistent in her exhortations that the situation was becoming uncomfortable for me. I provided two examples in (4.1 : 70–105), that supported her contention, thinking that this would convince her that I had taken her concerns to heart. I accordingly claimed in (4.1:96) that *yo sé también* 'I know too'. Because I had just entered the community and was unfamiliar with basic sociolinguistic patterns, I had not realized that taking such an active role in the argument and asserting that 'I know too' could be interpreted in this context as expressing a lack of *respeto* 'respect' (cf. Briggs 1986).

The proverb performance formed an effective means of dealing with both of these problems. Mrs. López used the horse beans proverb in suggesting that the antisocial behavior of the 'kids' is not an isolated problem. The elders often comment on the way that social and economic changes have led to a lack of adequate exposure of the children to the ways of the elders of bygone days, thus precipitating an insensitivity to the needs of other individuals and of the community as a whole. In other words, she broadened the scope of the discussion by referring to the ubiquity of the problem of 'bad kids.'

Widening the frame of reference of her argument also enabled Mrs. López to incorporate my examples directly into her "proof." By tying her contention—that I must be most circumspect and wary when I am approached by 'the kids'—to a proverb, she placed the weight of the elders of bygone days behind her argument. She apparently believed that she convinced me, because she dropped the subject after (4.1:134). On the rhetorical level, I could provide my own examples when the discourse consisted of unmarked speech. When she shifted to a proverb performance, however, the only available response (and the appropriate one) was to signify my agreement. The performance was thus effective in enabling her to regain her rightful control over the process of teaching me proper behavior in Mexicano society.

Mrs. López's status as my teacher and sponsor within the community had been brought into question in a much more serious way in (4.2). A religious, upstanding, elderly woman, Mrs. López had nevertheless told me what she considered to be a lie. (The semantic range of the term *mentira* includes both accounts that have been deliberately falsified as well as erroneous statements that the speaker believes to be true.) This was her third attempt of the day to extricate herself from an uncomfortable situation. A statement that she made during the previous exchanges on the subject of venison suggests that she feared that the implications of the incident might be more than rhetorical. She portrays a possible scenario in the following terms: "VENGA, Mrs. LÓPEZ," dile, "es la Mrs. LÓPEZ ⟨que⟩ DIJO que vendían CARNE," y luego que VENGAN los OFICIALES. ¡Ay DIOS de mi VIDA! NO, NO, NO, NO. . . . "I MY SORRY," yo voy a decir. '"COME ALONG, Mrs. LÓPEZ"; tell them, "it was Mrs. LÓPEZ ⟨who⟩ SAID that they were selling ⟨deer⟩ MEAT," and here COME the AUTHORITIES. Oh dear GOD! NO, NO, NO, NO. . . . "I AM SORRY," I am going to say.'

Comprehension of this statement and of the performance as a whole rests on two basic assumptions. As I noted in Chapter 2, loss of access to the uplands surrounding the community has deprived Córdovans of nearly all the subsistence they formerly derived from agriculture and pastoralism, and wage labor or government assistance has not filled the resulting economic gap. Some families have thus found it necessary to supplement their diet with venison. The State of New Mexico had, however, recently instituted a program entitled Operation Gamethief; anonymous informants were paid substantial sums for information leading to the conviction of persons taking game illegally. The possession of venison is thus a sensitive subject in the area.

Second, Anglo-Americans are stereotyped as being notoriously indiscreet, especially in term of revealing Mexicano secrets to other outsiders. I do not believe that Mrs. López ever thought that I would report the alleged possession of venison by the household; she was, however, afraid that I might repeat the venison story to another outsider, thus prompting the possible arrival of *los oficiales*. Note that Mrs. López makes it clear that she is addressing me at this point as an outsider by codeswitching into English—"I my sorry"—and by referring to herself as an outsider would—"Mrs. López."[6]

The proverb performance ingeniously extricates her from both types of threat. *Dios usa todas las personas* suggests that the truth came out, the lie came unraveled not by chance, but through divine mediation. The point is that God loves truth, not lies; he is thus loath to allow one of his faithful to remain in the status of a liar, even if the act was inadvertent. God thus used 'a person who has a good heart', the Lópezes' great-nephew, to expose the 'lie'. Mrs. López draws on the proverb in turning the situation around in her favor. It ultimately serves to identify her as a religious person rather than one who has a penchant for lying. The performance also provides me with a message for 'the outside world' to replace the potentially harmful announcement about the Lópezes' purported possession of venison. I am admonished to tell the world, in effect, that Mrs. López is a pious woman who quotes religious sayings, not a prevaricating purveyor of illegal venison.

THE ROLE OF PRESUPPOSITION AND CONTEXTUALIZATION

Those who are familiar with the literature on proverbs will surely see the heresy that emerged in the preceding description of Mexicano performances. I have shunned the conventional wisdom of proverb research by including a number of features in addition to the proverb text in my characterization of the genre. Moreover, four of the features (2, 5, 6, and 7) are not overtly marked in all performances. It thus becomes necessary to consider whether these features (excluding the text) are simply interesting verbal amenities that are irrelevant to the description of the genre. My analysis suggests that an adequate characterization of the Mexicano proverb genre must make reference to all eight of these features.

MEXICANO PERSPECTIVES ON PROVERB USAGE

Ben-Amos argues that "as the grammar of each language is unique and has its own logical consistency, so the native categorization of oral literature is particular and does not need to conform to any analytical delineation of folklore genres" (1976/1969:225). He accordingly suggests that definitions of ethnic genres must take into account the "grammar of folklore" that guides the production and interpretation of folkloric forms. This point is crucial for the analysis of Mexicano proverbs, because received scholarly definitions and their ethnic generic counterparts differ precisely on the question of the need to include extratextual features in characterizing the genre of la plática de los viejitos de antes.

As I noted in Chapter 1, my initial research on proverbs was thwarted by a failure to perceive the substantial gap that separates received analytical definitions of the proverb from the nature of the Mexicano proverb performance tradition. Although few modern scholars would deny the importance of "the context" of proverb performances, investigators simply assume that "the proverb" consists of the proverb text itself. Aurelio and Costancia Trujillo, Federico Córdova, and other Córdovans refused to identify *dichos* 'proverbs' with proverb texts. Once a proverb text has been stripped of the features that link it both to tradition and to the ongoing social interaction, it becomes 'just words.' Not only does it fail to count as a performance, but it is no longer seen as falling within the proverb genre. My consultants' perspective thus provides additional evidence for the view that the Mexicano proverb genre cannot be defined in isolation from other linguistic features that accompany the text in performance.

The question remains whether features that do not always appear in performances should be included in the definition of the genre. I will turn this problem around, arguing that the optional deletion of some of the features is a basic strength of the pragmatic model of proverb usage rather than an inherent limitation. The answer to this puzzle lies in the processes of presupposition and contextualization.

PRESUPPOSITION

Two types of variation are apparent in the manner in which these features are marked in performance. One axis is overt marking versus the absence of such marking; features 1, 5, 6, and 7 may thus be deleted. I use the term *deleted* rather than *omitted* because, as argued above for each feature, awareness of the status of all eight features[7] is necessary if a given token is to count as a performance. If a feature is not overtly marked, the information it conveys does not simply disappear but forms part of the background knowledge that is shared by the participants. The other axis is elaboration versus abbreviation; here we are concerned with the way that information is added to features 2–7 if the performer thinks that the audience will not grasp the meaning of the performance without it.

The location of a given performance along the axes is not random but is based upon the following rules: First, features 1, 5, 6, and 7 will only be made explicit when the speaker assumes that the members of the audience will not be able to infer this information from their knowledge of the proverb genre; their general social, cultural, and sociolinguistic background understandings; and their awareness of crucial parameters of the present interaction (and perhaps others that preceded it). Second, features 2–7 will only be elaborated to the extent that the performer believes is rendered necessary by the audience's lack of awareness of these three bodies of information. The way that performances relate to these two axes is summarized in Table 1. The same principle underlies both rules: Presuppose as many features as you can without interfering with your audience's ability to grasp the *sentido* of the performance.

This process points to two basic features of Mexicano communicative patterns. First, speakers base their performances on assessments of the sociolinguistic competence of their audience. This entails judging the degree to which they are knowledgable about the talk of the elders of bygone days, biographical and genealogical information on current residents, the geography of Córdova and its environs (including the historic and cultural associations of localities and landmarks), linguistic and sociolinguistic competence, and experience in interpreting proverbs.

Which elements are most important to any given assessment is obviously contingent in part on which proverb is selected. Who is being assessed is relative as well. If a given person, old or young, is being singled out as the chosen beneficiary of the

TABLE 1   *Summary of Proverb Performance Features*

Feature	Obligatory vs. Optional	Textual vs. Contextual [*]
1. Tying phrase	Op	C
2. Identity of "owner"	Ob	T
3. Quotative	Ob	T
4. Proverb text	Ob	T
5. Special association	Op	T
6. General meaning and/or hypothetical situation	Op	T
7. Relevance to interactional setting	Op	C
8. Validation	Ob	C

[*] Defined as the relative orientation of the feature as indexing an element of the textual tradition versus an element of the sociolinguistic setting of the performance.

performance, the competence of this individual in particular is at stake. If the proverb is directed at an audience as a whole, some "averaging" will be necessary. This process draws on the sum total of the performer's knowledge of the interlocutors and takes place, in the main, below the surface of consciousness.

A second facet of Mexicano sociolinguistic patterns explains the need to make such assessments. As I noted previously, verbal facility is an important determinant of individuals' reputations within the community. Accordingly, just as a person should not feign competence that she or he does not possess (cf. Briggs 1986), under-estimating someone else's competence is an insult. A higher degree of marking of proverb performance features than is warranted by the competence of the audience is thus likely to be an affront.

CONTEXTUALIZATION

The course of a given performance is certainly not entirely contingent upon the speaker's assessment of the audience before the performance begins. As Cook-Gumperz and Gumperz (1976) have argued, contexts are not solely defined on extralinguistic bases prior to the beginning of social interactions, and contextual features do not necessarily hold constant throughout conversations. Indeed, the verbal and visual cues that are provided by the audience during Mexicano proverb performances provide the speaker with information that is crucial to the success of the performance.[8]

Members of the audience who are familiar with the genre emit a number of visual signals at the beginning of the performance that indicate that they are aware that a performance has begun—for example, leaning forward, raising the eyebrows, smiling, and gazing intently at the speaker. The nonverbal behavior of the speaker and prosodic features of his or her speech are distinct during the utterance of the proverb text and the remainder of the discourse. The utterance of the text is generally set apart from the remaining features by a preceding pause as well as by changes in the speaker's facial expression and in the pitch, speed, and loudness of delivery. The anticipatory state of those members of the audience who are familiar with the genre correspondingly reaches a peak during the utterance of the text. Afterwards, they will smile, laugh, and settle back into their chairs.

One or more members of the audience may not be psychologically engaged with the speaker at the time of the performance or may be unfamiliar with the status of these eight features as perceptual cues of a stylistic shift and as indicators of the linear structure of the performance. The behavior of such persons may not change throughout the performance. Those who are listening but cannot understand the performance often change their facial expression to a look of confusion or even slight discomfort after the text is uttered, especially if the performance has been staged for their benefit. In either case, failure to emit the appropriate visual signals enables the speaker to perceive such gaps in the effectiveness of the performance.

With respect to verbal cues, Burns (1980, 1983:19–24) has noted that folkloric performances often exhibit a "dialogue nature." In the case of Mexicano proverbs, brief affirmatory interjections or reiterations of key words and phrases by a member of the audience provide the speaker with important cues as to the participation of the interlocutors—for example, my responses to Mrs. López in (4.2:3, 9, 26, 58, 64, 66, 68, 72, 82, 92). The speaker supplements these responses by periodically eliciting a response from the intended hearer(s), often using the term *¿ves?* 'you see?'. Mrs. López queried me in this fashion in (4.2:18, 33, 37, 42, 44, 46, 56, 61, 63, 67, 73, 75, 76, 93–94), and I responded auditorily in (64, 68), and (95–96). I suspect that I must have responded to the other queries with the most common signal of comprehension, a nod of the head. (In the absence of a video recording of the performance, I cannot verify this.)

These verbal and nonverbal cues affect the course of proverb performances in two major ways. First, the signals emitted by members of the audience (and especially by the intended hearer) provide the speaker with the opportunity to revise her or his a priori assessment of the audience's ability to interpret the proverb. This reassessment is reflected in decisions as to the realization of succeeding features as well as in possible reiterations of features that may not have been comprehended. In feature 2, for example, a speaker may simply note that the previous "owner" of the proverb was his or her *compadre* 'coparent'. If this does not elicit a verbal or visual signal that the hearer has correctly identified the referent, the speaker may proceed to supplement the relationship term with the "owner's" name, the fact that he has died, or the location of his former residence. In (4.1:105–06), for example, Mrs. López presupposed the identity of the "owner" of the horse beans proverb (all I learn is that the "owner" is male) and the special association between the horse beans proverb and the community of Truchas. I had no idea, however, that Truchas was a center of horse bean cultivation, and I did not know the Truchas elder who is associated with the horse beans proverb. Thus I gained little information and was far from achieving an understanding of the bearing of the proverb on the bad kids situation. Mrs. López accordingly makes this information explicit in (109–11). The rapidity with which the mind can decode and act upon such responses enables the speaker to use such signals in determining the course of a proverb performance.

Feature 8 provides the performer with a final opportunity to obtain a response. The intended hearer occasionally either responds negatively or simply gives the performer a puzzled or querulous look. The lack of an affirmatory response prompts a "recycling" of the performance. The speaker regains the floor and initiates the sequence anew, often beginning as early as feature 2. Such a communicative failure generally occurs because the speaker assumes that the intended hearer(s) is in command of more of the information needed to interpret the performance than is in fact the case. This gap can be "filled in" by elaborating the features that were abbreviated at first and making explicit those features that were presupposed. Features 6 and 7, the general meaning of the proverb and its relevance to the situation at hand, play particularly important roles in reversing such failures.

CONCLUSION

If we presume for argument's sake the validity of the preceding analysis, what insights can this description of the pragmatics of a single genre in a single dialect area provide us for the cross-cultural study of proverbs? The extension of these results to proverb performances as a whole or to other small genres must await research in other speech communities. I believe, however, that these findings do broaden our understanding of the nature of such speech events and their role in social life.

Hymes (1974:126) has charged that "almost never do [anthropologists and other social scientists] specify what one would need to know to recognize an instance of a verbal genre or to perform it." One of my consultants pointed to this sort of problem in stating that proverb texts were 'just words' in the absence of what Cook-Gumperz and Gumperz (1976:10) would call the proper contextualization. The present findings point to the complexity of the issues involved in meeting Hymes's challenge, even with respect to one of the smallest genres.

Studies of the importance of contextual factors in determining the meaning of proverb performances (cf. Abrahams 1968a, 1968b, 1972; Arewa and Dundes 1964; Bird and Shopen 1979; Gossen 1973; Jason 1971; Paredes 1982; Penfield 1983; Seitel 1972, 1977; Yanga 1977; Yankah 1985, 1986) certainly bring us closer to realizing this goal. The Mexicano data suggest that the success or failure of our efforts may rest in part on the need to question the a priori assumption that the proverb consists of the text alone. If other performance features are present in a given tradition, adopting this assumption will lead the researcher to create a false dichotomy between the social setting of performances and the text. The transformative properties of language and the emergent character of performance challenges the notion that "contexts" are preexisting molds that are constituted independently of fixed "texts." Both Mexicano "oral literary criticism" of proverb performances and my own analysis of form-function relationships in tape-recorded tokens suggest that contextual elements are part of the internal structure of both individual performances and of the genre as a whole.

To conclude that textual components are peripheral would similarly preclude our understanding of the nature of performances. The point is rather to grasp both the distinct role that contextual and textual features play in performances and the basis of their interdependency. Mukařovský (1971) clearly perceived the paradoxical nature of this relationship in a paper that was written in 1942–1943. Here he is concerned with the status of proverbs as quotations, a subject that is also taken up by Penfield (1983). Mukařovský argues that "a quotation at the same time attempts to be singled out in context and to merge with it." A quotation is "highlighted against its context" (1971:298) both stylistically and by virtue of the fact that it "allows a foreign subject to intrude into the utterance (someone else, a third person, speaks through the mouth of the speaker)" (1971:300).

This perception brings into focus the importance of three features of Mexicano proverb performances, namely the identity of the "owner," the quotative verb, and the proverb text. The fact that these features are obligatory suggests that all but one of the minimally essential components of proverb performances are the ones that call attention to the status of the proverb as speech that is drawn from outside of the current interaction. Pointing out the membership of the "foreign subject" in the ranks of the elders of bygone days and repeating the quotative verb calls further attention to this "intrusive" character of the proverb, just as the poetic features of the text emphasize its stylistic differentiation from the surrounding discourse. This helps us understand why proverb "specialists" nearly always use stylistically marked texts— they are particularly skilled in emphasizing the intrusive character of proverbs.

Mukařovský points to a number of communicative functions of this "foreign" character. First, proverbs are quotations that are drawn from a body of speech that is both old and generally recognized for its "truth or obligatoriness" (1971:302). This "collective acceptance" of the quote evokes another function, the "desubjectiviza-tion" of the discourse. Mukařovský uses the term to call attention to the fact that the speaker is not the originator of the quotation; the validity of what is said now rests on the shoulders of a third party. The "supra-subjective validity" that this fact confers on the utterance bears a great deal of force when the quote is attributed to a member of los viejitos de antes. Mukařovský also notes that "a proverb in and of itself is se-mantically incomplete. . . . it is ambiguous and only the incorporation into a con-text determines its sense" (1971:285, 287). This character affords the speaker the ability to use the proverbial quotation in evaluating the present situation; the proverb thus addresses the interaction as scolding, praise, ridicule, and so forth. The speaker thereby "takes a certain position to the matter at hand by virtue of the use of the quote and exhorts the listener to take that position" (1971:300).

Mexicano proverb performances provide speakers with powerful tools for trans-forming "semantically incomplete" proverb texts into powerful evaluative and ex-hortative speech acts—precisely the function of features 1, 2, 3, 5, 6, and 7. These features specify the bearing of the "desubjectivized" utterance—the text—on the situation at hand. This act of "depersonalization" (cf. Penfield 1983:5–6) is quite personal as well, because it simultaneously conveys the speaker's perception of what is happening and what should be happening in the present interaction. The relation-ship between the speaker, the audience, and the person(s) to whom the quote is at-tributed is thus highly ironic in that proverbs use the guise of indirectness and impersonality in permitting speakers to be unusually direct in articulating their view of the present and future. As Mukařovský (1971:298) notes, irony is also evident in the stylistic incorporation of the text into the interaction: "A quotation is an element which is highlighted against its context, it differs from it. This opposition is of course of a dialectic nature because it does not mean isolation within the context. A quotation at the same time attempts to be singled out in context and to merge with it." In the case of Mexicano proverb performances, the stylistic basis of this "dialectic nature" is lodged in the relationship between textual and contextual features; whereas the former emphasize the sociohistorical and stylistic differentiation of proverbs features that accompany texts in performance, the latter generate this stylistic and ideological merger. Note that the fourth obligatory feature, the validation, attests to both the textual distinctiveness of the proverb as well as the effectiveness with which the performer has connected it to the ongoing interaction.

Of course, Mexicano proverb performances may be unique in terms of the reliance that they place on other features in addition to the text itself. One of the most in-depth studies of oral proverb usage, Seitel's research on the Haya of Tanzania, mentions the importance of both introductory phrases and other elements that regularly accompany the text in performances and that frame the utterance as a proverb (1972:219–236). This usage suggests that proverb performances in other societies may also be characterized by a range of features. Even if textual and contextual features prove not to be stylistically marked in many traditions, Mukařovský's essay suggests that textual and contextual processes are both part of the business of performing proverbs.

The study of proverbs also points to additional facets of la plática de los viejitos de antes. Like pedagogical discourse and collective representations, proverbs are clearly conversational in nature. As is true of pedagogical discourse, proverb performances revolve around a systematic comparison of features of bygone days with elements of nowadays. The two are also alike in the degree to which their form and content are shaped by the performer's assessment of the audience's knowledge of the talk of the elders of bygone days and the way this knowledge is reflected in the course of the performance.

One crucial difference remains, nonetheless. In the case of proverbs, performers do not assume complete control over the process of interpreting this talk. The use of a quotation-framing verb, decía, brings the voices of elders of bygone days themselves into the discussion. Performers often foreground the status of the embedded utterance as direct or quoted discourse by repeating the quotative several times. In all cases, special voice characteristics set the quotation apart from the performer's own words. Performers use their voices artistically in trying to capture the style and meaning they attribute to the proverb "owner's" usage of the expression, not just the "owner's" words. Proverb performances thus bring the elders of bygone days to life in a way that is not possible in the absence of quoted speech. In performances, it is as if the speaker moves to the back of the stage while the spirit of a deceased elder briefly intervenes in contemporary affairs, a process that Mukařovský (1971:302) refers to as the "'dialogization' or even 'theatricalization' of an utterance by the use of a quote."

Proverb performances place strong constraints, however, on the participation of the elders of bygone days. Although these individuals may temporarily enter the stage of daily life, their role is limited to advancing the performer's perspective on a particular interaction. Most of all, los viejitos de antes are not free to develop a narrative, thus recreating a specific chain of events that led them to use the proverb. Proverb performances move phenomenologically between two worlds, bygone days and nowadays. The direction of this movement is quite clear—rather than draw performers and audience members into the world of antes, proverbs begin in the present (feature 1), appropriate a small fragment of antes (features 2–6), and then return to ahora (features 7–8). To use the analogy that I posed at the beginning of the chapter, proverb performances may open the door between the past and present, but they do not allow the living to enter the world of bygone days.

5

■■

SCRIPTURAL ALLUSIONS

The movement from proverbs to scriptural allusions is not abrupt. Both forms unfold in a conversational context, legitimizing the speaker's point of view. Each consists of a specifiable set of features that effect a rapprochement between past and present. But two differences are striking. First, one of the most important characteristics of historical discourse and proverbs is the use of the past habitual or past imperfect, an attribute that is not shared by scriptural allusions. This contrast is tied to a difference in the identity of the "foreign subject" that is introduced into the discourse through the use of a quotation. While historical discourse and proverbs are associated with the elders of bygone days, scriptural allusions draw on the other major source of legitimacy in the talk of the elders of bygone days—the words of Jesus Christ and God the Father.

SCRIPTURAL ALLUSIONS AND THE TRANSFORMATION OF EVERYDAY ENCOUNTERS

The range of social situations in which scriptural allusions are used is quite similar to that for proverb performances. They can occur during brief, casual exchanges that are not pedagogical in intent. In the instance in example (5.1), I met a friend, Melaquías Romero, on my way to the post office (see Plate 17). He lives next to the main road into Córdova (see Plate 18), and he greeted me as I walked past. I returned the greeting, then asked after the health of his brother Carlos, who had been quite ill. Melaquías noted that Carlos was improved, as witnessed by the fact that the family had been able to take him to the horseraces the previous Sunday. This prompted the comment on the outing quoted in example (5.1).

This text provides a good example of the use of conversational folklore outside a pedagogical situation; it is quite similar to performances of proverbs in such contexts. Such usage is related to pedagogical uses of scriptural allusions. The scriptural quote,

Plate 17. Melaquías Romero, 1984. Photograph by Charles L. Briggs

Plate 18. The Romero home, 1984. Photograph by Charles L. Briggs

(5.1) Melaquías Romero (70) and CLB (28); 28 July 1981, Córdova, New Mexico

CB ¿Cómo está mi tocayo? ⟨i.e., Carlos⟩[1]
MR Está bien.
CB   Oh, ¿sí?
MR   Sí,
      está bien.   5
      El Domingo lo llevaron ahi a las carreras.
      Ahi andaba a las carreras.
CB   Oh, ¿sí?
MR Estuvo muy bonito ahi en las carreras,
      no más es que al último se pelearon.   10
CB   Oh, ¿sí?
MR   Sí.
      Se dieron golpes.
      ¡Mira no más ((esa)) gente tonta!
              ¿Eh?   15
CB   Sí.
MR ¡Más que veas, que!
              ¿Eh?
CB   Sí.
      Quizás se animan tanto que/   20
              /Sí,
MR ¡mira no más!
      ((Hay buen tiempo y todo,))
      y se brincan al golpe.
      'Stá mal,   25
              ¿no?
CB Creo,
              ¿no?
MR   ¿Eh?
CB Muy fea la cosa.   30
MR Muy fiero.
      Este negocio no sirve,
              ¿no?
CB   Sí.
MR Ahi en la Biblia dice que, que "semos PRÓJIMOS,   35
      todos debemos tratar todos como HERMANOS."
              ¿Eh?
CB   Sí.
MR "Hermanos,"
      como hermanitos,   40
      semos de la misma sangre,
      todos.
      No importa el color ni nada.
              ¿Eh?
      Todos semos lo mismo.   45
CB   Sí.
MR   ¿No?
CB   Sí, es verdad.
MR   Sí, pos sí,
      ahi en la Biblia dice,   50
CB   Sí.

English translation

How is my namesake? ⟨i.e., Carlos⟩[1]
He's fine.
  Really?
  Yes,
he's fine.
On Sunday they took him to the horseraces
He was over at the horseraces.
  Really?
It was great over at the horseraces,
except that they had a fight at the end.
  Really?
  Yes.
They exchanged blows.
See how stupid these people are!
  Eh?
  Yes.
Just imagine!
  Eh?
  Yes.
Maybe they get so excited that/
  /Yes,
just imagine!
((Everything is going beautifully,))
and they jump into a fight.
That's bad,
  isn't it?
I think so,
  right?
  Eh?
What an ugly thing.
Very ugly.
This is no good,
  right?
  Yes.
There in the Bible it says that, that "we are fellow CREATURES,
We must all treat everyone like BROTHERS AND SISTERS."
  Eh?
  Yes.
"Brothers and sisters,"
like close brothers and sisters,
we're of the same blood,
everyone.
Not even ⟨skin⟩ color or anything else matters.
  Eh.
we're all the same.
  Yes.
  Right?
  Yes, that's true.
  Yes, well, yes,
in the Bible it says,
  Yes.

laughs

MR ((pos, e–, pro–)), como PRÓJIMOS.
CB   Sí.
MR Como mejor si fúeramos HERMANOS, que–.
            Sí,   55
      hasta los hermanos se dan golpes.
CB ¡Trabajoso!
MR 'Ora, hasta los hijos
      le brincan al papá.
CB   ¡Uuuh!   60
MR   ¿Eh?
CB ¿Cómo le gusta?
MR 'Stá loco.
            ¿Eh?
      Por eso los castiga mi tata Dios.   65
CB   Sí.
MR Dios los castiga.
            ¿Eh?
CB   Sí.
MR ¡Llega!   70
CB   Bueno/
MR   /y bueno/
CB /voy pa' abajo ahi.
            Bueno.
MR   Bueno,   75
      ahi te miro.
CB   Bueno, gracias,
      que le vaya bien.
MR   Bueno
      vamos a ver que hacemos ahora.   80
CB   Oh, ¿sí?
      ¿Ya van pa' arriba?
MR Vamos arriba y luego pa' allá abajo.
CB   Oh, ¿ sí?
MR   Sí. Bueno.   85
CB   'Stá bueno.
            Bueno.
      que le vaya bien,
            ¿eh?
MR   Bueno.   90

---

semos prójimos, todo debemos tratar todos como HERMANOS 'we are all fellow creatures, we must all treat everyone like BROTHERS AND SISTERS', is a variant of one of the most common—*todos semos hermanos* 'we are all brothers and sisters'. Mr. Romero used it on a number of occasions in pedagogical discussions with me, and it is frequently invoked by other Córdovan elders.

The thrust of the allusion is to emphasize Mr. Romero's point about the foolishness of the racetrack combatants. More than a mere reiteration, it provides a theo-

((well, e–, fel–)), like FELLOW CREATURES.
Yes.
It's more as if we were BROTHERS AND SISTERS, that–.
Yes,
even brothers and sisters hit each other.
That's awful!
laughs   Nowadays even the children
will start a fight with their father.
Uuuh!
Eh?
How do you like that?
It's crazy.
Eh?
My God the Father punishes them for that.
Yes.
God punishes them.
laughs   Eh?
Yes.
Come over!
Okay/
/that's okay/
I'm going below ⟨to the post office⟩.
Okay
Okay,
I'll be seeing you.
Okay, thanks,
take care.
Okay
let's see what's to be done now.
Oh, yes?
Are you going up ⟨i.e., into the mountains⟩?
We're going up and then down over there.
Yes? Really?
Yes. Okay.
That's good.
Okay,
take care
eh?
voice trails off   Okay.

---

logical interpretation of such actions. Mr. Romero broadens the critique to include all persons who engage in violence for violence's sake. The combatants are thus held responsible for far more than spoiling a 'very beautiful' day. They have broken a divine rule regarding the way one should treat one's 'fellow creatures'.

The underlying logic to this allusion runs as follows. We are all children of God; accordingly, we are all brothers and sisters. Because this relationship is spiritual, it imposes certain obligations on us, particularly the duty to render assistance to any

Plate 19. Costancia Apodaca de Trujillo, 1986. Photograph by Charles L. Briggs

Plate 20. The Trujillo home, 1986. Photograph by Charles L. Briggs

fellow human being who is in need. About forty percent of all scriptural allusions bear on this subject. This theme is encapsulated in the term *prójimo*. Prójimo thus stands as a synecdoche; an elder using it effectively introduces this entire argument into the discourse. The word prójimo is thus pragmatically charged.

Note the reference to the predominance of the prójimo principle over distinctions of race or ethnicity (*color*). Such uses apply the prójimo principle in asserting that the speaker would not allow my *gringo* origins to interfere with our friendship, and that I should follow suit. If this point is being subtly conveyed in this performance, then it constitutes a metacommunicative message regarding the present social situation. The same allusion was used in this regard in a quite direct fashion by Aurelio Trujillo. He embedded it in the first extended conversation that I had with the Trujillos, in 1972. (Costancia Apodaca de Trujillo is pictured in Plate 19, and the Trujillo house is visible in Plate 20; I have not been able to obtain a photograph of the late Aurelio Trujillo.) In the course of a long theological discussion, presented as example (5.2), Mr. Trujillo commented on the fact that many believers no longer attend Mass, maintain their devotional practices, or even make the sign of the cross.[2]

(5.2) Aurelio Trujillo (69), Costancia Apodaca de Trujillo (69), CLB (19); 8 October 1972, Córdova, New Mexico

---

AT	Pero al cabo que,	
	al cabo que Dios los los sabe premiar,	
	lo mismo que premia al ((pecador)),	
	porque dice	
	"perdonad al inocente,"	5
	dice,	
	"porque no sabe lo que hace."	
CB	Sí.	
AT	Y todos semos HIJOS,	
	todos semos *BROTHERS*,	10
	todos semos hermanos.	
CB	Sí.	
AT	Y muchos NO,	
	porque tiene un *nickel more* que el otro;	
	es ORGULLO.	15
	Mire,	
	la VANIDAD	
	se acaba,	
	no tiene fin.	
	El DINERO se acab	20
	no tiene fin.	
	De modo que hay tres cosas	
	que no tienen fin.	
	Y la, y la AMISTAD REINA EN LA VIDA.	

This scriptural allusion is metacommunicative in two major respects. The allusion is to Christ's invocation on behalf of his crucifiers (Luke 23:34). The term *inocentes* refers to those who lack the knowledge of good and evil and is generally applied to young children and imbeciles. The term is extended to all humans in the text, however, because we lack divine omniscience and our actions are fallible. God will accordingly forgive those who forget him just as he forgives sinners. Mr. Trujillo extends this logic here and in two subsequent allusions to suggest that humans must love their fellow inocentes, regardless of what wrongs they may commit against them. Mr. Trujillo also lists what he sees as the three greatest obstacles to the expression of such brotherly/sisterly affection—pride, vanity, and avarice.

The second major thrust of this allusion, its bearing on the situation at hand, is especially poignant. I had inaugurated my fieldwork in the community three weeks previously, and I met Mr. and Mrs. Trujillo four days before the present meeting. During this, our first extended conversation, my position was quite ambiguous. I was a stranger, an Anglo-American, who came with a tape recorder and wished to conduct research. As a member of the Anglo majority who wished to write about the

English translation

But in the end,
in the end God knows how to reward them
just as he rewards ((sinners)),
because he says
"pardon the innocent,"
he says,
"because s/he knows not what s/he does."
Yes.
And we are all CHILDREN,
we are all *BROTHERS,*
we are all siblings.
Yes.
But not for MANY,
because one has a *nickel more* than the other;
it's PRIDE.
Look,
VANITY
comes to an end,
it is pointless.
MONEY comes to an end,
it is pointless.
So there are three things
that are pointless.
And, and FRIENDSHIP REIGNS IN LIFE.

---

community, I possessed a high degree of status. On the other hand, I was only nine-teen, and I obviously sought the friendship of the Trujillos and wanted to learn from them. Mr. and Mrs. Trujillo's speech reflected this ambiguity. Although they used formal/deferential usted forms, they framed our conversation as pedagogical dis-course. The scriptural allusion thus emerged in the course of an asymmetric mode of interaction in which they occupied a preeminent position.

But Mr. Trujillo had an obvious interest in playing down the deference-to-hearer and emphasizing the solidarity-with-hearer dimension (cf. Silverstein 1981a:5). His speech was accordingly pronouncedly performative in that he sought to create a close friendship and be accorded the deference that he, being fifty years my senior, de-served. Like Mr. Trujillo's utterances in this conversation as a whole, a number of features of the scriptural allusion were carefully suited to this goal. His condemnation of pride, vanity, and avarice is not simply reflective of basic values. Anglo-Americans are commonly stereotyped as proud, vain, and avaricious, characteristics that are be-lieved to engender in Anglo-Americans a sense of superiority to Mexicanos and a reluctance to develop close friendships with them. Mr. Trujillo goes on to argue that friendship (*amistad*) conquers these obstacles.

Mr. Trujillo and Mr. Romero both use the same scriptural allusion—'we are all fellow creatures'—in arguing that this kinship through God and the social obliga-tions it engenders admit no racial barriers. Thirty-five seconds later, in (5.2 cont.: 49–53), Mr. Trujillo notes: *No importa quien SEA, no importa que sea NEGRO o que sea lo que FUERE o–, o AUSTRIACO o lo que fuere* 'It doesn't matter who it MIGHT BE, it doesn't matter if they're BLACK or what HAVE YOU o–, or a FOREIGNER or what HAVE YOU'. In both cases, the expression is used in commenting on the be-havior of individuals who are not participants in the conversation. Mr. Trujillo fo-cuses attention specifically on my duty in this regard by citing pride, vanity, and avarice and by code switching into English (5.2:10, 14). As you may recall from Mrs. López's proverb performance (4.2), the insertion of a few English words in such situations can index the status of the hearer as a native speaker of English. To adopt Mukařovský's (1971:302) terms, the code switching underlines that status of the quotation as "addressed speech" that extends an "evaluative element" to the speech situation, particularly to the position of the hearer within it.

Friendship did come to reign in the situation. The Trujillos became some of my best friends, central consultants, and major sponsors within the community. The Trujillos shifted to *tú* forms before long, and we adopted kin terms for use in address a year later. (I addressed them as *mamá* 'mother' and *papá* 'father', and they addressed me as *hijo* 'son'.)

Scriptural allusions provide metacommunicative commentary on the ongoing conversation in two primary ways. First, scriptural allusions draw upon a textual tradition that is shared by the speaker, her or his interlocutor(s), and their audience. Such phrases as *Dios dice* 'God says' or *dice mi Señor Jesucristo en sus evangelios* 'my Lord Jesus Christ says in His scriptures' tell the hearer "these are not my words, these are the words of Jesus Christ." Use of a scriptural allusion thus places the highest source of legitimacy in the society behind the speaker's words. Because the scriptural text is irrefutable, the legitimacy of the speaker's point of view can be disputed only by challenging the bearing of the text on the issue at hand.

The rhetorical force of scriptural allusions cannot be attributed entirely, however, to the connection of the discourse to this shared textual background. The effective use of a scriptural allusion draws on this source of legitimacy in advancing the speaker's view of an issue of present concern. Example (5.2) adumbrates the values that Mr. Trujillo deems central. It also affords insight into his perception of Mexicano–Anglo-American relations, our friendship, and of what was taking place on an interactional level that afternoon. The scriptural allusion thus functions as a blueprint or, in Peircean terms, a diagram of the speaker's view of a particular situation. This diagrammatic function is two-sided, so to speak, because it also includes an iconic condensation of one aspect of the talk of the elders of bygone days.

In anthropological terms, scriptural allusions connect an ideal model with a real, temporally bounded event, specifying how the former applies to the latter. Such speech events thus show great promise for ethnographers. Some fieldworkers collect extensive data on structural principles or decontextualized ideals. Others are less concerned with norms and meanings than with the details of "objectively" observable behavior. The ideal and the real are, however, never equivalent, and ethnographers encounter difficulties in relating the two. The study of such speech events thus provides the ethnographer with a large set of examples of how the people themselves envisage the relationship between cultural norms and concrete situations.

SCRIPTURAL ALLUSIONS AND PEDAGOGICAL DISCOURSE

When scriptural allusions are used in pedagogical discourse, as was the case in example (5.2), their rhetorical force emerges both from the structure of the performance and from the way in which the performance is embedded in the conversation as a whole. In analyzing these two facets of scriptural allusions, I will present an example that was used by George López just after the segment of pedagogical discourse transcribed in example (3.2). Immediately following that passage, Mr. López asserted the importance of three central religious values—faith, hope, and charity. Mr. López then noted that his father used to spend his winters up on the plaza and his summers in a *fuerte* 'log cabin' in the Quemado Valley next to his fields (see Plate

Plate 21. A fuerte owned by José Dolores López, located near his fields; chile peppers are drying in the foreground. Courtesy of the Museum of New Mexico, neg. no. 13790.

21). With the drastic curtailment of Córdovans' rights to graze livestock in the uplands, however, the Lópezes were forced to give their goats to Miguel Córdova in exchange for cattle. This prompted commentary, presented as example (5.3), on the transformation of Mexicano society that followed the loss of stockbreeding as part of the Córdovans' base of subsistence. I will analyze this example from two perspectives, that of the performance itself and that of its relation to the conversation as a whole.

PERFORMANCE FEATURES OF SCRIPTURAL ALLUSIONS

Scriptural allusions comprise a number of performance features, which are summarized in Table 2. Although these bear some resemblance to those associated with proverb performances, both a number of the features and the pattern as a whole are distinct. Initially, feature 1 provides a moral point of departure for the allusion, which can consist most simply of the statement of a basic principle of moral conduct. When the scriptural allusion is embedded in pedagogical discourse, this principle emerges from a contrast between antes and ahora. Although feature 1 is not always realized in the same way, it is closely tied to the discourse that precedes it (see below). The type of cohesiveness required to convey the sentido necessitates a greater flexibility.

Feature 1 is realized in a fairly complex manner in example (5.3). Mr. López begins with what he sees as a crucial fact that pertains to the contrast he is making between agriculture antes and ahora. His comment that it used to rain more than at present leads me to query him as to the basis for this change. He replies, most am-

TABLE 2   Summary of Scriptural Allusion Performance Features

Feature	Obligatory vs. Optional	Textual vs. Contextual[a]
1. Statement of initial moral principle(s)	Ob	T
2. Assessment of its applicability nowadays	Ob	C
3. Tying word or phrase	Op	C
4. Quotative	Ob	T
5. Source of quotation	Ob[b]	T
6. Scriptural allusion text	Ob	T
7. General meaning	Op	T
8. Relevance to interactional setting	Op	C
9. Additional moral principle(s)	Ob	T
10. Validation	Ob[b]	C

[a] Defined as the relative orientation of the feature as indexing an element of the textual tradition versus an element of the sociolinguistic setting of the performance.

[b] These features are obligatory in isolated performances of scriptural allusions. When several scriptural allusions are performed in a series, feature 4 is often marked overtly in a previous and feature 10 in a succeeding performance (see below).

(5.3) George López (83), CLB (30); 22 July 1983, Córdova, New Mexico

GL Ese Miguel Córdova vivía en LAS TRUCHAS. . . .
CB   Um hum. . . .
GL El tenía VACAS,
    y nosotros le cambiamos las cabras por VACAS. . . .
CB   Hm.   5
    Y, ¿él tenía 'onde PASTUREARLAS?
GL.   Bueno.
    Pos sí, allá en Las TRUCHAS
    tenían–, eran unos, un–, muy, lugares muy GRANDES,

    que hacían SIEMBRAS,   10
        ves.
CB   Mm hm. . . .
GL   Sí. . . .
    Pero ya 'ora NO.
    Ya 'ora no quieren,   15
    ya no hay quien SIEMBRE. . . .
        Nuh nuh.
CB   Hm.
GL Pienso que ya no hay ni uno que siembre en LAS JOYAS
        yo creo. . . .   20
CB   Falta que sí.
GL   Yo creo que NO. . . .
    Nosotros sembrábamos ahi en EL ALTO,
CB   ¿sí?
GL ahi, delante del Huachín,   25
    ahi SEMBRÁBAMOS. . . .
    Ahi cosechábamos,
    ahi cosechaba Empapá mucho FRIJOL.
CB   Hm.
GL Pero ya en esos tiempos llovía MUCHO.   30
    'ORA NO.
CB Pues, por qué?
GL Porque CAMBIÓ el TIEMPO.
CB   Hm.
GL Va cambiando,   35
    va cambiando
    el, el TIEMPO, · · ·
    hasta que se llegue el día que nos FUIMOS. . . .
CB   ¿Sí?
GL   Sí,   40
    porque no más QUIERE, no más,
    no más quiere mi Tata Dios,
    y se acabó TODO. . . .
    Porque dice la BIBLIA
    que, que, que se acabará el, se acabará el MUNDO,   45

    que LA GENTE va a acabar EL MUNDO. . . .
    ((Ha habido)) tan, tanta GUERRAS, . . .
CB   sí

English translation

	This Miguel Córdova used to live in Las TRUCHAS. . . .
nods	Um hum. . . .
	He used to have CATTLE,
	and we traded him ⟨our⟩ goats for CATTLE. . . .
nods	Hm.
points to Truchas	And he had a place to PASTURE THEM?
	Okay.
	Well, up there in Las TRUCHAS
lifts up both hands to	they used to have, there were some, so–, fields that were very
suggest tall plants	LARGE
	in which they planted CROPS,
	you see.
	Mm hm. . . .
shakes head	Yes. . . .
	But not any MORE.
	Nowadays they don't want to,
	there is no one who PLANTS. . . .
shakes head	Nh nh.
	Hm.
points	I think that there is no one who plants in LAS JOYAS,
	I believe. . . .
	I bet that's true.
shakes head	I think NOT. . . .
points and looks in	We used to plant up there in EL ALTO, ⟨The Heights⟩.
that direction	Really?
points and looks	there in front of the Huachín,
points	we used to PLANT THERE. . . .
	There we used to harvest,
	father used to harvest a lot of BEANS.
nods	Hm.
	But back in those days it used to rain A LOT.
shakes head	NOT NOWADAYS.
	But why?
nods	Because the WEATHER ⟨and the times⟩ have CHANGED.
nods	Hm.
rotates hands in circle	⟨It⟩ keeps on changing,
	keeps on changing,
CB nods	the, the WEATHER ⟨and the TIMES⟩, . . .
sweeping gesture	until the day should arrive that we're GONE. . . .
	Really?
	Yes,
	because as soon as ⟨he⟩ WILLS it, as soon,
	as soon as my Father God wills it,
sweeping gesture	everything comes to an END. . . .
CB nods	Because the BIBLE SAYS
	that, that, that the end will come, the end will come for the
	WORLD,
points toward 'outside	that THE PEOPLE will destroy THE WORLD. . . .
world'	((There have been)) so, so many WARS, . . .
nods	yes

```
GL  tantas GUERRAS no HA HABIDO,
          'mano. . . .                                                    50
CB          Pues, sí
GL  Y ahora DICEN
      que, que quieren hacer PAZ. . . .
      ¡Quién sabe!
CB  ¡Quién sabe!                                                          55
          ¿No?
GL  ¡Quién SABE! . . .
      Porque . . .
      esta la, esta la gente muy, muy ⟨de⟩ A TIRO. . . .
CB          Mm hm. . . .                                                  60
Gl. Pero, yo te DIRÉ,
      que si UNO PIERDE LA FE,
      nuh uh,
      no hermano. . . .
      Sin DIOS, no hay quien VIVA,                                       65
      nuh uh.
      Tiene uno que pidirle a DIOS,
      pa' que Dios le AYUDE.
CB          Pus, sí.
GL          Sí.                                                          70
            Sí,
            es VERDA',
            es CIERTÓ.
CB          Sí,
            es VERDA'.                                                   75
```

---

biguously, *Porque CAMBIÓ el TIEMPO. Tiempo* refers to the weather, but it can also be interpreted as referring to 'the times', that is, patterns of human conduct. He then suggests that this difference is part of an ever-accelerating process of change that will eventually lead to the destruction of humankind. This process is itself interpreted, yielding the proposition that God has complete control over this sequence of events. The climatic observation (*CAMBIÓ el TIEMPO*) thus occasions two principles, that the changing physical and social environment is a sign of the coming end and that God is directing this process.

Feature 2 follows closely from the initial feature. Here the principle set forth in feature 1 is applied to some feature of nowadays, which generally evokes a statement either that the moral value in question either no longer guides human conduct or that it is realized in a vastly different manner. In (5.2), this feature consists of a critical assessment of the lackadaisical way that many worshipers express their religious faith. The situation is more complex in (5.3); here the notion that *va cambiando el, el TIEMPO. . . . hasta que llegue el día que nos FUIMOS* '[It] keeps on changing, the, the WEATHER [and the TIMES]. . . . until the day should arrive that we're GONE'

points 'outside'	there HAVE BEEN so many WARS,
	brother. . . .
	Well, yes.
	And now they SAY
	that, that they want to make PEACE. . . .
shrugs	Who knows!
	Who knows!
	Right?
	Who KNOWS. . . .
	Because . . .
shakes head	the people are, are so, so FAR GONE. . . .
nods	Mm hm. . . .
	But I will TELL YOU,
	that if ONE LOSES FAITH ⟨IN GOD⟩,
shakes head and	nuh uh,
pointed finger	no, brother. . . .
	No one can LIVE without GOD,
shakes head	nuh uh.
	One must ask GOD,
nods	so that God will HELP HER/HIM.
nods	Well, yes.
nods	Yes.
	Yes,
	it's TRUE,
	it's CERTAINLY TRUE.
nods twice	Yes,
	it's TRUE.

revolves around the transition between *antes* and *ahora*. It is thus impossible to separate features 1 and 2 in this performance.

Feature 3 consists of a tying word or phrase. As in proverb performances, this element establishes a relationship of local coherence between the preceding discourse and the succeeding utterances. *Porque* 'because' creates an even stronger relationship, asserting that the following utterances will provide an interpretation of the basis, here in moral and religious terms, of what has come before.

The quotative appears in feature 4. While quotatives are generally marked for imperfective or habitual aspect in the case of proverbs, collective recollections, and pedagogical discourse, this aspectual marking is absent in performances of scriptural allusions. Quotatives in scriptural allusions are rather marked for past perfective ('He said') or the present ('He says' or 'the Bible says'). When the quotation is attributed to Jesus Christ, inflection is generally marked for past + perfective. This tense/aspect form frames the quoted utterance as an historical event, as recorded in scripture. When the present tense is used (as in 5.1, 5.2, and 5.3), the source is usually either God or the Bible. This does not, however, restrict the temporal applicability of the quotation. As Silva-Corvalán (1983:778) has argued, the present in Spanish "either relates events to the moment of speaking, or refers to events which are true at all times, including the moment of speaking." The latter sense provides a useful resource for performances of scriptural allusions, since it suggests that the truth of the scriptural quotation is not applicable to a single historical period alone, past or present. The past perfective and present forms thus provide important means of interpreting the nature and religious force of the quoted utterances.

The quotative generally appears in the same clause as feature 5, attribution of the source of the quotation. God, Christ, and the Bible are the most common. Most scriptural allusions are not drawn directly from the Bible by the speaker. Some are taken from catechisms and other religious texts. More commonly, however, they are transmitted orally. Another source is the words of local priests, both as uttered during the Mass (in the homily) and in conversation. I have labeled the quotative and the source as features 4 and 5 because they appear in this order in (5.3); which comes first in a given instance, however, varies.

Feature 6 consists of the quotation itself. As with proverbs, it is frequently given twice, first in elliptical and then in elaborated form. The quotes vary between simple one-sentence utterances and long passages in multiple voices. One allusion consists, for example, of a long discussion between Christ, Death, and Satan. The quote is marked by intonational changes, usually an increase in pitch and loudness and a change in voice quality. The emergence of the quotation often leads the audience to reinterpret what has come before. As I noted above, it was not clear whether Mr. López was using el tiempo in reference to 'the weather' alone or to both 'the weather' and 'the times' in (5.3:33, 37). He suggested in (46) that it is ultimately 'THE PEOPLE' who will bring on the apocalypse through the changes that have left humans *muy* ⟨*de*⟩ *A TIRO* 'so far GONE'. Because it is human conduct that is really in question, the quotation confirms our suspicion that the second meaning of el tiempo was indeed invoked. This connection is based on a number of biblical passages concerning the second coming of Christ (e.g., Matthew 24, Thessalonians 2, Revelation 12–22).

Seventh, the text is usually supplemented with an exegesis, which generally takes the form of a statement in the speaker's own voice on the meaning of the text. In longer quotations, the interpretation is contained in the quotation itself. This element is similar to feature 6 of proverb performances. It similarly remains implicit if the speaker thinks that the hearer will be able to interpret the general meaning of the quotation, as is the case in (5.3). Melaquías Romero marks this feature overtly in (5.1), when he begins by arguing that racial differences are superficial, because 'we're of the same blood, everyone' and 'we're all the same' (5.1:41–45). This feature may produce a lengthy theological discussion.

Feature 8 points to the bearing of the quotation on the present. Mr. López uses this element in a fascinating way in (5.3). He draws out one aspect of the scriptural basis of his argument; one of the signs that the end of the world is imminent is widespread war—"For nation will make war upon nation, kingdom upon kingdom" (Matthew 24:7). The time of the performance, 22 July 1983, lends special significance to both this scriptural allusion and Mr. López's skeptical assessment of present attempts to obtain peace. Mr. López had listened to the five-minute summary of the news in Spanish that morning on a radio station in nearby Española. As Middle Eastern and Central American conflicts were escalating, President Reagan had just dispatched special ambassadors to these two regions. Mr. López's allusion is thus quite timely. He goes on to suggest that the basis of these hostilities is moral and religious decay—"the people are so, so FAR GONE."

The ninth feature consists of the statement of another moral and religious principle. Because one or more principles appear in feature 1 and another is expressed as a scriptural quotation in feature 5, this feature presents minimally a third principle. Generally, all three will involve related themes. The point is to use each sequentially to interpret the moral and religious basis of its predecessor. In (5.3), principle$_1$ (= feature 1) interprets the meaning and direction of this change in el tiempo. Principle$_2$, which is also contained in feature 1, asserts that the change process is divinely controlled. Principle$_3$, which is contained in the quotation (= feature 6), argues that it is human action that will motivate God to use his power to destroy the world. Principle$_4$ (= feature 9) advances the notion that it is faith in God, as expressed by asking for God's help, that can keep both individuals and society as a whole from falling victim to this destructive process.

The final feature consists of a validation of the certitude of the scriptural allusion—*sí, es VERDA', es CIERTÓ* 'yes, it's TRUE, it's CERTAINLY TRUE'. These validating phrases affirm the legitimacy of the text, acknowledging its "collective acceptance" (Mukařovský 1971:297), and assert its relevance to the ongoing social interaction. In pedagogical situations, it is equally important that the pupil provide a validating phrase, which signals the junior's comprehension of the allusion and an admission of its truth and applicability. Unlike proverb performances, the junior's validation frequently comes first. Additional validations may then be provided by the speaker who presented the allusion or by other participants.

SCRIPTURAL ALLUSIONS AND THE GLOBAL STRUCTURE OF DISCOURSE

When viewed from the perspective of the individual performance, scriptural allusions appear to be quite analogous to proverbs. They emerge from an interactional context, and they are closely entwined with the surrounding discourse. They provide legitimation for the speaker's point of view by placing several basic principles of the talk of the elders of bygone days behind it. One of these is drawn from what is reckoned to be the highest source of legitimacy in the society—the words of God and

Jesus Christ. These elements of the past are then connected with some feature of the present. In example (5.3), basic moral and religious principles find their reflection in the most current events of global importance. Like proverbs and pedagogical discourse, then, scriptural allusions convey the speaker's interpretation of antes and ahora, and the way they relate.

When the two genres are performed outside of pedagogical discourse, such as in the type of encounters exemplified by (5.1), this structural similarity prevails. A notable difference emerges, however, when one turns to the way that each type of performance is integrated into pedagogical discourse. In (5.3) Mr. López had, from the beginning of the conversation, moved in dialectical fashion from describing antes to characterizing ahora to adducing an underlying principle. His focus thus far had been on the devotion of Córdovans to subsistence-oriented agriculture and pastoralism before 1915 versus their subsequent reliance on wage labor. His remarks had thus centered on the location and extent of their plantings and on the size of their herds. His rhetorical goal in the conversation was, however, to use these observations in drawing out the changes in the nature of social relations that accompanied this economic transformation. He notes that 'the people were much poorer in bygone days', but that 'the people lived more happily'. His point in this conversation is not simply that a higher level of material prosperity, as measured by possession of consumer goods, is morally reprehensible. Here, as well as in numerous previous pedagogical discussions, he is asserting that this process will have disastrous effects on Mexicanos if it leads to the displacement of corporatism and religiosity. This tendency is encapsulated in the term *el estilo*.

Before the beginning of (5.3), the discourse had consisted of a rapid movement between antes and ahora, punctuated by references to el estilo and statements of underlying principles. Mr. López's scriptural allusion does not bring this movement to a close, as would be the effect of a proverb performance. It rather appropriates the dialectical rhythm as part of its own structure—and then intensifies it. In doing so, it sums up the meaning of these differences and of the moral values they reflect. The quotation, exegesis, and application to ahora comment metacommunicatively on the preceding discourse, including the series of antes/ahora comparisons and the accompanying principles. Having taken the rhetorical movement one step further, revealing an underlying theological basis, Mr. López moves to a more detailed description of various periods of Córdovan history.

Having examined three performances of scriptural allusions and analyzed their features, we are in a position to make an initial assessment of the similarities and differences between proverbs and scriptural allusions. The two genres each revolve around the stylistic and ideological intrusion of a third party into the speech event; whereas the elders of bygone days enter the proverb performance, God or Christ emerges in the scriptural allusion, often through the mediation of a sacred text. In both cases, the quotation addresses the audience and evaluates the social interaction.

This latter statement is, however, truer of proverbs than of scriptural allusions. Comparison of Tables 1 and 2 suggests that the movement between textual and contextual features is somewhat different:

Proverbs:	C→T→C
Scriptural allusions:	T→C→T→C→T→C

Proverbs move from an initial focus on contextual elements to a concern with textual elements, only to return to the contextual sphere once again. Indeed, the textual sphere generally disappears entirely following a proverb, because such performances generally bring that particular token of the talk of the elders of bygone days to a close.

In contrast, scriptural allusions center first on textual elements (the statement of one or more moral principles), then move into the contextual realm (features 2 and 3), only to return to a textual focus in presenting the quotative, source, text, and general meaning (features 4–7). Explicating the relevance of the scriptural allusion for the situation moves the performance back into the contextual realm, while the statement of an additional moral principle reverses this trend once again. A focus on the audience's comprehension of the scriptural allusion and the applicability of the allusion to the situation at hand places us once again in the contextual realm. In the case of brief performances that are not embedded within larger discussions of la plática de los viejitos de antes, we may indeed end here. This is generally not the case, because most performances are followed either by another scriptural allusion (see below) or by some other form of the talk of the elders of bygone days. In either case, we move quickly back into a consideration of the textual realm. This is indeed the general effect of most performances of scriptural allusions—leading the participants deeper into the world of antes.

The processes of presupposition and contextualization affect the performance features of scriptural allusions in the same way that they do proverbs, operating in such a way as to make explicit only as much information as the audience needs to make sense of the performance. The sequence of features and the degree of stress that is accorded to each are also subject to another major constraint in the case of scriptural allusions. The latter ride on a movement between antes and ahora, appropriating and intensifying its dialectical structure. As such, the way that the features will be realized in a given performance is partially contingent on the nature of the contrasts between bygone days and nowadays that have been developed in the discourse and the place at which the scriptural allusion is inserted. True, this same statement could be made for proverb performances that occur in discussions of antes. Scriptural allusions are much more dependent, however, upon the global structure of the discourse; the vagaries of the preceding discourse thus produces greater variation in the structure of performances of scriptural allusions.

SCRIPTURAL ALLUSIONS AND TEXTUALITY

The three examples that we have examined thus far do not provide an overwhelming body of evidence to support the claim that scriptural allusions constitute a distinct genre of la plática de los viejitos de antes. Based on these data, one might equally argue that scriptural allusions are a type of proverb, albeit one with different features, a distinct performance pattern, and a different relationship between textual and contextual spheres. We have, however, only examined more conversationally focused examples. I believe that the distinctness of the genre becomes more apparent when we consider performances in which the "addressed" character of the scriptural allusion and its "evaluative" orientation toward the interactional setting are increasingly displaced by a focus on the performance of a scriptural allusion as an event in and of itself. This displacement takes place when the text leaves behind the pithiness of a proverb-like form and assumes narrative form, and when scriptural allusions are juxtaposed to create long series in which one scriptural allusion provides the setting for performance of another.

The continuation of example (5.2) illustrates both processes. It comes from a pedagogical discussion between Costancia Trujillo, Aurelio Trujillo, and myself that took place in 1972. One segment of this discussion was presented as the second example in this chapter (5.2). The continued transcript begins precisely where the previous segment ended (5.2:24). The recorded portion of this conversation is two and

(5.2 continued) Aurelio Trujillo (69), Costancia Apodaca de Trujillo (60), CLB (19); 8 October 1972

AT	Pues, si yo quiero a usted	25
	LO AMO	
	de CORAZÓN,	
	como si fuera a MÍ MISMO.	
	Si USTED me de–, si USTE–,	
	si YO le digo a usted	30
	"Yo no lo quiero a usted,"	
	((yo desairarlo)) a ÉL,	
	a usted,	
	a mí,	
	el PRÓJIMO.	35
	Pero si yo le deseo a usted BIEN,	
	y, y, y en mí CAE,	
	y luego a usted le van los favores MÍOS	
	a usted pa' que usted VIVA lo mismo que VIVO YO,	
	y HABLAMOS 'ondequiera que nos VEANOS,	40
	asina,	
	¿ve?	
	Y muchos NO.	

one-quarter hours in duration. The Trujillos devoted most of the time to teaching me a number of *alabanzas* 'hymns of praise' (primarily for the Virgin and the saints) and *alabados* 'hymns commemorating the passion of Christ' (see Chapter 8). Mr. Trujillo had taken out two of his *cuadernos* 'notebooks' that contained texts for the hymns and prayers. In the course of singing each hymn, Mr. Trujillo would stop periodically to interpret and expand upon the import of the text. Mrs. Trujillo also produced an old catechism and examined a few passages; she gave the book to me at the end of the conversation.

Mr. Trujillo performed ten scriptural allusions on this occasion. The examples in (5.2) were preceded by a scriptural allusion that explained the relationship between agriculture and faith in God (cf. Briggs 1983): *La voluntad de mi Dios dice claro, en su evangelio, que dice mi Señor Jesucristo en su evangelio que "no, no sea hombre de poca fe. Que tire su semilla, para que levante y lo asista. Y de ahi vivirá el pecador, vive el hombre,"* *dice. Y es verdad.* 'The will of my God says clearly, in His gospel, that my Lord Jesus Christ says in His gospel, "don't, don't be a man of little faith. Spread your seeds, so that they will come up, and care for them. And this is how sinners will live, how man lives," he says. And it's true.' He used the first scriptural allusion in arguing that by planting, a person expresses faith in God, because only God can determine whether one's efforts will end in success or failure. This practice is contrasted with the failure of people nowadays to sow the fields.

English translation

Well, if I care about you,
I LOVE YOU
from my HEART,
as I would MYSELF.
If YOU were to sa–, if YOU–,
if I were to say to you,
"I don't care about you,"
((I would snub)) HIM,
you,
me,
my NEIGHBOR.
But if I wish you WELL,
and, and, and this returns to ME,
and then you receive my HELP
for you, so that you might LIVE the same as I LIVE,
and we SPEAK wherever we SEE EACH OTHER,
like this,
        see?
But many people aren't LIKE THIS.

"Mi mano no es NADA,
(( )))" se van,   45
pero no.
La habla es de mi DIOS,
de mi Señor JESUCRISTO. . . .
No importa quien SEA,
no importa que sea NEGRO   50
o sea lo que FUERE
o–, o AUSTRIACO
o lo que FUERE.
Si aquella persona no le HABLA,
a USTED,   55
DÉJELO. . . .
El tendrá que pagar a la ((presencia)) de Dios por ESO. . . .
Y cada quien tiene que hacer UNO
pa' SÍ MISMO. . . .
            ¿Ve?   60
Por eso nosotros–, nosotros tenemos que eh, estar llendo a misa
para a CUMPLIR a DIOS
los pecados mortales que tenemos;
Él nos los PERDONA.
Porque, porque hay una cosa   65
que si nosotros la IGNORAMOS,
dice mi Señor Jesucristo en sus, en sus EVANGELIOS,
que "PERDONARI . . .
al que no SABE,
porque son inocentes,   70
y PERDONAR," dice
"a TODOS nuestros LADRONES."
Yo perdonari a usted,
usted perdonari a mí,
ESE es el PRÓJIMO.[3]   75
Pero muchos NO, . . .
con mucho ORGULLO
que no, no QUIEREN,
            hombre. . . .
CB   "Yo puedo buscar."   80
AT   Sí,
            es VERDAD.
Pero,
la PERSONA
que, que ENTIENDE las cosas . . .   85
y las AGARRA en su CORAZÓN, . . .
le TIEMBLAN sus CARNES,
LLORA UNO.
Porque le tiene uno que dar el ALMA
a mi DIOS,   90
la tiene PRESTADA. . . .
Y muchos NO,
"Yo no miro a DIOS, no ESTÁ."
Aquí MISMO, ahora MISMO está ÉL co–,
en mero de NOSOTROS,   95
aquí ESTÁ. . . .

spoken as if
intoxicated
	"My brother is NOTHING,
	(( ))," they go,
	but no.
	The words are of my GOD,
	of my Lord Jesus CHRIST. . . .
	It doesn't matter who it MIGHT BE,
	it doesn't matter if they're BLACK
	or what HAVE YOU
	o–, or a FOREIGNER
	or what HAVE YOU.
	If that person doesn't SPEAK
	to YOU,
	FORGET HIM. . . .
	He will have to pay in the ((presence)) of God for THIS. . . .
	And EVERY PERSON must do THIS
	For HERSELF OR HIMSELF. . . .
	      You see?
	This is why we–, we must go to Mass
	and ANSWER to GOD
	for the mortal sins that we have ⟨committed⟩;
	HE FORGIVES us FOR THEM.
	Because, because there is one thing
	that if we IGNORE,
	my Lord Jesus Christ says in his, in his GOSPELS,
	to "PARDON . . .
	those who DO NOT KNOW,
	because they are inocentes,
	and PARDON," he says
	"ALL of our TRESPASSERS" [lit. thieves].
	I pardon you,
	you pardon me,
	THAT is BROTHERLY LOVE.[3]
	But NOT for LOTS OF PEOPLE, . . .
	they have so much PRIDE
	that they don't, don't WANT TO,
	      man.
	"I can take care of myself."
	      Yes,
	       that's TRUE.
	But,
	the PERSON
	who, who UNDERSTANDS ⟨these⟩ things . . .
	and TAKES them to HEART, . . .
	so that her/his BODY QUAKES,
	and S/HE CRIES.
	Because one must give her/his SOUL
	to GOD,
	it is ON LOAN. . . .
	But many aren't LIKE THIS.
	"I don't see GOD, He doesn't EXIST."
	Right HERE, right NOW HE is wi–,
	in the midst of US,

knocks on table	He IS HERE. . . .

Dice,
"Si CINCO se JUNTAN en mi NOMBRE,
Yo ESTARÉ," dice
"en el MEDIO de ustedes, un espíritu puro."   100
No lo MIRAMOS,
pero es ESPÍRITU,
es DIOS,
      ve.
Por eso, él no se da VISTAR,   105
porque posible aquí en el mundo
haiga unos con RIFLES,
diga,
"pos, a mí me hicistes POBRE,"
LO VAN A MATARI.   110
      ¿No?
CB   um h–/
AT   /No, no, sí.
CB   Pues, sí/
AT /Por eso no se da VISTARI. . . .   115
Lo mismo que este AIGRE que está AHI,
((dice que está haciendo)) aigre,
no lo VEMOS,
pero está SOPLANDO. . . .
Y DONDEQUIERA ESTÁ DIOS con uno. . . .   120
Eso sí te puedo decir la mera verdad,
      ((Carlos)).
Pero muchos no lo COMPRENDEMOS.
Muchos no se arriman ni a MISA,
no se arriman   125
ni hacer la SEÑAL ni NADA, . . .
como HEREJES.
TIENE MÁS CONOCIMIENTO UN ANIMAL
que ARRODILLE
cuando vea una procesión,   130
      mire.
Se queda MIRANDO . . .
como ha–, ha–, haciendo ORACIONES MISMO,
      mire,
que es un ANIMAL. . . .   135
Es ÁNIMA, como dicen.
Y que mejor que un CRISTIANO.[4]
Porque la MULA cuando FUE al PESEBRE,
    y lo llamó mi Señor Jesucristo a la mula pa', . . .
    pa' que FUERA a tomar la HOSTIA, . . .[5]   140
      y le, y tenía que ir en AYUNA la MULA.
        Y, y, pa' acá, y que pa' que CREYERA la GENTE

    en el–, en el–, como en una IGLESIA,
    les dijo,
    "Traigan la MULA,"   145
    les decía mi Señor Jesucristo, . . .
    "y TRAÍGANLE mucho MAIZ,
    mucho AVENO", . . .

He says,
"If FIVE GATHER in my NAME,
I WILL BE," he says,
"in the MIDST of you, in spirit only."
We don't SEE HIM,
⟨because⟩ he is a SPIRIT,
he's GOD,
   you see.
That's why he doesn't become VISIBLE,

laughs   because here in the world it is possible
that there might be some ⟨people⟩ with RIFLES,
who might say,
"well, you made me POOR,"
THEY'LL KILL HIM.
   Right?
   um h–/
   No, no, yes.
   Well, yes/
/This is why he doesn't become VISIBLE. . . .
It's the same as the WIND over THERE,
((they say it's blowing;))
we don't SEE IT,
but it's BLOWING. . . .

knocks on table AND GOD IS WITH US EVERYwhere. . . .
I can tell you that this is the very truth ,
   ((Carlos)).
But many of us don't UNDERSTAND THIS.
Many don't even go to MASS,
they don't go
or make the SIGN OF THE CROSS or ANYTHING, . . .
like PAGANS.
AN ANIMAL HAS MORE UNDERSTANDING
when it KNEELS
if it sees a procession,
   you see.
It keeps WATCHING . . .
as if it were REALLY PRAYING,
   you see,
even though it's an ANIMAL. . . .
It's a SOUL, as they say.
And it's better than a CHRISTIAN.[4]
Because when the MULE WENT to the MANGER,
   and my Lord Jesus Christ called the mule so, . . .
  so that he could TAKE the HOST, . . .[5]
   and the, and the MULE had to be FASTING.
    And, and so that, and so that the PEOPLE would
     BELIEVE
    in the, in the—, like in a CHURCH,
    he said to them,
    "Bring the MULE,"
    my Lord Jesus Christ said to them, . . .
    "and BRING IT lots of CORN,
    lots of OATS," . . .

                            todo que recogió al templo
                            'onde están los imagenes.   150
                                Esa mula,
                                reclaman y está ahi, ele,
                                que DOBLÓ su RODILLA,
                                una,
                                asina,   155
                                y le ponían en el pesebre el grano AQUÍ.
                                ((De sentada)) donde está el padre hablando
                                el predicadore,
                                o mi Señor Jesucristo,
                                    y NO TOMÓ,   160
                                    no tomó AVENO,
                                    y ¡no había COMIDO!
                                    ni MAIZ,
                                    hasta que ya pasó la MISA,
                                    que le arrimaron a quedar–   165
                                    le dijo el padre,
                                    "AHORA, SÍ,"
                                    eh, eh, ah, le echó la BENEDICIÓN,
                                    que se levantara uno.
                                    Entonces,   170
                                    ya entonces COMIÓ LA MULA.
    Pa' que yo te–,
    ¡tiene más conocimiento una mula
    que un CRISTIANO!
    ¡SÍ TIENE!   175
            Y ve,
    uno MACHO, MACHO,
            ve.
    ¡Un BRUTO!
    Y, y yo creo más bien que fuera uh, uh, un ANIMAL   180
    l.acer mejor que un CRISTIANO.

The first scriptural allusion of (5.2), *perdonar al inocente,* appears thirteen minutes later. Example (5.2:25–41) provides additional explication of the point of the second allusion. Here Mr. Trujillo argues that because the obligation to treat each other as brothers and sisters is ordained by God, God will punish us for mistreating each other or will reward us for acts of kindness. After noting the tendency ahora to disregard this tenet (5.2:43–45), he asserts the preeminence of this principle over racial or ethnic differentiation. Mr. Trujillo returns in (61) to the importance of going to Mass and asking God's forgiveness as a way of staying "very close" to him. This leads him in (5.2:65–72) to reiterate the second scriptural allusion, adding a slight expansion of the text (y *perdonar . . . a todos nuestros ladrones*). He asserts in (75) that this is the true meaning of el prójimo.

After reiterating the incompatibility of this attitude with pride (76–78), he goes

all that they brought to the temple
where the images are ⟨kept⟩.
      That mule,
      it is said, and it's there ⟨in scripture⟩,
      that it KNEELED,
      on one ⟨knee⟩,

indicates with gesture   like this,
points to location of   and they put the grain in the manger HERE.
grain and mule   ((Seated)) where the priest was talking
      the preacher,
knocks on table   or my Lord Jesus Christ,
            and IT DIDN'T EAT,
            it didn't eat OATS,
            and it hadn't EATEN,
            or CORN,
            until the MASS was OVER,
            they brought it over to stay–,
            the priest said to it,
            "YES, NOW,"
            eh, eh, eh, he gave the BLESSING,
            so that everyone could get up.
            Then,
            so then THE MULE ATE.
      So to you I—,
      a mule has more understanding
CB laughs   than a CHRISTIAN!
      SURE IT DOES!
            And look,
      a HE-MULE, HE-MULE,
            you see.
      A BRUTE!
      And, and I think that an ANIMAL
      can do better than a CHRISTIAN.

on to describe the state of mind of the person who understands these principles. This description is immediately contrasted with the doubt of the agnostic or atheist. Mr. Trujillo attempts to refute the latter attitude with the third scriptural allusion. This passage supports Mr. Trujillo's contention by reiterating Christ's promise to appear to his faithful, but not in visible form. He then suggests that it is human wickedness that prevents Christ from becoming visible. The "present but invisible" theme is addressed once again through an analogy between divine presence and the wind. Mr. Trujillo concludes in (120) that God always watches over his faithful.

Note that the validation in (121)—*eso sí te puedo decir la mera verdad* 'I can tell you ⟨that this is⟩ the absolute truth'—is the only validation evident in (5.2).[6] Although this pattern is not in keeping with that evinced by isolated performances, such as (5.1) and (5.3), it is the norm for serial performances, such as (5.2). It indicates that Mr. Trujillo is not simply providing one self-contained scriptural allusion after another but rather is weaving them into a larger whole. The second and third scriptural allusions possess all the characteristic features of the genre, minus the validation. The beginning of the fourth allusion, however, is provided by features 6–8 of the third allusion. Given the high degree of coherence between the two allusions, Mr. Trujillo simply presupposes features 3 and 5 (the tying phrase and the source). This text illustrates the way in which a number of scriptural allusions that are used in the same conversation will be woven together to such an extent that they cease to be individual performances. The nature and the location of the validation reflect this amalgamation. Not only does the validation follow (and thus further consolidate) several scriptural allusions, but it is longer and more emphatic.

Quoted speech often plays a special role in such discourse. Scriptural allusions gain their force by framing a moral principle as the words of Christ, God, or the Bible. Changes in pitch, volume, and the speed of delivery signal the audience that "these are not my words—it is Christ (or God) who is speaking." In Mukařovský's (1971) terms, they mark the intrusion of a "foreign subject" into the discourse; here this foreign subject is Christ or God. As (5.2) progresses, Mr. Trujillo begins juxtaposing these quotations with the words of contemporary mortals who have missed the point. In (44–45), he decreases the speed of his delivery and "slurs" his words to such an extent that several words are unintelligible. This creates the impression of an extremely intoxicated and belligerent individual. A sudden drop in pitch, a decrease in speech, and a slightly "guttural" quality occur in (93), suggesting an argumentative, skeptical tone. This contrasts with the higher pitch, careful enunciation, longer pauses, and sonorous quality used in the quotations attributed to Christ and God.

As Mr. Trujillo turns from scripture (5–7) to sacrilege (13–14, 43–45) to scripture (68–73) to sacrilege (93) to scripture (98–100) to sacrilege (109) and so forth, he is not simply *describing* this contrast in values. Embodying sacrilegious and antisocial attitudes in quotations does not signal the fact that they are accorded "collective acceptance" by the community. By framing them as quoted speech, Mr. Trujillo is able to use stylistic devices (those used in producing the voice characteristics attributed to the sinner or agnostic) to the task of interpreting the way people act nowadays. The performance now features three voices—the voice of the interpreter/performer (Mr. Trujillo), that of God and Christ, and that of the modern agnostic and sinner. Here antes, ahora, and the interpretive process that mediates between them have become much more fully "dialogized" and "theatricalized," because each speaks with a stylistically distinctive voice. The discourse is now "dialogical" in Bakhtin's (1981) sense of the term as well, because the discourse has begun to be "stratified" by a meeting of distinct voices, each of which seeks to dominate the discourse in ideological as well as stylistic terms.

Now the stage is set for the emergence of a narrative in (138–71). This is the first performance that has been examined thus far in which a clear progression of prosodically defined discourse units is tied to the unfolding of a set of sequentially arranged events. Mr. Trujillo begins with a typical backdrop for the performance of a scriptural allusions. He states that some humans are so reluctant to use their mental capabilities to comprehend the word of God that they are no more enlightened than animals; he presents the narrative as evidence for the validity of this assertion. The emergence of a narrative scriptural allusion on the heels of a number of other allusions is characteristic and points to the possibility that the rhetorical complexity that develops in the course of performing a series of scriptural allusions is a necessary prerequisite for performance of a scriptural allusion that assumes narrative form.

CONCLUSION

The preceding example illustrates the point at which scriptural allusions contrast maximally with proverbs. Although the latter possess internally coherent patterns of features, their relationship to the issue at hand remains clear. Scriptural allusions are able to break out of the interactional setting that gave rise to them and become the raison d'etre of the discourse. This potential is realized in scriptural allusions that assume narrative form, some of which are much longer and more complex than the mule story. In one example, the allusion includes a lengthy discussion between Christ, Death, and Satan. In such cases, the quoted material and the exegesis extend far beyond the problem that they originally addressed. The differences that distinguish proverbs and scriptural allusions may not have been strikingly apparent when the latter are seen in isolated performances; the distinguishing features of the two genres are more clearly visible in performances that contain a series of scriptural allusions, particularly if one of these takes the form of a narrative. Extended performances in this genre thus take us one step farther along the road from contextual to textual orientations. Although such scriptural allusions may have been occasioned by a given social interaction, the performance begins to transcend this focus and to create a setting of its own—namely, an opportunity to tell a biblical story.

Scriptural allusions cover a greater range of the textual-contextual continuum than is the case with proverbs. Example (5.1) is quite similar to a proverb performance. A tiny slice of another world—the textual world of the Bible—is recreated in the present. This world, however, does not come alive; we have no descriptive or narrative portrait of how this expression came into being and only a fleeting glimpse of the way it was used antes. In the case of the mule in the manger, the direction is reversed. This scriptural allusion may indeed help prove a point, and Mr. Trujillo's narrative is structured in such a way as to show that this is the case (cf. Sacks 1974;

Wolfson 1976). It can accordingly be said that the scriptural allusion is contextualized vis-à-vis the setting in which it emerged. This mode of contextualization differs substantially from Mr. López's reference to world politics or Mr. Trujillo's earlier (5.2:1–24) model of how we should relate to each other. The narrative is contextualized with respect to an element of the discourse that is itself textually based.[7] It does not foreground the social interaction (in terms of time, place, social roles, etc.); the phenomenological movement of the performance rather lies in the opposite direction. We begin to move outside of a particular kitchen in a certain community at a given time and to step into an imaginary realm. The narrative presents characters (Christ, the mule, the crowd, etc.) and specific events (obtaining the mule, preparing for the Last Supper, testing an animal's respect for the divine, and preaching). As the narrative begins to penetrate the discourse, contextualization cues (e.g., response queries, back-channel cues, validations, references to the social interaction) recede into the background. The quotation is still "addressed," but this orientation is more toward the specifics of a theological discussion than toward the social interaction.

Most of the scriptural allusions we examined lack a narrative element. When Mr. Trujillo does move into a narrative mode, he presents us with more of a narrative sketch than a well-developed story. Setting, characters, and events are alluded to, but narrative detail and development are held to a minimum. Although scriptural allusions may be characterized by a narrative tendency that is lacking in proverbs and historical discourse, this proclivity operates within narrow limits. A narrative may rise to the surface but only for a moment. Even such a hesitant movement toward a textual orientation begins to displace the emphasis on contextual features that so dominated proverbs and historical discourse. It also witnesses the beginnings of a stylistic stratification of the discourse that is tied to the ideological conflict that divides bygone days and nowadays. *Chistes,* which are analyzed in the next chapter, give much broader rein to such stylistic and ideological heterogeneity. Here both antes and ahora are subjected to a much more penetrating ideological examination, a process that parallels the emergence of a different set of stylistic devices to be used in effecting this interpretive exploration.

6

■■

JESTS, ANECDOTES, AND HUMOROUS TALES

The flexibility and incipient narrative structure encountered with scriptural allusions become greater in the realm of *chistes*. The term covers a broad range of analytic (cross-cultural) types, including what are generally termed jokes, jests, anecdotes, humorous tales, and numbskull stories. Chistes are thus quite varied both in their form and in the ways they relate to performance settings. The formal and interactional characteristics accordingly present a challenge to the capacity of ethnopoetics and discourse analysis.

Freud began his classic study of *der Witz* by noting, "Anyone who has at any time had occasion to enquire from the literature of aesthetics and psychology what light can be thrown on the nature of jokes and on the position they occupy will probably have to admit that jokes have not received nearly as much philosophical consideration as they deserve in view of the part they play in our mental life" (1960/1905:9). The period that extends from the time of Freud's statement to the present has witnessed the publication of numerous works on jokes and related speech forms; the problem thus rather becomes one of organizing the diversity that is apparent in the literature. Jokes have been studied under the guise of humor and laughter,[1] play,[2] social structure,[3] ritual and religion,[4] psychoanalysis,[5] politics and ethnicity,[6] gender roles,[7] as well as speech play and discourse.[8] This body of literature points to a number of crucial dimensions of Mexicano performances.

First, many authors have commented on the fact that jokes and related forms closely reflect the values that constitute central components of the collective identity of social groups. This relationship is frequently indirect, taking the form of comments on deviations from social norms (e.g., Gossen 1974a:91–92) or characterizations of populations that are socially, culturally, religiously, occupationally, or geographically distinct. Basso (1979), for example, has detailed the manner in which Western Apaches articulate their own cultural values by mimicking the ways "the Whiteman" violates Western Apache patterns of social interaction. Much ethnic hu-

mor, on the other hand, reflects derogatory stereotypes that often bear little relationship to the cultural patterns of the target group (cf. Abrahams 1970, 1972; Abrahams
and Dundes 1969; Apte 1985:114; Dundes 1971b, 1975b; Raskin 1985:180–221;
Zenner 1970).

Second, a large body of research has demonstrated that the relationship between
jokes and cultural identity does not always take the form of a simple affirmation of in-
group norms and values. Jokes that seem to derogate an entire ethnic population may
be performed by the target group as a means of articulating differences (of generation,
immigrant status, occupation, etc.) between members (cf. Ben-Amos 1973; Oring
1981; Paredes 1968) or of redistributing power (cf. Dundes 1985; Limón 1982) between members. Even "ethnic jokes" can be used in expressing ambivalence, as
is amply demonstrated by Paredes's (1966, 1968) discussion of how middle-class
Mexican-Americans in Texas both ridicule and express affection for aspects of their
cultural heritage and at the same time articulate their resentment of Anglo-American
prejudice and exploitation. (See also Jordan 1981; Limón 1977, 1982; Reyna 1973,
1978.) Oring (1981) has similarly analyzed the way that the *chizbat* humor of the
Palmah, a group of Jewish guerrillas in pre-1948 Palestine, heightened rather than
resolved the contradictions inherent in their collective identity.

Third, these findings affirm Douglas's (1968) characterization of jokes as meta-
physical interpretations of dominant patterns of social relations; she argues that jokes
provide means of challenging and temporarily overcoming their binding force. Abrahams (1980, 1982a, 1986b) and Bauman (1986) draw inter alia on Bakhtin (1968/
1965, 1981), Burke (1941, 1969/1950), Goffman (1974, 1981), Huizinga (1955),
and Turner (1969, 1974) in arguing that jokes, anecdotes, and other forms invoke a
play dimension that enables participants to embrace "a kind of skepticism and relativism that takes pleasure in refusing to take ideal, normative moral expectations too
seriously" (Bauman 1986:75). Play creates "a zone at the boundaries of the community" (Abrahams 1986b:4) in which rules and conceptual schemata are dissected,
reorganized, and negotiated. Levine (1977:338) argues that the capacity of humor to
reveal absurdities, unmask hypocrisies and double standards, and play with stereotypes enabled blacks "to turn American racism on its head." Limón (1982) challenges the psychological or sociological functionalism that underlies most discussions
of jokes—that is, the notion that this "anti-structural" (cf. Turner 1969) process
ultimately succeeds in strengthening the status quo. He analyzes jokes performed by
Chicano students at the University of Texas between 1966 and 1975 in suggesting
that joking played a key role in producing a distinct ideology and social formation.

These findings are compatible with the portrait of Mexicano verbal art that has
begun to emerge in the preceding chapters, in which I suggest that performances of
historical discourse, proverbs, and scriptural allusions provide interpretations of a
broad range of underlying features that shape and are shaped by daily life. The literature on jokes also provides us with an initial insight into the special character that

such interpretive processes assume when they are subjected to the ludic transformations that emerge within the play frame. The overall thrust of the present work points to the need to transcend one common limitation of analyses of jokes. As Raskin (1985:30) has noted, most studies focus on a single dimension (e.g., social or psychological functions) of a single type of humor (e.g., "dirty jokes"). Moreover, most researchers analyze the referential content of jokes, treating questions of form and contextualization en passant if at all. Accordingly relatively few studies consider specific performances of jokes to analyze how their meaning is conveyed as particular aspects of style and content emerge in the course of an ongoing social interaction. A number of studies have brought us much closer to overcoming this hiatus (see particularly Abrahams 1964, 1970, 1976, 1983b: 55–76; K. Basso 1979; Bauman 1986:54–77; Limón 1982; Sacks 1974, 1978).[9]

This approach to Mexicano jokes is necessary in this study as we continue to consider the ways textual and contextual elements come together in performance, and will help us adequately to address a number of basic issues regarding chistes. The Mexicano materials suggest the importance of two considerations. First, the chiste genre includes a particularly wide range of speech forms; it is accordingly necessary to account for this diversity in form, function, and content. Second, given the focus of this study on the nature of the competence that underlies la plática de los viejitos de antes, I will analyze the role of chistes in acquiring the ability to participate in performances of this talk. I will suggest that the placement of chistes with respect to the textual-contextual continuum accords the genre a crucial role in the acquisition process.

CHISTES AND CONVERSATION

In examining the different ways in which the forms of chistes are situated with respect to their interactional context, an important distinction can be drawn between performances that are motivated by a specific social interaction and those that emerge in chiste-telling sessions. Although many chistes can be used in both types of situations, each makes different formal requirements on the performer. Let us begin with chistes that bear the greatest similarity to scriptural allusions. Here, a chiste, like a proverb or scriptural allusion, is used in conversation because of its coherence with respect to the topic of the discussion. At first glance, such performances appear to be identical, in pragmatic terms, to pedagogical uses of historical discourse and scriptural allusions. The chiste is closely integrated with the surrounding discourse, and it provides an interpretation of what has been said. The nature of this interpretation, however, is different from those associated with scriptural allusions and proverbs.

The performance presented in example (6.1) emerged in a pedagogical discussion with Federico Córdova and Lina Ortiz de Córdova (Plate 22). The chiste invoked

Plate 22. Federico Córdova, who died in 1974, and Lina Ortiz de Córdova, with one of their grandchildren. Courtesy of Lina Ortiz de Córdova.

Plate 23. The Córdova home, 1986. Photograph by Charles L. Briggs

(6.1) Federico Córdova (78), Lina Ortiz de Córdova (ca. 78), Samuelito Córdova (ca. 16), CLB (19); 3 October 1972, Córdova, New Mexico

FC Tenía que ser asina,
       ¿ves?
   Ya verás tú, ¿ya ahora qué?
   Está tan ((fregado)) ya.
   Ya está todo, TODO—.   5
   ESTÁ, ESTÁ COMO,
      una vez aquí estaba un hombre
      que se llamaba Antonio RICO,
      muy RICO.
            Venía siendo su abuelo de, de mano Emilio.   10
            Ese era hijo de un Pedro Córdova
            que era el más rico;
            'izque manejaba aquí TODO,
            (('izque sí tenía?)),
            manejaba pa' acá todo él. . . .   15
      Y tenía un INDIO,
            porque entonces COMPRABAN NAVAJOSES
            o los ROBABAN.
CB   Mm hm.
FC   Y un Navajo que se llamaba "CHICO."   20
        Y este, 'izque lo enseñó a rezar el Padre Nuestro ÉLE.

        Rezaba "Padre nuestro, que estás en el cielo,"
        hasta que llegaban ahi 'onde dice,
        "Danos el pan de cada DÍA."
            Y ahi 'izque le DECÍA,   25

            | el, el ri-, el Antonio, se llamaba,
        "SIGUE, SIGUE, Chico."
        "Oh NO, padre Antonio,
        pus de AHI PA' ALLÁ
        está TODO ENREDA'O,   30
        TODO ENREDA'O."
        (('Izque le dicía,))
        (("así está, padre 'Tonio,)) . . .
        de AHI PA' ALLÁ,"
        "padre Antonio,   35
        está TODO ENREDA'O. . . ."
   Y ese dicía que de ahi pa' allá no ENTENDÍA,

      porque estaba TODO ENREDA'O.
CB   Yah.
FC   No más decía 'onde dicía   40
        "El pan de cada, de cada día,"
        dicía.
            Y luego 'izque le dicía "SIGUE, SIGUE."

        "No, querido papá ANTONIO,
        de ahi pa' allá está TODO enreda'o,"   45
        'izque dicía él.

English translation

It had to be this way,
    you see?
Soon you'll see, and now what?
Things are so ((screwed up)) already.
Everything is already all, ALL—.

laughs   IT'S, IT'S LIKE,
    once there was a man here
    named Antonio the WEALTHY,
    ⟨he was⟩ very WEALTHY.

        | He was the grandfather of brother Emilio.
        | He [Antonio] was a son of Pedro Córdova
        | who was the richest of all;
        | it is said that he used to run EVERYTHING HERE,
        | ((it is said that he used to have?))
        | everything around here used to be run by him. . . .
    And ⟨Antonio⟩ had an INDIAN,

        | because then they USED TO BUY NAVAJOS,
        | or they USED TO STEAL THEM.
            Mm hm.
    And ⟨he used to have⟩ a Navajo named "CHICO."
        And it is said that he taught ⟨Chico⟩ how to pray
            the Our FATHER.
        He used to pray "Our Father who art in heaven,"
        until he used to come to where it says,
        "Give us this day our daily BREAD,"
            And then it is said that ⟨Antonio⟩ used to
            TELL HIM,
           | the, the weal–, Antonio, he was called,
           "GO ON, GO ON, Chico."
           "Oh NO, father Antonio,
           well, FROM THERE ON
           it's ALL MIXED UP,
LO laughs   ALL MIXED UP."
SC and CB laugh   ((It is said that he used to tell him,))
           (("that's it, father 'Tonio,)) . . .
everyone laughs   from THERE ON,"
           "father Antonio,
           it's ALL MIXED UP. . . ."
And he was saying that from there on HE COULDN'T
    UNDERSTAND,
because it was ALL MIXED UP.
        Yah.
    He used to say it only to where it would say
    "Our daily, daily bread,"
    he used to say.
        And then it is said that he used to tell him
            "GO ON, GO ON,"
        "No, dear papa ANTONIO,
        from there on it's ALL mixed up,"
everyone laughs   it is said that he used to tell him.

	De modo que "Pa' allá está todo enreda'o."	
	¿Ve?	
LO	¡Ay que Padre Nuestro!	
FC	¿Ve?	50
	¿Ven? . . .	
CB	Sí.	
	¡Válgame Dios! . . .	
FC	Sí,	

todas estas cosas PASAN,   55
    ve.
Y ya estamos pasando a otro SIGLO, ya. . . .
Ya estamos en otro SIGLO. . . .
Ya estamos pasando otros eh—, otros— . . .
otro MODO de VIVIR. . . .   60

---

is popular with local elders and involves Córdova's most noted historical figure, Pedro Córdova (see Chapters 2 and 7). This chiste usually emerges in discussions of Pedro Córdova and his era of the community's history, *más antes*. In this case, however, Federico Córdova's concern was with more recent events. The conversation took place in the Córdova home (Plate 23) at the end of a six-hour period during which a number of family members had come, talked, eaten, and exchanged chistes (see example (6.5)). The part of the recording presented in (6.1) was made at about 11:00 PM; by this point, everyone had left except Mr. Córdova and his wife, Lina Ortiz de Córdova, their grandson Sammy, and myself. Having spoken about the community's past, Mr. Córdova was now discussing the difficulty of living in accordance with these values in the present. Mr. Córdova then continued to develop his contrast between the world of the viejitos de antes that he and his wife had experienced as children and that of the present.

This short chiste appeared in the midst of a serious conversation, producing a hearty laugh from the teller and his interlocutors. The exchange then quickly resumed its more serious tone. Two questions come to the fore: What does one need to know in order to appreciate its humor, and what role did it play in the conversation?

The humor hinges on knowledge of a historical allusion and of stereotypic conceptions of Native Americans. The allusion is drawn from the material on Pedro Córdova, whom we met briefly in Chapter 2. Córdova is said to have been so wealthy that he owned *Indios*, a term that refers in this context to captured or ransomed members of "nomadic" tribes, particularly Navajos, Utes, Apaches, and Comanches. The chiste alludes to an Indio who belonged to the richest of Córdova's sons, José Antonio. Indios were generally baptized and incorporated into Mexicano households (cf. Swadesh 1974). The chiste purportedly captures one part of this process, Antonio's efforts to teach his charge how to say the Lord's Prayer.

So then "From there it's all mixed up."
You see?
My what an Our Father!
You see?
You see? . . .
Yes.
God save us! . . .
Yes,

everyone stops   all these sorts of things HAPPEN,
laughing   you see.
And now we are moving toward another CENTURY already. . . .
We are already in a another CENTURY. . . .
We are already moving toward new eh—, new— . . .
another WAY of LIFE. . . .

Three stereotypes come into play in interpreting why Chico stopped at this point in the prayer. First, Chico had just finished the passage that refers to eating. Indios, captive and otherwise, are seen as being always hungry and perpetually oriented toward food. A particularly striking embodiment of this facet of the stereotype is evident in a legend that credits two Córdovans with escaping from potential ambush by Indios in the mountains; the Mexicanos offered the Indios a stack of tortillas, thus gaining enough time to devise a means of escape (see example (7.1)). Second, Indios were born as *infieles* 'infidels', raised in the worship of "pagan" religions. These religions are believed to provide them with supernatural powers, which is why captive Indios are often credited with having enchanted buried treasure (see Chapter 7). Mexicano efforts to convert Indios are often believed to have been only marginally successful—the Indios are said to have retained their pagan ways under a facade of Christianity. The succeeding lines of the Lord's Prayer deal with transgressions against fellow human beings and with deliverance from evil. The chiste implies that Chico did not want to continue because utterance of the passages regarding sin and evil might have forced him to renounce his evil powers. The third part of the stereotype is the notion that Indios were only partially successful in learning Spanish. Inadequate competence in Spanish is thus another reason behind Chico's feeling that everything gets 'mixed up' later in the Lord's Prayer.

Mr. Córdova begins to use the phrase *todo enreda'o* in characterizing ahora (6.1:5). As soon as he does so, however, it reminds him of the chiste, and he begins to laugh. He starts to provide me with an index of the chiste in (6.1:6), but he realizes in midsentence that neither his grandson nor I would be likely to have heard it previously. He thus starts over, turning to a performance of the chiste (in 7). This concern with our ability to comprehend the chiste extends to providing genealogical information on Antonio in (10–11) and a capsule summary of the career of Pedro Córdova

(12–15). He similarly explains the presence of the Indio in (17–18), introduces Chico in (20), and gives a partial explanation of the chiste in (37–47). He repeats the punchline in (33–36, 44–45, 47). Both these concerns, providing enough background information for the audience to get the *sentido* and repeating the punch line, are characteristic of performances in the genre.

Mr. Córdova immediately proceeds to use the chiste as an analogy for the way things are getting 'all mixed up' in contemporary society. In (55), he connects the chiste performance with the statement that occasioned it (5–6), noting that this chiste originated the formula *pa' allá está todo enreda'o* 'from there on it's all mixed up'. The fact that the chiste comments metacommunicatively on both the topic under discussion and a phrase that is used to represent it (*todo enreda'o*) suggests a similarity with proverbs and scriptural allusions. But let the interpreter beware! It is "just a joke," and the commentary is somewhat oblique.

Although the chiste is drawn from antes, it hardly provides evidence of the veracity of the principles that it represents. It illustrates the concept of being 'all mixed up' by jocularly referring to the difficulties than an Indio encountered in internalizing part of Mexicano culture. This use of the Indio stereotype certainly qualifies the chiste as an example of ethnic humor. As Apte (1985:114) has noted, such jokes presuppose the existence of a set of "readymade and popular conceptualizations of the target group(s)." Let us recall, however, Paredes's (1966, 1968) demonstration that jokes told by middle-class Mexican-Americans in Texas both ridicule the "ignorance" and "backwardness" of lower-class Mexican nationals and Mexican-Americans and at the same time identify with aspects of their cultural values and sociopolitical situation.[10] Indeed, Mr. Córdova's chiste does not revolve around a simple validation of the in-group through a denigration of the target population. The chiste rather plays on an ambiguity that is apparent in the English gloss, the idea that the mix-up may be in the mind of the beholder *or* in the phenomena in question. It is thus intentionally unclear whether Chico is asserting that his knowledge of the Lord's Prayer is 'all mixed up' after this point or whether the prayer itself is 'all mixed up.'

This example provides us with an initial clue to the way that chistes differ from the genres explored in previous chapters. At this point in the conversation, Mr. Córdova could have drawn on a very common scriptural allusion regarding Christ's prediction that an abandonment of moral values would constitute a sign of his second coming. He rather provides an example of what we would describe in analytic terms as an anecdote—"a short, humorous narrative, purporting to recount a true incident involving real people" (Bauman 1986:55). My citation of Bauman's work on Anglo-Texan anecdotes in this vein is not coincidental; the communicative functions of Mr. Córdova's anecdote are remarkably similar to those identified by Bauman for the Anglo-Texan examples. Bauman argues that the anecdotes he analyzes revolve around the role of the punch line in transcending a moral polarity that is set up in the opening lines. This sudden reversal not only redistributes the dramatis personae in moral terms but provides a "subversive" and critical perspective "that takes pleasure in refusing to take ideal, normative moral expectations too seriously" (1986:75).

One could hardly ask for a better character to effect such a transformation than Chico. As an Indio, he is marginal in social, cultural, and political-economic terms, having been forcibly incorporated into Mexicano society at the lowest rung. As Douglas (1968:366) has argued, however, in jokes "a dominant pattern of social relations is challenged by another." Chico not only refuses to proceed with the acculturative task, but he asserts that the remaining lines of the Lord's Prayer are 'all mixed up'. Chico stops just at the point at which the Lord's Prayer addresses the question of the worshipers' willingness to treat one another as we ask God to treat us; Chico's statement thus seems to reflect skepticism with regard to the way that members of the community he associates with the prayer are able to embody this ideal in their own conduct. Remember that the person who is trying to teach Chico the prayer is the individual who was primarily responsible for his forced incorporation into Mexicano society, his owner. Recall as well that Antonio's father, the late Pedro Córdova, formerly 'owned' most of his fellow Córdovans, albeit in a rather different sense ('they were like slaves'), and that Antonio carried on the role of *rico* to a greater extent than his siblings. This information may contribute to the Córdovans' enjoyment of Chico's transformation from an underclass, ignorant heathen to a trickster-like exposer of moral duplicity.

Another element of the joke seems to contribute to this process of satirizing the social inequality represented by the figure of 'Antonio the WEALTHY'. On three occasions, Chico refers to his master as *padre* Antonio (28, 35) or *padre* 'Tonio (33). *Padre* plus first name is generally used in Spanish to address or refer to a priest, and it would be highly unusual to address one's father (or foster father) in this way. The oddity of the form is highlighted by its repetition, its placement within the punch line (and a replaying of the punch line), and its similarity to the title (and the opening line) of the prayer, *Padre Nuestro*. Chico's use of this highly ambiguous mode of address seems to place Antonio in the role of the priest, implying a playful and biting criticism of the way in which *ricos* such as Pedro and Antonio Córdova extended political-economic domination of their fellow villagers into religious control as well.[11] It is nonetheless true, however, that Chico also addresses Córdova as *papá* Antonio (44), and that parents assumed the role of catechists within their families until recent decades. Thus, while the sociolinguistic abnormality of *padre* Antonio points to the probable validity of the foregoing interpretation, it should be regarded as tentative.

As Fry (1963:153) notes, the punch line becomes "a meta-communicative message regarding the joke content in general (as a sample of communication)." The Lord's Prayer, a culturally central text, thus stands as a perfect model of Mexicano culture, society, and religion. Mr. Córdova's index-plus-performance of the chiste shows us how 'everything' can get 'all mixed up'. The anecdote goes far beyond this simple task, thus moving the audience towards a basic goal of la plática de los viejitos de antes—prompting the participants to think in critical and reflexive terms about moral and religious values and the way they relate to action. Anecdotes and other humorous forms use a particularly indirect means of achieving this end, the creation of a ludic vantage point from which the community and its workings can be critically examined.

A second example points to different dimensions of the oblique character of chistes. In this case, I was visiting two friends, Fabiola López de Domínguez and her husband Benjamín Domínguez, who live in Chamisal, a community north of Córdova (see Map 1 and Briggs 1985). They were sitting in an open-air garage next to their house. Shortly after we began talking, they were joined by Mrs. Domínguez's parents, Leonarda Lovato de López and José Paz López.

The conversation consisted of collective recollections, most of which were ori-

(6.2) Fabiola López de Domínguez (ca. 65), Benjamín Domínguez (ca. 65), Leonardo Lovato de López (79), José Paz López (83), CLB (30); 24 July 1983, Chamisal, New Mexico

---

LL	MUCHA FE tenía la gente antes.
BD	Siempre guardaban un día para REZAR,
	para—. . . .
CB	Hm.
LL	Y, . . . 5
	y los CATÓLICOS . . .
	paseaban los santos cuando estaba el tiempo muy SECO,
	pa' que LLOVIERA. . . .
	'Ora la gente católica no, pu's,
	yo no me acuerdo que, . . . 10
	que la gente católica/
BD	/Sacaban los SANTOS de la IGLESIA,
	y los paseaban en los *FIELDS* para que,
	que LLOVIERA.
	'Izque SACARON . . . 15
	al SANTO NIÑO, . . .
	y lo PASEARON
	pa' que cayera agua, . . .
	y cáeles un GRANIZAL. . . .
	Y otro día 'izque andaban con la, . . . 20
	con la/
JL	/Esos eran los indios,
	¿qué no?/
BD	/Mm hm,
	con la SANTA MARIA, 25

ented towards a common theme. The two men (along with Mr. López's nephew) had been arrested by employees of the National Forest Service for cutting fuelwood on grant lands adjacent to the community. Their ancestors had obtained wood in this area for two centuries. A number of illegal actions on the part of Anglo-American land speculators had, however, resulted in the sale of the grant to speculators; it was eventually traded to the U.S. Forest Service (cf. deBuys 1981, 1985). The Forest Service thus claimed that residents had to secure permits to cut fuelwood and abide by regulations greatly limiting where wood, particularly live or "green" wood, could be harvested. Given the usufruct that had been enjoyed by local residents, the arrest of Mr. Domínguez, Mr. López, and the nephew came as quite a shock. At the time of the discussion (1983), the case was still pending; most of the conversation accordingly centered around the case. The Domínguezes and Lópezes alluded to the many ways that their ancestors had used the grant lands in bygone days. The chiste presented in example (6.2) emerged quite suddenly in the midst of a collective recollection.

       English translation

    The people had A LOT OF FAITH in bygone days.
    They would always keep a day for PRAYER,
    for—. . . .
        Hm.
    And, . . .
    and the CATHOLICS . . .
    used to take the images of the saints around when the weather was
       very DRY,
    so that it WOULD RAIN. . . .
    Nowadays Catholic people don't, well,
    I don't remember that, . . .
    that the Catholic people/
    /They used to take the IMAGES out of the CHURCH,
    and they used to take them around the *FIELDS* so that,
    that it WOULD RAIN.
        It is said that they TOOK OUT . . .
        the HOLY CHILD, . . .
            and they TOOK HIM AROUND
            so that it would rain, . . .
            and down came a HAILSTORM. . . .
                And the next day it's said that they were
                   going around with, . . .
                with the/
                     | /They were [Pueblo] Indians,
                     | right?/
                     | /Mm hm,
                with the VIRGIN MARY,

```
CB                          | sí
BD                          pasearon a la Santa María.
                            'Izque les dijieron,
                            "¡PA' QUÉ?
                            ¿Pa' qué traen 'ora a la Santa MARÍA?"           30

                            "¡Pa' que vea la MIERDA que hizo su HIJO!". . . .

LL                          Ese hijo ((ese)) de la Santa María
                            era DIOS,
                                   ¡ves!
BD                          El Santo Niño.                                   35
LL                          E–, era el nie–/
FL   Y luego antes también la gente
     no—,
            ¿qué no?
     también/                                                               40
BD   /Eran muy religiosos.
FL   Yah.
```

At first glance, this popular chiste[12] follows the pattern that emerges from performances of proverbs and scriptural allusions. In discussing the religious faith of the elders of bygone days, Mrs. López exemplifies this religiosity with reference to the practice of taking the image of the patron saint and perhaps other images through the fields in times of drought (cf. Briggs 1983; Brown 1941; Brown et al. 1978:185–86; J. E. Espinosa 1967; Rael 1942). This leads Mr. Domínguez to provide an interpretation of this subject by performing a chiste about a specific, if fictive, procession.

Such a description would, however, fail to "get the joke," and it would misconstrue the way the chiste relates to the surrounding discourse. The chiste does not reiterate the truth of the talk of the elders of bygone days, nor does it bring the wisdom of los viejitos de antes to bear in legitimizing the preceding point about the religiosity of the deceased elders. To the contrary, the chiste provides all four elders with a means of *distancing* themselves from one element of this cultural tradition.

The discord begins to emerge in Mrs. López's reference to *los católicos* (6.2:6). Thus far in the discourse, all four elders have focused on the talk of one or more of their community's elders of bygone days. As is to be expected, the two couples cite la plática de los viejitos de antes as setting a legal and historical precedent for such actions as cutting fuelwood, farming, and herding. In (6, 9, and 11), however, Mrs. López refers to the procession participants as los católicos. Although all four elders were baptized in the Catholic Church, they have converted to an Evangelical sect. Their church forbids veneration of the Virgin and the saints and of holy images. When she uses the phrase *la gente católica* 'the Catholic people' (9 and 11), Mrs.

| yes
they took the Virgin Mary around.
It's said that they asked them,
"WHY?
Why are you now carrying around
the Virgin MARY?"
"so that she'll see the SHIT that her
SON DID!". . . .
That son of the Virgin Mary
was GOD,
you see!
The Holy Child.
He was the so–/

everyone laughs

And then in bygone days the people
didn't—,
            right?
also/
/They used to be very religious.
Yah.

López looks at the other three family members. Her words effect a realignment of the Lópezes and Domínguezes with respect to Mexicano social and religious structure; by distancing themselves from los católicos, these individuals step out of their roles as elders who assert traditional values and identify themselves as members of another religion. Mr. Domínguez's utterance of the term *MIERDA* 'SHIT', the only use of a taboo word during this conversation, underlines his critical and ludic departure from his role as a representative of the elders of bygone days.

The coherence between Mrs. López's statement and Mr. Domínguez's chiste is thus more than topical. Mr. Domínguez not only focuses on his mother-in-law's point, but takes this distancing process much further. This is a popular chiste, one familiar to all present. When performed by Mexicano Catholics, it pokes gentle fun at the once serious belief that such processions made in times of crisis would gain the Virgin's or the saints' intercession. It also plays on the tendency to interact with holy images as if they were rather like human beings (cf. Brown et al. 1978: 131–32).[13] One of the major points of differentiation between Protestants and Evangelicals on the one hand and Catholics on the other has been the assertion by members of the former groups that the veneration of images is idolatrous and superstitious.[14] Such attempts "to show the saint ⟨or the Virgin⟩ the condition of the fields" are cited as the height of religious naïveté.

The humor of the chiste plays precisely upon such naïveté. It takes the process of attributing human qualities to holy images to the logical extreme of casting the images of the Holy Child and the Virgin in the roles of naughty child and remonstrative mother. In her interpretation of the punch line ('so that she'll see the SHIT that her SON DID!') Mrs. López suggests that the participants in this apocryphal procession went so far as to forget that "that son of the Virgin Mary was GOD, you see!" When told by members of an Evangelical church, the chiste can be used to support the view that Catholicism promotes an idolatrous and naïve form of Christianity. Mr. Domín- guez was interested in convincing me of the strong points of his faith; on a previous visit he had tried to convert me, feeling that it was his religious duty. The chiste performance enabled the four elders to express their lack of identification with this element of their own past despite their solidarity with most of the talk of the elders of bygone days.

Mr. Domínguez's performance shows, as Douglas (1968:373) put it, how "the joke consists in challenging a dominant structure and belittling it." Levine's (1977) powerful analysis of black folklore and political struggle demonstrates the way that jokes can play a key role in creating and recreating a collective self-image and expos- ing prejudice and discrimination, while at the same time permitting "the articulation of criticism concerning characteristics of the race that troubled and often shamed certain members" (1977:330). Levine argues that jokes that ridicule religion and black preachers reflect both affection for and a critical perspective on the role of reli- gion in Afro-American life (1977:329). Catholicism similarly enjoys an important although not unchallenged role among Mexicanos. It is closely connected with a number of elements (such as carved images, wakes for saints and for the dead, pro- cessions and feast days, etc.) that were and to some extent continue to be central "cultural emblems" (Singer 1984) or representations of collective identity. As sym- bols of a "folk religion" (cf. Yoder 1974), images, wakes, processions, and feast days have faced strong challenges from Mexican and American ecclesiastical officials and, during the past hundred years, from Protestant and Evangelical groups (cf. Rendón 1953; Walker 1983; Weigle 1976).

The Mexicano population is thus stratified and often divided in religious terms, and these divisions have produced social and political repercussions. Mr. Domínguez's performance provides an example of a chiste that reflects and comments on these schisms, while at the same time subtly articulating the location of himself and his family within this socioreligious matrix. This process forms part of a larger process of using the ludic space of the joke to cope creatively with the conflicting loyalties that are part of being a Spanish-speaking member of American society (cf. Jordan 1981; Paredes 1966, 1968).

CHISTE-TELLING SESSIONS

I have argued that chistes seldom relate directly to the topic under discussion by straightforwardly asserting its validity. In some instances, the chiste's relation to the topic is oblique, and in others it states a contrary view. In either case, the chiste bears an important similarity to performances of scriptural allusions and proverbs in that the chiste is selected in accordance with the tenor of the situation at hand.[15] Another type of setting departs even further from a contextual focus. Here the orientation toward the folkloric text becomes so strong that it begins to generate a context of its own. This process occurs with different levels of intensity. In the less pronounced type, a discussion that lacks a pedagogical focus will give rise to a situation in which a number of chistes are inserted at various points. Here the chistes are separated by conversational interludes, and at least some of them are selected for their relevance to the current topic of the conversation.

An excellent example is provided by an exchange between my New Mexican colleague, Julián Josué Vigil, and his parents, Lilia Pacheco de Vigil and Lázaro Vigil. I had known Julián for some years but had not met his parents before this occasion. The videotape was made in front of their home in Guadalupita, located near Mora on the other side of the Sangre de Cristo Mountains from Córdova (see Map 1). Although I was sitting with the family at the time of the conversation, I was not an active participant in the telling of chistes.

Much of the preceding conversation had focused on Mrs. Vigil's fears about being left alone while her husband was employed as a shepherd in Colorado. Mr. Vigil had just returned from picking choke cherries from one of their trees, and Julián and I were eating them. Julián then asked me if I knew the chistes concerning Count Manchado. (The surname means 'soiled'; the chistes are modeled on those about the eighteenth-century Baron von Münchhausen.) I replied in the negative, and Julián then narrated a chiste concerning one of Count Manchado's hunting trips. Lacking bullets, he packed his muzzle-loader with choke cherry pits and fired. *No, no le hizo nada, pero el siguente año, andaba un venado con un arbolito en la cabeza* 'No, it didn't do anything to it, but the following year there was a deer with a little tree on his head'.

Mrs. Vigil was not paying much attention to her son's performance of the chiste, and she did not laugh after Julián uttered the punch line. Shortly afterwards, however, she told one of her own. While her son and husband were away for a few minutes, Mrs. Vigil again took up the subject of her isolation. (See example (6.3).)

Mrs. Vigil later related a similar tale in which she and another woman were alone on the ranch in which her husband herded sheep. A Mexican national who was employed on the ranch acted menacingly and refused to leave the ranchhouse. When the boss arrived, Mrs. Vigil asked him to force the man to leave before she had to shoot him.

The anecdote about the matches had two important effects on the course of the conversation. First, Mrs. Vigil transformed my perception of her, which had a profound impact upon our later interactions. When first introduced to her, I had gained the impression that she was somewhat helpless. She had broken both of her feet, and she talked at some length about how difficult it was for her to walk. Her husband had

(6.3) Lilia Pacheco de Vigil (68), Lázaro Vigil (69), Julián Josué Vigil (37), CLB (30);
18 August 1983, Guadalupita, New Mexico

LP Aquí en esta casa . . .
vive un BORRACHO.
Tiene una pensión de VETERANO. . . .
Y ahi se JUNTAN—. . . .
'Ora no está.   5
Sí, 'ora se lo llevaron sus hijas
pa' salvarle poco dinero,
porque lo dejaron hasta SIN QUE COMER. . . .
Se junta TODA LA BORRACHERA,
y ahi venden MARIHUANA.   10
¡Oh, es una cosa TERRIBLE cuando él está aquí! . . .
JV ¡No estés hablando de Fernando!
LP Y cuando yo estaba SOLA,
la primavera,
que había TANTO GARRERO,   15
unos *CHARACTERS* tan BRUTOS caen de 'ONDEQUIERA,
da miedo,
hasta en el DÍA les tiene uno miedo, . . .
Y no me—. . . .
Tenía mi perrito ahi . . .   20
cerquita,
y la perrita que ladrara siquiera
si alguien llegaba. . . .
No me venía acostando algunas noches . . .
hasta como las dos de la mañana.   25
Ahi me acostaba en el sofas vistida
CB   sí/
LP /del MIEDO que les tenía. . . .
JV No sabe uno de 'onde llegan a la borrachera/
LP /Y si quiénes, quién, quiénes SERÁN/   30
CB   /¡trabajoso!/
LP /a la MARIHUANA.
Sí, to[d]avía los borrachos no son tan MALOS. . . .
Y había NOCHES,
hubo como TRES NOCHES que yo no me acosté hasta después las dos de la mañana,   35

que no se empezaban ir CARROS y se AQUIETABA. . . .
Y tenía mis perritos ahi.
Sí una noche LLEGÓ EL VECINO . . .
│ *he's harmless,*
│ pero tiene un *PARASITE* ahi   40
│ que . . .
│ es mal.
│ Ese se le prende SIEMPRE; . . .
│ ese es MAL MUCHACHO. . . .
Y una NOCHE estaba caendo AGUA, . . .   45
eran las diez y media dc la NOCHE . . .
cuando tocó en la puerta.
"¿QUIÉN?"

English translation

---

points	Here in this house . . .
	lives a DRUNKARD.
	He has a VETERAN'S PENSION. . . .
	And there get TOGETHER—. . . .
	He's not ⟨there⟩ now.
	Yes, now his daughters took him away
	to save him some money,
	because ⟨his buddies⟩ even leave him WITHOUT FOOD. . . .
CB nods	ALL THE DRUNKARDS get TOGETHER,
	and over there they sell MARIHUANA.
JV comes	Oh, it's just TERRIBLE when he's here! . . .
JV laughs	Don't go talking about Fernando!
	And when I was ALONE
	this past spring,
	there was SO MUCH RIFF-RAFF,
	some REALLY ROUGH *CHARACTERS* come from ALL OVER,
	they frighten you,
	you're even afraid of them in the DAYTIME, . . .
JV sits down	And I wouldn't— . . . .
LP points with head	I had my little dog there . . .
	close by,
	and at least ⟨its mother⟩ used to bark
	if someone approached. . . .
	I wouldn't go to bed some nights . . .
	until around two in the morning.
	I would lie down fully dressed on the sofa,
	yes/
	/I was SO afraid of them. . . .
turning to CB	You don't know where the drunkards come from/
	and what, what, what they'll BE LIKE/
	/that's hard!/
	/on MARIHUANA.
	Drunkards alone aren't so BAD. . . .
	And there were NIGHTS,
	there were maybe THREE NIGHTS that I didn't
	get to bed until after two in the morning,
	when CARS started leaving and things GOT QUIET. . . .
	And I had my little dogs here.

Yes, one night THE NEIGHBOR CAME . . .

> *he's harmless,*
> but he has a *PARASITE* there
> who . . .
> really is bad.
> He hangs around ALL THE TIME; . . .
> he is a BAD FELLOW. . . .

And one NIGHT it was RAINING, . . .
it was around ten-thirty at NIGHT . . .
when he knocked on the door.
"WHO'S THERE?"

"YO, BEN."
"¿QUÉ QUERÍA?" . . .   50
"Vinía a que me prestara unos FÓSFOROS." . . .
     Y le dije, "Yo no puedo abrir la puerta cuando estoy SOLA,"

     le dije. . . .
     Por ahi por la RENDIJA

     cuando estaba aquel otro,   55
     la otra TRANCA,
     por ahi por la rendija le di unos FÓSFOROS.

          "Y NO ME TENGA MIEDO, COMADRE."

          "No, no le tengo MIEDO," le dije,

          "pero yo no ABRO."   60
          "NO TENGA MIEDO.
          Anda el Sammy CONMIGO."
          "NO," les dicía,
          yo estaba en el oscuro,
          "NO, no tengo miedo.   65
          Yo traigo la PISTOLA en la MANO,"
          le dije. . . .

JV   ¡EL CUENTO de la pistola de LUPE
                es la cosa más bonita! . . .
CB   ¡Ni que MIEDO! . . .   70
JV   Habiendo PISTOLA,
                ¿quién tiene MIEDO?
LP   No la TRAIBA,
                pero ahi la tenía CERQUITA
                pa' si se me iban a METER.   75

                No los iba a dejar ENTRAR. . . .
          Pues, asina me dijo,
          "NO TENGA MIEDO, comadre."
          "No, no tengo MIEDO," le dije,
          "traigo la PISTOLA en la MANO.   80
          "Vamos," le dijo,
          y se FUE. . . .
     Un día de estos juntamos capulín,
     y hago un poquita de *jelly*. . . .
JV   Como e–, José, ¿qué no andaba?   85
     No, no la, . . .
     la mujer de José.
LP   La mujer, 'izque traiba una pistolita aquí/
JV   /yah/
LP   /en el seno. . . .   90
JV   Andaba uno ahi medio ENAMORA'O con ella,
     y . . .
     feeling his way around,
          tú sabes,

"ME, BEN."

"WHAT MIGHT YOU WANT?" . . .

"I came to borrow some MATCHES." . . .

And I told him, "I can't open the door when
  I'm ALONE,"

I told him. . . .

Through the CRACK THERE ⟨between door
  and frame⟩

where there was another,

another LOCK,

through the crack there I gave him some
  MATCHES.

"AND DON'T BE AFRAID OF ME,
  COMADRE."

No, I'm not AFRAID OF YOU," I told
  him,

"but I won't OPEN UP."

"DON'T BE AFRAID.

Sammy is WITH ME."

"NO," I told them,

where I stood it was dark,

"NO, I'm not afraid.

JV and CB laugh   I've got my PISTOL in my HAND,"

I told him. . . .

> The STORY about LUPE's PISTOL
> is the most beautiful thing! . . .

CB laughs   No FEAR THERE! . . .

> Having a PISTOL,
> who's AFRAID!
> I didn't HAVE IT,

JV and CB laugh
> but it was NEARBY
> in case they wanted to FORCE THEIR
>   WAY IN.
> I wasn't going to LET THEM IN. . . .

Well, this is what he said to me,

"DON'T BE AFRAID, comadre."

"No, I'm not AFRAID," I told him,

"I've got my PISTOL in my HAND."

subdued tone of voice   "Let's go," he said

and he LEFT. . . .

One of these days we'll gather choke cherries,

And I'll make a little bit of *jelly*. . . .

Like, uh, wasn't it José?

No, no, his, . . .

José's wife.

points to chest   His wife, it's said, had a pistol here/

  /yah/

/by her breast. . . .

Along came someone kind of IN LOVE with her

and . . .

feeling his way around,

  you know,

y pega en la PISTOLITA,   95
ya no quiso NA'A con ELLA. . . .
CB   Ahí se hizo. . . .
LP   Una vez que fue un MEXICANO allá en Antonito—. . . .
     Yo no les tenía miedo a los mexicanos de México. . . .

---

continued working on a sheep ranch in southern Colorado, thus leaving her alone for extended periods. She had recently asked him to retire in order to keep her from having to remain alone in Guadalupita.

The beginning of the chiste invoked this impression with, as I see in hindsight, great artistry. She noted that she had been left alone in the spring, living in fear of the drunkards who lived nearby. After describing the way this situation had affected her, to the point of sleeping, fully clothed, on the couch and staying awake until two in the morning, she related her moment of maximum vulnerability, when the worst rogue of all came to her door late at night. The set up of the chiste thus greatly reinforced my portrait of Mrs. Vigil as weak and vulnerable.

Instead of succumbing to her fear, however, Mrs. Vigil responded with one of the strongest images of power throughout the Spanish-speaking Southwest United States—the portrait of the isolated Mexicana, defending her home and honor 'with ⟨her⟩ pistol in ⟨her⟩ hand.' An important work by Paredes (1958) demonstrates the saliency of this phrase and the richness of the cultural, political, and folkloric associations that it bears. The corrido 'ballad' of Gregorio Cortéz accords the phrase great prominence; although this corrido centers on cultural conflict in the border region of southern Texas, it is also sung in northern New Mexico. As Paredes notes, the corrido evokes an image of unusual strength and a willingness to risk one's life in order to protect key values. Interestingly, Mrs. Vigil later notes (73–74) that the pistol was not really in her hand but was nearby, which suggests that her statement "*traigo la PISTOLA en la MANO*" "'I've got my PISTOL in my HAND'" constitutes a literary trope and not just a literal account of the facts.

The strength of this image served her well. I laughed quite heartily at the time, as did Julián. I realized immediately that she had been playing the role of a poor and pathetic little old lady for comic effect. Her artistry was also revealed in the ingenious way she disguised the chiste, which at first I thought was a personal narrative that would highlight Mrs. Vigil's vulnerability, not a humorous anecdote that forms part of her repertoire of chistes. By carefully leading me into this trap, she maximized the incongruity between the initial image of weakness and the strength of the pistola allusion. Julián, of course, had heard the story numerous times; his appreciation of the performance emerged from awareness of the way his mother had beguiled me (as he later informed me). He immediately suggested to his mother that she tell a similar

and he hits the LITTLE PISTOL,
then he didn't want to have ANYTHING to do with HER. . . .
    So much for that. . . .
One time a MEXICAN came over in Antonito ⟨Colorado⟩—. . . .
I wasn't afraid of the Mexicanos from Mexico. . . .

---

tale, the account of Lupe's pistol (68–69, 85–96). She returned instead (in 83) to her preoccupation with her choke cherry trees. Mrs. Vigil did not discard the weakness/strength dialectic at this point but juxtaposed the two again in a narrative concerning the way she stood up to a threatening ranch hand in Colorado (98ff.).

The existence of a connection between women's humor and gender roles is hardly confined to Mrs. Vigil's performance. Research by Johnson (1973), Mitchell (1978), and Spradley and Mann (1975) shows that joking provides women with strategies for gender interactions. The surprise that I experienced on hearing the punch line emerged from the way that it succeeded in transforming my image of Mrs. Vigil. Note that the anecdote deals with gender issues; the female protagonist reverses the direction of the gender-based asymmetry, such that she becomes the controlling and potentially violent force. Mrs. Vigil stands in the roles of performer of the anecdote and participant in the interaction. The power of the performance lies in the extension of the gender-role transformation from the anecdote to the interaction.

Douglas's (1968) work on jokes prompts us to examine the way that chistes are "expressive of the social situations in which they are occur" and the way they relate to broader patterns of social relations and cultural epistemology. Beyond its immediate social interactional effects, the anecdote produced a small-scale inquiry into contradictions in gender relations. Male-female asymmetry is by no means absent in Mexicano society; nevertheless, as Swadesh (1974) has argued, gender roles exhibit a surprising degree of flexibility. Indeed, the feminine ideal of being *muy mujerota* 'a very brave and strong woman' is based not on passivity and deference to males but on demonstrating physical strength and the ability to stand up for one's own rights as well as those of one's family and community.

Mrs. Vigil clearly presents both images of women and both sets of gender roles in the anecdote; women's ability to subvert domination and reveal personal independence and power certainly triumphs. Douglas (1968:366) has characterized jokes as "the image of the levelling of hierarchy." As Limón (1982:157) has pointed out, Douglas concludes that the joke "is frivolous in that it produces no real alternative, only an exhilarating sense of freedom from form in general" (1968:365). Mrs. Vigil's performance provides a demonstration of the way that women's humor tell can engender critical examinations of gender roles that bear the potential for producing real and lasting changes.

The question remains as to how this process is rooted in the form of the performance. Sherzer (1985) notes that the initial "set up" of a joke implicitly invokes one or more sets of presuppositions. The punch line brings these assumptions to the surface by reframing the point of view that was established in the set up. Bauman (1986) points to a number of reasons that quoted speech plays such a crucial role in punch lines. The use of quoted speech allows the narrator not only to invoke the words used by the characters but to represent (through prosody, voice quality, gestures, etc.) the ideological basis of what was reportedly said. Bauman (1986:70) similarly argues that "the punch line contains within it two voices—its own and that of the preceding speaker upon which it has wrought a transformation." Note how carefully Mrs. Vigil sets up these two voices, repeating the lines *NO ME TENGA MIEDO* and *No, no le tengo MIEDO* twice before springing *Yo traigo la PISTOLA en la MANO* on her audience. The "double-voicedness" of the punch line is underlined by the protagonist's appropriation of the would-be intruder's own words (as appropriately modified grammatically). The surprise lies in the realization that the two denials of fear are motivated by entirely different sets of motives. Although the male

(6.4) Lilia Pacheco de Vigil (68), Julián Josué Vigil (37), CLB (30); 18 August 1983, Guadalupita, New Mexico

---

LP	Una vez teníamos un PATO . . .	
	que PISABA las PATAS,	
	y luego PISABA las GALLINAS;	
	y TODAS gallinas que pisaba el pato/	
JV	/oh, pobrecito/	5
LP	/¡LAS MATABA!	
	¡ERA UN DIABLO!	
	¡HE WAS A SEX MANIAC!	
JV	No, pus,	
	se necesitaba una PATA,	10
	el POBRE.	
LP	No, pus, TENÍA.	
JV	No TENÍA.	
LP	Sí TENÍA PATAS,	
	sí TENÍA.	15
JV	Oh, yah, yah,	
	pero ya cuando se murieron las pobres.	
	Bueno,	
	no eran más que dos,	
LP	sí,	20
	bueno,	
	es suficiente/	
JP	/*they, they need a HAREM,*	
	los POBRES.	
LP	¡SÍ!	25

voice implies that Mrs. Vigil can trust (read depend on) him, her words bear the unstated assumption that she is capable of defending herself without relying on anyone. Mrs. Vigil has hidden this presupposition all along just as carefully as she had concealed her pistol.

Another effect of the performance was to transform the conversation into a chiste-telling session. Although Julián is an excellent performer of chistes, his mother's performances remained centerstage. When Mrs. Vigil fails to follow up Julián's invitation to tell about Lupe's pistol, he provides a report rather than a performance of the story. Mrs. Vigil then relates an account that is structurally quite analogous to the anecdote, 'I've got my PISTOL in my HAND.' Although it elicits some laughter, the response is much more subdued this time, because the process of transforming an image of weakness into one of strength had already taken place. However, Mrs. Vigil had not exhausted the potential of the chiste for shattering personae. Mrs. Vigil is a devout Catholic, and her behavior is quite circumspect. Her piety provided a fitting backdrop for the performance of two chistes, presented in example (6.4).

Mrs. Vigil plays upon a juxtaposition of two sets of roles or social images in these

English translation

One time we had a DUCK . . .
that used to "GET" the FEMALE DUCKS,
and then used to "GET" the CHICKENS;
and ALL the chickens that the duck used
to "get,"/
/oh, the poor thing/

CB *laughs*   /HE KILLED THEM!
HE WAS A DEVIL!
HE WAS A SEX MANIAC!
No, well,
he needed a FEMALE DUCK,
the POOR THING.
No, well, he HAD ONE.

drops head   He did NOT HAVE ONE.
nods   Yes, he HAD FEMALE DUCKS,
he DID HAVE SOME.
Oh yeah, yeah,
but after the poor things died.

points with 2 fingers   Okay,
there were only two,
yes,
okay,
that's enough/

looks at CB   /*they, they need a HAREM*,
JV and CB laugh   the POOR THINGS.
YES!

L⟨ueg⟩o que SÍ que mataba las GALLINAS,
TODAS.

JV	El pobre las lastimaba.	
LP	Y las pescó LUIS—,	
	lo pescó LUIS,	30
	y lo ENCERRÓ en una JAULITA, . . .	
	y lo ASISTIÓ	
	pa' matarlo pa' COMÉRNO(S)LO. . . .	
	Y venían	
	y les decía	35
	que si POR QUE estaba ese pato AHI. . . .	
	"*For* RAPE,"	
	les decía. . . .	
JV	Y, al fin, ¿se murió de viejo?	
LP	NO,/	40
JV	/¿Hasta no(s) lo comimos ése?/	
LP	/le, le, le dieron mucho MAIZ,	
	y lo ENGORDARON,	
	y un día no(s) COMIMOS.	
JV	Ya ni me acuerdo yo.	45
LP	¡No(s) lo COMIMOS, POR DIABLO!	
JV	Yah.	
LP	Estaba como el CHUPILOTE/	
JV	/¡*For* RAPE!/	
LP	/como el GALLO AQUEL.	50
JV	Sí.	
	¡*For* RAPE!	
LP	¿No oístes tú el CUENTO del GALLO? . . .	
	Tenía un RANCHERO un GALLO, . . .	
	que ya no HALLABA que hacer con ÉL;	55
	pisaba las GALLINAS de ÉL,	
	LAS de los VECINOS,	
	las PATAS,	
	las GANZAS,	
	y TODO.	60
	¡NO HALLABA QUE HACER	
	CON ÉL! . . .	

	Y . . .	
	dijo que lo iba a MATAR,	
	¿qué no?	
JV	No.	65
	"Te vas a MATAR de. . . ."/	
LP	/Oh, sí,	
	que se iba a MATAR,	
	le dijo.	
JV	Yah.	70
LP	Y se hizo él MUERTO, . . .	
	se acostó y parecía que estaba MUERTO. . . .	
	Y fue un GALLO,	
	y lo dijo, "¿qué pasa?"	
	—otro gallo. . . .	75

So then, he DID kill the CHICKENS,
ALL OF THEM.
The poor thing used to injure them.
And Luis caught THEM—,
Luis caught HIM,
and he SHUT HIM UP in a CAGE, . . .
and he TOOK CARE OF HIM,
so that we could kill him and EAT HIM. . . .
And [people] would come,
and they would ask
WHY that duck was ⟨in⟩ THERE. . . .
"*For RAPE,*"
all laugh   he would tell them. . . .
And, finally, did he die from old age?
shakes head laughing   NO/
/You mean we ate him?/
/they, they, they gave him lots of CORN
and FATTENED HIM UP,
and one day we ATE HIM.
I'd forgotten about that.
We ATE HIM for ⟨being such a⟩ DEVIL!
to CB   Yeah.
He was like the BUZZARD/
/*For RAPE!*/
/like THAT ROOSTER.
Yes.
to CB   "*For RAPE!*"
CB shakes head   Did you hear the STORY about the ROOSTER? . . .
A RANCHER had a ROOSTER, . . .
and he no longer KNEW what to do with HIM;
he would 'get' the CHICKENS,
the NEIGHBORS' ⟨CHICKENS⟩,
the DUCKS,
the GEESE,
and EVERYTHING.
HE DIDN'T
KNOW WHAT
TO DO WITH
HIM! . . .
leans forward   And . . .
he told ⟨the rooster⟩ that he was going to KILL HIM,
turns to JV | right?
No.
"You're going to KILL YOURSELF by. . . ."/
leans back |/Oh, yes,
that he was going to KILL HIMSELF,
⟨the rancher⟩ told him.
| Yah.
stiffens body   And he played DEAD, . . .
he lay down and it looked like he was DEAD. . . .
raises head   And along came a ROOSTER
and asked him, "What's wrong?"
—another rooster. . . .

"¡Shush!"
le dijo.
    Andaba unos CHUPILOTES arriba,

    pensaron que estaba MUERTO.
| Y que él lo que QUERÍA—   80

        "Lo que QUIERO es que abajen
        las CHUPILOTAS

        pa' PISARLAS,"
        le dijo. . . .

CB   ¡Ay qué!
        ¡Shush!   85
JV   ¡Shush!
                 ¡Gallito muy POTENTE! . . .

LP OH, ¡ese pato estaba TERRIBLE!/
JV   /Yah.
    ¡Daba hasta VERGÜENZA con él!/   90
JV   /Yah. . . .
    ¡Ése sí era un COSA MALA! . . .
JV Oh, pobrecito necesitaba—. . . .
    Hasta un toro tiene de CIEN VACAS ahi en su–,
    SUELTAS. . . .   95
LP Y luego cuando venía llegando su *GRANDMA*
    parecía que ADREDE,/
JV /ADREDE, sí/
LP /ADREDE parecía;
    le daba hasta VERGÜENZA con él.   100

---

chistes. I had gained an impression of her as being religious and circumspect. Her conversation until this point had revolved around her family and her domestic concerns (her house, garden, fruit trees, pets, etc.). Although the pistola anecdote had dispelled the illusion of weakness, her piety and modesty remained unchallenged. The first of these two chistes emerged from the domestic domain as well, focusing on a pet duck that had belonged to the Vigils. The opening formula *una vez* 'one time' signaled the beginning of a narrative. The status of the story as a humorous anecdote, and a ribald one at that, became apparent once Mrs. Vigil used the verb *pisar*. The verb is generally used in the sense of "to run over" or "to step on." When used in reference to sexual relations, it euphemistically conveys an aggressive sexuality on the part of the male. The humor of both chistes is also aided by the fact that the objects of the duck's and the rooster's attacks are consistently marked + female and + plural with the suffix *-as*. This also sets up a relationship of grammatical parallelism between series of lines that refer to the female birds.

each "shush!"
accompanied by
raising of index finger
to lips, then looking up
and pointing to sky

"Shush!"
he told him.
　Some BUZZARDS were
　　⟨flying⟩ overhead;
　they thought he was DEAD.
　And what ⟨the rooster⟩
　　WANTED —
　　　"What I WANT is for
　　　the FEMALE BUZ-
　　　ZARDS to DESCEND
　　　so I can 'GET' THEM,"
　　he told him. . . .
　　　　Imagine that!

all laugh
points to sky
points to sky laughing

Shush!
Shush!

　　　What a VIRILE
　　　　young
　　　ROOSTER! . . .

Oh, that duck was TERRIBLE!/
　/Yah.
We were even ASHAMED of him!/
　/Yah. . . .

shakes head
He really was AWFUL! . . .
Oh, the poor little thing needed—. . . .

JV and CB laugh
Even a bull has A HUNDRED COWS in his—,
ON THE LOOSE. . . .
And then when your *GRANDMA WOULD ARRIVE,*
it looked as if [he did it] ON PURPOSE, yes/

nods
/ON PURPOSE,
/[he did it] ON PURPOSE, it seemed;
we were even ASHAMED of him.

Code switching helps create the humor of the first chiste. Reference to aggressive sexuality is expressed both in Spanish (*¡ERA UN DIABLO!*) and English ('HE WAS A SEX MANIAC'). The humor of the punch line is created in a similar fashion. Luis, Julián's older brother, penned the duck in a cage. Luis provides visitors to the Vigils' with an explanation of the duck's encarceration. A naïve interpretation of *que si POR QUE estaba ese pato AHI* 'WHY that duck was ⟨in⟩ THERE' would concern the family's plans with respect to the duck, the fact that they were fattening him up in order to eat him. However, the punch line, *'For RAPE!'* provides a translation of *POR QUE* as 'for what ⟨reason⟩,' that is, "what has he done." The term *rape* reinterprets his actions in English in keeping with a legal code. His enclosure in the cage thus constitutes encarceration for a capital offense, for which he would soon be executed.

This provides a fine example of the "double-voicedness" that Bauman (1986 : 70) describes as the key to the form and meaning of punch lines. A high degree of cohesion is apparent between the set up (the duck's propensities, his capture, the arrival of unnamed friends and relatives, and the question they pose) and the punch line. Framing a punch line as an answer is an excellent way to establish such cohesion, given the fact that the posing of a question-answer sequence leads the listener to expect that the answer will consist of the information that has been requested (or will at least relate to the question; cf. Levinson 1983:105–107). A number of studies show, however, that the relationship between questions and answers is by not always simple and direct (cf. Briggs 1986; Churchill 1978; Cicourel 1974b; Goffman 1981:40–48; Halliday and Hasan 1976:206–17; Herzfeld 1981; Jefferson 1972; Levinson 1983:293, 303–07). A question-answer sequence thus provides an ideal frame for the punch line of an anecdote or joke; it creates a strong relationship of cohesion between the punch line and the set up, yet without specifying exactly what relationship the two units of discourse will bear.

Bauman argues that "double-voicedness" revolves around the punch line's appropriation of the preceding line. The character that utters the punch line incorporates the words of another character in order to transform the meaning of those words. How does Mrs. Vigil accomplish this? Raskin (1985) argues that jokes revolve around the production of utterances that could be interpreted in keeping with two (or more) *scripts,* opposing bodies of "knowledge of certain routines, standard procedures, basic situations, etc." (1985:81). Most jokes have a "semantic-switch trigger" that prompts the listener to discover a second, generally hidden script.

The duck chiste revolves around three major sets of scripts. First, much of the conversation concerns the activities that relate to the physical setting—the Vigils' home and its surroundings, which we might term a domestic script. The appearance of *PISABA* 'USED TO "GET"' in (2) shifts the discourse to a sexual script. The dangers of excessive sexuality provide an interpretive frame throughout the remainder of the set up. 'For RAPE' then prompts a shift to a legal script in which the duck's actions are reinterpreted as a criminal offense. The humor comes from imposing two additional sets of scripts (sexual and legal) on a series of actions (fattening and eating a duck) that would ordinarily be seen as an unremarkable domestic event. The listener's assumptions are also violated with respect to the relationship between discourse and event. The meaning of the question (*Que si POR QUE estaba ese pato AHI*) hangs on future events as carried out by humans (i.e., "What do you plan to do with the duck?"); the meaning of the punch line, however, directs the listener towards the duck's actions in the past. This incongruity is heightened by the fact that one of the basic presuppositions of legal scripts is that they generally apply to humans, not ducks.

This prompts Mrs. Vigil to perform the rooster chiste. I must admit to having exercised what might be termed "folkloristic license" in shaking my head in response to Mrs. Vigil's query (53); Julián had related the chiste to both his mother and myself on separate occasions. Mrs. Vigil frames the chiste by providing a classic introductory formula—*estaba como el* . . . '[he? it?] was like the . . .' (cf. Reyna 1973:227–28). The punch line of this chiste also involves forcing the audience to reinterpret the meaning of an event. Having been led to believe that the rooster was going to kill himself through excessive sexual activity (66–69), we discover that he is playing dead in order to catch a female buzzard. Mrs. Vigil is less facile with this chiste. Her version is shorter than that of her son (which I do not have on tape), and she fails to note the presence of the circling buzzards before giving the punchline. She is thus forced to explain the rooster's "Shush!" after uttering the punchline. She also partially "gives away" the nature of the rooster's actions before uttering the punch line by noting that the rooster "played dead." This joke also circulates in English throughout the United States; in other Spanish and English versions that I have heard, the rooster is described as having been "found dead."

By this point in the interaction, Mrs. Vigil has clearly established her identity as an independent, strong personality who is capable of using humor in creating and transforming her social persona and reflecting on societal values. She explored another means of transforming my perception of her in performing these sexual chistes. Research by Green (1977) suggests that the performance of "bawdy" humor by older women is not uncommon; the postmenopausal phase of a women's life brings greater license in a number of societies (cf. Jacobs 1959:177, 1960; Weigle 1978:4). Reyna (1973:255) notes that women often tell sexual jokes in Texas. I have also heard sexual chistes performed by young and middle-aged women in northern New Mexico. Although impiety outside the play frame might endanger a woman's status as a respected *viejita* or *anciana*, chistes create a ludic sphere in which speakers may bring sexual mores and moves to the fore with relative impunity.

However, the humor goes far beyond a simple exploitation of the opportunity to broach sexual topics. Note that Mrs. Vigil does not leave her modesty and piety behind altogether. She uses the euphemism, *pisar*, to refer to coitus. Mrs. Vigil also ends the second chiste by reiterating her condemnation of the duck's behavior in even stronger terms and by noting that his behavior shamed her. This suggests that both chistes extend a process that played a central role in the anecdote about the 'matches'—the exploration of conflicting cultural values—into the sexual sphere. An insatiable sexual appetite and a willingness to have relations with anyone of the opposite sex are characterized as criminal ("For RAPE") and as possibly leading to death, either at one's own hands or as retribution. On the other hand, sexuality, even when taken to extremes, is celebrated in these chistes. Although the oversexed duck is killed and eaten, the rooster used sexuality in attempting to overcome the buzzard, a potent and repulsive symbol of death. These conflicting visions of excessive sexuality as potential threat to self and society versus sex as a powerful source of gratification are dialectically engaged—one does not merely replace the other.

The interactions that take place between Mrs. Vigil and Julián in the course of the performance provide an interesting problem. Julián interrupts his mother's narration in (9–11) to comment on the duck's need for additional mates. In (23–24) he seems to aggrandize the duck in suggesting that 'they, they need a HAREM, the POOR THINGS'. The exchanges between Mrs. Vigil and her son in (9–25) are prosodically and syntactically marked as an argument. Julián counters Mrs. Vigil's claim in (93–95) that the duck was 'TERRIBLE' and 'a BAD THING!' by reiterating the 'poor little thing' theme and comparing the duck to a bull with one hundred cows. In these exchanges, mother and son seem to be assuming gender-specific roles with Julián taking the side of the male duck while Mrs. Vigil asserts that two female ducks should have been enough.

However, the two roles do not divide quite so neatly along gender lines. Julián also expresses sympathy for *las pobres* 'the poor [female] things' and the way the duck 'would injure them'. He replays each of the punch lines; he also agrees with his mother that the duck was 'TERRIBLE!' (88), that he caused them shame (91), and that the duck seemed to have done this 'ON PURPOSE' (97). Most important, not only did Mrs. Vigil learn the chiste from her son, but she solicits his collaboration when she is unclear about a crucial element of the setup (64). Julián is thus not simply playing a role that is opposed to the one assumed by his mother; his alternations between opposition and collusion rather enhance Mrs. Vigil's ability to move dialectically between the voices of sexual constraint and sexual gratification.

In Bakhtin's (1981) terms, these chistes produce an internal dialogism in Mrs. Vigil's discourse. The voice that she initially adopts in our interaction, that of the pious and rather frail elderly woman, has been invaded and dissected by the voice of feminine strength and independence and that of sexual explicitness and license. The creation of this polyphony works in the other direction as well; the more restrained persona invades the last two chistes stylistically through the use of a sexual euphemism (pisar), the condemnations of the duck's behavior, and the farmer's statement that 'HE DIDN'T KNOW WHAT TO DO' with the rooster. Julián's participation superimposes an external dialogism (one involving alternating turns at talk) over the internal dialogism.

CHISTE CYCLES

Some of the most popular chistes form part of cycles that revolve around a central comic figure. Such chistes are generally longer, and the narrative element is predominant, permitting them to be classed as either *chistes* or *cuentos* 'jokes' or 'stories'. Those concerning Pedro de Ordimalas[16] as well as Don Cacahuate and his wife, Doña Cebolla (cf. Córdova 1973; Rael n.d.:357–58, 538), are two of the most popular. The central figures possess stereotypic personalities, the roguish good-for-nothing and the arrogant. Although they are quite widely distributed, the chistes are generally told as if these characters used to live in the performer's own community. In chiste-telling session, each participant will invoke another fictitious incident in the life of the principal character. After a number of chistes within the same cycle have been performed, the exchange will shift to another cycle or to chistes that do not form part of any cycle.

I participated in a chiste-telling session that centered on two joke cycles during my first conversation with Lina and Federico Córdova. After we had spoken for several hours, one of their sons, a daughter-in-law, and several grandchildren converged on the Córdovas' house. A conversation that began in the living room was dominated initially by family concerns. Then I asked them if they had heard of Pedro de Ordimalas. After noting that his Uncle José Dolores was *muy chistoso* 'a great jokester', Mr. Córdova related a chiste concerning Pedro de Ordimalas that he learned from his uncle, presented as example (6.5).[17]

Two questions arise immediately upon examination of this performance. What is the answer to the second question, and why did Mr. Córdova omit it? Resolution of the first issue is facilitated by another presentation of this chiste nearly a year later, when I elicited a number of chistes from Mr. Córdova. I wanted to see how the performance of a chiste in a chiste-telling session that included the extended family was different from a performance elicited by a collector. I left the selection of the chistes up to Mr. Córdova, who provided me with three, including the chiste about Pedro de Ordimalas and the three questions. Here the order of the questions is changed, with the time needed to go around the world given first. Example (6.6) provides Pedro de Ordimalas' response.

But why did Mr. Córdova omit this answer from the first performance of the chiste? Given Mr. Córdova's command of pedagogical discourse, proverbs, and chistes, I doubt that he simply forgot. Note that the first and third answers in (6.5) are linked by the statement *Y luego cuando vino la PREGUNTA, "¿Qué cosa ES. . . .* 'And then when he got to the QUESTION, "What IS IT. . . . ?"' This suggests that any number of questions might have intervened between the two at the time, but they have been left out of the performance. Why, nevertheless, does Mr. Córdova omit this answer? This is part of a systematic deletion of narrative detail in the second half of the first performance. Interestingly, the first performance is 3 minutes and 50 seconds long, whereas the elicited version is 5 minutes and 12 seconds in duration (i.e., 36 per cent longer).

The "hurried" character of (6.5) follows from the problems that Mr. Córdova encountered in maintaining contact with his audience. Two more grandchildren entered the living room at line (64). An older grandchild, who was raised by the Córdovas, knocked on the door at (133), entered, and greeted the assembled relatives. A side conversation then started between Lina Córdova, the grandson, and the daughter-in-law. Mr. Córdova was thus encountering more and more difficulty holding his audience. He reacted to this situation by repeating *'izque le dijo* 'they say that he said to him' five times. The third *'izque le dijo* was preceded by OYES 'LISTEN', a remark that was addressed to the competition. The side conversation con-

(6.5) Federico Córdova (78), Lina Ortiz de Córdova (ca. 78, designated LO), son (designated S), daughter-in-law (designated DI), Samuelito Córdova (designated SC), other grandchildren, CLB (19); 2 October 1972, Córdova, New Mexico

FC Yo tenía un TÍO,
    que ese tío,
    mi tío, un tío, un Tío José DOLORES,
    papá del GEORGIE ⟨López⟩,
    era MUY CHISTOSO,   5
CB   Yah
FC muy chistoso era.
    Sí.
  Y una vez platicaba un CHISTE,
     'izque, 'izque   10
    una vez 'izque andaba ahi,
    andaba Pedro de ORDIMALAS . . .
    cuidando las CABRAS, . . .
        | ¿ve?
      Y iba el PADRE,   15
      un PADRE,
        | ¿ve?
      Y este–.
        Y HABÍA UN REY,
        'izque HABÍA UN REY.   20
           | Allá puso la historia corre–,
           | había ahi ((como)),
           | ¿ve? . . .
       Había un REY, . . .
        'izque, 'izque tenían que adivinarle a éle,   25

        éle, éle, éle un, . . .
        uni, uni, uni, uni, . . .
        una PREGUNTA que les estaba haciendo a TODOS,

          y al que no sabía,

          lo sentenciaba a la MUERTE. . . .   30

    Y luego
      le TOCÓ al PADRE. . . .
      Y luego el Padre 'izque iba ahi en su boguecito a misa, y–,

      como ahi en EL ALTO ⟨junto a Córdova⟩,

      ((yendo)) ahi, pa', pa' allá pa' Truchas,   35

        Y ahi encontró a Pedro de Ordimalas. . . .

    Y,
    Y ENTONCES, . . .
      'izque, 'izque le DIJO,
      se paró con él,   40
      ya lo conocía,
        'izque le dijo,

English translation

I used to have an UNCLE,
⟨and⟩ that uncle
my uncle, an uncle, an Uncle José DOLORES,
the father of GEORGIE ⟨López⟩,
was a GREAT JOKER,

laughs   Yeah
he was a great joker.
Yes.
And one time he told a JOKE,
            it is said that, it is said that
            once upon a time it is said that over there was,
            over there was Pedro de ORDIMALAS · · ·
            herding GOATS,
                        | you see?
            And along came the PRIEST,
            a PRIEST,
                        | you see?
            And this–.
                        AND THERE USED TO BE A KING,
                        it is said that there USED TO BE A KING.
laughing | Now I've got the story––,
                                        | it used ((to be possible)),
                                        | you see? · · ·
                        There used to be a KING,
                                it is said that, it is said that they
                                    had to answer for him,
                                him, him, him a, · · ·
                                a, a, a, a, · · ·
                                a QUESTION that he was asking
                                    EVERYONE,
                                        and anyone who didn't know
                                            ⟨the answer⟩,
                                        he would sentence him to
                                            DEATH. · · ·
            And then
                    it was the PRIEST'S TURN. · · ·
                        And then it is said that the priest was going
                            in his buggy to Mass up there, and–,
                        up there around THE HEIGHTS ⟨by
                            Córdova⟩,
                        ((going)) up there, ⟨going⟩ up there to
                            Truchas,
                                and there he came across Pedro de
                                    Ordimalas. · · ·
            And,
            AND THEN, · · ·
                    it is said, it is said that he TOLD HIM,
                    he stopped next to him,
                    having recognized him,
                            it is said that he asked him,

"¿Por qué va tan triste, padre?"
'izque el dijo ((éste)).
"¿Por qué usted está tan triste?"   45
'Izque le dijo Pedro al padre,
          "¿CÓMO NO?" 'izque;

          "mira, allá está el REY,"
          'izque le dijo,
                    "ya ha mata'o a TANTOS   50

          que, que pa' estás PREGUNTAS que les está
          HACIENDO." . . .

Y

'izque le dijo el Pedro,
          "DÍGAME las PREGUNTAS,"
          'izque le dijo. . . .   55
          "Pues," 'izque le dijo éle,
          "pues ÉSTAS," 'izque le dijo,

          "son,
                    'Dime qué tantos, . . .
                    qué tantos . . .   60
                    CABELLOS tengo en mi,
                    ((el mío)),
                              que tantos cabellos tengo en mi
                              CABEZA'. . . .
                    La SEGUNDA," 'izque le dijo,

                              "'¿CUÁNTAS i–,   65
                              CUÁNTAS i–,
                              CUÁNTO me ESTARÉ',"

                    'izque le dijo,

                    "'pa' dar VUELTA a la, la–,

          ALREDEDOR de la TIERRA?'" 70

                    ¿ve?
          "Y la OTRA," 'izque le dijo,

                    "'¿Qué cosa estoy PENSANDO

          que no ES?'
                    Ésa es la MÁS,"   75

                    'izque le dijo,

          "la mási, . . .
          DIFICULTOSA."/
LO   Yah, ¡oye!

"Why are you so sad, father?"
it is said that he was asked by ((this fellow)),
"Why are you so sad?"
It is said that Pedro asked the priest.
            "WHO WOULDN'T BE?" it is said
            ⟨that he told him⟩;
            "look, there is the KING,"
            it is said that he told him,
                    "he has already killed SO
                    MANY
                    on, on account of these QUES-
                    TIONS that he is ASKING
                    THEM." . . .

    And
            it is said that Pedro told him,
                "TELL ME the QUESTIONS,"
            it is said that he told him. . . .
                "Well," it is said that he told him,
                "well, THESE," it is said that he told
                him,
                "they are,
                        'Tell me how many, . . .
                        how many . . .
                        HAIRS I have on my,
                        ((my own)),
                                how many hairs I have
                                on my HEAD.' . . .

two grandchildren   The SECOND," it is said that
enter room   he told him,
                        "'HOW MANY i–,
                        HOW MANY i–,
                        HOW LONG ⟨would⟩ it
                        TAKE ME,'"
                        it is said that he told
                        him,
                                "'to GO
                                AROUND
                                the, the–,
                                AROUND the
                                WORLD?'"
                                you see?
                "And the OTHER," it is said
                that he told him,
                        "'What thing am I
                        THINKING
                        that's NOT ⟨TRUE⟩,'
                                "That one is the
                                MOST,"
                                it is said that he
                                told him,
                                "the most,
                                DIFFICULT."/

laughing   Yeah, just
                                        listen!/

FC Y luego,   80
      'izque le dijo,
      "¡OH! ¡QUÉ!
¡Piense usté'!"
        Pues se acabaron de–.
'Izque le dijo,   85
        "Si quiere, QUÉDESE con mis CABRAS,"
      'izque le dijo,
        "pero es pa' cada una de diferentes DUEÑOS. . . .
            Allá cuando llegue al corral de 'Mano GRACIA,

            de 'Mano EUSEBIO,   90
            ahi les dice, '¡'FUERA, 'FUERA, CABRAS!'

            Y ellas se APARTAN SOLAS,

            y ((van pa' acá, 'onde andan)),

        la ENTRIEGA."
            "Y PRÉSTAME," 'izque le dijo,   95

        "tus, tu VESTIDO y TODO,

            y luego voy a dar MISA,

            ALLÁ,"
        'izque le dijo,
        "a Las TRUCHAS." . . .   100
Y BUENO,
      se acostó el PADRE,
      pu's, muy CONTENTO,
          ve.
      El dijo,   105
      "Aquí me dejas saber,"
          y ⟨Pedro de Ordimalas⟩ se FUE. . . .

Luego ya, ...
   ALLÁ ASINA,
'izque, 'izque, 'izque, 'izque VINO,   110

     'izque le DIJO, . . .
     le dijo,
"¿va a misa?"
        "NO,"
             | era misa, . . .   115
"NO," 'izque le dijo, y se levantó.
"Misa, como todas las misas.
VÁYANSE!
VÁYANSE!
VÁYANSE!   120
VÁYANSE! PA' SUS CASAS!"
     'izque le dijo . . . ,
Pedro de Ordimalas,
        ¿ve?

And then,
>it is said he told him,
>>"AH! WHAT THE HECK!
>>Think!"
>>>Well they finishing de–.
>>It is said that he told him,
>>>"If you wish, STAY here with my GOATS,"
>>>it is said that he told him,
>>>"but each one goes to a different OWNER. . . .
>>>>Over there ⟨in Córdova⟩ when you get to
>>>>Brother GRACIA's CORRAL,
>>>>Brother EUSEBIO's,
>>>>then tell them, 'GO AWAY, GO AWAY,
>>>>>GOATS!'
>>>>>And they will SPLIT UP BY
>>>>>>THEMSELVES,
>>>>>and ((they will go over here where
>>>>>they belong)),
>>>>>the HANDING OVER."
>>>>>>"And LOAN ME," it is said
>>>>>>that he told him,
>>>>>>"your, your CLOTHING and
>>>>>>EVERYTHING,
>>>>>>and then I am going to say
>>>>>>MASS,
>>>>>>UP THERE,"
>>>>>>it is said that he told him,
>>>>>>"in Las TRUCHAS." . . .
>>>>AND OKAY,
>>>>>the priest lay DOWN,
>>>>>well, very CONTENTEDLY,
>>>>>>you see.
>>>>>He said,
>>>>>"let me know over here,"
>>>>>>and ⟨Pedro de Ordimalas⟩
>>>>>>LEFT. . . .

Then already, . . .
>UP THERE ⟨it was⟩ IN THIS WAY,
>it is said that, it is said that, it is said that, it is said that he
>>CAME,
>it is said that ⟨someone⟩ ASKED, . . .
>⟨someone⟩ said,
>"Are you going to Mass?"
>>"NO,"
>>>| it was ⟨time for⟩ Mass,
>>"NO," it is said that he told him, and he got up.
>>"Mass, like all Masses,
>>GO!
>>GO!
>>GO!
>>GO HOME!"
>>it is said that he told them, . . .
>>Pedro de Ordimalas,
>>>you see?

Dijeron,   125
"¡Ya el padre está enfermo QUIZÁS!"
'izque dijeron,
"¡Quién sabe qué tiene!
Ya no quiere darnos misa HOY."

> No más no era el PADRE,   130
>
>   ¿ve?
> era Pedro de ORDIMALAS. . . .

Y luego se FUE,
    se fue pa' casa del REY. . . .
SC | Jaló.   135
OTROS | Jaló.
FC   Entonces'izque le dijo el REY,
      "BUENO,"'izque le dijo el rey,
      al padre;
> él pensaba que era el PADRE,   140
> el REY,
>   ¿ve? . . .

    'Izque le dijo,
    'izque le dijo,
> OYES,   145
> Qué bonito!

LO
FC   'izque le dijo, . . .
     'izque le dijo ASINA,
        "¿CUÁNTAS,"
          'izque le dijo,   150
        "ESTRELLAS hay en el CIELO,
        pa' contarlas?" . . .
          Y, y'izque le dijo,
          y haciéndole muchas rayas ⟨en un papel⟩.

> "¿Puede contar esas RAYAS?" . . .   155
> 'izque le dijo él al rey.
> "No."
>   "Pus, asina son las estrellas;
>   no hay nadie que las pueda contar." . . .

>   ¿Ve? . . .   160

> "Y luego TAMBIÉN,
> el cabello TAMBIÉN,
> pues, es la misma COSA."

Y luego cuando vino la PREGUNTA,
     "¿Qué cosa ES,   165
     que no ES, . . .
     que estoy PENSANDO?" . . .

LO laughs

They said,
"MAYBE the father is ILL!"
it is said that they told ⟨each other⟩.
Who knows what's wrong with him!
Now he doesn't want to say Mass for us
TODAY."

 | The thing is that it wasn't the
 | FATHER,
 | you see?
 | it was Pedro de
 | ORDIMALAS. . . .

[There is a knock at the door; SC enters; a conversation begins; FC continues to talk]

And then he WENT,
    he went to the house of the KING. . . .

 | Hello.
 | Hello.

Then it is said that the KING SAID,
"OKAY," it is said that the king said,
to the priest;

 | he thought that it was the PRIEST,
 | the KING,
 | you see? . . .

It is said that he asked him,
it is said that he asked him,

loudly, to stop side
conversation

 | LISTEN,
 | How pretty!

touching baby

it is said that he asked him, . . .
it is said that he asked him LIKE THIS,
"HOW MANY,"
    it is said that he asked him,
"STARS are there in the SKY,
⟨if you were⟩ to count them."

 And, and it is said that he asked him,
 making some lines there ⟨on a piece of
     paper⟩.
 "Can you count these LINES?" . . .
 it is said that he asked the king.
 "No."

  "Well, the stars are like this;
  no one would be able to count
      them." . . .
          You see?

[The side conversation begins again]

 "And then IT'S THE SAME,
 with hair IT'S THE SAME,
 well, it's the same THING."
And then when he got to the QUESTION,
 "What IS IT;
 that is not TRUE, . . .
 that I am THINKING?" . . .

y luego'izque le dijo Pedro de ORDIMALAS,

"¡SABE usted que está PENSANDO usté, REY?

que está HABLANDO con el PADRE;   170

está HABLANDO con Pedro de

ORDIMALAS,"
'izque. . . .

DI   Ahi salió,

                                        ¿ve?

(6.6) Federico Córdova (79), CLB (20); July 1974, Córdova, New Mexico

FC   Ya que FUE,
        'izque le dijo,
        'izque dijo el REY,
            "¿CUÁNTO me tomaré YO
            pa' ir ALREDEDOR del MUNDO?"   5
                'Izque le dijo Pedro de Ordimalas,
                "SEÑOR REY,
                si se SUBE en el SOL,
                    en 24 HORAS VOLTEAS,"
                'izque le dijo.   10
                    "BUENO,
                    está BIEN,
                    está BIEN," dijo.

---

tinued unabated. In (148), Mr. Córdova followed the 'izque le dijo with ASINA 'LIKE THIS', which was uttered slowly, deliberately, with greater force, and with a pronounced falling tone. This succeeded in silencing the audience temporarily. The side conversation became quite audible again at (161), and Mr. Córdova knew that he could not hold his audience for much longer, so he abbreviated the performance.

The point is that the form of the chiste is shaped by Mr. Córdova's attempt to construct a narrative and to gain his audience's participation in this process. The performance features point less to the preceding conversation or to a concrete interactional goal than to the structure and meaning of the narrative. The performance is framed by the opening formula *una vez* 'one time', which is repeated. The chiste is

and then it is said that he was
told by Pedro de
ORDIMALAS,
"DO YOU KNOW what you
are THINKING, KING?
that you are SPEAKING with
the PRIEST;
you are SPEAKING
with Pedro de
ORDIMALAS,"
it is said ⟨that he told
him⟩. . . .
That's how it
came out,
you see?

everyone laughs

English translation

Once he had GONE,
it is said that he asked him,
it is said that the KING ASKED HIM,
"HOW LONG would it take ME
to go AROUND the WORLD?"
It is said the he was told by Pedro dc Ordimalas,
"YOUR MAJESTY,
if you CLIMB up on the SUN,
in 24 HOURS YOU'LL GO AROUND,"
it is said that he told him.
"OKAY,
that's FINE,
that's FINE," he said.

---

presented as the quoted speech of an elder of bygone days, José Dolores López. A closing formula, *ahi salió* 'that's how it came out', is also used. Another phrase that marks the status of the discourse as narrative, *'izque* 'it is said that', appears 46 times. *'Izque* is derived from *dizque*, from the verbum diciendi *decir* 'to say' or 'to tell' plus the relative pronoun *que* 'that' (Espinosa 1946:99–100). It functions as an evidential frame, signaling that the information is derived from verbal evidence. As Espinosa (1946:99) notes, it also functions (like simple *que*) as a conjunction. *'Izque* thus serves as a means of establishing cohesion between the segment and the discourse that precedes it and the reported speech that follows. When used repeatedly and in association with other performance features, it signals the audience that the performance of a narrative is taking place. In the course of negotiating a new discourse frame, the performer asserts the right to a different quantity and type of control over the conversational floor.

The chiste begins with what Labov and Waletzky (1967:32) refer to as an "orientation section." Chistes that involve such fictional or supernatural characters as Christ, kings, or the saints utilize devices for creating a frame in which the participation of these figures is believable. The opening formula invokes a "storyrealm," in Young's (1983) terminology, in which the normal canons of truth and falsity do not apply. The quotation-framing verb *platicaba* (9) and repeated use of *'izque* suggests that truth and falsity of the chiste will be judged in relationship to other examples of the talk of the elders of bygone days. Note the way in which Pedro de Ordimalas, the priest, and the king are introduced (12, 15, 19). These verb phrases use past + imperfective in placing the events in a time period (*una vez*) in which the fictional Pedro de Ordimalas and kings existed in the area and in setting the stage for Pedro's meeting with the priest. Federico Córdova once noted in the course of a chiste performance that 'in those days there were kings here.'

Once the three questions have been mentioned (25–30), the stage is set for the beginning of the chiste's action. The plot is developed through a series of episodes, the priest's assignment to the task of answering the questions, his encounter with Pedro de Ordimalas above Córdova, Pedro's assumption of the priest's burden (and clothing), Pedro's masquerade as the priest in Las Truchas, and his meeting with the king. Note that the beginning of each of the episodes is signaled by a formal element—*y luego* 'and then' (31, 80, 133), *luego ya* 'then already' (108), or *y entonces* 'and then' (38). In each case, one of these episodic boundary markers occurs at the beginning of a line. In addition to delineating a boundary between episodes, these phrases delineate the linear structure of the narrative, marking the passage of narrative time and weaving together the events that they separate into a coherent story.

After Mr. Córdova's performance, I took the floor and related another Pedro de Ordimalas chiste. (I had acquired a repertoire of chistes by this time as a result of having listened to a number of chiste-telling sessions in Córdova and other communities.) Here Pedro de Ordimalas is approached by a very old man who lived above Córdova, who is actually Christ in disguise. Christ asks Pedro for 'two bits'. Doing the only good deed in his entire life, Pedro gives Christ the two bits. Christ then reveals his true identity; surprised and pleased with Pedro's actions, Christ grants the rogue three wishes. Pedro thinks for a moment, then replies *Bueno, primero, por favor, deme los dos reales* 'Okay, first please give me ⟨back⟩ the two bits'. The tape ends here, with a chorus of laughter, and the remainder of the chiste was lost. Numerous variants of this chiste are performed in New Mexico and Colorado (see for example Rael n.d.: 234–237 and J. M. Espinosa 1937:127–130), and each presents a different set of wishes. I believe that I related requests for a magic drum, one which a person cannot stop beating until released by Pedro, and a chair that similarly imprisons all who sit in it. Pedro uses the drum and chair to trap Death (which is represented as a feminine character) when she comes to take him, thus bargaining for additional years of life.

The second side of the tape starts at the beginning of the punch line of another chiste, this one performed by Mr. Córdova. Fortunately, my colleague Julián Josué Vigil is familiar with the chiste. A promiscuous woman goes to confession; she tells the priest euphemistically that she has had a *trompezón* 'stumbling' with a long list of men. The priest responds to each tale with ¡YYY!, a sound that can signal both surprise and fright. When she has finished, the priest told her, '"If you were a mare, you'd be very clumsy (*muy trompezadora*)." And she answered, "And if you were a *macho* (he-mule), you wouldn't be so easily frightened (*espantón*)."'

This provides an example of jokes, popular among Mexicanos and in countless folkloric traditions as well, that center on outwitting priests or parsons. Mr. Córdova follows this performance with another confessional chiste. A man goes to the priest to confess that "he had intended to rob a cow from his neighbor." The priest tells him that the cost of absolution would be 'paying for a mass', arguing that the intention is more important than the actual commission of the act. So the parishioner brought 'about ten dollars' to the priest but then refused to give him the money, noting that the priest had told him that the intention was of equal value to the act itself.

Mr. Córdova's son then tells a slightly off-color chiste, transcribed below as example (6.6.) A woman farts once, then says '"This is MONDAY"'. She walks a short distance, farts again, and says '"TUESDAY"'. She walks a bit further, farts, and says '"This is WEDNESDAY"'. A man has been following behind her; she turns and asks him, '"How long have you been following me?" "Since Monday," it is said that he said to her'. The son then immediately tells a chiste about Pedro de Ordimalas and the priest. As the priest was counseling Pedro, the latter was staring at a point above his interlocutor's head. 'The priest then said "Pedro, I bet that you don't know what, even a word of what I told you." "The same with you," it is said that he said to him, "I bet you that you don't know how many ants came out of an anthill (and through the window)"'. Federico Córdova noted: 'He was watching the ants!' (See Robe 1977:186 for a variant on this chiste.)

I then shifted to the cycle of chistes regarding Don Cacahuate 'Sir Peanut' (cf. Córdova 1973; Rael n.d.:357–58, 538). The family laughed at the mention of his name, which is the usual response to a reference (within a chiste-telling session) to the designation for a popular chiste cycle. Don Cacahuate and his wife Doña Cebolla 'Lady Onion' are portrayed as being so haughty and pretentious that they place themselves unknowingly in ludicrous situations. The couple is generally described as having lived in the speaker's community around the turn of the century. In the chiste that I performed, the couple attempt to adopt modern ways by identifying with the growing Anglo-American presence in the area; Don Cacahuate and Doña Cebolla accordingly provide a prototype for *agringados,* Mexicanos who behave like or want to be considered *gringos* (cf. Limón 1977). In order to display their identification with the growing Anglo-American presence in the area, the couple decides to give its first child an English first name. Lacking competence in English, they assume that the word that is most frequently used by English speakers must be a popular name. Their child is thus christened *Sonovabish* (a New Mexican Spanish borrowing of Son-of-a-bitch).[18]

The chorus of laughter that followed the chiste suggests that it met with some success. I then performed another Don Cacahuate chiste. A fictionalized setting is created in which, at the turn of the century, cars are unknown but motorcycles are common. Don Cacahuate is quite proud of owning the newest and largest motorcycle around. Once (*una vez*) he sees two lights in the middle of the road. Thinking that these were misbehaving adolescents on motorcycles, he decided to frighten them into acquiescence. He thus drove at top speed between them, only to discover that this was the first car to visit Abiquiú.[19] The punch line elicited only minimal laughter. The problem seems to be that I lacked fluency in New Mexican Spanish at the time (after four weeks of fieldwork). I thus substituted *coche* for *carro,* *motocicleta* for *moto* or *baika,* and *camión* for *troca.* These dialectal differences appear to have confused some members of the audience and to have decreased their level of participation in the chiste. Once the son explained the chiste and reiterated the punch line, this time using dialectally appropriate forms, more laughter emerged, but far less than in the previous case.

The son then regained the floor and related another Don Cacahuate chiste. Don Cacahuate, in the bar as usual, agrees to watch a woman's "German Shepherd police dog." Don Cacahuate becomes more and more intoxicated, and he allows the dog to escape. Noting his absence, Don Cacahuate goes into the street and brings back a small dog to put in its place. Upon returning, the woman refuses to accept the small dog in lieu of her own. *"Don Cacahuate, ¿el perro?" "Ahi está." "NO,"* 'izque le dijo *ella, ésta, "NO,"* 'izque le dijo ella, *"MI PERRO ERA POLICE DOG." "¡Shhhh!"* 'izque le dijo, *"éste es detective."* '"Don Cacahuate, [where's] the dog?" "There it is." "NO," it is said that she told him, this [woman], it is said that she told him, "MY DOG WAS A POLICE DOG." "Shhhh!," it is said that he told her, "this one is a detective."' This elicits a great deal of laughter.

The oldest grandson, who I believe was sixteen at the time, then asked about Don Cacahuate: 'Were they people or what?' Mr. Córdova noted that these chistes constitute *historia de los pinates* 'story of the pinates' (see later discussion). Mrs. Córdova then replied *historia; no es más de chiste* 'story; it's only a chiste'. The conversation then turned to two publications that feature numerous chistes, Cervantes' *Don Quixote* and a volume of chistes about Bartolo. This constitutes the first point since Mr. Córdova's initial performance of the chiste concerning the three questions that more than a few lines of discourse have fallen outside the chiste frame. Mr. Córdova's son then indicated his desire to return home, and a series of leave-takings commenced.

In the middle of this process, the son states "Mr. Peanuts" (in English). This elicits both laughter and a metacommunicative comment on the chiste-telling session from both Mrs. and Mr. Córdova—*muy bonito salió* 'it came out very well'. This phrase is repeated by the daughter-in-law and the oldest grandson. The son then provides a very short chiste. Doña Cebolla (Don Cacahuate's wife) was quite ill, so Don Cacahuate left in search of a doctor, a task he pursued for an entire year. Just as he was about to return, he fell down in the road. '"This ⟨business⟩ of being in such a hurry," it is said that he said, "is not good"'.

The grandson then asks, 'So when Don Cacahuate died, only nine *peanuts* were left?' After a chorus of laughter, Mrs. Córdova mentions: *los empinates*, a reference to the pun that constitutes the classic synecdochic index of the Don Cacahuate/Doña Cebolla cycle. Doña Cebolla and Don Cacahuate's ten children are referred to as *los diez pinates* 'the ten peanuts'. Peanut, a loanword in New Mexican Spanish, is pronounced *pinate*, which sounds, however, like the second person singular imperative of the verb *empinarse* that is used to describe the action of tipping a bottle (to drain its alcoholic contents), getting down on all fours (often to be spanked), and moving into a position in which either the vagina or anus is exposed for phallic penetration. So, once Don Cacahuate and Doña Cebolla died, the "ten peanuts" were sold for ten cents (i.e., were forced into prostitution). The phrase "ten *pinates* for ten cents" is often inserted into conversation, generally uttered as if it were an advertisement; as such it provides a miniperformance of the Cacahuate cycle.[20]

THE SPECIAL POWER OF CHISTE CYCLES

Note that chiste cycles, particularly the ones associated with Pedro de Ordimalas and Don Cacahuate, are more prevalent in chiste-telling sessions than in conversations in which chistes are periodically inserted. Why is this the case? The emergence of a successful session depends on the ready availability of a substantial number of chistes and on the ability of the participants to string them together with minimal interruption. Invoking the name of the principal figure in a chiste cycle immediately indexes a large collection of chistes; such pronouncements are immediately followed by laughter. Chiste cycles also lend a great deal of cohesion to the discourse. The individual chistes differ greatly in terms of content and length; as long as the next contribution consists of another chiste in the same cycle, its appropriateness is virtually assured. Given their wide distribution, persons who participate in Mexicano chiste-telling sessions are virtually certain to be familiar with a number of chistes in each cycle. This facilitates the process of gaining access to the floor.

A concept presented by Labov in his study of ritual insults provides a useful means of conceptualizing the discourse properties of such chistes. Drawing on a suggestion by Goffman, Labov notes that "a sound opens a *field*, which is meant to be sustained" (1972:160; emphasis in original). The performance of a *sound* or ritual insult by one participant carries two expectations, namely, that at least one other participant will respond with a sound and that the second may be based in part on the properties of the first. In the case of chistes that form part of cycles, the performance of one chiste conveys the expectation that another participant will tell a chiste that is drawn from the same cycle. Accordingly, if a person wants to create a chiste-telling session, the best approach is to open a field by performing a chiste that is drawn from a popular cycle. A chiste that is not drawn from a cycle may create such a session, but it does not produce the *expectation* that this will be the case. The peculiar appeal of cycles thus seems to derive in part from the fact that their constituent chistes possess meta-communicative properties that are not present in the case of unrelated chistes; performing a chiste that focuses on Pedro de Ordimalas or Don Cacahuate thus provides the performer with a greater degree of control over the nature and the content of the discourse that follows.

Such cycles are important in another respect. I have argued that chistes provide playful commentaries on topics of substantial cultural relevance; they afford a particularly good means of exposing contradictory cultural values. If one examines the two cycles from this perspective, the fact that they focus on Pedro de Ordimalas and Don Cacahuate becomes highly significant. These characters are tricksters, masters of deceit and symbolic inversion.[21] They similarly embody contradictory traits. In the opening chiste, Pedro de Ordimalas is assigned the role of a simpleton, an adult who cannot be trusted with greater responsibility than watching the goats. He is able nonetheless to take on a task that terrifies the local priest, and he outsmarts the king. Don Cacahuate similarly strives to be the most modern and sophisticated person in town; the punch lines of most Don Cacahuate chistes focus, however, on revealing the fact that his social pretensions are really intended to mask his laziness, drunkenness, ignorance, and egocentricity.

If performances of chistes concerning Don Cacahuate and Pedro de Ordimalas provide "a playful restructuring of the world" (Abrahams 1983:73) that exposes cultural contradictions, what is the range of their targets? Gender and sexuality are at issue in the confession of the woman who 'stumbles'. The main thrust of these two chiste cycles, however, centers on social inequality, and each chiste cycle has its own particular way of generating social commentary.

Pedro de Ordimalas launches his attack from a position of social inferiority. In the story of the three questions, he gives the priest a lesson on the skills that are required to assume the task of goatherd. Interestingly, the priest does not seem to think it necessary to train Pedro in sacerdotal duties, even when Pedro declares that he plans to offer Mass. Pedro demonstrates his capacity for assuming the role of the priest, which is associated with education and high social standing as well as with religious authority. He even outsmarts the paragon of wisdom and power, the king. This act of social inversion, in which the lowest defeats the highest, seems to be all that Pedro is seeking; Pedro wins neither gold nor the right to marry the king's daughter. Pedro similarly uses the wishes that Christ grants him not to gain wealth and power, but to prove that Christ himself can be mistaken, and to outsmart Death.

The last Pedro de Ordimalas chiste in this session juxtaposes two types of information, the priest's exhortation on religious and social values and the observation that a large number of ants have abandoned their anthill and entered the priest's quarters. The social order places more weight on the priest's knowledge of religious mores and social norms. In his rejoinder, Pedro ("I bet you that you don't know how many ants came out of an anthill"), appropriates some of the syntax and lexicon as well as all of the prosodic features, including increased volume, of the priest's accusation ("I bet that you don't know what, even a word of what I told you"). The stern, exhortative character of Pedro's voice in the punch line underlines his claim that his words are just as important as the priest's.

Pedro's ability to outsmart priests emerges in a host of other tales. Priests are frequently the butts of his coarse jokes. One of Pedro's favorite tricks is to trade a pile of feces, which is hidden under a hat, for a priest's clothing and donkey, telling the latter that underneath the hat is a bird of seven colors, and even subverts the bishop's orders while masquerading as a priest (cf. A. M. Espinosa 1910–16/1914: 126, 127, 129–30). Numerous tales recount Pedro's adventures in the afterlife. He is thrown out of hell for tormenting devils, banished from purgatory for abusing the souls there, and recalled from limbo for baptizing babies by throwing them in the river. He enters heaven, generally by tricking St. Peter. At this point Pedro is finally punished by being turned to stone; getting in one last trick, he manages to retain eyes with which to see all who enter. These episodes are generally preceded by Pedro's procurement of additional years of life by outsmarting Death (see A. M. Espinosa 1910–16/1914: 128–29; J. M. Espinosa 1937:124–30; Rael n.d.: 232–34, 236–37, 253, 254–55; Robe 1977:71–76).

Another series of tales focus on Pedro de Ordimalas's relations with employers. He often has an older brother, Juan, who leaves in search of work. The employer is generally termed a *rico* or *patrón* (A. M. Espinosa 1910–16/1914:121–24), and in one case he is the king (J. M. Espinosa 1937:121–23). The boss imposes a contract: whoever loses his temper first must suffer the loss of a strip of flesh from his back. Juan loses both skin and wages, but Pedro turns all of the employer's tricks back on the master himself. The exchanges (in direct discourse) between Pedro and his superior reflect the social asymmetry clearly: Pedro uses deferential titles, and his verbs and pronouns are highly marked for deference: "*Sí, patronsito* [sic]," *asina com' uste dise* [sic], *asina sí hará*" "'Yes, beloved master, just as you say it shall be done'" (A. M. Espinosa 1910–16/1914:123). The *rico* not only first-names Pedro and uses non-deferential forms, but the words he addresses to Pedro generally take the form of highly explicit directives. Pedro's wits enable him to subvert these exploitative relationships. In one version Pedro not only deprives the king of four strips of flesh and a sum of money, but 'then the other kings make Pedro king because of his cleverness and valor and because of the traps that he used to lay' (J. M. Espinosa 1937:123; translation mine).

Don Cacahuate rather considers himself to occupy the uppermost rung of the social ladder. The way he attempts to achieve upward mobility is crucial. In the sonova-bish chiste, Don Cacahuate and Doña Cebolla's desire to be modern and to advance in social position lead them to seek out an English name for their child. The police dog chiste and the one in which Don Cacahuate spends a year searching for a doctor point to the fact that his efforts at social climbing do not include the use of hard work to achieve this goal. His strategy is rather to align himself with the Anglo-American majority by attempting to appropriate linguistic and technological accouterments that symbolize the newcomers' presence. The failure of this strategy is encapsulated in the pun that describes Don Cacahuate and his children, los pinates. The Don Cacahuate cycle provides quite pointed social criticism of a type that can be found throughout the Southwest—*agringado* 'Gringoized' individuals who stand apart from their own cultural tradition as well as from their neighbors and relatives (cf. Limón 1977). The history of los pinates suggests that those who adopt this course eventually, as the pun goes, "get screwed."

UNDERSTANDING CHISTES

The preceding description may have provided the reader with a sense of why chistes are difficult to characterize from a communicative perspective. Although the features of specific performances can be isolated, it is nearly impossible to adduce a set of features shared by all examples of the genre. In terms of referential content, chistes embrace fictionalized experience (*mentiras* 'lies'), anecdotes, and jests, as well as humorous and picaresque tales that are enjoyed in many parts of the Spanish-speaking world (e.g., Pedro de Ordimalas) and beyond (e.g., the three questions). They present a very broad range of ways in which performances are contextualized. Some chistes emerge from a given conversation, commenting metacommunicatively on the preceding segment of the discourse. Nevertheless, they seldom directly validate moral principles or other aspects of the ongoing discourse. Some chistes, such as (6.2), are used to make fun of tradition, perhaps even to call it into question. Others create a context, that of a chiste-telling session.

One of the most striking features of performances of chistes is their apparent violation of the rules that constrain who can perform them and what they can say. In (6.2), Benjamín Domínguez stole the floor from his elderly mother-in-law and performed a segment of the talk of the elders of bygone days. In (6.4), an elderly woman told chistes that focused on excessive sexuality. In the Córdova family chiste-telling session, a son in his forties exchanged chistes with his elderly father. I myself, only nineteen years of age and a newcomer, would have clearly lacked the competence to perform a proverb or scriptural allusion; such an act would in any case have been quite pretentious. My chistes, on the other hand, were accepted by the family, and even provoked laughter when my ignorance of the dialect did not interfere.

Because the task of identifying and defining a genre generally focuses our attention on features that are *shared* by individual tokens, the range of variation evident in performances of chistes poses a real challenge. What is needed is to discover the factors that motivate including such different forms under the aegis of a single genre, and to show why the observed range of variation forms an intrinsic part of the genre. My analysis addresses four questions. First, why are these apparently anomalous forms included under the aegis of la plática de los viejitos de antes? Second, how do we account for the unusual degree of variation in the form and content of chistes? Third, what do all the performances we have examined hold in common? Finally, why is the range of speakers who can perform chistes so much broader than is the case with the other genres? Particularly, why are youths free to perform chistes, even in front of elders?

CHISTES AND LA PLÁTICA DE LOS VIEJITOS DE ANTES

I have argued that chistes differ from historical discourse, proverbs, and scriptural allusions in that they do not focus on the identification and explication of moral principles. Chistes are indeed more likely to parody elements of antes, such as religious processions, and to focus on flatulation and uncontrolled sexuality, than they are to exhort participants to obey the will of God. One might accordingly suggest that chistes do not form part of la plática de los viejitos de antes; I would argue, however, that this proposition is at odds with the nature of the talk of the elders of bygone days and chistes in particular. I have tried to show that this talk does not simply reify the past and the values it represents. It rather consists of a dialectical engagement of past and present designed so as to foster critical thinking about the nature of human experience and the needs of the social community. Thus, although the fact that chistes fall within a ludic frame may indeed foster a particularly indirect relationship with moral values, challenging performers and audiences alike to discover meanings that lie below the surface lies at the heart of this talk.

Such indirect relationships between values and humor can assume a variety of forms.[22] One of the most common is social inversion; Abrahams (1982b, 1983b, 1986b), Babcock (1978), and others have argued that inversion is a key feature of play in general. K. Basso (1979:76) provides us with a striking example of the systematicity with which jokes can adumbrate central cultural ideals "by dramatizing . . . conceptions of what is 'wrong'." The way that Don Cacahuate and Pedro de Ordimalas embody laziness, gluttony, ignorance, egoism, and selfishness suggests that social inversion plays a key role in performances of chistes. But the subversion of existing orders is not confined simply to pointing out what is clearly good by denigrating what is clearly bad. The spirit of the chistes that we have examined in this chapter is more akin to the spirit of the chizbat of the Palmah described by Oring (1981) or the Mexican–American border humor analyzed by Paredes (1966, 1968).

In each case, jokes that ridicule the behavior of both in-group and out-group members critically explore contradictions in the collective identity of the participants and their community just as they expose the foibles of nonmembers.

Many researchers have argued that jokes present a contradiction or incongruity; the punch line then resolves the opposition. Douglas (1968:373), however, suggests that "the joke consists in challenging a dominant structure and belittling it." Although this takes us a step further, Douglas accepts a widely held view of social structures and conceptual patterns as objectified systems that stand apart from and are prior to the communicative acts of individuals. This view obscures the ways that humor can go beyond reinterpreting social structure and assist in transforming it. Abrahams, Bauman, and Limón rather share Bakhtin's (1968/1965, 1981) concern with the way that ideology, culture, and history both shape and are shaped by communicative processes; they argue that this dialectical relationship is particularly evident in such activities as jokes and festivals, where creative and critical restructurings of social reality are celebrated.

This process is evident in la plática de los viejitos de antes as a whole and in chistes in particular. I argued above that historical discourse, proverbs, and scriptural allusions provide potent critiques of contemporary reality. Given the fact that antes and ahora stand in dialectical relationship and that the manner in which each is interpreted is negotiated in performance, antes itself is a dynamic entity. Chistes give particularly free rein to this process of critically reexamining bygone days. Nothing, including the words and actions of Christ, Death, the Devil, the elders of bygone days, and one's own parents and grandparents, is exempt from criticism. Even the words of the Lord's Prayer are vulnerable to comic examination and interpretation.

TEXTUAL-CONTEXTUAL VARIATION IN CHISTES

In turning to the second issue, I have argued in previous chapters that the genres that we have examined thus far can be arranged along a continuum from textual to contextual poles. This spectrum is represented graphically in Figure 4. Historical discourse lies closest to the contextual pole, because its form and content are firmly rooted in the contextualization process and there is no narrative development. Proverbs combine a very close reading of the ongoing interaction with the encapsulation of a textual tradition (the talk of the elders of bygone days) in a widely recognized text. Scriptural allusions emerge from a given conversational setting, but the biblical content is sometimes developed into a complex narrative. Legends, as we shall see later, involve a further step in the direction of narrativity; here the performance foregrounds the structure of the legend and the speaker's relationship to it.

Having examined the way that the genre as a whole is situated with respect to the textual-contextual continuum, let us focus on the way that performances differ in this regard. Some performances are contextually focused, emerging from some ele-

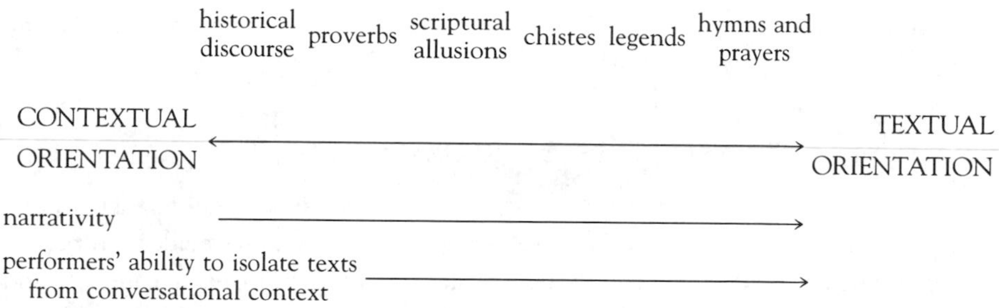

| historical discourse | proverbs | scriptural allusions | chistes | legends | hymns and prayers |

CONTEXTUAL ORIENTATION ←———————————————————————→ TEXTUAL ORIENTATION

narrativity ———————————————————→

performers' ability to isolate texts from conversational context ———————————————————→

Figure 4. Relationship Among Genres of the Talk of the Elders of Bygone Days

ment of what has just been said. Here the chiste provides a metacommunicative comment on the topic, and the conversation then returns to its prior focus. In contrast, chiste-telling sessions are similar to occasions when lengthy legends are recounted. Even if the first chiste may be related to the preceding topic of conversation, this association soon recedes into the background as the narrative element comes to the fore. Although the performance is still contextualized vis-à-vis the competence and knowledge of the audience, the formal features point less toward the interaction than toward delineating the internal structure of the narrative and creating ludic and critical relationships between form and sociocultural content. Some chistes are framed as anecdotes, lacking features (such as '*izque*) that point to their evidential status as objects of verbal transmissions; other chistes form part of widely distributed narrative cycles.

I am thus suggesting that the range of variation evident in chiste performances reiterates the range of text-context relations (if not all of the specific component features) of proverbs, scriptural allusions, and legends. Thus, the contextual-textual continuum reveals two different axes of contrast. Genres differ in terms of their placement along this continuum; chistes as a whole thus stand between scriptural allusions and legends in terms of the role of textual and contextual elements in performances. If the analysis stopped at this point, however, it would be impossible to account for textual-contextual variation within performances of chistes or the way that the genre overlaps with both more contextual and more textual genres. This would, in short, simplify the picture in such a way as to reify the nature of the genre.

A more adequate picture emerges once the second axis of contrast is taken into account. This dimension contrasts genres with respect to the breadth of the span of the continuum that they cover (i.e., the extent of their internal variation in terms of textual-contextual focus). Among the genres that constitute the talk of the elders of bygone days, chistes are unique in that they span an extremely wide segment of the continuum. Here we see an increase in such flexibility as we move from the narrowly focused historical discourse and proverbs to the substantially broader scriptural allusions to the maximally flexible chistes. Interestingly, with legends we take a large step in the direction of less variation, a trend that is even more pronounced in the case of hymns and prayers.

COMMON FEATURES OF CHISTE PERFORMANCES

Given the fact that more internal variation is apparent in this genre than in any other, it is the hardest to define with respect to features that are evident in performances. The term chiste is, nevertheless, an important metalinguistic category, and the examples that are included under its aegis are clearly distinct from both "just words" and from other genres of the talk of the elders of bygone days. A number of features aid in the identification of chiste performances; some are evident in all of the examples that have been examined in this chapter, while others appear in only part of them. These features are summarized in Table 3.

As was the case with proverbs and scriptural allusions, tying words or phrases (feature 1) appear only in some performances. In the case of highly contextualized performances, the tying phrase connects the performance with the ongoing interaction. In (6.1), for example, *ESTÁ, ESTÁ COMO* 'IT'S, IT'S LIKE' links the Lord's Prayer chiste to Mr. Córdova's characterization of nowadays. In chiste-telling sessions, however, tying phrases connect one chiste with another, as was the case when Mrs. Vigil began the virile rooster chiste by noting that *estaba como el CHUPILOTE* 'he was like the BUZZARD'. Feature 1 can accordingly be either contextual or textual in focus, depending on the textual-contextual focus of the performance as a whole.

The most important characteristic that is shared by all performances is the presence of a tripartite narrative structure. Each chiste opens with what we may refer to,

TABLE 3   *Summary of Chiste Performance Features*

Feature	Incidence in Sample
1. Tying word or phrase	54% *
2. Opening formula—*una vez* 'one time'	69% *
3. 'Izque	62% *
4. Past + imperfective → past + perfective	100%
5. Quotative	93%
6. Punch line	100%
7. Punch line replayed	31% *
8. Explication of meaning	62% *

* Based on a sample of thirteen performances rather than the fifteen discussed above. Pedro's three wishes and the woman's "stumbling" are not considered because of the lack of a complete tape recording.

following Labov and Waletzky (1967:32), as an orientation section. Here we meet the principal characters and discover the time frame of the event(s). The minimally essential elements of the orientation are apparent in the opening lines of the shortest chiste that has been considered in this chapter, the one concerning the woman and her farts that Mr. Córdova's son performed in the chiste-telling session. This section of the transcript (example (6.5) cont.) begins with Federico Córdova's explanation of the punch line of his chiste concerning the man who intended to rob his neighbor's cow.

También, the tying phrase, connects this chiste with the preceding one; this is significant in that the two are separated by the beginning of the leave-taking sequence. *Una VEZ* is an opening formula used for performances of narratives. When *una VEZ* is used without any other temporal markers (as in this case), it also points to the fact that the event(s) could have taken place practically anytime. '*Izque* stands both as a narrative marker and as an evidential frame. It tells us that the basis of the performer's knowledge is verbally transmitted information that is known to the community as a whole.

Next let us examine the tense/aspect characteristics of the verbal elements. *Había* 'there used to be' is marked for past + imperfective. Next comes *mira* 'see'; it does not refer to the narrative development but is an imperative that addresses the audience. *Mira* is accordingly marked for mood. *Tiró* does form part of the sequence of events; it is marked for past + perfective. This tense-aspect shift is apparent in all of the chistes in the sample. While verbs that form part of the orientation section are marked for past and for either habitual or imperfective, the shift to the next section is signaled by the inflection of at least one verb with past + perfective.[23] This moves us from a characterization of the general setting of the action to the relation of the specific event or events that led up to the punch line. I will refer to this second section as the *action setting.*

The shift from past + (habitual or imperfective) to past + perfective provides a particularly effective means of effecting this transition. As Hopper (1982) has argued, aspect performs crucial discourse functions in narrative. In particular, the perfective/imperfective distinction tells the listener how a particular action relates to other actions and to the narrative structure as a whole. Past + imperfective (or habitual) is inclusive, meaning that one such action does not have to end before another can begin. In the chiste on the three questions, for example, Pedro de Ordimalas can be tending goats, the priest can be traveling, and the king can be requiring his subjects to answer the three questions all at the same time. Here imperfective and habitual point to the status of the information that they accompany as being *conditions* and as holding true for a *period* of time. Actions that are marked by past + perfective are contrastively characterized as *events,* and the *point* at which they occur in the temporal sequence of the narrative is crucial. Pedro's conversation with the priest

(6.5 cont.) Continuation of chiste-telling session in Córdova home; 2 October 1972

FC Valió la INTENCIÓN,
    no más INTENCIÓN,
        ves;
    pues el mismo PADRE tuvo la CULPA
    de ((su dispensorio en el confesionario)).   5
S ¡VAMOS!
LC ¿Por qué se van tan presto?
S También, una VEZ,
        'izque habia una mujer ASINA,
            mira, . . .   10
      que . . .
      tiró un PEDO, . . .
      'izque dijo,
      "este es LUNES. . . ."
        Y luego caminó otro POCO,   15
        'izque tiró otro PEDO,
        'izque dijo,
        "MARTES. . . ."
          Y luego caminó otro POCO,
          'izque tiró otro PEDO,   20
          'izque dijo,
          "Este es MIÉRCOLES. . . ."
          Y luego venía un hombre ATRÁS.

        Le decía,
        "Oiga, señor,   25
        ¿desde cuándo, desde cuándo se iba siguendo a mí?"

        "Desde LUNES,"
        'izque le dijo. . . .

Y 'izque una vez que estaba el PADRE
    aconsejando a . . . Pedro de ORDIMALAS.   30

would have assumed a quite different significance if it had preceded rather than followed the moment in which it became 'the PRIEST'S TURN'. Note that Silva-
Corvalán (1983:764–65) has argued that this function of the Spanish imperfective
is particularly suited to presenting the background for events, and that the "orientation section" of narratives often contains a high proportion of imperfectives (also see
Hopper and Thompson 1980).

    The third section contains the punch line and whatever may follow it. In all the
chistes in our sample except one (Don Cacahuate and the motorcycle), the punch
line is framed as quoted speech. As Bauman (1986:68) notes, punch lines contribute

English translation

What counted was the INTENTION,
the INTENTION ITSELF,
    you see,
well the PRIEST himself was to BLAME,
for ((his dispensation in the confessional)).
LET'S GO!
Why do you have to leave so soon?
Also, one TIME.
    it is said that there used to be a woman LIKE THIS,
        see, . . .

3 sec. pause   who . . .
followed by 6 sec.   FARTED, . . .
laughter   it is said that she said,
"this is MONDAY. . . ."
    And then she walked a bit FURTHER,
    it is said that again she FARTED,
    it is said that she said,
"TUESDAY. . . ."
    And then she walked a bit FURTHER,
    it is said that again she FARTED,
    it is said that she said,
"This is WEDNESDAY. . . ."
    And then a man was FOLLOWING
    HER.
    She said to him,
    "Listen, mister,
    how long, how long have you been fol-
    lowing me?"
        "Since MONDAY,"
followed by 19 sec.   it is said that he said to
laughter   her. . . .
And it is said that one time the PRIEST
  .was giving some advice to . . . Pedro de ORDIMALAS.

a strong sense of closure to the story; this effect is achieved by developing multiple relations of cohesion (cf. Halliday and Hasan 1976) between the punch line and what has come before. In the chistes discussed in this chapter, except two of my own (about the motorcycle incident and the name sonovabish), one central technique is used in creating this coherence. In each case, the punch line segment of the chiste consists of one or more conversational exchanges. One character utters the first part of a two-part discourse unit, and the punch line comes as the second part. Questions and answers are used in the chistes concerning the Christ Child, the duck, the rooster, the king's three questions, and the farts. In others, such as the "stumbling" woman's confession or Pedro de Ordimalas and the ants, the characters trade insults; in others, the sequence is imperative-response (e.g., the chistes about being 'all mixed-up' and Mrs. Vigil's pistol). In all the chistes except my own, the first part is delivered as reported speech. Mrs. Vigil frames the words of the visitors who asked about the duck as indirect discourse—she does not quote them directly. All of the other first parts take the form of quoted speech, as do all of the punch lines (second parts) as well.

Why quotations? I argued in my interpretation of Mrs. Vigil's pistol anecdote that the use of quoted speech, particularly in the punch line, provides a powerful tool for exploring contrastive sets of ideologically motivated assumptions. Quoted speech is important in formal terms as well. What is quoted is not just words, but conversational exchanges. These exchanges organize the discourse into larger units (such as question-answer sequences), creating structural expectations regarding what will come next. They also place the relationship between the characters into a recognized interactional frame.

The cohesion relations established by these two-part pairs also extend backwards to the words and actions that have been described in the orientation and action-setting sections of the chiste. In most of the chistes the first part (the question, command, etc.) refers anaphorically to the events that led up to that moment. In some chistes, the quote sums up everything that has come before. In (6.2), for example, the participants in the procession are asked, "*¿Pa qué traen'ora a la Santa MARIA?*" '"Why are you now carrying around the Virgin MARY?"'. While 'carrying around the Virgin MARY' describes their current actions, 'now' points back anaphorically to the original procession. In others, the quote provides a synecdoche, using an element what has come before to evoke the whole. In the three questions, the king repeats the questions; not only were they presented earlier, but the chiste is structured around them. Here the questions enable us to anticipate the chiste's end, just as the answers enable us to look back on what has come before.

The punch line completes this retrospective movement. As a second part, it refers back to the preceding question, imperative, or insult, appropriating the referents and often part of the syntax and lexicon of the first part. As I noted in my remarks on the pistol chiste, the punch line does not simply reiterate what comes before—it transforms it. The punch line calls into question one or more of the presuppositions of the utterance that it subverts. The king learns that he has falsely assessed the identity of his interlocutor, Mrs. Vigil's character has been incorrectly assessed by the would-be intruder, Antonio's social and religious superiority is questioned, and so forth. Recall that the first part stands for the events of the orientation and action-setting sections of the chiste. By subverting the first part, the punch line imposes a new interpretation on the whole of what has come before. In some chistes, such as Mrs. Vigil's pistol, the punch line transforms not only the interpretation of the narrative but the relationship between the performer and audience as well.

The punch line is sometimes followed by one or more replayings of the punch line and by an explication of or comment on the chiste; these can be presented by either the performer or another participant. If the performer fails to establish adequate coherence relations, the audience may need reiterations of the punch line or explications of its meaning in order to make sense of the chiste. An example of the use of an explication in repairing a lack of coherence is apparent in Mrs. Vigil's rooster joke. She failed to note the presence of the circling buzzards before she uttered the punch line; "¡Shush!" (and its gestural complement) accordingly did not convey the rooster's intention to seduce the female buzzards. Mrs. Vigil thus notes the presence of the buzzards, and she goes on to frame an explanation of the rooster's "¡Shush!" as the quoted speech of the rooster.

Whereas Mrs. Vigil's rooster chiste may evince a structural flaw, my rendition of Don Cacahuate and his motorcycle provides an example of a complete failure. Interestingly, it is also the only chiste in our sample that does not contain quoted speech in its punch line. The exception may, as the saying goes, prove the rule. My failure to use dialectally appropriate terms was partly responsible for this situation. The problem was, however, not simply a failure to understand the content of the chiste. The punch line elicited no response, and my audience simply continued to stare at me. Although I had portrayed a series of events that led up to a climax, the lack of a two-part pair and of reported speech as a whole deprived the audience of any cues of the imminence of the punch line and then of its arrival. This is not to say that any chiste will necessarily fail if its punch line does not contain quoted speech. It does, nonetheless, underlie the importance of this feature to the formal structure and rhetorical effectiveness of chistes.

Chistes clearly illustrate the veracity of Goffman's (1974:559) observation that "tales told about experience can (and tend to) be organized from the beginning in terms of what will prove to be the outcome." Cues are provided all along the way that enable the audience to identify the punch line and to grasp how it brings closure to the form and sense of the chiste. But this is only half of the story. The dialectical relationship between the punch line and everything that comes before also looks backwards. The form and meaning of the chiste remain incomplete until we reach the punch line. The latter not only affords the closure we have been seeking, but provides us with a basis for grasping the role of heretofore enigmatic words and for reinterpreting elements that we thought we understood. The punch line similarly plays a crucial role in the interactional structure of the performance, because it marks the point at which other speakers may lay claim to the role of performer.

CHISTES, VARIATION, AND RHETORICAL COMPETENCE

The final question about chistes concerns why virtually anyone can assume the role of performer. Chistes differ in this regard from all the other genres of la plática de los viejitos de antes. Two conclusions regarding the communicative structure and function of chistes provide us with insight into these issues.

First, I have argued in this chapter that performances of chistes provide forums for launching ludic and critical explorations of social experience and noted Limón's (1982) observation that jokes demonstrate the power of folklore to contribute to the creation of new ideologies and social formations. This invites the observation that the lack of restrictions on the role of performer opens up this crucial reflexive process to all sectors of the community, young and old, female and male. I have argued that the talk of the elders of bygone days constitutes a dialectical examination of past and present, not a conservative reification of tradition. If this process were restricted to those persons who are most closely associated with the elders of bygone days—the contemporary elders—the creative and critical capacity of chistes would be unlikely to achieve its full impact.

Second, Gossen (1974b:106) has argued that the Chamula genre of "truly frivolous talk" is "extremely important to the socialization process in general and to the learning of the language [Tzotzil] in particular," and students of other humorous traditions have reached similar conclusions. A number of factors point to the importance of performances of chistes in acquiring competence in la plática de los viejitos de antes. Access to the role of performer is severely limited for other genres. Specifically, the right to perform historical discourse, proverbs, scriptural allusions, and legends that deal with bygone days is primarily reserved to elders; the few attempts I have witnessed by younger persons to perform in these genres were regarded as presumptuous. One might accordingly wonder how an individual gains competence in these genres, given the fact that opportunities for practicing them are so restricted.

Chistes provide excellent means of developing such abilities. Anyone may try, and younger persons are free to perform chistes in the company of peers and older persons alike. Chistes provide performers with a chance to interpret antes and ahora, and the relationship between them. The values associated with bygone days are not represented directly; they rather disguised through the use of parodization, stereotypification (e.g., the priest, the Catholics, an Indio), fictionalization (e.g., through the appearance of kings and Christ in northern New Mexican communities and the creation of anthropomorphic roosters and other creatures), the embodiment of character traits and sociocultural processes in such trickster figures as Pedro de Ordimalas and Don Cacahuate, and other transformations. As Abrahams (1982a) has argued, the ludic frame enables performers to criticize and even mock cultural elements without having to face the consequences that such behavior would engender outside of the world of play.

Pedagogically, chistes are ideal. Each performance is assessed immediately, publicly, and almost quantitatively through the volume, duration, and character of the laughter it produces. My consultants suggested that laughter provides an essential criterion for judging performances as well as for defining the genre. A performance that does not make the audience laugh is, in their eyes, a failure. They note that performances of proverbs sometimes prompt a few laughs. In the case of chistes, however, generating laughter is crucial, while this is not true for proverbs. Success has its rewards, gaining the person a reputation for being *muy chistoso* 'a great jokster'. Federico Córdova once characterized the nature of this ability in the following terms: *Bueno, hay personas que tienen como un modo, como un ESTILO, que cae, que cae muy, muy, muy bien* 'Okay, there are persons who have a way, like a STYLE, that comes across, that comes across very, very, very well'. The enjoyment that this *modo* or *estilo* affords the audience places such individuals in great demand within the community.

Chistes differ from the other genres not so much in the consequences of success but in those of failure. Attempting to perform a proverb when one lacks the competence to do so constitutes a serious loss of face, to use Goffman's (1959) term. The stakes are particularly high in competitive situations, because one person's less-than-adequate performance will be subverted by a competitor. Public displays of rhetorical ability in competitive exchanges of proverbs or historical vignettes continue to form a major conversational resource in the community for several days.[24] Performances of chistes are free from such negative side-effects. If a performance elicits confusion rather than laughter, the situation is likely to embarrass the would-be performer. It is, however, not regarded as an affront or presumption, and it is very unlikely to engender ridicule, either at the time of the performance or afterwards. Another participant generally engages in some repair work (cf. Churchill 1978), providing missing information or correcting misinformation, and then the conversation proceeds to a new topic or, in a chiste-telling session, to a new performance.

I have argued throughout this book that the ability to use language artistically and persuasively is a central concern in Mexicano culture. Chistes provide an important means of demonstrating one's competence in this regard. Chiste-telling sessions constitute occasions in which rhetorical ability is celebrated. This relationship between communicative competence and performances of chistes appears to be an important feature of Mexicano culture in the Southwest in general. Reyna (1973:261) notes, for example, that the jest and anecdote provide the "most important vehicle" for realizing "an immense desire to be verbally adequate."

This does not provide us with any special insight into the nature of chistes, because performances in other genres of la plática de los viejitos de antes also foreground rhetorical competence. The special character of chistes is, however, apparent in the lack of restrictions on access to the role of performer, the indirectness with which chistes relate to the values embodied in bygone days, and the fact that performing chistes does not put one's reputation on the line to such a great extent. But perhaps the most important characteristic of chistes in this regard is the breadth of the genre vis-à-vis the contextual-textual continuum. Some chistes, such as (6.1),

embed a ludic frame in the midst of a serious discussion, and the relationship between the chiste and its conversational setting are foregrounded. Chistes can also
generate their own setting, that of the chiste-telling session. In such cases the structure of the interaction is patterned by the narrative structure of individual performances; the structure of the genre as a whole, as containing groups of chistes that are
organized according to content (e.g., sex, religion, Anglo-Americans, etc.) or principal character (Pedro de Ordimalas or Don Cacahuate), also contributes to the organization of such sessions.

The point is that the textual-contextual variation that is apparent within the
genre reiterates the textual-contextual relations that underlie performances of both
highly contextual genres, such as proverbs, and more textual ones, such as legends.
Gaining skill in telling chistes, which begins early in life, thus provides a means of
mastering the communicative processes that can be used in demonstrating virtuosity
in performances of historical discourse, proverbs, scriptural allusions, and legends.
Chistes are accordingly crucial collectively, as tools for critically examining social
reality; interpersonally, in their capacity for defining and transforming roles and social relations; and individually, by virtue of the broad access that they provide to the
process of acquiring communicative competence.

7

■■

LEGENDS AND TREASURE TALES

Chistes provide a transition between the highly contextualized genres and those that evince a more narrative focus. Although some chistes take the form of short performances that are solidly lodged in a given conversational setting, others create many of the elements of the interaction in the course of developing a narrative. In this chapter we find performances in which the urge to narrate not only predominates, but generates lengthy stories that sometimes take more than an hour to tell. Here we discover that the basic process underlying performance—the ability to assess the elements of a given interaction and then select a folkloric form, shaping it to fit that interaction—is reversed. As I noted previously, proverbs and scriptural allusions invite the elders of bygone days into the midst of the conversation. In the case of legends, the performer begins with a narrative representation of a given set of events and then reaches out of the story, as it were, to bring the audience into the world that is evoked by the narrative.

I will deal in this chapter with the two basic types of legends that form part of la plática de los viejitos de antes. The first provides a narrative representation of a given set of events. Because such legends are of substantial length, I will be forced to limit the number of examples that are presented in full and are accorded detailed analysis. I will thus focus on one of these event-centered legends, an account of a narrow escape from an encounter with Native Americans in the mountains above Córdova. Legends of the second type, which concern the provenance of treasure caches and gold mines and attempts to find them, are related frequently by Córdovans, and evoke intense interest on the part of some residents.

LEGENDS OF HISTORICAL EVENTS

I noted previously that legends are most similar to chistes among the genres discussed so far. This congruity is apparent in the way that performances relate to their social settings. Legends are sometimes used as evidence in support of a particular point of view. More often, they illustrate a topic under discussion, providing a detailed account that fleshes out a more general point. Like chistes, performances of legends can also begin with the urge to tell a story for the story's sake, where an explicit relationship to the topic of the preceding discourse is absent.

This might suggest that the way legends and chistes effect a rapprochement between textual traditions and the social settings of performances is roughly the same.

(7.1) Melaquías Romero (74) and CLB (30); 24 August 1983, Córdova, New Mexico

CB	Pos, pos, ¿cómo era la vida	
	cuando andaban aquí los INDIOS?	
	¿O cuándo, cuándo,	
	pues,	
	cuando andaban atacando aquí los INDIOS?	5
MR	Bueno, pues,	
	YA cuando,	
	AQUÍ cuando,	
	cuando, cuando yo estaba MEDIANO,	
	me acuerdo que,	10
	t[od]avía estaba yo MEDIANO,	
	venían indios pa' ACÁ,	
	pa' acá pa' la SIERRA,	
	y la GENTE les tenían MIEDO a los INDIOS,	
	cuando	15
CB	sí	
MR	cuando	
	veían pasar INDIOS pa' allá pa' la SIERRA,	
	pues, le, le, les daba MIEDO con ELLOS,	
	porque quizás PELEABAN los INDIOS con los MEXICANOS,	20
	¿ves?	
	Y, y había un hombre AQUÍ,	
	había un hombre aquí en CUNDIYÓ;	
	se llamaba ANTONIO VIGIL.	
	Y ése no les tenía MIEDO a los INDIOS;	25
	se peleaba con ellos y los MATABA.	
CB	¿Sí?	
MR	Ese Antonio VIGIL,	
	ves,	
	él los MATABA. . . .	30
	Y una vez,	
	platica–, platicaba mi abuelito,	
	el [di]junto Ramón ROMERO,	
	que, que habían ido como, como DOCE,	
	como doce PERSONAS,	35
	doce HOMBRES . . .	
	a dar una VUELTA	
	por aquí por Los OJITOS,	

To the contrary, however, they involve quite different processes, and they achieve distinct communicative effects. The differences between chistes and legends are apparent in example (7.1). This legend was recorded during a videotaped conversation with Melaquías Romero. Because he mentioned the presence of *Indios* 'Indians' around Córdova antes, I asked him about the quality of life during the days in which Mexicanos exchanged hostilities with Apaches, Comanches, Utes, Navajos, and other groups.

	English translation
	Well, well, what was life like
nods	when the INDIANS used to be HERE?
	Or, when, when,
	well,
	when the INDIANS used to ATTACK?
	Okay, well,
	BACK when,
	HERE when,
	when, when I was A CHILD,
	I remember that,
	I was still a CHILD,
	Indians used to come HERE,
points with head	here in the MOUNTAINS,
	and the PEOPLE were AFRAID of the INDIANS,
	when,
nods	yes
	when
	they used to see INDIANS going by up there in the MOUNTAINS,
	well, they, they, they were AFRAID of THEM,
	because I guess the INDIANS used to FIGHT with the MEXICANOS,
CB *nods*	you see?
	And, and there was a man HERE,
	there was a man here in CUNDIYÓ;
	his name was ANTONIO VIGIL.
	And this fellow wasn't AFRAID of the INDIANS;
	he used to fight with them and he used to KILL THEM.
CB *nods*	Really?
	This fellow Antonio VIGIL,
	you see,
	he used to KILL THEM. . . .
	And one time,
	my grandfather said–, used to say,
	the late Ramón ROMERO,
	that about TWELVE,
	about twelve PERSONS,
	twelve MEN had gone OUT . . .
	to take a LOOK
looks and points	over here by Los OJITOS,

CB   sí
MR   a dar la vuelta por aquí por Los OJITOS,   40
                 y volvieron–
         y jueron hasta ALLÁ,
     hasta Borde'e Tierra AMARILLA,
               y luego de allá se VOLVIERON.
                     Y cuando se volvieron pa' atrás,   45
                     le–, había uno,
                     mi abuelito mío,
                     se llamaba Ramón ROMERO,
                     y, y el otro, el otro se llamaba, . . .

                     se llamaba, . . .   50
                     éste,
                     el otro se llamaba . . .
                     José RAFAEL ROMERO,
CB   ¿oh sí?
MR   José Rafael ROMERO.   55
                     Y ellos le DIJERON a, al DIFUNTO,

                     ellos le dijeron al DIFUNTO
                     Vicente, Vicente MONDRAGÓN,

                     porque este hombre, Vicente Mondragón,
                     los LLEVÓ   60
                     a dar una VUELTA
                     a ver si no se vieran INDIOS,
                     pa' allá pa' la SIERRA,
                     porque les tenían MIEDO,
                         ¿ves?   65
CB   Sí.
MR   Y este Vicente MONDRAGÓN
                     era el juez de BARRIO,
                     y el/
CB   /oh, ¿sí?/   70
MR   /y el juez de barrio en esos tiempos, . . .
                       | esos son los que mandaban
                       | como un gobernador,
                       | porque en ese tiempo,
                       | en ese tiempo,   75
                       | e–, e–, era aquí TERRI-
                       | TORIO,
                       | t[od]avía le llamaban
                       | TERRITORIO,
                       | ¿ves?
                       | Nuevo México no vino a,
                       | a ser hasta,   80
                       | a ser hasta el '912 PA' ACÁ,
                       | vino à ser/
                       | [[/oh sí]]
                       | vino a ser ESTA'O,
                       | ¿ves?   85

nods

          yes

to take a look over here by Los OJITOS,
    and they returned–,

gesture indicates
continued movement

and they went as far as up THERE,

as far as Yellow Earth DAM,
      and then they came back from up THERE.
        And when they came back again,
        he–, there was one,
        my own grandfather,
        was named Ramón ROMERO,
        and, and the other, the other's name
           was, . . .
        his name was, . . .

pauses and looks up
while thinking of name

        this one,
        the other's name was . . .
        José RAFAEL ROMERO,

nods

             oh, really?
        José Rafael ROMERO.
           And they SAID to, to the
           LATE,
           they said to the LATE
           Vicente, Vicente
           MONDRAGÓN,

because this man, Vicente Mondragón
TOOK THEM
to have a LOOK
to see if there were any INDIANS,

sweeping gesture

up there in the MOUNTAINS,
because they were AFRAID of THEM,
      you see?
      Yes.
And this Vicente MONDRAGÓN
used to be the local MAGISTRATE,
and the/
      /oh, yes?/
/and the local magistrate in those days, . . .
      those are the ones who ruled
      like a governor,
      because in those days,
      in those days,
      t–, t–, this used to be a TERRITORY,

      it was still called a TERRITORY,

        you see?
New Mexico didn't come into,
into being until,
into being until '912 ONWARDS,
came into being/
     [[/oh, yes]]
became a STATE,
      you see?

Y cuando ya fue esta'o,
tuvieron que tener GOBER-
  NADORES;
pero antes de eso,
e–, ponían en cada PLAZA
un, un JUEZ DE
  BARRIO,   90
y ése era–,
un JUEZ DE BARRIO
  era como una,
como uni, como un
  GOBERNADOR.
    [[Sí.]]
Era como un GOBER-
  NADOR.   95

Y ahi cuando,
  y ahi cuando VOLVIERON,
  que ya iban a volver por 'onde MISMO,
  por ahi por La Cuchilla de Los OJITOS,
  venían a salir, a salir en 'onde esta el *campground* 'ORA, . . .   100

    pus, ahi se le apalancó mi abuelito,
          | Ramón Romero,
          | y el difunto Rafael,
          | Rafael,
          | ROMERO,   105
    se le apalacaron a ELLOS
    que los dejaran venir por aquí por Los BRAZOS,

    pa' pescar TRUSHAS ahi en LOS BRAZOS.
CB   Sí.
MR   Sí.   110
        Y no, y no los querían DEJAR,

    pero al FIN
    los dejaron VENIR,
        y se VINIERON . . .
            y pescaron trushas ahi en Los BRAZOS,   115

            y, y ahi en el, en la subida del, del,
              del, del VALLE pa' ARRIBA, . . .
            ahi iban SUBIENDO,
                  | es una SUBIDA
                  | que va uno SUBIENDO,
                  | viene uno SUBIENDO   120
                  | pa' ARRIBA,
                  | y, y, y luego que YA,
                  | ya subes,
                  | ya queda PAREJO,
                  | un remendito ((queda))
                  | PAREJO,   125

            ahi estaban dos APACHES,
            o INDIOS,

emphatic gesture	And once it was a state, they had to have GOVERNORS;
	but before that,
emphatic gesture	every TOWN had a, a LOCAL MAGISTRATE,
emphatic gesture	and he was–, a LOCAL MAGISTRATE was like a, like a, like a GOVERNOR.
	[[Yes.]] He was like a GOVERNOR.

points toward Los
Ojitos

And then when,
    and then when THEY CAME BACK,
    they were going to come back the same WAY,
    over there by Los OJITOS RIDGE,

points with head

    they were coming out, coming out where the *campground* is
      NOWADAYS, . . .
        well, there my grandfather insisted,
              | Ramón Romero,
              | and the late Rafael,
              | Rafael,
              | ROMERO,
        they INSISTED

points with head

        on being allowed to come over here by Los
          BRAZOS,
        in·order to catch FISH there on LOS BRAZOS.

nods

                Yes.
                Yes.
        And they didn't, and they didn't want to LET
          THEM,
        but FINALLY
        they let them COME,
          and they CAME, . . .
             and they caught fish there in
              Los BRAZOS,

points with head
motions upward with
head
indicates degree of
incline with hands

and, and there at the, at the slope that, that, that that comes
  UP out of the VALLEY, . . .
they were coming UP THERE,
       | it's a SLOPE
       | it takes you UP,
       | you climb UP,
       | on UP,
       | and, and, and then ONCE,
       | once you are on top,
       | then it's FLAT,

indicates incline
indicates flatness
points to one side of
flat area

       | an area that is FLAT,
    there were two APACHES,
    or INDIANS,

esperándolos a ELLOS,
¿ve?

CB   ¿sí?   130

MR   de un la'o de la VEREDA,
¿ves?
Estaban ESPERÁNDOLES,
y viéndoles cuando iban
SUBIENDO,
¿ves?   135

Y antonces,
el dijunto José Rafael traiba torti–,
traiba una servilleta con TORTILLAS, . . .
y se quitó la SERVILLETA
de–, se desat–, se desató la servilleta de, de la CINTURA,   140

y les dió las TORTILLAS que TRAIBA . . .

CB   sí
MR   y
CB   a los INDIOS
MR   a los INDIOS.   145

Eran INDIOS o APACHES,
no sé que serían,
si serían indios apaches ellos; . . .
pero eran INDIOS o APACHES,
[[¿ves? . . .]]   150

Y,
y estos, y estos INDIOS
traiban mucho ⟨sic⟩ HAMBRE,
¿ves?
Pu's, de una vez agarraron las TORTILLAS   155

con mucho GUSTO, . . .
y se pusieron a comer TORTILLAS

de una vez ahi con ELLOS. . . .
Y ellos, y ellos, que e–, y ellos hasta TEMBLA-
BAN de MIEDO,
no más los VIERON a ELLOS.   160
Por eso sacaron las tortillas y les DIERON,

porque DIÓ mucho MIEDO.
Tenían MIEDO
de que los INDIOS fueran a MATARLOS
a ELLOS.

CB   Sí.   165
MR   Pero como les DIERON las TORTILLAS,
ellos las RECIBIERON con mucho GUSTO,
y se pusieron a comer TORTILLAS.
Y luego les DIJERON,
"¿TÚ con QUIÉN VENIR!   170
¿TÚ con QUIÉN VENIR?"
Antonces le, les dijeron ELLOS,
"Nosotros venimos con, . . .

waiting for THEM,
            you see?
            really?
        on one side of the TRAIL,
            you see?
        They were WAITING FOR THEM,

gestures and looks up   and watching them as they were
                                COMING UP,
                                    you see?

    And then,
                the late José Rafael was carrying torti–,
            was carrying a handkerchief with TORTILLAS, . . .

pantomines action   and he took off the HANDKERCHIEF
                    from–, he unti–, he untied the handkerchief from,
                        from his BELT,

pantomines action   and he gave the TORTILLAS that he WAS
                    CARRYING . . .

nods   yes
                        and

nods   to the INDIANS
                        to the INDIANS.

                    They were INDIANS or APACHES,
                    I don't know what they were,
                    if they were Apache Indians; . . .

motions to one side   but they were INDIANS or APACHES,
                        [[you see? . . .]]
                    And,
                    and these, and these INDIANS

motions to side   were very HUNGRY,
                            you see?

grabbing gesture   Well, immediately they grabbed the
                                TORTILLAS
                                EAGERLY . . .
                            and immediately they started to eat
                                the TORTILLAS

shows flat area   there with THEM. . . .

                    And they, and they, that th–, and they were even

shakes hand   TREMBLING with FEAR
                    as soon as they SAW THEM.

pantomines action   That's why they took out the tortillas and handed
                        them OVER,
                    because they BECAME quite AFRAID.

brings hand from side They were AFRAID
to center   that the INDIANS might KILL THEM.

nods   Yes.
extends hand   But since they HANDED OVER the TORTILLAS,
pulls hand back   they TOOK them EAGERLY,
                    and began eating the TORTILLAS.

                        And then they ASKED THEM,

shakes fist   "YOU with WHO to COME?
                        YOU with WHO to COME?"
                            Then he, they told THEM,
                            "We came with, . . .

con Antonio VIGIL,
con Antonio VIGIL."   175
Tan pronto como les dijimos
    "Antonio VIGIL,"
que les dijimos NOSO-
    TROS,
que les dijie–, que les
    dijeron,
no,
que les dijeron ELLOS, 180
"Antonio VIGIL,
AQUÍ VIENE."
"¿'Ónde VIENE?"
"Aquí viene SUBIENDO.
Aquí viene SUBIENDO."
                                    185
De una vez ARRANCARON JUYENDO
    pa' ARRIBA,
pa' allá pa' la LADERA JUYENDO

a todo lo que SABÍAN
con ti TORTILLAS ,
se fueron.   190
Y se fueron JUYENDO to[d]a la vere–,

toda la ladera DERESHO pa' ARRIBA.

Y ellos ⟨los Romeros⟩
    se vinieron
        toda la VEREDA
corriendo a todo lo que
    SABÍAN. . . .
Y,   195
  y cuando llegaron AQUÍ
  al, al–, a 'onde está ahora el CAMPGROUND

        'onde abaja la vereda pa' 'l,
        pa', pa' 'l Río en Medio,
    ahi estaban ya ellos ESPERÁNDOLOS   200

    en lo, la–, el dijunto José–,
    el dijunto . . .
    Vicente MONDRAGÓN
    y los demás que fueron con ellos. . . .
        Y AHI   205
        les dijeron que por que sa habían TARDA'O pa' VOLVER;

        ya les DIJERON
        que, que se habían ENCONTRA'O con los INDIOS,
CB   sí
MR   los INDIOS.   210
                Y ya dijeron,

CB laughs
shakes head

with Antonio VIGIL,
with Antonio VIGIL."
As soon as we told them,
"Antonio VIGIL,"
as WE told THEM,

as they tol–, as they told them,

no,
as THEY told THEM,
"Antonio VIGIL,

points behind himself

HERE HE COMES."
"Where is HE COMING?"

points behind himself

He's coming UP HERE
He's coming UP HERE."

brings hands up/CB
laughs
extends hands forward

At once they FLED
UPWARDS,
up there towards the RIDGE
they FLED
as fast as they KNEW HOW,

extends hands forward
extends hands forward
extends hands forward

taking along the TORTILLAS,
they went away.
And they FLED up the entire
tra–,

extends hands forward

STRAIGHT up the length of
the RIDGE.

extends hands on
diagonal

And they (the Romeros)
came down the
length of the TRAIL
running as fast as they
KNEW HOW. . . .

And,

points

when they arrived HERE
at the, at the, where nowadays one finds the
CAMPGROUND,

where the trail starts down to,
to, to the Río en Medio,
they were already over there WAITING FOR
THEM,
in the, the, the late José–,
the late . . .
Vicente MONDRAGÓN
and the others who went with them. . . .
And THERE
they asked them why they had taken SO
LONG to RETURN;
and so they TOLD THEM

points upward with
head

that they had MET UP with the INDIANS,
yes
the INDIANS.
And right away they asked,

"Pero, ¿cómo ESTUVO
que no los MATARON?"
  "Pues, no nos MATARON,"
  'izque les dijo,   215
  porque les dimos las TORTILLAS.

  Sa–, saqué yo,"
  'izque les dijo el difunto José Rafael,

  "me DESATÉ la, la SERVILLETA,

  y les DI las TORTILLAS. . . .   220

   Y luego se pusieron a comer TORTILLAS.

   Y tan pronto como, como, como se pusie-
    ron ELLOS a comer las TORTILLAS,
   que traiban mucho ⟨sic⟩ HAMBRE, . . .
   di–, nos dijeron que,
   '¿USTEDES con QUIÉN
    VENIR?' . . .   225
   Y les dijimos NOSOTROS
   que, 'Con . . .
   ANTONIO VIGIL.' . . .
   'Y 'ÓNDE VIENE ANTONIO VIGIL?'

   'AQUÍ VIENE SUBIENDO',"   230
   'izque les dijeron. . . .
     Pu's, de una vez arrancaron
      JUYENDO
     TODA la LADERA
     pa', pa'–, TODA la LADERA,
     pa' arriba arrancaron
      JUYENDO   235
     TODA la LADERA
     pa' arriba juían TODO lo que
      SABÍAN.
     Y ELLOS pa' ARRIBA la LADERA
     y NOSOTROS PA' ACÁ"

CB
MR
         sí   240
     "TODA la VEREDA.
       Y por eso nos TARDAMOS,"
     les dijo.
  "De modo que USTEDES tuvieron SUERTE,"
  'izque les dijejron la–, los DEMÁS, GENT–,   245

  los demás HOMBRES
  y el, y el, y, y el, y este VICENTE
  MONDRAGÓN,
       que era el juez de barrio en esos tiempos,

"But HOW IS IT
that didn't they KILL YOU?"
                    "Well, they didn't KILL US,"
                    it is said that they told them,
CB nods   because we gave them the
                        TORTILLAS.
                    I, I took,"
                    it is said that the late José
                        Rafael told them,
pantomines action   "I UNTIED the, the
                        HANDKERCHIEF,
pantomines action   and I GAVE them the
                        TORTILLAS.
And then they started to eat the
    TORTILLAS.
points   And as soon as, as, as THEY began eating the
points   TORTILLAS
points   being very HUNGRY, . . .
sa–, they asked us,
"YOU with WHO to COME?"

And WE told THEM,
'With . . .
ANTONIO VIGIL.' . . .
'AND WHERE IS ANTONIO VIGIL
    COMING?'
points behind him   'HE IS COMING UP HERE',"
it is said that they told them. . . .
speaks rapidly/CB laughs   Well, at once they FLED

extends arm upwards   the LENGTH of the RIDGE
extends arm upwards   up, up–, the LENGTH of the RIDGE,
                              upwards they FLED

extends arm upwards   the LENGTH of the RIDGE
                              upwards they fled as FAST as they
                                  KNEW HOW.
extends arm upwards   AND THEY ⟨went⟩ UP the RIDGE
extends arm on diagonal   and WE ⟨came down⟩ HERE"
nods   yes
                              "the LENGTH of the TRAIL.
                                  And that's why we're LATE,"
                                  he told them.
CB nods   "So then YOU were LUCKY,"
             it is said that the–, they were told by the
                 OTHERS,
points with head   the other MEN
and, and, and, and, and this VICENTE
MONDRAGÓN,
                              | who was the local
                              | magistrate in those
                              | days,

	él que mandaba.	250
	Sí.	
MR	Y estaban muy CONTENTOS,	
	porque los INDIOS no les hicieron NADA.	
CB	SÍ, seguro que sí.	
MR	Si no más no han lleva'o las TORTILLAS,	255
	y los MATAN.	
	Pero las TORTILLAS	
	fue la SALVAVIDA de ELLOS.	
CB	Sí.	
MR	Sí.	260
CB	Ahi está.	
MR	Sí.	

Y luego ((ELLOS))
  ya se vinieron JUNTOS pa' ACÁ,
   y AQUÍ   265
   les platicaron a, a la GENTE
   lo que habían PASA'O.

CB	Sí.	
MR	Sí.	
	Y asina PASÓ.	270

This legend provides a rich encapsulation of my Córdovan consultants' perception of Native American–Mexicano conflict. This portrait is quite similar to the one that emerges from the material, which includes legends, that Lorin Brown collected in Córdova between 1936 and 1941 (cf. Brown et al. 1978). The Apaches, Utes, Comanches, and Navajos with whom Córdovans exchanged hostilities until the mid-nineteenth century are characterized as being exceedingly fierce, good marksmen, and cunning fighters.[1] As I noted in Chapter 6, they are also stereotyped as being perpetually hungry and as speaking Spanish very badly. We find in the narrative that the Córdovans used to be afraid of Navajos, Apaches, Comanches, and Utes, even in the time of Mr. Romero's youth.

The Mexicanos' ability to hold their own in such warfare is traced in part to the reputation of a few individuals who possessed legendary bravery, cunning, and physical ability. One of the most famous of these is Capitán Antonio Vigil of Cundiyó. His exploits are related in a number of narratives that were collected by Brown in Córdova (cf. Brown et al. 1978:46–48). When such figures were not present, Mexicanos are seen as having escaped certain death by outsmarting their opponents. Here the two Romeros played on the supposed hunger and gluttony of the Apaches and their fear of Vigil in effecting their escape.

Mr. Romero thus used the narrative in illustrating his portrait of life in Córdova

	the one who was in charge.
nods	Yes.
	And they were very HAPPY,
	because the INDIANS hadn't hurt
	THEM AT ALL.
nods	YES, that's right.
	If they hadn't taken the TORTILLAS,
CB nods	they would have KILLED THEM.
	But the TORTILLAS
	SAVED their LIVES.
nods	Yes.
	Yes.
nods	There you have it.
	Yes.
points	And then ((THEY))
	they came back HERE TOGETHER,
	and HERE
	they told the PEOPLE
points with head	what had HAPPENED.
nods	Yes.
	Yes.
nods	And that's how it HAPPENED.

before the cessation of Native American–Mexicano hostilities. The length and the complexity of the narrative suggest, however, that the meaning of this performance is hardly exhausted by Mr. Romero's desire to reiterate these basic points. He could have used a shorter form, such as a proverb, or simply pedagogical discourse. What, then, is the broader meaning of this narrative, and how are we to account for Mr. Romero's use of a legend in this setting?

I will return to the basic ethnopoetic strategy of examining a broad range of dimensions of the form of the performance in trying to discover its situated meaning. Examination of the videotape and transcript suggest that the structure of the performance emerges from the convergence of a number of different modes of grounding the action of the story. Place names, evidential frames, and gestures play central roles in this process.

PLACE NAMES

The legend is organized in keeping with a geographic frame of reference. The description that precedes the narrative places the Mexicanos safe within their fortified plaza watching the Indios pass through the high and untamed mountains (*sierra*) above. Mr. Romero then introduces Antonio Vigil; he does this both by mentioning his reputation as a fighter and by locating him *aquí en Cundiyó* 'here in Cundiyó'. (Cundiyó lies just south of Córdova; see Map 1.) The complication begins with the departure of the twelve men from Córdova. As they enter the sierra, their progress is traced through an upland meadow known locally as Los Ojitos; here Córdovans had "tamed" part of the wilderness by planting dry farms and building *fuertes* 'log cabins'. The trip takes them to a location high in the mountains, the Bordo de Tierra Ama-rilla, from whence they return to a well-traveled area that is currently the site of a campground established by the U.S. Forest Service.

The two Romeros leave this area of comparative safety within the sierra, taking steep, narrow trails in order to reach a popular fishing stream, Los Brazos. Their journey back to meet Vicente Mondragón and the others receives the most detailed geographic description that is apparent in the legend. The ascent enters into the development of the narrative in two ways. First, it points to the fact that the site affords an ideal location from which to launch a surprise attack. Second, the Indios' departure follows from the mistaken belief that Antonio Vigil is right behind the two Mexicanos. The episode concludes as the Indios make their escape up the ridge, while José Rafael and his companion take off just as quickly down the trail. We are then taken back to the campground. The legend ends with a return to the point from which the trip began and in which the narration is taking place (Córdova).

All of these sites are rich with history and appear frequently in performances of la plática de los viejitos de antes, usually in historical discourse or legends, and in nar-ratives that recount the trips that members of Mr. Romero's generation have made into this area. This history is closely associated with an exceedingly detailed system of place names that is known, by and large only to the residents of Córdova and neighboring communities. Mr. Romero knows that I have become familiar with this system and have a mental image of each of the places that he mentions in the narrative.[2]

The geographic images that play a key role in the narrative are more than recol-lections of the physical appearance of these sites. I noted in Chapter 2 that for rural Mexicanos the landscape is very much alive in cultural and historical terms. These places are, in Bakhtin's (1981:84–258) terms, *chronotypes*, points of intersection be-tween space and time. These locations are intimately associated with the roles that they have played in the history of the community and that accordingly form part of its self-image. As K. Basso (1984) has recently argued, such culturally significant sites enter into a dialectical relationship with narratives. Just as narrative perfor-mances contribute to the ongoing process of imbuing the landscape with cultural and historical meaning, they also draw on preexisting meanings. Even though members of the audience may not have heard a particular story before, they possess a set of geographic images rich in historical and cultural associations, and these images can be used in making sense of the narrative.

The same can be said for walking, riding, or driving in and around the community, particularly in the company of an elder. One's view of the place expands as a result of hearing the story; elders often note, for example, that 'it is said that this is where the Indios were waiting for the late José Rafael and the late Ramón to come up the trail'. This reference not only serves as an index of the legend, it also contributes to the process of imagining the narrative action. Other locations will be identified by their place name and by brief descriptions of the activities that were carried out there. 'This is where my grandfather used to plant beans; they grew in abundance up here'. Such references may permit the listener to make sense of various stories in the future.

SPEECH AND ACTION: EVIDENTIALS AND QUOTATIVES

Another set of narrative stages is created within the legend through changes in quotatives and other evidential frames. Mr. Romero begins his account by noting that his description pertains initially to the period *cuando yo estaba MEDIANO* 'when I was A CHILD'. The fact that personal experience is the source of his information is indicated by the frame *me acuerdo que* 'I remember that'. When Mr. Romero shifts from generalities to a specific narrative, he provides a new evidential frame: *y una vez, platica–, platicaba mi abuelito* 'and one time, my grandfather said– used to say'. This tells us that a specific set of events will be conveyed and that their portrayal will follow the manner in which a given individual recounted them.

The frame changes again in (169). With the emergence of quoted speech in the climactic scene; now the action is not represented solely through the voice of the narrator, but through the words of the participants as well. When the Romeros respond to Mondragón's question (214–43), a new frame emerges. Here Mr. Romero quotes José Rafael, and the latter quotes both his own speech[3] and that of the Indios. Note that this is the first point at which we encounter *'izque. 'Izque* appears less frequently in legends than in chistes; when used in legends, *'izque* highlights the status of the succeeding utterance(s) as reported speech (in addition to sustaining the narrative frame of the discourse).

The emergence of *'izque* in this context is far from surprising. The statements quoted in (225–30) represent quotations within a quotation, which appears in a conversation that is quoted in a legend that is itself the reported speech of the performer's grandfather. The changes in evidential frame enable Mr. Romero to move from his own perspective ('I remember that') to that of his grandfather's status as narrator ('my grandfather used to say') to that of the Romeros' role as central participants (101–194) to José Rafael's role as narrator (214–243) to that of Vicente Mondragón and the others (244–53). Mr. Romero never abandons his role of third-person narrator. In (176), Mr. Romero begins to assume the role of the participants, using first person pronouns for utterances that are not direct discourse. He quickly corrects himself, however, and he returns to the third person. Mr. Romero uses the narrator role in (255–58) to provide an interpretation of the events contained in the narrative: 'If they hadn't taken the TORTILLAS, they would have KILLED THEM. But the TORTILLAS SAVED their LIVES'.

The use of quoted speech imbues the legend with a more fully "dialogized" and "theatricalized" (again following Mukařovský) character than is evident in proverbs and scriptural allusions. Here the voices of the characters interact not just with that of the narrator, but with each other. In the dialogue between the Mexicanos and the Indios, Mr. Romero modifies his voice characteristics as he shifts from the personae of the terrified Romeros to those of the brave and cunning Indios. The ungrammatical form of the Indios' initial question, *¿TÚ con QUIÉN VENIR?* 'YOU with WHO to COME?', provides a formal representation of the stereotype of Indios as unable to speak Spanish properly. The voice characteristics that Mr. Romero uses to quote the Mexicanos' response are particularly rich. While the question is uttered rapidly, confidently, and with great force, the Mexicanos' response is slower, softer, and more hesitant. Mr. Romero's voice conveys more than fear in the latter. He pauses after *con* 'with' (173), then repeats *con* before saying *Antonio VIGIL,* then repeats *con Antonio VIGIL.* Here the words and prosodic characteristics represent a movement from fear to seeking an escape to deciding on a ruse to uttering the lie with greater and greater confidence. By the time they cap the lie by noting that Vigil is just behind them, the Mexicanos' voices have grown confident while the Indios' voices have weakened.

Mr. Romero uses reported speech as more than a means of telling us what happened. His voice characteristics convey the emotional states that lie behind the words and actions, contrasting the Indios' bravery, bellicosity, and cunning with the Mexicanos' combination of fear and vulnerability with astuteness. The quoted speech shapes the narrative into a perfect example of the way that Mexicanos and Indios related during this period, according to Mr. Romero, which is the raison d'etre of the performance. This points to an explanation for Mr. Romero's confusion in (176–81) as he speaks in the voice of the two Romeros ('As soon as as we told them'), corrects himself (*no*), and then resumes the role of the narrator ('as they told them'). The power of the quoted speech in evoking the scene of the confrontation becomes so great that it begins to erode Mr. Romero's distance, as narrator, from the characters and events. If he had done so, however, he would have lost the delicate balance that he has achieved between his interest in the narrative and the world it conveys as against his concern with highlighting the way that the narrative is contextualized within the interaction (i.e., the status of the performance as an illustration of Mexicano-Indio hostility).

GESTURE

Geographical references and quoted speech are often used in close conjunction with gestures. As he mentions the sierra and specific locations within in it, Mr. Romero points to the area in question with his head or hand. Beyond helping to specify the location of these sites, such gestures indicate the character of the action (e.g., a sweeping gesture for searching a large area). He also uses gestures in bringing us back to the story on completion of his remarks concerning Territorial political structure (72–95), thus pointing to the end of an aside and a return to the narration. As we approach the spot where the Indios lie in wait, the angle of the ascent is conveyed repeatedly with both hands, and then both hands indicate the flatness of the top.

Next, the Indios are visually placed on the right-hand side of the trail. Most references to the Indios or quotations of their lines are accompanied by gestures that point to the right or are made with the right hand. Actions or utterances attributed to the Romeros are made with the left hand. Gestures that involve two hands combine a locative significance with a representation of the characters' actions. When 'the late José Rafael' takes off his handkerchief, Mr. Romero pantomines this act by placing his hands behind his waist and then bringing them around to the front. Offering the tortillas to the Indios and their acceptance are similarly pantomimed.

The gestures convey more than the physical actions alone. As Mr. Romero notes that 'and immediately they started to eat the TORTILLAS there with THEM', he brings both hands together in front of him. The statement regarding the fact that the Indios grabbed the tortillas greedily is accompanied by a grabbing gesture. This evokes another major component of the Indio stereotype; because Indios are supposed to be perpetually hungry, they were willing to postpone the task of killing the Mexicanos in order to eat the tortillas. Mr. Romero provides an evaluation of the significance of this event toward the end of the story by stating that 'the TORTILLAS SAVED their LIVES' (257–58). The Indios' fierceness is indicated by the shaking fist that accompanies the question regarding the Romeros' companions (170–71), just as the Mexicanos' fear is highlighted by a quivering hand (159). The gift of the tortillas neutralizes this animosity for a moment, providing a common ground; this rapprochement is doubly signaled by the addition of a sentence-final prepositional phrase (*con ellos* 'with them') and by the double-hand gesture.

When the Romeros describe their encounter with the Indios to Vicente Mondragón (207–42), the gestures change. The alternation of left and right hand is omitted, although the action of removing the handkerchief and giving the tortillas to the Indios is retained. This follows from a change in the stage onto which the action is projected. José Rafael does not take Mondragón and the others back to Los Ojitos. He rather creates a new stage on which Mondragón and company are on the left, at the bottom of the trail, while the two Romeros arrive from the right. These positions are indexed in the succeeding lines by occasional head motions in the direction of the appropriate group. These motions are complemented by alternately taking on the spatial orientation of a member of one group when addressing the other. When quoting Mondragón, Mr. Romero tilts his head slightly to the left and then looks right; he reverses this orientation when taking on the part of José Rafael Romero.

Gesture plays two roles in the narrative. Bauman's (1986:66) statement regarding an important communicative function of reported speech points to the first function:

Reported speech, especially quoted speech, involves special problems of communicative management, because the narrator is actually speaking for other people in addition to himself. Accordingly, there is a need for ways of marking the difference between the voice of the narrator in the present storytelling context and the reported speech of the actors in the original event being reported . . . and of marking speaker change within the conversational dialogue that is the core of the narrated event.

In the case of this legend, Bauman's words are just as applicable to gesture. Quotatives often do not identify which party is speaking: *Y luego les DIJERON* 'and then they asked them' (169) does not specify whether the Indios are speaking to the *Mexicanos* or vice versa. This information is rather contained in the form (e.g., the lack of grammaticality of (170–71) and the accompanying prosodic features) and the content of the direct discourse as well as in the gestures. In each case, gesture, gaze, and head movement provide a clear sense of who is speaking.

Second, gestures and prosody go together in providing Mr. Romero with evocative tools for conveying the emotional character of the actions he describes and the changing tenor of the interaction. Mr. Romero uses these features in conveying his ongoing interpretation of the events as components of the narrative and in pointing to their relationship to the conversational setting of the performance. The visual cues thus provide rich sources of information on the manner in which the audience is drawn into the world inhabited by the Romeros, their companions, and the Indios.

TREASURE TALES

Treasure tales occupy a fascinating niche of la plática de los viejitos de antes. They are certainly the most popular legends in Córdova and one of the most widely used forms of verbal art. Some elders devote much time to discussions of buried treasures, lost mines, and the attempts that have been made to recover them. Not all Córdovan elders believe in the existence of such caches or even find the topic compelling; indeed, one of the most interesting aspects of treasure tales is that they are performed by ardent believers in asserting their veracity and by disbelievers in disputing such claims. Another compelling dimension is the fact that treasure tales add new chapters to the talk of the elders of bygone days each year, because contemporary treasure hunts, regardless of their success or failure, are incorporated into the oral tradition. Legends of this type accordingly offer us new insight into the way that past meets present in Mexicano verbal art.

Two different types of treasure tales are contrastive on both formal and functional grounds. One body of legends focuses on *entierros* 'buried treasures'. Such narratives generally discuss the person or persons who buried the treasure, how they acquired their wealth, the circumstances of the burial, and the attempts that have been made at recovery. Most of the legends of entierros that are told in Córdova focus on the treasure that was left, *'izque,* by 'the late' Pedro Córdova. His tremendous cache is reputed to have been buried on a hillside by the arroyo that lies just to the north of Córdova. Every Córdovan knows these legends, and many have looked for the treasure. These tales are, nonetheless, probably the most controversial items in the talk of the elders of bygone days, because many elders argue that the cache never existed.

Legends of lost gold mines are much less controversial. Few Córdovans deny the existence of some of the most famous gold mines in the area. Skepticism tends to focus on the inadvisability of 'wasting one's time' talking about and particularly looking for these mines. Performances focus on the location of the mine, the extent of its mineral wealth, the persons who have found and exploited it, how its secret came to be lost, and the attempts that have been made to recover it.

Tales of lost mines are generally longer than those dealing with buried treasure, with some performances lasting more than a hour. These provide examples of the most textually focused and complex legends. Melaquías Romero's account of the Lost Gold Mine of Juan Mondragón has been transcribed and translated by Julián Josué Vigil and myself, and I have compiled an extensive analysis of his performance. Due to the length of the transcription, translation, and analysis, it is being published separately (Briggs and Vigil 1989). The reader should consult this source in order to comprehend the full scope of the legend genre.

THE ENCHANTED TREASURE OF PEDRO CÓRDOVA

A brief summary of the career of Pedro Córdova and his wife Ramona Mondragón was given in Chapter 2. Born in 1796, Córdova was no wealthier than his fellows during the first half of his life. In the 1830s, however, he acquired a large proportion of the land and livestock in the community, and the majority of the other residents are said to have worked for him. His trading ventures took him north to Taos and as far south as Zacatecas. (See Briggs 1987a for archival evidence on Pedro Córdova.)

Some performances of the treasure tales relating to Pedro Córdova's cache include a description of the manner in which it was interred. Córdovans once fled the community when the United States government came 'to take soldiers'. Once everyone else had gone, Pedro Córdova and two of his Indian servants carried the gold and silver into a nearby canyon and buried it. Because it is widely believed that Christian baptism did not necessarily deprive Indios of the supernatural powers accorded to them by their 'infidel' origins, Indios are said to have been expert at enchanting treasures. Pedro Córdova is claimed to have instructed his Indios to place a spell on the treasure. This explanation conforms to a widespread formula for the recovery of buried treasure: the seeker(s) must contend with the spirit of the person(s) who interred the cache.[4]

I recorded the conversation presented as example (7.2) toward the midpoint of my 1978–79 research on Mexicano verbal art. The tape recording was made in the

(7.2) Two elders, Bernardo (B) and Juan (J), and CLB (25); 26 March 1979, Córdova, New Mexico

B	No puede uno tener nada ahora.	
J	Antes, estaba libre todo.	
	Estaba libre todo.	
	Ya 'ora no, ¡ya qué!	
B	Antes todo.	5
CB	¿Era más la gente,	
	más rica la gente antes que ahora?	
J	Oh, sí.	
B	Vivía más a gusto.	
CB	Sí.	10
J	Tenían todos sus ranchos,	
	pero 'ora no.	
CB	Yo creo que sí.	
B	Había muchas CABRAS, ¡uuuh!	
	un CABRILLO.	15
	Había pa' allá,	
	había pa' allá/	
J	/borregas y todo.	
B	Pero ya 'ora no.	
	Después de que vino el PARK,	20
	ya no.	
	Ya no dejan entrar animales pa' allá.	
J	Antes, había muchos burros aquí.	
B	Sí.	
CB	¡Burros, puros burros!	25
	¿No?	
J	¡Puros burros!	
CB	Yah.	
B	Se acabó TODO.	
J	Sí.	30
CB	Yah.	
B	¡Ay! que había muchas borregas, cabras, y/	
J	/mucho de TODO había aquí,	
	hombre.	
B	'Ora, ya no.	35
J	Pero ya se acabó todo.	
B	Estaba LIBRE pa' allá todo,	
	¿ves?	
	Pero ya no.	
CB	Sí.	40
J	'Ora no.	
	Hay el cerco,	
	y luego hay	
	el gobierno.	
CB	¿Cuándo lo cerraron?	45
J	¿Qué?	
CB	¿Cuándo cerraron este campo ahi ?	
J	Uh, hace mucho.	
B	Sí.	
CB	¿Cómo que año?	50

English translation

A person can't have anything nowadays.
In bygone days, everything used to be open.
Everything used to be open.
Not nowadays, now what!
In bygone days, everything.
> Were the people more,
> were the people richer in bygone days than nowadays?
> Oh, yes.
They used to be better off.
> Yes.
Everyone had their farmplots,
but not nowadays.
> I think so.
There used to be a lot of GOATS, uuuh!
GOATS EVERYWHERE.
Up there, there used to be
Up there, there used to be/
/sheep and everything.
But not nowadays.
After the PARK [national forest] CAME,
not any more.
Now they don't let animals in up there.
In bygone days, there used to be a lot of burros here.
> Yes.
Burros, nothing but burros!
> Right?
Nothing but burros!
> Yah.
EVERYTHING has ENDED.
> Yes.
> Yah.
So there used to be lots of sheep, goats, and/
/there used to be lots of EVERYTHING here,
> man.
Nowadays, not any more.
But now all that has ended.
Everything up there was OPEN,
> you see?
But not any more.
> Yes.
Not nowadays.
There's the fence,
and then there's
the government.
> When did they close it?
> What?
> When did they close this area up there?
> Uh, many years ago.
> Yes.
> In about what year?

B	No me acuerdo.	
J	Ya hay como cincuenta años,	
	yo creo.	
	Es mucho.	
B	Oh, aquí había muchos animales,	55
	oye.	
J	Estaba LIBRE todo.	
	Aquí estaba todo libre.	
B	Pa' acá y pa' allá había mucho.	
	Borregas, tenían muchas aquí y todo.	60
	'Ora no.	
J	Aquí,	
	aquí estaba,	
	estaba un hombre MUY RIQUOTE.	
	Era como un REY.	65
	Estaba MUY, MUY rico.	
	Se llamaba Pedro Córdova.	
CB	¿Pedro Córdova?	
J	Pedro Córdova.	
	Era un hombre MUY, MUY RIQUOTE.	70
	Oh, no sabe uno lo que tenía allá.	
	Se, se extendieron sus terrenos pa' allá pa' La–, pa' Las Joyas de Arriba.	
	No sabe uno lo que tenía pa' allá.	
CB	¿Sí?	
J	Y ese hombre, ese hombre tenía pa' acá también,	75
	¿no?	
CB	Sí.	
J	Sí,	
	estaba MUY RICO,	
	oye.	80
CB	¿Cuándo vivía?	
	¿Hace mucho?	
J	Uh, ya hace,	
	ya hace,	
	ya hace más que 100 años,	85
	yo creo.	
	Como 150 años yo creo.	
	De modo que,	
	todos los terrenos eran de él.	
	De modo que,	90
	allá en esta casa vivia él.	
	Estaba MUY RICO.	
B	Uh, ¡ya qué!	
J	Pos, al cabo que estaba muy,	
	MUY RICO.	95
	Ocupaba gente,	
	nunca trabajaba.	
	Nunca tenía que trabajar.	
	Muy rico.	
CB	¿Muy rico?	100
J	Sí.	

I don't remember.
It's been about fifty years,
I think.
A long time.
Oh, there used to be a lot of animals here,
  see.
Everything used to be OPEN.
Here everything used to be open.
There used to be a lot here and up there.
Sheep, they used to have a lot here and everything.
Not nowadays.
      Here,
      here there used to be,
      used to be a man who was VERY WEALTHY.
      He used to be like a KING.
      He used to be VERY, VERY rich.
      His name was Pedro Córdova.
              Pedro Córdova?
              Pedro Córdova.
      He used to be a VERY, VERY WEALTHY man.

pointing to Las   Oh, who knows what he used to have up there.
Truchas   His, his lands up there used to stretch up to, to
                  Upper Las Joyas.
              Who knows what he used to have up there.
                  Really?
              And that man, that man used to have [land] here
                  too,
                      right?
                      Yes.
                      Yes,
              he used to be VERY RICH,
                  you see.
                  When was he alive?
                  Was it a long time ago?
                  Uh, it's already been,
                  it's already been,
                  it's already been more than 100 years,
                  I think.
                  About 150 years, I think.
      So then,
      all of the land used to be his.
              So then,
              he used to live over there in that house.
              He used to be VERY RICH.
                  Uh, you bet!
                  Well, so then he used to be very,
                  VERY RICH.
                  He hired people,
                  he never used to work.
                  He never used to have to work.
                  Very rich.
                          Very rich?
                          Yes.

Era, este hombre,
era su, era su, era su, de mano Horacio,

¿cómo?

B   bisabuelo.   105

J   ¡Sí, no!

¡Sí, no!

Era su/

B   /bisabuelo

CB   ¿abuelo o bisabuelo?   110

B   ¿qué?

CB   ¿abuelo o bisabuelo?

B   bisabuelo

B   sí, ¿no?

de 'mano Horacio.   115

B   ((No era abuelo de nosotros)).

¡Uuh! Ya hacían–.

J   Y sus corrales iban hasta allá arriba.

Y luego, tenía muchos animales.

Estaba MUY, MUY rico.   120
Estaba muy RICO,
oye.
Como es que tenía una vaquería ahi arriba.

Era como un rey.

CB   ¿Era cómo un rey?   125

J   Como un rey,
sí.
Pos, él mandaba aquí,
mandaba Las Truchas,
mandaba Peñasco,   130
mandaba muchos LUGARES.

CB   ¿También mandaba otras plazas?

J   Sí.
Muy rico, muy riquote.
Tenía PEONES.   135

B   Sí.

CB   Peones, ¿muchos
peones?

J   Oh, sí.

CB   Sí.

J   Y luego tenía una vaquería.   140
MUCHOS,
oye.
Tenía ORO.

He was, this man,
he was the, he was the, he was the,
  brother Horacio's,
    what?
    great-grandfather.
    Yes, that's right!
    Yes, that's right!
He was his/
/great-grandfather
    grandfather or great-
      grandfather?
    what?
    grandfather or great-
      grandfather?
    great-grandfather,
    yes, right?
    of brother Horacio.
((He wasn't our grandfather)).
    Uuh! There used to be–.
    And his corrales used to go way
      up there.
    And then, he used to have a
      lot of livestock.
    He used to be VERY, VERY rich.
    He used to be very RICH,
      you see.
    He had a tremendous herd of
      cattle up there.
laughs   He used to be like a king.
        He used to be
          like a king?
    Like a king,
        yes.
Well, he used to run this place [Córdova],
he used to run Las Truchas,
he used to run Peñasco,
he used to run a lot of TOWNS.
        He used to run other towns as well?
laughs   Yes.
    Very rich, very, very rich.
    He used to have SERVANTS
      (*PEONES*).
        Yes.
        Servants, many servants?

        Oh, yes.
        Yes.
    And then he used to have a
      tremendous herd of cattle.
    LOTS,
        you see.
        He used to have GOLD.

	Esa CAMPANA que está AHI,	
	en la iglesia,	145
	¡ÉL la HIZO!	
	¡La hizo;	
	el oro y plata era de ÉL!	
CB	Sí,	
	se ve.	150
	Con una piedra la TOCAN/	
J	/sí.	
CB	¡Suena como ORO!	
J	¡SÍ!	
B	¡SÍ TIENE ORO ESA!	155

J   Ese hombre tenía TESORO,
      y lo enterraba aquí en este arroyo.
      Pero, cuando uno está escarbando,
    se va PA' ABAJO.

CB	Oh, ¿sí?	160
J	Ese hombre tenía MUCHO dinero.	
	Pero,	
	para hallarlo,	
	está TRABAJOSO.	
CB	Sí.	165
J	Pos AHI lo enterró ahi pa' ARIBBA.	
	Pos ahi lo han buscado pa' acá pa' arriba.	
	NO LO HALLAN.	
	Ese hombre, lo enterró por aquí	
	((junto al arroyo)).	170
CB	Oh sí.	
	¿[Han buscado] pa' 'l ALTO aquí?	
B	Sí.	
CB	¿Y también pa' 'l SUR?	
J	También pa' 'l sur.	175
	Pero no lo hallan.	
	Lo han buscado por allá ARRIBA.	
	Lo han buscado pa' 'l cerro.	
CB	¿También pa' 'l CERRO?	
J	Sí.	180
	No lo HALLAN.	
CB	¿No lo hallan? ¿Por qué?	
B	No,	
	pos, ellos buscan pa' ALLÁ–/	
J	/PA' ACÁ Y PA' ALLÁ.	185
	Y con una MAQUINA,	
	¿no?	
	Una buena MAQUINA que marca todo.	
	¡Pero, no sabe ni uno!	
CB	Pero la cosa es que no sabe uno	190

That BELL over THERE,

in the church,
HE MADE IT!
He made it;
the gold and silver were HIS!

Yes,
you can see it.
They RING it with a ROCK/

/yes.
It sounds like [it has] GOLD!
YES!
THAT ONE DOES HAVE
GOLD!

That man used to have TREASURE,
and he used to bury it here in this arroyo.
But, when you start to dig,
it DESCENDS.

Oh, yes?
That man used to have A LOT of money.
But,
finding it,
is DIFFICULT.

Yes.
Well, he hid it OVER THERE up on TOP.
Well, they've looked over here up on top.
THEY CAN'T FIND IT.
That man, he buried it here
((next to the arroyo)).

Oh, yes.
[Have they looked] on the HEIGHTS
here?
Yes.
And also to the SOUTH?
Also to the south.

But they can't find it.

pointing south   They've looked for it way up THERE.
They've looked for it on the hill
On the HILL, TOO?

laughs   Yes.
They can't FIND IT.
They can't find it? Why not?
No,
well, they look THERE–/

B and J laugh   /HERE AND THERE.
And with a METAL DETECTOR,
right?
A good METAL DETECTOR that marks
everything.

But none of them know!
But the thing is that one
doesn't know

que tanto pa' abajo está el TESORO,

porque hay unas que marcan como CUATRO,

cinco pies pa' abajo,
y otros como SIETE;
pues, si marca CUATRO,   195
y está a SIETE pies ahi, pues/

J   /Los viejitos de antes dijeron, . . .
           en tiempo santo, . . .
           se va pa' ARIBBA.
CB   ¿En tiempo santo?   200
J   Sí,
           en tiempo santo.
                Como AHORA,
                ahora estamos en TIEMPO SANTO,
                dicen ya que se va pa' ARRIBA.   205
                Ya cuando no es tiempo santo,

                se va pa' ABAJO.
                Asina dicen.
CB   ¿Quién dice?
J   Los viejitos.   210
B   Los viejitos de antes.
J   Sí.
CB   ¿De modo que
                            andaban buscando al tesoro antes?

J   Sí,   215
                ¡pero NO LO HAN HALLADO!

CB   ¿No han hallado ni un centavo?
J   De modo que hay muchos
                            que han ESCARBADO,
                                 oye,   220
                            muchos,
                            por 'onde quiera.
                            Pero ese hombre,
                            sí tenía tesoro ahi.
                            Era, era como un REY aquí.   225

CB   Sí.
J   Todo era de él.
CB   ¿Toda la gente eran peones
                               de él?
J   Pos, sí.
                            Sí,   230
                            todos necesitaban trabajo.
CB   Sí.
                            ¿Y él tenía todo,

                            el terreno y todo?
B   Oh, sí, todo/   235

how far down the TREASURE
IS,
because there are some that
mark about FOUR,
five feet down,
and others about SEVEN;
well, if it marks FOUR,
and it's at SEVEN feet there,
well/
/The old folks of bygone days said · · ·
during Lent, . . .
it comes UP.
During Lent?
Yes,
during Lent.
Like NOW,
now we're in LENT,
they say that now it comes UP.
Then when it is no longer
Lent,
it goes DOWN.
That's what they say.
Who says?
The old folks.
The old folks of bygone days.
Yes.
So then,
they used to look for the
treasure in bygone days?
Yes,
but THEY HAVEN'T FOUND
IT!
They haven't found even a cent?
So then a lot of people
have DUG [for it],
you see,
lots,
everywhere.
But that man,
he did have treasure there.
He used to be, used to be like a KING
here.
Yes.
Everything used to be his.
Everybody worked as servants
for him?
Well, yes.
Yes,
they all needed work.
Yes.
And he used to own every-
thing,
the land and everything?
Oh, yes, everything/

B and J laugh

J

/él tenía todo el terreno,
¡TODO!
¡TODO aquí era de él!

CB

Y aquí en el valle,
¿todo era de él
también?   240

J

Sí,
no más que, en esos tiempos,
no había tanta gente aquí.

Había muy poca,
pero, hace muchos
AÑOS,   245
oye.
Pero/

B

/Muchos animales, mucho terreno.

J

Tenía todo. . . .

J

De modo que este
HOMBRE   250
estaba muy RICO.
Tenía mucho TESORO,

y lo enterró ahi ARRIBA.
Y decían que está enterrado
ahi.
Sí señor.   255

B
J

Pero muchos no CREEN.
No creen que había aquí
un hombre tan rico ANTES.

CB

¿No creen?
¿Por qué no creen?   260

J

Muchos no CREEN.
Dicen, "¿cómo lo HACÍA?"
¿Cómo lo HACÍA?"
Tenía todo,
todo era de ÉL,   265
¿ves?

CB

¿Preguntan cómo hacía el dinero?

J

Yo creo que la vida estaba
MUY DURA cuando
estaban los INDIOS atacando.   270
Dicen, "¿cómo lo haría?"

CB

¿Lo que preguntan es cómo estaba tan rico?

J

"¿Cómo puede haber un RICO
en los tiempos de ÉL?
Sí.   275

CB

¿En SERIO?

J

¿Qué?

CB

¿En SERIO?

J

En serio, sí.

/he used to own all of the land,
EVERYTHING!
EVERYTHING here used to be his!
   And here in the valley,
   he used to own everything
      as well?
   Yes,
   except that, in those days,
   there didn't used to be as many

   There used to be very few,
   but it's been many YEARS,

   you see.
But/
Many animals, lots of land.
He used to own everything. . . .

[5 seconds are undecipherable]

So then this MAN

used to be very RICH.
He used to have a lot of
   TREASURE,
and he buried it up THERE.
And they used to say that it's
   buried there.
      Yes sir.
But many don't BELIEVE IT.
   They don't believe that there used to be
such a rich man here IN BYGONE DAYS.
         They don't believe it?
         Why don't they believe it?
Many don't BELIEVE IT.
They say, "how did he MAKE IT?
How did he MAKE IT?"
He used to own everything,
everything used to be HIS,
            you see?
         They ask how he made the money?
I think that life used to be
VERY HARD when
the INDIANS were attacking.
They say, "how could he have made it?"
            What they ask is how he got to
               be so rich?
"How could there be a RICH MAN
back when HE LIVED?"
         Yes.
         SERIOUSLY?
         What?
         SERIOUSLY?
         Seriously, yes.

	Y tenía monedas de ORO.	280
CB	¿De oro? ¿Y de plata?	
J	Plata también.	
B	Pero más de ORO.	

CB	Pero, ¿muchos no creen?	

J	No,	285

no creen.
"¿Cómo lo HACÍA? ¿Cómo lo HACÍA?"

Lo hacía porque tenía buena mente.
Sabía de todo.
Pues, todo aquí era de él.   290
Casas arriba tenía,
también eran de él.
Y todo; era como un REY.

J   Pues, MIRA TÚ.
El otro día andaba yo y ÉL [Bernardo],   295
y ESE HOMBRE [Epifacio].
Y como a unos CINCO PIES pa' abajo,
yo estaba escarbando,
y la pala TOCABA algo ahi.
Y ese hombre dijo,   300
"OH,
quiero CARRO NUEVO,
quiero este y el OTRO,"
y se fue PA' ABAJO.
B   ¡TRABAJOSO!   305
J   Mira, mira,
mira,
((esta es)) la COSA,
y la pala tocaba una CAJA,
y, ¡MIRA!   310
¡dijo que todo el dinero era de ÉL!
CB   ¡TrabaJOSO!
J   ¡Cuando íbamos a sacar al ORO!

Mira,
el otro día andaba yo,   315
este HOMBRE, y Epifacio.
Y EPIFACIO ANDABA, ANDABA–,
es como si DIJERA YO,
"Voy a comprar CARRO NUEVO,
voy a comprar una TROCA.   320
Y luego,
¡se fue PA' ABAJO!

And he had GOLD COINS.
Of gold? And of silver?
Silver too.
But more of GOLD.

[We then speak for twenty seconds about the current price of silver.]

But, many don't believe
it?
No,
they don't believe it.
"How did he MAKE it? How
did he MAKE it?"

He made it because he had a good mind.
He used to know about everything.
Well, everything here used to be his.
He used to have houses up above,
they used to be his too.
And everything; he used to be like a KING.

[We then speak for 2 minutes, 34 seconds, enumerating elders who do believe the legends about Pedro Córdova.]

Well, LOOK.
The other day I went out with HIM [Bernardo],
and THAT MAN [Epifacio].
And about FIVE FEET down,
I was digging,
and the shovel TOUCHED something.
And that man said,
"OH,
I want a NEW CAR,
I want this and the OTHER,"
And [the treasure] went DOWN.
WHAT A PAIN!
Look, look,
look,
((here's)) the THING,
and the shovel touched a CHEST,
and, LOOK!
he said that all of the money was HIS!
What a PAIN!
Right when we were going to take out
the GOLD!
Look,
the other day I went out with
this MAN [Bernardo], and Epifacio .
And EPIFACIO WENT AND, WENT AND–,
it's as if I WERE TO SAY,
I'm going to buy a NEW CAR,
I'm going to buy a TRUCK.
And then,
and it DESCENDED!

	¡se fue el cajón pa' abajo!	
CB	¿Cómo es que dice, del EPIFACIO?	

J	"MIRA,"	325

me dijo,
"si SACAMOS ese dinero,
voy a comprar un CARRO NUEVO,
voy a comprar troca nueva
y TODO." 330
Y YA CUANDO UNO ESTÁ BUSCANDO,

nada de eso.

CB	¿El tesoro?	
J	Sí.	
CB	¿Por qué?	335
J	Porque tiene uno que andar	

no más por mente de DIOS.
"Si SACAMOS, está BUENO."

CB	"Si no, pues–."/	
J	/"Si NO, es la misma."	340

Pero, ¡QUÉ!
ESE HOMBRE,
ESE HOMBRE,
cuando ya iba YO a SACAR
el ENTIERRO pa' ARIBBA, 345
ese hombre dijo,
"Voy a ser BIEN RICO.
Voy a ser RICO."
((Y no lo sacamos,
porque QUERÍA SER RICO. 350
Si no fuera por eso,
lo hubiéramos agarrado.))

J		

Cuando estaba yo ESCARBANDO,
la pala pegó un CAJÓN.
Un CAJÓN de esos que tenían DINERO. 355
Pero ya cuando lo íbamos a sacar PA'
ARIBBA,
DIJO que quería TERRENO,
quería CARRO NUEVO,
TROCA NUEVA,
y TODO. 360
YA cuando lo íbamos SACAR,
se fue pa' abajo.

CB	Y ¿cómo sopone pensar?	

J	¿Qué?	
CB	Un hombre que busca el	
	tesoro.	365

The chest descended!
What is it that you are saying,
about EPIFACIO?
"LOOK,"
he said to me,
"if we DIG UP that money,
I'm going to buy a NEW CAR,
I'm going to buy a new truck
and EVERYTHING."
AND WHEN A PERSON IS
SEARCHING,
none of that.
The treasure?
Yes.
Why?
Because one must go
with only GOD on his MIND
"If we RECOVER IT, that's
GOOD.
"If not, well–."/
/"If NOT, it's the same."

But, DAMN!
THAT MAN,
THAT MAN,
when I was just about to PULL
the TREASURE on UP,
that man said,
"I'm going to be GOOD AND RICH.
I'm going to be RICH."
((And we didn't get it,
because HE WANTED TO BE RICH.
If it hadn't been for that,
we would have gotten it.))

[9 seconds are undecipherable]

When I was DIGGING,
the shovel struck a CHEST.
A CHEST like those that used to have MONEY.
But right when we were going to pull it ON
UP,
HE SAID that he wanted LAND,
he wanted A NEW CAR,
A NEW TRUCK,
and EVERYTHING.
RIGHT when we were about to GET IT,
it descended.
And how is a person supposed to be
thinking.
What?
A man who is searching for the
treasure.

	¿Ser de buena mente y todo?	
J	SÍ, o se va pa' ABAJO.	
CB	Sí, ¿no?	
	Pero, como sopone pensar uno que está buscando al TESORO?	
J	Bueno pues, ES–,	370
	ES–, sopone de ir no MÁS por MENTE DE DIOS, ¿ves?,	
	"Si SACAMOS, ESTÁ BUENO."	375
	Pero NO puede uno decir, "Voy a COMPRAR ESTA COSA y la otra"; se va pa' abajo.	

kitchen of a house on the central plaza belonging to two elders, whom I will call Bernardo and Juan.[5] Although I had seen them many times during the previous six years, this was our first extended interaction. I suggested the main theme, Córdova in the days of los viejitos de antes, and I solicited material on some of the topics that I was currently researching. I did not attempt to focus the conversation on particular oral traditions or to elicit specific genres. It should be noted that the two men, who live alone, are known as two of the most ardent treasure hunters in the community. Although they denied ever having unearthed any loot, some Córdovans assert that Bernardo and Juan have not been entirely unsuccessful in their efforts.

LINEAR STRUCTURE OF THE NARRATIVE

This conversation was framed by our initial agreement *platicar de lo de antes* 'to talk about things of bygone days'. Given the discrepancy in age, this defined our interaction as pedagogical discourse. The discussion begins, as is usually the case, by setting up a basic contrast between contemporary and historical eras (cf. Chapter 3). Bernardo begins by asserting that Córdovans used to the more prosperous and self-sufficient—'better off'—in bygone days.

Both Bernardo and Juan point out that the viability of this way of life was contingent upon the fact that the surrounding uplands were 'free' or 'open.' The end of this freedom was signaled by the arrival of the Forest Service and the changes in grazing regulations that were put into effect around 1915. As outlined in Chapter 2, the loss of this vital pastoral element of the economy forced Córdovans and other Mexicanos to depend increasingly on wage labor employment outside the workers'

> Be without evil thoughts and
>   everything?
> YES, or it DESCENDS.
> Yes, right?
> But, how is a person who is searching
>   for the TREASURE supposed to be
>   THINKING?
> Well then, IT'S–,
> IT'S–, [one] is supposed to go with ONLY
> GOD ON ONE'S MIND,
>   you see?
> "If WE GET IT,
> THAT'S GOOD."
> But one CAN'T say,
> "I'm going to BUY THIS THING
> and the other";
> it descends.

home communities. This dispersal of the work force went hand in hand with the disruption of cooperative work patterns and the annual cycle of ceremonies and festivals, prompting Bernardo's remark that 'everything has ended.'

Juan then changes the topic in (62). He narrows the discussion of the community's former agricultural and pastoral abundance by bringing up the prime example of this fertility—the wealth of Pedro Córdova. This subject dominates the conversation in (62–124) and again in (225–51). Juan begins his enumeration of Córdova's wealth by alluding to the extent of his land resources. He then moves the discussion in (118) to Pedro Córdova's livestock holdings.

My reiteration of Juan's claim in (125) that Córdova 'was like a king' prompts him to move to a discussion of Pedro Córdova's position vis-à-vis his neighbors. Juan goes on to note that Córdova's relationship with the other residents was characterized by generosity, expressed through special allocations that he gave to those who were celebrating a wedding, baptism, or the like and by the sponsorship of community-wide events. This statement is illustrated in Juan's account as in all of the other accounts that I obtained by reference to Pedro Córdova's provision of a bell for the local chapel. In addition to hiring the caster, Pedro Córdova is said to have provided a great deal of gold and silver for the alloy, which is believed to lend the bell a sweeter, clearer tone. Córdova also sponsored a great feast following the christening of the bell (cf. Brown et al. 1978:99–105). Allusion to the contribution of gold and silver is frequently exploited in the treasure tales as a means of shifting to the topic of Pedro Córdova's treasure. In (149–53), I respond to Juan's reference to the use of Córdova's gold in making the bell by invoking the local belief that the precious metals in the alloy lend the bell a clear and pleasing tone. If we can judge from other accounts,

Bernardo and Juan would probably have gone on to talk of the bell's christening if I had not conveyed my awareness of this material. This points to my contribution to the course of the conversation in general.

As is the case with other forms of the talk of the elders of bygone days, junior interlocutors are free to ask for reiterations or further elaborations of what has been said. These frequently take the form of tag questions, placing an interrogative marker (such as *¿no?* 'isn't it?' or 'right?') after a statement. The younger person can use questions (e.g., *¿verdad?* or *¿sí?* 'really?') or such exclamations as *sí* 'yes,' um hum, and the like to signal the elder that the discourse is understood. I drew on these forms appropriately, for example, in (68, 74, 100, 125, 132, 137, 160, 179, 200, 217, 259–60, 267, 272, 333). Although I had learned how to use this device, I was far from being competent in the conversational rules pertaining to pedagogical discourse at this time. The questions I pose in (45–50 and 81–82) proved to be extraneous, because Córdovans generally segment the past according to basic oral historical periods and not chronologically (see Chapter 3).

Juan then shifts the discourse to the subject of the treasure as a whole—'that man used to have TREASURE.' He then turns quickly to the attempts that have been made to recover the treasure. Juan alludes to the difficulty of recovering the treasure. Bernardo then broaches the subject of the unsuccessful searches by other treasure hunters. Two reasons are cited in accounting for the failure of their efforts. First, although the location of the purported site is common knowledge among Córdovans, the 'others' have chosen to dig in various places. The implication is that they trust their own judgment more than local lore. Second, Juan notes that the others rely on a technological aid, the metal detector. These remarks on the other hunters' searches are interrupted by several pauses for laughter.

Wherein lies the humor? The other treasure hunters are seen as devoting themselves to overcoming the major physical obstacles to recovery, that is, *finding* the cache. This approach obviously appeals to my outsider's understanding of treasure hunting, conceiving of the project as a scientific and technological puzzle. In (197), Juan signals the irrelevance of the information that I am providing, and the fact that I am talking out of turn, by cutting off my remarks on metal detectors. He shifts the conversation from these issues to reveal the real problem in recovering the cache—overcoming the enchanted treasure's powers of self-concealment. Unless the treasure seekers observe the proper precautions, excavations at the site itself will prove futile. Juan's assertion that 'when you start to dig, it DESCENDS' (158–59) now becomes intelligible. The other seekers deem the process of locating the burial spot more important than fulfilling the supernatural preconditions that are described in the legends. Juan begins by asserting that recovery is most feasible during Lent, the most holy season of the year, because the forces of enchantment are weakest and those of the righteous strongest at this time, especially on Wednesday, Thursday, and Friday of Holy Week. Indeed, Bernardo and Juan generally attempt to recover the treasure each year at this time.

Beginning in (197), Juan moves from the presentation of this information as traditional knowledge to its citation as reported (or indirect) speech. His use of *decían* or *platicaban* 'they used to say' shifts the authority of his words to the elders of bygone days. Because I was researching the use of quotative verbs in discourse structure at the time, I asked Bernardo and Juan to clarify the presupposed referent of these clauses in (209). The effect of this question was to trigger one of the elders' central pedagogical tools. If the "pupil" fails to understand part of the discourse, the elder(s) will reiterate, generally returning to the preceding topic. I consciously exploited this device (along with the pupil's right to request reiterations) in (228–55) in order to obtain additional information on Pedro Córdova.

The topic that Juan addresses in (256–93) is pedagogically crucial. By framing their discourse as the talk of the elders of bygone days, Bernardo and Juan ground their "lesson" by connecting it to the highest source of earthly wisdom—the anonymous realm of traditional wisdom. After repeating this association in (254), Juan goes on to characterize the narrative as a source of ongoing disagreement among the contemporary elders. The skeptics not only deny the existence of the cache, but they assert that Pedro Córdova was wealthy in conventional terms—land and livestock—but lacked monetary resources.

A great deal is at stake here from the viewpoint of Juan and Bernardo. This doubt poses a challenge to the authority that Bernardo and Juan accord to the historical traditions and calls into question the central example of the former strength of the community. Pedro Córdova's success in acquiring wealth is said to have emanated from his fulfillment of God's will by extending acts of charity to his fellows. Juan adds in (288–89) that 'he made it because he had a good mind. He used to know about everything.' My consultants noted that this sort of wisdom or cleverness is a divine gift. Because the skeptics are well aware of these explanations, their challenge—'how could he have made it?'—calls into question this native theory of wealth, that riches are produced by astuteness, God's will, and hard work.

The discussion becomes even more specific at this point. Juan and Bernardo enumerate the community of believers; they also list the elders who reject them. Then Juan moves to the point of maximum specificity of the discourse, describing a single treasure hunt involving the two narrators and one of their peers. Note the sudden increase in the "density" of formal elaboration and narrative emphasis at this point. The longest utterances of the conversation are inserted into the dialogue. Direct or quoted speech, which first appeared in (262), similarly becomes the major narrative device. Juan quotes appropriate statements ('If we RECOVER it, that's GOOD. If NOT, it's the same.') as well as Epifacio's highly inappropriate assertions. (Epifacio is a pseudonym.) The plot focuses additional attention on Epifacio's words, because it is the speech act itself that instantly terminates a nearly successful expedition.

The dramatic tension of the discourse reaches a peak in this segment, and an ironic element is introduced. While treasure hunters are obviously motivated by the desire to acquire great wealth, their success is deemed contingent on the rejection of selfish motives. The disruptive effects of egoistic or individualistic motives is a major theme in this corpus of treasure tales. Juan and Bernardo stress one means of denying egoism—through concentration on God's will—in this segment of the conversation. Later in the dialogue, they emphasize another way to deny individualism in the treasure tales, involving the maintenance of harmony and unity within the community of seekers. The ideal participants were frequently described as being *de buen corazón*. This translates literally as 'good hearted', and is used in this context to refer to sociability, compassion, and generosity. Although the corporatism theme is not made explicit in this text, it is implied by the alternation between use of the first person singular in Epifacio's egoistic statements ('I want . . .') and the first person plural in appropriate utterances ('if we RECOVER it, that's GOOD.'). A central theme in these treasure tales is thus the need to reject individualism in favor of corporatism and religiosity.[6]

FROM STRUCTURE TO CONTEXT

Having commented on the smaller units, I now turn to the structure of the performance as a whole. As I noted earlier, the conversation in which the legend is embedded forms an example of pedagogical discourse. As such, it uses a dialectical movement between antes and ahora in adducing a number of key values. It similarly moves from general contrasts to more and more specific issues. This performance provides a good example of the way that this growing specificity often leads to the emergence of performances in any of the other genres that illustrate the point under consideration.[7] The legend or proverb generally comes at points of maximum specificity in the dialectical movement of the pedagogical discourse. Once the performance in the second genre has encapsulated discussion of the theme in question, the pedagogical discourse then shifts to a more general consideration of a related issue.

Like nearly all pedagogical dialogues, example (7.2) begins with a discussion of general, commonplace facts about the community's past. This general information does not bear directly on the participants. As is summarized in Figure 3, each change of topic moves the dialogue closer to the pole of specificity and contextual relevance. The progression is effected by the presentation of a topic, its illustration by an example, the derivation of a more specific topic from some feature of the example, and so on. This segment of the discourse thus culminates in the telling of a single treasure tale.

This progression is also apparent in the way the basis of Bernardo's and Juan's knowledge shifts in the course of the conversation. The material contained in (1–155) is common knowledge in the community. With respect to (156–222), however, the two men's particular longstanding interest in treasure hunting has led them to obtain all the information they could on attempts by others to recover the cache. This process has been facilitated by their employment by a number of 'outsiders' as assistants on treasure hunts. They are thus much more knowledgeable about these events than their peers. They are also well versed regarding the controversy regarding the existence of Pedro Córdova's treasure (256–93), having served as major participants in the dispute. In the case of the treasure hunt itself, very few Córdovans know anything about it, and only the participants (and perhaps a few close associates) are aware of the details. The linear structure of the conversation thus maps a series of changes in Juan's and Bernardo's relation to the events and the account itself. They move from the status of bearers of the talk of the elders of bygone times in general (past/present) to reporters (others' attempts) to participants (belief/skepticism) to major participants (final treasure hunt). The discourse thus increasingly reflects the expertise and personal involvement of the two elders.

This transformation of the pedagogues' relationship to the events and their recounting does not emerge from the referential content alone—it is also marked by changes in formal features. Their speech is relatively unmarked in terms of its prosodic features in (1–61). When the topic shifts to Pedro Córdova, however, Juan's voice rises slightly in pitch and volume. These changes become more marked when the subject of the treasure is introduced in (143). The speed of his speech increases markedly at both of these points, and it reaches the point of near unintelligibility as he quotes Epifacio. More important than the absolute values of pitch, volume, and rate is the fact that the range of variation (e.g., from soft to loud) both within and between utterances increases in the course of the conversation.

The discourse thus moves from reported action in the first part to indirect discourse in the middle, to quoted speech (direct discourse) in the recounting of the dispute and the final treasure hunt. As Bakhtin (1981; Vološinov 1973/1930), E. Basso (1985), Bauman (1986), Hymes (1981), Mukařovský (1971), Penfield (1983), Silverstein (1985), Urban (1984, 1985), and others have argued, the use of quotation-framing devices can provide important insight into both discourse structure and the communicative goals of the speaker. The elders seek to convince their juniors that Córdovans enjoyed prosperity in bygone days as a result of their adherence to the principles of corporatism and religiosity, the fact that they had not yet lost access to the uplands, and their willingness to work extremely hard. All of the topics that arise in (7.2) are commonly used by elders in illustrating these points. By ordering these topics in this sequence and by introducing these formal features, however, Juan and Bernardo have converted this material into a form in which its impact on the student will be the most pronounced. The action is not simply framed as the distant reflection of past events; it increasingly takes place in the speech situation itself. Juan uses quotative verbs in speaking on behalf of the absent actors, particularly the skeptics and Epifacio. The prosodic variation suggests that Juan is imitating the voices of these persons, transforming the pedagogical discourse into pedagogical drama.

The progression of the discourse is also marked through changes in tense-aspect forms. As is characteristic of pedagogical discourse, the passage is characterized at the beginning (1–61) by a repeated alternation between the use of past + habitual for references to bygone days and present for nowadays. The exception proves the rule: a past perfect construction that is used in (20, 29 and 36), *se acabó TODO* 'all that has ENDED', describes the consequences of the event (*vino el PARK* 'the *PARK* [national forest] CAME' (20)) that divides bygone days and nowadays. The next section (62–144) draws on past imperfective. These actions characterized a period within bygone days—the reign of Pedro Córdova. This material also prepares us for the emergence of the past perfective beginning in (146); here we learn of two specific events, the casting of the bell and the burial of the treasure, that provide evidence for the existence of the cache. Beginning in (167), nowadays comes to the fore as we turn to the efforts of the unsuccessful treasure hunters. We move back to the past imperfective in (223–48) as Juan and Bernardo reiterate information on Pedro Córdova's wealth. Then (256–93) juxtaposes present, characterizing currently held beliefs, and past imperfect, as the skeptics refer to Pedro Córdova. The climax of the tale brings us back to the past perfective as we witness another specific event—the unsuccessful treasure hunt of Bernardo, Juan, and Epifacio.

As is the case with chistes, tense-aspect alternations simultaneously possess referential and discourse-level functions. They are used to mark an action as durative or nondurative; perfective *LA HIZO* '[he] made it' (146) refers to an action that occurred during a period of several days (cf. Brown et al. 1978 : 101–05), while imperfective *tenía ORO* 'he used to have GOLD' (143) refers to a state of affairs that lasted several decades. Some actions are seen as having characterized the whole of antes; *tenían todos sus ranchos* 'everyone had their farmplots' refers to living off the land as a habitual feature of antes. Nonetheless, the temporal contours of the events themselves do not dictate which aspectual marking they will receive. The arrival of the park (*vino el PARK*) and the end of bygone days (*se acabó TODO*) also occurred over a period of time. Use of the perfective here reflects the interpretive functions of aspectual distinctions and the role they play in the structure of the discourse. The arrival of the *PARK* is a synecdoche for the political-economic transformation that brought bygone days to a close. This usage places the transformation, in Molho's (1975) terms, in the "sphere of transcendence," focusing attention on the effect it had on future events and on its location within a temporal sequence. It does not draw us into the "sphere of inmanence" in which we are placed in the middle of actions that are in the process of unfolding, as does the imperfective. The perfective rather maintains our distance from the event; we look back on the action from a later time.

Imperfective forms play three critical functions in legends. The past habitual is used in the case of actions and processes that characterize antes as a whole or at least a significant part of it; the past habitual vs. present alternation simultaneously distinguishes such features of bygone days from the state of affairs that is evident nowadays. Imperfective forms are also used in framing "supportive background information" that provides a "ground" for interpreting particular events (cf. Wallace 1982 : 209). This function of the imperfective has been documented for other dialect areas (cf. Silva-Corvalán 1983) as well as for other languages (cf. Hopper 1979, 1982; Hopper and Thompson 1980; Wallace 1982). It should be cautioned, however, that the directionality of this relationship can be reversed; for instance, the casting of the bell (past + perfective) provides evidence for the existence of Pedro Córdova's gold, thus enhancing the plausibility of assertions that he 'used to have TREASURE' (156) and that 'he used to bury it' (157). Finally, imperfective forms are also used in evoking the "sphere of inmanence," placing the audience in the middle of the action as it is unfolding. This is exemplified by Juan's use of the imperfective in referring to the actions that preceded Epifacio's ill-fated utterances and the descent of the chest.

Juan and Bernardo's tense-aspect alternations do not simply refer to different kinds of events, but effect interpretive and discourse functions as well. This grammatical alternation contributes to the process of interpreting the nature of these actions and their effects on rural Mexicanos. Tense-aspect alternations signal the performers' interpretations of the action in question, and they shift the way that performers and audience members relate to the phenomenological realms that are created in the narrative. Tense-aspect forms also specify the manner in which a given action enters into the structure of the discourse, i.e., as a general feature of antes, as a characteristic of ahora, as "supportive background information " for a particular event, or as a specific event that lies within a temporal sequence. The discussion brings these issues to the fore in an even more immediate situation, that of the conversation itself. Bernardo and Juan sought to change the situation from a conversation between two elderly Mexicanos and one gringo fieldworker to the creation of a community, albeit a tiny one, that was united by belief in the treasure tales and in the values they represent. Indeed, the conversation ended with a discussion of plans for the next treasure hunt, which now included me.

VARIETIES OF PERFORMANCE: THE SKEPTICAL KEY

One of the most striking features of (7.2) is the manner in which Juan incorporates reference to the fact that a number of Córdovan elders do not believe that Pedro Córdova ever buried or even possessed substantial amounts of gold and silver. These skeptics invoke a central paradox in the problem: If such treasures exist, and if so many people have been looking for them for so long, why have they not been found? Bernardo, Juan, and other believers are convinced that the problem lies in the social and moral disposition of the treasure seekers. Carlos Córdova stated this position succinctly while discussing the problems involved in recovering the Córdova treasure with Julián Josué Vigil, as shown in example (7.3).

On the other side of the belief spectrum, however, we find Córdovans who totally discount the veracity of legends regarding the cache. Such persons also recount the

(7.3) Carlos Córdova (ca. 50) and Julián Josué Vigil (38); 17 April 1984, Córdova, New Mexico

---

CC Que si uno anda buscando un tesoro,
    y tú traigas dos compañeros o uno,
    lo que sea,
JV   um hum
CC y si ese compañero te tiene envidia,   5
    ya no hallas nada.
    Se vuelve POLVO.
JV   Yah.
CC CENIZAS, en otra palabra.
JV En otra palabra,   10
    ser de buen corazón.
CC   Yah.
JV   Yah.
CC Pero ⟨si⟩ el otro te tiene ENVIDIA,
    ahi no hallate[s] nada.   15
JV   No.
CC Sí,
    desaparece.

(7.4) Francisca (F) and Estevan (E), two elders about 85 years of age, CLB (26); 9 October 1979, Córdova, New Mexico

---

CB Dicen que había un difunto Pedro aquí
    que era más rico que QUE.
          ¿Es verdad?
E   Asina DICEN/
F   /Platican HISTORIA,   5
          oiga.
    ¡Quién sabe si será verdad!
E   Andan, andan después de los ENTIERROS,
    dicen.
CB ¿Qué entierros?   10
E   'Izque hay un entierro por ahi en la ladera,
    dice la plebe.

---

legends, and the referential content of their renditions does not differ significantly from that of the believers. The facts remain the same. The manner in which they express their skepticism provides insight into the communicative structure of legends and their relationship with other genres of the talk. Example (7.4) is taken from a conversation with two direct descendants of Pedro Córdova, whom I will call Fran-

English translation

If a person is looking for a treasure,
and you take two companions or one,
whatever it may be,
     um hum
and if that companion is envious of you,
you won't find anything.
It turns to DUST.
     Yah.
ASHES, in other words.
In other words,
⟨you must⟩ be of good heart.
     Yah.
     Yah.
But ⟨if⟩ the other is ENVIOUS,
you won't find anything there.
     No.
     Yes,
it disappears.

English translation

	They say that there was a Pedro here
	who was richer than HECK.
	Is it true?
laughing	That what THEY SAY/
	/They tell STORIES,
	you see.
	Who knows if it's true!
laughing throughout	They go, they go after the BURIED TREASURES ,
	they say.
	Which treasures?
	It is said that there is a buried treasure up there on the ridge,
laughing	that's what the kids say.

cisca and Estevan. My reference to the wealth of Pedro Córdova did not, however, elicit the reaction that I had anticipated.

Pedro Córdova and his treasure were mentioned several times later in the conversation. On each occasion, Francisca and Estevan were careful to qualify their recitation of the legends with statements such as the following: *PLATICO no más lo que me han PLATICADO, no más, porque es mucha la historia de ANTES* 'I'm just TELLING you what they have TOLD me, no more, because a lot is told about BYGONE DAYS'; *No estoy cierto, no te puedo decir mucho de esto, porque . . .* 'I'm not sure, I can't tell you much about this, because . . .'; *Como será la HISTORIA, no sé. Yo estoy platicando no más lo que me han PLATICADO, oiga. Porque yo no vide nada de esto* 'What the STORY is, I don't know. I'm just telling you what they have TOLD me, because I didn't see any of this'.

Both have invoked a powerful device in expressing their skepticism. Even the most ardent believers must admit that, with the exception of the treasure hunts in which they have participated, the basis of their knowledge is verbal. The evidential frame for the material on Pedro Córdova is thus the familiar past + imperfective in-flection of *decir: decían*. Note that this frame is not used with great frequency in (7.2). Although Juan and Bernardo acknowledge that the *viejitos de antes* are the basis of their information, they background this fact, placing the narrative force of the legends and their moral underpinnings in the foreground. Exactly the opposite is true with Francisca and Estevan. They emphasize the fact the evidence concerning the existence of the mine is verbal, reiterating the evidential frame repeatedly (*dicen que* 'they say that', *platican HISTORIA* 'they tell STORIES', *'izque* 'it is said that', etc.) and stressing the inapplicability of other evidential frames (*no sé* 'I don't know', *no vide nada de eso* 'I didn't see any of this', etc.).

Note the reframing of the legends that occurs in (7.4:12). Here Estevan cites the legends not as the talk of the elders of bygone days, but as the talk of *la plebe*. Plebe is used to refer to children and youths; bearing etymological relationship to the Latin *plebs* (which translates as "the common people" and "the rabble"), plebe bears a negative connotation in New Mexican Spanish. The effect of Estevan's use of the term is doubly pejorative, because the Córdovans who perform treasure tales most frequently are elders, not misbehaved 'kids'.

MORAL VALUES AND NARRATIVE FOCUS

The skeptics' rendition of the material on Pedro Córdova points to two important facets of legends. First, I noted previously that performances provide believers with a stage for publicly stating their relationship to the talk of the elders of bygone days. I argued that the legends, like the genres we have encountered in previous chapters, constitute interpretations of basic Mexicano values, particularly corporatism and re-ligiosity. Performing the legends and actually looking for the treasure also provide interpretations of the relationship between *antes* and *ahora*, assertions that the moral tenets of the *viejitos de antes* continue to provide important principles for conduct at present. This viewpoint, however, represents only one end of the belief spectrum that, as Dégh and Vázsonyi (1976/1969) have shown, underlies perfor-mances of legends. The narratives about Pedro Córdova also provide vehicles for ex-pressing a negative interpretation of the legitimacy of these values.

The strongest skeptics adhere to values that opposingly stress self-reliance and a secular view of production, and they urge their fellow Córdovans to save money and to look for ways to reinvest their capital in the most profitable manner. This conflict of values has ramifications in social relations in general. The skeptics are often accused of being miserly and uncooperative, whereas the skeptics point to some of the most devoted treasure seekers as childish ('the kids'), backward, and unambitious. In terms of opinions on community affairs, the skeptics generally stress modernization and individual social advancement. The believers do not deny the value of these goals, but they emphasize the need to subordinate such pursuits to the maintenance of cooperation and community solidarity.

A second point that is underlined by the skeptical recitations pertains to the relationship between contextual and textual elements in legends. The communicative impact of recitations that adopt contrastive keys (cf. Goffman 1974; Hymes 1972), from utterly skeptical to enthusiastically positive, could not be more distinct. There are, nonetheless, no great differences between them with respect to content. Indeed, the skeptics' versions are equally detailed, and they even include material on the treasure and its burial that I have not collected in other versions. The way in which these differences in key are conveyed lies in the manner in which the formal features are used in framing antes and ahora and in relating them in the course of the performance.

This contrast can be brought into sharper focus through the application of a framework developed by Young (1983, 1987).[8] She analyzes narrative components into three different "realms," domains of experience that contrast with respect to their ontological and epistemological underpinnings. The "taleworld" consists of the realm invoked by the events themselves; for our purposes, this is the world of bygone days. Pedro Córdova, the Indios who helped him bury the treasure, and particularly the cache itself exist within this realm. Performances also draw on the "realm of conversation," those features of the social situation of the performance, including its physical setting, the relationship between the participants, and the present state of affairs in the community, that the performer uses in contextualizing the performance. The pedagogical character of my conversation with Bernardo and Juan is central in this regard. The "storyrealm" lies between these two spheres; it draws actors, actions, and words out of taleworld and realm of conversation alike. These elements are woven into narrative settings, events, and conversations that are organized by such stylistic devices as rhetorical particles, evidential frames, and prosodic patterns. The storyrealm appropriates elements of the other two realms and reconstitutes them in accordance with its own task—the need to build a coherent narrative.

Applying this model to the Córdovan treasure tales brings out the importance of *a radical shift in the relationship between these three realms that takes place in the course of the performance.* In the beginning, the narrators and the storyrealm itself stand at some distance from the taleworld. The elders of bygone days are invoked, but they never enter the scene directly as actors or speakers (through quoted speech). The gap narrows as the conversation turns to the efforts of others to secure the treasure. These actors never speak, but they do pass across the stage that has been created by the storyrealm as they traverse the community with their metal detectors.

The doubters stand firmly upon the stage, and they are accorded a few lines. With the emergence of quoted speech (262), the storyrealm no longer simply views the taleworld from a distance but brings it directly onto the stage. As the narrator simulates the skeptical tone of the original utterances, the doubters emerge from the tale-world to state their position. Quoted speech reveals not only what an actor said, but the character and attitude that lie behind the words.[9] Juan's adoption of the skeptical tone of the doubters brings this message home. The gap between taleworld, story-realm, and the realm of conversation diminishes once again as the narrative focuses on a specific utterance in one place and in one point in time. This section of the discourse brings together the roles of Juan and Bernardo as major participants in tale-world (as treasure hunters), storyrealm (as narrators), and realm of conversation (as the senior participants in a pedagogical interaction). Note that it is the speech event itself, Epifacio's exuberant statement, that brings both treasure hunt and legend to a close.

The centripetal direction is crucial. The elders are primarily concerned with what they describe as a growing divergence between the talk of the elders of bygone days and the words and actions of the present; this gap is evident in the preceived failure of many persons nowadays to use la plática de los viejitos de antes in interpreting the present and thinking about the future. This situation motivates Bernardo's and Juan's concern with the skeptics' position. The doubters' views on treasure and treasure hunts is not expressed exclusively by the believers; the skeptics also tell the treasure tales. Although the content does not differ significantly between the two sets of variants, the skeptics' renditions relate the taleworld and realm of conversation quite differently. The doubters seek to discredit the notion that the taleworld (as it is portrayed in the believers' performances) ever existed, arguing that Pedro Córdova lacked the resources to amass any significant stores of gold and silver. Their performances of the legends are geared to convincing their interlocutors that the latter should not believe the legends or, more important, waste their time searching for treasure. The skeptics thus attempt to drive a permanent wedge between the tale-world and the realm of conversation.

The performances of Bernardo and Juan operate in a diametrically opposed fashion. They use the storyrealm dialectically in creating a rapprochement between the taleworld and the realm of conversation. The movement from nowadays to bygone days is the most visible. The Córdovans of nowadays are seen as holding the potential to enrich their own world by reaching back into the resources of bygone days. The benefits of this process would accrue to the community of believers as a whole. I was told later in the conversation that should the treasure be recovered, all of us (including myself) would get a share. The ability of the present to appropriate the past is, however, not absolute. The failure to date of efforts to unearth the cache lies in the fact that they have been motivated by the values of the present—egoism, greed, and secularism. Treasure hunts will only succeed when the ethical basis of action has been transformed by embracing the values that are associated with bygone days.

The storyrealm does not, however, leave antes intact. The elders do not romanticize the past, asserting that it was perfect in every way. They are quick to point out that 'the elders of bygone days used to work like mules' and suffered from the precariousness of reliance on small-scale agriculture and pastoralism in a semiarid environment. The tales do not simply validate Pedro Córdova's actions; the accumulation of such treasures is viewed as having rested on the ascendancy of one individual as 'king' and the treatment of the remainder 'like slaves'.[10] Greed and egoism are, as I noted previously, seen as ethically contemptible and socially destructive. The moral of this component of the legend seems to lie in Pedro Córdova's untimely death and the resultant loss of the treasure to his widow and children. The point is that bygone days, like nowadays, cannot be accepted per se; they, too, must be interpreted vis-à-vis the storyrealm.

Performing a treasure tale thus involves an active process of analyzing the values that underlie the taleworld, discerning those that lie behind the realm of conversation, and interpreting the relationship between the two. It is precisely this dialectical unfolding of moral principles that constitutes the topical and global structure of pedagogical discourse. In the case of treasure tales, the believers effect this rapprochement by performing the legends as well as by looking for the cache. Treasure hunting operates simultaneously in two phenomenological worlds; the seekers play a significant role in the social life of their community just as they create taleworld events for subsequent incorporation in the storyrealm of treasure tales.

Both doubters and believers alike provide interpretations of the meaning of all three realms. The stylistic features of their performance index their own personal relationship to each sphere. Treasure tales also operate performatively, in Austin's (1962) sense of the term, vis-à-vis the younger participants. Performers seek to transform their interlocutors' relationship to each of these realms, albeit in opposite directions. This performative character also embraces the relationship between the interlocutors. Each group attempts to draw others into their respective circles. Treasure tales encapsulate basic perspectives on bygone days and nowadays; performing treasure tales in either skeptical or affirmative keys thus provides a powerful index of a person's relationship in both spheres and to the underlying values that are identified with each. Performing treasure tales accordingly constitutes a powerful vehicle for ascertaining whether another person shares one's estimation of basic cultural values or for attempting to bring another person's position in line with one's own.

Believers' renditions of accounts of buried treasure use formal features in drawing their interlocutors deeper into the taleworld and storyrealm. The skeptics, on the other hand, use these same devices to move in precisely the opposite direction. By citing the legends as *pura historia* 'just stories' and calling the believers 'kids', they index their distance from the event. Their recitations are not so much performances as reports of performances by others. Both gesture and intonation are used, but their effect is not to draw the audience into the story. The pitch is heightened, and the rhythm is modulated in a rolling fashion to lend a parodying tone. Such gestures as shrugs of the shoulders and wide, sweeping gestures with open palms point to the speaker's interpretation of the veracity of the legends. If the believers try to draw the audience into the taleworld and storyrealm, the skeptics seem determined to close all points of access to the world that is recreated by the narrative.

LEGENDS OF LOST MINES AND NARRATIVE COMPLEXITY

The narrative focus that is apparent in believers' performances of legends of buried treasure is even more pronounced in the case of legends of lost mines. The latter usually do not involve supernatural sanctions that render success contingent upon one's social and religious disposition, and actually finding the mine *is* a central concern. They are generally longer than tales of buried treasure, and some performances last well over an hour. The legend that enjoys the greatest popularity among Córdovans (and which is also told in many other parts of northern New Mexico) relates to a gold mine located high in the Sangre de Cristo Mountains above Córdova; it has been discovered and lost by 'the Spaniards,' the Sánchez family of Mora, three Germans who settled near Mora, Juan Mondragón (a Córdovan), and others. To provide a fuller view of the legend genre, I will briefly discuss a performance by Melaquías Romero of the legend of the lost gold mine of Juan Mondragón. Due to its length, the text is not reproduced here, but the reader can examine the transcript and a more detailed analysis in a separate publication (Briggs and Vigil 1988).

Legends of lost mines grant the performer more control over the process of turn-taking than any other form of the talk of the elders of bygone days. The most important elements of contextualization are back-channel signals, speaker requests for verification of audience comprehension (¿*ves?*, etc.), and presuppositional loops. Narratives move through intricate series of episodes in which the mine is discovered, worked, and then lost again. Intertextuality is crucial; performers often make reference to other legends of lost mines or to other variants of the same legend. Gesture serves various communicative functions. For example, each episode contains a unique configuration of gestures that play a fundamental role in the process of building distinct existential realms for each segment of the story. Crucial gestures, particularly those that iconically represent the structure of the mine, are nearly identical in each episode. These assist the audience in connecting the essential elements from the various episodes.

The formal features are oriented, in the main, toward assisting the audience in grasping the role of persons, places, words, and actions in the narrative structure. Prosodic patterns, gestures, rhetorical particles, and phonological, morphological, and syntactic parallelism are used in placing each utterance within hierarchically organized units of form and content. The performance does not center directly on issues of moral values, but on the wealth and beauty of the mine in question, how it was discovered, why it was lost, and how it can be located once again. Appreciation of the legend involves a willingness to enter the worlds that are created in each episode, the ability to recall a vast array of details, and a sensitivity to the performer's often subtle indications as to how the pieces fit together.

Mr. Romero's performance is particularly interesting in that it exemplifies a much further extension of the process of stratifying the taleworld and storyrealm. The narrative is initially stratified into distinct periods that correspond to the different epochs in which the mine has been discovered. In each temporal segment, Mr. Romero creates a sphere of action that is culturally and historically distinct. The periods also differ with regard to the directness with which the actors move from the taleworld into the storyrealm. This differentiation is largely created through quantitative and qualitative differences in the use of reported speech. Both direct and indirect discourse is absent in the case of the first two parties of prospectors (the Spaniards and the Sanchez family), and we accordingly gain little sense of who they are. We learn more about the next group, the Germans, through one quoted conversation and a number of passages of indirect discourse. The Córdovan protagonist, Juan Mondragón, is quoted at length, and his words are used in expressing a major point of the performance.

Mr. Romero is keenly interested in demonstrating the authenticity and the accuracy of his version of the legend. This concern is reflected in the care with which he traces each body of information back to its source, revealing who told it to him, where that person heard it, and when, where, and how it was performed. This focus on reported speech is reflected in the existence of a number of characters who never discovered the mine; their function is to report the words of the persons who did find it. Reported speech enables Mr. Romero to go beyond simply describing events in exploring the interpretive processes that underlie the transmission of this body of information. Mr. Romero goes to great pains to characterize the relationship between each intervening link, thus showing us why a particular person revealed the information to another. He thus provides his audience with a means of assessing some of the factors that led these individuals, including himself, to tell the story in the way that they did.

This process is not simply used in stratifying the narrative diachronically. Mr. Romero subtly uncovers the differences in class, culture, and character that differentiate persons who inhabit the same time frame. For example, Juan Mondragón decides to reveal the mine to his boss, García. The latter refuses the offer: "'HOW COULD YOU HAVE ANY MINES?" it is said that [García] told [Mondragón]. "IF YOU HAD RICH MINES, . . . you wouldn't be working for me for eighteen DOL-LARS'" a month. Mr. Romero comments: 'In those days, the rich, I guess, used to treat the poor just LIKE DIRT.' The power asymmetry between Mondragón and García is similarly evident in the use of asymmetrical pronominal and verbal forms; García uses *tú* with Mondragón, whereas the later deferentially grants García *usted*.

The use of form and content in stratifying the taleworld and storyrealm is more than a source of ornamentation. The fact that the mine is lost over and over again suggests that more than bad luck is at fault. The plot of the legend revolves around crucial junctures in which successfully negotiating a cooperative relationship could have led to the use of the mine's incredible wealth in enriching not only all of Córdova but the region as a whole. Sometimes greed and egoism lead to failure, as occurred when two Anglo-Americans planned to kill Ambrosio Romero, one of the last persons to find the mine, as soon as he revealed it to them. More often, however, it is the inability of characters to overcome the interpretive barriers that are imposed by their own personal, historical, cultural, and social spheres in order to form partnerships with persons who occupy distinct spheres. This stylistic and phenomenological stratification enables Mr. Romero to convey his sense of the structure of the narrative and the meaning of the events that it relates, just as it assists him in using the performance to take up issues that relate to human conduct and communication in general.

THE ROLE OF TEXTUAL AND CONTEXTUAL FEATURES IN LEGENDS

Legends are similar to proverbs and other genres in that they also connect textual and contextual spheres. Each performance takes a slice of la plática de los viejitos de antes. The status of such speech events as interpretations of things of bygone days is especially clear in treasure tales. A host of formal features, particularly gesture, prosody, tense-aspect, rhetorical particles, and evidential frames, provide speakers with the tools for constructing a running commentary on their view of what is being said. Treasure tales are so popular that nearly every member of the community knows them. What is revealed in a given performance is thus less a matter of conveying a body of referential content than of infusing basic questions of collective identity and survival with a polyphony of voices. Studies of narrative in a number of different societies suggest that Mexicano legends are not unique in this regard (see for example Bauman 1986; Glassie 1982; Hill 1983; Hymes 1985).

Nearly all of the performance features point inward, as it were, indexing the structure and meaning of the legend. I thus place legends to the right of chistes on the contextual-textual continuum (see Figure 4); however, I do not believe that the contextual process has ceased to exist in performances of legends. One of the functions of contextualization is to remove obstacles to the audience's ability to enter the world of the legend. If the listener has misunderstood part of the discourse or lacks the necessary background information, the extent of her or his participation will be limited. Speakers are continually monitoring such participation, and they use presuppositional loops and other devices to keep their audience as fully involved as possible in the development of the narrative.

The use of back-channel cues in performances of legends provides a case in which contextualization is subordinated to a focus on the text. Legends also possess another type of contextual orientation that is not so fully subordinated to textual features. Speakers do not index their relationship to this talk simply as a means of self-expression. The matter of belief versus skepticism is taken very seriously. Performers try to convince their interlocutors of the legitimacy of their position. The treasure seekers do not selfishly attempt to keep the potential spoils for themselves, but are rather interested in initiating new members into the circle of believers. The importance of banishing greed and egoism that plays such a key role in legends of buried treasure thus also dominates the performance process itself. The skeptics, on the other hand, believe that both talking about and searching for treasure is childish and a waste of time, distracting those afflicted with "treasure fever" from more important pursuits. In both cases, performers monitor their interlocutors' participation in gauging the degree to which the audience understands and empathizes with the speaker's interpretation, and the structure of the tale is shaped accordingly.

As is the case with the other genres, each performance of a legend springs from a unique juxtaposition of participants, a social setting, a particular time, and so forth. It never divorces itself from this human interaction; indeed, one of the goals of performers is to transform those social relations. In the case of believers such as Juan and Bernardo, this entails enlarging the circle of those whose speech and action is shaped, in part, by belief in buried treasures and lost mines. In contrast, skeptics seek to convince their interlocutors that both they and their community will benefit from a turning away from such pursuits to what they see as more productive endeavors. In either case, those who tell the legends are negotiating and renegotiating a relationship with their co-conversationalists and with their community.

Although performances of legends and of other genres may be rooted in similar human concerns, it is nonetheless true that legends approach this process from the opposite direction. In the case of proverbs and scriptural allusions, the element of the context that gave rise to the performance is readily apparent. Speakers articulate the bearing of the form on the present context, often overtly. The members of the audience are left with a clear sense of the performer's perception both of who they are at that moment and what they should do. Performers of legends rather invite the audience to accompany them on a journey. The reasons for embarking and the way this world relates to the social context can be as unclear as Alice's passage through the looking glass. The audience members' ability to find their way through this sphere is enhanced by the provision of stylistic devices that stand as signposts along the way, orienting the participants with respect to the topography of the narrative world, not vis-à-vis their point of departure.

The performer recreates this imaginative world in such a way that the audience members can gain new perceptions of themselves, their community, and how to cope with the challenges offered by the present and future. Unlike historical discourse, proverbs, and scriptural allusions, these "lessons" are seldom stated succinctly and explicitly. The audience is rather asked to take a more active role in the interpretation process. The performance features point the audience in the direction of the speaker's interpretation, but the conclusions are seldom laid out fully in advance. Concessions to context are made along the way, but the path leads squarely into the textual traditions of Mexicano society. With respect to the skeptics' treatment of treasure tales, the point of reference is similarly a textual world, although the path leads in the opposite direction.

Beginning with the most contextually focused genres, we have indeed traveled far. Inextricably conversational forms have given way to performances in which narrative detail and formal complexity have very nearly displaced turn-taking. Legends are far from monologic, in Bakhtin's sense of the term; the juxtaposition of voices comes, however, not so much from exchanges between participants in the speech event as between characters in the story. But our journey is not yet finished. In the next chapter, we consider a world that springs from a textual tradition with roots that extend far beyond Córdova and northern New Mexico. This tradition creates settings that match precisely its own rhetorical needs with respect to time, place, participants, utterances, and actions. Here the textual tradition reaches an apex in terms of its role in the performance process. This world, which is inhabited by prayers and hymns, images and ritual actions, reemerges each year in Lenten commemorations of the crucifixion of Christ.

for the late Aurelio Trujillo
teacher and friend[1]

8

■■

HYMNS AND PRAYERS

In a well-known essay on the magical power of words, Tambiah (1968) grapples with the somewhat mystical ability of ritual language to mystify ethnographers and other researchers. Many questions confront those who venture into this realm. Does the language of magic and religion (if one accepts the distinction) revolve around the supernatural accomplishment of specific practical effects or a cognitive (re-)structuring of the world? What is the relation between the words used in a given ritual and the actions that accompany them? To what extent does ritual language differ in form and function from other communicative modes? To these we may add an issue raised by Sapir (1949:349): Does ritual revolve around individual or collective experience?

Such enigmas pose particular problems for my analysis. Two genres of la plática de los viejitos de antes, hymns and prayers, fall under the aegis of ritual language. Although they form part of this talk, hymns and prayers prove exceptions to many of the generalizations that have emerged from the study of historical discourse, proverbs, scriptural allusions, chistes, and legends. Hymns and prayers are nevertheless recognized as models for expression and conduct in general, and most Catholics (and even many Protestants) believe that the Lenten rituals in which they are performed are the mainstay of social and cultural continuity. Others, Protestants and Catholics alike, boycott performances and ridicule the participants' intense religiosity. My analysis of these genres is also faced by a practical difficulty. Grasping the communicative processes that characterize performances of hymns and prayers requires a detailed description of a complex series of rituals that could easily produce a separate monograph.

I will attempt to reconcile these competing goals in the following manner. I will begin by distinguishing the two major types of hymns, *alabanzas* and *alabados*. The former are performed on the feast days of the saints that they eulogize, whereas the latter evoke the passion of Christ and the suffering of the Virgin Mary. My focus will be on the alabados, the *rezos* or *oraciones* 'prayers' that accompany them, and the Lenten rituals in which they are performed; the motive for my selectivity is that alabanzas are rarely performed at present. The first major section of the chapter describes the rituals that take place between Wednesday and Friday of Holy Week; here I will characterize the types of hymns and prayers used in each ritual and how they are performed. A detailed analysis of the textual and contextual dimensions of these performances follows.

The second section will present a detailed analysis of the most important of these cycles, *El Santo Rosario* 'The Holy Rosary'. Here a petition for the intercession of the Virgin Mary is combined with other rezos (the *Salve*, Our Father, Apostles' Creed, etc.) as well as with verses from alabados to form a complex union of chanted and sung styles; these are performed by groups of participants who assume such roles as those of prayer leader, hymn leader, and flutist. My analysis of this cycle concentrates on the complex sets of parallelistic relations that are evident in these texts and the way that these formal elements are tied to a symbolic unification of the worshiper, Christ, and the Virgin; the formal structure also patterns the manner in which worshipers interrelate. I will argue that the communicative structure of these rituals contrasts markedly with that associated with every other speech event in the society. The movement from a contextual to a textual focus reaches its limits in performances of alabados and rezos or oraciones. (Because both rezos and oraciones are used in reference to these prayers, I will use the two terms interchangeably.) The contextualization process is pushed so far toward the periphery that its character is radically transformed. These findings will force me to reexamine the picture that I have presented of the nature of la plática de los viejitos de antes, a task that I will take up in Chapter 9.

BASIC TYPES OF HYMNS

Although most scholars include alabanzas and alabados under the aegis of alabados, my consultants made a clear distinction, one that is also made by Mendoza (n.d.) and Robb (1980:612–13). Alabanzas are hymns of praise for the saints and commemorations of certain events in the lives of Christ and the Virgin (such as the Virgin's Immaculate Conception or Christ's apparition as the Holy Child of Atocha). Hymns that deal with the events of the passion and crucifixion are termed alabados. This thematic opposition is paralleled by substantial differences in musical style. The term alabado is used in an unmarked sense to refer to both types. Both alabanzas and alabados are sung a capella; one or more leaders sing the verses and the remainder of the worshipers take up the chorus. Other types of religious music, used in other contexts, are described by Robb (1980:680–735).

An equally important distinction lies in the social situations in which alabados and alabanzas are performed. Alabados were formerly used in wakes and funerals conducted by the Brothers of Our Father Jesus the Nazarene (cf. Brown et al. 1978: 230–32, 234–37; de Córdova 1972:13–16, 48–50; Weigle 1976:175–78). Wakes now take place on two consecutive nights in one of the funeral homes in Española or Santa Fe; unlike the all-night wakes that were formerly held in Córdovan homes, contemporary wakes are usually one to two hours in duration. Although most funerals are held in Córdova, the priest and funeral service personnel now fulfill many of the roles that were formerly undertaken by the Brothers. The most important setting for the performance of alabados was and continues to be the rituals of Lent and Holy Week, as will be described shortly.

Alabanzas are generally performed in the course of festivals that mark the feast day of Catholic holy personages. Throughout Latin America, local communities set aside one or more days each year for devotions, feasting, dancing, folk dramas, and other activities dedicated to their patron saint; celebrations are also held for other saints as well as for Christ and the Virgin. In some parts of Latin America, such ceremonial cycles play a major role in articulating the community's political-religious hierarchy (cf. Camara 1952; Cancian 1965; Reina 1966, 1967). In Mexicano New Mexico, *funciónes* 'feast days' are celebrated in honor of the Holy Cross (4 May), St. Isidore of Madrid (15 May), St. Anthony of Padua (13 June), St. John the Baptist (24 June), Our Lady of Mt. Carmel (18 July), St. James Major (25 July), St. Ann (26 July), and other religious personages (cf. Brown et al. 1978: 79–80, 185–89; Rael 1942).

Córdova similarly held its share of *velorios de santo* 'wakes for the saints' and funciones. Those dedicated to the community's patron, St. Anthony of Padua, and to St. Isidore, the patron of husbandmen, were the most important. Brown (1941) provided an excellent description of the wake for St. Isidore, which was discontinued about 1932 (cf. Briggs 1983). *Rezadores* 'prayer leaders' in Córdova, still know it; J. D. Robb recorded George López's version in 1950 (Robb 1980:668–69), and I taped Aurelio Trujillo's rendition (along with an exegesis) in 1972 (Briggs 1983).

The función for St. Anthony is still observed, although in a somewhat attenuated fashion; 13 June itself is marked by a Mass celebrated by one of the parish priests. *Mayordomos* 'sponsors' for the St. Anthony of Padua chapel are chosen each year by the pastor; these two couples are responsible for organizing the feast day and for maintaining the chapel. They generally clean and refurbish the chapel before this date. The feast day begins with a Mass. At the end of the Mass, the mayordomos place the image of St. Anthony in an *andita* 'processional platform' and lead one or more circumambulations of the chapel (see Plate 10). In the course of the procession, rezadores sing the verses of the alabanza to St. Anthony; the other participants respond with the chorus.

Attendance is usually sparse, particularly when 13 June falls on a week day. The feast has accordingly been postponed in recent years until the fall, generally until November, and held on a weekend, so that preparations can be more elaborate. The Mass and procession are repeated. The mayordomos then invite everyone to come to their houses afterwards to eat. Occasionally the celebration is extended by holding a dance, an ubiquitous feature of funciones in former years. In 1976, the year of the procession depicted in Plate 10, the mayordomos had arranged for a visit by a group from Albuquerque who perform a ceremonial dance called Los Matachines (cf. Jaramillo 1972:49–50; Robb 1961, 1980:741–80). Elders note that contemporary funciones are much less elaborate than they were before World War II.

THE BROTHERHOOD OF OUR FATHER JESUS THE NAZARENE

Alabados are performed during Lent and Holy Week in connection with the commemoration of the passion of Christ that is led by members of local chapters of The Confraternity of Our Father Jesus the Nazarene. It is thus impossible to analyze alabados and the oraciones or rezos that accompany them in performance without treating the Brotherhood and the ritual cycle of Lent and Holy Week. My concern in this chapter will not be with the history, organization, and practices of the Brotherhood per se, and I refer the reader to studies of the organization by Steele and Rivera (1985), Weigle (1976), and Woodward (1974/1935). Most publications on the Brotherhood have presented accounts, often sensationalized or unsympathetic, of the penitential exercises of Brothers (see Hollander 1985; Kenneson 1978:25–26; Weigle 1981 for research on Anglo-American views of the Brotherhood). The tone of many of the works, the presence of distortions and falsehoods in numerous publications, and the fact that they publicize private acts of devotion have led to a great deal of resentment on the part of many Mexicanos, including those not in the Brotherhood. I am concerned, however, with the one aspect of Brotherhood ritual that members are most interested in conveying to non-Brothers—their theological system and the way it is embodied in prayer, song, and other forms. Through an analysis of this information, an understanding of the structure and meaning of performances of alabados and rezos and their place in la plática de los viejitos de antes can be attempted.

I presented a brief summary of the Brotherhood and its history in Chapter 2. The structure of the organization includes a central council with representatives from local *moradas* (cf. Steele and Rivera 1985; Weigle 1976:121–38; Woodward 1974/1935). (The term morada is used in reference both to individual Brotherhood chapters as well as to the building that each chapter owns and maintains.) Each morada elects a group of officers annually. An *hermano mayor,* literally 'elder brother', oversees all aspects of the chapter's activities during the year. Another officer, the *celador* 'warden', is charged with keeping order, both among the Brothers and, during public processions and services, the public. The *maestro de novios* 'teacher of novices' makes sure that initiates receive instruction in prayer recitation and other areas. The rezador carries his *cuaderno* 'notebook' with the necessary alabados and rezo texts, leading in the singing of hymns and recitation of prayers during the rituals of Lent and Holy Week. Virtuoso *rezadores*, such as the late Aurelio Trujillo, are also in demand for wakes for the dead and memorial services among the public at large. A "second" or assistant is elected for many of the offices, so there are, for example, a first warden and a second warden each year.[2]

Membership is open only to men (cf. Steele and Rivera 1985:150; Wallrich 1950; Weigle 1976:144–46). In Córdova many of the Brothers' wives belong to the all-female sodality of La Sagrada Familia 'The Holy Family'. Individuals who wish to join the Brotherhood inform the hermano mayor, who then calls a meeting. A majority must support the petition. Boys are occasionally "promised" to the morada at an early age, when a mother vows to "give" her son to the morada if Christ heals him from a life-threatening illness. The final decision is still up to the boy. Candidates must obtain the permission of their mothers, if unmarried, or of their wives before they can join. Brothers must be members in good standing of the Catholic Church. If a Brother is divorced, he will be forced to leave the morada. Brotherhood officers stress the importance of obtaining the sacraments; going to confession and communion at least once a year is crucial. Members of the local morada meet at the Córdova chapel one Sunday during Lent for confession.

Once a candidate has been admitted, he undergoes an initiation rite known as the *entrada* 'entrance' (cf. Weigle 1976:154–57; Woodward 1974/1935:223–26). Initiates must swear that they will keep Brotherhood secrets, and this vow is taken quite seriously. Such secrecy certainly follows the need to avoid the type of sensationalized publicity that the Brothers have received. It also accentuates the sharpness of the distinction that divides the *cofrados* or *hermanos* from the *público* 'public' (i.e., non-Brothers). Initiates also ask forgiveness from any Brothers with whom they are not on friendly terms; help in learning the necessary prayers comes from a Brother who is designated as the initiate's sponsor.

HOLY WEEK RITUALS

Ash Wednesday is generally the first time that the Brothers will have gathered for some months, unless they have met to repair the morada or for some other special purpose. The Brothers convene each Wednesday night during Lent to hold a *Rosario* 'Rosary Service' and each Sunday at 3:00 PM to pray the *Estaciones de la Cruz* 'Stations of the Cross' or *Via Crucis*. These services do not differ significantly from the way they are offered during Holy Week. The Stations were formerly offered on Friday afternoons; because most Brothers are wage laborers at present, the Stations are now recited on Sunday afternoons, except during Holy Week. Brothers who are working in distant areas (Colorado, California, Nevada, etc.) seldom arrive before Holy

Wednesday. Brothers attempt to convince their employers to give them enough time off from work to be fully preoccupied with their devotions between Wednesday night and Friday night of Holy Week.

THE ROSARY SERVICE OF HOLY WEDNESDAY

As darkness descends upon Córdova in the evening of the Wednesday of Holy Week, it brings a tremendous collective sense of excitement. Relatives who live in other states and have not been seen for a year or more have begun returning home. This and many other signs indicate that Holy Week is, for Mexicano Catholics in communities such as Córdova, the most important religious holiday of the year. The morada has been opened, the lanterns have been lighted (the morada has no electricity), and the wood fires have begun to warm the building. Some of the Brothers' mothers, wives, and sisters will be busy preparing the meal that will be offered to the public around midnight. The morada is L-shaped. The back room functions as kitchen, dining room, and meeting room.

The front room is divided by a shoulder-high partition into a meeting room and an oratory. At the extreme right, elevated by about eight inches above the oratory floor, is a sanctuary. Here stand the religious images that are owned by the morada. Some were carved and painted by folk artists, such as José Rafael Aragón, during the nineteenth century,[3] while others are commercial plaster-of-Paris or metal-on-wood images. They represent the Virgin of Guadalupe, Our Lady of Sorrows, the Holy Child, St. Anthony of Padua, and St. Francis of Assisi, and several representations of Christ. The images that are generally taken out in procession are crucifixes and standing representations of the crucified Christ. These are clothed in blue, as is the altar table; with the exceptions of the crucifixes, the remainder of the wooden images are draped in black. The women and children sit on benches in the front, near the sanctuary, while the men and older boys sit or stand toward the back.

Members of the público begin to arrive at the morada shortly after 7:00 PM. Most Córdovans, cofrados and público alike, go to the altar shortly after entering the morada in order to pay their respects to the images. Worshipers kneel immediately in front of the sanctuary step, cross themselves, and recite a short silent prayer. Then the worshiper stands, touches the *estandarte* 'banner' of the morada that lies just outside the sanctuary, and makes the sign of the cross on her/his forehead and chest.

The individual then enters the sanctuary and repeats this series of gestures for each of the images, moving in a counterclockwise direction through the sanctuary. The worshiper touches the hem of the skirt of the statue or the feet of the crucifix; the person may touch three or four of the smaller images before making the sign of the cross. Most worshipers more than twenty-five years of age pick up the smaller metal-on-wood crucifixes and kiss them above the head and at each of the hands. Worshipers also bend down and kiss the hem of the skirt of Nuestra Señora de

Dolores 'Our Lady of Sorrows'. Although some of the children complete this ritual in a fairly perfunctory fashion, most worshipers proceed slowly, focusing meditatively for a few seconds on each of the images. Members of the público cross themselves before leaving the sanctuary, then walk toward the back of the oratorio. Brothers remain facing the altar, walking backwards. They make the sign of the cross as they pass each of the fourteen small plaster-of-Paris depictions of the Stations of the Cross that are hung at intervals along the side walls of the oratory.

The atmosphere is relaxed, as friends and relatives, Brother and público, greet one another; the seriousness that follows from intense concentration on Christ's death has yet to emerge. The Rosary service will not start for two or three hours. Small groups of Brothers leave periodically in procession, generally bound for the chapel. Two younger Brothers carry the images of Christ, and at least two Brothers carry lanterns or flashlights. They are accompanied by two rezadores, one bearing a cuaderno and the other a flashlight. More Brothers may join the procession as well. Their departure and return are marked by great ceremony. Officers take the images from the altar and place them in the hands of the kneeling Brothers; the company then backs out of the morada (i.e., keeping their eyes on the altar), their steps punctuated by the rhythm of such alabados as *Al pie de este santo altar* 'At the Foot of this Holy Altar'.

Two members of the público occasionally leave the crowd and sit on a small bench next to the altar. Such individuals are known for their virtuosity at singing alabados. Some used to be Brothers but were forced to leave the morada, generally following divorce. Although they are predominantly men, it is not uncommon for women to act as prayer leaders as well. Some prayer leaders use their own cuadernos, others borrow one from the Brothers. The usual practice is for a young Brother to copy his father's or sponsor's cuaderno by hand upon initiation or upon accession to an office that entails leading performances of alabados and oraciones. Printed texts are, however, becoming increasingly prevalent; Rael's *The New Mexican Alabado* (1951) is the most common. In 1984, I witnessed for the first time the use of photocopies of both handwritten and printed cuadernos. Once they decide upon a particular alabado, the two leaders intone the first stanza, which is repeated by most members of the público, particularly the women. This first stanza then becomes a chorus that is repeated after each new stanza is sung. *Jesucristo me acompañe* 'Jesus Christ Accompany Me' is often sung in this setting (cf. López 1942 : 42–46; Rael 1951 : 35–36; Robb 1980 : 623–25).

The celador or hermano mayor usually signals the beginning of the Rosary service shortly before 10 PM. Approximately fifty non-Brothers will have gathered by this point. The Brothers take their places in the sanctuary, with the exception of the celador. He remains in the rear of the oratory, watching the crowd and making sure that everything is in order. Two Brothers lead the rosario from the middle of the sanctuary, just in front of the altar. They alternate between standing and kneeling, with the remaining Brothers kneeling as they kneel and sitting back as they stand.

Some members of the público, mainly women, kneel with the Brothers, but most remain seated throughout. Two rezadores will stay near the rosary leaders; the former will lead the verses of the alabado, which is interspersed with the Hail Marys and other rezos. Another Brother plays a short instrumental melody on a *pito* before each intonation of the alabado as well as other points. Pitos used to be hand carved,[4] but small plastic recorders are currently used in Córdova. The cycle of oraciones and alabados that constitutes the Rosario is described and analyzed later.

The Rosary involves forty minutes, on the average, of intensely focused prayer, song, and meditation. Once the cycle has been recited, the Brothers regain their feet and place their rosaries around their necks. Beginning with the prayer leaders, the Brothers come, one by one, to the right-hand side of the front of the sanctuary. The Brothers again venerate the images, followed by the público. Because participants proceed singly, this ceremony takes about twenty minutes to complete. Afterwards, some of the women and children remain seated in the oratory, while others join the men of the público and the Brothers in the meeting area behind the partition at the back of the oratory; here a circle of benches is warmed by a bell-shaped corner fire-place. Some members of the público leave for home at this point, but most stay. All participants converse freely, enjoying the presence of friends and relatives whom they may not have seen for some time. Some of the older Brothers turn to religious topics, exhorting the young to contemplate the meaning of Holy Week and its cere-monies. One conversation I had with an elderly Brother at this time consisted of a stream of scriptural allusions.

The Brotherhood then provides a meal for all participants; it is prepared by the Brothers' wives, mothers, and sisters. Only about twenty persons can be seated at one time, so three to four settings are needed. Brief prayers precede and follow the meal, and each group of diners gathers in the oratorio immediately after eating to pray several cycles of the Our Father and the Hail Mary. The last members of the público leave by 12:30 or 1:00 AM. Prior to departing each member of the público shares a brief leave-taking ceremony with the Brothers. Nonmembers thank the Brothers for allowing them to participate in the service, while the Brothers thank them 'for having accompanied us in our devotion'.

MAUNDY THURSDAY—THE ROSARIO AND VISITA OF THE SAGRADA FAMILIA

A women's society that is dedicated to La Sagrada Familia 'The Holy Family' (i.e., Mary, Joseph, and Jesus) has gained in popularity in Córdova in recent years. The group's major devotional activity takes place during Holy Week, but La Sagrada Fa-milia also participates in processions and other events that are sponsored by the Holy Family Parish, which is centered in Chimayó.

La Sagrada Familia meets at 9:30 on Maundy Thursday morning for a Rosary service in the Córdova Chapel. The service is led by two of the Brotherhood's *rezadores*. Once the members of La Sagrada Familia are assembled in the Córdova chapel, the Brothers come in procession from the morada with a crucifix and a standing *Nazareno* 'Nazarene Christ'. The service is the same as that of the preceding night.[5] After the Rosario, the Brothers return to the morada, and the members of La Sagrada Familia make a *visita* to a morada or church in a neighboring community. The trip is open only to members.

Visitas are a common feature of Holy Week. The Brothers make visitas to the chapel, to a large cross near the community that is termed *El Calvario* 'Cavalry', and elsewhere. They also travel by either foot or car to moradas in neighboring communities. These rituals are private. At least one person is in the morada at all times to assist both Brothers from other moradas and members of the público who come on visitas. Other visitas are made to the shrines of Our Lord of Esquipulas and the Holy Child in the famous Santuario in Chimayó, four miles away (cf. de Borhegyi 1953, 1956). The Santuario has become a major pilgrimage shrine. Pilgrims travel in small groups, generally on Maundy Thursday and Good Friday. Travel by foot is de rigueur, and some pilgrims go barefoot. Visits to the shrine are accompanied by expressions of intense religious feeling, and they are a constant subject of conversation among non-Brothers during Holy Week.

MAUNDY THURSDAY—LOS MAITINES

The nights of Maundy Thursday and Good Friday are marked by ceremonies that generate much excitement in the community. Tenebrae services commemorate the darkness that fell over the earth upon the death of Christ. After the chapel lights have been turned out, periods of raucous noise alternate with the recitation of prayers for the dead. Children await the event with both timidity and eagerness, and even adults speak of it as an experience that is without parallel.

On Maundy Thursday the sacristan opens the chapel at about 7:00 PM, and participants continue to arrive for the next three hours. Five non-Brotherhood rezadores occupy the pews directly in front of the sanctuary. As was the case during the Rosario of the previous night, rezadores enter the sanctuary in twos, cuaderno in hand, to lead the público in singing alabados. As they begin to sing, most of the subdued conversations cease. The other participants have no way of knowing in advance which alabado will be sung; those who wish to sing must listen carefully to the first verse in order to be able to take up the chorus.

The rezadores' performances are sometimes interrupted by the entrance of Brothers on a visita. As the latter approach the chapel, the sound of their alabado becomes more and more audible. A period of cacaphony in which two different *alabados* are sung by the público and the Brothers ends as the sacristan and celador turn off the lights. The crowd then concentrates on the Brothers as the latter enter the chapel, traverse its length, and enter the sacristy. The Brothers' alabado, which they have been singing continuously, grows faint after the group closes the sacristy door behind them. Because they will exit the chapel through the sacristy, this is the end of the visita from the público's point of view. As the rezadores in the sanctuary take up their alabado once again, the emotional intensity of the singing and the state of excitement of the crowd diminish considerably. Once the alabado has ended, the rezadores will ask the other members of the público to join them in reciting a Hail Mary, Apostles' Creed, Our Father, or other oraciones. These are generally offered in memory of a deceased relative, but prayers are also recited by the rezadores or a sacristan 'for the life and health of all who are present.'

By this time some one hundred fifty persons will have crowded into the diminutive chapel. The beginning of the Maitines ceremony itself is marked by the entrance of the Brothers into the chapel without extinguishing the lights. The fact that they have not come on a visita is also evident in the fact that many of the Brothers are carrying the large wooden rachet noisemakers known as *matracas*. The Brothers gather in the sanctuary, take the rosaries from around their necks, and begin praying the Holy Rosary. This is followed by a number of Our Fathers, Apostles' Creeds, and other prayers.

Once the Rosary service has ended, the Brothers place their rosaries back around their necks and take their matracas in hand. The officers position each Brother in a different part of the chapel. Only the Brotherhood rezadores remain in the sanctuary. An alabado is intoned softly. One of the rezadores then delivers a short speech. On behalf of the Brothers, all are invited warmly. The participants are asked to clap their hands and whistle when it is time to make noise, but to refrain from pounding on the furniture. All are invited to offer *Sudarios* 'prayers for the dead' in memory of the community's deceased. In closing, the público is thanked for accompanying the Brothers *en este santo ejercicio* 'in this holy exercise'.

Thirteen candles have been placed on the altar and lighted, and the electric lights are now switched off. Two rezadores stand side-by-side on the left side of the altar, while a lone rezador stays on the right. Of the former, one holds a cuaderno and the other a flashlight. The two rezadores sing a verse of the *Miserere*, then extinguish one candle with their fingers. (I do not have a recording or written text of the *Miserere*, but one is presented by Rael 1951:84–86.) The rezador on the other side responds with a stanza from an alabado, then extinguishes a candle.[6] This is the *tinieblas* 'tenebrae' referring to the darkness that covered the world after Christ's death (Luke 23:44–45). The candles represent the flight of the twelve apostles from Christ's presence before the crucifixion.

Soon only the middle candle, which stands for Christ, remains lighted. Once it has been carried into the sacristy, near total darkness reigns in the chapel. One of the rezadores then calls out loudly ¡*Ave María!* 'Hail Mary!', and a deafening racket ensues. The Brothers whir matracas and play wild cadences on pitos while the público makes as much noise as it can.[7] The cacaphony provides an icon of the disturbances that marked the death of Christ; "the curtain of the temple was torn in two, from top to bottom; and the earth shook, and the rocks were split; the tombs also were opened, and many bodies of the saints who had fallen asleep were raised, and coming out of the tombs after his resurrection they went into the holy city and appeared to many" (Matthew 27:51–53). When the rezador calls out ¡Ave Maria! again, all becomes quiet.

The rezador then begins the process of offering Sudarios[8] for deceased relatives: *Un Sudario en nombre de Dios por el alma del difunto X* 'a Sudario in the name of God for the soul of the late X'. Sudarios are offered for individuals, often parents of the petitioner, most of whom have been dead for decades. All participants are free to offer Sudarios. After about five Sudarios have been requested and the prayers offered, the rezador calls out in a loud voice ¡Ave Maria!, and the noise-making is resumed. In all, four sets of Sudarios and four periods of cacaphony emerge. The end of the last disturbance is signaled by the sudden reappearance of the chapel lights. The lone candle reemerges from the sacristy, and the remainder are relighted. The Brothers pick up the images that they brought before the rosary, and they form a procession. Beginning an alabado, they return to the morada. Weary but exhilarated, the members of the público return to their houses.

EL ENCUENTRO OF GOOD FRIDAY

The morning of Good Friday marks one of the most moving rituals of Holy Week. *El Encuentro* 'The Meeting' symbolizes the encounter between Christ and Mary on the way to Calvary; this is the Fourth Station of the Via Crucis. El Encuentro commences in two different places. The público meets in the chapel at about 10:30 AM. Some variation is apparent in the composition of the público and the way it is organized for the Encuentro. The following description is based upon the 1979 performance of the ritual; on this occasion the major participants are the members of La Sagrada Familia and the sacristan. The latter serves as rezador for the público, even though he is a Brother. Other Brothers, including a rezador who leads the singing of alabados, accompany the público as well. The members of La Sagrada Familia carry nineteenth-century polychromed images of Our Lady of Sorrows and Verónica from the altar.[9] These are given to the women who will carry them in the procession. Another member carries the organization's banner. They are followed by the rezador, the other members of La Sagrada Familia, and then the members of the público who do not belong to the organization. Córdova (1973:45) suggests that this part was formerly taken by the members of the Order of Our Lady of Mount Carmel. Although this organization no longer exists in Córdova, a chapter remains in neighboring Truchas.

Once the público has assembled in the chapel, the rezador begins to recite the Stations of the Cross, and the público responds with the oraciones that appear in the text of the Via Crucis. Another rezador from the Brotherhood leads the participants in an alabado that commemorates the Virgin's anguish, *Madre de Dolores* 'Mother of Sorrows' (cf. Rael 1951:40–42; Robb 1980:658–59). Such assumption of key roles by Brothers is quite unusual. The group proceeds, in procession, out of the chapel, through the cemetery in the chapel courtyard, and out into the plaza toward the morada.

Meanwhile the rest of the Brothers have formed a procession in the morada. They bear the image of the standing Nazarene Christ, a crucifix, and the chapter's banner. Two rezadores carry a cuaderno, and they lead the Brothers in alabados devoted to the Passion of Christ, including *Mi Dios y mi Redentor* 'My God and My Redeemer' (cf. López 1942:22–32; Rael 1951:49–51; Robb 1980:617–19) and *Venid, pecadores* 'Come, Sinners' (cf. Rael 1951:44–46; Robb 1980:642–43). As the Brotherhood and the público approach each other, the two recitations of alabados and oraciones grow cacophonous.

El Encuentro itself generally occurs on the road to the morada just beyond *la puerta de la plaza* 'the gate of the plaza'. Timing is crucial here, because the rezador who is coming from the chapel should reach the beginning of the Fourth Station just at the time that the two groups meet. The images of the Virgin and Christ are brought together in an embrace; they are then held side-by-side. As the participants kneel on the rocky soil of the road, the rezador reads the Fourth Station, providing a textual concomitant to the visual unification. The focus is on the pain that Mary experienced as she saw Christ for the first time in the course of his passage to Calvary and, reciprocally, of the pain and compassion that this inspired in Christ. The passage quotes the Virgin as saying to Christ

My son and eternal God, light of my eyes and life of my soul, receive, Lord, this most sacred sorrow that I cannot alleviate the weight of the cross and take it myself so as to die on it for your love, like you want to die for the most ardent charity for mankind and for other tender and loving reasons.

These words deeply affect Brother and non-Brother alike, and many worshipers cry. As they stare fixedly at the images, the participants appear to feel the 'most bitter pain' and 'most sacred sorrow' themselves. As the Brothers turn again to singing the alabado, members of the público venerate the images. One at a time, they kiss or touch the feet of the two images of Christ, the base of the Holy Family, and the hem of the gown of the Verónica. After they cross themselves, most touch the two banners and make the sign of the cross again. This part of the procession takes quite some time. Given the fact that the weather is often cold and snow is not uncommon, participation in the ritual entails some physical hardship.

Once the público has passed through the line formed by the image carriers and the remaining Brothers, the latter lead a now unified procession toward the chapel. On arrival, the Brothers return the images to the altar and lead a series of oraciones for

Christ and the Virgin. The sacristan then speaks to the público, noting that El Encuentro was very beautiful. He thanks the público for its participation and invites everyone to return at 3:00 that afternoon for a recitation of the Stations of the Cross and at 7:00 in the evening for Las Tinieblas. The Brothers then leave in procession. As the crowd files out, warm and animated greetings are exchanged between members of the público. Visiting relatives join their extended families for lunch, an occasion of such importance that many Brothers are allowed to return home for the meal.

VIA CRUCIS OF THE AFTERNOON OF GOOD FRIDAY

The público gathers in the chapel again just before three, and the Brothers come in procession from the morada. Via Crucis were formerly held at this time during all the Fridays of Lent, corresponding to Christ's death on the afternoon of Good Friday. The Stations may be prayed out-of-doors, moving counterclockwise around the chapel, or inside, following the depictions of the fourteen Stations that adorn the side walls of the nave. Many Córdovans, both Brothers and público, walk barefoot as an expression of penance and identification with Christ's suffering. Historically, the Via Crucis provided a means of extending the indulgences gained by pilgrims who visited the sites of Christ's suffering in the Holy Land to those who could not make the journey (Brown 1967:832). The present Stations and the mode of practicing them were standardized by the monita issued under the authority of Pope Clement XII in 1731 (Brown 1967:833). Many Brothers have handwritten cuadernos which contain the Stations of the Cross and associated oraciones and alabados. They designate the Stations as follows:

1. *La sentencia de muerte* (Christ is condemned to death by Pilate)
2. *La cruz acuesta* (Jesus is made to carry the cross)
3. *Primera caída* (Jesus falls the first time)
4. *Encuentro de María Santísima* (Jesus meets his blessed Mother)
5. *El Sirineo* (the cross is laid on Simon of Cyrene)
6. *La Verónica* (Veronica wipes the face of Jesus)
7. *Segunda caída* (Jesus falls the second time)
8. *Llanto de las hijas de Jerusalem* (Jesus speaks to the women of Jerusalem)
9. *Tercera caída* (Jesus falls the third time)
10. *La desnudez y mirra* (Jesus is stripped of his garments and receives gall to drink)
11. *La crucificación* [sic.] *del Señor* (Jesus is nailed to the cross)
12. *La expiración del Señor* (Jesus dies on the cross)
13. *El descendimiento de la cruz* (Jesus is taken down from the cross)
14. *El santo sepulcro* (Jesus is laid in the sepulcher) [10]

The Stations of the Cross involve the cooperation of a number of rezadores. One or two rezadores chant the text associated with each Station, including both a description of the Station and an oración that is specific to it. This reflects the doctrinal basis of the ritual, namely that each Station is a halting or stopping point ". . . at which the soul of the onlooker is moved to sorrowful contemplation" of Christ's passion and death (Brown 1967:832). Córdovans follow the usual practice of praying one Our Father, Hail Mary, and Glory Be to the Father at each Station. Another pair of rezadores lead the remaining Brothers and the público in these rezos. A third pair sing a short musical prayer at the beginning of all Stations save the first. Another Brother plays the pito before each of these musical prayers.

The service begins with a few verses from an alabado that is also used in the Rosary Service of Holy Wednesday, *El llevando el Padre Eterno*. A pair of rezadores then chant a call to worship, which begins *En el monte murió Cristo; no murió por sus pecados* . . . 'Christ died on the hill [Calvary]; He did not die for his sins . . .'. After the response, all pray the Apostles' Creed.

The rezador who is reading the Stations begins the Via Crucis itself by chanting, *Primera estación, la sentencia de muerte* 'First Station, the sentence of death'. His chanting follows the three-tone patterns described below. The rezadores who sing the musical prayer of each Station intone the first rezo. The other participants respond, singing *Pues con tierno llanto todos, te rogamos, audinos* 'So all weeping tenderly, we beseech Thee, hear us'.[11] The principal rezador then chants an initial prayer of invocation, asking for all the indulgences that 'Our Holy Mother Church' has invested in the Via Crucis.

The rezador continues with the meditation that relates the event identified in the Station. These generally begin with the formula *contempla alma en esta X estación* . . . 'contemplate, soul, in this X Station'. . . . The other participants then respond with *bendito y alabado sea para siempre tan gran Señor* 'may you be blessed and praised forever, great Lord'. A prayer called the *Ofrecimiento* 'Offering' is then chanted by the principal rezador. All participants recite an Our Father, Hail Mary, and Glory Be to the Father at some stations and a Salve, Apostles' Creed, or Sudario at others. The principal rezador then announces the number and designation of the next Station, and the cycle is repeated.

The Via Crucis procession will have nearly encircled the chapel by the time that the Thirteenth Station has been recited, and the Fourteenth Station will be prayed inside. Once the last station has been completed, the principal rezador reads a summary of Christ's sufferings 'so that we should give praise (*alabemos*) and give thanks to the Lord because he wanted to suffer so much for us'. The other participants respond to each with *bendito y alabado sea para siempre tan gran Señor* 'may you be blessed and praised forever, great Lord'. These meditations provide a sequential summary of the passion, including the agony in the garden, the mockery and blows, the false testimony offered against Christ, the denuding and whipping, mock coronation, *ecce homo*, and so forth. These recall scenes of the crucifixion that are not included in the *Via Crucis*.

Then a prayer that asserts that 'our sins were the cause of so much pain' and asks for Christ's forgiveness is offered by the principal rezador. The other participants respond with *bendita y alabada sea la pasión y muerte* 'may the passion and death be blessed and praised'. The rezador recites a concluding prayer known as the *Ofrecimiento del Via Crucis* [sic] 'the Offering of the Way of the Cross'. The hope is expressed that the devotions will have been of sufficient merit to offer to the Eternal Father. The prayer continues, 'I beg you to confirm all of the indulgences that have been conceded to the Via Crucis by the pontiffs for the forgiveness of my sins'. The Via Crucis is also offered for the welfare of the souls in purgatory. It concludes with the words, 'I ask you to give me perseverance in this exercise so that you will reward me by giving me your glory'.

All participants then join in praying an Our Father, Hail Mary, Glory Be to the Father, and a Sudario for the souls in purgatory. Another rezador asks for a Sudario for the blessed souls. Next he offers a Salve for everyone who has accompanied the Brothers during the Via Crucis. The Brothers form a procession, and the two rezadores who sang the musical parts of the Stations then begin the alabado *Considera, alma perdida* 'Consider, Lost Soul' (cf. Rael 1951:70–71; Robb 1980:628–30). The Brothers prepare to go to the morada while singing the alabado, and the público follows them as far as the plaza, singing the chorus. The mood remains somber, in keeping both with the tone of the event and with the sense that this was the time that Christ was crucified.

LAS TINIEBLAS, THE TENEBRAE SERVICE OF GOOD FRIDAY NIGHT

The público returns home, eagerly anticipating the final ceremony, the Tenebrae service of Good Friday night. Although labeled differently from the *Maitines* 'Matins' of Maundy Thursday, the *Tinieblas* 'Tenebrae' is nearly identical to it. It is marked by the same reverence for this commemoration of the events that surrounded the death of Christ. Its conclusion signals, however, a lifting of the somber atmosphere and the ritual prohibitions (against drinking and dancing, dietary restrictions, etc.) that have characterized Lent.

The chapel begins to fill at about 7:00 PM, and the non-Brotherhood rezadores take turns leading alabados. Occasionally, these rezadores will ask the Brotherhood's permission to lead the público in an additional Rosary service prior to the beginning of the one led by the Brotherhood. The service is led from the sanctuary by the four rezadores of the público, beginning around 9:00. It follows the usual pattern and ends with requests for Sudarios and other prayers.

One difference between Maitines and Tinieblas services lies in the composition of the público. The chapel is even more filled on the latter occasion, leaving no room even for standing after about 8:30. Tinieblas ceremonies nearly always draw a number of outsiders. One or more of the nuns from the Holy Family Parish in Chimayó generally attend. Córdovans also sometimes ask Mexicanos from areas in which moradas no longer exist to come to Tinieblas with them. Córdovans invite a few Anglo-Americans each year. These are either fellow employees and their families or, in the case of the wood carvers, customers who are well known to the artists. A few Anglo-Americans simply learn of the ceremony and come on their own. Such newcomers are welcomed. The rezador generally provides a translation of the address that he gives before the Tenebrae ceremony itself. He makes a special point of welcoming the visitors, urging them to return again.

No differences are apparent in the structure of the Rosary or Tenebrae services. The way in which the participants leave the chapel, however, is distinct. One of the central features of Brotherhood comportment between Wednesday and Friday nights is that the Brothers do not recognize their friends and relatives before, during, or after ceremonies. Eye contact is avoided, and the Brothers generally maintain a most serious asocial stance vis-à-vis the público.[12] Their behavior remains somewhat reserved when they return home for meals or to sleep.[13]

The end of Tinieblas marks a change in their demeanor. The Brothers line up along the walk in the cemetery outside the chapel. Two Brothers hold the two crucifixes while others sing alabados softly, without responses from the remaining participants. As the público files past, friends and relatives are greeted personally and warmly, and smiles, laughter, and joking are common. Outsiders are greeted in English and asked to come back the following year. The seriousness that pervaded the atmosphere a short time ago is gone, displaced by the resurrectional symbolism of the return of the lone candle representing Christ from the sacristy and the relighting of the other candles. Once the público is gone, the Brothers leave in procession for the morada. After a few remaining visitas have made their way to the chapel, the Brothers' observance of Lent will have come to an end.

PATTERNS OF PERFORMANCE

Having characterized the ritual setting for Lenten performances of hymns and prayers, I now turn to a description and analysis of the central textual cycle that is used in Lenten and Holy Week rituals, the Holy Rosary. The central prayer is the Hail Mary, which consists of two parts. The first is derived from the salutations to the Virgin spoken by the Archangel Gabriel (Luke 1:28), "Hail ⟨Mary⟩ full of grace, the Lord is with Thee, blessed art thou amongst women" and by Elizabeth (Luke 1:42), "Blessed is the fruit of thy womb ⟨Jesus⟩." The second part is a formula of petition, "Holy Mary, Mother of God, pray for us sinners now and at the hour of our death. Amen." The Hail Mary is believed to have originated in the sixth century, and it was codified in its present form by Pius V in 1568 (de Marco 1967).

The Holy Rosary centers on praying decades (i.e., groups of ten) of the Hail Mary, preceded by an Our Father and followed by a Glory Be to the Father. The full

Rosary contains fifteen of these units, and each is tied to a meditation, termed a *mystery*. The fifteen mysteries are based on the lives of the Virgin and Christ. They are divided into three groups, the Joyful Mysteries (the Annunciation of Christ's incarnation to Mary, her visit to Elizabeth, Christ's birth, His presentation in the temple, and His discovery in the temple), the Sorrowful Mysteries (Christ's agony in the garden. His scourging, crowning with thorns, carrying His cross to Calvary, and crucifixion and death), and the Glorious Mysteries (the Resurrection, His Ascension into heaven, the coming of Holy Spirit, the Assumption of Mary into heaven, and her coronation as Queen of Heaven).

Rosary services commonly use only one set of mysteries; Rosary services during Holy Week obviously draw on the Sorrowful Mysteries. The mysteries are not spelled out in the text. The worshiper repeats the Hail Mary and related prayers, all the while meditating on the mystery that is associated with that part of the rosary cycle (Hinnebusch 1967:667). This Rosary is termed the Dominican Rosary due to the tradition that the Virgin revealed it to St. Dominic. The elements that formed the Rosary were recognizable from the early fifteenth century, and it was standardized in the mid-sixteenth century (Hinnebusch 1967). The Rosary was disseminated in the New Mexico by the Franciscan missionaries.

I have transcribed below one segment of the Rosary, including the verses of the alabado *Con un pesado madero* 'With a Heavy Cross', the Our Father, and other prayers. In this chapter, transcriptions follow a special set of conventions that are tied to the musical properties of the performances. Italicized words are chanted at higher pitch; all capitals indicates lower pitch; text that is not italicized or capitalized is recited at middle pitch. Lines that are sung are set in bold-face type. Alabados use far more than three tone levels. I use italics for marking the point at which the alabados reach a relatively high pitch and an increase in volume. Such points generally correlate with a elongation of the vowel, voiced consonant, or entire syllable and a glissando. (See the section on musical style.) A more detailed sense can be gained from the transcription of the first verse of the alabado, which I have included in Figure 6 below. PL stands for prayer leader, RZ for rezador(s) who leads the alabado, PT for the *pitero* 'flute player', OP for other participants, meaning the remaining Brothers and the público, and ALL refers to all participants. A new typographic line indicates a poetic line, marked both by prosody and semantic parallelism (see later discussion); a new line that is indented left signals the beginning of a breath group. Double-spacing marks the transition from one rezo to the next or from a rezo to a pito melody to an alabado (etc.).

A PERFORMANCE OF THE ROSARY SERVICE

The beginning of the Rosario is signaled by a ringing of the altar bell.[14] The leaders hold their rosaries in their hands (as do the other Brothers), which provides them with a mnemonic for structuring the service. All participants recite a series of oraciones in unison before starting with the decades of the Hail Mary.[15] These commemorate the power of Jesus Christ and the Virgin Mary to overcome evil, invoke their protection, call to mind the worshiper's own sins, and ask forgiveness, both for oneself and for one's enemies. After reciting the Apostles' Creed, the petitioner asks Christ to 'open our lips so that we can praise your Holy Name'; the Virgin is asked to 'cleanse our hearts, clease our thoughts . . . so that we will be worthy of praying the Rosary'.

The segment presented as example (8.1) comes after these initial prayers. The leaders chant the first part of the rezo, with the remaining Brothers and the público responding with the second. This order is reversed periodically. The recitation alternates between two main pitches and a third, lower pitch. The men adopt a tenor voice; all participants thus sing the same three notes.

The Hail Mary is recited identically nine more times. As the last "y en la *hora* de nuestra muerte, amen" is recited, one of the Brothers rings a bell. The Glory Be to the Father is then chanted by all participants. After a brief pause, the rezadores begin the next decade of the Ave Marias by changing "POR todo el mundo resuena. . . ." There is one variation from one decade to the next. After the other participants have chanted the Ave María, the prayer leaders do not begin the Padre Nuestro. Indeed, they say (rather than chant) "Padre Nuestro." This signals the remaining Brothers and the público that *they* are to begin the Padre Nuestro in this decade. The order is thus reversed throughout the decade, with the other participants reciting the salutations of the Hail Mary and the leaders providing the petition. The prayer leaders thus chant the first part in the first, third, and last decade.

The end of the last decade is marked in two ways. First, the alabado verses that follow the last decade are augmented by four additional lines. Second, the rezadores say (rather than chant) Ave María purísima, to which the people respond with Ave María, also in spoken form. This is followed, as usual, by the closing petition: *SEa para siempre*. . . . Next comes the oración that begins each decade, *POR todo el mundo* . . . , which is followed by a Padre Nuestro. In this case, however, we find

---

(8.1) Segment of Rosary Service of Holy Wednesday in Córdova

```
PL   POR todo el mundo resuena[16]
              el eco de esta doctrina
              de la gloria del mismo Dios
              y su madre, María.
OP   VIVA el nombre de Jesús                               5
              viva la fe y su doctrina
              viva por los siglos eternos
              la concesión de María.
                    Ave María.
```

three (rather than ten) Ave Marías, each of which contain a particular invocation of the Virgin (e.g., *Hija de Dios, Virgen purísima* 'Daughter of God, purest Virgin'). Next come two prayers that ask the Virgin and Christ to use their power over death and evil in granting the worshipper eternal life. After one more Padre Nuestro and Ave María, worshipers are called to pray for the souls that are in Purgatory. The prayer leaders and others ask all participants to accompany them in chanting Sudarios and other prayers for the welfare of all present and their deceased relatives; the same formula is used here as well as in the Maitines and Tinieblas rituals. The service closes with two more oraciones that echo the themes of Christ's defeat of death, the Virgin's and Christ's compassion, and the culpability of mortals; these prayers also request the assistance of Christ and the Virgin in following these divine models of grace, suffering, and compassion.

FORMAL STRUCTURE OF THE ROSARY SERVICE

I have summarized the organization of the Rosary service in Figure 5. I will begin with the smaller discourse units before attempting to analyze the overall structure. I will attempt to show that all levels of the structure of the Rosary Service revolve around the recurrent use of binary and triadic units, and that this can be seen in content as well as in form.

In analyzing these formal units, it is crucial to keep in mind that nearly all of the discourse that is uttered within the frame of the Rosary service is either chanted (the vast majority) or sung (the alabado). In forty-one minutes of speech, only nine words are spoken.[17] This has radical implications for the formal structure of the ritual discourse. For those who are actually reciting the rezos aloud (and this includes virtually everyone present), their use of breath and the prosodic characteristics of their voice are fixed. Moreover, no one breathes alone. The prayer leaders breathe simultaneously, and their prosodic patterns, particularly of pitch, volume, and rate are identical. This is true as well for the Brothers who lead the singing of the alabado. The

---

English translation

Throughout the world resounds[16]
　　　the echo of this doctrine
　　　of the glory of the same God
　　　and his mother, Mary.
Long live the name of Jesus,
　　　long live the faith and its doctrine,
　　　long live through the centuries eternally,
　　　Mary's concession.
　　　　Hail Mary.

PL *Pa*dre nuestro   10
    que est*ás* en el cielo
    *sa*ntificado
    sea tu nombre,
    venga a nosotros tu reino,
    haga Señor su voluntad   15
    así en *la tierra* como en el cielo.

OP EL pan nuestro de cada día
    danos hoy, Señor,
    y per*dona* nuestras deudas,
    así como nosotros perdamos   20
    a *nue*stros deudores.
   Y *no nos de*jes caer en tentación
    mas líbranos
    igual de todo mal. Amén.

PL DIos te salve, María,   25
    llena eres de gracia,
    el Señor es contigo;
    ben*dita e*res, Señora,
    entre *to*das las mujeres,
    *y bendi*to es el fruto   30
    de tu *vi*entre, Jesús.

OP SANTA MA*rí*a, madre de Dios,
    ru*ega* Señora
    por no*sotros* los pecadores,
    a*hora*   35
    y en la *h*ora de nuestra muerte. Amén.

ALL *Gloria al Pa*dre, gloria al Hijo, y al Espíritu Santo
    por los siglos de los siglos santos. Amén.

PL *Du*lc*í*simo Jesús mío,
    que en la cruz estéis por mí.   40
OP *En la vi*da y en la muerte,
    Señor acordéis de mí.

RZ **Con *un p*esado madero**
    y dolor extraor*di*nario,
OP **Camin*aba* para el Calvario**   45
    El hermosísimo Corde*ro*.
RZ **Al*ma, el* aliento apresura,**
    A María verás *llo*rando.
OP **Y con *lá*grimas regando,**
    la calle de a*margura.*   50

PL SEa para siempre bendito y alabado.
OP DUlc*í*simo misterio de Jesús sacramentado.

Our Father
who art in heaven
hallowed
be thy name.
Thy kingdom come,
thy will be done
on earth as it is in heaven.
Give us this day
our daily bread,
and forgive us our debts,
as we forgive
our debtors.
And lead us not into temptation,
but deliver us
from every evil. Amen.

Hail Mary,
full of grace,
the Lord is with you;
blessed art thou
among all women,
and blessed is the fruit
of thy womb, Jesus.
Holy Mary, mother of God,
pray
for us sinners,
now
and in the hour of our death. Amen.

[The Hail Mary is recited nine more times; a bell is rung at the close of the last Hail Mary.]

Glory be to the Father, glory to the Son, and to the Holy Spirit
for ever and ever. Amen.

My sweetest Jesus,
you are on the cross for me.
In life and in death,
remember me, Lord.

[PT plays pito for 8 seconds]

With a heavy cross
And extraordinary pain,
He was walking toward Calvary
The most beautiful Lamb.
Soul, how one's breath quickens
On seeing Mary crying,
And watering, with her tears,
the street of bitterness.

Blessed and praised forever.
Sweetest mystery of sacramental Jesus.

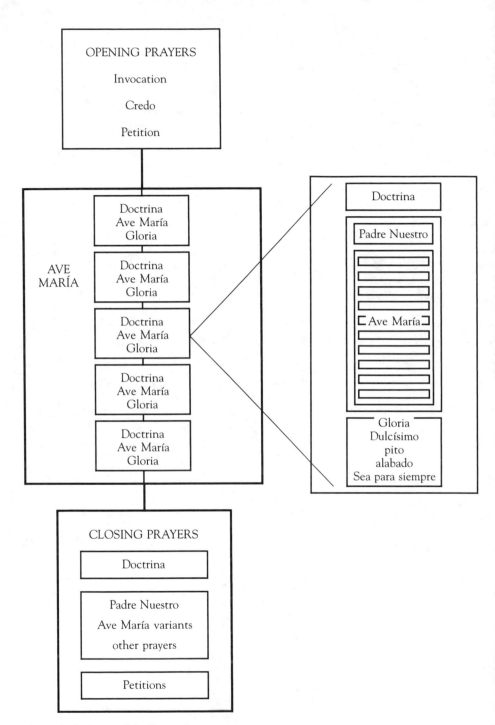

Figure 5. Structure of the Rosary Service

other participants similarly respond to the prayer leaders and alabado leaders in unison. Finally, in the case of some prayers, such as the Gloria, all present chant as with a single voice.

Just as important, these shared discourse features are not negotiated at the time of the performance; rather, they are dictated in large measure by the texts themselves. The qualifying phrase is appropriate, given the fact that some details of textual selection are variable. Such variations are, however, quite minor in comparison with the similarities from year to year in the way that the oraciones are chanted and the alabados are sung. Attending Holy Week ceremonies from childhood on provides one with a knowledge of more than the words used in the prayers and alabados; patterns of performance are learned as well. This shared stylistic competence enables a group of some fifty to one hundred fifty persons (depending on the ritual) to coordinate the production of a fairly complex array of verbal and musical forms by a number of distinct classes of participants to such a degree that everybody is saying that the proper thing in the appropriate way and in near perfect harmony.

What are the stylistic features that distinguish performances of alabados and oraciones and that enable participants in Lenten rituals to achieve this degree of coordination? Let us begin with the minimal unit, that of the poetic line. With regard to the prayers, lines are not differentiated through the use of pause; indeed, lines run directly from one to the next without any gap. Their unity rather lies in the creation of a single prosodic contour. This contour generally consists of the maintenance of the same pitch and volume throughout the line, except as broken by a dramatic rise in pitch and volume. A second pattern, one that commonly comes at the beginning of turns at talk, is of an initial decrease (one to three syllables) in pitch and volume, followed by a rise to the middle level. Whereas such descents are realized in the first one to three syllables of the line, rises may come either at the beginning of the line or one to three syllables later; in either case, however, the peak or valley comes at or near the beginning of the line.

The next level of organization consists of two to three lines that are marked as a unit. The features that are used in defining these groupings fall within patterns that have been observed in couplet formation in a wide range of oral traditions (cf. Fox 1974; Gossen 1974a: 142–44, 1974b; Jakobson 1960, 1966; Sherzer 1983: 128–31; Silverstein 1981b; Tedlock 1976; Urban 1986b). In some cases, the two lines form a single clause:

> (1–2)   POR todo el mundo resuena
> el *eco* de esta doctrina

Lines that are grouped together generally evince parallelism in content as well as in one or more formal features. In the couplet

(26–27) *Llena eres* de gracia,
el Señor es contigo;

the two lines are associated in terms of their referential content. "The Lord is with you" because the Virgin is "full of grace"; enjoying Christ's eternal presence reciprocally enhances Mary's position as a human who is free from sin and beloved by God; in other words, the two halves of the couplet go together in terms of the religious beliefs that are associated with the oración. The prosodic parallelism (a single rise in pitch and volume toward the beginning of each line) is matched by the lexical parallelism provided by present tense inflections of the same verb stem, *ser* 'to be'. The following provides an example in which three lines are linked by lexical and syntactic parallelism:

(5–7) VIVA el nombre de Jesús,
viva la fe y su doctrina
viva por los siglos eternos

Both the division of the discourse into lines and the formation of most lines into couplets and triplets create the basic rhythmic structure of the Rosary service. The lines provide a rhythmic pulse that divides the prayers into prosodically defined units that average 1.2 seconds in length. By linking most of these lines into couplets and triplets, this basic rhythm is augmented by a secondary pattern that provides semantic as well as formal associations between lines.

At the next level of organization, a larger number of lines are grouped together by virtue of their inclusion in the same breath group.[18] Learning how to chant entails learning when to breathe; this is of course true of singing as well. The formal importance of the breath group is increased by the fact that the rate of speech, like pitch and volume, are highly regulated; an average of 3.4 words per second is held virtually constant throughout the chanted portions of the service. Everyone accordingly speaks at the same time and at a constant rate, and pauses are evident only between breath groups (about one second) and turns at talk (approximately the same). Despite their important role in synchronizing speech and matching prosodic patterns, breath groups do not seem to be associated with units of referential content in the rezos.

In the case of the next level of organization, turns at talk, the form/content relationship is quite clear. With the exception of the Gloria, all the prayers that are included in the main (middle) section of the Rosary service consist of two parts, one for the prayer leaders and one for the other participants. The stanzas of the alabados are divided in this way as well. This unit is also marked in most cases by utterance of the initial one to three syllables at a lower pitch and volume. The change of speaker generally divides individual oraciones into two parts. For the prayers that make up the central section of the Rosary, the first part generally invokes Christ or the Virgin and commemorates one or more dimensions of their divine actions or attributes. The second part emphasizes a petition that the worshiper is addressing to Christ or Mary. The general movement is thus from invocation/commemoration to petition, with different sets of participants assuming responsibility for uttering the contrastive speech acts.

In the case of POR *todo el mundo* . . . (1–8), the *Ave María,* and *Dulcisimo Jesús mío* (39–42), this transition from one speech act to the other is marked by a change in modality from declarative to imperative or subjunctive (to use the traditional labels). This is not true of the *Gloria* (37–38) or the *SEa para siempre* (51–52). The Padre Nuestro provides only a partial exception. The change in modality occurs within the first part, but the movement is from declarative to optative; a true imperative in which the worshiper asks the Lord in a first person (plural) voice for specific actions does not in any case come until the second part. The status of first parts as invocations/commemorations and second parts as petitions is thus not hard and fast, but it does provide an important relationship between form, the social structure of Lenten rituals, and communicative function. (I will take up this question again later in the chapter.)

Another basic textual unit is that of the individual *oraciones.* This unit plays a major role in the process of acquiring the competence needed to participate in these rituals. Listening to Lenten performances does not provide the only means to this end. Córdovan children now attend catechism classes taught by nuns who visit the community from the parish church in Chimayó. The catechisms that are used in these classes provide texts of the Padre Nuestro, Ave María, Gloria, Credo, Salve, and other prayers. All of these texts must be memorized before the child will be allowed to take First Holy Communion, an important rite of passage. Men who wish to join the Brotherhood must demonstrate their knowledge of these *rezos* as a part of their initiation. The Trujillos gave me a missalette that contained these texts in the course of teaching me how to participate in ritual activities.

The notion of a prayer as forming a basic unit is also apparent at a later stage in the pedagogical process when one learns how to participate in rituals, whether in a leadership role or not. Such instructions as 'here you pray one Padre Nuestro and ten Ave Marías' are supplemented by lessons designed to aid in the memorization of *oraciones* that are not included in the basic catechism. I was not alone in receiving such explicit, if informal, training; as noted earlier, candidates for initiation into the Brotherhood work with a sponsor in order to ensure that they know the relevant prayers and learn to use these units in ritual sequences.

The largest units that are evident in the Rosary service involve various means of combining individual *rezos.* Some units are formed by simply repeating the same text, as is the case with the decades of Ave Marías. The closing prayers demonstrate another means; here three Ave Marías are recited, each one preceded by a distinct introductory formula. Similarly, a number of different prayers (some of which may be repeated) may be combined to form a larger unit. For example, the POR todo el mundo, Padre Nuestro, Ave María (ten repetitions), Gloria, pito melody, alabado, and SEa para siempre all combine to form one decade, while five decades jointly constitute the middle section of the Rosary service (see Figure 5).

Finally, the Rosary service itself operates as a unit in the constitution of a wide range of Mexicano Catholic services. Beyond the instances that I have described for Lent and Holy Week, the Rosary service is recited on some Sundays in Córdova when Mass is not read. (A priest from the local parish church in Chimayó generally offers Mass every other Sunday.) The local rezadores formerly led Rosary services every Sunday. Rosary services are also given on at least one of the nights preceding the burial of Catholics; these services usually take place in the chapel of one of the funeral homes in Española. Rosary services are also offered as memorial services for Córdovans, particularly on the anniversaries of their death. There is a basic contrast at this level: Rosary services constitute almost the entirety of some ceremonies (e.g., Wednesday night services of Lent and Holy Week) but form only one part of others (e.g., *Los Maitines* and *Las Tinieblas*).

MUSICAL PATTERNS

Most of the preceding analysis dealt with chanted discourse. Some of the generalizations that emerged from this body of material are applicable to the alabado verses, but others are not. It is accordingly necessary to examine the way each form is used in performance. The alabado verses that appear in Example (8.1) are transcribed in Figure 6.

The leading student of the musical form of alabados, J. D. Robb (1951, 1980), notes that alabados differ markedly from the styles associated with other Mexicano religious or secular songs, such as alabanzas and himnos (1980:644). Alabados often adopt minor modes; modulation from one mode to another, a common characteristic of medieval plainchant, occurs as well (cf. Robb 1951:254–55; 1980:624). Alabados are, in musical terms, generally unmeasured. In other words, unlike the even meter of most himnos and many alabanzas, the alabados sustain one rhythmic pace for several syllables, slow considerably for a few syllables, and so on. Although the meter is thus asymmetrical within and between lines, it is generally identical between stanz

This unmeasured quality complements the special way that words and music are associated in the alabado. Alabados follow a melismatic text setting, meaning that there is a many-to-one relationship between notes and syllables. Alabados are characterized by both the melismatic style (five or more notes sung for some syllables) or the neumatic (where two to four notes accompany some syllables). The melismas often follow a pattern that was common in early medieval chants, where a dramatic

REZADOR:

Con un pe- sa- do ma- de- ro y do- lor ex- tra- or- di- na- ri- o

OTHER PARTICIPANTS:

Ca- mi- na ba pa- ra el Cal- va- rio el her- mo- si- si- mo cor- de- ro

REZADOR:

Al- ma a- li- en- to a- pre- su- ra a Ma- ri- a ve- ras llo- ran- - do

OTHER PARTICIPANTS:

Y con la- gri- mas- re- gan- do la ca- lle de a- mar- gu- - ra

Figure 6. Alabado Used in the Rosario

rise in pitch is followed by a gradual descent (cf. Crocker 1980:106). Alabados also feature continuous modulation from one end of the pitch range to the other at the end of lines, and this may occur within lines as well.

St. Augustine noted about 400 A.D. that the essence of the melisma (*jubilus* or *jubilatio*) was the expression of an emotion that was too deep to follow the more common syllabic relationship between words and music (Crocker 1980:105). This statement seems to point to the basis of the almost uncanny power and emotionality of alabados. Their musical style corresponds to the intensity of the religious emotion that is expressed in the texts. The arabesques that are produced by the pito between text sections (and sometimes while the alabado is being sung as well) creates a powerful polytonal effect that augments the emotionality of the alabados (cf. Robb 1951: 252–53, 1980:612).

These features clearly distinguish alabados, both from rezos or oraciones and from other musical genres. On the other hand, the way that alabados and rezos are woven together in the course of Rosary services, Via Crucis, Maitines and Tinieblas, and other events of Holy Week generates a number of commonalities in the way that these rituals are performed. I noted previously that the formal structure of chanted texts imposes a number of constraints on the prosodic characteristics of the participants' voices. As one moves from chanting to singing, the prosodic "tune" becomes a melody, thus regulating pitch, volume, rate, and voice quality to a much higher degree. The distribution of the discourse between two sets of participants is apparent in the intoning of the alabado verses as well. We similarly find semantic couplets; here the second couple of the stanza is joined to the first semantically, through an extension of the same theme, and through an ab–ba rhyme scheme as well.

The relationship between alabados and oraciones thus involves a stylistic contrast that creates a deep unity. The inclusion of the alabado verses in performances of the Rosary adds to their stylistic diversity by creating a periodic movement from chanting to music; this is augmented through the instrumental music of the pito. One the effect of the transition from one form to the next is to heighten the poetic patterns of emotional expressivity that are evident in the chanted speech.

RECURRENT PATTERNS OF FORMAL STRUCTURE

Closer scrutiny of the formal characteristics of Lenten and Holy Weeks rituals thus provides us with a strong sense of unity underlying a complex sequence of diverse events. A single textual sequence, the Rosary service, is a central component of nearly all the rituals. The Via Crucis text similarly relates El Encuentro and Via Crucis ceremonies, although its distribution is more limited than the Holy Rosary. We have also seen how the Rosary service itself revolves around a parallelistic repetition of identical units as well as units that provide patterned variations. Such units are frequently repeated in one of two basic patterns. A triadic pattern is frequently evident in parallelistic sequences of three lines, in the three-part structure that is apparent in each decade of the Rosary, in the overall organization of the sequences of opening and closing prayers, and in the structure of the service as a whole. Whereas this triadic pattern is most apparent in the structure of larger textual units, a dyadic pattern dominates the structure of lines, couplets, and individual prayer texts. Drawing on Austin's (1962) term, we may note that these dyads and the formal changes that often accompany them (such as changes of modality) are closely tied to the performative structure of the oraciones—namely the constant movement between invocations of Christ's and the Virgin's presence and petitions for divine intercession. This textual movement between invocation and petition is also reflected in the way that the discourse is distributed among the worshipers, particularly between the prayer leaders and the other participants; it thus mirrors the social structure of the ritual.

These shared rhythms extend from the level of a single word or phrase (the line) to that of the major sections of the service. These recurrent patterns are not simply mnemonic aids, enabling the participants to sense where they are and what is to come next. They also provide powerful tools for creating collective speech as well as for structuring religious experience.

TEXTUALITY, SIGNIFICATION, AND THE NATURE OF RELIGIOUS EXPERIENCE

Readers who are familiar with the literature on the language of ritual will realize that the stylistic patterns that emerge from performances of hymns and prayers are hardly unique to this facet of la plática de los viejitos de antes. To cite just a few examples, E. Basso (1985:257) suggests that among the Carib-speaking Kalapalo of Brazil "the apparently banal and repetitive nature of the lexically meaningful songs emphasizes the crucial objects and attributes that make them distinctive, which the singers need to focus on during the performance." Speaking of Kuna (Panamá) curing rituals, Sherzer (1983:128) writes, "a pervasive feature of the structure of curing and magical *ikarkana* is parallelism—the patterned repetition of sounds, forms, and meanings." Gossen (1974b:188) similarly notes that the ritual language of the Tzotzil-speaking Chamula of southern Mexico centers on "highly loaded symbolic statements [that] are reinforced by the rhythm and the various repetitive devices used to express them"; speech that is stylistically marked in this way possess the ritual "heat" that "help men to transcend the temporal and spatial bounds of the mundane world" (1976:49). Hanks (1984:140) calls attention to the way that "parallelism establishes a background of equivalence relations superimposed on the sequential development of the discourse" in invoking the presence and intervention of spirits in another Mayan group, the Yucatec. Tedlock (1976) documents the use of a mid-low-high pitch contour by the Zuni of western New Mexico that marks speech as remarkable, invested with authority, and rhetorically strong, such that the words can be heard by the *ky'ápin áaho"i* 'raw people' (spirits).

We are faced, then, with a widespread association in ritual language between parallelism, repetition, semantic redundancy, and special prosodic patterns that organize speech into patterns of form and content. One important effect of these stylistic constraints is to reduce the importance of the referential function in the overall meaning of the discourse. Some ritual language accords a prominent role to forms that have little or no semantic value (cf. E. Basso 1985:243–311; Buckley 1984). In the case of Mexicano Lenten rituals, the forms clearly possess semantic meanings, and these meanings are interpretable by the participants. Indeed, Córdovan Catholics who have learned their catechisms all know the basic prayers that form the heart of the Rosary services. Even those portions of the texts that are chanted or sung by the rezadores are well known to the remaining participants. The latter may lack competence in leading performances of these texts but are quite capable of interpreting them (cf. Hymes 1981/1975). All participants know the story of the passion of Christ and the suffering of the Virgin that lies behind El Encuentro, the Via Crucis, Tenebrae services, and other rituals. This story is retold countless times in many different forms during these three days.

The participants are thus highly familiar with the texts that are used in Holy Week rituals and with the biblical events that they commemorate. The combined effect of familiarity and redundancy is to place the referential function in the background, relegating it to a peripheral role in these speech events. I use the term here in referring to use of the semantic value of lexemes and phrasal constructions in conveying information. The amount of information (in the technical sense of the term) that is derived from the referential content of the texts in the course of these rituals is accordingly nil.

A long scholarly tradition has asserted that highly formulaic prayer is only a degraded form of spontaneous prayer. This view holds that the recitation of formulaic prayer is a mechanical act that is motivated by a specific utilitarian effect—obtaining the blessings that are believed to accrue automatically to those who recite the given prayers. Even the classic modern work on the subject, Heiler's *Prayer* (1932), advances this position.

As Gill (1981) argues, this belief is based on a naïve and uncritical view of the communicative functions of prayer and rests on two crucial assumptions. First, because the content and even the form of the prayer are standardized, it is assumed that the individual does not play an active role in the creative process. Second, the purported lack of individual creativity is equated with the absence of personal involvement; the worshiper's motives for uttering the prayer are seen as extending only to the desire to obtain the benefits that are mechanically produced by the act of uttering the prayer. In other words, the communicative function of formulaic prayer is identified, as Reichard (1944) has phrased it, with the "magically compulsive" power of prayer. This view accordingly constitutes a theory of the relationship between the form and content of prayer and the structure of communicative events in which they are uttered. It will thus be necessary to place my analysis of the formal properties of Mexicano religious discourse in its ritual setting in order to evaluate its validity. In keeping with the goals of the present study, I will attempt to show how the distinctness of the features that are evident in performances of hymns and prayers (as compared with those evident in other genres) are tied to the rather different communicative process that takes place during Holy Week.

First, let us recall that worshipers are surrounded not only by words, but by material objects as well. One of the most important of these is the *rosario* 'rosary' or 'rosary beads'. (I will use initial capitals in English and Spanish to designate the *Rosario* 'Rosary', a set of prayers, and lower case *rosario* 'rosary' to refer to the material object.) The beads provide a tangible mnemonic for structuring the Rosary. Sequences of ten beads represent ten Ave Marías. The isolated beads are keyed to the prayers, such as the Padre Nuestros and Glorias, that precede and follow the decades as well as to meditations on the mysteries. The design of the rosary reflects widely distributed features of Rosary performances; alabado verses, POR todo el mundo, and several opening and closing oraciones are not represented by rosary beads.

Worshipers move from bead to bead with the fingers of one or both hands. This enables those who use rosaries (i.e., all of the Brothers and a few members of the publico) to "feel" their way through the Rosary service. Accordingly, even less conscious attention must be devoted to one's current position within the prayer cycle.

Other material items that are used in Holy Week rituals are not tied specifically to the Rosario. Principal among these are images of holy personages. Images are visible at all points in these rituals; most of the images will have been draped in black, signifying mourning, by the beginning of Holy Week. The images rest on the altars of the chapel and morada, facing the worshipers, and they are carried in procession by younger Brothers and, in the case of El Encuentro, by members of the público as well. Four images play a crucial role here; these consist of standing images of the Nazarene Christ,[19] Our Lady of the Seven Sorrows, and the Veronica, along with a crucifix. Our Lady of Sorrows pictures the Virgin as she suffered the anguish of Christ's passion and death.[20] The Veronica represents the woman who is believed to have wiped the sweat off Christ's face as he carried his cross toward Calvary; the imprint of the divine countenance remained on her kerchief. This act is memorialized as the Sixth Station of the Via Crucis (cf. Steele 1974:172, 196; Steele and Rivera 1985:199).

Two facets of these images are particularly important. First, all four were carved and painted in the nineteenth century by José Rafael Aragón and by one of his apprentices or followers. Aragón lived in Córdova until the time of his death in 1862, and his apprentice or follower was a native Córdovan.[21] These images appear to have been used in rituals within the community ever since;[22] they are accordingly closely connected in the eyes of worshipers with the religious practices of los viejitos de antes. As I have argued elsewhere, polychromed images of saints that reflect regional stylistic canons are considered powerful symbols of Mexicano identity in general (Briggs 1980).

Second, the relationship between the image and the holy personage it represents is hardly exhausted by an iconicity of physical resemblance. The images receive an initial sacralization when they are taken to the priest to be blessed. This process is extended through such devotional acts as burning candles in front of the images and asking the holy personage, in the guise of this particular image, to grant a supplicant's request (cf. Briggs 1980:16–19; Brown et al. 1978:131–32, 135–38; Espinosa 1967/ 1960:82–87; Steele 1974; Wroth 1979:29–30). Some images, such as those of Our Lord of Esquipúlas and the Holy Child in the Santuario in Chimayó, are believed to be particularly miraculous (cf. de Borhegyi 1956). Such reputations are extended once the miracles that are associated with the image are commemorated in legends. Taken as a whole, these acts of faith transform the image; rather than a sign vehicle that stands for the holy personage, the image becomes an index of the presence of the saint, the Virgin, or Christ.

A number of other material objects predominate in these rituals. Candles light the altar of the morada at all times between Wednesday and Friday, and the chapel sanctuary is lighted with candles much of this period. One or two Brothers also carry lanterns, now fueled by gasoline or kerosene, during processions, day and night. The candles and lanterns are characterized as symbols of Christ's light and of the presence of the Holy Spirit. Steele and Rivera (1985:193) quote a Brotherhood document on the subject: "The elder brothers and wardens are charged with seeing to it that there is a light during the exercises at the Calvario, since by this we recognize the presence of the Holy Spirit at our devotions." The association between lighted candles and Christ is particularly clear during the Tenebrae services of Maitines and Tinieblas. Here the extinguishing of the twelve candles explicitly stands for the flight of the apostles. The remaining candle is not extinguished; it is hidden from the people, just as Christ's light was hidden from the world before he rose from the dead.

Matracas, the hand-carved wooden noisemakers, are used during Tenebrae services to help simulate the chaos that ensued following Christ's death (cf. Steele and Rivera 1985:196–97). Pitos are likewise played in the course of Holy Week rituals, including processions. The tunes are traditional, and they provide an instrumental interlude between the chanted rezos and the verses of the alabado. The wailing quality of the pito melody echoes the emotionality of the alabado.

The use of space also plays an important role. Holy Week rituals revolve around the use of two spaces that are entirely devoted to seasonal ritual activities, the morada and the nearby *Calvario* 'Calvary', as well as a number of spaces that are normally devoted to other purposes, including the chapel and its environs and the narrow earthen roads and paths that stretch between morada, chapel, and Calvario (cf. Weigle and Lyons 1982:241). Even the paths that lead to communities that lie at a distance of two to seven miles become sacred spaces when used by Brothers on visitas (generally nocturnal) to neighboring moradas. All of these spaces become meaningful during Holy Week by virtue of their status as sites in which some part or parts of the passion are reenacted or as routes that provide access to these sites. Space, in short, becomes textual space. The meanings that are associated with life in the community at other times are transformed, because space is only meaningful insofar as it has been reincorporated into a textual world.

Time is similarly transformed. Leisure activities are prohibited, and only necessary work is performed. Wage laborers try to take off all of Holy Week if possible. In short, time is not punctuated by the usual round of activities but is measured in ritual terms. The major points of temporal reference are provided by the rituals. Greetings and leave-takings between members of the público are articulated vis-à-vis the ritual that will occur next and when it will take place: *¡Ya pronto nos vamos al Encuentro!* 'We'll be going to the Encuentro soon!' Within rituals, time is measured in terms of one's place within the oración-alabado cycles. Ritual time is, of course, textual time, because the rituals represent, both individually and collectively, the events surrounding the crucifixion.

The body itself is treated differently. Most households observe a prohibition against consuming meat on Fridays during Lent (as do Catholics in general); this is extended to all of Holy Week. *Tortas de huevo* are served in lieu of meat. These consist of small egg dumplings that are filled with either bran or, more recently, salmon, and stewed in a chile pepper sauce. Two special desserts, *panocha* and *sopa*, are eaten as well. Sopa is bread pudding. Panocha is prepared from whole wheat, which is sprouted, dried, ground, mixed with regular flour, and then baked for hours.[23] These foods not only mark the special character of the Lenten season (they are rarely prepared outside of it), but they also provide (according to worshipers) the stamina that one needs to participate in the rituals. Special patterns for the consumption and distribution of food also apply. The Brothers generally eat collectively in the morada; most of this food is brought there by the Brothers' mothers, wives, and sisters. Dishes of food are constantly being exchanged between members of the público during Holy Week, and beans, lentils, chile sauce, tortas de huevo, sopa, and panocha are always on hand for visitors.

Bodily processes are also modified in keeping with the change of activities. Córdovans generally go to bed early, because they rise quite early. Holy Week finds them out of their homes until midnight or later on Wednesday, Thursday, and Friday nights. This lack of sleep is much more acute for the Brothers; not only do they generally remain all night in the morada, but the majority of their processions (including those to moradas in neighboring communities) are conducted at night in order to ensure privacy.[24] Sleeplessness is complemented by the tremendous amount of physical exertion that is involved in participating in the long rituals and frequent processions. It should be borne in mind that these physical hardships are not incidental concomitants of ritual activity. Feeling some semblance of the pain that Christ endured in the passion is part of the process of identifying oneself with him. As A. M. Espinosa (1926:418) notes, this relationship can be particularly direct: "During Holy Week some of the ignorant women of New Mexico do not wash their faces or cut their finger-nails; for, if they do, they wash Christ's face and cut His finger-nails."

One of the most controversial expressions of this identification with Christ is the corporal penance that Brothers administer to themselves. This penance consists mainly of self-flagellation with yucca-fiber whips and dragging heavy crosses. Brothers who are engaging in such acts of penance wear only a black hood that obscures their identity and a pair of white trousers. A host of observers have documented these acts of penance (see for example de Córdova 1973; Darley 1893; Henderson 1937; Hernández 1963; Horka-Follick 1969; Lee 1910; Lummis 1893; Woodward

1974/1935). It is far from clear, however, that the meaning of such ritual acts has been clearly discerned.[25]

Because the Brothers refer to these exercises as *penitencia* 'penance', most observers have simply assumed that the goal of such punishment is to expiate one's sins through performing acts of penance (cf. Stark 1971:310; Weigle 1976:182; Woodward 1935:226). According to Hernández (1963:223), for example, these people "believe in a God who is merciful, but who also, through a very real Purgatory and Hell, can be merciless unless propitiated. Propitiation must be by prayer or 'active' penance, with 'active' penance the more efficacious." Indeed, the expiation of sin through penance plays an important role in Catholic observances of Lent in general. To go on to assert that expiation constitutes the sole motive of such activities, however, is to engage in the same type of reductionism that equates praying the Rosary with a mechanical process of obtaining indulgences.

A number of considerations suggest the inadequacy of this interpretation. First, Brothers are required to participate in the sacrament of reconciliation or confession;[26] members of the Córdova morada generally receive the sacrament together on a Sunday early in Lent. Second, penance is not carried out by the Brothers alone. Practicing Catholics in Córdova all engage in some form of penance during Holy Week, even if this is limited to fasting. Most will also walk to the Santuario, at a distance of four miles. Many will go barefoot during El Encuentro and the Via Crucis. In many years, Holy Week is characterized by cold weather, and snow is not uncommon. The combination of rocky earthen roads and inclement weather is hard on barefoot soles. Many Córdovan Catholics make an annual visita to the morada. These may be confined to venerating the images in the oratory. Other visitors come in fulfillment of a *promesa* 'religious vow', and this often involves a mild physical punishment, such as walking on one's knees while carrying a large image of Christ.[27] Note that these are seen as acts of religious devotion to Christ or the Virgin and not simply as penance for sins committed.

Most important, interpretations that equate such acts with the expiation of sin fail to appreciate their place within the ritual setting. Penance stands as one component of a complex array of ritual actions that are geared toward a common end— identification with Christ and the Virgin. Beginning on Ash Wednesday, dietary and behavioral prohibitions and prescriptions frame the Lenten season as a sacred time. Nightfall on Wednesday of Holy Week stands as a frame within a frame, marking the beginning of a forty-eight-hour period that is wholly given over to commemorating the passion. During this time, other indicators of social status lose their importance as roles within the ritual structure (as Brother, rezador, member of the Sagrada Familia, etc.) come to the fore. For the público, frequent exchanges of food and visits join with participation in rituals as a means of suspending individual differences in favor of emphasizing a corporate identity. This process becomes even more acute for the Brothers as they separate themselves from friends and family and live collectively in a group, one that is constituted in ritual terms (cf. Steele 1978; Weigle and Lyons 1982).

The rituals themselves play a twofold role in this process. The first of these is particularly evident in the constant movement between invocation and petition that is apparent in the texts. The performative character of both types of speech acts is emphasized in the form of the texts as well as in what people say about them. The invocational component is believed to prompt Christ and the Virgin to be spiritually present in the community. Recall the emphasis that is placed on Christ's words, "if two of you join your voices on earth to pray for anything whatever, it shall be granted you by my Father in heaven. Where two or three are gathered in my name, there am I in their midst" (Matthew 18:19–20). Invocations also commemorate those attributes or actions of Christ and the Virgin that point to the basis of their spiritual power. Oraciones and alabados thus describe the suffering that the Virgin and Christ experienced in the course of the passion.

This prompts the worshiper to meditate upon these experiences and upon the spiritual transcendence that they produced. The structure of these meditations is important here as well. The constant verbal and visual activity of these rituals locks the attention of the worshiper not so much on the individual words of the texts as on the events and the emotions that they evoke. Hinnebusch (1967:667) notes with reference to the Rosary that "While he recites the vocal prayers, the worshiper does not direct his attention to them but dwells on the mystery assigned to the decade he is reciting."[28] The overall effect of the invocations is to open up a channel; Christ and the Virgin are now spiritually present, and the worshipers are fully focused upon this presence.

This accomplished, the worshipers can now petition Christ, 'in life and in death, remember me, Lord' (8.1:41–42). The Virgin is similarly asked to 'pray for us sinners, now and in the hour of our death' (33–36). Worshipers are clearly concerned with gaining admission to heaven for themselves and their deceased relatives, but their petitions focus on the present as well as the hereafter. Worshipers often state that the basic goal of these rituals and of religious practice in general is 'to become very, very *close* to Christ'; this refers to a spiritual identification with the deity both in this life and, upon death, as eternal salvation.

A second dimension of these rituals suggests that the invocation/petition process is far from mechanical. Another basic theme in alabados and rezos is that of the social and religious consequences of sin. Sin is characterized as the essence of antisociability and egoism and is produced by placing one's own interests above God's will and the needs of one's fellow human beings. By sinning, we alienate God, thus losing both the power to invoke his presence and the spiritual openness that enables us to sense this presence. Communication with God is effectively blocked; the channel can only be reopened once the worshiper admits to being a sinner, feels remorse, and is granted forgiveness. Sin similarly creates tears in the social fabric; expiating sin is thus crucial for reestablishing harmony within the community.

Holy Week rituals attempt to remove sin in a number of ways. Rezos and alabados are frequently offered in the voice of 'us sinners'; the rezadores or the other participants similarly address either their fellow worshipers or Christians in general as sinners. One of the most popular alabados thus begins with *Venid, pecadores* 'Come, sinners'. These texts also constantly express remorse for sins committed. For example, the Thirteenth Station of the Via Crucis (when Christ is taken down from the cross) contains a prayer to the Virgin that reads, in part, 'O most sorrowful mother . . . I ask you to take pity on the sins that my soul has already committed, cause of the most bitter passion of your sweetest son and of your sorrow'. All forms of penance, including fasting, walking to the Santuario, and going barefoot are similarly offered as admissions that the penitent has sinned as well as attempts to obtain forgiveness. Carrying crosses and whipping oneself thus constitute means of personally and collectively highlighting a process that all worshipers undergo during Holy Week.

But even this interpretation of penance is incomplete, because it fails to account for another major facet of the communicative function of the practice. I argued in earlier chapters that the notion that each person acts in keeping with his or her own individually defined and mutually competing interests is often cited as underlying social divisiveness and a loss of God's blessing. Sin stands as an embodiment of these ever-present individualistic tendencies. Holy Week rituals concern themselves not only with the manifestation of individualism as sin, but with the social effects of individualism as well. Here one's own interests are not only subordinated to God's will, they are (insofar as the ritual is effective) obliterated by an attempt to internalize a divine consciousness. This deeper meaning of penance is thus clarified; penance expresses remorse for sin and attempts to expiate sin, the embodiment of individualism, because both sin and individualism preclude complete identification with Christ and the Virgin. Interpretations that isolate penance thus mistake the means for the end—penance is one of the means that is used in attempting 'to become very, very *close* to Christ.'

Another means to this end is apparent as well. Observers of the Brotherhood have long noted the emphasis on death symbolism in their rituals, but they have failed to account for its presence. Skulls were frequently placed in exposed places in Third Order of St. Francis chapels, and many moradas featured them as well until at least the 1930s (Boyd 1974:446; Woodward 1935:227). I found that many of the younger Brothers kept elaborate collections of skeletal representations of death in their homes.

The Brotherhood death icon par excellence is the carved figure of death, variously known as *La Muerte* 'Death', *Doña Sebastiana* 'Lady Sebastiana', or *la comadre Sebastiana* 'coparent Sebastiana' (Plate 24). The carving, replete with bow and arrow and possibly other instruments of death (knife, hatchet, etc.) formerly adorned all mo-

Plate 24. *Death cart, believed to have been made by Nasario López of Córdova in the nineteenth century. Courtesy of the Taylor Museum of the Colorado Springs Fine Arts Center; gift of Alice Bemis Taylor.*

radas, and it has been suggested that death carts replaced skulls as *mementi mori* (Boyd 1974:446–47, 462). The main ritual use of the figure was in Holy Week processions, where it was pulled in a heavy wooden cart by a Brother by means of thin ropes that cut into the neck or armpits (Henderson 1937:35; Hernández 1963:220). This task was undertaken voluntarily, usually in fulfillment of a vow. Legends recount occasions on which an arrow that was accidentally released kills either the person pulling the cart or a mocking bystander (Henderson 1937:32; Martínez 1937).

A widespread group of legends also features ghostly Brothers who have returned to earth as revenants. Such Brothers are often referred to as being *del otro mundo* 'from the other world', thus distinguishing them from those *de carne y hueso* 'of flesh and blood' (cf. Martínez 1940). These revenants appear most often during Holy Week, where they join processions and slip into moradas unnoticed. Ghostly Brothers whip skeletal backs in which candles burn, and they leave trails of blood but no footprints (Córdova 1973:51; de Córdova 1972:29–33, 41; Lummis 1893:72–73; Weigle 1974:183–85). A revenant is believed to be a Brother who failed to fulfill a vow during his lifetime, and "God had sent him back to earth to scourge himself properly, before allowing him to enter heaven" (Espinosa 1926:408). In some cases, either active penitents or Brothers in general were referred to as 'people of the dead' (cf. Branning 1967). Lorin Brown, who was raised by his Mexicano grandparents in the Taos area (cf. Brown et al. 1978), notes that "We had been inculcated with the notion that those figures wielding the disciplinas, hooded and streaming from scourged backs, were not of this world, but souls in torment sent back from the other world to fulfill unredeemed vows" (de Córdova 1972:29).

This plethora of death symbols demands explanation. Weigle (1977:136) points to the sociological function of revenant legends in protecting the Brotherhood from outside interference. Although such beliefs might have contributed to this end, our understanding of this phenomenon will remain incomplete until we have accounted for other communicative functions of this death symbolism. Brothers stress the New Testament passage, "Whoever loses his life for My sake will save it, but whoever insists on keeping his life will lose it" (Luke 9:24). The Thirteenth Station of the Via Crucis accordingly suggests that in memory of Christ's passion and Mary's suffering, the worshiper promises to live 'only for Him who gave His life for me, and I offer mine in return for such exquisite love'. Here life stands for the sum total of material and psychological attachments to the world that keep human beings from achieving total identification with Christ and the Virgin. Death symbolism and penance both phenomenologically strip worshipers of the cloak of their humanity, thereby readying them for invoking the presence of the Virgin and Christ and for petitioning their divine intercession. The rituals thus take a group of discrete individuals, each with her or his own identity, interests, and worldly involvements, and transform them into a unified body that is completely dedicated to a common goal.

THE "MAGICAL POWER" OF STYLE

This interpretation does not, nonetheless, explain the formal nature of performances of hymns and prayers. Lévi-Strauss's *Mythologiques* (1964, 1966, 1968, 1971) demonstrated the way in which myths create a textual world in which time, space, objects, food, actions, and other elements conform to special ontological and epistemological patterns, and recent studies have analyzed how such experiential shifts are realized in performance (cf. E. Basso 1985, 1986; Gossen 1974a; Hymes 1975, 1981). One might accordingly ask why a performance of a sacred myth could not take the place of the Holy Week ritual cycle. In answering this question, I will place the performance features of oración-alabado cycles vis-à-vis the communicative character of the rituals. I hope to show that the formal dimension is crucial to the success of this process of religious transformation.

I argued previously that the referential content of the texts and the use of sacred images focus the worshiper's attention on the events that characterized the lives of Christ and the Virgin at the time of the passion, the emotions that these events produced, and the spiritual results that emanated from this suffering. Note that the words and actions that make up these rituals are not seen as arbitrarily selected sign vehicles. They rather enjoy a special ontological and epistemological status. Worshipers assert that the texts have been handed down verbatim through the generations of los viejitos de antes. The words are believed to be ultimately derived from the words of Christ, the Virgin, and the apostles as preserved in the New Testament. The sign vehicles themselves thus bear an intrinsic connection with Christ and the Virgin and with the events of Holy Week; this status is not enjoyed by the referential content of the texts alone. The words, as sign vehicles, are considered to be powerful entities that are closely connected with the sacred.

As the texts are performed, a tremendous amount of formal elaboration is focused on these sign vehicles. As I noted previously, volume, pitch, rate, breath, syntax, lexicon, rhetorical structure, and other patterns are stylized and, in the process, set into a fixed form. Despite this tremendous emphasis on form, such performances are not poetic, in Jakobson's (1960) sense of the term, meaning that the poetic function of foregrounding the form is not the dominant communicative function. In performances of proverbs, scriptural allusions, jokes, and legends, the oral literary criticism (cf. Dundes 1966) that provides an evaluative aftermath to public speech events often focuses on the performers' success or failure in exploiting the formal properties of the genre.[29] In the case of Holy Week rituals, however, *estuvo muy bonito* 'it was very beautiful' refers to the success of the performances in generating profound religious feeling; form per se is not singled out for comment. The elaboration of linguistic form, visual features, and temporal and spatial elements provides the experiential basis for a total immersion in the acoustic, visual, temporal, and spatial features of Christ's and the Virgin's own experience. This elaboration of form in all these modalities provides the difference between referring to the words, actions, emotions, and spiritual effects of the passion and directly experiencing them. Formal elaboration also facilitates this internalization of the sacred by virtue of its ability to displace the behavioral, perceptual, and cognitive foci of daily life.

TRANSFORMING THE NATURE OF THE SIGN

Let us reflect for a moment on the nature of the signs that are used in effecting this transformation. Drawing on Peirce's second trichotomy of signs (1932), it is clear that the signs that constitute these rituals draw on symbolic, indexical, and iconic modes simultaneously.

In terms of symbolic meaning, the referential value of the words is preserved, and this content plays an important role in describing the events of the passion. Many of these same sign vehicles also stand as indexes. Two sets of indexical functions seem most important. First, as in the other genres, a host of stylistic devices index the generic status of the discourse and the location of particular utterances and actions within the structure of the speech event. Because this speech and action is collective, the indexical function of pointing to what is to come next in the oración-alabado cycle is important. Examples are provided by the entrance of the Brothers into the chapel with matracas, thus indexing their intention to begin a tenebrae service. Similarly, the rezadores' utterance (without chanting prosody) of Padre Nuestro indexes the fact that it is the other participants' turn to chant the first part of the Padre Nuestros and Ave Marías in the decade that has just begun. Second, indexes also point to the presence of the sacred and the religious-emotional state of the worshipers. This state is particularly revealed in prosodic features; one quickly notes a sudden increase in the sacred character of the discourse and the religious and emotional intensity with which it is received when the rezadores' alabados are drowned out by the Brothers' alabado as the latter enter the chapel during a visita. Behavioral indexes are also apparent in the treatment of images (as reflecting the presence of the holy personage) and the tears that are produced by El Encuentro.

Iconicity is certainly no less apparent. The rituals stand in an iconic relationship to the events of the passion; moreover, the effect of these rituals as a whole is to fashion the community into a textual world that provides a large-scale icon of the passion.

This characterization is compatible with Tambiah's (1968:188) interpretation of the linguistic basis of ritual. He argues that Trobriand magical language "is not qualitatively 'different' from ordinary language, but is a heightened use of it. The same laws of association that apply to ordinary language apply to magical language." Although Holy Week rituals may evince a "heightened" use of evocative symbols, indexes, and icons, this juxtaposition of communicative modes is characteristic of language in general (cf. Silverstein 1976). The fact that Holy Week rituals rest on the same basic sign types does not necessarily mean, however, that sign vehicles and objects (in Peirce's 1932:2.230–31 sense of the term) are related in the same fashion as in other speech events. I believe that the relationship between these sign vehicles and their objects differs radically from the way that this relationship is realized in other signs used in the speech community, and that herein lies a crucial way in which ritual and other uses of language are "qualitatively 'different'."

Wherein lies this difference? I noted previously that the overriding goal of Holy Week rituals is to achieve a symbolic identification with Christ and the Virgin. I also described the means that are adopted in achieving this end—a replication of the words, actions, emotions, and the spiritual state that Christ and the Virgin achieved in the course of the passion and crucifixion. I argued that the words and actions that make up these rituals do not simply function as sign vehicles that stand for a sacredness that lies beyond their reach; they are seen as having emanated directly from the original (i.e., biblical) words and acts and as having been faithfully transmitted from generation to generation. The sign vehicles, the words and actions that make up Holy Week rituals, are thus seen as having retained their sacred character. Insofar as the worshipers' words, actions, emotions, and spiritual states are qualitatively different from those of Christ and the Virgin, to that extent the ritual has proved ineffective and the goal of symbolic unification with Christ and the Virgin has not been achieved.

I am not suggesting that these ritual actions simply become icons, even perfect icons, of the objects that they represent. Extending the intimacy of the iconic connections certainly plays a role in the process; this is part of what lies behind the power of performing acts of penance, such as carrying crosses or simulating the crucifixion by having one Brother strapped to a cross for a short time on the afternoon of Good Friday (cf. de Córdova 1972:46; Henderson 1937:46–49; Weigle 1976:171–75). The physical resemblance of sign vehicle and object in these rituals is never perfect, nor is it most important. Rather the crucial element is that the worshiper experience her or his own words, actions, emotions, and spiritual states as matching those of Christ and the Virgin during the time of the passion to such an extent that the sense of symbolic unification is achieved.

The crucial transformation lies in the nature of the sign itself. Saussure (1959/1916:115) argues that the value of signs, linguistic and otherwise, is composed "(1) of a *dissimilar* thing that can be *exchanged* for the thing of which the value is to be determined; and (2) of *similar* things that can be *compared* with the thing of which the value is to be determined" (emphasis in original). This "paradoxical principle" gives rise to two oppositions that play a fundamental role in his theory of the sign, that between signified (*signifié*) and signifier (*signifiant*) and that between one sign and all the other signs of the system. We encounter no difficulty in accepting the applicability of this latter notion to the signs of Holy Week, because they occupy distinctive places in this communicative system. The idea that the sign unifies dissimilar entities also works for the other signs that make up the talk of the elders of bygone days and of speech events in general. But this is precisely what distinguishes the words and actions that emerge during Wednesday through Friday of Holy Week from the communicative repertoire as a whole: *the goal of the ritual progression of these three days lies in overcoming the opposition between signifier and signified.* Insofar as worshippers achieve symbolic unification, their words, actions, emotions, and spiritual states do not just represent those of Christ and the Virgin; they merge phenomenologically with the words, actions, emotions, and spiritual states that were realized some 2,000 years ago.

Some will argue that the semiotic basis of these rituals is simply the achievement of an identity between signified and signifier; the nature of the sign thus remains unchanged. My claim is that the basic duality between signified and signifier has been overcome. A perfect analogy to clarify the distinction is provided by the sacrifice of the Mass. A number of elements of the Mass resemble the ritual process that takes place during Holy Week. In the latter case, fasting, atoning for one's sins, and reconciling oneself with one's fellows were necessary. Both celebrant and communicants (those receiving communion) are similarly required to fast [30] and to be free from mortal sin. Fortescue (1912:225; 1943/1917:38–41) also notes that the priest must "be reconciled to all men." This preparatory cleansing is completed by a washing of the priest's hands before vesting for Mass and in the course of the Mass (before the communion) as well. The priest also offers a confession in preparing himself for the communion. The people recite a "Penitential Act" as part of the entrance rite; this includes the words *mea culpa, mea culpa, mea maxima culpa.* The reconciliation of the participants with all persons is represented by the "sign of peace," a descendant of the Roman kiss of peace; this act, performed just before communion, is associated with Christ's teaching concerning the need to settle differences with other persons before offering sacrifices to God (Matthew 5:23–24).

The most important parallel lies in the canon of transubstantiation; this central element of Catholic doctrine asserts that the wine and bread that are offered in the sacrifice of the communion are changed into *the* body and blood of Christ. According to Church doctrine, the physical appearance ("species" or "accidents") of the bread and wine is preserved (cf. Chrichton 1971:102). Note that it is not the case that the bread and wine *refer* to Christ's body and blood. The consecration of the bread and wine, as modeled on Christ's words and actions in the Last Supper, transforms the bread and wine from the status of substances that stand for Christ to the whole body and blood of Christ. If the signifier (bread and wine) and the signified (body and blood of Christ) remain distinct, then the communion has not been realized.

The rituals of Holy Week and the Catholic Mass are thus perfectly parallel in this fundamental respect. Without changing physical appearances, the worshipers' performance of words and actions that are modeled on Christ's words and actions generates an identity between the two. Similar felicity conditions—fasting, absence of sin, and reconciliation of interpersonal disputes—hold in the Mass and Lenten rituals. The desired effect, symbolic unification with Christ, is likewise the same. Semiotically, both rites involve the transformation of the signifier such that it is merged with that which it represents. This process may provide some insight into the history of the Brotherhood. The rituals that were performed by its members posed a threat to the Church in that they provided an alternative route to symbolic unification with Christ, one that did not directly require the mediation of the priesthood. The failure of the Church to suppress the Brotherhood effectively is partly due to the fact that the organization's doctrine and rituals contained no heretical elements; indeed, they were based on the same religious texts. Similarly, one of the measures that was used in attempting to control Brotherhood rituals was to instruct priests that recalcitrant Brothers "are to be deprived of the Sacraments until they submit to Church jurisdiction" and that Mass should not be celebrated in the chapels that were frequented by members of the organization.[31] Such measures would seem to be counterproductive, destined to force the Brothers to place greater reliance on their own rituals.

CONTEXTUALIZATION AND THE POWER OF THE RELIGIOUS TEXT

What roles do textual elements play in performances of hymns and prayers? First, nearly every word that is uttered within these rituals is determined in advance—almost nothing is composed in the course of the performance. This applies not only to the words themselves, but to the accompanying gestures and the prosodic characteristics of the participants' voices as well. The notable exception is the address that is offered during Maitines and Tinieblas. Second, the texts are tied to events, not all of which are mentioned explicitly in the referential content of the text. The standardized verbal content and the multiple layers of rhythmic patterns enable the worshiper to meditate on these events at the same time that she or he is saying the oraciones and singing the alabado verses. Indeed, such meditation is necessary if the performance is to be effective. As Hinnebusch has noted with respect to the Rosary, "while he recites the vocal prayers, the worshiper does not direct his attention to them but dwells on the mystery assigned to the decade he is reciting" (1967:667).

Third, the text also dominates aspects of the bodily processes of the worshiper, including both the general condition produced by fasting, less sleep, processions, exposure, and hours of prayer as well as the effects of the rhythms of the rezo-alabado cycles in regulating breath. In the case of persons carrying crosses or using whips, the textual enactment produces even greater changes in physiological processes. Note that either chanting and singing or engaging in active penance is effective in dominating the physical state of the worshiper—no one does both simultaneously. Finally, social interactions are also patterned by these textual rhythms. Roles are defined by the textual realm, not by the participants' status in the community. The distribution of turns at talk is similarly a function of the structure of the text; the nature of each person's contribution (as first or second part, chanted or sung, etc.) is likewise specified by the text. The text perfectly coordinates the utterances of persons who share the same part (as prayer leader, público, etc.), such that they say the same thing with the same prosodic features at the same time. The spatial location of the participants is similarly patterned.

These effects are achieved to some extent in all genres of la plática de los viejitos de antes. Even in the case of such flexible genres as that of historical discourse, some words and prosodic patterns are formulaic. The participants are likewise stimulated to contemplate events and processes that lie behind words. Each genre is characterized by particular rhythmic patterns that can affect breath and other physiological processes; posture, facial expression, gaze, and gesture are certainly modified as well. All of the genres pattern the social interaction; the *¿ves?* 'you see?', *sí* 'yes' provides a basic interactional unit. Nonetheless, the power of the text in performances of historical discourse, proverbs, scriptural allusions, chistes, and legends falls far short of the extent of its role in hymns and prayers. In the former case, the text generates a much smaller portion of the discourse; the process of contextualization contributes utterances that are not common to all performances. More important, the role of contextualization is not simply additive but dialectical as well; contextualization thus actively influences the way that the textual component will be realized in a given performance. Quite simply, performances in the other genres are composed in situ, albeit in keeping with a shared textual tradition. In the case of hymns and prayers, however, no composition takes place at the time of the performance; nearly everything that is said and done is dictated by the textual tradition. (The rezador's speech during tenebrae services again provides an exception.)

In comparison with the conversational genres, the relationship that hymns and prayers bear to la plática de los viejitos de antes contrasts sharply. The power of proverb performances, for example, lies in the ability of performers to shape the proverb in such a way that it is maximally reflective of the ongoing interaction. Exactly the opposite is true for hymns and prayers. Their power derives, in the eyes of their users, from their lack of susceptibility to situational variation. Proverbs draw on the talk of the elders of bygone days in focusing attention on some element of the situation at hand. Prayers and hymns are designed to fix the consciousness of the participants on another place and time.

TEXT AND TIME

Hymns and prayers lead backwards in time in two senses. First, both Brothers and nonmembers frequently state that the Holy Week rituals are *muy, muy viejo* 'very,

very old' and that they have been reenacted in the same way for a long time. The Brothers resist any form of modernization to the morada structure itself, such as electrification, on the grounds that 'we like to leave things here like they were in bygone days'. This stability is deemed essential not only to the continued vitality of the Holy Week rituals but to the perseverance of the Catholic faith in Córdova altogether. I have heard Brothers, members of the *público*, and even Protestants assert that *los hermanos guardan la fe* ('the Brothers guard the faith' of the community). They add that if the local chapter of the Brotherhood should collapse, *ya no vas a ver nada aquí* 'you're not going to see anything here'. The *nada* refers to religious practices; it is not altogether clear, however, that such statements do not also imply that Mexicano cultural traditions as a whole would disappear.

Second, the hymns and prayers in question are not practiced in Córdova alone. Textually speaking, the same hymns are sung throughout northern New Mexico and southern Colorado (cf. Robb 1980:613). With respect to the prayers, many of the fundamental *oraciones*, such as the Our Father, Hail Mary, Apostles' Creed, and Glory Be to the Father, are of importance to all Catholics. Thus, the textual background of the hymns and prayers of Holy Week and Lent is believed to extend not only through the generations of the Mexicanos' New Mexican forebearers, but to the testimonies left by the apostles. The sanctity of the texts is thus believed to emanate from their status as divinely inspired representations of the events themselves.

This emphasis on maintaining the texts intact provides us with insight into a most peculiar facet of hymns and prayers—the fact that they are objectified in writing. This is the central example of written transmission in the genres that constitute la plática de los viejitos de antes. The other major exception to the norm of oral transmission is, interestingly, the derivation of some scriptural allusions from readings of catechisms and other devotional books. In the case of alabados and oraciones, the act of writing is of prime significance. Brothers generally produce their own cuaderno once they are voted into an office in which cuadernos are used. The date on which they finished copying the cuaderno is generally given; if the notebook is loaned to another Brother for copying, this is often noted as well.

Inscription is thus of symbolic as well as of practical (mnemonic) significance. The older Brothers assert that complete memorization is the ultimate goal. Copying the text is viewed with favor, however, because it ensures textual stability. As I noted previously, the borrowing of a cuaderno is marked by a high degree of formality. This emphasis on the role of writing in securing the transmission of Brotherhood ritual is also apparent in the way in which the *reglas* 'rules', bylaws and regulations, are regarded. These stress the imitation of Christ and the avoidance of sinful conduct, providing both a guide for individuals' religious devotion and conduct as well as a set of procedures and regulations for the morada (cf. Steele and Rivera 1985; Weigle 1976:149–50; Woodward 1935:216, 311–21). The Brothers note that their reglas have been preserved since the morada's inception.

MOVEMENT TOWARD THE CONTEXT

This does not mean, however, that context plays no role in shaping the way these texts are realized in ritual performances. There are a number of points in the course of Holy Week rituals in which contextual factors prove significant.

First, a number of decisions are made each year with respect to the role that written texts will play in the services. Brothers over the age of seventy stress the need for rezadores to memorize prayers and alabados, whereas younger members seem to feel this is less crucial. Observation over a twelve-year period suggest to me that cuadernos are used more and more in the course of the services. Similarly, as little as a decade ago, nearly all cuadernos consisted of handwritten texts, copied from fellow Brothers. Printed texts, such as Rael's (1951) *The New Mexican Alabado* and printed versions of the Via Crucis, have become increasingly important during the intervening years. After an absence of five years from Holy Week observances, I noted in 1984 that many Brothers possess photocopies of both handwritten and printed cuadernos. This suggests that the way written texts are used reflects broad sociolinguistic patterns in Mexicano northern New Mexico, including changing rates of literacy, greater access to and interest in printed material, and technological advances in the dissemination of information.

Second, selections are made in certain cases with regard to which text(s) from a given source will be performed. This is particularly true for the singing of alabados by rezadores from the público before the beginning of the Rosary service of Holy Wednesday, Los Maitines, and Las Tinieblas. Of course, the individuals involved decide whether to move into the sanctuary and lead an alabado at all. Once two rezadores have seated themselves in the sanctuary, they generally spend a few moments looking through the cuaderno, deciding which alabado to sing. These decisions reflect the range of alabados with which they are familiar through oral performance, because none of the rezadores can read music.[32] Their choices are also affected by personal preferences and a knowledge of which alabados have already been sung in previous services. All of these decisions are constrained by the rules that specify which alabados should be used on a given Holy Week day.

Third, the enactment of some rituals or parts of rituals is optional. The addition of the Rosary service on Maundy Thursday morning reflects the rise of the society of the Holy Family. Similarly, a Rosary service was offered on the afternoon of Maundy Thursday in 1984 in memory of a deceased rezador, Aurelio Trujillo. Because it was sponsored by the family rather than the Brotherhood, it was led by rezadores from the público. The rezadores who are not Brothers can also petition the sacristan for permission to offer a Rosary service before the beginning of the Wednesday night Rosary service, Los Maitines, or Las Tinieblas. Such decisions reflect their own personal religious intentions as well as the degree of interest of other members of the público.

Fourth, some intertextual variation is present. In other words, choices are available to rezadores and other participants as to which texts will be performed together and in which order they will appear. Such variation is greatly limited, however, by the high degree to which intertextual associations are part of the rules shared by participants for the constitution of a particular service. In the case of written texts, cuadernos specify exactly which rezos or oraciones (Our Father, Hail Mary, Glory Be to the Father, *Sudario,* etc.) should follow a given portion of the text for the Stations of the Cross, El Encuentro, or other service.

One of the most important sources of contextualization pertains to the selection of participants. Much of the Brotherhood's recruitment of individuals to fill specific roles is determined by an election held at the end of the previous Good Friday (cf. Weigle 1976:175). Decisions as to who will go on a given visita, for example, follow both from individual intentions and from the instructions of the officers. The members of the society of the Holy Family make similar decisions as to the recruitment of persons for various roles, particularly for their annual visita and for El Encuentro.

With regard to the público, participation is contingent upon the religious conviction of each individual. While some Córdovans always participate in all or nearly all of the public services, other persons, including Catholics, take no part in them. Individuals can also be more or less active participants; they can, for example, make individual visitas to the morada, the Santuario de Chimayó, or elsewhere. Persons who have received training as rezadores may or may not choose to act in this capacity.

The presence of nonresidents, particularly Anglo-Americans, has some effect on services; this is most directly manifested in the separate address that is given, in English, to the newcomers during Las Tinieblas—the only occasion in which a word of English is used in the course of Holy Week services. Because English lexemes and phrases appear in all of the other genres of the talk of the elders of bygone days,[33] the absence of Spanish/English code switching in the hymns and prayers and its virtual exclusion from the services as a whole is another manifestation of the tremendous textual conservatism associated with Holy Week rituals.

The weather affects the course of Holy Week services as well. Córdova lies at an elevation of 6,900 feet, so the weather is never warm in the early spring. In some years, in fact, it is quite cold, and heavy snowfalls are not rare. In cases of severe weather, the Stations of the Cross are held indoors. Similarly, the Brothers will meet the público on the cement walkway just outside the chapel during the El Encuentro if the road is quite muddy. There are, however, clear limitations to such adaptation. For example, the Brothers still go barefoot in the processions in which this is appropriate, even if the ground is covered with snow.

Finally, errors or mishaps can affect the course of rituals in minor ways. Occasionally, for example, two rezadores will encounter difficulty in leading the público in an alabado. This generally results from the selection of a less-known alabado and a shortage of those members of the público, generally women, who are active in singing the chorus. Likewise, a rezador from either the Brotherhood or the público will occasionally falter, thus interrupting the flow of prayer and song. This sometimes elicits laughter from younger participants, Brothers and non-Brothers alike, which can temporarily lessen the religious intensity of the service. Similarly, a rezador sometimes comes to a word that he cannot make out immediately. The resulting pause will alter the prosodic structure of his chanting.

THE TEXTUAL CIRCLE

These points do not, however, evince the systematic contextualization of textual features to social setting that is apparent in the other genres. Texts are not shaped in such a way as to provide an interpretation of current events in the community or in the lives of the individual participants. Texts are similarly not altered in performance in order to enhance their comprehensibility (i.e., to reflect the level of competence of the participants). The only notable exception is the addition of the address in English during Las Tinieblas. The burden of comprehension is placed upon the individual; competence emerges gradually from learning prayers and doctrine well, primarily during childhood, and listening closely and participating as much as is possible during numerous Holy Weeks.

Contextualization is not absent. Holy Week ceremonies reflect the events of the New Testament as they have been codified by ritual patterns of the laity and religious (particularly the Franciscans) and by pontifical and conciliar decisions over the centuries. The hymns and prayers that I have described have developed from these sources along lines that reflect linguistic, folkloric, cultural, and religious patterns among Mexicanos. Although many commonalities are present, the way Holy Week is celebrated in Córdova differs in detail from the rituals that are enacted in other rural northern New Mexican communities. The course of the rituals during a given year similarly reflects such processes as recruiting participants, selecting texts, and compensating for the weather, as well as the way in which the outcome of one service affects the course of the next.

But this movement toward context is hardly the final step in the ritual process. The rezos or oraciones and alabados can only emerge through their adoption by a given social community in a certain location. Once the recruitment process is complete, however, the texts are used in transforming the social context that exists before Lent and Holy Week into a drama that emerges from the texts. The physical setting is transformed into a representation of Jerusalem, as the roads between the chapel and morada become part of the way to Calvary. Existentially, then, the recruitment process does not orient the participants toward the broader processes and events that fuel it; rather, it produces a social community that is partially devoted over a period of forty days and entirely focused for three on replicating in word, action, emotion, and spiritual state a series of scenes that are embodied in the text. Social structure becomes narrative structure. The movement toward context, never terribly pronounced, turns out to be one step on a road that leads back to the text.

ON THE INTERPRETATION OF HYMNS AND PRAYERS

This analysis returns us once again to Tambiah's characterization of "the magical power of words." I was forced to disagree with his conclusion that ritual language is not qualitatively different from "ordinary language," suggesting that the communicative basis of Holy Week rituals differs radically from that of other modes in the speech community—except the Mass and the sanctification of holy images. Nonetheless, the above findings leave me in strong agreement with his suggestion that all ritual "uses a technique which attempts to restructure and integrate the minds and emotions of the actors" (1968:202). I have tried to show how the performance of hymns and prayers during Holy Week exercises a powerful effect over the words, actions, emotions, and spiritual state of worshipers. This conclusion seems to align my approach with the mechanistic view of ritual language, the notion that participants play no creative role in the ritual process.

It is indeed true that worshipers have little say as to which words and actions they will produce during Holy Week. It is equally clear that the overall goal of the rituals—symbolic unification with Christ and the Virgin—is both collective and predetermined. Several facets of this process point to the fact that it is far from mechanical, however, and that individual creativity is important.

First, the goals of Holy Week rituals cannot be realized merely by producing the proper words and gestures. In Austin's (1962) terms, the mere locution of a particular set of illocutionary formulae is seen as utterly useless. To be successful in achieving symbolic unification with Christ and the Virgin, a worshiper must be fully engaged, physically, cognitively, and emotionally, in the rituals.

Second, the role of the interpreting subject vis-à-vis the object of interpretation has changed radically in keeping with a radical change in the nature of the sign. I argued in previous chapters that performers of historical discourse, proverbs, scriptural allusions, chistes, and legends maintain a critical distance from the aspects of antes and ahora that they are interpreting, which enables them to change their own relationship to the material in the course of the performance. We saw in example (7.2) how the performers shifted from bearers of the talk of the elders of bygone days to reporters of others' attempts to find the treasure to participants in a dispute over the validity of the legend to major participants in their own treasure hunt. This interpretive distance enables them to criticize nowadays in general, the actions of other treasure hunters, the lack of faith of the skeptics, and an aspect of bygone days (Pedro Córdova's enslavement of his fellow villagers).

I have also argued that this internal dialogicality is brought into being by a polyphony of stylistic devices, particularly the use of quoted speech. Interestingly, discourse that is framed as quoted speech plays an extremely minor role in rezo-alabado cycles. Quoted speech emerges only once in the course of the rezador's narration of the passion story during the Via Crucis.[34] The Virgin is quoted in the Fourth Station, the commemoration of her meeting with Christ on the road to Calvary, as offering, sotto voce, a prayer addressed to Christ; I presented a transcription of this prayer in the description of El Encuentro. Here, the one time that the Virgin speaks in her own voice, she draws on the same terms as the worshipers themselves—use of "second person" verb inflections and pronouns. These terms foreground the conative function (cf. Jakobson 1960:355), focusing on the addressee, Christ. Stylistically and ideologically, the performer does not stand apart from what is being interpreted. Once the presence of Christ and the Virgin has been evoked in relation to a particular set of words,[35] actions, emotions, and spiritual effects, the worshiper uses the same conative voice in petitioning Christ or the Virgin to enable the worshiper to experience these same words, actions, emotions, and spiritual states.

The interpreting subject is thus merged with the object of interpretation in the course of the rituals. The state of consciousness achieved by the interpreter is defined by the consciousness that lies in the object of interpretation—the words, actions, emotions, and spiritual states of Christ and the Virgin. Insofar as they achieve this state, the consciousness of each worshiper will be identical. This fact lies behind the symbolism that plays a major role in both Holy Week rituals and in the Catholic Mass—the unification of the body of worshipers by virtue of their common symbolic unification with Christ. It also gives rise to the perception that the community itself is renewed and unified each Holy Week (cf. Weigle and Lyons 1982).

If the final result of this interpretive process is the same for all worshipers, wherein lies the creativity? As I noted previously, achieving this state is predicated upon examining one's own involvement with the world. Individual worshipers must examine their own thoughts and actions during the past year in order to identify occasions on which they have gone against God's will (i.e., have sinned) or have offended other human beings. Once these thoughts and actions have been reinterpreted (as sin and antisociability), worshipers must feel remorse and seek forgiveness. Worshipers, Brothers, and members of the público all decide for themselves which act or acts of penance are most appropriate for this context.

This process goes hand-in-hand with the larger task of meditating upon the sum total of one's involvement with the world. A major focus of Holy Week rituals is on reinterpreting this involvement as secondary to one's primary commitment, following Christ. The rituals elaborately embody Christ's words "Whoever wishes to be my follower must deny his very self, take up his cross each day, and follow in my steps. Whoever would save his life will lose it, and whoever loses his life for my sake will save it" (Luke 9:23–24). Holy Week rituals contextualize this process via a yearly examination of the applicability of the concepts of sin and worldly attachment to one's own immediate experience. Note that this personalization and contextualization of the ritual discourse is not attached in any way to the form of the rezos or oraciones and alabados—it remains entirely implicit, internal, and private. No participant has the right or the ability to monitor, let alone guide, the way that any other participant contextualizes this ritual discourse.

Prayers, hymns, and the rituals in which they are performed thus provide us with a greater sense of the intimacy and the complexity of the relationship of textual and contextual elements in la plática de los viejitos de antes. The role of contextualization in the form and content of Holy Week rituals is not only minimal—it is suppressed. One of the major features of alabados and rezos is the emphasis that is placed on minimizing the degree to which contextualization produces textual variation, both geographically and historically, and the power of the written word is employed in this attempt. This overt suppression is paralleled by a reemergence of contextualization within the interpretive process. Here the individual's obligation to contextualize the textual world vis-à-vis her or his own life is complemented by tremendous interpretive freedom; the contextualization process is not constrained by style, content, or social interaction. Although the goal of these activities is textually defined, the textual component cannot be adequately performed without according a very real phenomenological space to its contextual counterpart. In maintaining its ground, however, the contextualization process does not root itself in any observable performance features but is transformed into a facet of the unspoken consciousness of the participants.

9

CONCLUSION

My analysis thus far has focused on isolating the features that identify the genres that constitute la plática de los viejitos de antes and analyzing the role they play in performances. I argued in Chapter 1 that these genres cannot be adequately analyzed apart from the process of contextualization, which entails detailed examination of the way in which the participants draw on elements of the social, physical, and verbal setting of particular interactions in negotiating a shared frame of reference. I also stressed the need to focus closely on formal features of the discourse, from the level of grammatical particles to that of the global structure of the performance. Information about Córdova in particular and Mexicano northern New Mexico in general has also been presented to reveal the rich layers of background information that inform the production and interpretation of performances. As a result, the reader has been confronted with a host of particulars; it is now time to face the general issues that are raised by these materials. In doing so, I will return to the basic question that I posed in Chapter 1: What is the nature of the competence that underlies performances of the talk of the elders of bygone days?

My interpretation has emphasized the diversity that is apparent in performances both within and between genres, which raises a more fundamental problem: Is it useful to attempt to ask the question of competence in this general form at all? Can we presuppose the existence of a common competence that is shared by the different individual performers and diverse genres? Or are we dealing with a range of discrete types of competence that characterize contrastive speech events, all of which happen to fall within the aegis of this talk? To examine both sides of this issue, I will begin by analyzing the differences that are apparent between the various genres in terms of the discourse processes that are evident in performances and then examine the commonalities that emerge from amidst the diversity.

DIVERSITY IN MEXICANO FOLKLORE

Many differences are apparent between the genres that fall under the aegis of the talk of the elders of bygone days. These are apparent in the types of occasions in which performances emerge, the length of performances, the number of people that they involve, and the types of restrictions that each places on the recruitment of performers. Analysis suggests, however, that one basis of differentiation looms far above the others in importance—the orientation of the performance in terms of the continuum from contextual to textual foci. This distinction lies at the heart of contrasts in stylistic features and the way that performances relate to tradition and to social interaction . Examining the various genres in relation to textual and contextual orientations is more a means of exploring the way that performances come into being and the meaning that they hold for participants than a process of scholarly classification.

PROVERBS VIS-À-VIS LEGENDS: A COMPARISON OF TWO PERFORMANCES

In comparing the role of textual and contextual processes in historical discourse, proverbs, scriptural allusions, chistes, legends, and hymns and prayers, I will initially examine performances of proverbs and legends. Each of these genres occupies a position that is one genre removed from either pole of the continuum (see Figure 4). I will draw on Mrs. López's venison proverb (4.2) and Mr. Romero's legend of his grandfather, the Indians, and the tortillas (7.1), contrasting the role of contextual versus textual processes in each performance.

An initial measure of the relative orientation of these performances along this axis can be provided by counting the number of lines in each that point toward textual and contextual spheres. The latter includes both the ongoing social interaction, specific interactions that preceded the performance (e.g., the venison 'lie'), and characterizations of nowadays as a whole. For the proverb, the percentages of lines pointing toward the textual and contextual spheres are twenty-seven and sixty-nine percent respectively; for the legend they are eighty-eight and twelve percent.

This rough quantitative measure suggests two conclusions. First, there is a vast disparity in the predominance of textual versus contextual elements in the two performances. Second, contextual elements appear to be more dispensable than textual elements; contextually oriented lines make up only twelve percent of the legend performance, while textually oriented lines remain at twenty-seven percent of the proverb performance. My data show that this quantitative disparity holds for all performances in these genres. Indeed, the preponderance of contextual elements diminishes as one moves throughout the range of genres from historical discourse to hymns and prayers (see Figure 4) just as the textual orientation of performances grows.

I believe, however, that this simple measure tells us relatively little about the differences between these genres. To comprehend the way that genres differ along the contextual-textual continuum, we must also examine differences in the role of both types of elements within performances, particularly because contextual and textual processes both include a wide variety of formal-functional relationships.

Let us begin with Mrs. López's proverb performance. Here we find evidence of a range of different contextualization cues. Mrs. López devotes twenty-four lines to interpretation of two recent events (the original 'lie' and its exposure by Elvis). She similarly uses seven lines just before the end of the performance in interpreting the future, telling me what I am supposed to tell outsiders about her. She also uses contextualization cues in interpreting a number of different aspects of the ongoing social interaction. She states her doubt about whether I am at that point (4.2:47) convinced of her account of the 'lie' or not. Mrs. López similarly draws on a host of contextualization cues that provide her with information as to whether I am comprehending what she is saying. As I noted in Chapter 4, these include visual signals (such as gaze and facial expressions) in addition to her queries (¿ves? 'you see', etc.) and my responses (sí 'yes', um hum, etc.).

With respect to textual elements, the proverb text relates one of the beliefs associated with the elders of bygone days. Mr. López interprets a basic value—the idea that 'God loves the TRUTH and not LIES'. Mrs. López does begin the process of bringing bygone days to life by framing this information as the words of a specific individual and by telling us where this person lives and what religion she practices. Access to the world of bygone days, however, ends at this point in the performance. The neighbor may be a voice, but she is not a character. We learn nothing about the sorts of experiences that led her to assert this principle. Bygone days remains a timeless sphere that is not differentiated through a succession of events or a series of contrastive voices.

Textual and contextual elements do not exhaust the range of forms that are evident in this or other proverb performances—a number of lines do not fall exclusively into either category. Proverb performances also contain metacommunicative features that articulate the relationship between textual and contextual spheres. I argued in Chapter 4 that validations, which appear in all proverb performances, do not simply assert that a given utterance is part of la plática de los viejitos de antes. Assertions by the performer, other elders, and younger persons also affirm the connection between this segment of the talk of the elders of bygone days and the performer's view of the situation at hand—that is, between textual and contextual spheres.

Other features of this performance have a similar metacommunicative function. Note that the words of the proverb text are inserted, both in the aggregate and individually, in Mrs. López's interpretation of nowadays. In (14), Elvis' role is summarized in the words of the text: *Dios usó la persona de ELVIS* 'God used Elvis'. In lines (15, 38, 43, 62, 65, 74, and 90), Mrs. López uses either *la verdad* 'the truth' or *la mentira* 'lies' in her characterization of the present. These words become synecdoches for the proverb text as a whole. The entire text is repeated in (89–90) as part of the words that I am to use in telling others about Mrs. López.

This process of inserting elements of the proverb text into other parts of the performance provides us with a clue to the directionality of the use of textual and contextual elements in this performance. Note that most of the lines that focus on the textual sphere come toward the beginning of the performance; the latter part focuses almost entirely on the present. I believe that this linear asymmetry (cf. Silverstein 1981b) at the formal level parallels an interpretive movement. We begin with a hazy glimpse into bygone days. Rather than fleshing out this vision, proverb performances soon turn toward an interpretation of nowadays. The transition is not abrupt, because this element of antes becomes a Leitmotiv for interpreting ahora. Proverb performances do not draw us into bygone days; rather, they draw tiny slices of bygone days into nowadays. Textual elements play an extremely important role in this process. Proverb texts are, as many pariemiologists have argued, pithy and formulaic. The words of the text thus serve as excellent synecdoches of the text as a whole. Thus, the performer can index the bearing of the text and the values of bygone days on the situation at hand repeatedly and most succinctly by reiterating key terms of the text throughout the performance.

Assertions of the validity of the performance and repetitions of the language of the text explicitly connect textual and contextual spheres. This process becomes even more overt toward the end of the performance. I have noted that Mrs. López used the proverb for its performative effect in transforming the situation. In her view, the impact of the text and its exegesis on the situation at hand was to transform her status from a 'lying' purveyor of illegal venison to a pious woman who can speak with authority about bygone days. Just to make sure that I make the connection between textual and contextual spheres, she summarizes the point of intersection in the form of a quotation of the words that I am to use in portraying her to 'the outside world'.

In the case of Mr. Romero's legend, we encounter fewer different types of contextual elements. I do provide a number of back-channel cues that signal my comprehension, and Mr. Romero asks me whether I am following the performance on nine occasions with a ¿ves? 'you see?'. The most striking hiatus in contextual elements as we move from the proverb to the legend is the lack of any explicit interpretation of nowadays. Mr. Romero presents no vision of contemporary society in the course of the performance. With the exception of his concern in assessing my level of comprehension, he similarly fails to interpret the ongoing social interaction.

This relative impoverishment in the complexity of the contextual sphere is matched by an efflorescence of textual layering in comparison to the proverb performance. Rather than a single, undifferentiated sphere of bygone days, we find a development of qualitatively distinct modes of experience within antes. In temporal terms, we can distinguish the time that the Indians passed through the mountains near Córdova (during Mr. Romero's childhood) from the epoch in which Mexicanos and Indians still exchanged hostilities (during his grandfather's youth). Temporal differentiation also follows the linear structure of the narrative. Use of the narrative frame *una vez* 'one time' carves a discrete portion of time out of bygone days. A shift from imperfective to perfective aspect reinforces this temporal differentiation, creating a series of discrete events.

Bygone days also shows geographic diversity in the legend. The first part of the performance places the Mexicanos in the Quemado Valley, when they watch the Indians pass through the mountains. Mr. Romero's grandfather and his companions then pass through the mountains themselves; the account of their journey provides a map of a number of the sites that figured significantly in the events of antes. The dialogue between the two Indios and two Mexicanos is placed on a specific spot, and each party occupies a particular part of this locale. When the two twosomes depart, their respective flights are defined geographically, with the Indians going over the ridge and the Mexicanos moving closer to Córdova.

The legend differentiates bygone days in social terms as well. It not only pits the Mexicanos against the Indios, but it interprets their respective cultural characteristics. The twelve members of the party are similarly differentiated from the rest of the community, just as the leader, Vicente Mondragón, is set apart socially from his fellow Córdovans. Mr. Romero's grandfather and his companion then boldly isolate themselves from the remainder of the reconnaissance force. Note that this social differentiation does not emerge from the referential content of the performance alone. Mr. Romero uses direct discourse in according a distinct voice to the two Mexicanos, the Indios, and Vicente Mondragón.

In short, the legend performance not only evokes the world of bygone days, it musters form and content in providing us with a blueprint of its temporal, geographic, and sociocultural texture. Proverb performances convey a sense of the values that are seen as having regulated social interaction antes. Legends provide us with characters, settings, and events that enable us to envision how people actually lived. Proverb performances level temporal and social distinctions within bygone days, and they create personae that are more embodiments of moral values than flesh-and-blood creatures. Legends bring these characters to life, pointing out a few warts amongst the strong backs and bowed heads.

How, then, do textual and contextual spheres come together in legends? I believe that performances of legends lack some of the features that operate in an explicitly architectonic fashion. There is no equivalent to the validations or the tying phrases of proverb performances. Still, there is some interaction between textual and contextual spheres in legend performances. Mr. Romero uses visual signals as well as queries (e.g., *¿ves?*) and back-channel cues in closely monitoring my comprehension of his words. When he thinks that I am unlikely to be aware of needed background information or that I look confused, he arrests the narrative flow and fills this hiatus. The prime example of such background loops is his analysis of political structure during New Mexico's territorial period (7.1:72–95). In other words, the exchange of contextualization cues closely affects the unfolding of information about bygone days.

The manner in which textual and contextual elements come together in legends provides a crucial point of comparison with proverb performances. The latter are characterized by features that explicitly link textual and contextual spheres, whereas such elements are lacking in legends. Proverb performances overtly interpret a number of features of nowadays; performances of legends contrastively provide an implicit interpretation of one element of the present social interaction—the audience's comprehension of what is being said. The important difference here lies in the directionality of the movement between textual and contextual spheres. Mr. Romero does comment on our interaction metacommunicatively through his queries and background loops. The role of these features, however, is hardly to present an interpretation of life in nowadays. Contextualization cues constitute means toward textual ends; they assist in the process of drawing the audience into the sphere of bygone days.

The interpretive movement of legends thus lies in the opposite direction from that of proverbs, because it proceeds from contextual to textual spheres. In some cases, a particular social situation will occasion a given legend. Even in this case, however, the narrative soon takes on a life of its own as the factors that prompted the performance fade and the events related in the legend become focal. Legends are similar in this regard with all save the most conversationally based chistes. Those scriptural allusions in which narrativity begins to emerge share this directionality as well. The movement from contextual to textual spheres is, of course, the most pronounced in the mélanges of hymns and prayers that mark Holy Week. Here the contextualization process itself becomes textually programmed as individuals assume roles in a textual universe.

BROADENING THE COMPARISON

Now let us generalize from these results in considering the role of contextual and textual spheres in all the genres that comprise la plática de los viejitos de antes. In terms of the role of the contextual realm, the picture that emerged from the comparison of proverbs and legends holds for the rest. The number of features that point toward the ongoing social interaction and toward nowadays as a whole diminishes as one moves from historical discourse to proverbs to scriptural allusions to chistes to legends to hymns and prayers. A reduction is similarly apparent in the range of dimensions of nowadays that are interpreted in the course of performances. The more conversational genres often provide interpretations of nowadays in general, recent interactions between the participants, and the social interaction in which the performance emerges.

As we approach the textual end of the continuum, contextual features focus on the participants' understanding of and relationship to information about bygone days. The point is that the contextual realm has been transformed from the role of a central focus of interaction to that of a means of assisting the participants in gaining access to the world of antes and in interpreting it. This tendency reaches its apex in the case of hymns and prayers; here the contextual elements are not tied to the roles that the participants ordinarily play in their community, but to the parts that they have assumed in a textual world.

This diminution in the importance of contextual elements is matched by a change in their form-function relationship. In the case of highly conversational genres, some features point explicitly to aspects of the social setting. The referential function plays a significant role here; in Mrs. López's venison proverb, she *described* what had taken place and what should come to pass. As textuality increases, the form-function relationship becomes increasingly indirect. Contextual features become, in Silverstein's (1981a) terms, less unavoidably referential, surface segmentable, and relatively presupposing as one moves toward the textual side. In other words, grasping the significance of such features depends more on nonreferential sign modes and less on the interpretation of lexically coded information. For example, nods of the head, smiles, pauses, queries, signals of comprehension, and other contextualization cues provide us with a picture of the audience's comprehension of a legend and of the way the performance relates to the ongoing interaction. This information is not conveyed through referentially coded lexemes that describe these aspects of the setting but through such "nonsegmental" features as prosody and visual signs and through pragmatically coded particles. Contextual features similarly rely less on indexing preexisting elements of the setting than on the creation of such elements. As Silverstein argues, features that lack the properties of unavoidable referentiality and surface segmentability and that are more creative than presupposing generally lie beyond the limits of awareness of native speakers. We would accordingly expect performers and audience members to exhibit much less conscious awareness of the role of contextual features in more textually focused genres than they will in the case of historical discourse, proverbs, and scriptural allusions.

If textuality suppresses awareness of contextual elements, it promotes consciousness of the way that textual features join in forming a discernible text. I noted in Chapter 1 that my consultants refused to identify proverb texts as proverbs. Only when textual and contextual elements joined in the process of trayendo el sentido did a given example count as a token of the genre. In the case of proverbs, scriptural allusions, and the more conversationally based chistes, this refusal to equate the text alone with the genre is matched by an inability to produce tokens of the genre outside a suitable social setting. My efforts to elicit examples from these genres met with such responses as 'I've heard proverbs all my life, but I can't remember any right now'. In the more conversational genres, then, the isolation of familiar textual elements is highly problematic.

Exactly the opposite is true of narratively focused chistes and of legends, hymns, and prayers. All of these forms can be elicited. Furthermore, those who are familiar with the talk of the elders of bygone days possess an awareness of the way that textual features combine to form texts that can be identified, summarized, and repeated apart from a specific performance. For these genres, texts have an existence of their own that holds from performance to performance. Melaquías Romero can thus speak of his parents' version of *la historia* 'the story' of the lost gold mine of Juan Mondragón. In one performance of this tale, he framed the end of the legend as his parents knew it by saying *y ahi se acabó la historia* 'and that's the end of the story'; he then performed sections of the narrative that his parents had never learned. At the point of maximum textuality within this tradition, Lenten performances of hymns and prayers, the texts are handed down as physical objects in the notebooks of rezadores.

As one moves toward the textual pole, an overall decrease in the range of diversity of the performance features is apparent. Rather than systematically developing both textual and contextual realms, the performance features produce a greater and greater complexity within the textual realm. This complexity is apparent in the role of features that metacommunicatively index the discourse structure of the text. As the performance assumes a more pronounced textual orientation, the sorts of form-function units that emerge from verse analysis (cf. Hymes 1981) become more prevalent. The emergence of a metatextual focus in performances is reflected in a change in the way I transcribed performances. Starting with the more textually complex scriptural allusions, I began to find evidence of lines, episodes, subsections, and other units; these units are represented in the transcriptions and translations by changes in the way lines are distributed horizontally on the page.

These narrative units are strikingly evident in Melaquías Romero's tale of the lost gold mine of Juan Mondragón. In such narratives we find that prosodic features, gesture, and the structure of repetitions demarcate the unfolding of the narration in distinct *lines;* many lines are marked by the placement of stress on the line-final word. *Groups of lines* are linked by a common prosodic contour, particularly of pitch and volume. *Episodes* are framed by the use of rhetorical particles (e.g., *y luego* 'and then'), prosodic and gestural junctures, and a rhetorical pattern that moves from statement of conditions that presage an event, the unfolding of the event, and lastly a comment on or recap of the event.[1] Episodes are contained within *subsections* that lend thematic unity and a temporal structure to a number of events. These are in turn woven together into *partes* 'parts'; partes join temporally disjunctive sets of events into major sections of the narrative that focus on a particular group of characters. A number of these partes are combined in forming a particular version of the legend, just as these versions, which are often presented by themselves, are woven together as *segments* of an extended narrative performance, such as the one by Mr. Romero (cf. Briggs 1989).

The growing complexity of the textual realm is also apparent in the changing role of tense and aspect. Both tense and aspect play an important role in keying each of these genres. The past + habitual and past + imperfect versus present contrast plays a central role in placing utterances in either antes or ahora. Beginning with chistes, aspect assumes a crucial role in discourse structure. While past + habitual points to the status of actions as general features of antes, past + perfective marks actions as events that are bounded in space and time. Antes thus becomes differentiated: specific events are highlighted as figures against the ground of antes as a whole (cf. Wallace 1982), and events contrast with one another as sequentially ordered, discrete entities (cf. Hopper 1982). This sets the stage for dialectical movements within bygone days (rather than simply between antes and ahora as opposing realms) as characters who embody differing ideologies clash in sequences of events. The legend of Pedro Córdova's treasure, for example, pits Mexicanos and outsiders, ricos and pobres, Mexicanos who believe in the talk of the elders of bygone days and those who do not, as well as egoistic and corporatistic treasure hunters in a struggle for the right to interpret the meaning of wealth and power.

One of the most powerful means of stratifying the textual sphere is reported speech. As Bakhtin (1981/1975; Vološinov 1973/1929) argued for the novel, reported speech creates both stylistic and ideological polyphony in discourse. Thus, stylistically speaking, historical discourse is seamless. Although pedagogical discourse and collective recollections explore differences between antes and ahora, the absence of reported speech leaves the characterization of these two realms to the voices of the participants in the speech event. In the case of proverbs, an initial stylistic contrast may appear between the performer's voice and that of the proverb "owner," but the elders of bygone days still speak with a single voice.

As we move farther into the textual realm, the participants' own voices become more and more displaced by those of the characters themselves. Note that the relationship between genres in this regard is paralleled by the linear structure of many of the narratives. In the case of Mr. Romero's legend of the Indios and the tortillas, we moved from Mr. Romero's narrative voice to the narrative voice of his grandfather to the reported speech of his grandfather, José Rafael Romero, and Vicente Mondragón to the direct or quoted discourse of the two Romeros and the two *Indios*. Here, as in other legends, the narrative climax is saturated with direct discourse.

Not only are the characters' voices formally distinct from that of the narrator, but these voices are differentiated from one another. The Indios' speech is thus ungrammatical and strident, and the accompanying gestures suggest the bellicosity and bravery attributed to them. In Mr. Romero's legend of the lost gold mine, the chief protagonist, Mondragón, offers to share the mine with his boss, García. Here Mondragón uses deferential, *usted* forms in addressing his boss, while García couches his refusal in condescending, *tú* forms (cf. Briggs 1989). Interestingly, the characters' own voices sometimes undergo transformation in the course of the legend. In the tortillas example, the Indios' defiant tone changes to one of fear once the Mexicanos invoke the name of the famous Indian fighter, Antonio Vigil, while the Mexicanos' own voices gain in confidence. Similarly, in the lost mine legend, once García discovers his foolishness in refusing Mondragón's offer, García himself offers *usted* forms to another character ('Sito Candelario), only to receive *tú* in return.

Increasing textuality thus combines with greater density and complexity in the use of quoted speech. As Bakhtin, the Prague "School," and other scholars have argued, however, style does not exist in a vacuum. Stylistic contrasts between reported utterances are tied to differences in ideologies that are embodied in the different characters. The *tú/usted* contrast between the utterances of Mondragón and García represent a conflict between two distinct *Weltanschauungs*. Mr. Romero characterizes García's attitude in the following terms: 'in those days the RICH, I guess, used to treat the POOR just LIKE DIRT' (cf. Briggs and Vigil 1989: lines 1104–05). Mondragón, on the other hand, 'out of the goodness of his heart wanted to show him one of his MINES. . . . ⟨Mondragón⟩ SURE LIKED HIM'.

This is not to say that such conflicts were purely ideological. As I argue in my analysis of the gold mine legend (Briggs 1989), Mr. Romero's performance points to the impact of political economic inequality on historical events. García stands as the archetype of the wealthy Mexicano sheep rancher of the nineteenth century. Mr. Romero notes that the rich 'used to have the POOR . . . working for eighteen dollars a MONTH'. It is precisely this exploitation of Mondragón that deprives García of the chance to become a multimillionaire, because it leads García to believe that Mondragón is too poor to be the owner of a gold mine.

Exploitation based on class is coupled with that based on ethnicity in an episode that comes later in the legend. Ambrosio Romero (no relative of Melaquías), who has also found the mine, is approached by two Anglo-American employees of the U.S. Forest Service. The Anglos promise to supply the horses, the food, and all the supplies and to split the gold fifty-fifty with Ambrosio and his friend if Ambrosio will show them the mine. Ambrosio accepts. When they get to the site of the mine, however, Ambrosio pretends that he cannot find it. He later explains to his Mexicano friend that he didn't like 'the manner' of the Anglos. He surmised that their true demeanor was greedy and deceitful and that 'HAD I ONLY SHOWN THEM THE MINE, THEY WOULD'VE KILLED BOTH OF US', a conclusion that Melaquías Romero heartily endorses.

This scene thinly disguises the historical experience of Mexicanos in New Mexico and southern Colorado. Although the Treaty of Guadalupe Hidalgo, which ceded the area to the United States, guaranteed the property rights of the (then) Mexican citizens, the past 130 years have witnessed a vast expropriation of Mexicano land holdings by Anglo-American land speculators and the U.S. government (cf. Briggs and Van Ness 1987). Loss of the common lands that surrounded communities like Córdova has spelled poverty and a loss of self-determination for many. Much of this land fell under the jurisdiction of the U.S. Forest Service, and Forest Service employees have been charged with enforcing policies that reduce or eliminate local residents' access to this area for grazing livestock, hunting and fishing, and cutting fuelwood and timber. The episode that pits Ambrosio Romero against the two Anglo Forest Service employees thus evokes contrastive ideologies and a very real political-economic conflict.

This brings us to a basic point. I have argued that the contextual realm plays a smaller and smaller role in the genres that lie more toward the textual pole of the continuum. This loss of contextual focus is balanced by an increase in the stylistic and ideological stratification of the textual realm. The preceding sketch of class and ethnic conflicts in Mr. Romero's legend of the lost gold mine suggest that legends, which are highly textual, are also concerned with the themes of arrogance, greed, exploitation, and egoism. The difference lies in the way that these concerns are expressed. In the more conversational genres, these concerns with the tenor of life nowadays are made explicit. In legends, such allusions are represented indirectly through the actions and the words of characters who dwell in a textual world. These contextual elements have thus been incorporated into the textual realm.

This discussion of the differences between the various genres does not, however, successfully account for hymns and prayers. These forms indeed provide something of an enigma. They are, on the one hand, maximally textual in the sense of being transmitted, interpreted, and performed as texts. They occupy the one facet of the talk of the elders of bygone days in which oral composition plays no role. These texts are memorized, not learned formulaically. Little variation is apparent either diachronically or geographically in the words, although alabado melodies do differ somewhat between communities (cf. Robb 1980:613). In the ritual performances of Holy Week, gaze, gesture, body position, and prosody are also fixed as participants coordinate their voices in accordance with the dictates of a textual world. Hymns and prayers rightly occupy the textual extreme of the continuum; few concessions are made to context.

We must note, on the other hand, that one of the three major markers of textuality—the predominance of reported speech—is less apparent in hymns and prayers than it is in legends. Reported speech is not absent; the Via Crucis, for example, quotes the words of Christ and others. But the major proportion of the discourse in hymns and prayers is framed as the words that the worshiper is addressing to God, which means that the stylistic and ideological polyphony of the legend, the chiste, and even of some scriptural allusions is lacking.

This absence should come as no surprise. I have argued that hymns and prayers move worshipers from a state of separation (human versus God, sinner versus redeemer, etc.) to one of unity (total identification with the deity and harmony with one's sisters and brothers). This is accomplished by a sustained coordination of words, prosody, gestures, and even breath itself vis-à-vis a textual invocation of the passion of Christ and the suffering of Mary; this process is sufficiently powerful to enable worshipers to enter that world psychologically. The textuality is clearly no less complete here than it is in the case of the legend: the opposite is rather the case. The difference is in the means. Whereas legends, chistes, and some scriptural allusions draw participants into the textual realm by creating stylistic and ideological diversity, hymns and prayers accomplish the same effect through a unity in which the community as a whole seems to move in keeping with the same rhythmic repetitions. This suggests the need for a refinement of a previous conclusion. While the stylistic and ideological differentiation that is embodied in reported speech is closely associated with a focus on the textual realm, it does not provide the only means to this end.

The genres that make up la plática de los viejitos de antes vary greatly in their power as means of critically examining imaginative realms that encapsulate historical events and processes or the world of the present that surrounds the performance. A number of studies have explored the generic distribution of the labor of communicative activity in other societies. Glassie (1982), Gossen (1974a, 1974b), and Sherzer (1983) provide detailed studies of the full range of speech genres that are evident, respectively, in Irish, Chamula (Tzotzil-speaking Mexican), and Kuna communities. As we found in the Mexicano case, genres are characterized by specific constraints and capacities with respect to the way that formal, content-based, and contextual elements enter into discourse. In a cross-cultural examination of the problem, Abrahams (1976/1969) argues that genres can generally be distributed along a continuum between the "total interpersonal involvement" of performer and audience, as witnessed in conversational genres (e.g., naming practices and proverbs), to the removal of speaker and hearer in favor of "symbolic role-playing in a time and place removed from real life," as in the case of fictive genres (e.g., cante fables, legends, and other narrative forms). Play genres, such as riddles, ritual, and folk drama, would lie between the two extremes. The insights that have emerged thus far point to the critical need for more systematic ethnographic studies in order to facilitate cross-cultural comparisons, not simply of specific genres, but of systems of genres. This will enable us to extend research such as that presented by Abrahams to a broader range of performance dimensions.

PANGENERIC PROPERTIES OF THE TALK OF THE ELDERS OF BYGONE DAYS

The previous section stressed the evident differences among the genres of la plática de los viejitos de antes; I argued that the most fundamental contrasts lie in the role that textual and contextual realms play in performances. Much evidence also supports the contention that these genres share a number of basic properties. These similarities are most apparent when one considers the nature of the competence that underlies performances in each genre.

The formal complexity of performances provides a basic commonality in the different genres. The talk of the elders of bygone days includes genres in which performances are relatively short (e.g., proverbs) and those whose formal properties bear a strong resemblance to "ordinary" conversation. It is clear, however, that there are no *simple* genres. Performance in any of the genres presupposes command of a complex set of features. Furthermore, these features range from forms that define the structure and frame the interpretation of individual lines to those that index the global structure of the performance. Performers are simultaneously operating at a number of levels of formal structure at the same time as they form each line, connect it with the preceding line, mark groups of lines as rhetorical units, segment the performance into episodes (in narratives), indicate the overall structure of the performance, and point to its relationship to other bodies of discourse (other performances, previous interactions, etc.).

Competence at the formal level is, however, hardly just a matter of repeating the sounds and gestures that characterize a given genre. In all genres except hymns and prayers, performance consists of an oral composition process. Performers thus bring together a rhetorical intent, a social and linguistic setting, and some segment of la plática de los viejitos de antes in a new way. This involves constant analysis of the formal-functional properties of formal features in selecting those that will successfully convey contextual and textual functions. The complexity of this process is apparent in the fact that features do not stand to communicative functions in preestablished one-to-one relationships. Features are not like signs in Saussure's (1959/1916) *langue*, where the meaning of forms is constituted through context-free, semantic relations between linguistic signs. In the case of performance features, connecting forms and functions is a pragmatic process that emerges from the participants' ongoing interpretation of the discourse. Of course, not any feature can convey any function. I have tried to show that formal features are associated with a particular range of elements of the performance process (e.g., as a tying element will connect a proverb performance with the preceding discourse). Yet such prefigured connections are far from rigid, and the business of relating form and function remains an active and interpretive task that is an integral part of the performance process.

The complexity of the competence that underlies use of the formal structure of performances is evident in three additional properties of performance features. First, multifunctionality is a basic property of performance features: a single form (a word, prosodic contour, gesture, etc.) can signal more than one function. For example, triplex signs form one of the central features of pedagogical discourse and collective recollections. Triplex signs refer to a given facet of bygone days, index a particular sphere of bygone days, and mark a change of topic to a discussion of this sphere. In the narrative genres, both tense/aspect and reported speech play central roles in structuring the discourse and interpreting the nature of antes. Not every use of every feature is multifunctional, but most of the features in all of the genres exhibit this character. Part of the reason that multifunctionality plays such an important role is that it is one of the properties of the language of verbal art that saturates performances with meaning and enhances their performative effect on social relations.

Second, performance features do not simply connect a given form with a given function. The formal complexity of performances also emerges from the intricate relations that obtain between features. In the case of the proverb, if a key member of the audience fails to respond to the performer's validation or signals a lack of comprehension, the performer is likely to loop back to the beginning of the performance. The preceding features will be elaborated in such a way as to bring the meaning of the performance home to the audience. As I noted above, validations and reiterations of words and phrases from the proverb text connect textually and contextually oriented features; their communicative function is thus explicitly relational. Such connections do not simply join pairs of features; in all of the genres, the features and their relations lend an architectonic structure to the performance.

Third, the formal structure of performances in each genre is dialogic in nature. In all genres except hymns and prayers, the performance is shaped in keeping with an ongoing exchange between participants. In most cases, this process consists of the control of the performance by one or more performers and the insertion of back-channel cues and responses by one or more members of an audience. In historical competitions, collective recollections, and other symmetrical exchanges (e.g., proverb competitions), the dialogue is apparent in frequent exchanges of performer and audience roles. With the exception of hymns and prayers, the verbal and visual cues provided by the audience significantly affect the form and content of the performance. This responsiveness of the form to the ongoing interaction greatly adds to the formal complexity of performances.

Another form of dialogism, one that has been studied by Bakhtin (1981; Vološinov 1973/1930) does not revolve around turn-taking. This type is rooted in the stylistic and ideological stratification of discourse, and it emerges primarily through the use of reported speech. This type of dialogism assumes different forms as one moves from the contextual to the textual pole of the continuum. On the contextual side it consists of dialectical movements between antes and ahora. In pedagogical discourse, for example, bygone days and nowadays are interpreted vis-à-vis each other and basic cultural premises. As one moves toward the textual pole, the dialectic focuses much more on the polyphony of voices that represent the texture of bygone days. In any case, all genres exhibit both an external dialogism that is inherent in the social interaction and an internal dialogism that springs from the talk of the elders of bygone days itself and the perspective it provides on the present.

The fact that dialogism provides a central common element in all of the genres should come as no surprise, since it is a feature of discourse in general. As Bakhtin (1986:89–92) has argued,

Our speech, that is, all our utterances (including creative works), is filled with others' words, varying degrees of otherness or varying degrees of "our-own-ness," varying degrees of awareness and detachment. These words of others carry with them their own expression, their own evaluative tone, which we assimilate, rework, and re-accentuate. . . . After all, our thought itself—philosophical, scientific, and artistic—is born and shaped in the process of interaction and struggle with others' thought, and this cannot but be reflected in the forms that verbally express our thought as well.

The dialogic character of communication plays a special role in la plática de los viejitos de antes. Here a host of crucial performance features, including reported speech, the antes/ahora dialectic, tense-aspect alternations, the verbal interaction of performer and audience, and the interplay of textualization and contextualization processes as a whole, build upon this dialogical character. The talk of the elders of bygone days greatly enhances consciousness of the way that our voices are shaped by those of other persons, and it transforms this awareness into an ongoing process of collectively and critically examining the world around us.

One may object that hymns and prayers are not characterized by these properties. Tokens of these genres are not composed in the course of the performance; their features are accordingly not selected at the time of the performance. It must be admitted, then, that hymns and prayers form a special case in the sense that participants do memorize texts. However, multifunctionality, architectonic relations between features, and dialogism are not unimportant in the case of hymns and prayers. Hymns and prayers are characterized by multifunctionality; most features simultaneously refer to some facet of the passion story, address Christ or the Virgin, and index the point that has been reached in the discourse structure of the performance. Features are similarly integrated into a formal architectonic that is no less complex than that associated with other genres.

The type of external dialogism that plays so important a role in other genres is clearly absent. If one of the participants cannot follow or does not understand some part of the performance, the leaders are not induced to elaborate or in any way change the structure or content of the text. A different sort of dialogism is apparent, however, in the relations between leaders and other participants. The participants as a whole sing the chorus of alabados, while the leaders intone the verses. The leaders similarly provide the longer narrative sections of prayers. Indeed, performances of hymns and prayers stand as long and complicated series of alternations between groups of participants. Turn-taking is of no less importance here; the difference lies in the fact that turn allocation is determined in advance by the alternation of parts within the text and decisions as to who will play each part.

Internal dialogism is apparent as well, although it takes a rather different course from that found in the other genres. Utterances stand in several types of dyadic relations. Many parts of hymns and prayers place the worshiper in the role of a sinner who is addressing Christ or the Virgin. Others, like *Ven, pecador, y verás* 'Come, sinner, and you will see', find worshipers addressing other worshippers. Other sections, many of which are sung or chanted by the leaders, narrate events of the passion. Finally, portions of quoted speech appear as well; here worshipers take on the roles of Christ, the Virgin, and other characters. Leaders and other participants thus alternate between entering into internal dialogues with silent interlocutors and standing as narrators.

Participating in performances of hymns and prayers does involve a rather different sort of competence. Sensitivity to the details of particular social interactions and the ability to select features that are pragmatically rich are of very little use here. What is needed is a facility at drawing on complex formal structures as guides for coordinating one's words and actions with those of the group as a whole and in producing an intense religious focus. Thus, competence in participating in such performances also requires a grasp on the multifunctionality of performance features, the complex relations between features, and the way that the discourse is textured through dialogism.

Hymns and prayers represent the point in la plática de los viejitos de antes where the textual realm saturates performance. Drawing on Silverstein's (in press) recent work, we can characterize the role of textuality here as a powerful regimenting force. Past performances are not simply reappropriated by performers as resources for possible use in effecting a new set of rhetorical goals. The Lenten rituals of former years, as preserved both in memory and in notebooks, provide a blueprint for constructing nearly the totality of contemporary performances. In the talk of the elders of bygone days as a whole, textuality is balanced against multifunctionality, contextualization, and the relations between features. Just as the structure and meaning of the textual realm is constituted through these properties of performance features, as we move toward the textual side of the continuum textuality exercises more and more effect on which features are selected and how they are used. As we reach hymns and prayers, textuality has suppressed the ability of these properties to affect the discourse-production process.

The only room left for the creative use of performance features lies in the way that the worshiper interprets the meaning of what she or he is saying and hearing. No one monitors the participation of anyone else to see whether that individual is following what is being said and to discern how the person is interpreting it. Each individual's level of participation in the interpretive process is thus contingent upon her or his competence in perceiving the performance features and their functions as well as the nature of her or his own life experiences and religious faith. Although textuality has largely displaced the composition process from performances, it has left the interpretive process relatively open.

COMPETENCE, TEXTUALITY, AND CONTEXTUALIZATION

What, then, is the nature of the basic similarity that underlies all these genres? Every performance of la plática de los viejitos de antes involves an interplay of contextual and textual forces. No text can be performed without being incorporated into human interaction, just as no interaction gains the legitimacy that is accorded to the talk of the elders of bygone days unless it bears some features that are recognizable from past performances. Even though they are indispensible to one another, contextual and textual realms are related in any given performance in a dialectic fashion. As one gains in prominence, it weakens the role of the other. More important, the dominant realm appropriates the subordinate one to its own rhetorical goals; this often results in a transformation of its communicative structure. Each performance thus stands as a unique synthesis of these two opposing forces.

To be judged competent as a performer, an individual must be able to produce a unique synthesis of contextual and textual realms. Of course, performers are not granted completely free rein in this process. To be counted as a token of the talk of the elders of bygone days, the discourse must fall within one or more genres of this talk. As I have argued, each of these genres is characterized by a number of features. These performance features frame a given stretch of speech as a token of a particular genre. Just as important, however, these features constitute textual and contextual realms as they are realized in a particular performance. They also create a rapprochement between these two realms.

Competence thus emerges from an intertextual process of reaching back into past performances, selecting a particular set of elements, and interpreting their meaning. It also entails a critical reading of the ongoing social interaction and perhaps other dimensions of modern society as well. As the two come together in performance, both are transformed. Certain elements of antes have come to be associated with new meanings, just as particular elements of ahora are now seen in a different light. Performers thus contribute with each performance to the ongoing process of preserving the talk of the elders of bygone days.

The object of this process, of course, is precisely trayendo el sentido. The elders assert that the transmission of this talk from generation to generation is requisite for the survival of Mexicanos, both collectively and individually. Simply repeating the same texts over and over is not what they have in mind. As the elders will tell you, performing la plática de los viejitos de antes is their way of preparing younger generations for the day that the teachers themselves will join the elders of bygone days. The elders' goal is not to get their descendants to memorize a set of texts but to convince their juniors to resist ideological domination by the society that exercises political-economic control over their lives.

The elders know, however, that they cannot control the pressures that will be brought to bear on succeeding generations or even, for that matter, foresee what conditions will prevail in the future. Their solution is to accord a central role in the sociolinguistic repertoire of the community to a critical, dialectical process through which tradition is continually reinterpreted through the eyes of the present, and the present echoes the words and the values of the past. La plática de los viejitos thus stands as a force that regiments the way people speak and act and, in the process, is itself transformed. Of course, Mexicanos do not invent their past. The referential content of the talk exhibits remarkable stability and historical validity (cf. Briggs 1987a). However, the dialectical nature of the process of interpreting that past ensures the continuing relevance of the talk of the elders of bygone days in a changing world.

THEORETICAL AND COMPARATIVE IMPLICATIONS

What, then, does la plática de los viejitos de antes have to teach us about the nature of communicative competence? The Mexicano case points with particular clarity to the limitations of Chomsky's (1965:3) identification of competence with "an ideal speaker-listener, in a completely homogeneous speech-community, who knows its language perfectly." I do not cite Chomsky here merely to discredit him. Even if one rejects his condemnation of performance, which he defines as "the actual use of language in concrete situations" (1965:4), it must be granted that Chomsky clearly articulated the importance of exploring the knowledge that is shared by all speakers of a particular language and, at a later state of the analysis, by all humans. He similarly pointed to the need to gain greater theoretical sophistication in explaining the linguistic creativity that emerges from this knowledge. My major problem with his particular response to these crucial questions is the notion that competence can only be understood as a purely abstract and homogeneous system. I rather claim that unless the analyst is willing to treat Mexicano speakers as real humans who occupy specific historical, political-economic, and personal niches the nature of the system that underlies the talk of the elders of bygone days will remain hidden from view.

I have emphasized the fact that linguistic heterogeneity lies at the heart of this system. Although all tokens of this talk share a common basis in the convergence of textual and contextual spheres, each performance is unique with respect to the way that this connection is articulated. Such differences are, however, far from random. Competence as a performer entails mastery of a complex system of basic strategies for linking past and present; these socially-constituted types form the genres that structure this heterogeneity. Beyond this diversity in the ways that form and communicative function are related lies the heterogeneity in the distribution of this knowledge. Contrary to Chomsky's vision of the ideal speaker-listener, no individual knows the system perfectly, i.e., can generate appropriate examples in all genres. Moreover, following Hymes (1981/1975:82–86) and Labov (as cited by Hymes), it should be emphasized that the competence that is needed to grasp the meaning of performances is quite different from what one must know in order to assume the role of performer. In short, pursuing Chomsky's well-founded challenge to the study of language has entailed violating the basic limitations that he places on linguistic research. In order to identify the knowledge that is shared by speakers, it becomes necessary to comprehend heterogeneity.

I want to stress that this heterogeneity is not purely stylistic. Performances relate textual and contextual spheres in different ways. The contextualization process relates tokens of the talk of the elders of bygone days to ongoing social interactions in a dialectical fashion. This means that performances are created by real individuals in the course of specific human encounters. One thing that performance features do is to select elements of the ongoing linguistic, social, cultural, political, historical, and natural environment and to accord them a meaning and role within the performance. Verbal art cannot exist without real people in real settings; nevertheless, recasting the situation into the language of the storyrealm transforms the "real world" itself. This transformative effect extends back from the performance to the broader social setting, since the performativity (here in Austin's sense) of verbal art holds the potential for changing the relationship between the participants and the way they perceive themselves and their environment.

COMPETENCE AND CREATIVITY IN DOMINATED COMMUNITIES

Accepting for the sake of argument that performances provide rich reflections of social life, let us ask some basic questions about the role of la plática de los viejitos de antes in Mexicano communities. Do performances affect more than the specific social interactions in which they are situated? Is the talk of the elders of bygone days an historical force that at least to some degree shapes the history of this people?

I will begin by widening the frame of the analysis to encompass the place of Mexicanos within American society. As the historical record shows, Mexicanos and Native Americans were forcibly incorporated into the United States through an expansionist policy. An imperialist ideology commonly known as Manifest Destiny rationalized the belief that the United States possessed the right and duty to expand its holdings to the Pacific coast (cf. Brack 1975; Billington 1963; De Voto 1943; Mares 1960; Merk 1963). With the outset of the Mexican-American War, New Mexicans surrendered to U.S. forces without offering resistance, apparently through the collusion of Gov. Manuel Armijo, but uprisings by Mexicanos and Native Americans occurred the following year in several areas. Anglo-American expansionism engendered much bitterness, and violent resistance has continued through the present (cf. Ortiz 1980; Romero 1980; Rosenbaum 1981; Rosenbaum and Larson 1987).

A number of researchers have documented the illegal and extra-legal actions of government officials and Anglo-American land speculators in appropriating grant lands (cf. Briggs and Van Ness 1987; Ortiz 1980; Van Ness and Van Ness 1980; West-phall 1983). I have described the impact of these actions on the residents of Córdova in the preceding chapters.[2] The loss of much of their land base had two major effects on Córdovans and other rural Mexicanos. The first was a collapse of their subsistence-based economy. Once the farmer/ranchers were unable to graze goats and sheep in the mountains, they also lacked fertilizer needed to enrich their fields. Second, this undermining of subsistence patterns rendered Mexicanos largely dependent upon the political economy of the dominant society. A group of land-owning farmer/ranchers was transformed into a rural proletariat for whom survival was contingent upon willingness to leave one's home community and migrate to locations where employment was available.

The pressure that is exerted on Mexicanos by the dominant society has not been limited to acts of direct economic intervention, such as land expropriation and regulations on the use of national forest lands. The more diffuse forms of control that are used by the dominant sectors of society are pin-pointed by Gramsci's (1970) use of the term *hegemony*. Gramsci's work in this regard, particularly as it has been extended by Williams (1977), is quite telling with respect to the Mexicano situation. As Williams (1977:108) notes, while rule (*dominio*) is directly exercised by the state, hegemony rather stands as "a complex interlocking of political, social, and cultural forces." Williams, following Gramsci, points to the way that hegemony extends the control of the dominant sector into the daily life of the society through diffuse elements that are generally termed "superstructural" or "ideological" in Marxist theory:

[Hegemony] is a lived system of meanings and values—constitutive and constituting—which as they are experienced as practices appear as reciprocally confirming. It thus constitutes a sense of reality for most people in the society, a sense of absolute because experienced reality beyond which it is very difficult for most members of the society to move, in most areas of their lives. It is, that is to say, in the strongest sense a 'culture', but a culture which has also to be seen as the lived dominance and subordination of particular classes. (Williams 1977:110)

The power of hegemony emerges from the fact that it does not simply seek to bring individuals in line with the interests of the dominant sectors of society through external, coercive pressure. "The true condition of hegemony is effective *self-identification* with the hegemonic forms: a specific and internalized 'socialization' which is expected to be positive but which, if that is not possible, will rest on a (resigned) recognition of the inevitable and the necessary" (Williams 1977:118; emphasis in original).

One of the crucial features of the diffuse and pervasive control exercised by the dominant society is the way that this "lived system of meanings and values" seeks to suppress competing points of view. How is this accomplished? From the perspective of a given hegemony,

the relations of domination and subordination, in their forms as practical conscious-ness, [are seen] as in effect a saturation of the whole process of living—not only of political and economic activity, nor only of manifest social activity, but of the whole substance of lived identities and relationships, to such a depth that the pressures and limits of what can ultimately be seen as a specific economic, political, and cultural system seem to most of us the pressures and limits of simple experience and common sense. (Williams 1977:110)

Ironically, such efforts to limit the ability of groups and individuals to perceive and articulate phenomena that are not in keeping with the hegemonic perspective fuel attempts to transform such elements in counter-hegemonic movements. A *counter-hegemony* organizes oppositional politics and culture into an alternative mode of per-ceiving and organizing social life. Hegemonic frameworks attempt to incorporate *residual* elements, which Williams (1977:122) defines in the following manner:

The residual, by definition, has been effectively formed in the past, but it is still ac-tive in the cultural process, not only and often not at all as an element of the past but as an effective element of the present. Thus certain experiences, meanings and val-ues which cannot be expressed or substantially verified in terms of the dominant cul-ture, are nevertheless lived and practiced on the basis of the residue—cultural as well as social—of some previous social and cultural institution or formation.

The past also includes the *archaic*, elements associated with former institutions or formations that have lost any direct connection with the present.

In developing the implications of the concepts presented by Gramsci and Williams for the Mexicano case, it should be recalled that a number of agencies of county, state, and national governments exert direct control on the lives of rural Mexicanos. The U.S. Forest Service is one of the most visible and deeply resented, because it is charged with regulating access to former grant lands. Mexicanos are accordingly forced to submit to rules that often favor commercial interests and urban recrea-tionalists or face possible fine and/or imprisonment. The school system similarly penetrates the day-to-day world of Mexicanos; local communities exercise virtually no control over where or how their children are educated (cf. Kutsche and Van Ness 1982:153–97). Social service agencies administer Aid to Families with Dependent Children, Food Stamps, unemployment benefits and workman's compensation, assis-tance for the elderly, and other programs. Checks, stamps, and meals all carry hid-den costs, including frequent and lengthy trips to government offices, required disclosures of personal information, visits by low-level officials designed to monitor compliance with regulations, and the labeling and stereotyping that are applied to recipients of public aid. Mexicanos similarly come under the direct control of the dominant society as employees, particularly when they work for state or federal agencies. Mexicanos also encounter the dominant hegemony as consumers and as members of television and radio audiences.

By virtue of the loss of their most crucial resources, Mexicanos have been forced into daily contact with representatives of the dominant society. This influence goes far beyond direct political domination; it is rather the constant bombardment with cultural, political, material expressions of the hegemonic perspective. As Williams notes, hegemonic processes are complex, diverse, and dynamic; it would accordingly be dangerous to present an abbreviated picture of the multitude of messages that are conveyed in this fashion. It would, however, be safe to argue that a basic theme is apparent: Survival in a modern capitalist society is predicated on a commitment to selling one's labor to institutions that represent the dominant society and, in turn, becoming a consumer of the goods and services sold by such institutions. Moreover, to occupy a socially legitimated position within this process one must be willing to act as an individual who competes with other individuals in attempting to sell one's labor for the highest price and to buy commodities that will satisfy one's own particular needs and desires at the lowest cost.

As I noted above, Mexicanos have made a number of attempts during the past 140 years to resist political-economic domination. Lacking access to an independent industrial base, they have been largely unsuccessful in reversing the land appropriation and proletarianization process. Nevertheless, the power of a "lived system of meanings and values" has been exploited by Mexicanos in forming a counter-hegemony that challenges the hegemonic pressures of the dominant society. One of the main forms that this has taken is the development of a collective self-conception as a community that is linguistically and culturally distinct from the English-speaking majority. Before the beginning of the Anglo influx in 1821, the collective self-identity of impoverished native speakers of Spanish was tied to class relations and ethnic relations within the region as well as the relationship between settlers on the northern frontier and officials in Spain and central Mexico. With the establishment of Anglo-American hegemony in the region, *Mexicanismo* was increasingly defined vis-à-vis this new population and the political economy that it championed. As Rodríguez (1987:314) argues forcefully, ethnic identity became a means of focusing the struggle for "cultural survival and social self-determination." Just as this counter-hegemony adapted creatively to changes in the character of the dominant society's hegemonic pressures, it transformed cultural and artistic elements into conscious symbols of counter-hegemony. Land and water have been of central political-economic and cultural importance throughout the history of the region. As Rodríguez argues, the ongoing expropriation of land and water resources "have, in concert with various local, regional, and macrosocial factors, intensified rural Hispano resistance to further usurpation and displacement, and stimulated the crystallization of land as a symbol of Hispano cultural survival" (1987:382).

I argued in a previous work (Briggs 1980) that locally-produced, polychromed images of the saints have been closely connected with Mexicano Catholicism for more than two centuries. The commercialization of the region during the second half of the nineteenth century brought the local production of images to a virtual standstill, although images continued to be used in worship. Members of the Anglo-American intelligentsia in the region purchased eighteenth- and nineteenth-century images, and, beginning in the 1920s, they "encouraged" Mexicanos to produce unpainted images as well as secular carvings for sale. These works reflected the cultural and aesthetic categories of the dominant society, including stereotypes of Mexicanos, to a greater extent than they did the cultural and religious convictions of the artists and their communities. The ethnic awareness movement of the 1960s and 1970s sparked Mexicano concern with the expropriation of the art form by the dominant hegemony; a new group of artists began producing polychromed images that responded to contemporary aesthetic, cultural, and religious needs of Mexicanos.

The situation with respect to land and water and images of the saints presents intriguing parallels. All three are visible objects that can be easily perceived by Anglo-American and Mexicano, rich and poor. They have similarly been the focus of exchanges between poor Mexicanos and rich Anglo-Americans during at least the past sixty years. Even those Anglo-Americans who know little or nothing about the meaning of land, water, or images to Mexicanos can, if they can muster the economic resources, buy land, water rights, and images. This appropriation is accomplished as much through cultural hegemony as it is through outright acquisition; by incorporation in the dominant hegemony, land, water, and images move from the status of inalienable community resources that serve locally-defined economic and cultural needs to commodities that are bought and sold by individuals as well as state institutions and exploited in ways that often run counter to the patterns of thought and action characteristic of their former owners.

Important differences and similarities are apparent in the case of la plática de los viejitos de antes. This talk is not a physical object, and it is not as amenable to expropriation by the dominant sectors of society. Appreciating performances of Mexicano verbal art is predicated on a thorough knowledge of New Mexican Spanish and on detailed cultural, historical, geographic, biographic, and other types of knowledge about specific Mexicano communities. Learning the talk of the elders of bygone days thus involves spending a great deal of unhurried time listening to contemporary elders. Unlike land, water rights, and images of the saints, this talk cannot be expropriated through theft or sale, and Mexicanos never lost control over this talk. Since the dominant society was unable to expropriate, perform, or even understand the talk of the elders of bygone days, these genres escaped incorporation into the dominant hegemony.

I do not mean to imply that this talk currently bears no relationship to the dominant hegemony. At the time of the United States conquest, Mexicano verbal art was independent of the dominant hegemony. As the latter penetrated more and more facets of Mexicano life and began to exercise a forceful cultural hegemony, the talk of the elders of bygone days increasingly assumed the role of a counter-hegemonic force.

Several basic characteristics of la plática de los viejitos de antes render it a particularly effective means of representing this struggle between hegemonic and counter-hegemonic processes. First, as I have argued all along, this talk does not simply reflect a variety of social worlds, past and present—it interprets them. A host of generic formal features foreground this dialectic. In historical discourse, the performer selects a feature that is associated with Mexicano historical experience (*lo de antes*) and contrasts this with the way that this same phenomenon is manifested ahora. In legends, the voice and actions of one or more characters (e.g., Juan Mondragón) represent the counter-hegemonic forces, while the dominant hegemony is embodied in the voice and actions of other characters (e.g., Mondragón's boss and the Anglo-American forest service employees). Such features as tense/aspect markers, prosodic characteristics, gesture, and facial expression are used in highlighting the contrast between the two sets of voices.

But I would hardly want to suggest that the hegemony/counter-hegemony dialectic is manifested in stylistic terms alone. One of the major theses of this book is that la plática de los viejitos de antes musters these stylistic tools to the task of exam-

(9.1) Aurelio Trujillo, Costancia Trujillo, CLB; 8 October 1972 (continued)

AT: De ahi pa' acá no,
     ves.
No hay FE,
se acaba la fe.
Muchos dicen,   5
"Oh, yo no siembro, porque se seca."
Pero NO.
La voluntad de mi Dios dice claro,
a los arcobispos ahi en su evangelio,
que dice mi Señor Jesucristo en su evangelio   10
que NO, no sea hombre de poca FE.
Que tire su semilla,
para que levante, y lo asista.
Y de ahi vivirá el PECADOR,
vive el HOMBRE,   15
dice.
Y es verdad.
Y ahora no quiere sembrar NADIE,
no más,
     ¿sabes qué?   20
alfalfa, pa' 'l CABALLO,
por la VACA.
Pues, no más.
De modo que está muy DIFERENTE a aquellos TIEMPOS.

ining Mexicano historical experience, particularly with respect to key political-economic transformations. This talk is quite concerned with expropriation of the common lands that formed the backbone of Mexicano communities and the way that this loss has transformed the production process. We must be wary, however, of the prevalent tendency to identify production with material production. One of the central themes of the viejitos is that production is not a purely mechanical and material process; antes, production was as much social and spiritual as it was material.

Let us take the central example that is offered of the social and religious dimension of agricultural production antes—the feast day celebrated in honor of St. Isidore (cf. Briggs 1983). On the eve of the saint's day, the image of St. Isidore (along with that of the community's patron, St. Anthony) was taken through the fields and placed in a bower in the upland fields of Las Joyas. After an all-night wake and a communal meal at midnight, the image was carried back through all the fields so that his blessing would render them fertile. After noting that the feast day has not been celebrated for over fifty years, Mr. Trujillo made a comment that is recorded in example (9.1) (Briggs 1983:106):

English Translation

Since then no,
 you see.
There is no FAITH,
the faith is being lost.
Many say,
"Oh, I don't plant, because it dries up."
But NO.
The will of God clearly says,
to his archbishops in his gospel,
my Lord Jesus Christ says in his gospel not,
NOT to be a man of little FAITH.
Cast your seeds,
so that they will come up, and take care of them.
And that's how the SINNER WILL LIVE,
how MAN LIVES,
he says.
And it's true.
And now NOBODY wants to PLANT,
they only [plant],
 you know what?
alfalfa, for HORSES,
for CATTLE.
Well, that's all.
So [now] it's very DIFFERENT from those DAYS.

For those of us who were raised in urban areas within modern capitalist societies, such talk about St. Isidore and the religious underpinnings of agriculture initially appears to be a romantic metaphorization of an economic process. It is easy to read such statements as reflecting a "magical" view of reality, viz. the belief that religious thoughts and acts of devotion can miraculously produce an abundant crop. This response is, however, a symptom of our internalization of the dominant hegemony. The French structuralist-Marxists, such as Godelier (1966, 1973), have forcefully developed Marx's insight that humans reproduce themselves socially and culturally as well as physically through the production process. Bourdieu's *Outline of a Theory of Practice* (1972) provides a striking analysis of the way that the symbolic underpinnings of social life, including power relations, are reproduced in all facets of social life.

The perspective of los viejitos thus parallels recent social scientific discourse in emphasizing the way that production reproduces a social and cultural system just as it produces a handful of wheat. This discourse about religious devotion, collective feasting, and agricultural production reflects less a magical view of the relationship between humans and their environment than a way of emphasizing the fact that Mexicano agricultural production was not seen as a separate domain that obeyed purely "natural" laws; such talk rather emphasizes the cultural and historical implications of the way that production has become increasingly severed from social life in general.

The difficulty that we experience in understanding this message is telling. As Williams (1977:90–94) argues, one of the major ideological changes that is part of the rise of modern capitalism is to identify production with material production and, in a further transformation, with "heavy industry." The Mexicano conception of production is accordingly doubly alien to us, both in its emphasis on non-industrial (primarily agricultural, pastoral, and "handicraft" production) and in its refusal to isolate the purely material components of the production process. In capitalist society, production becomes a sphere that has a life of its own, one that is cut apart from areas of our experience (work versus play, job versus home, occupation versus religion, etc.). As Marx (1867, 1939; Marx and Engels 1947), Polanyi (1957), Weber (1958) and a host of others have argued, the "rationalization" of production formed a major prerequisite for the development of capitalism. This involved severing the production process from social and religious constraints and orienting production toward the exertion of control over natural processes (through technology) and the maximization of profit. A final element of this logic is apparent: once the infrastructure has been abstracted and conceptually cut off from the superstructure, the former is seen as shaping social relations and ideologies. As Sahlins (1976), Williams (1977), and others have argued, this view, which has also been adopted by certain forms of Marxist criticism, oversimplifies the complex interlinkages and modes of mutual determination that link material and other dimensions of social reproduction. As Williams stresses, this historically-specific view of production has come to seem so "natural" that we are hard pressed to see social life through any other lens.

This is precisely why the viejitos' emphasis on agriculture, pastoralism, and other features of production antes provides such an effective counter-hegemonic discourse. The manner in which agricultural production was related to other dimensions of Mexicano life antes contrasts with the view of production that is promoted by the dominant hegemony on nearly every count. Discussions of the wake for St. Isidore and the connection between faith and planting in general are used in suggesting that agriculture was not set apart from the rest of social life antes and that agricultural production was controlled by social, cultural, and religious premises as well as by natural processes, technology, and economic calculations. The talk of the elders of bygone days also stresses the fact that the labor process and distribution of its fruits were conceived of primarily in collective rather than individual terms; this is why elders emphasize the fact that farmers worked together in such tasks as harvesting and that persons in need were taken care of by the community. Elders go on to note that labor is currently treated as a commodity that can be bought or sold: 'Nowadays there is no one who would help out anyone else. "If you want me to work, pay me," they tell you'. This common expression points to the fact that the fruits of labor are now seen, to adopt Marx's useful distinction (1867:36), as exchange values, commodities to be sold for profit, rather than as use values, goods to be used in satisfying the needs of the community.

The productive relations that are described in the talk of the elders of bygone days have very little to do with the way that Mexicanos make their living today. Although some individuals still farm or keep a small herd of cattle, far more are employed in Los Alamos National Laboratory and similar facilities. Land expropriation deprived most Mexicanos of the right to articulate a counter-hegemonic position through their labor. The view of production and social life that is articulated by the viejitos might simply have become archaic, treated as a way of life that is the object of romantic evocation but lacks relevance to the present. By virtue of its incorporation into la plática de los viejitos de antes, this view of production rather became what Williams (1977:122) refers to as a residual element of culture, one that "has been effectively formed in the past, but is still active in the cultural process." Since performances of the talk of the elders of bygone days necessarily involve both textualization and contextualization, they revolve around a reinterpretation of the past in keeping with its relevance to the present and future. The elders' explicit goal is to enhance their juniors' awareness of the dangers posed by the dominant hegemony to the political-economic and cultural survival of Mexicanos. They continually note that their efforts would be unsuccessful if they simply induced their juniors to memorize a body of facts about the past.

Williams's work points strikingly to the wisdom of this position; if the past is not systematically related to the present, the former becomes static, archaic, and politically impotent. The elders' approach is rather to provide a critical reading of the present, specifically of the impact of the dominant hegemony on their communities, by constantly rereading the past, selecting those elements that speak in dialectical fashion to the current manifestation of hegemony. The structure of la plática de los viejitos de antes thus guarantees the continuing vitality of the past as a dynamic force that plays a vital role in contemporary Mexicano experience. I have tried to show that becoming competent in this talk involves much more than learning a body of content; elders encourage their juniors to use the past as a lens for systematically and critically examining the present. Recall Williams's (1977:110) analysis of hegemony as a specific view of social life that seeks to generate "a sense of reality for most people in the society, a sense of absolute because experienced reality beyond which it is very diifficult for most members of the society to move." The talk of the elders of bygone days provides an effective counter-hegemony by virtue of its position as an alternative lens for viewing and evaluating experience, one that attaches alternative meanings to facets of social life and that reveals elements that the dominant hegemony has overlooked or suppressed. Becoming a competent performer of la plática de los viejitos de antes is thus as much a political as an aesthetic process, because it involves internalizing an approach to experience that is intentionally at odds with the dominant hegemony.

The dialectical relationship between hegemonic and counter-hegemonic views should not simply be equated with an Americano-Mexicano opposition. Recall Williams's (1977:118) words, quoted earlier, to the effect that hegemonic processes become powerful not as purely external forces, but through a process of internalization in which individuals come to identify themselves with the dominant hegemony. Performers do comment on the way that Anglo-Americans bring hegemonic pressures to bear on Mexicanos; take, for instance, the incident in which the Anglo-American forest service employees planned to kill Romero once he revealed the location of the mine. The richness of this image lies in the fact that the forest service has played a major role in enforcing the expropriation of Mexicano common lands that followed the United States annexation of the region in 1848.

Nonetheless, performers do not focus simply on the way that others, Mexicanos or Americanos, have internalized the dominant hegemony—the performers also point their fingers at themselves and their communities. Much more attention is devoted in the talk of the elders of bygone days to Mexicanos who have aligned themselves in one way or another with the dominant hegemony than to Anglo-Americans. In some cases, such self-identification is inadvertent. An example is provided by Epifacio's desire to profit from the recovery of Pedro Córdova's treasure: "'if we DIG UP that money, I'm going to buy a NEW CAR, I'm going to buy a new truck and EVERYTHING'" (7.2). In other cases, Mexicanos explicitly state that performing la plática de los viejitos de antes is not a worthwhile pursuit; they rather urge their relatives and neighbors to spend their time working for wages, saving their money, and investing it in profit-making endeavors. When Francisca and Estevan (7.4) dismiss the legends regarding Pedro Córdova's treasure as simply 'what the kids say', for example, they are rejecting both the talk of the elders of bygone days and the view of production that it entails. Such individuals are generally regarded as stingy or even exploitative by their neighbors because they refuse to participate in patterns of collective production and redistribution. For them production is seen in individual and economic terms, while others view it as a collective process that responds to social and religious as well as economic considerations.

One crucial element is still lacking in my analysis of the way that the talk of the elders of bygone days forms a counter-hegemony. Williams (1977:112) warns of the danger of casting hegemony in singular, static, and monolithic terms. Like any other dominant hegemony, the pressures that have been brought to bear on Mexicanos are themselves diverse and dynamic, and they are shaped by a host of internal and external contradictions. The Mexicano counter-hegemony that they have catalyzed has similarly emerged from a population that is diverse socially and linguistically (especially in terms of relative competence in different varieties of Spanish and English) and that spans both rural and urban areas. The counter-hegemonic response has thus been complex and heterogeneous as well.

Legends in particular emphasize the fact that Mexicanos express themselves in a variety of voices. Such dialogicality is built into the structure of la plática de los viejitos de antes, because each performer assumes responsibility for selecting elements of past and present and connecting them interpretively. This process accordingly reflects the creative and interpretive ability of the performer just as it reflects the interests and knowledge of the audience as well as current social and historical circumstances. The flexibility inherent in the talk of the elders of bygone days is such that it can also be turned on elements of Mexicano historical experience that are much less closely connected with the Anglo-American conquest of the region. Recall that Pedro Córdova, who enslaved his fellow Córdovans and expropriated most of their resources, was unable to reclaim his treasure or to pass it along to his descendants. His son Antonio was ridiculed by the Indio, Chico, who he tried to dominate in religious as well as political-economic terms. Moving close to the present, Mondragón's boss, García, was denied riches beyond belief as a result of his arrogance. Pedro de Ordimalas and Don Cacahuate are masters at exposing the superiority complexes of the better-to-do and of pretentious priests. Finally, women's humor offers us important insights with respect to the use of wit in subverting stereotypic gender roles and male claims to dominance. The lesson here is that la plática de los viejitos de antes stands ready as a counter-hegemonic tool in countering social inequality and forms of domination that exist within Mexicano communities as well as between Mexicanos and the dominant hegemony.

HEGEMONY, SCHOLARSHIP, AND INTERPRETATION

One runs the risk of restating the obvious by noting that scholars are human beings. I am not convinced, however, that linguists, folklorists, anthropologists, and other practitioners have adequately appreciated the implications of this fact. Like any other humans, scholars are socialized into particular political-economic niches of society, and the same hegemonic and counter-hegemonic pressures affect the way they perceive and act within the social world. As has been argued of late with increasing eloquence and clarity, interpreting the words and actions of other human beings accords a crucial role to the consciousness of the interpreter (cf. Clifford and Marcus 1986; Crapanzano 1977, 1980; Gadamer 1979; Geertz 1983; Rabinow and Sullivan 1979), and the consciousness of scholars is shaped by their gender, social class, ethnic group, and geographical region. If a researcher's socialization and subsequent experience aligns her or him with the dominant hegemony and does not include direct contact with counter-hegemonies, this is likely to limit the degree to which counter-hegemonic forces within a particular social milieu will prove to be comprehensible. Given the fact that scholars tend to be urban, middle or upper-middle class, and white, bias in favor of the dominant hegemony is a real danger.

Paredes (1978), Romano-V. (1968a, 1968b), and Vaca (1970a, 1970b) have pointed clearly to the way that ethnographic research can contribute to a reification of prejudicial stereotypes of Mexican-Americans; the study of folklore has similarly been used in presenting scholarly legitimations of the hegemonic perspective. The work of Espinosa (1910–16, 1946–47, 1985) and Edmonson (1952) provide two illustrations of this process.

Espinosa's research during the early part of the twentieth century on the Spanish-language folklore of New Mexico and southern Colorado was monumental in scope, extremely systematic, and informed by the latest theoretical and methodological work of his day. Espinosa summarized his assessment of these materials in the following terms:

After I began publishing my New-Mexican Spanish folk-lore material, some four years ago, I made the somewhat sweeping assertion, that in my opinion most of the material was traditional, that is Spanish. Further study has strengthened this opinion more and more. The traditional material—whether it be ballads, nursery rhymes, proverbs, riddles, folk-tales, or what not—may have sometimes undergone some modifications and amplifications, but it has survived, and not only has it survived, but it has remained practically untouched by foreign influences (1914:211).

In other words, a host of genres were transported from Spain through Mexico, existed for three centuries in a frontier region where contact with Native Americans was extensive, and then remained virtually unaffected by nearly half a century of political-economic domination by English speakers. Espinosa bolsters his thesis by downplaying and in some cases simply overlooking examples of legends, ballads, and other forms that commemorate historical processes and events (see for example Batchen 1972; Lamadrid 1987; Robb 1950–51). Espinosa's conclusion constitutes a blatant denial that New Mexican folklore bears any significant relationship to history, thus negating the possibility of studying the way that folklore can enable dominated groups to articulate their own history (cf. Paredes 1958), let alone to change it (cf. Limón 1982).

Edmonson focuses on cultural values. He follows Kluckhohn (1941; Kluckhohn and Strodtbeck 1961) in suggesting that "*Hispano* culture is not only traditional; it is dramatically, personally, paternalistically traditional. It is oriented towards the present, but towards a dramatic, yet fatalistically accepted present" (Edmonson 1952: 227). Not surprisingly, an examination of humor provides him with empirical evidence to support these stereotypes: "In *Hispano* culture clear joking patterns appear in relation to familism and paternalism (marital joking, flirtation), traditionalism (the *pachuco*), personalism (the *Gesellschaft-Gemeinschaft* joking), and dramatism (drinking, courtship)" (1952:268). I have tried to show in preceding chapters that Mexicano values involve a striking integration of concern with the past, present, and future, that familial relations are far from rigid. Most importantly, my analysis leads me to conclude that folkloric performances hardly provide evidence for a fatalistic acceptance of the status quo; they rather represent a critical examination of the way things are, a systematic exploration of how things could be different, and the belief that this process can influence the future.

My point is not that Espinosa and Edmonson are "bad guys." Both of these scholars have contributed substantially to their fields, and I am sure that they saw themselves as conducting unbiased research that would promote understanding of the Spanish-speaking population of New Mexico and the Southwest. One can similarly not cite Anglo bias or outsider misunderstanding as the root of the problem: Aurelio Macedonio Espinosa was born in 1880 in the San Luis Valley, and he traced his genealogy back to a soldier who came to New Mexico at the time of the first Spanish settlement in 1598 (J. M. Espinosa 1985:6–13). Such distortions rather reflect a much more serious and pervasive process by which the tenets used in scholarly research both emerge from and contribute to the authority of the dominant hegemony. While linguistics, folkloristics, and anthropology have often fallen victim to such cooptation, a number of recent developments in these and other disciplines hold great promise as means of redressing scholarly difficulties in identifying and critically examining both hegemonic and counter-hegemonic perspectives.

With respect to the study of verbal art, text-centered approaches that held sway until recent years provided a powerful tool for hegemonic cooptation of the self-expression of dominated peoples. When texts are divorced from contexts, folklore is reduced ipso facto to the archaic as a relic of past ages that is cut off from life in the present. Such perspectives construe folklore as conservative, passive, and inert, lacking the potential for retaining a vital connection with the present. If one believes that folklore lacks the inherent capacity to change in keeping with shifting historical circumstances, it is easy to conclude the folkloric traditions will soon die out. Limón (1983c) has noted that this identification of folklore as the hollow voice of the past is shared by many Marxist scholars as well. The Mexicano data suggest that such a view of folklore is a scholarly (and popular) fabrication rather than an accurate description of the nature of expressive culture and its role in social life. La plática de los viejitos de antes is creative and dynamic, and its ability to provide a systematic critique of the dominant hegemony is remarkable. As Limón (1982) has argued for Texas Mexican folklore, verbal art does not merely reflect changing historical circumstances but holds the potential for playing a leading role in creating new social formations. Spanish-speakers in the Southwestern United States are hardly alone in this respect; Chevalier (1982), Levine (1977), Taussig (1980), and Wachtel (1977) document cases in which verbal art plays a central role in resisting the dominant hegemony.

Clearly, the emergence of contextual and performance-based approaches is crucial, since they point to the status of contextual elements as central elements of the performance, not just external conditions. This step is crucial. When "the text" is separated from "the context," the latter is likely to be relegated to a set of external forces that can exert pressure on an inherently passive and static text. Such an approach fails to appreciate the intrinsic dynamism and creativity of tradition. It similarly falls short of illuminating the dialectical relationship between textual and contextual elements, particularly the potential of the text for transforming the social situation. Unless the contextualization process is studied vis-à-vis the way it is represented in the formal features of the performance, the scholar has no way of knowing whether her or his view of the social setting and its role in the performance bears any relation to the participants' own perspectives. Reifications of "the context" thus provide a means of writing the social setting into the analysis without considering the intrinsic connection between textual traditions and the historical situation of the participants. Such approaches thus provide new means of preserving the same old view of verbal art as inherently archaic and powerless.

This brings me back to my qualms regarding placing too much emphasis on distinguishing communicative events that are framed as performances from those that are framed in other ways. That is not to say that performances of legends, for example, are just like conversations regarding one's favorite television program. The danger emerges when the analysis focuses so much on the difference between the two that the fuzzy fringes of performance are overlooked. Similarly, such an orientation may well lead collectors to dwell more on types of performances that are maximally contrastive with "ordinary" conversations (in my terms, the most textually oriented); if researchers overlook the more contextually-focused genres they will fail to benefit from the insights into the contextualization process that are offered by performances that emphasize the continuity between performances and other types of communicative events. The overall effect of placing too much stress on this distinction will be the restriction of our ability to fully appreciate the dialectical relationship between past and present and, consequently, the way that verbal art can articulate counter-hegemony.

Ethnopoetics presents us with similar opportunities for revealing or obscuring counter-hegemonies. Ethnopoetic techniques assist transcribers, translators, and analysts in identifying the aesthetic properties of performances. The danger here lies in the possibility that some may use such insights as a means of presenting texts as purely aesthetic objects. (I am using the term "aesthetic" here in one of its vernacular senses as a thing of beauty that is set apart from the world of functionality.) My concern in this regard becomes particularly acute when I encounter collections of texts that are presented in "ethnopoetic" format (arranged in lines, marked for prosody, and so forth) and are not accompanied by analysis of their stylistic features, the social setting of the performance, and the meaning that these words hold for the participants. The "form for form's sake" mode can provide a particularly effective way of suggesting (however implicitly) that verbal art bears no direct connection with the everyday concerns of performers and audiences.

I would argue, however, that a more sophisticated view of ethnopoetics leads one in precisely the opposite direction. I have criticized the belief that the bearers of tradition, like the native speakers of a language, lack insight into the structure and significance of their own words; interpretation thus remains the exclusive purview of the scholar. I have argued throughout this book that performers embed interpretations in performances and that stylistic features play a special role in conveying these interpretations to audiences. The role of scholarly criticism is accordingly to extend the participants' interpretive efforts rather than to begin the process of interpretation. The data point strongly to the fact that performers interpret a broad range dimensions of social life, including the ongoing social situation, recent events both within and outside the community, and broad societal changes. Close attention to the way that performers use stylistic details in interpreting social life provides a powerful antidote to unwitting imposition of the hegemonic perspective, because it forces the research to focus systematically on the participants' own interpretive frameworks.

I remarked critically in Chapter 2 on a common assertion that the most appropriate methodology for collecting data on verbal art is to record performances in which the researcher is either absent or extremely peripheral, a premise that has lead some practitioners to use hidden tape recorders. The dangers posed by the scholar's unwitting identification with the dominant hegemony provide me with a stronger reason for rejecting this approach. Even if the fieldworker is entirely absent from the scene of the performance, her or his hand is at work throughout the research process—choosing the problem and theoretical framework; selecting a research site; deciding when, where, and who to record; choosing which recordings to transcribe and translate and how to go about doing this; and interpreting the performances in such a way as to render them comprehensible to the scholar's community. If removing oneself from the performance serves as a rationale for refusing to face difficult issues regarding the researcher's role in the research, then the critical process of reflectively examining the way that hegemonic and counter-hegemonic pressures have shaped our understanding of the data will be obscured.

The problem here is not simply one of eliminating bias but one of utilizing a rich source of data (cf. Briggs 1986). Recall the ways in which performers pointed clearly (if generally implicitly) to my involvement in performances. In some cases, performers provided general critiques of the problems faced by a middle-class Anglo-American researcher in Mexicano communities. Silvianita Trujillo de López exemplified the manner in which 'the outside world' misinterprets Mexicano messages and divulges community secrets in example (4.2). Aurelio Trujillo warned me about the pride, vanity, and avarice that sometimes conditions the way that Anglo-Americans treat Mexicanos in the course of our first extended visit (5.2). In both cases, code switching from Spanish into English signaled the special relevance of these statements to Anglo-Americans, present company included. The legend concerning Pedro Córdova's cache (7.2) pointed directly to the way that I was misinterpreting Bernardo's and Juan's words in the course of the performance by imposing the same materialist and positivistic assumptions regarding treasure hunting that had led the other outsiders astray in their efforts to locate the loot.

What were the performers trying to tell me? I argued earlier that such episodes provide commentaries on the history of relations between Anglo-Americans and Mexicanos. Note, however, that performers are characterizing more than the actions of Anglo-Americans—they are pointing to features of the dominant hegemony and the way it interprets the social world. In other words, the performers have anticipated the problems that I will face as a young, middle-class, Anglo-American in discerning the counter-hegemonic perspective that is embedded in la plática de los viejitos de antes. The metal detectors incident (7.2:190–96) demonstrates the fact that performers were often quite accurate in their assessments as to where my unconscious alignment with the dominant hegemony placed the counter-hegemonic perspective beyond my conceptual reach.

My experience points to the tremendous value of treating the collector's role in performances as a rich source of information rather than as an embarrassing contamination of the data. I have argued for the importance of discerning both hegemonic and counter-hegemonic processes in studying the self-expression of dominated groups. I also pointed to the way that researchers' unwitting imposition of the hegemonic perspective systematically distorts the data and blocks comprehension of the way that counter-hegemonic discourses provide alternative interpretive systems. The single most effective means of identifying such misinterpretations that I encountered in this study was listening to the way that performers used the stylistic features of the talk of the elders of bygone days in characterizing my involvement in performances.

This should come as no surprise: who would be in a better position to discern the points at which an outsider is likely to impose a hegemonic perspective on minority discourse than the people who have a long history of seeing their words misinterpreted by outsiders. Writing oneself out of the performance thus provides a convenient means of refusing to face the social criticism of one's consultants.

Scholarly comprehension of these issues has been thwarted by models of linguistic as well as social and cultural patterns that relate competence to static and homogeneous systems and reject the significance of individual voices. Here diversity, conflict, and struggle within and between human communities—in short, history—have often been hidden from view by a seamless view of the "ideal speaker-listener" or a monolithic view of culture. The critiques that have been offered by Paredes (1978), Romano-V. (1968a, 1968b), and Vaca (1970a, 1970b) provide potent lessons regarding the way that the unwitting imposition of the dominant hegemony on minority groups can produce caricatures that bear little resemblance to the perspective of the people studied. As Gramsci (1970), Williams (1977), and a host of others have warned us, scholars can easily become the ideological wing of the dominant sectors of society if their work simply imposes a hegemonic perspective on literature, verbal art, language, culture, or other aspects of dominated groups.

The problem is particularly acute in the case of verbal art, since scholars are often the only outsiders to gain intimate exposure to this facet of the group's self definition. Since scholarship transforms this intimate and private knowledge into public knowledge and renders it comprehensible to other outsiders, the way that one goes about this task is crucial. Unless the participants' own interpretations of the meaning of their words are taken seriously, researchers are likely to look to the dominant hegemony for an interpretive framework. If this occurs, the possible emergence of a critical and possibly counter-hegemonic voice will be replaced by a reaffirmation of the *Weltanschauung* of the dominant sectors of society. When scholarly interpretations fail to appreciate the struggles and the complexities of life in dominated groups, the members of such communities are likely to react with frustration and rage, and they will henceforth have good reason to mistrust any semblance of sensitivity offered by fieldworkers.

There are alternatives. In the early decades of this century, Sapir and Bakhtin (to name just two) presented models of language, culture, and society that portrayed systems of meaning as heterogeneous, dynamic, and intrinsically historical. Recent theoretical and methodological advances have enabled us to draw on such insights with greater clarity and systematicity, and they have placed us in a position to be able to appreciate the interpretive and poetic sophistication of the members of dominated groups. With respect to the study of verbal art, this step is crucial. The creative capacity of tradition to provide a critical perspective on changing experience frequently stands as a central asset of communities that have been stripped of their natural resources and of control over their own destinies. Here verbal art provides one of the central ways that voices of resistance and persistence can be clearly, if often indirectly, articulated. If scholars appropriate this discourse in the name of the dominant hegemony, their scholarship will have helped the controlling sectors complete the process of coopting the basic resources of the dominated group. If performers' interpretative efforts succeed in exercising some authority over scholarly discourse, however, studies of verbal art will demonstrate their capacity for greatly increasing the range and diversity of the voices that provide critical perspectives on discourse and social life.

NOTES

CHAPTER 1: INTRODUCTION

1. Hill and Hill (1986) use the term *Mexicano* with reference to Native Americans who live in the Valley of Pueblo-Tlaxcala in central Mexico and to the language they speak; the latter is also termed *Aztec* or *Nahuatl*. Spanish-speakers in northern New Mexico call themselves Mexicanos in recognition of the fact that they are descended from citizens of the Republic of Mexico, not because of any direct connection with the language documented by Hill and Hill.

2. I had undertaken study of folk music, particularly the hymns that commemorate the passion of Christ or praise the saints and the Virgin Mary, prior to 1974, but material culture had formed the focus of my research. I am grateful to Marta Weigle for suggesting that I investigate the way Mexicano proverbs are used in context.

3. A study by Arewa and Dundes (1964) provided a model for my procedure here.

4. This example is taken from a transcript of a performance by Fernando Medina, *Kobenahoro* 'Governor' of Murako, a Warao community located near San Fernando de Guayo, recorded in the course of fieldwork by the author in the Territorio Federal Delta Amacuro of Venezuela in November 1986.

5. This is not to say, however, that all studies that draw on ethnopoetics have focused exclusively on such narrative types as myths and tales. Clearly Glassie's (1982) research on an Irish community, Gossen's (1974a) study of Chamula Tzotzil, and Sherzer's (1983) work on the Kuna of Panamá provide notable exceptions; these authors are concerned with a broad range of genres, and each discusses conversational forms.

6. A striking exception to this lack of concern with the fuzzy fringes of performance is provided by Hanks's (1984) work on shamanistic discourse in Yucatec Maya.

CHAPTER 2: NORTHERN NEW MEXICO

1. I am including workers who are employed in other locations within Los Alamos and neighboring Whiterock as well; Córdovan men often work on construction or public works in the city, while the women are frequently employed as domestics in the scientists' houses.

2. Documents recording the exact date of the community's settlement have not come to light. The Pueblo Quemado is mentioned as constituting the northern boundary of the Santo Domingo de Cundiyó Grant in 1743 (Spanish Archives of New Mexico I: no. 211). A grant of land in the Cundiyó area in 1725 (later revoked) does not refer to the Pueblo Quemado (ibid.: no. 1041). The name was changed to Córdova when a post office was established in 1900 (Dike 1958). For a more detailed treatment of the history of the community, see Briggs (1987a).

3. This information is taken from both Córdovan oral testimony and the Mexican Archives of New Mexico (Hacienda Records, Aduana, *fracturas, guías,* and *tornaguías* for 1838, 1844, and 1845).

4. The wealthy and well-known José Antonio Vigil of neighboring Cundiyó, for example, had an estate valued in 1861 at $1,682.63 (Río Arriba County Clerk's Office, *Testamentos,* pp. 384–94).

5. This information is based on publications documenting the history of the Forest Service and of the sheep industry (cf. Forest Service 1936; Gillio 1979; Peffer 1951; Pinchot 1947; Roberts 1963; Steen 1976; Wentworth 1948), correspondence and conversations with officials of the Santa Fe National Forest, research in the History Section of the Forest Service, U.S. Department of Agriculture, Washington, D.C., and the Forest Service *Use Books* and grazing manuals for these years.

6. In 1935 the number of persons finding work outside the state had dropped to fewer than 2,000, and their earnings were estimated at $350,000 (Harper, Córdova, and Oberg 1943:77). Although earnings rose in the following years (Soil Conservation Service 1937:5), a large gap remained between the income of most villagers and the amount needed for subsistence. This gap was filled by relief dollars from the Work Projects Administration, Soil Conservation Service, Civilian Conservation Corps, the Farm Security Administration, Water Facilities Administration, Rural Rehabilitation Administration, and many other governmental relief projects. Estimated relief income for Mexicanos in the Middle Rio Grande Valley in 1936 was $1,143,051 (Soil Conservation Service 1937:5).

7. This information was provided by Charles Hart (personal communication, 1973) on the basis of a public voucher for work performed under provisions of the Federal Aid and Federal Highways Acts, as amended. The voucher was filed with the New Mexico State Highway Commission in 1955.

8. Córdova (1979) provides a detailed study of the pedagogy of missionization in the *genizaro* community of Abiquiú, New Mexico.

9. Some of the most important studies of New Mexican Catholic imagery are Boyd (1946, 1974), J. E. Espinosa (1967/1960), Mills (1967), Shalkop (1969), Steele (1974), Wilder with Breitenbach (1943), and Wroth (1979, 1982).

10. Don José Antonio Laureano de Zubiria y Escalante was appointed Bishop of Durango in 1831, and he made three episcopal visitations to interior New Mexico, in 1833, 1845, and 1850 (Weigle 1976:24–25). On the first of these visitations, Zubiría reported that "beyond a doubt, there is in this Villa [Santa Fe] a Brotherhood of Penitentes, already in existence for a number of years, but without authorization or knowledge of the bishops, who certainly would not have given their consent to such a Brotherhood, even if it had been asked" (Weigle 1976:242).

11. This date is taken from the cornerstone of the Presbyterian church that lies on the west side of the Córdova plaza. Rendón's (1953) history of the Presbyterian church in northern New Mexico mentions the presence of "a lay preacher, Mr. José Emiterio Cruz" in Córdova, but no date is given (1953:93).

12. Note that dialectal features account for the absence of accents in the transcription of such words as *ahi* (which is generally written as *ahí*).

13. These recordings are contained in the John Donald Robb Collection of Folk Music Recordings that is housed in the John Donald Robb Archive of Southwestern Music in the Fine Arts Library of the University of New Mexico. Robb's recordings are listed as numbers 244–55, 259–70, and 2147–70, and the Fishers' are 1017–34. I am indebted to Robb for loaning me a copy of his collection of folk music recordings in 1973.

14. The "Principles of Professional Responsibility" adopted by the Council of the American Anthropological Association in May 1971 state that "the aims of the investigation should be communicated as well as possible for the informant. . . . Those being studied should understand the capacities of such devices [camera, tape recorders, and other data-gathering devices]; they should be free to reject them if they wish; and if they accept them, the results should be

consonant with the informant's right to welfare, dignity and privacy" (American Anthropological Association 1973). The Statement on Ethics of the American Folklore Society, adopted in October 1987, suggests that "the aims of the investigation should be communicated as well as is possible to the informant" (American Folklore Society 1988:8).

15. I am concerned here with the way that calls for rejection of data on performances in which the collector is a participant may be linked to a positivist conception of verbal art. I am not suggesting, however, that this position necessarily leads to a lack of awareness of reflexivity and contextualization. Similarly, I am not claiming that such authors as Dégh, Vázsonyi, or Goldstein have used a concern with data collected in their "natural context" in advancing a false objectivity; this is certainly not the case.

CHAPTER 3: HISTORICAL DISCOURSE

1. I have suggested elsewhere (1986:83) that "'the talk of the elders of bygone days' emerges in three main types of social situations," namely, exchanges between elders, discussions by middle-aged persons, and pedagogical discourse. The fact that I describe four basic types of encounters in this chapter thus warrants comment.

The reasons for the change are twofold. First, the two statements apply to different levels of description and analysis. The three main types of social situations provide settings for performances of all genres of la plática de los viejitos de antes, save hymns and prayers; this chapter contrastively focuses on a much more detailed description of one domain of this 'talk'. Second, I long suspected that important stylistic differences existed between competitive and non-competitive performances, but my data were not systematic enough to explore such variation in depth, and my tape recordings of the non-competitive type of speech event were fragmentary. (Due to reasons that I discuss below, it was never possible to tape record competitive exchanges.) Additional fieldwork conducted in 1985 and 1986 provided me with more systematic data, including the tape recording of a non-competitive performance that is transcribed, in part, below (see example (3.1)). These materials strongly confirmed my belief that competitive and non-competitive types are stylistically distinct.

2. As I noted in the Preface, persons who appear in the transcripts and translations were given the option of being associated with their real names or with pseudonyms. In all cases, the participants requested use of their own names. I have been quite happy to comply with this request. The individuals who have contributed to this study stand more as highly skilled practitioners of Mexicano verbal art than anonymous "informants"; it thus seems only fair to give them recognition for their expertise and their contribution to the project. In some cases, it was not possible to contact one or more participants in a given performance due to death or serious illness. In such instances, I have used pseudonyms; this is the case in (3.1).

3. I use the terms "imperfective" and "perfective" because this is the way that the distinction between such forms as *hablaba* 'was speaking' and *habló* 'spoke' is generally phrased. Note, however, "perfective" and "imperfective" point to the quality of completion, whether or not an action was brought to an end. In Russian, for example, *Ja čital roman* and *Ja pročital roman* both mean 'I read a novel'; the latter, which is perfective, suggests that the speaker actually finished the book, while the imperfective (*čital*) does not tell us whether the book was finished or not.

4. It should be noted that recent research shows that the distinction between tense and aspect is far from water-tight (see for example Lyons 1977 and references therein).

5. This conclusion is based on nearly six hours of recorded collective recollections and on observation of a larger body of unrecorded examples.

6. I am grateful to Dan Ben-Amos for suggesting this comparison.

CHAPTER 4: PROVERBS

1. It should be noted that Taylor modified his position slightly in this recent restatement: "I am as doubtful today as I was then [in 1931] about the usefulness of a *brief* definition" (1967) (emphasis added). Does this imply that a longer, more detailed definition might provide us with "a touchstone" in accounting for this "incommunicable quality"? One way or the other, Taylor does not go on to compile such a definition.

2. This brief overview of the proverb literature is illustrative rather than comprehensive in intent, and I am concerned here only with studies of orally communicated proverbs. See Mieder (1982) for an extensive bibliography.

3. The standard Spanish term for the proverb, *proverbio*, is not used in New Mexican Spanish. Although Espinosa (1913:97) suggests that *refrán* appears in the dialect, my consultants never used it and they claimed to have never heard it before. *Chiste*, which generally refers to short humorous stories and jokes, was applied to proverbs by some nonspecialists. The proverb specialists made exclusive use of the term *dicho*.

4. The term *compadre* 'coparent' is used by a man or woman to address or refer to a man who either sponsored the speaker's child in baptism, confirmation, or marriage; or whose child was sponsored in one of these events by the speaker. A number of writers, such as Foster (1953), Mintz and Wolf (1950), Ravicz (1967), and Reina (1959, 1966), have described the system in Latin America. "Coparenthood" in Mexicano society has been treated by Swadesh (1974:189–92) and Vincent (1966).

5. Seitel (1972:147) refers to this feature as the "context situation"; his discussion of both this and the following feature (in my schema) in proverb performances of the Haya of Tanzania is quite useful.

6. This effect is achieved by Mrs. López's reference to herself as "Mrs. López." Córdovans use first names, nearly always prefaced by '*mano* (a contraction from *hermano* 'brother') for men and '*mana* (from *hermana* 'sister') for women, when conversing with each other. When further clarification is needed to specify a female referent, the woman's maiden name is cited. Further specificity may be obtained in the case of a married woman by stating *la que está casada con el* X 'the one who is married to X' plus (the husband's first and possibly last name). Córdovans are familiar, however, with the American English naming system. Thus, Mrs. López's hypothetical quotations from both "the authorities" and myself used the latter system in respectively addressing and referring to Mrs. López.

7. An obvious exception to this statement is provided by proverbs that lack any special association (feature 5).

8. I am indebted to Dell Hymes for pointing out the relevance of Cook-Gumperz's and Gumperz's (1976) concept of contextualization.

CHAPTER 5: SCRIPTURAL ALLUSIONS

1. *Tocayo* is used as a term of reference and address by persons who share the same first name. 'Namesake' does not provide an adequate gloss, since the English term implies that one person was named after the other, while *tocayo* does not.

2. This text was first published in Briggs (1986:85), and some of the discussion is taken from this publication as well.

3. Mr. Trujillo seems to be referring here to Christ's "Golden Rule" to "love one's neighbor as oneself."

4. The term *cristiano* is used in distinguishing Christians from either believers of other religions or "pagans," to distinguish Mexicanos from Native Americans, and to distinguish humans (*cristianos*) from animals. Mr. Trujillo seems to be using the term in this allusion in reference to both Christian (versus pagan) and human (versus animal) dimensions.

5. The reference is to Christ's instructions to two of his disciples, given as they journeyed

to Jerusalem: "Go to the village opposite, where you will at once find a donkey tethered with her foal beside her; untie them, and bring them to me. If anyone speaks to you, say, 'Our Master needs them'; and he will let you take them at once" (Matthew 21:2). Mr. Trujillo's remark, 'so that he could take the host', refers to Christ's anticipation of the Last Supper.

6. Mr. Trujillo does utter a phrase that is often used in validations (*sí, es verdad* 'yes, it's true') prior to this point (5.2:82–83). Given the fact that it follows my remark, it appears to function as a means of validating my contribution to the discourse and its relevance to Mr. Trujillo's message rather than as a validation of the performance as a whole.

7. The reference to the respect that animals sometimes show for the sacred emerges from Mr. Trujillo's claim that 'Christians' frequently fail to demonstrate an awareness that God is spiritually present everywhere, which is in turn derived from the third scriptural allusion ('if FIVE GATHER IN MY NAME').

CHAPTER 6: JESTES, ANECDOTES, AND HUMOROUS TALES

1. See for example Apte (1985), Chapman and Foot (1976), Fry (1963), McGhee (1979), and McGhee and Goldstein (1983).

2. See for example Abrahams (1982, 1983b, 1986b), Bauman (1986), McDowell (1979), and Manning (1983).

3. See for example Eggan (1955), Freedman (1977), Griaule (1948), Handelman and Kapferer (1972), Kennedy (1970), and Radcliffe-Brown (1940, 1949).

4. See for example Bricker (1973), Crumrine (1969), Ortiz (1972), and Parsons and Beals (1934).

5. See for example Abrahams and Dundes (1969), Brandes (1980), T. A. Burns (1984), Burns and Burns (1976), Legman (1968, 1975), and Wolfenstein (1954).

6. See for example Abrahams (1970), K. Basso (1979), Ben-Amos (1973), Burma (1946), Dundes (1971b, 1975b), Edmonson (1952), Levine (1977:298–366), Limón (1977, 1982), Oring (1981), Paredes (1966, 1968), Reyna (1973, 1978), and Zenner (1970).

7. See for example Dundes (1985), Farrer (1975), Green (1977), Jacobs (1960), Johnson (1973, 1977), Mitchell (1975, 1977, 1978), Spradley and Mann (1975), Weigle (1978), and Weinstein (1974).

8. See for example K. Basso (1979), Bauman (1986), Bricker (1976), Brukman (1975), Gossen (1974a:96–106, 1976b), Kirshenblatt-Gimblett (1976), Labov (1972b), Mitchell-Kernan (1972), Sacks (1974, 1978), and Sherzer (1978, 1985); also see Conklin (1959), Dundes (1977), Fromkin (1973), Hocket (1967, 1972), and Raskin (1985) on other linguistic facets of humor.

9. The work of Bricker (1973, 1976), Brukman (1975), Gossen (1974a:91–122, 1976b), Labov (1972b), Mitchell-Kernan (1972), Oring (1981), Paredes (1966, 1968), and Reyna (1973, 1978) warrants mention in this regard as well.

10. Brandes (1980:61) has made a similar case for the ambivalent attitude expressed by Andalusians in Gypsy jokes.

11. Legends recorded by Brown in Córdova in 1936–1941 point to Pedro Córdova's leadership in local religious affairs and his close association with the parish priest (Brown et al. 1978:101–5).

12. See DeHuff (1943) for a variant of this chiste.

13. Brown's collection of Córdovan folklore from 1936–41 includes another joke that plays upon this theme; see Brown et al. (1978:131–32).

14. Note that Mexicano veneration of locally produced wooden images of Catholic personages has similarly promoted ridicule from ecclesiastical authorities and, later, from Anglo-Americans (cf. Applegate 1932; Espinosa 1967/1960; Jaramillo 1972/1941).

15. For a discussion of the way that conversations key performances of jokes in Texas, see Reyna (1973:227–28).

16. A number of writers, including Campa (1947:332–34), A. M. Espinosa (1910–16/ 1914:119–34), J. M. Espinosa (1937:121–30), Lucero-White Lea (1953:200–201), Rael (n.d.:228–58), and Robe (1977:71–76) present tales that center on this character. Variation is apparent in the case of Pedro de Ordimalas's name. It is variously rendered as Pedro, él de Malas (Robe 1977), Pedro di Urdemales (A. M. Espinosa 1910–16/1914), Pedro de Urdemalas (J. E. Espinosa 1937), Pedro de Ordimalas (Rael n.d. and the Córdova variants I collected). He is similarly often referred to simply as Pedro (Robe 1977:71) or as Pedro Jugador 'Pedro the Gambler' (Rael 1937:127). Pedro Malasartes 'Pedro Evilarts' is used in Spain (A. M. Espinosa 1926:361–63). See A. M. Espinosa (1914:220–21) for a historical and comparative note on this character and an interpretation of the meaning of his name.

17. Folklorists will recognize this narrative as a version of tale type 922, "The Shepherd substituting for the Priest Answers the King's Questions"; it is the subject of a well-known monograph by Anderson (1923). Another variant collected in New Mexico is presented by Otero (1936:179–84).

18. Córdova (1973:32–33) presents the same chiste with a different rendering of the English loanword (*Sonufbitch*). In a variant presented by Rael (n.d.:357), "Don Cacaguate" suggests the name *Sanmagán* 'Son-of-a-Gun'. Note the variant spelling of Cacahuate. In Rael's variant, Don Cacaguate's wife is referred to as Doña 'Lady' Cacaguata.

19. Córdova (1973:70–75) presents this chiste in quite similar form, although the ill-fated protagonist is Bavitas, Don Cacahuate's oldest son.

20. For similar uses of titles, place names, and other elements of myths as textual indexes, see K. Basso (1984), Hymes (1981:322), and Silverstein (1985).

21. See Abrahams (1968b), Apte (1985:212–236), and E. Basso (1986) for surveys of the vast literature on tricksters. Also see Babcock (1978) and Turner (1967, 1969, 1974) on symbolic inversion.

22. In discussing Mexicano humor and cultural values, it should be noted that Edmonson (1952) devoted his dissertation to precisely this subject. His thesis is that humor will be taboo with respect to core cultural values, particularly "Lent and Holy Week, the Penitentes and the Eucharist, and perhaps also in relation to certain things symbolic of '*Hispanidad*'" (1952:244). Humor will be "institutionalized, rigidly patterned as to time, place, content, and agent" when it bears on values that are closely related to the core. Edmonson found relatively few "rigid" forms, such as jokes; in fact, excluding the jokes he himself told, his corpus contained only seven performances that he classified as "clearly in joke form" (1952:204). Most of the humor that he observed fell into a third category, that of "flexible patterns" of humor that related to less central value areas, such as "marital status, roles involving *Gesellschaft-Gemeinschaft* contact, flirtation, drinking, and a sex-bound pattern of the 'dirty joke'" (1952:245). Edmonson concludes that the "flexibility" of Hispano humor has afforded it a functional role in culture change: "We may suggest that humor has aided in this adjustment by furnishing a kind of forum on which the consensus on cultural values may be constantly tested, and the individual adjustments to changing culture may be made relatively painlessly" (1952:233). I will evaluate Edmonson's argument in Chapter 9.

23. Note, however, that the action setting may include verbs that are not inflected for past + perfective as well as those marked by past + perfective. In (6.4), for example, the duck is "caught" (perfective) by Luis, visitors "would come" and ask why the duck was there. Here *venían* and *decían* are iterative; they form specific events (coming, asking) that must occur in a particular order, but they are apparently repeated each time a new group of visitors arrives.

24. This is true as well for a type of discourse that does not fall under the aegis of the talk of the elders of bygone days, political rhetoric (see Briggs 1986:77–83).

CHAPTER 7: LEGENDS AND TREASURE TALES

1. The two passages in which Mr. Romero discusses the status of the potential assailants as *dos APACHES, o INDIOS* 'two Apaches, or INDIANS' (126–27; 146–49) may seem confus-

ing or even contradictory at first glance. The problem is simply that Indio is used in New Mexican Spanish in an "unmarked" or general sense to refer to a member of any Native American group, much as *Indian* functions in American English. Indio is, however, also used in a marked sense to refer to the members of such "nomadic" groups as the Comanches, Apaches, Navajoes, and Utes. Mr. Romero thus uses the term in the marked sense when he contrasts *Indios o Apaches* (meaning either Apaches or members of another "nomadic" group) and in the unmarked sense when he notes, *no sé que serían, si serían Indios Apaches ellos* ('I don't know what they were, if they were Apache Indians').

Warfare between Mexicanos and Pueblo Indians had long been a thing of the past by the time of Melaquías Romero's birth in 1909; nevertheless, because Navajo, Apache, Ute, and Comanche resistance was not entirely suppressed until the late nineteenth century, Mr. Romero's grandparents must certainly have remembered the days of Mexicano-Indio warfare.

2. I was quite familiar at the time with Los Ojitos, Los Brazos, and the Borrego Mesa Campground. I had heard of El Bordo de Tierra Amarilla, and I had a fair idea of its location; I had not visited it, however, and was not able to pinpoint it exactly.

3. More accurately, José Rafael quotes utterances that are attributed to both him and to Ramón Romero (cf. 226–30).

4. This theme is echoed in other Mexicano tales (see for example Robe 1980:472–73, 478–79; Dobie 1930:222–38), Spanish narratives from Texas (González 1927; Parks 1931: 737; Pérez 1951:96) and California (Miller 1973:110–40), and in Anglo-American treasure tales as well (cf. Dobie 1930; Hurley 1951:199–200).

5. Because Bernardo became quite ill before I was able to ask whether he would like to be cited by name, and he has unfortunately not recovered, I omitted the names from this text.

6. The treasure tales that Brown collected in Córdova between 1936 and 1941 are nearly identical to the versions that I collected nearly forty years later (Brown et al. 1978). His raconteurs also firmly believed that treasure hunts were doomed if any of the participants harbored selfish or evil thoughts (1978:107–08). Similar interdictions are quite common in treasure tales from other Hispanic communities in New Mexico (see for example Batchen 1939, 1972; Brown 1938; Campa 1963; De Huff 1943; Dobie 1930:222–38; Hurt 1940; La Sociedad Folklórica 1973; Martínez 1938; Otero 1936; Robe 1980:470–85; Tolman 1961) and throughout the Southwest. Lights, noises, ghosts, and the like frequently indicate the location of treasure (Dobie 1930; González 1927:14; Miller 1973:110–40; Pérez 1951:96). Spirits can either guard the treasure or aid the hunters in recovering it. The position that a spirit adopts vis-à-vis a given set of seekers is often tied to the latter's moral disposition. Participants are frequently enjoined to free themselves of "avaricious thoughts or ideas" (Pérez 1951:97). A tale collected in California relates the death of a woman at the hands of a guardian skeleton for her refusal to share the money with the child who had discovered it (Miller 1973:132–134).

7. The sole exception is provided by hymns and prayers. A report or repetition of a hymn or prayer is used for pedagogical purposes, but performances generate rather than respond to contexts. Pedagogical discourse accordingly would not provide a suitable setting for performing a hymn or prayer (see Chapter 8).

8. Young (1983:102) notes that the term *taleworld* was coined in collaboration with Barbara Kirshenblatt-Gimblett and was based on work by Jason (1975:208–15). The reader should note, however, that I use the terms *storyrealm* and *realm of conversation* in different senses than does Young.

9. Gesture also assumed a significant role in the performance. Unfortunately, because (7.2) is recorded on audiotape alone, I cannot provide a detailed analysis of this facet of the performance.

10. The phrase *como esclavos* 'like slaves' appears in legends of Pedro Córdova's cache collected from other Córdovan treasure hunters.

CHAPTER 8: HYMNS AND PRAYERS

1. This chapter is dedicated to the memory of Aurelio Trujillo, an extremely good rezador who taught me a great deal about hymns, prayers, and the meaning of life. I wish to thank his wife, Costancia Trujillo, and son, Manuel, for their help in clarifying several of the texts that appear in this chapter and for giving me one of Mr. Trujillo's cuadernos.

2. See Steele and Rivera (1985), Weigle (1976), and Woodward (1974/1935) for descriptions of other offices and their duties.

3. See Briggs (1980) for a study of the production and use of religious imagery in Córdova.

4. Wooden pitos are shown in Rael (1951:14).

5. This is based on observation. Because I did not tape record the Thursday morning Rosary service, I cannot rule out the possibility that the two Rosaries may differ in some details.

6. Rael (1951:16) notes that the second rezador's part draws on alabados connected with the passion of Christ.

7. Rael (1951:16) reports that the length of th^{o} clamorous interval is determined by the time it takes the rezador to recite the Apostles' Creed three times. The prayer may be recited silently, and it would, in any case, be inaudible in the face of the clamor. My sense is that the time lapse would permit only one recitation. See Steele and Rivera (1985:196−97) on the symbolism of the Tenebrae services.

8. Steele and Rivera (1985:198−200) provide an account of Sudarios.

9. This polychromed image of Our Lady of Sorrows has been replaced in recent years by a set of miniature images of the Holy Family (Jesus, Mary, and Joseph) enclosed in a wood and glass case. This image is owned by La Sagrada Familia, and it is closely identified with their collective identity. This substitution points to the rise in importance of La Sagrada Familia and its assumption of a leading role in the Encuentro.

10. The English summaries of the Stations are taken from Brown (1967:833).

11. As Thomas J. Steele, S.J. (personal communication, 1984) pointed out to me, this phrase derives from the Latin invocation *te rogamus, audi nos*. It is, however, rendered phonetically as Spanish.

12. An exception is provided by the relatively unconstrained conversations that follow the *Rosario* of Holy Wednesday.

13. The mothers and wives of the Brothers bring food to the morada during Holy Week. The Brothers eat some meals and sleep some nights at the morada and others at home.

14. The major communicative functions of the bell in the Rosary service are to frame the beginning of the service and to mark the end of each decade of Ave Marías. Note, however, that the use of the bell in Rosary services is optional.

15. Some variation is evident in the selection of these opening prayers.

16. I found it impossible to convey accurately the prosodic markings to the English translation without either creating a translation that is so literal that it is nonsensical or seriously distorting the prosodic structure. They have accordingly been omitted from the translation.

17. As I have noted, spoken words are used in two ways. First, the prayer leaders say Padre Nuestro to signal the other participants that they (the latter) are to chant the first part of the Padre Nuestros and Ave Marías during the current decade. Secondly, the prayer leaders say Ave María Purísima after the close of the last decade, and the other participants respond with Ave María.

18. Recall that new breath groups are indicated on the transcript by lines that are indented left.

19. Lange (1974b:24) suggests that this image represents the Man of Sorrows, who "always bears evidence of the wounds of the Crucifixion (*stigmata*) in spite of a living posture. He is dead as Man yet living as God, thus His eyes are open."

20. This image is often referred to as Our Lady of the Seven Sorrows in keeping with the seven heads that are painted on her garment (see Briggs 1980, Plate 10 for a photograph of this image). According to Brown, this image was identified as Our Lady of Sorrows in the 1930s

(cf. Brown et al. 1978:222–23). Steele (1974:175) notes that images of Our Lady of Sorrows are commonly used in El Encuentro in the region.

Scholarly iconography differs from attributions made by the users of the image in the case of this image. Lange (personal communication, 1978) suggests that the image would be identified by academic iconographers as the Seven Brothers and St. Felicity, Symphorosa and her Seven Sons, or the Holy Machabees.

21. See Briggs (1980:26–29) for information on Aragón, his apprentice, and the images that they created. Also see Boyd (1974:392–407) and Wroth (1982:129–69) on the life and work of Aragón.

22. Oral historical documentation of this point has been complemented by a description of the chapel and its contents written by Lorin Brown in the 1930s (Brown et al. 1978:210–26) and by a ca. 1935 photograph by T. Harmon Parkhurst of the interior of the chapel. The original negative lies in the Photo Archives of the Museum of New Mexico, Santa Fe, no. 9031; the date was supplied by the archivist, Arthur L. Olivas (personal communication, 1976).

23. See de Córdova (1972:24–26) for a description of Lenten foods and recipes for panocha and tortas de huevo.

24. The nocturnal execution of these rituals can be traced in part to the adverse publicity and the ridicule that resulted from the observation of daytime processions by newcomers, particularly Anglo-Americans (cf. Hollander 1985; Kenneson 1978:25–26; Weigle 1976:90–94, 1981). One of the changes that permitted a reconciliation between the Brotherhood and the Church hierarchy (achieved in 1947) was a stipulation that "The Elder Brothers are ordered and required not to allow any exercise [of penance] within view of the public; all this will take place at night with concealment and Christian charity." (This passage is taken from the "Certificate of Ordinance" that Miguel Archibeque, as Elder Brother of the newly formed Supreme Ministerial Council, sent Archbishop Edwin V. Byrne on 27 January 1946; it is reprinted in bilingual form in Steele and Rivera 1985:68–70.)

25. It should be noted, however, that Weigle (1976:179–92) presents a symbolic analysis of Brotherhood rituals that constitutes a major step in this direction; her interpretation draws on the work of Eliade (1959/1957, 1965), Turner (1969), and Van Gennep (1960/1909).

26. This rule was adopted in the "Certificate of Ordinance" of 27 January 1946 (cf. Steele and Rivera 1985:68).

27. See Turner and Turner (1978) on Christian pilgrimage in Latin America and elsewhere.

28. This point is stressed in a missalette that is commonly used among Córdovan Catholics. In a short passage on the praying of the Rosary, the editor notes that *para ganar las indulgencias concedidas, es necesario meditar los principales acontecimientos. Los misterios Gozosos, Dolorosos y Gloriosos en la vidas de nuestro Señor y de nuestra Señora.* 'In order to gain the conceded indulgences, it is necessary to meditate on, the principal events. The Joyful, Sorrowful, and Glorious mysteries in the lives of our Lord and our Lady' (Hoever 1943:489; translation mine).

29. Such commentary on formal elements is generally part of evaluations of the overall rhetorical persuasiveness of performances.

30. The fast formerly extended to the previous midnight for celebrant and communicants alike (cf. Fortescue 1943/1917:38), but this period has been shortened. Communicants are now required to fast only one hour before receiving communion.

31. Archbishop Salpointe, one of the Brotherhood's severest ecclesiastical critics, issued such instructions in 1888 and 1892. See Lee (1910:4) and Weigle (1976:60, 62, 210–16).

32. One of the printed sources that is used by Brothers, Rael's *The New Mexico Alabado* (1951), includes musical transcriptions.

33. I noted in Chapter 4 that English does not appear in proverb texts (feature 4). This does not mean, however, that English lexemes and phrasal constructions are not used in other features, particularly in explications of the proverb's relevance to the context.

34. Quoted speech is used more extensively in some alabados, particularly those that narrate the passion story. In the course of a pre-Maitines performance of *Ven , Pecador, y Verás* 'Come, Sinner, and You Will See', for example, Christ speaks to his disciples and to the Pharisees; the Pharisees, Pilate, and an angel (who tells Mary that Christ has risen from the dead) are also quoted. The voices of the dramatis personae do not enter into a dialectical relationship with that of the narrator, however, and they do not create stylistic and ideological polyphony.

35. The words that were exchanged in the events that led up to the crucifixion figure prominently in rezos and alabados. The point is that these words are reported, usually in quite general terms, rather than quoted. For example, a meditation is offered at the end of the Via Crucis *por las siete palabras que en cruz habló* 'for the seven words that He spoke while on the cross'. The text does not go on to quote those words or paraphrase their content.

CHAPTER 9: CONCLUSION

1. Note the similarity between this episodic pattern and those that Hymes (1981) has discovered in Northwest Coast myths.

2. See Kutsche and Van Ness (1982), Leonard (1943), Swadesh (1974), Van Ness (1979b, 1987a) for studies of the effects of the loss of grant lands on other Mexicano communities.

BIBLIOGRAPHY

Abrahams, Roger D. (1964). *Deep down in the jungle: Negro narrative folklore from the streets of Philadelphia*. Chicago: Aldine.

—— (1967). On proverb collecting and proverb collections. *Proverbium* 8: 181–84.

—— (1968a). Introductory remarks to a rhetorical theory of folklore. *Journal of American Folklore* 81: 143–58.

—— (1968b). A rhetoric of everyday life: traditional conversational genres. *Southern Folklore Quarterly* 32: 44–59.

—— (1968b). Trickster, the outrageous hero. In Tristram P. Coffin (ed.), *Our living traditions: an introduction to American folklore*, pp. 170–78. New York: Basic Books.

—— (1970). The Negro stereotype. *Journal of American Folklore* 83: 229–49.

—— (1971). Personal power and social restraint in the definition of folklore. *Journal of American Folklore* 84: 16–30.

—— (1972). Proverbs and proverbial expressions. In Richard M. Dorson (ed.), *Folklore and folklife: an introduction*, pp. 117–27. Chicago: University of Chicago Press.

—— (1976). *Talking black*. Rowley, Mass.: Newbury House.

—— (1976/1969). The complex relations of simple forms. *Genre* 2: 104–28. Reprinted in Dan Ben-Amos (ed.), *Folklore genres*, pp. 193–214. Austin: University of Texas Press.

—— (1978). Towards a sociological theory of folklore: performing services. *Western Folklore* 37: 161–84.

—— (1980). Play. In Venetia Newall (ed.), *Folklore studies in the twentieth century: Proceedings of the Centennial of the Folklore Society*, pp. 119–22. Woodbridge, Suffolk.

—— (1981). In and out of performance. *Narodna Umjetnost*, pp. 69–78.

—— (1982a). Play and games. *Motif: International Newsletter of Research in Folklore and Literature* 3: 1, 5–7.

—— (1982b). Storytelling events: wake amusements and the structure of nonsense on St. Vincent. *Journal of American Folklore* 95: 389–414.

—— (1983a). Interpreting folklore ethnographically and sociologically. In Richard M. Dorson (ed.), *Handbook of American folklore*, pp. 345–50. Bloomington: Indiana University Press.

—— (1983b). *The man-of-words in the West Indies: performance and the emergence of Creole culture*. Baltimore: Johns Hopkins University Press.

—— (1985). Pragmatism and a folklore of experience. *Western Folklore* 44: 324–32.

—— (1986a). Complicity and imitation in storytelling: a pragmatic folklorist's perspective. *Cultural Anthropology* 1: 223–37.

—— (1986b). The play of play: the human encounter. Paper presented at the Annual Meeting of the American Anthropological Association, Philadelphia.

Abrahams, Roger D., and Barbara Babcock-Abrahams (1977). The literary use of proverbs. *Journal of American Folklore* 90: 414–29.

Abrahams, Roger D., and Alan Dundes (1969). On elephantasy and elephanticide. *Psychoanalytic Review* 56:225–41.

American Anthropological Association (1973). *Professional ethics: statements and procedures of the American Anthropological Association.* Washington, D.C.: American Anthropological Association.

American Folklore Society (1988). A statement on ethics for the Society. *The American Folklore Society Newsletter* 17:8.

Anderson, Walter (1923). *Kaiser und Abt, die Geschichte eines Schwanks.* Folklore Fellows Communications, no. 42. Helsinki: Suomalainen Tiedeakatemia.

Appaduri, Arjun (1981). The past as a scarce resource. *Man* 16:201–19.

Applegate, Frank G. (1932). *Native tales of New Mexico.* Philadelphia: J. B. Lippincott.

Apte, Mahadev L. (1985). *Humor and laughter: an anthropological approach.* Ithaca, N.Y.: Cornell University Press.

Aranda, Charles (1975). *Dichos: proverbs and sayings from the Spanish.* Santa Fe, N. Mex.: Sunstone Press.

Arewa, E. Ojo (1970). Proverb usage in 'natural' context and oral literary criticism. *Journal of American Folklore* 83:430–37.

Arewa, E. Ojo, and Alan Dundes (1964). Proverbs and the ethnography of speaking folklore. In John J. Gumperz and Dell H. Hymes (eds.), *The Ethnography of communication. American Anthropologist* 66(6), pt. 2: 70–85.

Arora, Shirley L. (1968). Spanish proverbial exaggerations from California. *Western Folklore* 27:229–53 (1968) and 30:105–18 (1971).

——— (1972). Proverbial exaggerations in English and Spanish. *Proverbium* 18:675–83.

——— (1977). *Proverbial comparisons and related expressions in Spanish.* Berkeley: University of California Press.

——— (1982). Proverbs in Mexican American tradition. *Aztlán* 13:43–69.

Austin, J. L. (1962). *How to do things with words.* Cambridge, Mass.: Harvard University Press.

Babcock, Barbara (1977). The story in the story: metanarration in folk narrative. In Richard Bauman (ed.), *Verbal art as performance,* pp. 61–79. Prospect Heights, Ill.: Waveland Press.

——— (1980). Reflexivity: Definitions and discriminations. *Semiotica* 30(1–2): 1–14.

——— (ed.). (1978). *The reversible world: symbolic inversion in art and society.* Ithaca, N.Y.: Cornell University Press.

Bakhtin, M. M. (1968/1965). *Rabelais and his world* (Helene Iswolsky, trans.). Bloomington: Indiana University Press.

——— (1981). *The dialogic imagination: four essays* (Michael Holquist, ed.; Caryl Emerson and Michael Holquist, trans.). Austin: University of Texas Press.

——— (1984/1929). *Problems of Dostoevsky's Poetics* (Caryl Emerson, ed. and trans.). Minneapolis: University of Minnesota Press.

——— (1986). *Speech genres and other late essays* (Caryl Emerson and Michael Holquist, eds.; Vern W. McLee, trans.). Austin: University of Texas Press.

Bakhtin, M. M./P. M. Medvedev (1985). *The formal method in literary scholarship: a critical introduction to sociological poetics* (Albert J. Wehrle, trans.). Cambridge, Mass.: Harvard University Press.

Barakat, Robert A. (1980). *A contextual study of Arabic proverbs.* Finnish Folklore Communications, No. 226. Helsinki: Suomalainen Tiedeakatemia.

Barley, Nigel (1972). A structural approach to the proverb and maxim. *Proverbium* 20:737–50.

——— (1974). 'The proverb' and related problems of genre-definition. *Proverbium* 23: 880–84.

Barral, P. Basilio María de (1964). *Los indios guaraunos y su cancionero: historia, religión y alma lírica.* Madrid: Consejo Superior de Investigaciones Científicas, Departamento de Misionología Española.

Basso, Ellen (1985). *A musical view of the universe: Kalapalo myth and ritual performances.* Philadelphia: University of Pennsylvania Press.

—— (1987). *In favor of deceit: a study of tricksters in an Amazonian society.* Tucson: University of Arizona Press.

Basso, Keith H. (1976). 'Wise words' of the Western Apache: metaphor and semantic theory. In Keith H. Basso and Henry T. Selby (eds.), *Meaning in anthropology,* pp. 93–121. Albuquerque: University of New Mexico Press.

—— (1979). *Portraits of "the whiteman": linguistic play and cultural symbols among the Western Apache.* Cambridge: Cambridge University Press.

—— (1984). 'Stalking with stories': names, places and moral narratives among the Western Apache. In Edward M. Bruner (ed.), *Text, play, and story: the construction and reconstruction of self and society* (1983 Proceedings of the American Ethnological Society), pp. 19–55. Washington, D.C.: American Ethnological Society.

Batchen, Lou Sage (1939). The panic of 1862. Unpublished manuscript in the files of the W.P.A. New Mexico Federal Writers' Project, History Library, Museum of New Mexico, Santa Fe.

—— (1972). *Las Placitas: historical facts and legends.* Placitas, N. Mex.: Tumbleweed Press.

Bateson, Gregory. (1972/1955). A theory of play and fantasy. Reprinted in *Steps to an ecology of mind,* pp. 177–93. New York: Ballantine Books.

—— (1972). *Steps to an ecology of mind.* New York: Ballantine Books.

Bateson, Gregory, Don D. Jackson, Jay Haley, and John H. Weakland (1972/1956). Toward a theory of schizophrenia. Reprinted in Gregory Bateson (ed.), *Steps to an ecology of mind,* pp. 201–27. New York: Ballantine Books.

Bateson, Gregory, and Jurgen Ruesch (1951). *Communication: the social matrix of psychiatry.* New York: W. W. Norton & Co.

Bauman, Richard (1971). Differential identity and the social base of folklore. *Journal of American Folklore* 84:31–41.

—— (1977/1975). Verbal art as performance. *American Anthropologist.* 77(2):290–311. Revised and expanded in *Verbal art as performance* (1977). Prospect Heights, Ill.: Waveland Press.

—— (1982). Conceptions of folklore in the development of literary semiotics. *Semiotica* 39:1–20.

—— (1983). The field study of folklore in context. In Richard M. Dorson (ed.), *Handbook of American folklore,* pp. 362–67. Bloomington: Indiana University Press.

—— (1986). *Story, performance, and event: contextual studies of oral narrative.* Cambridge: Cambridge University Press.

Bauman, Richard and Roger D. Abrahams (eds.) (1981). *"And other neighborly names": social process and cultural image in Texas folklore.* Austin: University of Texas Press.

Bell, Michael J. (1983). *The world from Brown's Lounge: an ethnography of Black middle-class play.* Urbana: University of Illinois Press.

Ben-Amos, Dan (1971). Toward a definition of folklore in context. *Journal of American Folklore* 84:3–15.

—— (1973). The "myth" of Jewish humor. *Western Folklore* 32:112–31.

—— (1976/1969). Analytical categories and ethnic genres. In Dan Ben-Amos (ed.), *Folklore genres,* pp. 215–42. Austin: University of Texas Press.

—— (1977). The context of folklore: implications and prospects. In William Bascom (ed.), *Frontiers of Folklore,* pp. 36–53. AAAS Selected Symposium 5. Boulder, Colo.: West View Press.

—— (ed.) (1976). *Folklore genres.* Austin: University of Texas Press.

Ben-Amos, Dan, and Kenneth S. Goldstein (eds.) (1975). *Folklore: performance and communication.* The Hague: Mouton.

Bergson, Henri (1950). *Le rire: essai sur le signification du comique.* Paris: Presses Universitaires de France.

Billington, Ray Allen (1963). *Words that won the west, 1830–1850.* San Francisco: Foundation for Public Relations Research and Education.

Bird, Charles, and Timothy Shopen (1979). Maninka. In Timothy Shopen (ed.), *Languages and their speakers*, pp. 59–111. Cambridge, Mass.: Winthrop Publishers; pbk. rpt. Philadelphia: University of Pennsylvania Press, 1987.

Blacking, John (1961). The social value of Venda riddles. *African Studies* 20:1–35.

Blaustein, Richard (1983). Using video in the field. In Richard M. Dorson (ed.), *Handbook of American folklore*, pp. 397–401. Bloomington: Indiana University Press.

Bloom, Lansing B. (1913–1915). New Mexico under Mexican administration, 1827–1846. *Old Santa Fe* 1(1913):3–49, 131–75, 235–87, 347–68; 2(1914–1915):3–56, 119–69, 227–77, 351–80.

Bourdieu, Pierre (1977). *Outline of a theory of practice*, (Richard Nice, trans.). Cambridge: Cambridge University Press.

Bowen, J. Donald (1952). The Spanish of San Antonito, New Mexico. Ph.D. dissertation, University of New Mexico.

––––––– (1976). A structural analysis of the verb system in New Mexican Spanish. In J. Donald Bowen and Jacob Ornstein (eds.), *Studies in southwest Spanish*, pp. 93–124. Rowley, Mass.: Hewbury House.

Boyd, E. (1946). *Saints and saint makers*. Santa Fe, N. Mex.: Laboratory of Anthropology.

––––––– (1974). *Spanish Colonial popular arts*. Santa Fe: Museum of New Mexico.

Brack, Gene M. (1975). *Mexico views Manifest Destiny, 1821–1846*. Albuquerque: University of New Mexico Press.

Brandes, Stanley H. (1974). The selection process in proverb use: a Spanish example. *Southern Folklore Quarterly* 38:167–86.

––––––– (1977). Peaceful protest: Spanish political humor in a time of crisis. *Western Folklore* 36:311–46.

––––––– (1980). *Metaphors of masculinity: sex and status in Andalusian folklore*. Philadelphia: University of Pennsylvania Press.

––––––– (1988). *Power and persuasion: fiestas and social control in rural Mexico*. Philadelphia: University of Pennsylvania Press.

Branning, Don (1967). Behind closed doors, simple villagers called Penitentes relive Good Friday. *Albuquerque Tribune* 24 March 1967, pp. A-1, A-4.

Bricker, Victoria Reifler (1973). *Ritual humor in Highland Chiapas*. Austin: University of Texas Press.

––––––– (1974). The ethnographic context of some traditional Mayan speech genres. In Richard Bauman and Joel Sherzer (eds.), *Explorations in the ethnography of speaking*, pp. 368–88. Cambridge: Cambridge University Press.

––––––– (1976). Some Zinacanteco joking strategies. In Barbara Kirshenblatt-Gimblett (ed.), *Speech play: research and resources for the study of linguistic creativity*, pp. 51–62. Philadelphia: University of Pennsylvania Press.

Briggs, Charles L. (1980). *The wood carvers of Córdova, New Mexico: social dimensions of an artistic "revival."* Knoxville: University of Tennessee Press.

––––––– (1983). A conversation with St. Isidore: the teachings of the elders. In Marta Weigle with Claudia Larcombe and Samuel Larcombe (eds.), *Hispanic arts and ethnohistory in the southwest: new papers inspired by the work of E. Boyd*, pp. 103–16. Santa Fe, N. Mex.: Ancient City Press, and Albuquerque: University of New Mexico Press.

––––––– (1985). Remembering the past: Chamisal and Peñasco, New Mexico in 1940. In William Wroth (ed.), *Russell Lee's photographs of Chamisal Peñasco, New Mexico*, pp. 5–15. Santa Fe, N. Mex.: Ancient City Press.

––––––– (1986). *Learning how to ask: a sociolinguistic appraisal of the role of the interview in social science research.* Cambridge: Cambridge University Press.

––––––– (1987a). Getting both sides of the story: oral history in land grant research and litigation. In Charles L. Briggs and John R. Van Ness (eds.), *Land, water, and culture: new perspectives on Hispanic land grants*, pp. 217–65. Albuquerque: University of New Mexico Press.

––––––– (1987b). Power and performativity in Warao women's funerary laments. Paper presented at the Annual Meeting of the American Folklore Society, Albuquerque, N. Mex., 21–25 October 1987.

——— (1989). The meaning of the tale of the lost gold mine: an interpretive essay. In Charles L. Briggs and Julián Josué Vigil (eds.), *The tale of the lost gold mine of Juan Mondragón: a New Mexican legend performed by Melaquías Romero.* Tucson: University of Arizona Press.

——— (in press). Form, consciousness, and functional diversity in verbal art. In John A. Lucy (ed.), *Reflexive language: reported speech and metapragmatics.* Cambridge: Cambridge University Press.

Briggs, Charles L., and John R. Van Ness, (eds.) (1987), *Land, water, and culture: new perspectives on Hispanic land grants.* Albuquerque: University of New Mexico Press.

Briggs, Charles L., and Julián Josué Vigil (eds.) (1989). *The tale of the lost gold mine of Juan Mondragón: a New Mexican legend performed by Melaquías Romero.* Tucson: University of Arizona Press.

Bright, William (1979). A Karok myth in "measured verse": the translation of a performance. *Journal of California and Great Basin Anthropology* 1 : 117–23.

——— (1984). *American Indian linguistics and literature.* Berlin: Mouton.

Bronner, Simon J. (1984). "Let me tell it my way": joke telling by a father and son. *Western Folklore* 43 : 18–36.

Brown, B. (1967). Way of the Cross. In *New Catholic encyclopedia,* vol 14, pp. 832–35. New York: McGraw-Hill.

Brown, Lorin W. (1938). Treasure of New Mexico. Unpublished manuscript in the files of the W.P.A. Federal Writers' Project, New Mexico State Records Center and Archives, Santa Fe.

——— (1941). Fiestas in New Mexico. *El Palacio* 48 : 239–45.

Brown, Lorin W., with Charles L. Briggs and Marta Weigle (1978). *Hispano folklife of New Mexico: the Lorin W. Brown Federal Writers' Project manuscripts.* Albuquerque: University of New Mexico Press.

Brukman, Jan (1975). "Tongue play": constitutive and interpretive properties of sexual joking encounters among the Koya of South India. In Mary Sanches and Ben Blount (eds.), *Sociocultural dimensions of language use,* pp. 235–68. New York: Academic Press.

Buckley, Thomas (1984). Yurok speech registers and ontology. *Language in Society* 13 : 467–88.

Burke, Kenneth (1941). Literature as equipment for living. In *The philosophy of literary form: studies in symbolic action,* pp. 293–304. Baton Rouge: Louisiana State University Press.

——— (1945). *A grammar of motives.* Berkeley: University of California Press.

——— (1969/1950). *A rhetoric of motives.* Berkeley: University of California Press.

Burma, John H. (1946). Humor as a technique in race conflict. *American Sociological Review* 11 : 710–15.

Burns, Alan F. (1980). Interactive features in Yucatec Mayan narratives. *Language in Society* 9 : 307–20.

——— (1983). *An epoch of miracles: oral literature of the Yucatec Maya.* Austin: University of Texas Press.

Burns, Thomas A. (1984). Doing the wash: cycle two. *Western Folklore* 43 : 49–70.

——— with Inger H. Burns (1976). *Doing the wash: an expressive culture and personality study of a joke and its tellers.* Folcroft, Penn.: Folcroft.

Campa, Arthur L. (1939). Mañana is today. *New Mexico Quarterly* 9 : 3–11.

——— (1946). *Spanish folk-poetry in New Mexico.* Albuquerque: University of New Mexico Press.

——— (1947). Spanish traditional tales in the southwest. *Western Folklore* 6 : 322–34.

——— (1963). *Treasure of the Sangre de Cristos: tales and traditions of the Spanish southwest.* Norman: University of Oklahoma Press.

——— (1979). *Hispanic culture in the southwest.* Norman: University of Oklahoma Press.

Cancian, Frank (1965). *Economics and prestige in a Maya community: the religious cargo system in Zinacantan.* Stanford, Calif.: Stanford University Press.

Carey, George (1976). The storyteller's art and the collector's intrusion. In Linda Dégh, Henry Glassie, and Felix J. Oinas (eds.), *Folklore today: a festschrift for Richard M. Dorson*, pp. 81–91. Bloomington: Research Center for Language and Semiotic Studies, Indiana University.

Carson, Xanthus (1974). *Treasure! Bonanzas worth a billion bucks*. San Antonio, Tex.: Naylor.

Casares, Julio (1950). La locución, la frase proverbial, el refrán, el modismo. In *Introducción a la lexicographía moderna* (Reprinted, 1969), pp. 165–242. Madrid: S. Agrurre Torre.

Catron Papers, Special Collections, University of New Mexico, Albuquerque, Case 212.

Chapman, A. J., and H. C. Foot (eds.) (1976). *Humor and laughter: theory, research, and applications*. New York: John Wiley & Sons.

Chávez, Fray Angélico (1954). The Penitentes of New Mexico. *New Mexico Historical Review* 29:97–123.

Chevalier, Jacques M. (1982). *Civilization and the stolen gift: capital, kin, and cult in Eastern Peru*. Toronto: University of Toronto Press.

Chomsky, Noam. (1957). *Syntactic structures*. The Hague: Mouton.

————— (1965). *Aspects of the theory of syntax*. Cambridge, Mass.: M.I.T. Press.

————— (1968). *Language and mind* (enlarged edition, 1972). New York: Harcourt, Brace, Jovanovich.

————— (1975). *Reflections on language*. New York: Pantheon.

Churchill, Lindsey (1978). *Questioning strategies in sociolinguistics*. Rowley, Mass.: Newbury House.

Cicourel, Aaron V. (1974a). *Cognitive sociology: language and meaning in social interaction*. New York: Free Press.

————— (1974b). *Theory and method in a study of Argentine fertility*. New York: Wiley Interscience.

————— (1982). Language and belief in a medical setting. In Heidi Byrnes (ed.), *Contemporary perceptions of language: interdisciplinary dimensions*. pp. 48–78. Washington, D.C.: Georgetown University Press.

————— (1985). Text and discourse. In Bernard J. Siegel, Alan R. Beals, and Stephen A. Tyler (eds.), *Annual Review of Anthropology*, vol. 15, pp. 159–85. Palo Alto, Calif.: Annual Reviews.

Clifford, James and George E. Marcus (eds.) (1986). *Writing culture: the poetics and politics of ethnography*. Berkeley: University of California Press.

Cobos, Rubén (1973a). New Mexican Spanish folktales. *New Mexico Folklore Record* 13: 11–18.

————— (1973b). *Southwestern Spanish proverbs—refranes españoles del sudoeste*. Cerrillos, N. Mex.: San Marcos Press.

————— (1983). *A dictionary of New Mexico and southern Colorado Spanish*. Santa Fe: Museum of New Mexico.

Comrie, Bernard (1976). *Aspect*. Cambridge: Cambridge University Press.

Cohen, David William (1977). *Womunafu's Bunafu: a study of authority in a nineteenth-century African community*. Princeton, N.J.: Princeton University Press.

Conklin, Harold C. (1959). Linguistic play in its cultural context. *Language* 35:631–36.

Cook-Gumperz, Jenny, and John J. Gumperz (1976). *Papers on language and context*. (Working Paper No. 46, Language Behavior Research Laboratory, University of California, Berkeley.)

Córdova, Gilberto Benito (1973). *Abiquiú and Don Cacahaute: a folk history of a New Mexican village*. Los Cerrillos, N. Mex.: San Marcos.

————— (1979). Missionization and Hispanicization of Santo Thomas Apostol de Abiquiú, 1750–1770. Ph.D. dissertation, University of New Mexico, Albuquerque.

Corsaro, William A. (1985). Sociological approaches to discourse analysis. In Teun A. Van Dijk (ed.), *Handbook of discourse analysis*. Vol. 1: *Disciplines of discourse*, pp. 167–92. London: Academic Press.

Court of Private Land Claims, New Mexico Land Grants Collection of the State Records Center and Archives, Santa Fe, Case No. 212.

Crapanzano, Vincent (1977). On the writing of ethnography. *Dialectical Anthropology* 2:
69–73.

———— (1980). *Tuhami: portrait of a Moroccan.* Chicago: University of Chicago Press.

Crichton, J. D. (1971). *Christian celebration: the mass.* London: Geoffrey Chapman.

Crocker, Richard L. (1980). Melisma. In Stanley Sadie (ed.), *The new Grove dictionary of
music and musicians,* vol. 12, pp. 105–106. London: Macmillan.

Crumrine, N. Ross (1969). Capakoba, the Mayo Easter ceremonial impersonator: explanations of ritual clowning. *Journal for the Scientific Study of Religion* 8:1–22.

Darley, Alexander M. (1893). *The passionists of the southwest, or the Holy Brotherhood: a revelation of the "Penitentes"* (reprinted, 1968). Glorieta, N. Mex.: Rio Grande Press.

Darnell, Regna (1974). Correlates of Cree narrative performance. In Richard Bauman and
Joel Sherzer (eds.), *Explorations in the ethnography of speaking,* pp. 315–36. Cambridge:
Cambridge University Press.

Deane, Inigo, S. J (1884). The new flagellants: a phase of New-Mexican life. *The Catholic
World* 39:300–11.

De Beaugrande, Robert, and Wolfgang Dressler (1981). *Introduction to text linguistics.* London:
Longman.

De Borhegyi, Stephen F. (1953). El Cristo de Esquipúlas de Chimayó, Nuevo México. *Antro-
pología e historia de Guatemala* 5:11–28.

———— (1956). *El Santuario de Chimayó.* Santa Fe, N. Mex.: Spanish Colonial Arts Society.

De Buys, William (1981). Fractions of justice: a legal and social history of the Las Trampas
Land Grant, New Mexico. *New Mexico Historical Review* 56:71–97.

———— (1985). *Enchantment and exploitation: the life and hard times of a New Mexico mountain
range.* Albuquerque: University of New Mexico Press.

De Caro, Rosan Jordan (1972). Language loyalty and folklore studies: the Mexican-American.
Western Folklore 31:77–86.

De Córdova, Lorenzo (Lorin W. Brown) (1972). *Echoes of the flute.* Santa Fe, N. Mex.: Ancient City.

Dégh, Linda (1976). Symbiosis of joke and legend: a case of conversational folklore. In Linda
Dégh, Henry Glassie, and Felix J. Oinas (eds.), *Folklore today: a festschrift for Richard M.
Dorson,* pp. 101–22. Bloomington: Research Center for Language and Semiotic Studies,
Indiana University.

Dégh, Linda and Andrew Vázsonyi (1976/1969). Legend and belief. In Dan Ben-Amos (ed.),
Folklore genres, pp. 93–123. Austin: University of Texas Press.

DeHuff, Elizabeth Willis (1943). *Say the bells of old missions: legends of old New Mexico churches.*
St. Louis: B. Herder.

De Marco, A. A. (1967). Hail Mary. In *New Catholic encyclopedia,* vol. 6, p. 898. New York:
McGraw-Hill.

Denning, Greg (1980). *Islands and beaches, discourse on a silent land: Marquesas 1774–1880.*
Honolulu: The University Press of Hawaii.

De Voto, Bernard (1943). *The year of decision: 1846.* Boston: Little, Brown and Company.

Dewey, John (1925). *Experience and nature.* Chicago: Open Court.

Dike, Sheldon Holland (1958). *The territorial post offices of New Mexico.* Albuquerque: privately printed.

Dobie, J. Frank (1930). *Coronado's children: tales of lost mines and buried treasures of the southwest.* New York: Literary Guild of America.

Dorson, Richard M. (1972). Introduction: concepts of folklore and folklife studies. In Richard
M. Dorson (ed.), *Folklore and folklife: an introduction,* pp. 1–50. Chicago: University of
Chicago Press.

Douglas, Mary (1968). The social control of cognition: some factors in joke perception. *Man*
3:361–76.

Duncan, Starkey (1972). Some signals and rules for taking speaking turns in conversation. *Journal of Personality and Social Psychology* 23(2):283–92.

———— (1973). Towards a grammar for dyadic conversation. *Semiotica* 9(1):29–46.

———— (1974). On the structure of speaker-auditor interaction during speaking turns. *Language in Society* 3(2):161–80.

Duncan, Starkey, and G. Niederehe (1974). On signalling that it's your turn to speak. *Journal of Experimental Social Psychology* 10:234–47.

Dundes, Alan (1964). Texture, text, and context. *Southern Folklore Quarterly* 28:251–65.

———— (1966). Metafolklore and oral literary criticism. *The Monist* 50:505–16.

———— (1971a). Folk ideas as units of worldview. *Journal of American Folklore* 84:93–103.

———— (1971b). A study of ethnic slurs: the Jew and the Polack in the United States. *Journal of American Folklore* 84:186–203.

———— (1975a). On the structure of the proverb. *Proverbium* 25:961–73.

———— (1975b). Slurs international: folk comparisons of ethnicity and national character. *Southern Folklore Quarterly* 39:15–38.

———— (1977). Jokes and covert language attitudes: the curious case of the wide-mouth frog. *Language in Society* 6:141–47.

———— (1980). *Interpreting folklore*. Bloomington: Indiana University Press.

———— (1985). The J.A.P. and the J.A.M. in American jokelore. *Journal of American Folklore* 98:456–75.

Dyer, Brainerd (1946). *Zachary Taylor*. Baton Rouge: Louisiana State University Press.

Ebright, Malcolm (1980). *The Tierra Amarilla grant: a history of chicanery*. Santa Fe, N. Mex.: Center for Land Grant Studies.

———— (1987). A legal history of land grants. In Charles L. Briggs and John R. Van Ness (eds.), *Land, water, and culture: new perspectives on Hispanic land grants*, pp. 15–64. Albuquerque: University of New Mexico Press.

Edmonson, Munro S. (1952). Los Manitos: patterns of humor in relation to cultural values. Ph.D. dissertation, Harvard University.

———— (1966). Play: games, gossip, and humor. In Manning Nash (ed.), *Handbook of Middle American Indians*, pp. 191–206. Austin: University of Texas Press.

Eggan, Fred (1955). The Cheyenne and Arapaho kinship system. In Fred Eggan, *Social anthropology of North American tribes*, pp. 35–98. Chicago: University of Chicago Press.

Eliade, Mircea (1959/1957). *The sacred and the profane: the nature of religion*, (Willard R. Trask, trans.). New York: Harcourt, Brace.

———— (1965). *Rites and symbols of initiation: the mysteries of birth and rebirth*, (Willard R. Trask, trans.). New York: Harper and Row.

Erlich, Victor (1955). *Russian formalism: history—doctrine* (4th ed., 1980). The Hague: Mouton.

Ervin-Tripp, Susan (1972). On sociolinguistic rules: alternation and co-occurrence. In John J. Gumperz and Dell Hymes (eds.), *Directions in sociolinguistics: the ethnography of communication*, pp. 213–50. New York: Holt, Rinehart, & Winston.

Espinosa, Aurelio M. (1909–1914). Studies in New-Mexican Spanish. *Revue de Dialectologie Romane*, Part I: Phonology 1:157–239, 269–300 (1909); Part II: Morphology 3:251–86 (1911), 4:241–56 (1912), 5:142–72 (1913); Part III: The English Elements 6:241–317 (1914).

———— (1910–1916). New Mexican Spanish folklore. *Journal of American Folklore* 23(1910):395–418; 24(1911):397–444; 26(1913):97–122; 27(1914):105–47; 28(1915):204–6, 319–52; 29(1916):505–35.

———— (1911). Penitentes, Los Hermanos (The Penitent Brothers). *The Catholic encyclopedia*, vol. 11, pp. 635–36. New York: Robert Appleton.

———— (1914). Comparative notes on New-Mexican and Mexican Spanish folk-tales. *Journal of American Folklore* 27:211–31.

———— (1917). Speech mixture in New Mexico. In H. Morse Stephens and Herbert E. Bolton (eds.), *The Pacific Ocean in history*, pp. 408–28. New York: Macmillan.

———— (1923–26). *Cuentos populares españoles, recogidos de la tradición oral de España y publicados con una introducción y notas comparativas.* (3 vols, published in 1923, 1924, and 1926). Stanford, Calif.: Stanford University.

———— (1926). Spanish folklore in New Mexico. *New Mexico Historical Review* 1:135–55.

———— (1930). *Estudios sobre el español de Nuevo Méjico*, vol. 1, *Fonética* (A. Alonso & Angel Rosenblat, trans. and eds.). Buenos Aires: Biblioteca de Dialectología Hispanoamericana, Instituto de Filología, Universidad de Buenos Aires.

———— (1946). *Estudios sobre el español de Nuevo Méjico*, vol. 2, *Morfología* (A. Alonso & Angel Rosenblat, trans. and eds.). Buenos Aires: Biblioteca de Dialectología Hispanoamericana, Instituto de Filología, Universidad de Buenos Aires.

———— (1953). *Romancero de Nuevo Méjico.* Madrid: Revista de Filología Española-Anejo LVIII.

———— (1985). *The folklore of Spain in the American Southwest: traditional Spanish folk literature in northern New Mexico and southern Colorado* (J. Manuel Espinosa, ed.). Norman: University of Oklahoma Press.

Espinosa, José Edmundo (1967/1960). *Saints in the valleys: Christian sacred images in the history, life and folk art of Spanish New Mexico* (revised edition). Albuquerque: University of New Mexico Press.

Espinosa, J. Manuel (1937). *Spanish folk tales from New Mexico.* (Memoirs of the American Folklore Society, 30) New York: G. E. Stechert.

———— (1985). Aurelio M. Espinosa: New Mexico's pioneer folklorist. In Aurelio M. Espinosa, *The folklore of Spain in the American southwest.* (J. Manuel Espinosa, ed.) Pp. 3–64. Norman: University of Oklahoma Press.

Evans-Pritchard, E. E. (1962). *Sanza*, a characteristic feature of Zande language and thought. In *Social anthropology and other essays*, pp. 330–54. New York: Free Press of Glencoe.

Falassi, Alessandro (1980). *Folklore by the fireside.* Austin: University of Texas Press.

Farrer, Claire R. (1975). Women and folklore: images and genres. *Journal of American Folklore* 88:v–xv.

Feld, Stephen (1982). *Sound and sentiment: birds, weeping, poetics, and song in Kaluli expression.* Philadelphia: University of Pennsylvania Press.

Fine, Elizabeth C. (1984). *The folklore text: from performance to print.* Bloomington: Indiana University Press.

Fine, Gary Alan (1985). Rumors and gossiping. In Teun A. van Dijk (ed.), *Handbook of discourse analysis.* Vol. 3: *Discourse and dialogue*, pp. 223–37. London: Academic Press.

Finnegan, Ruth (1967). *Limba stories and story telling.* Oxford: Oxford University Press.

———— (1970). *Oral literature in Africa.* Oxford: Clarendon Press.

———— (1977). *Oral poetry: its nature, significance and social context.* Cambridge: Cambridge University Press.

Firth, Raymond (1926). Proverbs in native life, with special reference to the Maori. *Folk-Lore* 37:134–53, 245–70.

Forastieri-Braschi, Eduardo, Gerald Guiness, and Humberto López Morales (eds.) (1980). *On text context: methodological approaches to the contexts of literature.* San Juan: University of Puerto Rico.

Forest Service, U.S. (1936). *The Western range* (74th Congress, 2nd Session, Document No. 199). Washington, D.C.: U.S. Government Printing Office.

Fortescue, Adrian (1912). *The mass: a study of the Roman liturgy.* London: Longmans, Green and Co.

———— (1943/1917). *The ceremonies of the Roman rite described.* London: Burns Oates and Washbourne Ltd.

Foster, George M. (1953). Cofradía and compadrazgo in Spain and Spanish America. *Southwestern Journal of Anthropology* 9:1–28.

Fowler, Roger (1985). Power. In Teun A. van Dijk (ed.), *Handbook of discourse analysis.* Vol. 4: *Discourse analysis in society,* pp. 61–82. London: Academic Press.

Fowler, Roger, Bob Hodge, Gunther Kress, and Tony Trew (1979). *Language and control.* London: Routledge & Kegan Paul.

Fox, James J. (1974). 'Our ancestors spoke in pairs': Rotinese views of language, dialect, and code. In Richard Bauman and Joel Sherzer (eds.), *Explorations in the ethnography of speaking,* pp. 65–85. Cambridge: Cambridge University Press.

Freedman, J. (1977). Joking, affinity, and the exchange of ritual services among the Kiga of Northern Rwanda: an essay on joking relationship theory. *Man* 12:154–65.

Freud, Sigmund (1960/1905). *Jokes and their relation to the unconscious* (James Strachey, trans.). New York: W. W. Norton.

Friedrich, Paul (1979). *Language, context, and the imagination: essays by Paul Friedrich.* (Anwar S. Dil, ed.) Stanford, Calif.: Stanford University Press.

—— (1986). *The language parallax: linguistic relativism and poetic indeterminacy.* Austin: University of Texas Press.

Fromkin, Victoria A. (1973). Slips of the tongue. *Scientific American* 229:110–17.

Fry, William F. (1963). *The sweet madness: a study of humor.* Palo Alto, Calif.: Pacific Books.

Gadamer, Hans-Georg (1979). The problem of historical consciousness. In Paul Rabinow and William M. Sullivan (eds.), *Interpretive social science: a reader,* pp. 103–60. Berkeley: University of California Press.

Garfinke , Harold. (1967). *Studies in ethnomethodology.* Englewood Cliffs, N.J.: Prentice-Hall.

—— (1972). Remarks on ethnomethodology. In John J. Gumperz and Dell Hymes (eds.), *Directions in sociolinguistics: the ethnography of communication,* pp. 301–24. New York: Holt, Rinehart & Winston.

Garvin, Paul L. (ed.) (1964). *A Prague School reader in esthetics, literary structure, and style.* Washington, D.C.: Georgetown University Press.

Geertz, Clifford (1973). *The interpretation of cultures.* New York: Basic Books.

—— (1983). *Local knowledge.* New York: Basic Books.

Genette, Gérard (1980). *Narrative discourse.* Ithaca, N.Y.: Cornell University Press.

Georges, Robert A. (1969). Toward an understanding of storytelling events. *Journal of American Folklore* 82:313–28.

Gill, Sam D. (1981). *Sacred words: a study of Navajo religion and prayer.* Westport, Conn.: Greenwood Press.

Gillio, David "A" (1979). *Santa Fe National Forest area: an historical perspective for management.* (Cultural Resources Report No. 30.) Albuquerque: USDA Forest Service, Southwestern Region.

Giovannini, Maureen J. (1978). A structural analysis of proverbs in a Sicilian village. *American Ethnologist* 5:322–33.

Glassie, Henry (1982). *Passing the time in Ballymenone: culture and history of an Ulster community.* Philadelphia: University of Pennsylvania Press.

Godelier, Maurice (1966). *Rationality and irrationality in economics.* (Brian Pearce, trans., 1972) New York: Monthly Review Press.

—— (1973). *Perspectives in Marxist anthropology.* (Robert Brain, trans., 1977). Cambridge: Cambridge University Press.

Goffman, Erving (1959). *The presentation of self in everyday life.* New York: Anchor.

—— (1974). *Frame analysis.* New York: Harper & Row.

—— (1981). *Forms of talk.* Philadelphia: University of Pennsylvania Press.

Gold, Peter (1972). Total transcription. *Alcheringa* 14:1–14.

Goldstein, Kenneth S. (1963). Riddling traditions in Northeast Scotland. *Journal of American Folklore* 76:330–36.

—— (1964). *A guide for field workers in folklore.* Hatboro, Penn.: Folklore Associates.

—— (1968). The induced natural context: an ethnographic folklore field technique. In June Helm (ed.), *Essays on the verbal and visual arts: Proceedings of the 1966 annual spring meeting of the American Ethnological Society*, pp. 1–6. Seattle: American Ethnological Society.

Goldstein, Judith L. (1986). Iranian Jewish women's magical narratives. In Phyllis Pease Chock and June R. Wyman (eds.), *Discourse and the social life of meaning*, pp. 147–68. Washington, D.C.: Smithsonian Institution Press.

González, Jovita (1927). Folklore of the Texas-Mexican vaquero. *Publications of the Texas Folklore Society* 6:7–22.

Goodenough, Ward H. (1956). Componential analysis and the study of meaning. *Language* 32:195–216.

Goodwin, Charles (1981). *Conversational organization: interaction between speakers and hearers.* New York: Academic Press.

Goodwin, Paul D., and Joseph W. Wenzel (1979). Proverbs and practical reasoning: a study in socio-logic. *The Quarterly Journal of Speech* 65:289–302.

Goody, John Rankin (1977). *The domestication of the savage mind.* Cambridge: Cambridge University Press.

Gossen, Gary H. (1973). Chamula proverbs: neither fish nor fowl. In Munro S. Edmonson (ed.), *Meaning in Mayan languages*, pp. 205–34. The Hague: Mouton Publishers.

——— (1974a). *Chamulas in the world of the sun: time and space in a Maya oral tradition.* Cambridge, Mass.: Harvard University Press.

——— (1974b). To speak with a heated heart: Chamula canons of style and good performance. In Richard Bauman and Joel Sherzer (eds.), *Explorations in the ethnography of speaking*, pp. 389–413. Cambridge: Cambridge University Press.

——— (1976a). Language as ritual substance. In William J. Samarin (ed.), *Language in religious practice*, pp. 40–60. Rowley, Mass.: Newbury House.

——— (1976b). Verbal dueling in Chamula. In Barbara Kirshenblatt-Gimblett (ed.), *Speech play*, pp. 121–46. Philadelphia: University of Pennsylvania Press.

——— (1985). Tzotzil literature. In Victoria Reiffler Bricker and Munro S. Edmonson (eds.), *Supplement to the handbook of Middle American Indians*. Vol. 3, *Literatures*, pp. 64–106. Austin: University of Texas Press.

Gramsci, Antonio (1970). *The prison notebooks.* London.

Green, Reyna (1977). Magnolias grow in dirt: the bawdy lore of Southern women. *Southern Exposure* 4:29–33.

Griaule, Marcel (1948). L'alliance carthartique. *Africa* 18:242–58.

Gumperz, John J. (1982). *Discourse strategies.* Cambridge: Cambridge University Press.

Habermas, Jürgen (1971). *Knowledge and human interests,* (Jeremy J. Shapiro, trans.). Boston: Beacon Press.

Hacienda Records, Mexican Archives of New Mexico, Hacienda, Aduana, *fracturas, guías,* and *tornaguías* for 1838, 1844, 1845, State Records Center and Archives, Santa Fe.

Halliday, M.A.K., and Ruqaiya Hasan (1976). *Cohesion in English.* London: Longman.

Hamilton, Holman (1941). *Zachary Taylor: soldier of the republic.* Indianapolis: Bobbs-Merrill.

Hammond, George P., and Agapito Rey (eds. and trans.) (1940). *Narratives of the Coronado expedition, 1540–1542.* Albuquerque: University of New Mexico Press.

Handelman, Don, and Bruce Kapferer (1972). Forms of joking activity: a comparative approach. *American Anthropologist* 74:484–517.

Hanks, William (1984). Sanctification, structure, and experience in a Yucatec ritual event. *Journal of American Folklore* 97:131–66.

Harding, Susan (1975). Women and words in a Spanish village. In Rayna R. Reiter (ed.), *Toward an anthropology of women*, pp. 283–308. New York: Monthly Review Press.

——— (1978). Street shouting and shunning: conflict between women in a Spanish village. *Frontiers* 3:14–18.

Haring, Lee (1972). Performing for the interviewer: a study of the structure of context. *Southern Folklore Quarterly* 36:383–98.

——— (1985). Malagasy riddling. *Journal of American Folklore* 98:163–89.

Harper, Allan G., Andrew R. Córdova, and Kalvero Oberg (1943). *Man and resources in the Middle Rio Grande Valley.* Albuquerque: University of New Mexico Press.

Havelock, Eric (1963). *Preface to Plato.* Cambridge: Belknap Press.

——— (1982). *The literate revolution in Greece and its cultural consequences.* Princeton, N.J.: Princeton University Press.

Haviland, John Beard (1977). *Gossip, reputation, and knowledge in Zinacantan.* Chicago: University of Chicago Press.

Havránek, Bohuslav (1964). The functional differentiation of the standard language. In Paul Garvin (ed. and trans.), *A Prague School reader in esthetics, literary structure, and style,* pp. 3–16. Washington, D.C.: Georgetown University Press.

Heath, Shirley Brice (1982). What no bedtime story means: narrative skills at home and school. *Language in Society* 11:49–76.

Heiler, Frederick (1932). *Prayer: a study in the history and psychology of religion* (Samuel McComb, trans.). New York: Oxford University Press.

Henderson, Alice Corbin (1937). *Brothers of light: the Penitentes of the Southwest.* New York: Harcourt, Brace and Company.

Hernández, Juan (1963). Cactus whips and wooden crosses. *Journal of American Folklore* 76:216–24.

Herzfeld, Michael (1981). An indigenous theory of meaning and its elicitation in performative context. *Semiotica* 34:113–41.

——— (1985). *The poetics of manhood: context and identity in a Cretan mountain village.* Princeton, N.J.: Princeton University Press.

Herzog, George, and C. G. Blooah (1936). *Jabo-proverbs from Liberia.* London: International African Institute.

Hill, Jane H. (1983). The voices of Don Gabriel. Paper presented to the Annual Meeting of the American Anthropological Association, Chicago, Ill.

——— (1985). The grammar of consciousness and the consciousness of grammar. *American Ethnologist* 12:725–37.

Hill, Jane H., and Kenneth C. Hill (1986). *Speaking Mexicano: dynamics of syncretic language in Central Mexico.* Tucson: University of Arizona Press.

Hinnebusch, W. A. (1967). Rosary. In *New Catholic encyclopedia,* vol. 12, pp. 667–70. New York: McGraw-Hill.

Hobbes, Thomas (1651). *Leviathan* (C. B. MacPherson, ed., 1968). Harmondsworth: Penguin.

Hockett, Charles F. (1958). *A course in modern linguistics.* New York: Macmillan.

——— (1967). Where the tongue slips, there slip I. In *To honor Roman Jakobson.* Janua Linguarum, Series Maier, No. 32:910–36. The Hague: Mouton.

——— (1972). Jokes. In M. Estellie Smith (ed.), *Studies in linguistics in honor of George L. Trager,* pp. 153–78. The Hague: Mouton.

Holbeck, Bengt (1970). Proverb style. *Proverbium* 15:54(470)–56(472).

Hollander, Margot (1985). The Brotherhood and the Press: Anglo-American distortion of a Hispanic religious organization, 1872–1908. B.A. thesis, Vassar College.

Hoopes, James (1979). *Oral history: an introduction for students.* Chapel Hill: University of North Carolina Press.

Hopper, Paul J. (1979). Aspect and foregrounding in discourse. In Talmy Givón (ed.), *Discourse and syntax,* pp. 213–60. *Syntax and Semantics* 12. New York: Academic Press.

——— (1982a). Aspect between discourse and grammar: an introductory essay for the volume. In Paul J. Hopper (ed.), *Tense-aspect: between semantics and pragmatics,* pp. 3–18. Amsterdam: John Benjamins.

———. (ed.) (1982b). *Tense-aspect: between semantics and pragmatics.* Amsterdam: John Benjamins.

Hopper, Paul J., and Sandra Thompson (1980). Transitivity in grammar and discourse. *Language* 56:251–99.

Horka-Follick, Lorayne Ann (1969). *Los Hermanos Penitentes: a vestige of medievalism in the Southwestern United States.* Los Angeles: Westernlore Press.

Howell, Richard W. (1973). *Teasing relationships* (Addison-Wesley Module in Anthropology, No. 46). Reading, Mass.: Addison-Wesley.

Hurley, Gerald T. (1951). Buried treasure tales in America. *Western Folklore* 10:197–216.

Hurt, Wesley R. (1940). Spanish American superstitions. *El Palacio* 47:193–201.

Huizinga, Johan (1955). *Homo ludens: a study of the play element in culture.* Boston: Beacon Press.

Hymes, Dell H. (1964). Introduction: toward ethnographies of communication. In John J. Gumperz and Dell Hymes (eds.), The ethnography of communication. *American Anthropologist* 66(6), pt. 2:1–34.

——— (1971). The contribution of folklore to sociolinguistic research. In Américo Paredes and Richard Bauman (eds.), "Toward new perspectives in folklore." *Journal of American Folklore* 84:42–50.

——— (1972). Models of the interaction of language and social life. In John J. Gumperz and Dell H. Hymes (eds.), *Directions in sociolinguistics: The ethnography of communication,* pp. 35–71. New York: Holt, Rinehart and Winston.

——— (1974). *Foundations in sociolinguistics: an ethnographic approach.* Philadelphia: University of Pennsylvania Press.

——— (1975). Folklore's nature and the sun's myth. *Journal of American Folklore* 88:346–69.

——— (1981/1975). Breakthrough into performance. Reprinted in Dell Hymes, *"In vain I tried to tell you": essays in Native American ethnopoetics,* pp. 79–141. Philadelphia: University of Pennsylvania Press.

——— (1981). *"In vain I tried to tell you": essays in Native American ethnopoetics.* Philadelphia: University of Pennsylvania Press.

——— (1985a). Language, memory and selective performance: Cultee's "salmon myth" as twice told to Boas. *Journal of American Folklore* 98:391–434.

——— (1985b). Some subtleties of measured verse. Paper presented at the Annual Meeting of the American Anthropological Association, Washington, D.C.

Hymes, Virginia (1985). Verse analysis as heuristic. Paper presented at the Annual Meeting of the American Anthropological Association, Washington, D.C.

Irvine, Judith T. (1974). Strategies of status manipulation in the Wolof greeting. In Richard Bauman and Joel Sherzer (eds.), *Explorations in the ethnography of speaking,* pp. 167–91. Cambridge: Cambridge University Press.

Jacobs, Melville (1959). *The content and style of an oral literature.* Chicago: University of Chicago Press.

——— (1960). Humor and social structure in an oral literature. In Stanley Diamond (ed.), *Culture in history: essays in honor of Paul Radin,* pp. 180–89. New York: Columbia University Press.

Jakobson, Roman (1957). *Shifters, verbal categories, and the Russian verb.* Cambridge, Mass.: Harvard University Russian Language Project.

——— (1960). Closing statement: linguistics and poetics. In Thomas A. Sebeok (ed.), *Style in language,* pp. 350–77. Cambridge, Mass.: M.I.T. Press.

——— (1966). Grammatical parallelism and its Russian facet. *Language* 42:398–429.

James, William (1978/1907). *Pragmatism* (reprinted, 1978). Cambridge, Mass.: Harvard University Press.

Jameson, Fredric (1972). *The prison-house of language: a critical account of structuralism and Russian formalism.* Princeton, N.J.: Princeton University Press.

——— (1981). *The political unconscious: narrative as a socially symbolic act.* Ithaca, N.Y.: Cornell University Press.

Jansen, William Hugh (1957). Classifying performance in the study of verbal folklore. In W. Edson Richard (ed.), *Studies in folklore,* pp. 110–18. Bloomington: Indiana University Press.

——— (1983). Ethics and the folklorist. In Richard M. Dorson (ed.), *Handbook of American folklore,* pp. 533–39. Bloomington: Indiana University Press.

Jaramillo, Cleofas M. (1955). *Romance of a little village girl.* San Antonio, Tex.: Naylor.

—— (1972/1941). *Shadows of the past (Sombras del pasado)*. Santa Fe, N. Mex.: Seton Village Press. Reprinted 1972: Santa Fe, N. Mex.: Ancient City Press.

Jason, Heda (1971). Proverbs in society: the problem of meaning and function. *Proverbium* 17:617–23.

—— (1975). *Studies in Jewish ethnopoetry*. Taipei: The Orient Cultural Service.

Jefferson, Gail (1972). Side sequences. In David Sudnow (ed.), *Studies in social interaction*, pp. 294–338. New York: Free Press.

—— (1974). Error correction as an interactional resource. *Language in Society* 3:181–99.

Johnson, Ragnar (1975). The semantic structure of the joke and riddle: theoretical positioning. *Semiotica* 14:142–72.

—— (1976). Two realms and a joke: bisociation theories of joking. *Semiotica* 16:195–221.

—— (1978). Jokes, theories, anthropology. *Semiotica* 22:309–34.

Johnson, Robbie David (1973). Folklore and women: a social interactional analysis of the folklore of a Texas madam. *Journal of American Folklore* 86:211–24.

—— (1977). 'Women have no sense of humor' and other myths: a consideration of female stand-up comics, 1960–1976. *American Humor* 4:11–14.

Jordan, Rosan A. (1972). Language loyalty and folklore studies: the Mexican-American. *Western Folklore* 31:77–86.

—— (1981). Tension and speech play in Mexican-American folklore. In Richard Bauman and Roger D. Abrahams (eds.), *"And other neighborly names": social process and cultural image in Texas folklore*, pp. 252–65. Austin: University of Texas Press.

Jordan, Rosan A., and Susan J. Kalčik (1985). *Women's folklore, women's culture*. Philadelphia: University of Pennsylvania Press.

Kalčik, Susan (1975). '. . . like Ann's gynecologist or the time I was almost raped': personal narratives in women's rap groups. *Journal of American Folklore* 88:3–11.

Karp, Ivan, and Martha B. Kendall (1982). Reflexivity in field work. In P. F. Secord (ed.), *Explaining social behavior: consciousness, human action, and social structure*, pp. 249–73. Beverly Hills, Calif.: Sage.

Keenan, Elinor Ochs. (1973). A sliding sense of obligatoriness: the polystructure of Malagasy oratory. *Language in Society* 2:225–43.

—— (1974). Norm-makers, norm-breakers: uses of speech by men and women in a Malagasy community. In Richard Bauman and Joel Sherzer (eds.), *Explorations in the ethnography of speaking*, pp. 125–43. Cambridge: Cambridge University Press.

Kennedy, John G. (1970). Bonds of laughter among the Tarahumara Indians: toward the rethinking of joking relationship theory. In Walter Goldschmidt and Harry Hoijer (eds.), *The social anthropology of Latin America: essays in honor of Ralph Leon Beals*, pp. 36–68. Berkeley: University of California Press.

Kenneson, Carol Reyner (1978). Through the looking-glass: a history of Anglo-American attitudes towards the Spanish-Americans and Indians of New Mexico. Ph.D. dissertation, Yale University.

Kirshenblatt-Gimblett, Barbara (1973). Toward a theory of proverb meaning. *Proverbium* 22:821–27.

—— (1974). The concept and varieties of narrative performance in East European Jewish culture. In Richard Bauman and Joel Sherzer (eds.), *Explorations in the ethnography of speaking*, pp. 283–308. Cambridge: Cambridge University Press.

—— (1975). A parable in context: a social interactional analysis of a storytelling performance. In Dan Ben-Amos and Kenneth S. Goldstein (eds.), *Folklore: performance and communication*, pp. 105–30. The Hague: Mouton.

Kirshenblatt-Gimblett, Barbara, and Joel Sherzer (1976). Introduction. In Barbara Kirshenblatt-Gimblett (ed.), *Speech play*, pp. 1–16. Philadelphia: University of Pennsylvania Press.

Kluckhohn, Florence Rockwood (1941). *Los Atarqueños: A study of pattern and configuration in a New Mexico village*. Ph.D. dissertation, Radcliffe College.

Kluckhohn, Florence R., and Fred L. Strodtbeck (1961). *Variations in value orientations.* Evanston, Ill.: Row, Peterson.

Kochman, Thomas (comp.) (1972). *Rappin' and stylin' out: communication in urban Black America.* Urbana: University of Illinois Press.

Koestler, Arthur (1964). *The act of creation.* London: Hutchinson.

Kress, Gunther (1985). Ideological structures in discourse. In Teun A. van Dijk (ed.), *Handbook of discourse analysis.* Vol. 4: *Discourse analysis in society,* pp. 27–42. London: Academic Press.

Kress, Gunther, and Robert Hodge (1979). *Language as ideology.* London: Routledge & Kegan Paul.

Krikmann, Arvo (1974a). *On the denotative indefiniteness of proverbs: remarks on proverb semantics 1.* Talinn: Academy of Sciences of the Estonian SSR.

——— (1974b). *Some additional aspects of semantic indefiniteness of proverbs.* Talinn: Academy of Sciences of the Estonian SSR.

Kroeber, Karl (ed.) (1981). *Traditional American Indian literatures: texts and interpretations.* Lincoln: University of Nebraska Press.

Kuipers, Joel C. (1984). Place, names, and authority in Weyéwa ritual speech. *Language in Society* 13:455–66.

Kussi, Matti (1969). Southwest African riddle-proverbs. *Proverbium* 12:305–11.

——— (1972). *Towards an international type-system of proverbs* (FF Communications, No. 211). Helsinki: Suomalainen Tiedeakatemia.

Kutsche, Paul, and Dennis Gallegos (1979). Community functions of the *Cofradía de Nuestro Padre Jesús Nazareno.* In Paul Kutsche (ed.), *The survival of Spanish American villages,* pp. 91–97. Colorado Springs, Colo.: Colorado College.

Kutsche, Paul, and John R. Van Ness (1982). *Cañones: Values, crisis, and survival in a Northern New Mexico village.* Albuquerque: University of New Mexico Press.

Labov, William (1972a). *Language in the inner city: studies in the Black English vernacular.* Philadelphia: University of Pennsylvania Press.

——— (1972b). Rules for ritual insults. In David Sudnow (ed.), *Studies in social interaction,* pp. 120–69. New York: Free Press.

——— (1972c). *Sociolinguistic patterns.* Philadelphia: University of Pennsylvania Press.

Labov, William, and Joshua Waletzky (1967). Narrative analysis. In June Helm (ed.), *Essays on the verbal and visual arts: Proceedings of the 1966 annual spring meeting of the American Ethnological Society,* pp. 12–44. Seattle: American Ethnological Society.

Lamadrid, Enrique (1987). "*La indita de Plácida Romero*": history, legend and performance tradition of a nineteenth century New Mexico captivity ballad. Paper presented at the Annual Meeting of the American Folklore Society, Albuquerque, N.M., 21–25 October 1987.

Lange, Yvonne (1974a). Lithography, an agent of technological change in religious folk art: a thesis. *Western Folklore* 33:51–64.

——— (1974b). The santos of New Mexico, the Man of Sorrows, and the origins of the Penitente Brotherhood. In *Europe in Colonial America,* pp. 23–24. Williamsburg: Antiques Forum.

La Sociedad Folklórica (1973). *Compendio de folklore Nuevo Méjicano.* Santa Fe: La Socieded Folklórica.

Lavandero, Padre Julio (1972). Lamento fúnebre guaraúno. *Venezuela Misionera* 34:340–47.

——— (1983). Folclore guarao. *Venezuela Misionera* 45:9–13.

Lea, Aurora Lucero-White (1936). *Old Spain in our southwest.* New York: Harcourt, Brace and Company.

——— (1953). *Literary folklore of the Hispanic southwest.* San Antonio: Naylor.

Lee, Laurence F. (1910). Los Hermanos Penitentes. B.A. thesis, University of New Mexico.

Legman, G. (1968). *Rationale of the dirty joke: an analysis of sexual humor.* New York: Grove.

——— (1975). *No laughing matter: rationale of the dirty joke.* New York: Breaking Point.

Leonard, Olen E. (1943). *The role of the land grant in the social organization and social processes of a Spanish-American village in New Mexico.* Ann Arbor, Mich.: Edwards Brothers.

Levine, Lawrence W. (1977). *Black culture and Black consciousness: Afro-American folk thought from slavery to freedom.* New York: Oxford University Press.

Levinson, Stephen C. (1983). *Pragmatics.* Cambridge: Cambridge University Press.

Lévi-Strauss, Claude (1964). *Le cru et le cruit* (Mythologiques 1). Paris: Plon.

—— (1966). *Du miel aux cendres* (Mythologiques 2). Paris: Plon.

—— (1968). *L'Origine des manières de table* (Mythologiques 3). Paris: Plon.

—— (1971). *L'Homme nu* (Mythologiques 4). Paris: Plon.

Limón, José E. (1977). Agringado joking in Texas-Mexican society: folklore and differential identity. *The New Scholar* 6:33–50.

—— (1981). The folk performance of "chicano" and the cultural limits of political ideology. In Richard Bauman and Roger D. Abrahams (eds.), *"And other neighborly names": social process and cultural image in Texas folklore,* pp. 197–225. Austin: University of Texas Press.

—— (1982). History, Chicano joking, and the varieties of higher education: tradition and performance as critical symbolic action. *Journal of the Folklore Institute* 19:141–66.

—— (1983a). Folklore, social conflict, and the United States–Mexico border. In Richard M. Dorson (ed.), *Handbook of American folklore,* pp. 216–26. Bloomington: Indiana University Press.

—— (1983b). Legendry, metafolklore, and performance: a Mexican-American example. *Western Folklore* 42:191–208.

—— (1983c). Western Marxism and folklore: a critical introduction. *Journal of American Folklore* 96:34–52.

—— (1987). Aurelio M. Espinosa's romantic view of folklore. Unpublished paper presented at the Annual Meeting of the American Folklore Society, Albuquerque, New Mexico, 21–25 October 1987.

Limón, José E., and M. J. Young (1986). Frontiers, settlements, and development in folklore studies, 1972–1985. In Bernard J. Siegel, Alan R. Beals, and Stephen A. Tyler (eds.), *Annual Review of Anthropology,* vol. 15, pp. 437–60. Palo Alto, Calif.: Annual Reviews.

Loeb, E. (1952). The function of proverbs in the intellectual development of primitive peoples. *Scientific Monthly* 74:100–104.

Lomax, Alan (1968). *Folk song style and culture.* Washington, D.C.: American Association for the Advancement of Science.

—— (1968). Special features of the sung communication. In June Helm (ed.), *Essays on the verbal and visual arts: proceedings of the 1966 annual spring meeting of the American Ethnological Society,* pp. 109–27. Seattle: American Ethnological Society.

López, George (1942). Photocopy of his handwritten cuaderno (indexed and introduced by J. D. Robb, 1960). Special Collections, University of New Mexico Library, Albuquerque.

Lord, Albert Bates (1960). *The singer of tales.* Cambridge, Mass.: Harvard University Press.

Lounsbury, Floyd G. (1956). A semantic analysis of Pawnee kinship usage. *Language* 32:158–94.

Lummis, Charles Fletcher (1893). *The land of poco tiempo* (reprinted, 1966). Albuquerque: University of New Mexico.

Lyons, John (1968). *Introduction to theoretical linguistics.* Cambridge: Cambridge University Press.

—— (1977). *Semantics* (2 vols). Cambridge: Cambridge University Press.

McCrossan, Sister Joseph Marie, I.H.M. (1948). *The role of the church and folk in the development of the early drama in New Mexico.* Philadelphia: Dolphin Press.

McDowell, John (1982). Beyond iconicity: ostension in Kamsá mythic narrative. *Journal of the Folklore Institute* 19:119–39.

—— (1983). The semiotic constitution of Kamsá ritual language. *Language in Society* 12:23–46.

—— (1985a). The poetic rites of conversation. *Journal of Folklore Research* 22:113–32.

———— (1985b). Verbal dueling. In Teun A. van Dijk (ed.), *Handbook of discourse analysi* Vol. 3: *Discourse and dialogue*, pp. 203–11. London: Academic Press.

McGhee, Paul E. (1979). *Humor: its origins and development*. San Francisco: Freeman.

McGhee, Paul E., and Antony J. Chapman (1980). Children's humor: overview and conclusions. In Paul E. McGhee and Antony J. Chapman (eds.), *Children's humor*, pp. 281–305. Chichester, Eng.: John Wiley & Sons.

McGhee, Paul E., and Jeffrey H. Goldstein (eds.) (1983). *Handbook of humor research*. New York: Springer.

McLendon, S. (1982). Meaning, rhetorical structure, and discourse organization in myth. In Deborah Tannen (ed.), *Analyzing discourse: text and talk* (Georgetown University Round Table on Languages and Linguistics, 1981). pp. 284–305. Washington, D.C.: Georgetown University Press.

Malinowski, Bronislaw (1923). The problem of meaning in primitive language: In C. K. Ogden and I. A. Richards (eds.), *The meaning of meaning*. London: Routledge and Kegan Paul.

———— (1935). *Coral gardens and their magic* (2 vols.). London: Allen and Unwin.

Manning, Frank (ed.) (1983). *The world of play* (Proceedings of the 7th Annual Meeting of The Association for the Anthropological Study of Play). West Point, N.Y.: Leisure Press.

Mares, José Fuentes (1960). *Poinsett: historia de una gran intriga* (third edition). Mexico: Libro Mex.

Martínez, Oscar J. (1978). Chicano oral history: status and prospects. *Aztlán* 9:119–31.

Martínez, Reyes (1937). Death makes a hit. Unpublished manuscript in the files of the W.P.A. New Mexico Federal Writers' Project, History Library, Museum of New Mexico, Santa Fe.

———— (1938). The padre's mine at Cañon de la Soledad. Unpublished manuscript in the files of the W.P.A. New Mexico Federal Writers' Project, History Library, Museum of New Mexico, Santa Fe.

———— (1940). *La morada de los muertos:* the lodge-house of the dead. Unpublished manuscript in the files of the W.P.A. New Mexico Federal Writers' Project, History Library, Museum of New Mexico, Santa Fe.

Marx, Karl (1867). *Capital: a critique of political economy.* Vol. 1, *The process of capitalist production.* (Samuel Moore and Edward Aveling, trans., 1967). New York: International Publishers.

———— (1939). *Grundrisse: foundations of the critique of political economy.* (Martin Nicolaus, trans., 1973). New York: Vintage Books.

Marx, Karl, and Frederick Engels (1947). *The German ideology.* (C. Dutt, W. Lough, C. P. Magill, trans.). New York: International Publishers.

Matejka, Ladislav, and Krystyna Pomorska (eds.) (1978). *Readings in Russian poetics: formalist and structuralist views* (Michigan Slavic Contributions, 8). Ann Arbor: Michigan Slavic Publications.

Matejka, Ladislav, and Irwins R. Titunik (eds.) (1976). *Semiotics of art: Prague School contributions.* Cambridge, Mass.: M.I.T. Press.

Mendoza, Vicente T. (n.d.) Estudio y clasificación de la música tradicional hispanica de Nuevo México. Unpublished manuscript on file in the Fine Arts Library, University of New Mexico, Albuquerque.

Merk, Frederick (1963). *Manifest Destiny and mission in American history: a reinterpretation.* New York: Knopf.

Messenger, John C., Jr. (1959). The role of proverbs in a Nigeria judicial system. *Southwest Journal of Anthropology* 15:64–73.

Mieder, Wolfgang (1982). *International proverb scholarship: an annotated bibliography.* New York: Garland.

Mieder, Wolfgang, and Alan Dundes (eds.) (1981). *The wisdom of many.* New York: Garland.

Miller, Elaine K. (1973). *Mexican folk narrative from the Los Angeles area* (Publications of the American Folklore Society, Memoir Series, Vol. 56). Austin: University of Texas Press.

Mills, George (1967). *People of the saints.* Colorado Springs, Colo.: Taylor Museum.

Milner, G. B. (1969). Quadripartite structures. *Proverbium* 14:379–83.

———— (1971). The quartered shield: outline of a semantic taxonomy. In Edwin Ardener (ed.), *Social anthropology and language*, pp. 243–69. London: Tavistock.

———— (1972). Homo ridens: towards a semiotic theory of humor and laughter. *Semiotica* 5:1–30.

Mintz, Sidney W., and Eric P. Wolf (1950). An analysis of ritual co-parenthood. *Southwestern Journal of Anthropology* 6:341–68.

Mitchell, Carol (1975). *The difference between male and female joke telling as exemplified in a college community.* (2 vols.) Ph.D. dissertation, Indiana University.

———— (1977). The sexual perspective in the appreciation of jokes. *Western Folklore* 26:303–29.

———— (1978). Hostility and aggression toward males in female joke telling. *Frontiers* 3:19–23.

Mitchell-Kernan, Claudia (1972). Signifying and marking: two Afro-American speech acts. In John J. Gumperz and Dell Hymes (eds.), *Directions in sociolinguistics: the ethnography of communication*, pp. 161–79. New York: Holt, Rinehart and Winston.

Moerman, Michael (1972). Analysis of Lue conversation: providing accounts, finding breaches, and taking sides. In David Sudnow (ed.) *Studies in interaction*, pp. 170–228. New York: Free Press.

———— (1988). *Talking culture: ethnography and conversation analysis.* Philadelphia: University of Pennsylvania Press.

Molho, Mauricio (1975). *Sistemática del verbo español: aspectos, modos, tiempos* (2 vols.). Madrid: Biblioteca Románica Hispánica, Editorial Gredos.

Mukařovský, Jan (1971). 'Prislovi jako soucást kontextu' (The proverb as a part of context). In *Cestami poetiky a estetiky*, pp. 277–359. Praha: Edice Dilna. (Passages translated by Paul Garvin have been published in Joyce Penfield, *Communicating with quotes: the Igbo case*, pp. 96–104. Westport, Conn.: Greenwood Press.)

———— (1977a). *The word and verbal art: selected essays by Jan Mukařovský* (John Burbank and Peter Steiner, trans. and eds.). New Haven, Conn.: Yale University Press.

———— (1977b). *Structure, sign, and function: selected essays by Jan Mukařovský* (John Burbank and Peter Steiner, trans. & eds.). New Haven, Conn.: Yale University Press.

Murphy, William Peter (1976). A semantic and logical analysis of Kpelle proverb metaphors of secrecy. Ph.D. dissertation, Stanford University.

Norrick, Neal R. (1986). A frame-theoretical analysis of verbal humor: bisociation as schema conflict. *Semiotica* 60:225–45.

O'Kane, Eleanor S. (1950). On the names of the refrán. *Hispanic Review* 18:1–14.

Okezie, Joyce Ann (1977). The role of quoting behavior as manifested in the use of proverbs in Igbo society. Ph.D. dissertation, State University of New York at Buffalo.

Ong, Walter J., S. J. (1967). *The presence of the word: some prolegomena for cultural and religious history.* Mineapolis: University of Minnesota Press.

———— (1971). *Rhetoric, romance, and technology.* Ithaca, N.Y.: Cornell University Press.

———— (1977). *Interfaces of the word.* Ithaca, N.Y.: Cornell University Press.

———— (1982a). *Orality and literacy: the technologizing of the word.* London: Methuen.

———— (1982b). Oral remembering and narrative structures. In Deborah Tannen (ed.), *Analyzing discourse: text and talk* (Georgetown University Round Table on Languages and Linguistics 1981), pp. 12–24. Washington, D.C.: Georgetown University Press.

Opland, Jeff (1983). *Xhosa oral poetry: aspects of a Black South African tradition.* Cambridge: Cambridge University Press.

Oring, Elliot (1981). *Israeli humor: the content and structure of the chizbat of the Palmah.* Albany: State University of New York.

Ornstein, Jacob (1951). The archaic and the modern in the Spanish of New Mexico. *Hispania* 34:137–42.

Ortiz, Alfonso (1969). *The Tewa world.* Chicago: University of Chicago Press.

———— (1972). Ritual drama and Pueblo world view. In Alfonso Ortiz (ed.), *New perspectives on the Pueblos*, pp. 135–62. Albuquerque: University of New Mexico Press.

Ortiz, Roxanne Dunbar (1980). *Roots of resistance: land tenure in New Mexico*. Los Angeles: Chicano Studies Research Center Publications, University of California at Los Angeles and the American Indian Studies Center.

Otero, Nina (1936). *Old Spain in our southwest*. New York: Harcourt, Brace.

Paredes, Américo (1958). *"With his pistol in his hand": a border ballad and its hero*. Austin: University of Texas Press.

———— (1961). On "gringo," "greaser," and other neighborly names. In Mody Boatright, Wilson Hudson, and Allen Maxwell (eds.), *Singers and storytellers*, pp. 285–90. Dallas: SMU Press.

———— (1966). The Anglo-American in Mexican folklore. In Ray Browne (ed.), *New voices in American studies*, pp. 113–28. Lafayette, Ind.: Purdue University Studies.

———— (1968). Folk medicine and the intercultural jest. In June Helm (ed.), *Spanish speaking people in the United States: Proceedings of the 1968 annual spring meeting of the American Ethnological Society*, pp. 104–19. Seattle: University of Washington Press.

———— (1970). Proverbs and ethnic stereotypes. *Proverbium* 15:511–13.

———— (1973). José Mosqueda and the folklorization of actual events. *Aztlán* 4:1–30.

———— (1978). On ethnographic work among minority groups: a folklorist's perspective. In R. Romo and R. Paredes (eds.), *New directions in Chicano scholarship*, pp. 1–32. La Jolla, Calif.: Chicano Studies Center, University of California, San Diego.

———— (1982). Folklore, lo Mexicano, and proverbs. *Aztlán* 13:1–11.

Paredes, Américo, and Richard Bauman (eds.) (1971). Toward new perspectives in folklore. *Journal of American Folklore* 84, no. 331.

Parker, Carolyn Ann (1974). Aspects of a theory of proverbs: contexts and messages of proverbs in Swahili. Ph.D. dissertation, University of Washington.

Parks, H. B. (1931). Buried in Texas County. In J. Frank Dobie (ed.), *Southwestern lore* (Publications of the Texas Folk-Lore Society, No. 9), pp. 133–41. Dallas: Texas Folklore Society.

Parmentier, Richard J. (1985). Diagrammatic icons and historical processes in Belau. *American Anthropologist* 87:840–52.

Parry, Milman (1930). Studies in the epic technique of oral verse-making. I: Homer and Homeric style. *Harvard Studies in Classical Philology* 41:73–147.

———— (1932). Studies in the epic technique of oral verse-making. II: The Homeric language as the language of an oral poetry. *Harvard Studies in Classical Philology* 43:1–50.

———— (1971). *The making of Homeric verse: the collected papers of Milman Parry* (Adam Parry, ed.). Oxford: Clarendon Press.

Parsons, Elsie Clews, and Ralph L. Beals (1934). The sacred clowns of the Pueblo and Mayo-Yaqui Indians. *American Anthropologist* 36:491–514.

Peffer, E. Louise (1951). *The closing of the public domain: disposal and reservation policies, 1900–1950*. Stanford, Calif.: Stanford University Press.

Peirce, Charles Sanders (1932). *Collected papers of Charles Sanders Peirce*. Vol. II, *Elements of logic* (C. Hartshorne and P. Weiss, eds.). Cambridge, Mass.: Harvard University Press.

Peñalosa, Fernando (1980). *Chicano sociolinguistics: a brief introduction*. Rowley, Mass.: Newbury House.

Penfield, Joyce (1983). *Communicating with quotes: the Igbo case*. Westport, Conn.: Greenwood Press.

Pérez, Soledad (1951). Mexican folklore from Austin, Texas. *Publications of the Texas Folklore Society* 24:71–127.

Permyakov, G. L. (1979). *From proverb to folk-tale: notes on the general theory of cliché* (Y. N. Filippov, trans.) (Studies in Oriental Folklore and Mythology, U.S.S.R. Academy of Sciences). Moscow: "Nauka" Publishing House.

Pinchot, Gifford (1947). *Breaking new ground*. New York: Harcourt, Brace and Company.

Polanyi, Karl (1957). *The great transformation*. Boston: Beacon Press.

Polanyi, Livia (1985a). Conversational storytelling. In Teun A. van Dijk (ed.), *Handbook of discourse analysis*. Vol. 3: *Discourse and dialogue*, pp. 183–201. London: Academic Press.

———— (1985b). *Telling the American story: a structural and cultural analysis of conversational storytelling*. Norwood, N.J.: Ablex.

Price, Richard (1983). *First-time: the historical vision of an Afro-American people*. Baltimore: Johns Hopkins University Press.

Río Arriba County Clerk's Office (1852–1862). *Libro de testamentos, etc.* Record Book No. 1, in the Office of the County Clerk, Río Arriba County, Tierra Amarilla, New Mexico.

Rabinow, Paul, and Sullivan, William M. (eds.) (1979). *Interpretive social science: a reader*. Berkeley: University of California Press.

Radcliffe-Brown, A. R. (1940). On joking relationships. *Africa* 13:195–210.

———— (1949). A further note on joking relationships. *Africa* 19:133–40.

Rael, Juan B. (1937). A study of the phonology and morphology of New Mexican Spanish, based on a collection of 410 folktales. Ph.D. dissertation, Stanford University.

———— (1939). Associative interference in New Mexican Spanish. *Hispania Review* 7: 324–36.

———— (1942). New Mexican Spanish feasts. *California Folklore Quarterly* 1:83–90.

———— (1951). *The New Mexican alabado* (Stanford University Publications, University Series, Language and Literature, Vol. 9, No. 3). Stanford, Calif.: Stanford University Press.

———— (n.d.). *Cuentos españoles de Colorado y de Nuevo Méjico* (2 vols.). Stanford, Calif.: Stanford University Press.

Raskin, Victor (1985). *Semantic mechanisms of humor*. Dordrecht: D. Reidel.

Ravenhill, Philip L. (1976). Religious utterances and the theory of speech acts. In William J. Samarin (ed.), *Language in religious practice*, pp. 26–39. Rowley, Mass.: Newbury House.

Ravicz, Robert (1952). Compadrinazgo. In Robert Wauchope and Manning Nash (eds.), *Handbook of Middle American Indians*, vol. 6, *Social Anthropology*, pp. 238–52. Austin: University of Texas Press.

Reichard, Gladys Amanda (1944). *Prayer: the compulsive word* (Monograph of the American Ethnological Society, No. 7). New York: J. J. Augustin.

Reina, Rubén E. (1959). Two patterns of friendship in a Guatemala community. *American Anthropologist* 61:44–50.

———— (1966). *The law of the saints: a Pokomam pueblo and its community culture*. Indianapolis, Ind.: Bobbs-Merrill.

———— (1967). Annual cycle and fiesta cycle. In Manning Nash (ed.), *Handbook of Middle American Indians*. Vol. 6, *Social anthropology*, pp. 317–32. Austin: University of Texas Press.

Rendón, Gabino (1953). *Hand on my shoulder* (recorded by Edith Agnew). New York: Board of National Missions, United Presbyterian Church in the U.S.A.

Reyna, José Reynaldo (1973). Mexican American prose narrative in Texas: the jest and anecdote. Ph.D. dissertation, University of California, Los Angeles.

———— (1978). *Raza humor: Chicano joke tradition in Texas*. San Antonio: Penca Books.

Robb, John Donald (1951). Review of *The New Mexican alabado* by Juan B. Rael. *New Mexico Historical Review* 26:250–55.

———— (1950–51). The sources of a New Mexico folksong. *New Mexico Folklore Record* 5:9–16.

———— (1954). *Hispanic folk songs of New Mexico*. Albuquerque: University of New Mexico Press.

———— (1980). *Hispanic folk music of New Mexico and the southwest: a self-portrait of a people*. Norman: University of Oklahoma Press.

Robe, Stanley L. (1977). *Hispanic folktales from New Mexico: narratives from the R. D. Jameson Collection* (Folklore Studies, 30). Berkeley: University of California Press.

———— (1980). *Hispanic legends from New Mexico: narratives from the R. D. Jameson Collection* (Folklore and Mythology Studies. Vol. 31). Berkeley: University of California Press.

Roberts, Paul H. (1963). *Hoof prints on the forest ranges: the early years of national forest range administration.* San Antonio, Tex.: Naylor.

Rodríguez, Sylvia (1987). Land, water, and ethnic identity in Taos. In Charles L. Briggs and John R. Van Ness (eds.). *Land, water, and culture: new perspectives on Hispanic land grants,* pp. 313–403. Albuquerque: University of New Mexico Press.

Romano-V., Octavio Ignacio (1968a). Social science, objectivity, and the Chicanos. In Octavio Ignacio Romano-V. (ed.), *Voices: readings from El Grito: a journal of contemporary Mexican American thought, 1967–1973,* pp. 30–42. Berkeley, Cal.: Quinto Sol.

———— (1968b). The anthropology and sociology of the Mexican-Americans: the distortion of Mexican-American history. *El Grito* 2:13–26.

Romero, Mary (1980). Transformation of culture through appropriation. Ph.D. dissertation, University of Colorado, Boulder.

———— (1983). *Los ancianos* speak about the transformation of land ownership and usage in northern New Mexico. Paper presented at the annual meeting of the Western Social Science Association, Albuquerque, New Mexico, 28 April–1 May, 1983.

Rosaldo, Michele (1973). I have nothing to hide: the language of Ilongot oratory. *Language in Society* 2:193–223.

Rosaldo, Renato (1980). *Ilongot headhunting 1883–1974: a study in society and history.* Stanford, Calif.: Stanford University Press.

———— (1985). Chicano studies, 1970–1984. In *Annual Review of Anthropology* 14:405–427.

Rosenbaum, Robert J. (1981). *Mexicano resistance in the southwest: the sacred right of self-preservation.* Austin: University of Texas Press.

Rosenbaum, Robert J., and Robert W. Larson (1987). Mexicano resistance to the expropriation of grant lands in New Mexico. In Charles L. Briggs and John R. Van Ness (eds.), *Land, water, and culture: new perspectives on Hispanic land grants,* pp. 269–310. Albuquerque: University of New Mexico Press.

Rothenberg, Jerome (1969). Total translation: an experiment in the presentation of American Indian poetry. *Stony Brook* 3/4:292–301.

Ruby, Jay (1980). Exposing yourself: reflexivity, film, and anthropology. *Semiotica* 30(1–2): 153–79.

———— (ed.) (1982). *A crack in the mirror: reflective perspectives in anthropology.* Philadelphia: University of Pennsylvania Press.

Russell, Louise (1977). Legendary narratives inherited by children of Mexican-American ancestry: cultural pluralism and the persistence of tradition. Ph.D. dissertation, Indiana University.

Sacks, Harvey (1967). Unpublished lecture notes. University of California, Irvine.

———— (1973). On some puns: with some intimations. In Roger W. Shuy (ed.), *Sociolinguistics: current trends and prospects* (Monograph Series on Language and Linguistics), pp. 135–44. Washington, D.C.: Georgetown University Press.

———— (1974). An analysis of the course of a joke's telling in conversation. In Richard Bauman and Joel Sherzer (eds.), *Explorations in the ethnography of speaking,* pp. 337–53. Cambridge: Cambridge University Press.

———— (1978). Some technical considerations of a dirty joke. In Jim Schenkein (ed.), *Studies in the organization of conversational interaction,* pp. 249–69. New York: Academic Press.

Sacks, Harvey, Emanuel A. Schegloff and Gail Jefferson (1974). A simplest systematics for the organization of turn-taking for conversation. *Language* 50:696–735.

Sahlins, Marshall (1976). *Culture and practical reason.* Chicago: University of Chicago Press.

———— (1982). *Historical metaphors and mythical realities: structure in the early history of the Sandwich Islands Kingdom.* Ann Arbor: University of Michigan Press.

———— (1985). *Islands of history.* Chicago: University of Chicago Press.

Salpointe, Most Rev. J. B., D.D. (1898). *Soldiers of the cross: notes on the ecclesiastical history of New Mexico, Arizona and Colorado.* Banning, Calif.: St. Boniface's Industrial School.

Samarin, William J. (1976). The language of religion. In William J. Samarin (ed.), *Language in religious practice,* pp. 3–13. Rowley, Mass.: Newbury House.

Sanches, Mary, and Barbara Kirshenblatt-Gimblett (1976). Child language and children's speech play. In Barbara Kirshenblatt-Gimblett (ed.), *Speech play*, pp. 65–110. Philadelphia: University of Pennsylvania Press.

Sapir, Edward (1921). *Language: an introduction to the study of speech.* (reprinted, 1949) New York: Harcourt, Brace and World.

—— (1949). *Selected writings of Edward Sapir in language, culture, and personality* (David G. Mandelbaum, ed.). Berkeley, Calif.: University of California Press.

Saussure, Ferdinand de (1959/1916). *Course in general linguistics* (Charles Bally and Albert Sechehaye, eds.; Wade Baskin, trans.) New York: McGraw-Hill Book Company.

Sbarbi, José María (1891). *Monografía sobre los refranes, adagios y proverbios castellanos.* Madrid: Huérfanos.

Schegloff, Emanuel A. (1968). Sequencing in conversational openings. *American Anthropologist* 70:1075–95.

—— (1972). Notes on a conversational practice: formulating place. In David Sudnow (ed.), *Studies in social interaction*, pp. 75–119. New York: Free Press.

—— (1982). Discourse as an interactional achievement: some uses of 'uh huh' and other things that come between sentences. In Deborah Tannen (ed.), *Analyzing discourse: text and talk* (Georgetown University Round Table on Languages and Linguistics, 1981), pp. 71–93. Washington, D.C.: Georgetown University Press.

Schegloff, Emanuel A., and Harvey Sacks (1973). Opening up closings. *Semiotica* 8:289–327.

Schenkein, James N. (1972). Towards an analysis of natural conversation and the sense of *heheh. Semiotica* 6:344–77.

Scheub, Harold (1971). Translation of African oral narrative-performances to the written word. *Yearbook of Comparative and General Literature* 20:28–36.

—— (1972). Body and image in oral narrative performance. *New Literary History* 8:345–67.

—— (1975). *The Xhosa Ntsomi.* New York: Oxford University Press.

Schiffrin, Deborah (1981). Tense variation in narrative. *Language* 57:45–62.

—— (1985). Everyday argument: the organization of diversity in talk. In Teun A. van Dijk (ed.), *Handbook of discourse analysis.* Vol. 3: *Discourse and dialogue*, pp. 35–46. London: Academic Press.

Schutz, Alfred (1967). *The phenomenology of the social world* (George Walsh and Frederick Lehnert, trans.). Evanston, Ill.: Northwestern University Press.

Schwartzman, Helen B. (1976). The anthropological study of children's play. *Annual Review of Anthropology* 5:289–328.

—— (ed.) (1980). *Play and culture* (Proceedings of the 4th Annual Meeting of The Association for the Anthropological Study of Play). West Point, N.Y.: Leisure Press.

Searle, John R. (1969). *Speech acts: an essay in the philosophy of language.* Cambridge: Cambridge University Press.

Segal, Dmitri (1976). Folklore text and social context. *PTL: A Journal of Descriptive Poetics and Theory of Literature* 1:367–82.

Seitel, Peter I. (1969). Proverbs: a social use of metaphor. *Genre* 2:143–61.

—— (1972). Proverbs and the structure of metaphor among the Haya of Tanzania. Ph.D. dissertation, University of Pennsylvania.

—— (1977). Saying Haya sayings: two categories of proverb use. In J. David Sapir and J. Christopher Crocker (eds.), *The social use of metaphor: essays on the anthropology of rhetoric*, pp. 75–99. Philadelphia: University of Pennsylvania Press.

—— (1980). *See so that we may see: performances and interpretations of traditional tales from Tanzania.* Bloomington: University of Indiana Press.

SG (Surveyor General) File No. 227, Spanish and Mexican land grants in New Mexico, in the New Mexico State Records Center and Archives, Santa Fe.

Shalkop, Robert L. (1969). *Arroyo Hondo: the folk art of a New Mexican village.* Colorado Springs, Colo.: Taylor Museum.

Sherzer, Joel (1976). Play languages: with a note on ritual languages. In *Exceptional languages and linguistics*, pp. 175–99. New York: Academic Press.

———— (1978). "Oh! That's a pun and I didn't mean it." *Semiotica* 22:335–50.

———— (1982). The interplay of structure and function in Kuna narrative, or: how to grab a snake in the Darien. In Deborah Tannen (ed.), *Analyzing discourse: text and talk* (Georgetown University Round Table on Language and Linguistics 1981, pp. 306–220). Washington, D.C.: Georgetown University Press.

———— (1983). *Kuna ways of speaking: an ethnographic perspective.* Austin: University of Texas Press.

———— (1985). Puns and jokes. In Teun A. van Dijk (ed.), *Handbook of discourse analysis.* Vol. 3: *Discourse and dialogue*, pp. 213–21. London: Academic Press.

Siegel, Bernard J. (1959). Some structure implications for change in Pueblo and Spanish New Mexico. In Verne F. Ray (ed.), *Intermediate societies, social mobility, and communication* (Proceedings of the 1959 Annual Spring Meeting of the American Ethnological Society, pp. 37–44. Seattle: American Ethnological Society.

Silva-Corvalán, Carmen (1983). Tense and aspect in oral Spanish narrative: context and meaning. *Language* 59:760–80.

———— (1984). A speech event analysis of tense and aspect in Spanish. In Phillip Baldi (ed.), *Papers from the XIIth linguistic symposium on Romance languages*, pp. 229–51. Amsterdam: John Benjamins.

Silverstein, Michael (1976). Shifters, linguistic categories, and cultural description. In Keith Basso and Henry A. Selby (eds.), *Meaning in anthropology*, pp. 11–55. Albuquerque: University of New Mexico Press.

———— (1979). Language structure and linguistic ideology. In Paul R. Clyne, William Hanks, and Carol L. Hofbauer (eds.), *The elements: a parasession on linguistic units and levels*, pp. 193–247. Chicago: Chicago Linguistic Society.

———— (1981a). *The limits of awareness* (Sociolinguistic Working Paper 84). Austin, Texas: Southwest Educational Development Laboratory.

———— (1981b). Metaforces of power in traditional oratory. Unpublished manuscript.

———— (1985). The culture of language in Chinookan narrative texts; or, on saying that . . . in Chinook. In Johanna Nichols and Anthony Woodbury (eds.), *Grammar inside and outside the clause*, pp. 132–71. Cambridge: Cambridge University Press.

———— (1986). The diachrony of Sapir's synchronic linguistic description; or, Sapir's 'cosmographical' linguistics. In William Cowan, Michael K. Foster, and Konrad Koerner (eds.), *New perspectives on Edward Sapir in language, culture, and personality*, pp. 67–106. Amsterdam: John Benjamins.

———— (in press). Metapragmatics and metapragmatic function. In John A. Lucy (ed.), *Reflexive language: reported speech and metapragmatics.* Cambridge: Cambridge University Press.

Simmons, Marc (1969). Settlement patterns and village plans in colonial New Mexico. *Journal of the West* 8:7–21.

Singer, Milton (1984). *Man's glassy essence: toward a semiotic anthropology.* Bloomington: Indiana University Press.

Soil Conservation Service, U.S. Department of Agriculture (1937). *Village livelihood in the Upper Rio Grande area and a note on the level of village livelihood in the Upper Rio Grande area* (Regional Bulletin No. 44, Conservation Economics Series No. 17). Albuquerque, N. Mex.: Soil Conservation Service.

Spanish Archives of New Mexico. Unpublished documents. Vol. I, Wills and land transfers, nos. 211, 1041. State Records Center and Archives, Santa Fe, New Mexico.

Spradley, James P., and Brenda J. Mann (1975). The joking relationship. In *The cocktail waitress: woman's work in a man's world*, pp. 87–100. New York: John Wiley & Sons.

Stanislawski, Dan (1947). Early Spanish town planning in the New World. *Georgraphical Review* 37(1):94–105.

Steele, Thomas J., S.J. (1974). *Santos and saints: essays and handbook*. Albuquerque: Calvin Horn.

——— (1978). The Spanish passion play in New Mexico and Colorado. *New Mexico Historical Review* 53:239–59.

Steele, Thomas J., and Rowena Rivera (1985). *Penitente self-government: Brotherhoods and councils, 1797–1947*. Santa Fe, N. Mex.: Ancient City Press.

Steen, Harold K. (1976). *The U.S. Forest Service: a history*. Seattle: University of Washington Press.

Stevens, P., Jr. (1978). Bachama joking categories: toward new perspectives in the study of joking relationships. *Journal of Anthropological Research* 34:47–69.

Suárez, María Matilde (1968). *Los Warao: indígenas del delta del Orinoco*. Caracas: Instituto Venezolano de Investigaciones Científicas.

Sudnow, David (ed.) (1972). *Studies in social interaction*. New York: Free Press.

Sutton-Smith, Brian (1983). Play theory and cruel play of the nineteenth century. In Frank Manning (ed.), *The world of play* (Proceedings of the 7th Annual Meeting of The Association for the Anthropological Study of Play). West Point, New York: Leisure Press.

Swadesh, Francis Leon (1974). *Los primeros pobladores: Hispanic Americans of the Ute frontier*. Notre Dame: University of Notre Dame Press.

Tambiah, S. J. (1968). The magical power of words. *Man* ns. 3. 3:175–208.

——— (1976). *World conquerer and world renouncer*. Cambridge: Cambridge University Press.

Tannen, Deborah (ed.) (1982). *Spoken and written language: exploring orality and literacy* (Advances in Discourse Processes, Vol. IX). Norwood, N.J.: Ablex.

Taussig, Michael T. (1980). *The devil and commodity fetishism in South America*. Chapel Hill: University of North Carolina Press.

Taylor, Archer (1931). *The proverb*. Cambridge, Mass.: Harvard University Press.

——— (1967). The collection and study of proverbs. *Proverbium* 8:161–76.

Tedlock, Dennis (1972a). *Finding the center: narrative poetry of the Zuni Indians*. Lincoln: University of Nebraska Press.

——— (1972b). On the translation of style in oral narrative. In Américo Paredes and Richard Bauman (eds.), *Toward new perspectives in folklore*, pp. 114–33. Austin: University of Texas Press.

——— (1975). Learning to listen: oral history as poetry. In Ronald J. Grele (ed.), *Envelopes of sound: six practitioners discuss the method, theory, and practice of oral history and oral testimony*, pp. 106–25. Chicago: Precedent.

——— (1976). From prayer to reprimand. In William Samarin (ed.), *Language in religious practice*. Rowley, Mass.: Newbury House.

——— (1979). The analogic tradition and the emergence of a dialogical anthropology. *Journal of Anthropological Research* 35:387–400.

——— (1983). *The spoken word and the work of interpretation*. Philadelphia: University of Pennsylvania Press.

Toelken, Barre (1979). *The dynamics of folklore*. Boston: Houghton Mifflin.

Tolman, Ruth B. (1961). Treasure tales of the caballeros. *Western Folklore* 20:153–74.

Turner, Edith and Victor (1978). *Image and pilgrimage in Christian culture*. New York: Columbia University Press.

Turner, Victor W. (1967). *The forest of symbols: aspects of Ndembu ritual*. Ithaca, N.Y.: Cornell University Press.

——— (1969). *The ritual process: structure and anti-structure*. London: Routledge and Kegan Paul.

——— (1974). *Dramas, fields, and metaphors*. Ithaca, N.Y.: Cornell University Press.

Urban, Greg (1981). Agent- and patient-centricity in myth. *Journal of American Folklore* 94:322–44.

——— (1984). Speech about speech in speech about action. *Journal of American Folklore* 97:310–28.

———— (1986a). Ceremonial dialogues in native South America. *American Anthropologist* 88:371–86.

———— (1986b). Semiotic functions of macro-parallelism in the Shokleng origin myth. In Greg Urban and Joel Sherzer (eds.), *Native South American discourse*, pp. 15–57. Berlin: de Gruyter.

———— (in press). How to do things with words within words. In John A. Lucy (ed.), *Reflexive language: reported speech and metapragmatics.* Cambridge: Cambridge University Press.

Vaca, N. C. (1970a). The Mexican-American in the social sciences, 1912–1970. Part I: 1912–1935. *El Grito* 3:3–24.

———— (1970b). The Mexican-American in the social sciences, 1912–1970. Part II: 1936–1970. *El Grito* 4:17–51.

van Dijk, Teun A. (1985). Introduction: the role of discourse analysis in society. In Teun A. van Dijk (ed.), *Handbook of discourse analysis*. Vol. 4: *Discourse analysis in society*, pp. 1–8. London: Academic Press.

Van Gennep, Arnold (1960/1909). *The rites of passage*. (Minika B. Vizeda and Gabrielle L. Caffee, trans.) Chicago: University of Chicago Press.

Van Ness, John R. (1979a). Community and multicommunity in Hispano northern New Mexico. In Paul Kutsche (ed.), *The survival of Spanish American villages*, pp. 21–44. Colorado Springs, Colo.: Colorado College.

———— (1979b). Hispanos in northern New Mexico: the development of corporate community and multicommunity. Ph.D. dissertation, University of Pennsylvania.

———— (1987a). Hispanic land grants: ecology and subsistence in the uplands of northern New Mexico and southern Colorado. In Charles L. Briggs and John R. Van Ness (eds.), *Land, water, and culture: new perspectives on Hispanic land grants*, pp. 141–214. Albuquerque: University of New Mexico Press.

———— (1987b). *Hispanos: ethnic identity in Cañones*. Working Paper Series, No. 20. Stanford, Calif.: Stanford Center for Chicano Research.

Van Ness, John R., and Christine Van Ness (eds.) (1980). *Spanish and Mexican land grants in New Mexico and Colorado*. Manhattan, Kan.: Sunflower University Press.

Vansina, Jan (1965). *Oral tradition: a study in historical methodology* (H. M. Wright, trans.). Chicago: Aldine.

———— (1985). *Oral tradition as history*. Madison: University of Wisconsin Press.

Vincent, María (1966). Ritual kinship in an urban setting: Martíneztown, New Mexico. M.A. thesis, University of New Mexico.

Vološinov, V. N. (1973/1930). *Marxism and the philosophy of language* (Ladislav Matejka and I. R. Titunik, trans.). New York: Seminar Press.

Wachtel, Nathan (1977). *The vision of the vanquished: the Spanish Conquest of Peru through Indian eyes, 1530–1570*. New York: Barnes and Noble.

Walker, Randi Jones (1983). Protestantism in the Sangre de Cristos: factors in the growth and decline of the Hispanic Protestant churches in Northern New Mexico and Southern Colorado, 1850–1920. Ph.D. dissertation, Claremont Graduate School.

Wallace, Stephen (1982). Figure and ground: the interrelations of linguistic categories. In Paul Hopper (ed.), *Tense-aspect: between semantics and pragmatics*, pp. 201–23. Amsterdam: John Benjamins.

Wallrich, William (1950). Auxiliadoras de la Morada. *Southwestern Lore* 16:4–10.

Watzlawick, Paul, Janet Helmick Beavin, and Don D. Jackson (1968). *Pragmatics of human communication: study of interactional patterning, pathologies, and paradoxes*. London: Faber and Faber.

Weber, Max (1958). *The Protestant ethic and the spirit of capitalism*. (Talcott Parsons, trans.) New York: Charles Scribner's Sons.

Weigle, Marta (1976). *Brothers of light, Brothers of blood: the Penitentes of the southwest*. Albuquerque: University of New Mexico Press.

———— (1978). Women as verbal artists: reclaiming the sisters of Enheduanna. *Frontiers* 3:1–9.

———— (1981). The Penitente Brotherhood in Southwestern fiction: notes on folklife and literature. In Sam B. Girgus (ed.), *The American self: myth, ideology, and popular culture.* Albuquerque: University of New Mexico Press.

———— (1982). *Spiders and spinsters: women and mythology.* Albuquerque: University of New Mexico Press.

———— (1983). The Southwest: a regional case study. In Richard M. Dorson (ed.), *Handbook of American folklore,* pp. 194–200. Bloomington: Indiana University Press.

Weigle, Marta, and Thomas R. Lyons (1982). Brothers and neighbors: the celebration of community in Penitente villages. In Victor Turner (ed.), *Celebration: studies in festivity and ritual.* pp. 231–51. Washington: Smithsonian Institution Press.

Weinstein, Sharon (1974). Don't women have a sense of comedy that can call their own? *American Humor* 1:9–12.

Wentworth, Edward Norris (1948). *America's sheep trails.* Ames: Iowa State College.

Westphall, Victor (1983). *Mercedes reales: Hispanic land grants of the Upper Rio Grande Region.* Albuquerque: University of New Mexico Press.

Whorf, Benjamin Lee (1956). *Language, thought, and reality: selected writings of Benjamin Lee Whorf.* (John B. Carroll, ed.) Cambridge, Mass.: M.I.T. Press.

Wilbert, Johannes (1972). Tobacco and shamanistic ecstasy among the Warao Indians. In Peter T. Furst (ed.), *Flesh of the gods,* pp. 55–83. New York: Praeger.

———— (1987). *Tobacco and shamanism in South America.* New Haven, Conn.: Yale University Press.

Wilder, Mitchell A., with Edgar Breitenbach (1943). *Santos: the religious folk art of New Mexico.* Colorado Springs, Colo.: Taylor Museum.

Wilgus, D. K. (1983). Collecting musical folklore and folksong. In Richard M. Dorson (ed.), *Handbook of American folklore,* pp. 369–75. Bloomington: Indiana University Press.

Williams, Raymond (1973). *The country and the city.* New York: Oxford University Press.

———— (1977). *Marxism and literature.* Oxford: Oxford University Press.

Wolfson, Nessa (1976). Speech events and natural speech: some implications for sociolinguistic methodology. *Language in Society* 5:189–209.

Wolfenstein, Martha (1954). *Children's humor: a psychological analysis.* Glendale: Free Press.

Woodbury, Anthony (1985). The functions of rhetorical structure: a study of Central Alaskan Yupic Eskimo discourse. *Language in Society* 14:153–90.

Woodward, Dorothy (1974/1935). *The Penitentes of New Mexico.* New York: Arno.

Wroth, William (ed.) (1977). *Hispanic crafts of the southwest.* Colorado Springs, Colo.: Taylor Museum of the Colorado Springs Fine Arts Center.

———— (1979). *The chapel of Our Lady of Talpa.* Colorado Springs, Colo.: Taylor Museum of the Colorado Springs Fine Arts Center.

———— (1982). *Christian images in Hispanic New Mexico.* Colorado Springs, Colo.: Taylor Museum of the Colorado Springs Fine Arts Center.

Yanga, Tshimpaka (1977). Inside the proverbs: a sociolinguistic approach. *African Languages/ Langues Africaines* 3:130–57.

Yankah, Kwesi (1985). The proverb in the context of Akan rhetoric. Ph.D. dissertation, Indiana University.

———— (1986). Proverb rhetoric and African judicial processes: the untold story. *Journal of American Folklore* 99:280–303.

Yoder, Don (ed.) (1974). Folk religion: a symposium. *Western Folklore* 33 (no. 1) (special issue).

Young, Katherine Galloway (1983). Taleworlds and storyrealms: the phenomenology of narratives. Ph.D. dissertation, University of Pennsylvania.

———— (1985). The notion of context. *Western Folklore* 44:115–22.

———— (1987). *Taleworlds and storyrealms: the phenomenology of narrative.* Dordrecht: Martinus Nijhoff.

Zenner, Walter P. (1970). Joking and ethnic stereotyping. *Anthropological Quarterly* 43: 93–113.

Zijderveld, Anton C. (1968). Jokes and their relation to social reality. *Social Research* 35: 286–311.

Zolkovskij, A. K. (1978). At the intersection of linguistics, paremiology and poetics: on the literary structure of proverbs. *Poetics* 7: 309–32.

INDEX

■■■

Abrahams, Roger D., 8, 11, 12, 15, 21, 102, 103, 121, 132, 172, 173, 218, 221, 222, 230, 352
Action setting, of jokes, 225, 228
Address, by *rezador* in tenebrae services, 298, 304, 335, 336
Affect, and alabados, 315–16; and gesture, 251; and reported speech, 250; and hymns and prayers, 300, 323, 327, 328
Afro-Americans, 98, 172, 186
Age, 83, 118–89, 126, 148, 280; and background knowledge, 87–91; and gender, 201; and jokes, 172, 220, 230, 231–32; and performance, 8, 23, 49, 59, 60, 64
Agriculture, 34, 37; and collective labor, 30–31, 38; and hegemony, 364–67; displacement of, 75, 85 ln.22–33; 87 ln.67–78, 360; and ecological diversity, 120; and historical discourse, 63–64, 87; and religiosity, 43, 151, 161; and self-sufficiency, 87 ln.71–78; as triplex sign, 80, 92
Agringado 'Gringoized', 215–16, 220
Alabados 'hymns', 20, 22, 24, 43, 52, 63, 289–339, 386 n.1; basic types of, 290–92; compared with pedagogical discourse, 161; contextualization of, 332, 334–36, 339; defined, 290; and dialogism, 355–56; dyadic patterns in, 355–56; musical style of, 290; and the textual-contextual continuum, 224, 351–52; transcription of, 57, 305; in wakes, 43; as written texts, 333, 334. *See also* Prayers
Alabanzas 'hymns of praise', defined, 290; musical style, 290–91; and pedagogical discourse, 161; in wakes, 43, 52, 289
Anaphoric relations, in jokes, 227–28
Anecdotes, 171, 193, 220; definition of, 180; humorous, 192, 198, 223

Anglo-Americans, 350, 363; and hegemony, 362, 368; at Holy Week rituals, 304, 335; as seen by Mexicanos, 374; and *agringados*, 215–16, 220; prejudice towards Mexicans, 146, 147–48, 172, 286; stereotypes of, 127, 147–48; views of the Brotherhood, 292
Antes 'bygone days', 34–36; as communicative frame, 65, 72, 73, 80, 83, 86, 92; defined, 72, 73
Anthropology, 99, 375
Apaches, 42, 178, 235, 246
Apostles' Creed, 290, 298, 302, 306, 313, 333
Appaduri, Arjun, 97
Apte, Mahadev L., 172, 180
Aragón, José Rafael, 39, 42, 294, 319, 385 n.21
Aranda, Charles, 119, 121
Archaic elements, of culture, 361, 367, 371, 372
Arewa, E. Ojo, 102, 103, 132, 377 n.3
Arora, Shirley L., 102
Artificial context, 53
Asymmetry, social, 86, 172, 286
Audience, 8, 16, 19, 63, 97, 121, 124, 248; communicative competence of, 96–97, 129–32, 135, 216, 336, 347; versus performer, 93, 201–02; and historical discourse, 61, 62, 63, 64–65, 81, 82; and legends, 233; and length of performance, 203, 212; and methodology, 55, 56; and proverbs, 104, 121, 124, 128–32; roles within, 97, 123–24; and scriptural allusions, 157; and treasure tales, 285, 287, 288. *See also* Contextualization
Austin, J. L., 8, 14, 283, 316, 337
Authenticity, 8–9, 285
Authority, and performance, 8–9, 63; and quotatives, 273; of proverbs, 118, 122, 124–25; of scriptural allusions, 148–48
Ave María. See Hail Mary

Babcock, Barbara, 102, 221
Back-channel cues, 16, 53, 56, 332, 354; in his
torical discourse, 63, 81, 86, 96–97; in
legends, 272, 284, 285, 287, 344, 345; in
proverbs, 124, 130–32; in scriptural allusions,
170. *See also* Contextualization
Background information, in collective recollections, 87–91; and communicative competence, 363; genealogy as, 57, 63, 107, 129,
179; in jokes, 180; in legends, 345–46; in
proverbs, 104, 128–30; stratification of, 19;
and tense/aspect, 276–77; and topical progression, 94–96; in treasure tales, 287. *See also*
Contextualization
Bakhtin, M. M., 168, 172, 202, 222, 248, 275,
288, 349, 350, 354–55, 375
Basso, Ellen B., 8, 10, 15, 275, 317, 327
Basso, Keith H., 11, 15, 38, 171, 173, 221, 248
Batchen, Lou Sage, 371, 383 n.6
Bateson, Gregory, 9, 14
Bauman, Richard, 8–9, 10, 11, 15, 17, 21, 54,
172, 173, 180–81, 199, 200, 222, 226, 251,
275, 286
Belief, and treasure tales, 277–84, 287
Ben-Amos, Dan, 7, 8, 11, 13, 15, 102, 128, 172
Bilingualism, 45–46, 369, 382 n.18; and ethnic
identity, 220. *See also* Code switching
Bird, Charles, 132
Body position, 56, 97, 351
Bourdieu, Pierre, 366
Bowen J. Donald, 46
Boyd, E., 324, 385 n.21
Brandes, Stanley H., 381 n.10
Breath, 307, 312, 332
Bright, William, 10, 15
Brotherhood of Our Father Jesus the Nazarene.
See Confraternity of Our Father Jesus the
Nazarene
Brown, Lorin W., 60, 120, 184, 185, 246, 271,
290, 291, 301, 321, 326, 329, 381 n.11,
383 n.6, 385 n.22
Brukman, Jan, 16
Buckley, Thomas, 317
Buried treasure, legends of, 23, 252–84. *See also*
Legends; Treasure tales
Burke, Kenneth, 11, 102, 172
Burns, Alan F., 16, 131

Cacahuate, Don 'Sir Peanut' (character), 202,
215–17, 218, 219–20, 226, 230
El Calvario 'Calvary', 297, 320
Campa, Arthur L., 3, 383 n.6
Cancian, Frank, 291

Caridad 'charity', 34, 36, 149, 273
Catechisms, 156, 161, 181, 313, 317
Catholicism, vis-à-vis Pentecostalism, 113–15,
120; vis-à-vis Protestantism, 182–86
Catron, Thomas Benton, 36
Cattle, 75, 151, 153 ln.4. *See also* Grazing;
Livestock
Cebolla, Doña 'Lady Onion' (character), 202,
215–17, 218, 219–20
Chamisal, New Mexico, 52
Chapel. *See* San Antonio de Padua del Pueblo
Quemado Chapel
Chevalier, Jacques M., 372
Chicanos, and humor, 172. *See also* Mexicanos
Chimayó, New Mexico, 31, 45, 296, 297, 313,
314
Chistes. See Anecdotes; Humorous tales; Jokes;
Jests
Chomsky, Noam, 6, 358, 359
Chronotypes, 248
Churchill, Lindsey, 200, 231
Cicourel, Aaron V., 11, 16, 19, 200
Class, social. *See* social class
Clifford, James, 370
Closing formulae, 9, 213
Cobos, Rubén, 119, 121
Code switching, 304, 382 n.18; and audience,
148; in Holy Week rituals, 335, 336; in jokes,
199, 216; in proverbs, 119, 127; and transcrip-
tion, 56. *See also* Bilingualism
Cohen, David William, 98
Coherence, 17, 173, 227, 229
Cohesion, and *'izque*, 213; in jokes, 199–200,
217, 227; in pedagogical discourse, 92–96; in
proverbs, 122; in scriptural allusions, 158,
168; and tying phrases, 105–06
Collective labor, 271, 369
Collective recollections, 64–82; defined, 64; vis-
à-vis pedagogical discourse, 91; problems in
identifying, 17
Comanches, 42, 178, 235, 246
Commercialization, 34, 36–39, 75, 77, 158,
281, 350–51, 359–60, 361–62; and hegemony, 366; and religious values, 94
Common lands, 31, 39; loss of, 350–51,
359–60, 361–62
Communicative competence, 6–7, 52; as assessed during performance, 130–32; and
dynamism of tradition, 99; and ethnic identity,
46; of fieldworker, 124, 126, 216, 229; and
hymns and prayers, 311, 313, 336, 356; and
jokes, 179–80, 220, 231; pan-generic features
of, 353; and the past/present dialectic, 216;

political dimensions of, 368; and proverbs, 104, 106, 121, 126, 128–30; scriptural allusions, 159; and *el sentido*, 2–4, 12, 18, 21–22, 82–83, 93, 123, 128–30, 151, 357; and social status, 60, 130; and stereotypes, 179, 250; and textual-contextual continuum, 21, 357; and topical progression, 94–96. *See also* Linguistic competence

Communicative resources, 19, 20

Competence. *See* Communicative competence; Linguistic competence

Competitive performances, 59, 231

Composition in performance, 6, 332, 351

Comrie, Bernard, 73

Confraternity of Our Father Jesus the Nazarene, 43–45; 292–93, 293–304 passim, 313, 321, 322, 324, 330–31, 333; Anglo-American reactions to, 292, 293, 385 n.24; election of officers, 292–93; initiation, 293; role in cultural survival, 333; role of secrecy, 293, 385 n.24. *See also* Alabados; Holy Week Rituals; Prayers

Context, 11; as contextualization, 14–16; problems in defining, 12–17, 54–55, 103, 104, 132; versus text, 14–15, 103, 104. *See also* Textual-contextual continuum

Contextual approach, in folkloristics, 11, 372

Contextual sphere, dialectical relationship with textual sphere, 21, 159; of legends, 233; proverb performances, 102–03, 132, 133

Contextualization, 359; and back-channel cues, 124; and background information, 91; of collective recollections, 87–91; defined, 14–15; of hymns and prayers, 332, 334–36, 339, 356; of jokes, 173, 180, 203, 212, 220, 223, 232; of legends, 250, 272, 275, 344; of legends versus proverbs, 345–46; and methodology, 54; of pedagogical discourse, 82–83, 96–97, 274, 277; of proverbs, 2, 105–06, 120, 122–24, 128, 130–32, 342–43, 347; role of triplex signs, 81, 86–91; of scriptural allusions, 159, 169–70; and topical progression, 274, 277; of treasure tales, 287. *See also* Textual sphere; Textual-contextual continuum

Contextualization cues, 14–15, 20, 128; and audience comprehension, 96–97; in legends, 347; in proverbs, 130–32, 343; variation in the range of, 344–47, 348

Cook-Gumperz, Jenny, 14–15, 130

Córdova, 30–39, 60, 259, 270, 291, 296, 299, 319, 335, 360, 377 n.2, 378 n.8, 383 n.6; archbishop visits, 60, 300; author's involvement in, 47–52; and Catholic Church, 42; early history

of, 30–31, 377 n.2; economic transformation of, 36–39; loss of grant lands, 36–39; and New Mexican Spanish, 46; plaza of, 28 pl.2, 29 pl.3, 31, 33 pl.5, 77, 79 pl.13, 113 ln.3; and warfare in bygone days, 30, 31, 247–48. *See also* Pedro Córdova; San Antonio de Padua del Pueblo Quemado Chapel

Córdova, Antonio José (Pedro Córdova's son), 20, 177, 178, 179

Córdova, Carlos (performer), 277, 278–79

Córdova, Federico (performer), 3, 4, 52, 106, 116–17, 121, 128, 173, 174 pl.22, 175 pl.23, 178, 180, 203, 214, 215, 225, 231

Córdova, Gilberto Benito, 42, 202, 215, 326, 382 n.18

Córdova, Lina Ortiz de (performer), 52, 173, 174 pl.22, 175 pl.23, 178, 203

Córdova, Pedro, 30–34, 177, 253, 256–60, 262–67, 369; criticism of, 283; death of, 34; exploitation of Córdovans by, 181; as *inteligente*, 31; and jokes, 178, 179; land holdings, 31; livestock holdings, 34; skepticism regarding his legacy, 278–80; and trading, 34; treasure, 34; wealth of, 271

Córdova, Samuelito (performer), 178, 204

Corporatism, 34–36, 38, 77, 94, 275, 322, 349; and architecture, 77; as a cultural value, 158 and counter-hegemony, 367, 368–69; and Holy Week rituals, 338; and Mexicano history, 30–31; and political-economic change, 126; and religious values, 148; and scriptural allusions, 143, 144; and sin, 323–24, 326; and treasure, 280–84; and treasure hunting, 274–75

Counter-hegemony, 362–64; and Mexicano identity, 362; and verbal art, 357–58, 359–76. *See also* Hegemony

Couplets, 312, 316

Court of Private Land Claims, 36

Crapanzano, Vincent, 370

Creativity, and hegemony, 369; in hymns and prayers, 318, 337; in language use, 6–7; linguistic, 358; and tradition, 372, 375

Cuadernos 'notebooks', 52, 295, 297, 298, 300, 301, 348, 356; and literacy, 333, 334; and pedagogical discourse, 161

Cultural values, and hegemony, 361; and rhetorical structure of pedagogical discourse, 283; and jokes, 171, 172, 178, 180–81, 185, 201, 221, 230; and tense/aspect categories, 74; and treasure, 280–84. *See also* Moral principles

Cundiyó, 248, 377 n.2

Darley, Alexander M., 321
Death, and Holy Week rituals, 324–26; as character, 215, 218, 219, 222
DeBeaugrande, Robert, 20
DeBorhegyi, Stephen F., 297, 319
DeBuys, William, 36, 183
Deference, 219, 349–50
Dégh, Linda, 53–54, 55, 280, 379 n.15
DeMarco, A. A., 304
Denning, Greg, 98
Depression, Great, 37–38, 378 n.6
Dewey, John, 12
Dialectical relation of past and present, 82, 83, 91, 92–96, 123, 158–59, 216, 230, 274–77; and dialogism, 355, 373; in proverb performances, 134–35, 354; in treasure tales, 280–84. *See also* Interpretation
Dialogicality (internal), 337; in jokes, 202; and pan-generic properties, 354–56; in pedagogical discourse, 96; in scriptural allusions, 168; in treasure tales, 288. *See also* Heterogeneity; Reported speech
Dialogicality (as turn-taking), of collective recollections, 64, 81–82; in jokes, 202; in legends, 250; and pan-generic properties, 354–56; and pedagogical discourse, 96; in proverbs, 131; and transcription, 16, 56
Dichos 'proverbs'. *See* Proverbs
Direct discourse. *See* Quoted speech; Reported speech
Discourse structure, 348; and tense/aspect, 225, 275–77; and topicality in pedagogical discourse, 92–96; as indexed by triplex signs, 80; of jokes, 228; and triplex signs, 86–91
Dobie, J. Frank, 383 n.6
Domínguez, Benjamín (performer), 182, 183, 184, 185, 220
Domínguez, Fabiola López de (performer), 182
Don 'gift', 2, 7, 101
Double-voicedness, 199–200
Douglas, Mary, 172, 181, 186, 193, 222
Dressler, Wolfgang, 20
Duncan, Starkey, 16, 63
Dundes, Alan, 8, 11, 13, 102, 103, 132, 172, 327, 377 n.2
Dyadic pattern, in hymns and prayers, 316, 355–56

Ebright, Malcolm, 36
Edmonson, Munro S., 370, 371, 382 n.22
Egoism, 221, 274–75, 283, 323, 349
Employment. *See* Wage labor
Encuentro, El 'The Meeting' of Good Friday, 299–301, 316, 318, 319, 322, 328, 335

Ervin-Tripp, Susan, 122
Española, New Mexico, 45, 52, 72, 157, 314
Espinosa, Aurelio M. Sr., 3, 46, 213, 219, 321, 326, 370–71, 380 n.3
Espinosa, José Manuel, 3, 214, 219, 371
Espinosa, José Edmundo, 184, 319
Estaciones de la Cruz, Las 'The Stations of the Cross'. *See Via Crucis*
Ethics, of fieldwork, 53, 54, 378 n.14
Ethnicity, 8; and exploitation, 350–51, 359–60, 361–62; and jokes, 171; and language use, 45–46; and prejudice, 146–48
Ethnopoetics, xv–xvi, 10, 247, 348, 373
Eucharist, 165 ln.140, 330–31
Evaluation, of performances, 61, 160, 217, 251. *See also* Communicative competence
Evangelical churches, 45, 184
Evans-Pritchard, E. E., 102
Evidentials, as frames, 213, 223, 225, 249–50, 273, 279–80, 286; in historical explorations, 62, 63; in legends, 279–80; and quotations, 251–52, 273; and personal experience, 249; and topical progression, 274. *See also* Framing; *'Izque*
Exhortation, 93, 118, 125
Exploitation, by Anglo-Americans, 172; Mexicano resistance to, 357–59, 362–64; of Mexicanos, 350–51, 359–60, 361–62

Face loss, 126, 127, 231
Facial expression, 61, 97; and transcription, 56, 57; as contextualization cue, 130, 343
Faith, as cultural symbol, 149, 365 ln.3–4
Fasting, 321, 324, 330, 385
Feast days, 186, 271, 289, 291–92, 365
Festivals, 34, 42–43, 45, 50, 51 pl.10, 222, 291–92; and agriculture, 94; and corporatism, 38; displacement of, 39, 271
Fictive kinship, 106–07, 117, 131, 380 n.4
Fieldwork, 47–55, 147–48, 370–76
Fine, Elizabeth C., 56
Finnegan, Ruth, 98–99, 102
Firth, Raymond, 102
Fisher, Reginald, 52
Fisher, William R., 52
Folkloristics, 4, 53–55, 99, 371–72
Foodways, and cultural identity, 36; and Holy Wednesday service, 296; and Holy Week rituals, 321, 322; and Lenten rituals, 301
Forest Service, U.S., 37, 75, 183, 255 ln.21–44, 270–71, 350–51, 360, 361, 378 n.5
Form-meaning covariation, 10
Formulaic prayer, 318, 337
Fortescue, Adrian, 330

Framing, 9, 17–18; and belief, 281; of collective recollections, 65, 72; and espisodic structure, 214; and evidentials, 249–50, 251–52, 273, 275; of historical explorations, 62, 63; in hymns and prayers, 328; of jokes, 198, 216; of proverbs, 105, 118, 119, 124; and scripts, 200; and sexual license, 201; and triplex signs, 80; and turn-taking, 214; and validation, 214. *See also* Contextualization

Franciscan Order of Friars Minor, 39–42, 305, 336

Freud, Sigmund, 171

Fry, William F., 181

Fuelwood, 31, 37, 50, 77, 351; as hauled with burros, 71 ln.109–19

Fuertes 'log cabins', 35 pl.6, 149, 150 pl.21, 248

Funciónes 'feast days'. *See* Feast days

Funerals, 43, 314

Gadamer, Hans-Georg, 370

Garfinkel, Harold, 11

Gaze, 50, 332; as contextualization cue, 343; in hymns and prayers, 351; in legends, 251–52, and transcription, 56, 130; and turn-taking, 63. *See also* Body position; Gesture; Head movement

Geertz, Clifford, 370

Gender, 8; and hegemony, 369; and jokes, 171, 187, 192–93, 218

Genealogy, 57, 63, 107, 129, 179

Genre, and communicative competence, 7–8, and contextualization, 15–16; indexes of, 107, 118–19; and methodology, 16; and repertoire, 3; and rhetorical strategy, 47; terms for, 118; and the textual-contextual continuum, 22; versus analytical types, 7, 102. *See also* Framing

Geography, 57, 129, 247–49, 272, 345

Georges, Robert A., 11

Gesture, 50, 332; and audience comprehension, 97; and discourse structure, 251; in hymns and prayers, 351; and jokes, 194; in legends, 250–52, 284, 285, 286, 348, 349; in relation to prosody, 252; and ritual, 294; as signaling performance, 9; and speaker's perspective, 284; and transcription, 56, 57; and voice, 364

Gill, Sam D., 318

Giovannini, Maureen J., 102

Glassie, Henry, xvi, 8, 11, 14, 98, 286, 352, 377n.5

Glory Be to the Father, 302, 303, 304, 312, 313, 314, 333, 335

Goats, 31, 64, 67 ln.2–10, 76 pl.11, 83, 360; as triplex signs, 75, 80, 92; herded by boys, 69

ln.54–66, 71 ln.120–40, 79 pl.13, 209 ln.85–94; loss of, 151; in pedagogical discourse, 87. *See also* Grazing; Livestock

Godelier, Maurice, 366

Goffman, Erving, 9, 11, 14, 72, 172, 200, 217, 229, 231, 281

Gold, Peter, 56

Goldstein, Kenneth S., 8, 11, 53, 54, 55, 379n.15

Goodwin, Charles, 19

Good Friday, 297, 299–304

Gossen, Gary H., xvi, 10, 15, 98, 102, 132, 171, 230, 311, 317, 327, 352, 377n.5

Gramsci, Antonio, 360–61, 375

Grazing, 31, 36–37, 270–71. *See also* Goats; Livestock, loss of; Sheep

Greed, 266–71, 274–75, 283

Green, Reyna, 201

Guadalupita, New Mexico, 52, 187

Gumperz, John J., 14–15, 19, 130, 132

Habitual. *See* Past habitual

Hail Mary, 296, 298, 302, 303, 304, 306, 307, 313, 314, 333, 335

Halliday, M. A. K., 200, 227

Hanks, William, 16, 21, 317, 377n.6

Hasan, Ruqaiya, 200, 227

Head movement, 251–52

Heart, as cultural symbol, 115, 127, 161 ln.27, 274

Hegemony, defined, 360; vis-à-vis land and water, 362; and images of the saints, 362–63; and verbal art, 363–76; and scholarship, 366, 370–76

Heiler, Frederick, 318

Henderson, Alice Corbin, 321, 326, 329

Hernández, Juan, 321, 322, 326

Herzfeld, Michael, 200

Heterogeneity, and performance, 358–59; in cultural values, 201, 218; in hymns and prayers, 338, 351; religious, 186; in scriptural allusions, 168, 170; stylistic, 21, 202; in treasure tales, 285, 286; and voice, 202. *See also* Dialogicality

Hill, Jane C., 286, 377n.1

Hinnebusch, W. A., 305, 323, 331

Historical competitions, 60–62, 63

Historical discourse, 22, 50, 56, 59–99; and the textual-contextual continuum, 222, 223, 224; compared with hymns and prayers, 332, 337; basic types of, 59, 379n.1; dialectical nature of, 92–96; compared with scriptural allusions, 170; place names in, 248. *See also* Collective recollections; Dialectical relation of past and present; Pedagogical discourse

Historical explorations, 62–64

History, as central concerns of performers, 19; critical reflection upon, 82–83; and performance, 370–72, 375–76; and the talk of the elders of bygone days, 30

Hobbes, Thomas, 30, 59

Hockett, Charles F., 73

Hollander, Margot, 292, 385 n.24

Holy Family (women's lay society), 43, 293, 296–97, 300, 334, 335; role in El Encuentro, 299

Holy Family Parish, 296, 303, 313, 314

Holy Rosary. *See* Rosary service

Holy Wednesday, rituals of, 294–96

Holy Week, 45, 50, 293–304; and alabado-prayer cycle, 292; and treasure hunting, 272. *See also* Alabados; Prayers

Hopper, Paul J., 81, 225, 226, 277, 349

Horka-Follick, Lorayne Ann, 321

Huizinga, Johan, 172

Humorous tales, 202–220

Hymes, Dell, 7, 10, 15, 16, 17, 56, 63, 132, 275, 281, 286, 318, 327, 358

Hymes, Virginia, 21

Hymns. *See* Alabados; Alabanzas

Ionicity, 149, 319, 328, 329–31

Identity, Mexicano, 98–99, 172, 186, 319, 362

Ideology, and jokes, 172; and scriptural allusions, 168, 170; and style, 349; and reported speech, 194, 228; differentiation of, 168, 170, 349

Images of the saints, 39, 42, 45, 47, 299, 319–20, 322, 328, 378 n.9, 381 n.13; contemporary, 47–48; in El Encuentro, 300; and lay societies, 43; and Lenten rituals, 294–95, 296; and Mexicano identity, 362–63; in processions, 182–85

Imperfective. *See* Past imperfective

Indexicality, 80, 249; and communicative competence, 62, 97; and gesture, 250–52; in hymns and prayers, 328; in legends, 249, 286; and awareness, 103. *See also* Contextualization; Signification

Indios 'Indians'. *See* Native Americans

Indirect discourse, and structure of performances, 275, 281–82; in jokes, 228; in treasure tales, 285. *See also* Direct discourse; Reported speech

Individualism, and hegemony, 362, 367; and change, 39, 126; and religion, 94, 323–24, 326, 338; and verbal art, 59; and treasure tales, 274–75, 281. *See also* Corporatism

Induced natural context, 54

Inequality, 34, 219, 286, 350–51, 366; and gender, 193; and hegemony, 360–61; and jokes,

181, 215, 218, 219; and legends, 345; and wage labor, 91. *See also* Hegemony

Inocentes 'innocent persons', 147, 163, 166

Interpretation, and background information, 87–91; and belief, 280; dynamic nature of, 283, 353; and form-function relationships, 353; and framing, 80; and hegemony, 306, 364, 370–76; and heterogeneity, 168, 359; as historical criticism, 283; of hymns and prayers, 338–39, 356; of jokes, 172–73, 180, 222, 228; of legends, 233, 283; limits on, 286; of pedagogical discourse, 92–96; performers' role in, 18–19, 21, 286–88; and poetics, 373; of proverbs, 118, 125; and reflexivity, 53–55; and reported speech, 132–34, 285; rights to, 349; role of the fieldworker in, 54–55, 373; and gesture, 252; and scripts, 200; of scriptural allusions, 158; and tense/aspect, 72–74, 225; theological, 142–43

Intertextuality, 19, 284, 348, 357

Introductory formula, 200–01

Invocation, in hymns and prayers, 313, 316, 323

'Izque 'it is said that', 212, 213, 214, 225, 249. *See also* Evidentials; Reported Speech

Jacobs, Melville, 201

Jakobson, Roman, 9, 57, 60, 120, 311, 327, 338

Jason, Heda, 102, 132, 383 n.8

Jefferson, Gail, 11, 16, 200

Jests, 171, 220. *See also* Anecdotes; Humorous tales

Johnson, Robbie David, 193

Jokes, 20, 22, 23, 171–232, 380 n.3; and communicative competence, 230, 231–32; compared with hymns and prayers, 327, 332, 337, 352; compared with legends, 234–35; performance features of, 224–29; and politics, 171, 180, 186; reflexive character of, 230; and tense/aspect, 349; and the textual-contextual continuum, 222, 223, 224, 231, 234, 346

Joke cycles, 202–20

Joke-telling sessions, 186–220

Jordan, Rosan A., 172, 186

Karp, Ivan, 53

Kendall, Martha B., 53

Kenneson, Carol Reyner, 292, 385 n.24

Kirshenblatt-Gimblett, Barbara, 8, 102, 103, 121, 383 n.8

Kluckhohn, Florence Rockwood, 371

Krikmann, Arvo, 101, 103, 121

Kroeber, Karl, 10

Kuipers, Joel C., 38

Kussi, Matti, 102
Kutsche, Paul, 361

Labov, William, 7, 11, 72, 214, 217, 225, 358
La Cofradía de Neustro Padre Jesus Nazareno
   'The Confraternity of Our Father Jesus the
   Nazarene. *See* Confraternity of Our Father
   Jesus the Nazarene
Lamadrid, Enrique, 371
La Muerte 'Death'. *See* Death
Land grants, cultural importance of, 38–39; es-
   tablishment of, 30–31; and hegemony, 362,
   367; loss of, 36–39, 127, 151, 158, 183,
   270–71, 350–51, 359–60, 361–62, 368; and
   verbal art, 38–39. *See also* Uplands
Landscape, 87, 129, 248
Lange, Yvonne, 385 n.20
Larson, Robert W., 359
La Sagrada Familia 'The Holy Family'. *See* Holy
   Family
Las Joyas, 31, 43, 71 ln.132, 87 ln.59, 94, 95
   pl.16, 153 ln.19, 257 ln.73, 365
Las Tinieblas, 'The Tenebrae', 301, 303–04, 314,
   316, 320, 334. *See also* Alabados; Prayers;
   Tenebrae services
Las Trampas, New Mexico, 31, 61
Las Truchas, New Mexico, 31, 45, 50, 61, 65,
   67 ln.7, 85 ln.19–21, 106, 113 ln.111, 120,
   131, 153 ln.1–3, 205, 209, 259 ln.131, 299
Las Vegas, New Mexico, 52
Laughter, 171, 215, 216, 217, 230–31
Lee, Laurence F., 321
Legends, 22, 23, 233–88; compared with hymns
   and prayers, 332, 337, 352; compared with
   jokes, 234–35; compared with proverbs,
   342–46; contextualization of, 223, 234; and
   hegemony, 369; and Holy Week rituals, 326;
   about saints, 320; and methodology, 53–54; of
   Mexicano-Native American hostilities, 179,
   234–52; and pedagogical discourse, 274–77;
   and the textual-contextual continuum, 222,
   223, 224, 342–43, 344–46; use of place
   names in, 247–49. *See also* Treasure tales
Legitimacy, of divine speech, 149; of jokes, 184;
   past as source of, 98–99; and proverbs, 118,
   120, 122, 124–25; and reported speech,
   132–34; of scriptural allusions, 157; of treasure tales, 287. *See also* Authority
Lent, and Holy Week rituals, 44, 292, 293–304;
   and treasure hunting, 263 ln.198–208, 272.
   See also Alabados; Confraternity of Our Father
   Jesus the Nazarene; Holy Week; Prayers
Levine, Lawrence W., 98, 172, 186, 372
Levinson, Stephen C., 200

Lévi-Strauss, Claude, 327
Limón, José E., 172, 173, 193, 216, 220, 222,
   230, 372
Linear structure, of performance, 275, 344, 348,
   349
Line, 56, 214, 311–12
Linguistic competence, 6, 358
Linguistics, 5, 6–7, 375
Literacy, 42, 103; and hymns and prayers, 24,
   333, 334; and scriptural allusions, 23, 156;
   and textuality, 348
Livestock, 34, 67 ln.1–10, 75, 254 ln.14–34;
   loss of, 36–37, 151, 255 ln.21–44, 270–71,
   350–51, 359–60, 361–62; of Pedro Córdova,
   259 ln.118–129, 271; as triplex sign, 92. *See
   also* Cattle; Goats; Grazing; Sheep
Loan words, 46, 216. *See also* Bilingualism
Lomax, Alan, 8
López, George (performer), 47–48, 52, 83, 87,
   88 pl.14, 89 pl.15, 105, 106–17, 149, 151,
   152–55, 170, 183, 291, 295
López, José Dolores (deceased elder), 92, 109,
   118, 149, 150 pl.21, 184, 203, 204, 213
López, José Paz (performer), 182
López, Leonarda Lovato de (performer), 182,
   184, 185, 186
López, Silvianita Trujillo de (performer), 47–48,
   52, 83, 88 pl.14, 89 pl.15, 105, 106–17, 118,
   127, 131, 186, 342
Lord, Albert Bates, 6, 11
Lord's Prayer, 177 ln.21–48, 178, 179, 180, 181,
   224–25; in Holy Week rituals, 290, 296, 298,
   302, 303, 304, 307, 314, 333, 335
Los Alamos, New Mexico, 25, 38, 39, 75, 91,
   377 n.1
Los Alamos National Laboratory, 25, 38, 367
Los Maitines, 314, 316, 320, 334
Lost mines, legends of, 24, 252, 253, 284–86,
   348–51. *See also* Tale of the Lost Gold Mine
   of Juan Mondragón
Loudness. *See* Volume
Lucero-White Lea, Aurora, 3, 383 n.16
Ludic frame, 186, 221, 230, 232
Lummis, Charles Fletcher, 321, 326
Lyons, Thomas R., 320, 323, 338

Malinowski, Bronislaw, 12, 13, 16
Mann, Brenda J., 193
Marcus, George E., 370
Markedness, of *antes* 'bygone days', 72
Martínez, Filiberto (performer), 63
Martínez, Rubel, 49, 63, 326
Marx, Karl, 366, 367
Mass, 314; and saints' days, 291; and Holy Week

Mass (*continued*)
  rituals, 330–31; and scriptural allusions, 156, 166
Matracas 'wooden rachet noisemakers', 298, 320, 328
Maundy Thursday, rituals of, 296–99. *See also* Holy Week
Mayordomas 'sponsors', 291
McLendon, Sally, 10, 15, 56
Medanales, New Mexico, 52
Melodic structure, and transcription, 57, 305
Memorization, 333, 334, 355
Mendoza, Vicente T., 290
Messenger, John C. Jr., 102
Metacommunication, 9, 14, 46, 47; and contextualization, 15; in jokes, 180, 181, 218, 220, 223; in proverbs, 343; in scriptural allusions, 148–49, 158; and textual features, 348
Methodological problems, and context, 12–15; and hegemony, 373–75; and proverbs, 102, 103; and tape recording, 53–54, 63
Mexican-Americans of Texas, 192; and jokes, 172, 180, 201, 221, 372, 381
Mexicanos, defined, xvi, 2; identity as, 25, 39, 59, 171, 172; and language use, 46; hostility with Native Americans, 30–31, 234–47
Mieder, Wolfgang, 102, 380 n.2
Milner, G. B., 102
Misinterpretation, 374–75
Mitchell, Carol, 193
Moccasins, 69 ln.67–83, 74, 77, 85 ln.6; as triplex signs, 80
Modality, 313, 316
Moerman, Michael, 11, 105
Molho, Mauricio, 73–74, 276
Mondragón, Juan (character), 253, 284, 285–86, 348, 349, 350
Mondragón, Ramona (character), 31, 253
Mondragón, Vicente (character), 236 ln.56–95, 248, 249, 251
Mora, New Mexico, 284
Moradas 'local chapters', 44, 292, 296, 300, 303, 319, 320, 321, 322, 333, 336; description of, 294; images of the saints in, 294–95; processions to, 297. *See also* Confraternity of Our Father Jesus the Nazarene
Moral principles, and jokes, 220, 221; and pedagogical discourse, 94; and proverbs, 121; and scriptural allusions, 151, 157, 158, 168. *See also* Cultural values
Mucho más antes (initial period of Córdova's history), 30–31, 72, 73
Mukařovský, Jan, 102, 103, 121, 132–35, 148, 157, 168, 250, 275

Multifunctionality, 72, 74–81, 353, 356
Münchhausen, Baron von, 187
Musical form, of alabados, 290, 314–16; and transcription, 57

Narrative structure, and historical discourse, 80, 91; of jokes, 225; of scriptural allusions, 160, 169, 170; and transcription, 56–67; of treasure tales, 285; units of, 72
Native-Americans, 234–47, 382 n.1; as captives, 34, 178; and treasure, 253; and hegemony, 369; hostile relations with Mexicanos, 30–31, 234–47, 383 n.1; stereotypes of, 178–79, 180
Natural context, 53, 54, 372–73
Navajos, 42, 177, 178, 235, 246
Nazareno 'Nazarene Christ' (image), 297, 300, 319
New Mexican Spanish, 46, 216, 217
Nonverbal communication, 9, 15. *See also* Body position; Facial expression; Gaze; Gesture; Head movement; Prosody
Notebooks. *See Cuadernos*
Numbskull stories, 171

Opening formulae, 9, 198, 212, 225, 248
Oraciones 'prayers'. *See* Prayers
Oral composition, 6, 332, 351
Oral literary criticism, 46–47, 231; of competitive performances, 61; of hymns and prayers, 327; of proverbs, 103, 132
Ordimalas, Pedro de (character), 202, 203, 204–15, 218, 230, 382 n.16
Orientation section, 72, 214, 225
Oring, Elliot, 172
Ornstein, Jacob, 46
Ortiz, Alfonso, 38, 359, 360
Our Father. *See* Lord's Prayer

Padre Nuestro 'Our Father'. *See* Lord's Prayer
Parallelism, in treasure tales, 285; in jokes, 194, 198, 228; in hymns and prayers, 290, 311–12, 316; linguistic, 9; in proverbs, 119–20
Paredes, Américo, 102, 132, 172, 180, 192, 221, 370, 375
Parry, Milman, 6
Past habitual (tense/aspect category), 74, 137, 349; in scriptural allusion, 155; in jokes, 225; in legends, 276–77; in proverbs, 107, 118–19. *See also* Present; Tense/aspect
Past imperfective (tense/aspect category), 214, 228, 370 n.3; in collective recollections, 72–74; in jokes, 225, 226; in legends, 276–77; in scriptural allusions, 155; in textually-oriented genres, 348. *See also* Present; Tense/aspect

Past perfective (tense/aspect category), 81, 349, 379n.3; in collective recollections, 72–74; in jokes, 225; in legends, 276–77; in scriptural allusions, 155. *See also* Present; Tense/aspect

Pauses, 61, 130, 168

Pedagogical discourse, 59, 63, 82–97; defined, 83; discourse structure of, 274–77; and interpretation, 96; and legends, 270; problems in identifying, 17; and proverbs, 104–05; and scriptural allusions, 137, 142, 149, 157, 158; and topicality, 274–77. *See also* Historical discourse

Peirce, Charles Sanders, 80, 328, 329

Peñalosa, Fernando, 46

Penance, 43, 321–23, 324, 330, 331, 338

Peñasco, New Mexico, 52, 259

Penfield, Joyce, 102, 121, 132, 133, 275

Pentecostalism, 113–15, 120, 121

Perfective. *See* Past perfective

Performance, 50; as an active process, 18–19; authoritativeness of, 7–8, 17; collective recollections as, 65; and communicative competence, 7–8; defined, 7, 63; as defined by Chomsky, 358; degrees of intensity in, 9; disclaimers of, 9–10; and interpretation, 18–19; versus reports, 63, 284; scholar's versus performer's definitions of, 18; segmentation of, 372–73

Performance theory, xv–xvi, 5, 7–10, 12, 13, 14, 17–22, 372

Performativity, 8, 132, 359; in hymns and prayers, 313, 316, 323, 337; in Mass and Holy Week rituals, 330–31; and multifunctionality, 354; in proverbs, 344; in treasure tales, 283

Permyakov, G. L., 102

Picaresque tales, 220

Pitch, as contextualization cue, 130; and linear structure, 275, 281–82; and musical form, 316; in prayers, 306, 307, 311, 312; in scriptural allusions, 156, 168; and speaker's perspective, 284; and transcription, 56, 57. *See also* Prosody

Pito 'flute', 296, 298, 314, 315, 316, 320

Place names, 87, 247–49

Play, 172, 201, 230

Plaza. *See* Córdova plaza

Poetic structure, in hymns and prayers, 311, 316, 327, 348; and performance, 9; in proverbs, 120; and transcription, 56. *See also* Style

Polanyi, Karl, 366

Political discourse, 47, 62

Polyphony, 202

Positivism, 14, 53–55

Prague "School", 350

Prayers, 22, 24, 62, 289, 292, 336, 339; and dialogism, 355–56; and moral disposition, 123; and the textual-contextual continuum, 224, 351–52; and transcription, 57; as performative utterances, 312–13; communicative functions of, 318; dyadic patterns in, 355–56. *See also* Alabados; Holy Week

Presbyterians, 45, 378n.11. *See also* Protestantism

Present (tense/aspect category), 74; in legends, 276–77; in proverbs, 107, 118–19; in scriptural allusions, 155–56. *See also* Tense/aspect

Presupposition, and contextualization, 347; in jokes, 192–94, 195, 200–01, 228; in proverbs, 104, 106–07, 128–30; in scriptural allusions, 159. *See also* Background information

Price, Richard, 98–99

Priests, as characters in jokes, 204–12, 214, 218, 219; role of, 291, 330, 331

Processions, 296, 299, 365; in El Encuentro, 300; in festivals, 61; of Holy Week, 295, 297, 319, 326; and saints' days, 291; use of images in, 182. *See also* Festivals

Production, hegemonic view of, 362, 366–67, 369; Mexicano views of, 365–67; secular view, 281; transformation of, 38–39. *See also* Agriculture; Livestock

Prójimo 'brother/sister', 141–43, 146, 147, 160–63

Pronouns, and social inequality, 148, 286, 349–50

Prosody, and audience, 97, 212; and contextualization cues, 130; and dialogism, 252; and framing, 72; and gesture, 252; in hymns and prayers, 31, 307, 351; in jokes, 194, 219; in legends, 348; and linear structure of performances, 275, 281–82; and musical form, 316; and narrative structure, 169; and performance, 9; and reported speech, 250; in scriptural allusions, 156, 168; and transcription, 56, 57, 384; in treasure tales, 285, 286; and voice, 284. *See also* Pauses; Pitch; Rate of speech; Voice quality; Volume

Protestantism, 45, 186, 289, 378n.11

Proverbs, 16, 22, 50, 56, 101–35; abbreviation of features, 129, 131–32; compared with hymns and prayers, 327, 332, 337; compared with jokes, 180, 184, 224, 231; compared with legends, 250, 287, 342–46; compared with scriptural allusions, 151, 155, 156, 157, 158–59, 160, 169, 170; contextualization of, 3–4, 347; creation of, 120; definitions of, 101–03; dialogic nature of, 131; elaboration of

Proverbs (*continued*)
features in, 119, 121, 123–24, 127–28, 129, 131–32; and evidential frames, 118; as "owned" by individuals, 106–07, 118, 131, 133; and pedagogical discourse, 274; problems in identifying, 17, 128; settings for, 104–05; specialists in, 3, 120, 123, 130; terms for, 380 n.3; and the textual-contextual continuum, 222, 223, 224, 342–44

Público 'public' (i.e., non-Brothers), 293, 294, 297, 298, 303, 304, 319, 320, 322, 332, 335; role in Brotherhood ceremonies, 44, 299

Pueblo Quemado Chapel. *See* San Antonio de Padua del Pueblo Quemado Chapel

Punch line, 194, 199, 201; and discourse structure of jokes, 181, 226; and reflexivity, 218; repetition of, 180, 229. *See also* Jokes

Question-answer pairs, 200, 203, 214, 227–28, 272

Quotatives, in humorous tales, 214; in legends, 249–50, 252, 273; and linear structure of performances, 275, 281–82; in proverbs, 105, 107, 118–19; in scriptural allusions, 155

Quoted speech, in alabados, 386 n.34–35; in hymns and prayers, 337–38, 356; in jokes, 194, 226; in legends, 249–50, 251–52, 273; and linear structure of performances, 275, 281; performance framed as, 213; in proverbs, 132–34; in scriptural allusions, 168. *See also* Indirect discourse; Reported speech

Rabinow, Paul, 370

Race, and religious values, 140, 141, 146–48, 163 ln.49–53

Rael, Juan B., 3, 46, 184, 202, 214, 215, 219, 291, 295, 298, 300, 303, 334, 385 n.32

Ranchos 'farms/ranches', 25, 31, 39, 40 pl.7

Raskin, Victor, 172, 173, 200

Rate of speech, 10, 168, 275, 281–82, 307, 312, 316. *See also* Prosody

Realm of conversation, defined, 281, 282, 283. *See also* Contextualization

Referential function, 8, 60; and contextualization, 347; and text, 103; in hymns and prayers, 327, 331; in legends, 345; and tense/aspect, 74; and triplex signs, 80. *See also* Signification

Reflexivity, 182; and hegemony, 369, 373–75; and jokes, 172, 218, 221; and methodology, 53, 373–75

Reichard, Gladys Amanda, 318

Reina, Rubén E., 291, 380 n.4

Religiosity, 45, 158, 275; and emotion, 315, 323;

and hegemony, 364–67; and Holy Week rituals, 322, 326, 329–31, 333, 337–38; and inequality, 181, 218; and jokes, 171, 184–86, 198; and scriptural allusions, 143–49, 156, 157, 161, 166–69; and treasure tales, 274–75, 280–84; and veracity, 113–17

Rendón, Gabino, 186, 378 n.11

Repair procedures, 216, 229, 231, 273; in pedagogical discourse, 94–96

Repetition, as framing device, 181; in hymns and prayers, 316, 352; in legends, 348; in proverbs, 119, 343–44; of punch line, 180, 229. *See also* Parallelism

Reported speech, communicative functions of, 251–52; and dialogism, 355; and discourse structure, 275, 281–82; foregrounding of, 132–33; in historical discourse, 349; in hymns and prayers, 337, 351, 386 n.34–35; and ideology, 228, 349–50; in jokes, 226–29; in legends, 249–50, 251–52, 273, 345; in proverbs, 103, 105, 132–34, 349; in scriptural allusions, 155, 158; in treasure tales, 285. *See also* Indirect discourse; Quotatives; Quoted speech

Respeto 'respect', 49, 123, 126, 148

Responsibility, of performers, 8, 64, 72

Reyna, José Reynaldo, 172, 201, 231, 381 n.15

Rezador 'prayer leader', 292, 317, 332, 335; and Rosary services, 42, 295, 296, 311, 312; and El Encuentro, 299; and tenebrae services, 297–98; and wakes for the saints, 291; and written texts, 334, 348. *See also* Alabados; Prayers

Rezos 'prayers'. *See* Prayers

Rhetoric, competence in, 3, 47, 59, 60, 83, 118–19, 123; at festivals, 62; and history, 98–99; and historical discourse, 59, 60; and jokes, 23; and legends, 348; and proverbs, 103, 120, 121, 124–25; structure of, 22–23

Rhetorical particles, 56, 285, 286, 348

Ricos 'rich persons', 34, 181, 219, 349–50

Riddles, 16, 17

Rio Chiquito, New Mexico, 45

Ritual language, 289, 317, 328–29

Rivera, Rowena, 292, 293, 319, 320, 333

Robb, John Donald, 3, 52, 290, 291, 295, 300, 303, 314, 315, 333, 371, 378 n.13

Robe, Stanley L., 219

Rodríguez, Sylvia, 362

Romano-V., Octavio Ignacio, 370, 375

Romero, Carlos (performer), 137

Romero, Melaquías (performer), 137–43, 138 pl.17, 139 pl.18, 235, 248, 251, 284, 342, 348, 350, 359, 383 n.1

Romero, Vicente (character in legends), 248
Rosaldo, Renato, 98
Rosaldo, Michele, 105
Rosario 'Rosary service', 42, 44, 290, 293,
    294–97, 298, 302, 303, 304–17, 334. *See also*
    Alabados; Prayers
Rosary (beads), 296, 298, 318–19
Rosenbaum, Robert J., 359
Rothenberg, Jerome, 56

Sacks, Harvey, 11, 16, 105, 169, 173
Sahlins, Marshall, 98, 366
St. Isidore, wake for, 43, 94, 291, 365, 366
Salve (hymn of praise to the Virgin), 290, 302,
    303
San Antonio de Padua del Pueblo Quemado
    Chapel, 29 pl.3, 39, 41 pl.8, 61, 261
    ln.143–55, 271, 291, 292–99, 320; casting of
    bell, 271. *See also* Córdova
Sangre de Cristo Mountains, 25, 187, 284
Santa Fe, New Mexico, 38, 52
Santa Fe National Forest, 37, 75, 255 ln.21–44.
    See also Forest Service, U.S.
Santo Rosario, El 'Holy Rosary'. *See* Rosario
Santuario El (Chimayó), 297, 319, 322, 324,
    335
Sapir, Edward, 375
Saussure, Ferdinand de, 18, 329, 353
Schegloff, Edmanuel A., 11, 16
Scheub, Harold, 56
Schutz, Alfred, 14
Scripts, 200
Scriptural allusions, 17, 22, 23, 56, 137–70;
    compared with hymns and prayers, 327, 332,
    337, 352; compared with jokes, 180, 184, 187,
    224; compared with legends, 250, 287; global
    structure of, 159; performance features of, 151,
    157, 159; and the textual-contextual con-
    tinuum, 222, 223, 224, 346; written sources
    for, 23
Sebastiana, Doña 'Lady Sebastiana', 324
Secularism, 59, 94, 283
Segal, Dmitri, 53
Seitel, Peter I., 11, 102, 103, 132, 134, 380n.5
Self-sufficiency, 31–39, 75, 77
Semiotics, 80, 328–331, 337
Sexuality, 195–202, 218, 220
Sheep, 31, 35 pl.35, 360; in historical discourse,
    67 ln.3, 87; loss of, 37; economic importance
    of, 34–36, 83; as triplex signs, 75, 80, 92. *See
    also* Grazing; Livestock
Sherzer, Joel, xvi, 10, 11, 15, 21, 311, 316, 352,
    377n.5
Shopen, Timothy, 132

Signification, in hymns and prayers, 327, 328–
    31; in pedagogical discourse, 86–87, 91
Silva-Corvalán, Carmen, 156, 226, 277
Silverstein, Michael, 15, 21, 103, 148, 275,
    311, 329, 344, 347, 356
Sin, 147, 167, 178, 324–26
Singer, Milton, 186
Social class, 46, 285, 350, 362, 369. *See also*
    Inequality
Social criticism, 99; in jokes, 220, 221, 230
Social inequality. *See* Inequality
Social relations, and jokes, 171, 172, 181, 186,
    218, 222; and Holy Week rituals, 322, 336; as
    transformed in performance, 148, 193, 228,
    287, 359
Speech acts. *See* Performativity
Spradley, James P., 193
Stations of the Cross. *See Via Crucis*
Steele, Thomas J., 292, 293, 319, 320, 323, 333,
    384n.11
Stereotypes, 202; of the *agringado* 'Gringoized',
    215–16; of Anglo-Americans, 127, 147–48;
    and communicative competence, 179, 250;
    and fieldworkers, 370–71; and gender, 192–
    94, 369; and jokes, 171, 172, 230; of Native
    Americans, 178–79, 180, 246, 250, 251, 253
Storyrealm, 214, 281–84
Style, and belief, 281; and communicative com-
    petence, 133; and contextualization, 15;
    foregrounding of, 18–19; heterogeneity in,
    158, 202, 290; and ideology, 349; and inter-
    pretation, 5, 281; and legends, 288; and peda-
    gogical discourse, 83; and performance, 9–10,
    17–18, 64, 72; and performer, 275, 283; and
    proverbs, 118, 133–34; and transcription, 56,
    57; and scriptural allusions, 168. *See also*
    Genre
Sudarios 'prayers for the dead', 298, 299, 302,
    303, 307, 335
Sullivan, William M., 370
Supernatural, 179, 253, 272
Swadesh, Francis Leon, 178, 193
Synecdoche, and jokes, 217, 228; and discourse
    structure, 80, 81, 92–96, 146; historical, 276;
    in proverbs, 344

Taboo words, 119, 185
Tale of the Lost Mine of Juan Mondragón, 253,
    284–86, 348–51 passim. *See also* Treasure
    tales
Taleworld, 281–84
Tambiah, S. J., 43, 289, 328, 337
Taussig, Michael T., 372
Taylor, Archer, 101, 380n.1

Tedlock, Dennis, 10, 15, 16, 19, 56, 311, 317

Tenebrae services, 297–99, 303–04, 318, 320. *See also* Alabados; Las Tinieblas; Prayers

Tense/aspect, 72–74, 379 n.3; and dialogism, 355; in legends, 275–77, 345, 348; in proverbs, 107, 118–19; in treasure tales, 286; and voice, 364. *See also* Past habitual; Past imperfective; Past Perfective; Present

Terms of address, 219, 286, 380 n.6

Textual features, and transcription, 53; defined, 20; of proverbs, 128

Textual sphere, 21, 347, 348; and audience, 130; defined, 20; vis-à-vis contextual sphere, 14–15, 21; of historical discourse, 59; of hymns and prayers, 327; of jokes, 212–14; of legends, 233, 344; and performance theory, 21; of proverbs, 102–03, 119–20, 132–33, 344; of scriptural allusions, 156, 159, 169, 170; stratification of, 349. *See also* Literacy

Textual-contextual continuum, 342–59; and hegemony, 367–68; and hymns and prayers, 331–336; and jokes, 187, 222, 224, 231–32; and legends, 233; and scriptural allusions, 169–70; and treasure tales, 286

Theatricalization, in legends, 134–35, 168, 250

Theology, 23, 156, 158, 292

Thompson, Sandra, 226, 277

Time, and chronotypes, 248; and cultural values, 371; and legends, 344–45; and jokes, 225; and proverbs, 343, 345; and Holy Week rituals, 320

Tinieblas, Las 'The Tenebrae'. *See Las Tinieblas*

Toelken, Barre, 13

Topicality, and audience, 97; and collective recollections, 81; and framing, 72; and pedagogical discourse, 83, 86, 92–96, 274–76, 283–84; and proverbs, 104, 105, 125; and the textual-contextual continuum, 223; and triplex signs, 80, 81, 353; and tying phrases, 106

Tradition, 99, 367–69, 370–71, 372, 375–76

Transcription, and back-channel cues, 16, 53; and poetic patterns, 348; and performance, 17; and theory, 10; of hymns and prayers, 305; methods used, 55–57. *See also* Methodological problems

Treasure hunting, contemporary, 252, 270, 273, 282, 283

Treasure tales, 233, 252–88; and pedagogical discourse, 93–94; discourse structure of, 285. *See also* Legends

Tricksters, 181, 218, 219, 230. *See also* Jokes

Triplex signs, 74–81; and audience, 97; in collective recollections, 74–81; and multifunctionality, 353; in pedagogical discourse, 86–91

Trujillo, Aurelio (performer), 3, 4, 8, 52, 128, 145 pl.20, 160, 161, 168, 169, 170, 291, 334, 364, 384 n.1

Trujillo, Costancia (performer), 3, 52, 128, 144 pl.19, 145 pl.20, 160, 161, 364

Turn-taking, in historical discourse, 61, 63, 64; and dialogism, 354; in hymns and prayers, 312, 316, 332, 355; in joke cycles, 217, 229; in legends, 272; in proverbs, 124; and triplex signs, 80

Turner, Edith, 385 n.27

Turner, Victor W., 172, 385 n.27

Two-part pairs, 227–28, 229, 312

Tying elements, in jokes, 213, 224–25; in proverbs, 105–06; in scriptural allusions, 155. *See also* Cohesion

Uplands, 32 pl.4, 36, 365; and agriculture, 94, 95 pl.16; economic importance of, 31; and grazing, 75; loss of, 36–39, 127, 151, 153 ln.12–31, 183, 255 ln.21–44, 270–71, 350–51, 359–60, 361–62. *See also* Land grants

Urban, Greg, 11, 15, 16, 21, 275, 311

Utes, 42, 178, 235, 246

Vaca, N. C., 370, 375

Validation, of jokes, 180; of proverbs, 124–25, 131, 134, 343, 344, 354; of scriptural allusions, 157, 167–68, 170

Van Ness, John R., 38, 350, 360, 361

Vansina, Jan, 98

Variation, between genres, 222–23, 232; in jokes, 173, 221; linguistic, 11

Vázsonyi, Andrew, 53, 280, 379 n.15

Velorios para los difuntos 'wakes for the dead', 43, 186, 290–91, 293, 314

Velorios para los santos 'wakes for the saints', 42, 43, 186, 291–92, 365

Veracity, and jokes, 180; as disputed, 273; performers' concern with, 113–17, 118, 124, 126, 127

Vergüenza 'shame', concept of, 199 ln.99

Via Crucis 'Stations of the Cross', 44, 293, 299, 300, 301–03, 316, 318, 319, 322, 324, 326, 334, 335, 337, 351

Videotaping, 50, 57. *See also* Methodological problems

Vigil, Antonio Capitán (character), 235 ln.22–30, 240 ln.173–246, 247, 378 n.4

Vigil, Julián Josué, 52, 187, 188, 195, 201, 202, 215, 253, 277, 278–79, 284, 350

Vigil, Lázaro (performer), 187, 188

Vigil, Lilia Pacheco de (performer), 187, 188, 195, 198, 200, 202

Virgin Mary, 44, 304, 307, 312, 322, 323, 326, 338

Visitas 'ritual processions', 44–45, 297–98, 335

Voice, 354, 364; and dialogization, 250; and jokes, 194–219; of the narrator, 250, 252; and prosodic variation, 275. *See also* Prosody; Reported speech

Voice quality, 156, 168, 284, 316. *See also* Prosody

Vološinov, V. N., 275, 349, 354

Volume, 156, 158; in hymns and prayers, 307, 311, 312; and linear structure, 275, 281–82; and musical form, 316; and transcription, 56, 57. *See also* Prosody

Wachtel, Nathan, 372

Wage labor, 91, 360, 378 n.6; daily, 25, 37, 38, 39; and hegemony, 361, 362, 367; migratory, 37, 39, 75, 127, 270; and religious rituals, 94, 293–94

Wakes. *See Velorios para los difuntos; Velorios para los santos*

Walker, Randi Jones, 186

Wallace, Stephen, 277, 349

Wallrich, William, 293

Waletzky, Joshua, 72, 225

Warao (Venezuela), 9, 377 n.4

Warfare, 31, 153 ln.47–57, 157, 246

Weber, Max, 366

Weigle, Marta, 44, 186, 201, 290, 292, 293, 320, 322, 323, 326, 329, 333, 335, 338, 385 n.24, 385 n.25

Westphall, Victor, 360

Williams, Raymond, 360–61, 362, 366, 367, 368, 369, 375

Wittgenstein, Ludwig, 98

Wolfson, Nessa, 170

Women's humor, 189–202. *See also* Gender; Jokes

Woodbury, Anthony, 11, 15, 16

Woodward, Dorothy, 292, 293, 321, 322, 324, 333

Work, and contemporary youth, 69 ln.85–119, 82; of children, 77, 78 pl.12; for oneself, 85 ln.29, 91; for someone else, 85 ln.26, 91, 94. *See also* Agriculture; Production; Wage labor

Wroth, William, 319, 385 n.21

Yanga, Tsimpaka, 132

Yankah, Kwesi, 102, 132

Yoder, Don, 43

Young, Katherine Galloway, 14, 21, 214, 281, 383 n.8

Zenner, Walter P., 172

University of Pennsylvania Press
Conduct and Communications Series

Erving Goffman and Dell Hymes, *Founding Editors*
Dell Hymes, Gillian Samkoff, and Henry Glassie, *General Editors*

Erving Goffman, *Strategic Interaction*. 1970
William Labov. *Language in the Inner City: Studies in the Black English Vernacular*. 1973
William Labov. *Sociolinguistic Patterns*. 1973
Dell Hymes. *Foundations in Sociolinguistics: An Ethnographic Approach*. 1974
Barbara Kirshenblatt-Gimblett, ed. *Speech Play: Research and Resources for the Study of Linguistic Creativity*. 1976
Gillian Sankoff. *The Social Life of Language*. 1980
Erving Goffman. *Forms of Talk*. 1981
Dell Hymes. "In Vain I Tried to Tell You." 1981
Dennis Tedlock. *The Spoken Word and the Work of Interpretation*. 1983
Ellen B. Basso. *A Musical View of the Universe: Kalapalo Myth and Ritual Performances*. 1985
Michael Moerman, *Talking Culture: Ethnography and Conversation Analysis*. 1987
Dan Rose. *Black American Street Life: South Philadelphia, 1969–1971*. 1987
J. Joseph Errington. *Structure and Style in Javanese: A Semiotic View of Linguistic Etiquette*. 1988
Charles L. Briggs. *Competence in Performance: The Creativity of Tradition in Mexicano Verbal Art*. 1988